Lost Mountain Spirit

James Montgomery

PublishAmerica
Baltimore

First printing

ISBN: 1-60474-183-X
PUBLISHED BY PUBLISHAMERICA, LLLP
www.publishamerica.com
Baltimore

Printed in the United States of America

This book is dedicated to the love of my life, Toni, for her patience and personal sacrifices of the time that we share.

God be with you
and your family.
Jim Montgomery

Chapter 1

The cold, steel-gray winter skies hadn't changed for weeks, and freezing temperatures were a close companion to the slate-colored cosmos, riding on every blast of air from the north. The frigid air currents pierced the body like vengeful daggers deep into the hearts and attitudes of every living soul throughout the small community of Springville, South Dakota.

Zen Bragg always had his share of problems in the winter months and paid little attention to the problems of anyone else, especially the people of Springville. Compassion and general concern for others declined with his later years, as did his youthful outlook on life and mankind in general. The blood in his veins no longer carried warmth to his own body and mind, how could he possibly feel the slightest concern of others. He lived by himself, and pretty much stayed to himself. He seldom left the log house that he built as a refuge, and fortress, shielding him from the rest of the world. He never seemed to be able to understand and cope with people, the same way most others did. All his life he could see that he was different, but the lack of desire to conform to others ways made little difference in the paths that he chose for his own life. Zen was a loner, a hermit, to those who thought they knew him. Though no one in Springville really knew Zen, and most people would admit that Zen never really gave them the opportunity.

Zen was not the kind of person that shared himself, his ideas, or anything for that matter. His only contact with the people of Springville was during his rare excursions to the trading post to barter the tradable items that he gathered, trapped, or made; for the necessary sustenance to required by his lifestyle. His needs were few; for the only things he had to care for other than himself, were his two horses. Zen's cabin was situated beside the Aninandak River, named by the Chippewa Indians for the balsam fir trees that lined its banks at the rocky shoreline. He stumbled onto this site by following a small animal trail along the river to where a steep cliff practically surrounded a five-acre flat. The river's oxbow around the flat completely sealed the area off from potential intruders. The only access was the small path that Zen was sure to keep concealed from the outside world and anyone who might happen to the area.

This was perhaps the most perfect hideaway the territory had to offer. The high, sheer rock wall nearly surrounded the cabin on three sides, to the north and around each side. The spring sun, through early fall always appeared from mid-morning to late afternoon from the southern exposure. There were always uplifting air currents that worked much like a chimney, always carrying the smoke up and out of the natural sanctuary, quickly dissipating from sight. The Aninandak was just wide enough and deep enough to discourage anyone from crossing. Its swift current and rocky channels made canoe travel nearly impossible across that particular oxbow. Due to the higher elevation of Zen's chosen flat, flooding was never a concern. Travelers seeing the cliffs beyond the Aninandak banks would be discouraged to attempt such a purposeless crossing.

The country was much too big and traveled so seldom that the fear of someone finding the shelter no longer bothered Zen. His chosen place was natural, unspoiled by the ways of man, and Zen wanted to keep it that way. This was Zen's twenty second winter in his Black Hills sanctuary. Each year was becoming a little harder to endure.

The river was abound with rainbow trout, and many dens of beaver in all its tributaries and backwaters. The banks of the Aninandak were lined with lush wild berry bushes and aromatic herbs. Bears often frequented the area, drawn by the sweet smell of the aromatic plants, as a fly to an open jar of honey. The trail into the flat was always productive for woods critters such as deer, squirrels, coon, turkey, sheep and goats.

Zen took advantage of this and became an opportunistic self provider, but protected and enjoyed nature's bounty with his own definition of conservation. He took only what he needed. It was his personal code and moral ethics that guided his life style, perhaps the only code for of his simple lifestyle. The only thing that had any meaning to Zen was his surroundings, nature, and his ability to survive and live with it, not to change it. Zen despised change. Everyone that ever encountered Zen probably heard him say at one time or another, "Things 'er as they 'er, and 'er to be lived with as they ere to remain." Somewhere, Zen probably had those words carved in stone.

Zen reminisced, having said those words to his long-time friend Isaiah Griffin, one day many years prior, as they were preparing to go their separate way for the fall hunting season. He knew when he said it, by the puzzled look on Isaiah's face, that Isaiah didn't fully understand what he had said. It wasn't in Zen's character to explain himself, and Isaiah was a man much too proud to question his friend's statement in search for some deep-seated understanding.

At the time, Isaiah was a bit taken back and baffled at Zen's inquisitive summation about how things ought to be. Isaiah became preoccupied by Zen's comments, and that too, was rare for him. He thought knew Zen. He thought he knew Zen perhaps better than anyone else in their limited world of outside contacts.

"So wher' ya headed fer, Pilgrim?" inquired Isaiah as they both mounted their horses.

"Don't rightly know," replied Zen. "Somewher's wher' ther's nobody to spor'l it."

Isaiah understood that clearly enough. He grunted and nodded his head in concurrence, raised his rifle in a waving gesture and rode in the opposite direction from Zen. It would be more than a year before the two would meet again.

Isaiah Griffin was Zen's best friend for some ten years plus. Isaiah met Zen on the plains hunting in the fall of 1851 in the Oklahoma

Territory. Both men were apprehensive at their first encounter and approached each other slowly and with considerable hesitation and concern. Both felt as if the other had trespassed and momentarily intruded on their intended plans.

"Lost, pilgrim?" asked Isaiah.

"Nope, ain't ever been lost," he hesitatingly replied. "Just kinda been misplaced fer a few days, at most," Zen quipped back.

Isaiah and Zen continued to size each other up through short needling remarks, aimed more at the character than the man. But, after several short volleys of meaningless dialogue, they found themselves gaining a kind of respect for each other, perhaps because they were two of a kind.

Both men were clad and weather-worn buckskins. They were both somewhere in their early twenties, although neither knew exactly how old they were. They recognized the fact that they were both a part of the dying breed of humanity called the "mountain man."

"What brings ya out her'?" inquired Isaiah.

"Buffler," said Zen. "Thur gettin' harder to find, ain't they?"

"Yep, they sure 're," answered Isaiah.

"That a .50 caliber Hawkin ya got ther', Pilgrim?" Isaiah inquisitively asked.

"Ya sure gotta lotta questions," snipped Zen.

Isaiah took a closer gander at the Zen's rifle, and without the slightest hesitation he blurted, "That looks like Crazy Jack's rifle!"

"'Twas," replied Zen.

"How'd ya come ta have that, Pilgrim?" asked Isaiah.

"Traded a Blackfoot squaw even up," Zen responded.

"Ya got 'im good on that'n," snickered Isaiah. "Don't surprise me none. He always did like them womenfolk. Guess that's why they called him Crazy Jack."

From the time on, Isaiah always referred to Zen as "Pilgrim."

Zen also gave Isaiah the nick-name of Buffler. He chose that name because of some of the wild stories Isaiah told concerning some of his past buffalo hunts.

At that moment, a strong friendship had emerged. Neither man was aware at that time that their friendship would last a lifetime. The two men stayed together for several years hunting buffalo, and roaming the great plains, always in search of something better. Hunting was their way of life, and if one got the urge to move on, the other would take the initiative to decide which direction they would go. Neither man could be satisfied with where they were at any one time for any length of time. They continually had the feeling that there was always a better place to be than where they were at the present.

Spring always seemed to cheer their spirits and provided them new opportunities. They welcomed the new season, offering change by allowing them to go high into the mountains. There they would stay until the winter weather forced them back down. When the game moved out of one area, they would move with it or to a new area altogether.

Spring brought with it great opportunities and yet spawned a certain unrest and personal discontentment, especially for those who were always looking for something better. So it was Buffler and Pilgrim, in the spring of 1867. They couldn't agree as to where to go, so they agreed to temporarily part ways, in order to find those things in their life that could meet their expectations and complete their personal dreams.

Buffler was planning to head north for some trapping before the thaw took hold. Pilgrim thought best to go east onto the plains to find the buffalo. They briefly shared their plans and reasoning and agreed to rendezvous during the hunters moon where they had first met each other.

It was at that parting moment, when Pilgrim contributed the puzzling comment about the way things ought to be.

Chapter 2

Buffler got to thinking about the last thing Pilgrim had said about going where there wasn't anybody to spoil it. The longer he dwelled on Pilgrim's comment, the more offense he took to the statement. Buffler pondered on it for some time, thinking that he meant that Buffler himself was the one that was spoiling things. When you're by yourself for long periods of time, a man does a lot of thinking and soul-searching. Most of that type of thinking concerns the most recent conversations and attitudes of the people you've been around recently. And in Buffler's case that person was Pilgrim. Buffler headed on his northern trek. He dropped down from the foothills to the plains in order to cover more ground at a faster pace. His plans were never written in stone and were subject to change at his slightest whim. He was the kind of person that was often distracted by any event that offered something different.

Three days into his excursion and the weather broke. The temperature warmed rapidly and stayed warm for several days. The spring melt caused much flooding of the lowland plains. For three days Buffler found himself land-locked between two raging, flooded river basins. The sudden rise of the basins drove Buffler to highest ground he could find.

Buffler knew that he was cut off from where he had planned to go and that it appeared he would be imprisoned until the floods subsided. It would be some time before he could continue.

This temporary hold up, caused by the sudden change in the weather, would be enough to ruin his chances of trapping any quality late-winter furs.

He decided to make the most of a bad situation and set up his temporary camp on a high knoll to wait it out. Less than a week had gone by since Pilgrim had headed east. With any luck, Buffler thought that he might be able to catch up with Pilgrim. He thought for a minute, and then recalled Pilgrim's statement about spoiling things that reignited his anger like a fire from a single ember. He lay on his buffalo hide blanket, chewing on a piece of elk jerky, becoming quite restless and crazed by his thoughts. He mumbled to himself about being stuck in God forsaken territory with flood waters locking him in from the rest of the world.

He visualized Pilgrim standing out on the sun-stricken plains surrounded by mile-long herds of buffalo, and laughing at Buffler's bad luck. The thoughts ate at his soul and took hold of his mind like a bottle of whiskey.

Buffler threw himself back in rage, nearly slamming his head into a bolder that his supplies rested on. His ears locked to the sounds of rattles on a coiled rattle-snake as eyes locked on the movement. His heart skipped a beat and the realization of his predicament, instantly sent a shockwave of adrenaline, causing a sudden hot flash and tensed every muscle in his body.

The snake was inches from face, coiled and ready to strike. Fear took over, and Buffler's instant reflex to jerk away was no match for the striking snake. The snake drove its fangs deep in his upper arm of his right shoulder. With little thought and a subconscious gesture, he grabbed the rattler with his left hand and his knife with the right hand, and with one continuous flow of motion he slapped the snake to the ground and decapitated it.

"Danged varmint. Gotta mouthful did ya?" he said with a trembling voice.

Buffler sat there quietly thinking for a minute, looking at the rattlesnake. He silently wiped the knife across his leg and laid it aside. He stood up and struggled a bit to get his shirt over his head.

"Dang it," he uttered under his breath as he reached for the knife. He cut a fairly deep slit over each bite mark. The area started to bleed profusely. Grabbing his supply bag, he reached in and took out a chunk of salt pork. He nervously sliced off a thin piece of the pork and laid it over his wound. Then he took handfuls of dirt and mixed in a bit water from his water pouch to make a mud pack. He slapped a handful of mud over the top of the salt pork, took a strip of green elk hide from his possibles bag and wrapped it tightly around the wound and under his arm pit. He cut two pieces of fringe from his shirt, tied them together, and wrapped it around his arm several times to hold the poultice in place.

"Now, varmint, it's my turn," he said with half a grin.

He took his skinning knife and ran it under the skin of the rattler's belly, pulling the skin from the snake as he went the entire length. He cut the rattles off and counted them twice. There were twelve. He thought to himself that if he lived through this, those rattles would bring a nice price in barter. He put them in his bag and sat down against the rock to rest.

Buffler was quite aware of the fact that he could die from such a bite. He knew that to live could be one heck of a lot harder than dying, and that dying would not be without one heck of a lot of pain. The only thing he could do to prepare for what was coming, was to eat something; anything that would build his strength for the misery that he would surely experience.

He moved slowly and methodically so as not to speed the effects of the poison. With flint and steel, he struck a spark to his tinder and blew softly until it ignited. The flaming tinder was laid to the ground and sprigs of sage brush and bark were gently added until he had a usable fire. Slowly he roasted the meaty strips peeled from the snakes carcass.

The poison was beginning to affect his movement as well as his vision. He ate two strips of the rattlesnake and drank a lot of water from his leather water bag. He was exhausted. He lay back and instantly fell into a deep sleep.

There were brief moments that he regained consciousness, during the first night. He was sweating, yet un-controllably shaking from the cold. Heat radiated from his upper body and his head was pounding in pain. His thoughts were inconsistent and unpredictable, and his dreams came from a very dark side. A crazing fever had taken hold as his body fought the spreading invasion of the serpents venomous poison.

A buffalo's got me pinned to the ground. It's standin' on my chest. I can see Pilgrim over there. Yes, it's him a standin' over there by his packhorse. Help, Pilgrim! I'm yellin' out, but he can't hear me. The weight of the buffalo is pushin' the wind outta my lungs. I can't move, he thought. Then he passed out.

The fever caused delirium and took total control of his every thought. His body jerked with involuntary muscle spasms. The victim was writhing in agonizing pain.

Two full days had passed, and Buffler was still unconscious and in a deep sleep. Both of his horses had pulled free from the brush from which they were tied, and were feeding near by on some of the skimpy grasses the prairie had to offer.

At mid day on the third afternoon following the incident, Buffler began to resume consciousness. Slowly he opened his eyes and rolled over on his back. He moaned from the pains of muscle stiffness attributed to the hard ground, rather than the poison. Cognition was slow to enter his mind, until he realized he had messed his trousers. That spurned urgency to grasp his thoughts and make sense of his situation.

"Well, I'm still alive," he commented with some surprise in his voice.

His shoulder was now the center of his pain and the smell that came from his poultice gave him reason for his concern. He cut the poultice free and carefully lifted it from the wound. The blackened wound turned his stomach. It was apparent that the rotting flesh around the bite had provided a perfect environment for onset of his infection. Without hesitation, Buffler built a small fire to burn off his knife. He changed his leathers and cleaned the excrement from his trousers with a bit water and a handful of prairie grasses. He laid the trousers over a rock to dry as the knife reddened in the fire. With dreaded pause, he took the red-hot steel blade of the knife and laid it against the open wound. The pain was unbearable. Buffler fell to the ground and once again fell unconscious.

When he regained consciousness, the pain from the cauterization remained. He was slow to collect his thoughts and rested for several hours before he attempted to catch his horses and prepare a meal for the void that caused a rumbling in his stomach. He toiled assiduously over both tasks.

The next morning, Buffler gathered his belongings and headed east. The thoughts he had during his feverish state, stuck in his head like a bad dream. He was distraught by the thought that Pilgrim had made accusations that he was in some way ruining Pilgrim's life.

Buffler was bound and determined to straighten things out with Pilgrim. He knew where exactly where Pilgrim was headed, and set off in the direction of the morning sun. He held that course for the next ten days. He was obsessed with finding Pilgrim.

Chapter 3

Pilgrim stayed on an easterly trail for eighteen days after leaving Buffler at the foothills on the east side of the Rocky Mountains. The weather allowed him quick and easy travel, since the spring weather brought little rain, just warm temperatures.

Supplies were running short by the seventh day. His need to replenish his supplies took precedent over all other matters. He knew of a trading outpost that was only a four-day ride away. There he would be able to trade the furs that he trapped the previous winter.

Pilgrim eased upon a mesa overlooking a large rocky coulee. At the bottom of the coulee was a water hole that would surely entice the wiliest of animals. He left his horses at the top of the mesa and with his Hawkin rifle in hand, dropped over the edge of the mesa rim and crept his way to within a hundred yards of the water hole. He found a boulder on the down wind side of the water hole that allowed for the perfect ambush point to take an unsuspecting animal.

He waited with consequential patience and determination. The sun was on its afternoon descent in the western sky. Soon, the animals would be on the move and the area around the water would soon be transformed into an oasis of animal activity. A small antelope was the first to appear, followed by two larger ones. A buck antelope sojourned the trail of the does, but was disinclined to come in as quickly.

Pilgrim slowly readied his Hawkin rifle in the direction of the water hole. He anticipated the movements of the buck and took aim, placing the iron sights in line with the antelope's front shoulder. He waited for the best broadside shot that the buck might offer, and at the closest yardage. Cautiously, and with reluctance similar to that of a snail in a forest fire, the buck eased his way closer to the boulder where Pilgrim concealed himself. Seventy-five yards seemed to be the best shot opportunity that he was going to get, so he put a fine sight on the animal, pulled the set trigger and squeezed ever so lightly for the shot. The muzzle flared with smoke and caterwauled a loud blast that thundered through the coulee abruptly breaking the silence. Pilgrim raised his rifle and dropped his head slightly to peer under the rising smoke to see if the shot had met its intended mark. The antelope almost instantly fell topsy-turvy on its haunches and tried in last effort to regain its footing. The other antelopes were scuttling and bouncing for the open range in their usual startled stot.

Pilgrim vaulted to his feet and straightaway went for his powder horn to reload. After shoving the round ball into the muzzle, he drove it home with his ram-rod, yet never once took his eyes off his quarry as he approached. The antelope was down and by the time he reached it, he was sure it would remain.

Pilgrim stood over the buck for a moment and mumbled a few words of thanks to God, the Great Spirit, Creator of all things that allowed this for him. He looked the animal over and knelt to its side, pulled his knife from its beaded sheath and removed the animals entrails, keeping only the heart and liver and discarding everything else. He hoisted the limp carcass to his shoulders and started up the animal trail from the bottom of the coulee to the mesa edge where he left his horses.

When he reached the top of the coulee rim and looked for his horses, but they were nowhere in sight. The tracks in the area where the horses were left showed signs of other horses. He counted tracks of at least three other horses and the moccasin tracks of two. He contemplated the theft of his belongings and concluded that a Cheyenne hunting party had heard the retort of his rifle and approached from the mesa. Having seen the horses, they helped their savage, thieving selves to his goods.

Pilgrim knew he had to move, and move fast if he was going to get his horses back. He begrudgingly dropped the antelope to the ground and hoped that some hungry coyote would feast on it rather than have it just lie there and rot away.

They could have had as much as a two-hour head start, he thought. He wasn't sure when or how long ago they were there.

Darkness was swiftly closing, concealing any sign left by the horses. Pilgrim had the direction well established and decided to continue on the same course. If he could just reach their camp before daylight he'd have a chance to get it all back. He also knew that if he did find them, they would fight to the death to keep their take.

Pilgrim paced himself at a fast walk and half run, not stopping even momentarily. He knew that he had to push hard through the night, all night, if he wanted to retrieve his possessions. The only rest he got were short breathers when he slowed his gait to an enduring walk while coercing his mind to allow him the extra energy and wind that his body and lungs needed.

Hours into his hard jaunt, and driven by his self-motivated determination, Pilgrim was beginning to feel the tension build in his shoulders and neck. At the same moment that his mind balked at his determined quest and he lapsed in hope of ever finding the thieves, his nose detected the faint odor of burning sage and the smell of horses. He knew he was getting close to the camp of villainous scoundrels whomever they might be.

As he closed in on the camp, he unremittingly was developing a plan to get his belongings by whatever means it took. He closed in from the downwind side of the camp. He could see the fire embers in the pitch of darkness surrounding the camp. One of the horses stirred, by his approach.

Pilgrim backed off and went to the east side of the camp for his approach. This would serve a two fold strategy; the horses wouldn't spook, and he'd wait for the morning sun to be in the faces of his adversaries.

First light was creeping its way just over the eastern horizon. It seemed like hours before he could barely make the outlines of four motionless figures around the smoldering remains of the campfire. Pilgrim studied the camp over for any unseen dangers that might be encountered before he went trouncing in for retaliation.

He wanted to strike when the sun was up and shining, but the horizon was to high for an early sunrise, and he could see that they were already showing signs of movement and beginning to wake. About the time he was finalizing his plans, a turkey cut loose with a gobble within fifty paces of the camp. This stirred the camp with silent commotion. They rolled from their blankets and reached for their bows without a verbal sound. The action surprised Pilgrim, and it all happened so quickly that without even thinking, he too, jumped to his feet. He bolted right straight into the camp, flaring his arms in all directions, and yelling obscenities about stupid thievin' Injuns.

The closest brave was so taken and surprised that he got his feet twisted up in his blanket, lost his balance, and fell, face first into the smoldering fire. The one on the far side of the camp had already reached his bow and was in the process of knocking an arrow when Pilgrim lowered his rifle and pulled the trigger. The Indian was catapulted against a tree, from the force of the muzzle-loader's ball as it pierced his beaded chest plate.

Pilgrim kept going and never let his eyes stray. He was seeing the whole thing unfold as if he were on the outside looking in. He pulled his pistol from his belt, cocked, aimed, and fired at the youngest brave, to his right. The shot was to the face. His head exploded from the forceful impact.

He dropped his rifle and reached for his throwing knife and with unremitting motion hurled it at the chest of the third long-haired savage. The knife hit its mark and buried itself handle deep in the heart of its victim.

The fat, awkward Indian that stumbled, was still trying to get his feet untangled. Pilgrim, grimaced a threatening stare at the last remaining thief. The Indian, yelling wildly, attempted to swing his tomahawk at Pilgrim. Pilgrim stepped aside as he clutched his arm on the down stroke, and twisted the buck's arm behind his back. He tore the tomahawk from the hand of his opponent, and made a full swing, forcing the cutting edge under the ribs on the Indians left side.

He fell silently as the air rushed from his lung at the site of the wound. Pilgrim dropped to his knees, sighed a deep breath, and wiped his brow.

"Dang thievin' fools," he said with a gasp.

Pilgrim went through the camp, picking up everything that was his. He found several fur hides that belonged to the Indians, and felt that the furs and the fresh venison hanging in the tree were now his. They wouldn't need it, and besides they owed it to him for the trouble they had caused.

He packed his horse, stripped the Indian ponies and turned them loose. No white man ever had a use for the wild streak that all Indian ponies possessed. The Redskins trained their ponies with bad habits that could never be changed, especially by a white man.

Pilgrim mounted his horse and headed toward the rising sun. He followed a shallow stream for several miles, making sure that the horses kept their footing in the creek. He half-heartedly tried to cover his tracks just in case a scouting party came across the ravaged Indian camp. He knew that when it was discovered that retribution would be ordered on the trespasser. Pilgrim rode hard for three days, stopping only to eat and when nature called. He put as much time and distance between him and that camp as possible. He wanted to forget the entire incident.

Pilgrim finally entered what he thought was the western edge of the Oklahoma Territory, at least he'd always thought of it as the Territory. He felt confident that his trail was cold enough that not even the best trackers could have kept up with him. He had about half a day's ride to reach the trading outpost.

Pilgrim slowed his pace for peace of mind and rest for his horses. The skies were clear, and for the first time since the weather broke.

He noticed the clean, fresh smell of spring, and the new life in nature that was there for his pleasure, if a person would take the time to observe and enjoy it.

When he reached the outpost, he wasted no time hitching his horses to the tie posts, and advanced toward the front door. The front door swung open as a deep voice called out from within. "Well, if it ain't Zen Bragg. Hain't seen ya fer near two year," said the burley proprietor.

"Been out West," Pilgrim replied.

"Where's yer squaw?" the owner asked.

"Traded 'er," Pilgrim replied.

"Hell, you'd trade yer soul if ya thought there'd be a profit in it," wisecracked the proprietor.

Pilgrim ducked his head as he entered the dark confines of the trading post. He glanced around the room and saw three, obscure figures setting around the table in the center of the room. Without being too obvious he tried to focus his eyes to the dimly lit room by gazing around at the shelved merchandise.

"Got any powder, Ulysses?" Pilgrim asked the proprietor, knowing that he always had a supply of powder.

"Sure do; the finest grade ther' is in this here part a' the territory," replied Ulysses, as he pointed out the window to a small shed behind the post. "Got it in one-, three-, five-pound bags, and 20- pound hogsheads."

Pilgrim's eyes were adjusting to the light. "How 'bout some hot vittles?" he inquired. He then took the last available seat at the table.

"I'll fix ya right up," responded Ulysses.

The other patrons remained mute as each chagrined, glances at the newcomer. Pilgrim too, was examining each of the three with bold and intense stares, in a way that most people would find discomfiting, as did the three sitting at the table.

The older lady finally spoke out. "May I help you, young man?" she said in an incensed tone.

"Reckon not, ma'am," Pilgrim calmly countered.

Pilgrim remained quiet as several uncomfortable moments of silence passed. He continued to gape around the table, especially gawking at the young lady that sat across from him. The other immigrant was an older man that Pilgrim logically assumed was the husband of the older lady that seemed to be infuriated by Pilgrim's apparent lack of manners.

Ulysses broke the awkwardness of the moment when he brought a steaming-hot bowl of beans and a big chunk of cornbread to Pilgrim.

"Ther' ya go, Zen," Ulysses said. He placed the bowl in front of him.

Pilgrim crumbled the cornbread in the bean bowl and stirred it slightly before taking the first bite. He no more put the that first bite in his mouth when he asked the old man if they were Easterners.

The old man pushed his plate aside, looked at Pilgrim, and started in, "Well, no, not exactly. We're from Minnesota. We lost our farm when it burned to the ground about two months back. We lost everything we owned. My brother wrote last year about the farm he has in Texas and how open the land is and how easy it is to homestead. We decided to pack up what was left and go there for a new start. We haven't been properly introduced," the farmer interjected.

"This here is my wife, Pauline," the old man said as he motioned in the direction of his wife across the table. "This is my daughter Rebecca. I am Gabe Coleman," he said, as he offered his hand to the pilgrim.

Pilgrim's head nodded approval, but his eyes remained on his bowl of beans. He scooped up another bite, and ignored the offer. The farmer showed some concern as he cast a look at his wife.

When Pilgrim finished his meal, he slowly raised his head and focused his attention to Rebecca. "This is pretty rough country fer a young lady such as you," he remarked.

Gabe, looking a bit withdrawn and concerned by his comment, responded by saying, "We'll do all right for ourselves."

"What's your name, young man? I seem to have forgotten what Mr. Ulysses called you," Pauline blared out.

"My friends call me Pilgrim; but my given name is Zen, Zen Bragg ma'am. Just don't see many farmers from Minnesota in these parts. No disrespect intended," Pilgrim said.

The conversation seemed to die at that point.

"What you got to trade, Zen?" inquired Ulysses. He seemed to be obviously interested and anxious to get on with the trading. Ulysses thrived on trading. It was his quest in life to get the best deal possible and obtain more in dollar value than he ever gives in return. Ulysses was a shrewd trader and was known throughout the Territory as a hard man to best when it came to trading. Pilgrim had heard it said that Ulysses was tighter than round ball in a shrunken barrel.

"Got some furs, herbs, and a few nuggets," Pilgrim hesitantly responded. He pushed away from the table and sauntered toward the door without uttering another word.

Pilgrim returned with one large pack bundled in a single elk hide and bound with a hemp rope. He threw it onto the merchant's counter top, pulled his knife and cut the tie rope to one side of the knot. The bundle expanded from released tension. He unfolded the hide, exposing his collection of trade worthy merchandise.

As Ulysses poked through the pack scrutinizing every item, Pilgrim went from shelf to shelf gathering the a few of the commodities that he would need for the next several months. Pilgrim gathered up 20 pounds of sugar,20 pounds of flour, two 40 pound bags of beans, fifteen pounds of salt pork, two twenty pound bags of salt, .550 caliber lead balls, one yard of pillow tick for rifle patches, 20 pounds of coffee beans, five bottles of whiskey, 10 plugs of chewing tobacco, and a jar of sorghum.

"I'll need a twenty-pound cask of yer powder," he added.

"Whoa there, Bragg!" hollered Ulysses. "You ain't got near enuff goods ta put a lid on this barter."

"What's it goin' ta take, Ulysses?" mused Pilgrim.

"Well, let's see. Ya got two brain-tanned elk, one elk hide with hair. Two deer hides with hair, four brain-tanned deer, eight beaver, two Cheyenne tomahawks, three Cheyenne beaded chest straps, three Cheyenne hunting knives, and four Cheyenne pony blankets. I figure you still owe me about forty dollars worth of trade items," commanded Ulysses.

"How much in gold?" questioned Pilgrim.

"Aw, I'd hafta have at least two ounces," Ulysses demanded.

"One," Pilgrim shouted without hesitation.

Ulysses was caught off guard. He didn't expect that response so quickly and was dumbstruck at the offer. Pilgrim now had the upper hand of the deal.

"One ounce, or I start pullin' the Injun stuff back!" threatened Pilgrim. He added nonsense arm gestures, making the threat seem even more serious than it sounded.

"Oh, okay," agreed Ulysses. "Ya caught me on a good day."

Pilgrim pulled a small leather bag from under his belt, untied the leather thong that held it in place, and proceeded to pull the pouch open. He held it over Ulysses' scales and proceeded to shake the glittering gold dust in the scale tray. He stopped when the scale arm started to lower.

"Keep going, keep going," Ulysses repeated several times.

The scales finally tipped to the point of perfect balance, and Ulysses' expression turned to disappointment at such a small-looking ounce of gold.

Pilgrim on the other hand, cinched the top of his pouch and perceived the scales to have tipped with far too much of his cache.

Neither man disagreed with the scales. The measured offer sealed the deal and was accepted by both men with a final shake of the hands in agreement.

"Let's have a round a drinks ta ratify it," Ulysses offered, as he reached for one of the bottles that Pilgrim had picked from the shelf for his stock.

Pilgrim's hand was faster to the bottle. "Sure, let's do have that drink, but let's have it frum a bottle that's owned by the man thet offered it," Pilgrim said in haste.

"Yaw, yaw, 'tis what I meant," Ulysses cautiously responded, as he gazed into the stern facial expression that Pilgrim displayed so masterfully.

"Mr. Bragg, are those real Indian things?" Rebecca questioned. Her voice wavered as if she had trouble searching for the courage to ask.

"Yeah, thievin' Injuns at that," retorted Pilgrim.

"Did you ka…kill them?" asked Rebecca. She turned away and lowered her head as if she was afraid to hear the answer.

"Had to," was Pilgrim's quick response. He showed no emotion or remorse.

"Had to. You had to," Pauline repeated herself. "You stole their belongings and killed for your own personal gain, and say you had to."

"You're hell bound for your sins, young man," Pauline intensely interjected as she waved her hand above her head and pointed to the sky. "Vengeance is mine, sayeth the Lord."

She no more got the last word out when Pilgrim's rebuttal came quickly, calmly. In a soft, low tone he said, "Maybe so, ma'am, and when I get ther', I'll let ya show me around. I'm sure at yer age you'll git ther' first, and if fer no other reason, be it fer the judgment yer a makin' on me now."

Her resounding gasp fully demonstrated her perplexity. She jerked her head back and rested her frail body back in her chair, as revolt and astonishment cleared the expression on her face.

"No offense meant, Mr. Bragg. Pauline didn't mean any disrespect," Gabe apologetically replied as he perused Pauline with a scowl of disapproval.

"None taken," countered Pilgrim.

"Pauline, you and Rebecca better pick out a few supplies so we can get on our way," said Gabe. It was obvious that he was changing the course of the conversation.

Both Pauline and Rebecca silently acquiesced by politely excusing themselves from the table. They both walked to the merchandise shelves and proceeded to sift through the wares.

Pilgrim gathered his procurement and toted several loads outside to his packhorse. He carefully positioned every item in order to distribute the weight evenly on his pack horse's back. Ulysses went around back to get the twenty-pound hogshead of powder that was included in Pilgrim's trade. Gabe went to his Conestoga, with a two-horse team, to check the rig for any needed repairs.

Pilgrim was the first to complete his preparations. He took one last look around the post for anything he may have forgotten. He was content with his purchases, but momentarily hesitated when Gabe approached.

"You all watch yerselves. 'Tis a unsettled country out ther'," Pilgrim said in a voice loud enough for the women to hear.

"Sure will, and you take care of yourself, too," replied Gabe.

Pilgrim nodded his head and turned for the door. He sauntered his way to his horses, made a few final adjustments to his packhorse's cargo, raised his head as if testing the wind. He mounted his horse and looked at the farmers covered wagon. His insensate thoughts were justification for shaking his head as he tugged the reins to turn his horse.

Chapter 4

Pilgrim headed south from the post, at a steady even pace. In a short time he found himself in his buffalo hunting area, and wasn't in need of thing other than buffalo migration to begin. He scouted in a large half-circle pattern for several days, looking for buffalo sign. This area had always produced buffalo in past seasons, and he saw no immediate reason or cause for concern. The buffalo had be somewhere in the area this time of the year. All he had to do was locate them.

Several hours into his search, Pilgrim stopped next at a prairie stream flowing with clear, fresh water trickling over its pebble pathway. He had a growing disconcerted feeling and couldn't understand why it was taking him such a long time to find the buffalo herd.

As he reached in his pack for a chunk of pemmican, he bumped one of the whiskey bottles that he so carefully packed away at the post. Pilgrim pulled it out with a smile, he thought to himself that the day was much too pleasant to be waste away by negative thoughts.

Pilgrim sat by the cascading brook, held the top of the bottle to his mouth, grabbed the cork stopper between his teeth and popped it open. As he took his first sip from the bottle, he thought to himself that if he went further west, he'd surely cut a migratory path of the buffalo possibly within less than two-days' ride. Then he could follow it north or south, depending on the tracks left by the herd. He was about to take his third sip of libation when he observed a single column of smoke over the distant rise to the west. The smoke was rising to a black cloud that was forming at the top of the column and being carried off by the subtle prairie breezes. This brought him to his feet posthaste. He thoughtlessly tucked his things back into his pack, jumped on his horse, and rode in the direction of the billowing smoke. As he approached the final little rise between him and the source of the smoke, he hesitated with a sense of caution that was building inside him with increased anxiety. He jumped from his horse before it came to a halt. Vigilantly he advanced to the crest of the rise just in time to see half a dozen Indian ponies running to the summit of the far hill on the horizon.

Between Pilgrim and the departing band Indians he could see the source of the black smoke. Without question he recognized the burning remains of farmer Coleman's Conestoga wagon. Pilgrim vaulted to his horses back and bolted toward the blazing wreckage.

The wagon was swallowed in smoky flames. Both horses were down, with several arrows protruding from their carcasses. They were contorted and grotesquely positioned in a mass of twisted harness. Pauline lay half naked, next to an open trunk and piles of strewn clothing and other scattered personal effects that lay smoldering from the hot ashes that had fallen from the burning wagon. Pilgrim protected his face from the heat with his arm and pulled Pauline's body from the inferno.

Gabe Coleman was about fifty yards away with ten or more arrows projecting from his torso. Both Gabe and Pauline were grotesquely cut from the forehead to the top of the head, scalped, as the Indians had been taught by French trappers.

Pilgrim tried to examine the inside of the blazing wagon for any sign of Rebecca. He didn't think that the savages would have killed her. She was young and worth more to them alive. Pilgrim's grim thoughts took him back to his comment to Pauline back at the trading post. He remembered telling her that she might just beat him to hell. If he had ever had a Christian thought run through his heart it was at that moment. His penitence was unclear to him, but he silently hoped he was wrong about that. He wanted desperately to give the farmer and his wife a Christian burial, but if he was ever to get Rebecca back from the Indians, he had to pursue their murderers straightway.

He headed in pursuit with the same speed that the assailants left the scene. He rode his horses long and arduously until a lather of sweat and strained breathing made it obvious that the horses were being overworked. His desire to catch the marauders nearly overwhelmed his obligation to walk his weary horses for a short breather. He knew that they wouldn't be pushing their ponies as hard as they could, but if he could press on at a steady pace, he'd catch up with them sooner or later.

During the slow forward progress of his stalking and trailing efforts, the thought of even a short lead seemed an endless pursuit and an eternal chase. His packhorse was having the hardest time carrying the fresh load of supplies. For a moment Pilgrim considered leaving her behind, so that he could move at quicker pace. If he did, he took the chance of losing her on the prairie, or worse yet, someone could once again happen along and steal her. He knew that he'd catch them soon. He persisted the antagonizing pursuit of Rebecca's captors and often found himself contemplating what mighty lie in wait and the terrible things the Indians would do to her.

Pilgrim couldn't see anything ahead of him but rolling prairie. *Perhaps they're in a low area,* he thought. At times he thought he tasted their dust, and from the tracks left in the soft sands on the trail, he sensed their nearness. He could see by the tracks that the group of Indian ponies had finally slowed to walk. *They've slowed their pace,* he thought.

Pilgrim would have to surprise them, and that was going to be very difficult on an open prairie. He turned his horse and angled away from trail. The Indians would watch their back trail. If he could catch up to them from the side, or better yet circle around them, he might get the opportunity to lie in wait and surprise them in ambush.

Pilgrim finally saw their dust. Now was the time to keep a low profile and ride as hard as he could to cut them off. He knew the area. About a half hour's ride would put them at a water hole near a grove of scrub pine and boulders, where they most likely would set up camp.

Pilgrim stopped only long enough to tie his packhorse off to a clump of sage. He had to move fast. He got around the primal party and took his stronghold at the water hole using the surrounding boulders as his bulwark. In short time the throng of unsuspectingly riders appeared, and advanced single file. Rebecca was on the third of seven horses in the queue. A strong, bronze-skinned Indian held her tight around the waist in front of him on his horse. The second and fifth riders each held lances with the scalps of her murdered parents tied to the shafts. Pilgrim waited for them to dismount their horses and group up. He had accounted for all them.

Rebecca's hands were tied in front. She fell to the ground when the Indian halfheartedly assisted her dismount by holding tight to the front of her blouse. Once she fell loose from his hold, she scooted herself to one side, as far as she could, away from her aggressor. Now was Pilgrim's chance.

Pilgrim's first shot was with his pistol; cleanly placing the shot in the chest of the closest bronze-skinned Indian. Before any of them could react to the attack, Pilgrim raised his rifle and shot another Brave through his chest, and a third man also fell when the ball passed cleanly through the chest of the man standing in front of him, and lodged deep his vitals. As the two simultaneously fell to the ground, Pilgrim reloaded, and took yet another before the remainder of the Indians cleared their minds enough to grasp the surprise attack.

One of the savages ran at Pilgrim, with tomahawk raised and yelling wildly, as Pilgrim strove to load his rifle again. Pilgrim thrust his gun barrel into his combatant's chest throwing him off balance and to the ground. The Indian was shuffling to gain a foothold, but Pilgrim kicked him in the face, and the Indian fell back crashing his head into a boulder, sounding like that of a dry stick breaking. His lifeless body fell limp. Pilgrim fell behind some rocks from his lack of balance. He lost sight of the other two momentarily, and a lapse in time with a sudden calm allowed him time he needed to reload his pistol.

Pilgrim started to move toward Rebecca's location when he heard movement to one side. He turned with his pistol at his side just in time to shove it in the stomach of the on-comer.

He pulled the trigger and the muffled blast sent the Indian to his knees, then face down to dusty ground. The last Indian mounted his pony and attempted to escape the commotion. His direction of his escape was partially blocked from Pilgrim's view by the fortress of boulders.

Pilgrim readied his rifle, took careful aim and lightly squeezed the trigger. The primer ignited, but the anticipated blast did not transpire. His Hawkin rifle misfired. The Indian fled unscathed.

Pilgrim went to Rebecca and offered her his hand as she tried to get to her feet. Her fear was so deeply imprinted in her expression that Pilgrim was apprehensive in his approach. His solacing attempts were slowly and calmly spoken. "Yer okay now," he assured her. "They can't hurt ya now."

Rebecca's woebegone expression guided Pilgrim's consoling efforts into compassionate dialect based primarily with concern for her well-being. This was unfamiliar territory for Pilgrim, and he handled it somewhat awkwardly.

"Did they hurt ya?" he uttered without really thinking. "We gotta go. One of 'em got away, and he'll bring 'em all back lookin' fer us," Pilgrim advised.

He led one of the Indian ponies to her side. He cut the rawhide strips that bound her hands, and assisted her to the horse's back. "Kin ya ride?" he asked, with a disconcerted expression.

Rebecca nodded a promise of assurance. He wasn't sure how the pony would take to being led, so he held the lead strap in his hand. If there were troubles, he would be able to react better to the situation. The horse, after a few minor objections, clearly demonstrating the typical obstinate signs common to that of a well trained Indian pony, began to accept the circumstances.

Pilgrim took a direction opposite the fleeing Indian. He back-tracked on the same trail from where the had come. He left the main trail just long enough to pick up his packhorse. Time and distance were their only hope of eluding an avenging attack by the Indians who were sure to return with more braves than Pilgrim could handle by himself. Their only chance for survival would be in their ability to flee to safety.

Pilgrim and Rebecca traveled at a steady pace throughout the night and all the next day. The second night they took refuge from a hard spring rain among some deadfall cedars. Pilgrim threw a couple of hides over the downed tree tops and both sojourners crawled into the improvised shelter. Rebecca was gradually gaining her composure, and was cognizant of what was taking place around her. Pilgrim felt at ease when she meekly related her hunger to him. He rolled his pack around searching for a variety of foods to offer her. Pemmican, elk jerky, and a handful of dried apples were the best that he could offer without chancing a camp fire.

"Sorry I ain't got somethin' better," he uttered apologetically, as he handed her a bit of each.

"Thank you, sir," she responded.

Rebecca huddled tightly inside the blanket that Pilgrim wrapped around her and blankly gazed off into the darkness. She subconsciously picked at the jerky, and tears started streaming down her cheeks.

Pilgrim sat quietly he had no words of comfort for Rebecca. He didn't know what to say. He thought about the events of the day and contemplated long into the night about what the approaching day would bring. He glanced over at Rebecca and saw that she had fallen asleep, still clutching the jerky. He, too, was exhausted. He pulled the wool blanket up around his shoulders, slumped forward, and rested his head on his arms that were folded across his knees.

Morning seemed slow in coming. The rain proceeded to deluge the countryside. Even though the cold rain was discomforting and miserably dispiriting, Pilgrim felt at ease knowing that the rain was washing their tracks from the prairie trail.

He realized that a direction of travel they first set would establish a general direction. It was time to change direction while the rain could obscure any traces of their tracks. They headed northwest and remained on that course for several days. The rain continued.

Chapter 5

Buffler was approaching the Oklahoma Territory just about the time the rains ceased. He was headed for the outpost when he blundered upon the decomposed bodies of the four Indians. Had it not been for the fragrant spring rains of the prairie, the odor surrounding that camp would have been dreadful. He could only surmise that the attack on this camp came as a surprise to the Indians. Coyotes, buzzards, and porcupines had ravaged the bodies. He also determined that their defeat was accomplished by white-men. He knew that because they all had their scalps.

Buffler could tell from their leathers that these Indians were Cheyenne Dog Soldiers. What he couldn't understand was why they were so far to the east. Black Kettle, the Cheyenne Chief, declared peace in 1864 and had settled in the Colorado Territory.

Buffler reached the outpost by midmorning two days later. The post seemed to be securely closed. He remained mounted on his horse and yelled out for Ulysses. There was no immediate answer. Nothing stirred. He looked around and noticed that there wasn't a single horse or any other animals that normally roamed his property. The post's door was closed tight and the window shutters were secured. He dismounted and tied his horses to a post nearest the front door. The door was bolted from the inside, as were the windows.

Buffler walked around back, and noticed the little powder shed, privy, and chicken shed. He started toward the powder shed when Ulysses came busting out. It startled Buffler so badly that he lunged like a heart-shot buck.

"What the hell?" yelled Buffler.

"I'm glad ta see yooou!" Ulysses bellowed.

"What's goin' on, Ulysses?" asked Buffler.

"Injuns!" he replied. "Dad blame Injuns. They came a stormin' in here and found all that stuff I traded yer partner fer."

"What stuff ya talkin' about, and what partner ya referrin' to? Pilgrim?" Buffler asked.

"Yeah, Zen Bragg, Pilgrim, that be him," Ulysses responded. "Them Indians walked out with it all. I thought sure they'd kill me, burn me out, or somethin'. Guess they figgered I'd be easy pickin's if they just let me live. They took the stuff en' left; took my horses, too."

"So what's the problem now? Thur gone, ain't they?" quipped Buffler.

"Well, don't rightly know. Two of 'em's been stayin' round, and that was three days ago. I locked the post up and crawled through the tunnel to the chicken house. I figgered they'd burn the post. Ain't never heard of 'em burnin' a chicken shed. Let me go back in and open up, an' I'll tell ya the rest a' the story," said Ulysses as he walked to the shed where the tunnel led him back to the post.

He opened the back door and let Buffler in. Ulysses wasted no time telling him about Pilgrim, the farmer, Gabe Coleman, his wife, Pauline, and their daughter, Rebecca; and how he traded for Indian belongings. He told Buffler that Pilgrim and the others left at different times, but he added that they all ended up going in the same basic direction.

Buffler knew exactly where Pilgrim was headed. *Three-days' ride,* he thought, Buffalo Pass. He decided to spend the night; dry some of his things out in the afternoon sun, put a couple of good hot meals under his belt, sleep in a real bunk. He thought the sound of a hot bath in a real tub might help too.

Buffler woke up the next morning to a cabin full of black choking smoke. When he gathered his senses he jumped to his feet and called for Ulysses. The post was apparently burning from the outside. Both Ulysses and Buffler scrambled for their belongings and headed for the back door. When they flung the door open, there were two Indians ransacking the powder shed. Buffler instinctively took one with his rifle and the other with his pistol. Buffler and Ulysses ran for cover behind the powder shed.

"'Re these them Injuns ya tellin' me about, Ulysses?" Buffler asked.

"Nope, them were Cheyenne. These is Sioux," Ulysses said. "Must be thet yer partner's out ther a-takin' a stick ta ther' hive. He's got all of 'em stirred up like hornets."

The fire was nothing more than some old bean sacks soaked in some coal oil, and it quickly burned itself out.

"'Twern't much of a fire," Ulysses observed.

"Naw, jest a lot a smoke to get us out. Ther's too much useable stuff in ther' for them Injuns to burn it all up," responded Buffler. Buffler walked straight through the post to the front door to see if his horses were still there.

"Ya think ther's more out ther'?" queried Ulysses.

"Naw," Buffler stated matter of factly. "If they was more, they'd a-taken my horses. Prob'ly be more come later, though. Sioux 're determined folks; send only one er two at a time, but keep at it 'til they git what they want. Meaner than rattlesnakes, en' they's a lift yer hair in a heartbeat, iffen ya let 'em. Ulysses, maybe ya oughtta go with me."

"Nope, can't do it. Been her' twenty-some years and ain't lettin' no fool Injuns run me offen my own place. Why, I'll have 'em stacked out ther' like cordwood fer a fireplace," boasted Ulysses.

Buffler gathered a few supplies and settled up with Ulysses.

"Watch yer backside," Ulysses said.

"You too," replied Buffler. He walked out the front door of the post and proceeded to mount his horse and leaned over to untie his pack horse. He wrapped the lead around his saddle horn and made his departure.

Word traveled rather slowly in the West, and what information did get around was generally outdated and almost always exaggerated.

Buffler was right that Black Kettle had declared a peace with the whites in 1864, but soon after that a white soldier by the name of Chevington was led to Black Kettle's encampment on the Sand Creek in the Colorado Territory. Chevington's Indian guide was a Cheyenne named Robert Bent. Bent was lied to about Chevington's intentions.

Chevington rode into the camp on a cold and icy night late in 1864 with 700 soldiers and massacred some 200 Cheyenne men, women, and children. Black Kettle escaped the massacre and went north to the Dakota Territory with the other survivors. Robert Bent, after that incident, joined the Cheyenne Dog Soldiers who had joined forces with the Sioux and Arapaho, thus declaring that all whites were enemies.

Buffler was being followed at a distance. He had sensed it for several hours. When he reached a rocky, sage-covered wash, he hid his horses and back-trailed through some vegetative cover along the trail. There he waited to see who was following and for what purpose.

Two braves were so riveted to Buffler's tracks that they paid little attention to the trail in front of them. Buffler let them get to within pistol range before he made his move. When the sound of his rifle rang out, one of the Indians took the fall. Both horses danced to the report of the shot.

The other brave charged in Buffler's direction, and having spotted him, established his mark.

Buffler raised his pistol and fired the round in the direction of the approaching enemy. His shot missed. The brave leaped from his sprinting horse and pounced on Buffler before he could react.

The force of the body contact knocked Buffler's guns to the ground. They both jostled for position and struggled to gain a solid foothold. Their strength extended through their arms and fingers to the grasp on their opponents' leather shirts. The Indian's tomahawk was tied to his wrist, but swung free and out of control.

Buffler let go of the Indian's shirt and grabbed the tomahawk with both hands and lifted his arms as high as he could reach. His healing shoulder drastically limited his movements. At the same time he swept his leg from behind, catching the Indian's legs from the backside, he pulled his leg in as he pushed his opponent back, knocking him to the ground with a resounding thud.

Buffler hit him twice with the flat side of the tomahawk. He twisted his hands slightly and drove the bladed head of the weapon deep in the braves neck. Blood gushed from the Brave's fatal wound and spurted all over Buffler's forearms and left knee. The Indian's arms fell limp. His strength dissolved as quickly as the blood flow pulsed with the final few heartbeats.

Buffler paused momentarily and perused his arms as he sat straddle the braves chest. He unconsciously rubbed his strained shoulder as he stared at the Indian for a moment.

"Arapaho, Arapaho, dad blamed Arapaho. What ta heck is goin' on with these Injuns?" Buffler asked himself.

He jumped to his feet and started grabbing bits of sagebrush sprigs to wipe the blood from his arms and leg before it had a chance to dry. He washed his blood spotted leathers with water from his water pouch, until the scarlet stains had dissipated, leaving only the darkened color spots of wet leather.

He paused only long enough to survey the surrounding horizon for signs of other Indians in his pursuit, but realized that his anguish was created by his fears and not based on good judgment and an understanding of the ways of the Arapaho. They hunted in groups of twos, and it didn't matter if it were animals or enemies. It's not the way of the Arapaho to send more of their warriors in so soon, and once the word got back to them, Buffler would be considered a worthy enemy, respected and revered. He had just defeated two of their strongest braves, and so doing, deserved to be hunted in an orderly, well-planned, cautiously executed chase, much like the fox after the rabbit.

Buffler knew what to expect and thought he had best be making tracks away from these relentless pursuers. He hadn't seen any sign of Pilgrim, buffalo, or anything that held his particular interest to that part of the country any longer. He figured that if Pilgrim were in these parts, that he, too, had had some run ins with the Indians and for all he knew his partner could be laying somewhere out there with his hair already lifted.

He headed toward the setting sun, gave his horse a nudge in the ribs, and set out for the Rockies.

"Well, Pilgrim, iffen yer still alive, I'll see ya back at this 'ere rendezvous spot come fall," he said to himself.

Chapter 6

Pilgrim and Rebecca had traveled for three days when they came upon a small fort-like settlement comprised primarily of lost Easterners and gold-seeking prospectors. It was clear to him that this temporary settlement had been there for a considerable length of time. They appeared troubled, and the community was rife with signs of permanency. A wooden framed saloon, as in most Western settlements, was the first permanently constructed building; the rest of the town was normally built around it. Two sets of wooden sidewalks went out in each of the four directions, and each was lined with threadbare canvas tents. A wagon-wide, rutted trail extended between the walkways to the timbered walls that surrounded the camp's perimeter. As they passed through the corridor of tents Pilgrim noticed the variety of odors that wafted from all directions and changed with each step the horses took. The aroma of frying bacon was the first smell that heightened his awareness to the odors' presence. The dank fetor rising from the wagon path was a musty combination of mud and manure that was instantly supplanted by the pleasing scent of someone's hickory-chip cook fire. As they approached the tavern, Pilgrim picked up on the sour smell of whiskey and the fragrance of the perfumes worn by the ladies of the saloon.

Pilgrim and Rebecca approached the hitching post to the side of the saloon where Pilgrim's sluggish, rigid body seemed to strain just getting off his horse. He tied the horses to the post and helped Rebecca off her mount. Both weary travelers seemed to linger as they glanced around the encampment as if they were arduously resolving their next move.

"I think we need some good hot grub," he uttered.

Rebecca momentarily deliberated, but followed his lead to the front of the saloon. The couple drew immediate attention the minute they walked through the swinging doors, and Rebecca's pale color went flush from the embarrassment of feeling out of place. Pilgrim wasn't bothered by what people thought of him and had the attitude that he had as much right to be there as anyone else. They walked to a table on the far side of the room and both took a seat.

The rest of the patrons continued with their prior activities, but most of them often glanced at both Pilgrim and Rebecca, as if a coyote were dining with a prairie chicken. They were awestruck by their appearance; and puzzled at their differences as unlikely companions.

One of several parlor ladies strolled to the table with an ostentatious twist in her walk. What'll it be, Mister? A lady for you and a milk for the youngin'? The whole place seemed to break out in a clamor of laughter that lasted only a few seconds, but to Rebecca, it seemed to unease her already nervous situation and heightened her uncontrollable blush.

Pilgrim gave a solemn stare around the room to all that were amused by the parlor maid's jest. The guffaw subsided with each new set of eyes that met Pilgrim's quizzical expression. Pilgrim's reply was a softly spoken whisper in the ear of the parlor maid, so soft that not even Rebecca could hear his reply. The parlor maid's response was one of surprise and embarrassment, and everyone including Rebecca wondered what was said. The lady solemnly went on with her duties and started preparing their meals without uttering another word to anyone.

Just as the meals were being served, a gentleman sitting at an adjacent table introduced himself as Oliver Loving. "This is my friend and cohort Charles Goodnight," Loving added.

For some unknown reason, Pilgrim seemed to looked at them both with considerable interest. He seemed intrigued. Perhaps he took interest in the way they presented themselves or the intellectual tones of their speech, or maybe it was the they were dressed; nevertheless, Pilgrim welcomed them to his table, and introduced Rebecca.

Oliver Loving started the conversation with several questions directed to Pilgrim's knowledge of the territory. Mr. Goodnight followed Loving's questions with a series of his own, but Goodnight seemed to be more interested in what the Indian situation was. Pilgrim and Rebecca listened to the gentlemen, and responded to the questions, but Pilgrim finally responded more in line with his character.

"Hold on ther' just a minute; whut's all this got ta do with Injuns, and whut railroad?" Pilgrim spouted off. He fidgeted uncomfortably in his seat.

"Why, Mr. Bragg, you don't know about the railroad coming West?" said Loving. Mr. Loving continued to tell about the railroad, starting with what had taken place in the last five years. "In 1862 the railroad coming West was held up at the Missouri River, and the Central Pacific Railroad coming out of Sacramento going east was hung up trying to get through the Sierra Nevada Mountains. Most everything was at a standstill for a couple of years; you know, with the unsettled Union States and the Confederacy States not seeing eye to eye on issues and the like.

"But, soon, after the end of the Civil War in 1865, the government decided there should be a US Continental Railroad crossing the states from the Atlantic Coast, through the territories, all the way to Sacramento on the Pacific Coast. The Central Pacific made little headway. In fact, they still haven't broken through the Sierras. The Chinese are doing most of the work. I heard that this last winter they lost over 1200 Chinamen to snow drifts. I also hear that it's a good possibility that they'll break through the mountains in the next six to nine months.

"The railroad out East, once it crossed the Missouri River, became known as the Union Pacific Railroad. Times were pretty hard after the war in '65, and the Confederate States had a lot of disease, little to eat other than flour and water biscuits called hardtack.

"Whiskey became a curse of the south; some of the out-of-work soldiers would sit around and pit red ants against black ants just to get things stirred up. The lucky boys were the one's that got jobs building the railroad. They started in 1865 and are still building as we speak. Here it is 1867, and they've gotten as far as Baldwin City, Kansas. This is what brought Charles and me here. We're cattle drivers. We've driven cattle from the north all the way to Texas and back up to the railroad for shipment back East. Last year Charles and I worked a herd of 2000 cattle with only sixteen other cowboys.

"Do you know anything about cattle, Mr. Bragg?" asked Charles. "No, I don't suppose you've spent much time around cattle, have you?" Charles said. He was shaking his head as he realized how stupid the question must have seemed.

"Well, Charles, what Mr. Bragg doesn't know about cattle I'm sure is more than compensated by his knowledge of the Indians and buffalo. Isn't that true, Mr. Bragg?" Oliver said with considerable assurance.

Pilgrim responded with a rather curious nod directed at both gentlemen. Mr. Loving continued with his accounts of recent happenings:

"The Indians have been stirred up ever since Chevington went on his Indian-killing rampage in 1864. Some people feel that it was justifiable, but I think he would be hard pressed to prove it. Chevington, along with his group of Colorado volunteers, called the Bloodless Third, literally massacred some two hundred men, women, and children at Sand Creek in the Colorado Territory, but Black Kettle escaped.

"Other so-called Indian fighters and buffalo hunters are causing even more unrest among the Indians. George Custer, Phillip Sheridan, Nelson Miles, and a buffalo hunter named Frank Mares are all storming the West for their own gains, both financially and politically.

George Custer does what he wants, when he wants, and seems to gain the approval of the government even for his mistakes. Custer is from Ohio and graduated from West Point at the bottom of his class. He was assigned as Commander of the 7th Cavalry. He violated the Fort Laramie Treaty in 1864 when he went to the Black Hills in the Dakota Territory and found gold, and that's why we have many settlements like this one moving into this area," stated Oliver.

"Custer's a wild horse without reins," interjected Charles Goodnight.

"We got word from one of his own men that just last week he shot his own horse in the back of its head while he was chasing a herd of buffalo," added Loving.

Oliver Loving continued with his story. "Sheridan and Miles are men who do what they're asked to do, but always seem to take things into their own hands, and both would rather fight than talk. They despise the Indians and won't rest until they're all dead or driven out. They are the kind of soldiers that will find someone or something to fight even after the Indians are gone.

"Frank Mare is another strange breed that really bothers us. He has made himself a business killing hundreds of buffalo, starting first to feed the railroad workers and then sending the carcasses back East on the railroad. Mare calls the buffalo his walking gold pieces. He gets three dollars a piece for a buffalo carcass and brags about his profit of two dollars and eighty cents each, since a single cartridge costs less than a single bit. Mare once boasted of having taken only 300 shots to kill 289 buffalo.

"In the last two years since the railroad has passed through the plains, over three million buffalo have been killed. And now Mare takes Easterners on hunting trips for buffalo and his business is doing well.

"Sheridan just recently got the Indian campaign started. About two weeks ago Lt. William Featherman, under Ferrington's command, led eighty of his men into a trap set by the Sioux, Arapaho, and the Cheyenne. The thoughts of an Indian war stimulated Featherman, and in his zeal, fell for the two Indian decoys that led him into a crushing battle, just a short ways from here.

"They were all killed and mutilated. Their ears, nose, and scalps were cut off, their skulls were crushed, and their internal organs were spread all over the area."

Rebecca winced at Oliver's story, and her eyes immediately filled with terrified tears. Pilgrim calmly explained that Indians savagely killed her parents, and that she was abducted less than a week ago.

Oliver expressed his sympathy, hesitated only momentarily, and continued. "There was one soldier whose body was not defiled, perhaps because he was the bugler and carried no weapons. His name was Adolph Metzger. The Indians laid a buffalo skull next to his body showing respect for his courage.

"After this latest incident Sheridan has had no problem convincing the government to allow him to do whatever is necessary to stop the so-called barbaric Indians. So Sheridan, along with Sherman, has now hired George Custer to administer an all-out campaign to stop the Indians."

There was a pause in Loving's story.

"The stories yer tellin' 'er 're like a bad dream," said Pilgrim.

"Yes," replied Charles. "What Oliver is telling you is that this is no dream. It is as real as life itself."

"I need ta git this girl outta here fer her own protection," Pilgrim responded. "Could you gentlemen help me git her to her Texas relatives, or at least back East to a safe town or school?" asked Zen.

"Sure, Mr. Bragg," responded Oliver. He glanced at Charles as if to seek his approval, then added, "We can take Rebecca to either the railroad for passage back East, or we can take her with us to Texas. We're headed that way tomorrow to pick up some cattle for another drive. We've got twenty-three…

"Twenty-one," interjected Charles.

"Oh, yes, twenty-one of the toughest cowboys this side of the Mississippi River that can dog a steer through the eye of needle; surely they can get this pretty young thing to safety," added Mr. Loving.

"How's that sound to ya, Rebecca?" questioned Pilgrim.

Rebecca didn't verbally respond to either the offer or Pilgrim's question, but she nodded her approval as she shrugged her shoulders.

"Well, good; it's settled then," declared Oliver. "We'll all get a good night's sleep and head out first thing in the morning."

Pilgrim thanked the two gentlemen for their hospitality as he settled his account for the meals and asked about a room for Rebecca. The lady assured Pilgrim of her well-being for the night, so Pilgrim, Oliver, and Charles bid them a good evening and left the saloon.

Pilgrim asked the gents if they knew where he could care for his horses, and they directed him to the far end of the camp where he could get the horses fed and throw his bedroll out for the night.

Chapter 7

The morning sun sifted through the wooden fence slats on Pilgrim's bedroll, giving him a warm and peaceful sense of security not often felt by a man who contends with nature's ways. His sleep was good and the comfort that he experienced was unusual and something he hadn't experienced for a very long time. He readied his horse and bundled his belongings and was equipped to ride at a minute's notice. His first duty of the day was to get Rebecca squared away with Goodnight and Loving for her trip to safety. He felt an obligation to the girl.

Pilgrim entered the saloon to where Rebecca was being entertained and waited upon by the maids that were caring for the girl as if she were a helpless, woebegone child. She had a breakfast set at her place that would surely feed Custer's 7th.

"Mind if I join ya?" Pilgrim politely asked Rebecca.

All the ladies welcomed him and interrupted any attempt that Rebecca may have had in trying to answer Pilgrim's question.

"Did ya git a good night sleep?" he asked.

"Yes, very nice, thank you," replied Rebecca.

"Goodnight, did I hear someone call my name?" Charles jokingly broke in as he and Oliver approached their table.

"Good morning, folks," Oliver spoke out.

"Are you about ready to head for Texas, young lady?" inquired Charles. He looked directly into Rebecca's innocent face.

"Yes, sir, I'm looking forward to it, sir," Rebecca replied.

"You gentlemen want to join us fer some breakfast?" asked Pilgrim.

After accepting the invitation both Goodnight and Loving pulled up a chair and shared in conversation and ate their breakfasts. A short time had passed and when they all had finished, they decided it was time to leave.

Pilgrim saw that Rebecca was safely in Charles and Oliver's care before he mounted his horse and headed west. Pilgrim felt the sudden urge to confirm the stories that Oliver Loving had shared with him the night before. He felt the need to visit an old friend of his in the Cheyenne Nation. If all the stories were true that Loving had told, he may no longer be welcome.

For weeks he traveled slow and steady toward the Cheyenne village of Rock Forehead. As he traveled his thoughts and memories were of the days prior to the problems caused by gold seekers, the railroad, and the white man's desire to take that which isn't rightly his.

He remembered the day that he and Rock Forehead met. Both were young men in their peak years, probably not separated by more than a year of age. Each man upon seeing the other felt a respect for character without having uttered a word.

It was a sun filled fall day in the Colorado Territory about fifteen years prior, that Pilgrim was hunting on the eastern slope of the Rockies. He had a giant bull elk in the sights of his rifle. As he was steadying his rifle, he saw the magnificent red-skinned brave silently stalk his way closer to the elk. The stealthy figure with long, black hair moved with a silent elegance, much like the hawk in flight. He watched in complete admiration as the Indian took his silent aim with his bow and released the arrow that found the heart of the big bull. The bull ran through the spruce with unleashed force, using its last burst of energy from his life-giving blood, as it drained from the wound.

Pilgrim remembered watching the scene as if it were happening in slow motion. The Indian silently marked the trail of the fleeing giant and calmly studied the trail marked by the blood-letting wound.

From Pilgrim's position he could see where the animal fell. He visually marked the spot and silently, and without drawing attention to himself, sneaked to where the big-bodied bull lay motionless. Pilgrim pulled the arrow from the animal and knelt behind the animal waiting for the hunter to appear.

The Indian followed the blood trail to its end, spotting Pilgrim, several yards away. He hesitated at first, then realized that Pilgrim was not threatening him but paying homage to the skill and prowess of the hunter's savvy. Pilgrim extend his arm toward the Indian with the killing arrow in hand, offering it to its rightful owner. The Indian stepped forward and accepted it. They looked at each other with great respect.

Pilgrim learned that his name was Rock Forehead, and since he couldn't explain his name, Pilgrim accepted the name given to him by the Indian, Elk Arrow.

Pilgrim spent the better part of two years with the Cheyenne in their camp, learning their ways, and most of all living in harmony with nature. His memories of those days were happy, full of new things and peaceful times; the memory was distancing him even further from the melancholy of his world today. He began to wonder why he had left such a perfect place, when the memory of Lame Horse became vivid.

Lame Horse rejected the fact that Rock Forehead took a stranger in and was given all the rights that Elk Arrow received. Many incidents involving Lame Horse finally forced Pilgrim's hand. Pilgrim no longer felt like he belonged, and the fact was, he knew he didn't. Pilgrim reached the area close to where Rock Forehead's band usually hunted in the fall. He felt uneasy about what to expect, but it was something he had to do. He had an inner urgency to find out the truth about the Indians, white soldiers expansion, and most of all the buffalo.

An arrow whizzed in front of his face and stuck in Balsa Fir less than an arms length away. His forced reaction was to stay calm. Pilgrim recognized the arrow's markings. Pilgrim called out, "Lame Horse, it is I, Elk Arrow!"

Pilgrim didn't even look to see from where the arrow had come. The arrow markings were the same that Lame Horse once used.

Lame Horse once vowed to kill him, and the memory made the hair on his neck stand up.

"Lame Horse, is that you? I come in peace, brother!" shouted Pilgrim. He felt his voice quaver as he yelled his greeting message. He heard the horse approach from behind, but Pilgrim continued to face away from the oncoming rider as to not show any fear or aggression.

"It is me. What is it that you want, white eyes of little truth?" answered Lame Horse.

"I come in peace for only a short stay," responded Pilgrim. "I want to talk with you and Rock Forehead."

Pilgrim thought to himself, *Of all the dad blame Indians out here, I had ta go and run inta this one.*

"I will take Elk Arrow to see the people; there are many that still talk of you," said Lame Horse.

Pilgrim wasn't quite sure of what to make of Lame Horse's offer. He didn't say a word, just nodded his head and followed his lead. Lame Horse offered no conversation. Pilgrim thought it best not to question Lame Horse until he had had a chance to see if Lame Horse's attitude had changed toward him. The ride was very quiet and lasted several hours long.

When they reached the camp, Lame Horse rode through the center of camp followed by every young kid and stray dog in the camp. Pilgrim drew a lot of attention. The squaws were beginning to take notice as they rode up to Rock Forehead's lodge.

"Rock Forehead, it is I, Lame Horse. I have found your white brother, Elk Arrow."

The squaws began gathering and whispering amongst themselves.

Rock Forehead appeared at his lodge entrance. "Elk Arrow, you have gotten older," he said.

Pilgrim dismounted his horse and approached the Cheyenne leader. They clasp each other's arms as a traditional Cheyenne greeting. The chief looked at the squaws that were gathered near and said, "This is a friend from my past. Go and prepare a feast, for we have much to speak of."

The chief then turned and addressed the newcomer. "Come, Elk Arrow, come to my lodge, and we will smoke the pipe of friendship. Lame Horse, you come, too, so we can tell Elk Arrow our stories."

The three of them went into the lodge, but before they were settled, an outside disturbance caused the men to jump to their feet. One of the young boys came running to the lodge to report a white man soldier with long yellow hair was approaching the camp, with two more riders at his side. Rock Forehead motioned to let them pass.

Pilgrim had no idea of what was happening; yet both Rock Forehead and Lame Horse knew exactly what was taking place. They both were expecting the visitor. Pilgrim could see that Lame Horse was disturbed by the imposition caused by the approaching soldiers. Rock Forehead stood expressionless and appeared rather calm. The three soldiers rode through the camp to where Pilgrim stood beside the chief and Lame Horse. Pilgrim needed no introduction to this white leader of the soldiers. Though he had never met him, Oliver Loving's description, was quite accurate enough for Pilgrim to ascertain that this man was Custer.

"Rock Forehead, I have come here today to offer you a land of your own, and with it peace between our peoples," said Custer. His tone was arrogant and demeaning to the people before whom he stood.

Rock Forehead calmly stated, "You speak as if the land can be owned."

"The US government owns the land where you now stand. They will give you land of your own in another territory. We must have your answer now!" Custer demanded.

"The decision is to be made by all our people and is much too great to be made in haste now, as you demand. My people will meet on this issue, and we will have your answer tomorrow. Return tomorrow, and you will know our people's decision then," Chief Rock Forehead explained.

Pilgrim remained silent to the issue at hand since it did not directly involve him. Custer accepted the chief's answer, but warned him that if the offer was not accepted, that the army was ordered to remove them from the land with force. Before he turned to leave, Custer looked at Pilgrim and said, "I'm George Armstrong Custer, Commander and Chief of the 7th Cavalry. I don't believe we've met."

Custer's arrogance made Pilgrim's blood run cold. So without hesitation or much forethought, he answered Custer by simply saying, "I am Elk Arrow, friend and brother to the Cheyenne."

Custer openly displayed his disapproval with a sneer as he jerked his horse's head around and rode out of the village. The village elders, warriors, and chief called a meeting later that day. Pilgrim was invited to take part and share his thoughts and ideas. Rock Forehead thought it would be helpful to have a white-man's assessment, especially through Pilgrim's eyes.

The meeting lasted the remaining daylight hours and into the early evening. As in most community issues there were two sides, two choices, and no clear right or wrong answer. The village was clearly divided on the issue. Rock Forehead favored the acceptance of the new land.

He didn't look at it as surrender but an opportunity for his people and their future and the promise of a peaceful way of life.

Lame Horse seemed to lead the dissension. His people's argument was based on the previous lies of the white man. They had broken their promises in the past. They have not spoken the truth. They do not own the land; no one owns the land for himself.

When Pilgrim was asked to share his thoughts, he told only of what he had heard. He agreed that the whites are pushing a way west in great numbers and that they are a greedy, arrogant people that take without asking. They have broken many promises of the past. Pilgrim's only warning to the village was to beware of the yellow hair, who is sent to make more promises.

Rock Forehead's decision was to allow Lame Horse to take those people who agreed with him to the north. Lame Horse and many others prepared and left that very night.

The next morning, Custer returned to the village.

Rock Forehead asked Custer to enter his lodge along with Pilgrim and two other braves of puissance. Custer was seated under the sacred arrows, which represented the place of honor.

Custer started to say something, but Rock Forehead stopped him with a firm look and a hand gesture. Rock Forehead slowly, and with purpose, pulled a stick from the fire that had glowing embers at one end. He used it to light the pipe of friendship. He first passed the pipe to Pilgrim, and he returned it to the chief. The chief then offered it to each of the other braves seated on each side of him. They both returned the pipe to the chief, for it was the chief who offered it, not another. Rock Forehead finally offered the pipe to Custer as he gave Custer his reply to the demands that Custer had previously presented.

"I offer you this pipe of friendship not to represent our relationship, but in the hopes for the future relationship between your people and my children's children. My people will go to your reservation, but if the trust is ever broken, the blood shed will never end for your people."

Custer was getting what he wanted, and his eyes gleamed with the lies on his tongue as he repeated all his idle promises.

The chief tapped the ashes of the pipe on Custer's boots to signify his lack of trust. Rock Forehead, from that moment on, somehow lost that glowing strength and power that had always been a part of his character. Though he never admitted it, the perspective of defeat seized the strength in his heart. He began the preparation of his people's journey to the reservation with Army escort.

Chapter 8

Buffler rode for several weeks headed for the Rockies. The days were once again getting shorter and the nights were much cooler. The spring started out so wet, but the summer turned into one of the driest he could remember. The plains grasses were stunted and much of the area was barren where once the sage and prairie grasses were waist high. Buffler blamed the drought for the lack of buffalo. To him the dry summer meant a cold hard winter could be expected. The hunter's moon had passed nearly a month prior, and Pilgrim hadn't showed up at the agreed rendezvous spot. For all Buffler knew, the Indians probably got him.

His plan was to get to the mountain cabin that he and Pilgrim had built several years earlier, and settle in for the winter. He thought that if Pilgrim were still alive, he might have headed there since the fall weather was coming so much earlier than normal.

Buffler worked his way to the cabin early one snowy morning in November. The snow was soft and already to the horses fetlocks. He approached with caution when he saw smoke rising from the chimney. Then he recognized the packhorse as Pilgrim's. Buffler went inside and stoked the fire with some of the wood that had been gathered and stacked along the outside wall. He knew that Pilgrim would be returning soon.

A couple hours had passed, enough time for Buffler to put together some hardtack biscuits, fry up some salt pork, and make a watery gravy from the left-over grease. Pilgrim flung open the cabin door, catching Buffler oblivious to his presence, and yelled like a wild man.

Buffler was so surprised he jumped back and fell over a chair. He lay on his back in a cowering position with his hands covering his face, then he realized it was Pilgrim. "It's a good thing I saw ya comin', ya dang fool, er ya might-a scared me," blurted Buffler. His comments were similar to that of an embarrassed child.

"How the heck ya been?" Pilgrim said with friendly concern.

"Well, let's see. I been snake bit, half drowned, almost killed by Injuns, and got saddle sores as big as eagle eggs. Pretty good, I reckon," Buffler jested. "How 'bout yerself?"

Pilgrim took on serious expression and started jabbering to Buffler about Rebecca and her parents, his run-in with the Indians, the things that Oliver Loving had told him about; and rumors concerning Custer's visit to Rock Forehead's village.

Buffler told him to slow down and grab a bite to eat. Pilgrim gathered his composure and picked up a plate. He filled it with several large biscuits, slapped on some of the salt pork gravy, grabbed a unopened bottle of his whiskey from the shelf, and grabbed a chair. The whole time he never stopped talking about the things he'd seen and been through.

Buffler saw a different Pilgrim than he'd remembered. He was usually quiet and reserved and let the others to do the talking. Buffler was pleased that Pilgrim had returned was glad to see him. They spent the rest of the day swapping stories and drinking whiskey.

The weather soon turned from early fall snows to a blustery winter blizzard that hung on for nearly four months. It snowed every day for a month, and the winds howled and screamed with the fury of demons. Luckily, the two men had sufficient supplies to pull them through.

They spent their days trying to gather fire wood, and build some kind of protection for their horses. Buffler's packhorse froze to death in the last blowing blizzard. The sight of her lying there in the icy snow brought tears to Buffler's eyes. "The ole nag's been with me a long time," he sobbed. "I'll sure as hell miss 'er."

They gathered twigs and peeled bark off trees, to feed to the other horses. It was the roughest winter either ever had to deal with.

When spring finally broke, they were so exhausted by the extreme bitter cold winter, that decided to recoup. Hunting was extremely good, and the trout in the streams were easy to trap. Life was once again peaceful and fulfilling. Pilgrim and Buffler stayed on there for two more years. The winters were milder and there just didn't seem to be a reason to leave.

In the summer of 1869, Pilgrim and Buffler, were on their annual trek to get their yearly supplies. The trip in years past took them about three weeks to make, but for the last two years, it had taken them twice as long. The loss of Buffler's pack horse made that part of their lives a little harder, and it took them a little longer. They really didn't care; it gave them a chance to actually see the things they had always taken for granted.

They reached a small mining town that was northeast of Denver. The extra three days that it would have taken them to get to Denver wasn't worth the effort. Neither of the two liked the small towns, and had no desire or need to see a town as big as Denver.

Their first job when they got to town was to go to the fur trader and turn their pelts into cash.

These days there wasn't much quibbling or fuss concerning pelt prices. Quality seldom brought a better price. The fur companies in the East already had their control on the fur buyers in the West. Specific pelts brought standard prices.

Pilgrim and Buffler had never had any problems meeting needs with what they trapped, their needs were so few that they always had a surplus. If they hadn't been left with a surplus, they simply would have done without. The fur trader, after counting out the pelts and inventorying the total sale, offered them what they considered to be a fair price, considering the overall drop in fur prices. They accepted his offer, collected their money and were on their way in a very short time.

Buffler looked at Pilgrim and said, "What now, partner?"

The men both had had previously discussed plans for a good hot meal, a hot bath, a stiff drink, and a good night's sleep in a bed with a down filled mattress; therefore, Pilgrim didn't feel the need to respond to Buffler's question. He simply pointed at the Miner's Café, and started walking in that direction.

The talk in the Café was about the railroad. Buffler and Pilgrim remained quiet since neither of them knew anything of the modern-day news, but they each listened with unsurpassed interest. The patrons were laughing at both of the Railroad Companies that were supposed to meet, but continued building rail right past each other for a hundred or more miles. The government finally stepped in and put the thing together at Promontory Summit. The thought of being able to go from the Pacific Ocean to the Atlantic Ocean in a week or so was more than most could comprehend. Pilgrim sat quietly through his meal thinking of what this so called progress and growth would do, where it was going, and actually wondering where it would stop. The westward expansion worried Pilgrim and in many ways he was feeling the same pressures as the Indians. Pilgrim looked at the table next to his and quietly asked the gentleman about any reported trouble with the Indians.

"Injuns," the man repeated. "No, haven't had too much trouble with the Injuns. Custer rounded most of 'em up and sent 'em all to different reservations. There was that incident last fall."

"What incident?" Pilgrim asked.

"Well, it was November 23rd, I remember, because that's my wife, Hattie's, birthday. It snowed all night. Black Kettle's band took four white captives back to their camp along the Quachita River in Oklahoma. Custer got wind of it and was able to follow the pony tracks to Black Kettle's village. Almost four years to the day after the Sand Creek Massacre, two days after the anniversary, Custer rode in with his soldiers on November 27th and nearly wiped the village out. They said that a few Indians may have survived by hiding in the tall grasses that surrounded the camp, but for the most part, all the Indians were killed, including the women and children. Black Kettle himself was one of the victims."

Buffler commented, "At least he died for what he believed in."

"Yeah, suppose so," replied one of the strangers. "Sure beats gettin' killed and bein' left to rot like that cowboy Loving."

Pilgrim spoke up, "What cowboy? Was his name Oliver?"

"Yeah, Oliver, Toliver, or something like that," the stranger replied. "Caused a real stir with the cattlemen."

"Mr. Loving and his friend, Goodnight..."

"Yes, Charles Goodnight," interrupted Pilgrim.

"Yes, I believe yer right, Charles Goodnight. Well, they were pretty big in the cattle business. You've surely heard of the Shawnee and Chisholm Trails, haven't ya? Well, it seems to me that these two fellas developed a trail every bit as important as the others. It's called the Goodnight Loving Trail, and goes from Texas to the far northern part of the territories. The Comanche's attacked Loving and left his body along the railroad to be seen by the travelers passing by. Goodnight ended up taking his friend's body back to Texas."

"Thank ya, sir, fer that information," Pilgrim quietly murmured. His thoughts went back a couple of years, to the evening at the French Saloon when Loving told his stories to him and Rebecca. He remembered Rebecca and wondered whether she reached Texas safely.

Then he was interrupted by Buffler. "Hey, ya goin' ta mope all night or 're we goin' ta git that drink ya promised?"

Pilgrim conceded with a silent nod. They both spent the rest of the evening taking pleasure with the ways of progress and growth and became a part of the city and its people that evening.

Pilgrim slept on the floor that night, where his conscience allowed him temporary freedom from his feeling of being unclean, dirty, and guilt ridden. The previous night's activities caused him to feel that he had taken part in something that he shouldn't have. He wouldn't say a word to Buffler about his feelings, but couldn't wait to roust him from his bed so they could leave town and get back to what he knew and understood...the mountains.

Buffler was hung over and didn't share the same enthusiasm as Pilgrim in wanting to leave so soon. Pilgrim seemed so emphatic in wanting to leave that he thought it would be less of a hassle to humor his friend than to argue, so he complied with his wishes. They spent little time getting the supplies they needed, packed their horses, and headed out.

Pilgrim talked Buffler into buying another packhorse in order to speed the trip back. Buffler knew that something was really eating at him.

"Want ta talk about it, Pilgrim?" asked Buffler straight out.

"Talk about what?" Pilgrim abruptly came back.

"Why yer in such a dad blame hurry to git back."

"Remember when I set out a couple of year ago and told ya I wanted to go where things weren't so messed up?" asked Pilgrim. "Well, I think I was there and just didn't know it then. It took me this long ta find it out."

"Hell, I thought ya left meanin' I was messin' things up fer ya," said Buffler.

"No, but yer right, though; yer always messin' things up," responded Pilgrim as he kicked his horse in the side and at an easy pace passed Buffler by.

Buffler thought about it for a minute, and mumbled to himself, "Danged fool." He then nudged his own horse to a gallop to catch up with Pilgrim.

Six days later they arrived back at their modest little cabin tucked away on the eastern Rockies slopes. Both men went about their business and seldom talked about or even wondered what was happening in the world around them.

Another year had passed, and they had entered another decade. It was the spring of 1870, and as always, they got a little fidgety when the weather broke. It was the easy time of the year when their hard winter chores took a turn to the simple less demanding and much more enjoyable time, and allowed them to once again become an active part of their surroundings. Their appreciation for nature was deep rooted in the hearts of both men.

It was the spring days that the two men would sit along the banks of the mountain stream and talk about their past. They discussed the growth of the country and its sudden expansion westward. They discussed their concerns for the Indians and the buffalo, but never, before this day had either of them questioned the other about his family. Buffler brought the question up, and asked Pilgrim where he was from and if he had any family.

Pilgrim, responded quickly, as if he, too, had been thinking about it. "When I wuz 'bout ten or 'leven years old, my pa wuz one of them folks that thought he'd git a fortune in gold if he wuz to pack up and move his whole darn family from Virgini' ta Californi'. So he did. 'Twern't no time at all, 'bout two weeks inta the trip I reckon, the whole wagon train started ta fall right apart. First it wuz broken wheels and dyin' horses, then it turned to people dyin' off one by one from the fever. Both my ma and pa died from the fever. Far as I know'd that wagon train never did git ta Californi. A man by the name of Uriah Patrick rode as guide fer the wagon train company that Pa signed up with. Well, when the train fell part, Uriah more less let me go with him; mind ya, he didn't take me ta raise. I didn't know of any kinfolk anywheres, so I pretty much follered Uriah. He taught me most a' what I know, and he treated me fair.

"'Bout three year later his horse throw'd him offin' a steep slope up at Carter's Pass. Broke his leg bad. The bone was stickin' outta his leg in two places. We got the bleedin' stopped, but poison set in, and he died a slow painin' death bout two weeks later."

Buffler conceded with a long pause, then with concern on his face said, "That's a lot' a burden fer a youngin' ta hafta go through, huh?"

Pilgrim didn't even respond to Buffler's comments, not that Buffler expected him to. "Well, I never know'd my pa, and I ain't sure my mama did either. She, my mama, God rest her soul, never spoke of my pa when I wuz growin' up. Hell, I didn't even know ya needed one 'til I wuz twelve or so. She raised me in Tennessee. She wuz the only woman I ever knew that liked bein' alone and didn't need much ta keep her happy. She died when I wuz bout fifteen I reckon. I buried her there and headed out this way on my own. When I got ta the mountains I figgered I wuz as close ta God as I was goin' ta get in this life, so I stayed right here."

"Ya ever have a woman, Pilgrim?" Buffler coyly asked.

"I been with some; ya know that. But could never bring myself ta gittin' hitched up with one permanently," responded Pilgrim.

"Me, too," Buffler agreed.

Their conversations about such issues were rare. Seldom did they pry into the minds of each other especially concerning personal issues and feelings. Probably because their thoughts were so closely matched that they didn't have to.

Chapter 9

The next couple of years were kind, as far as the weather goes. The winters were exceptionally easy to cope with and the hunting season looked promising. Especially the season of the fall of 1873. Buffler and Pilgrim limited their hunting to deer and elk, and no further than a day's ride from the cabin.

Buffalo were no longer a necessity to Pilgrim and Buffler. They had plenty of food without them, and the robes didn't trade as well as they used to. Man-made blankets replaced the buffalo robes, though they didn't provide nearly as much warmth as a well-tanned buffalo hide in Buffler's opinion. Besides, between the two of them, they had held onto enough buffalo robes to last them the rest of their lives. Considering the plight of the buffalo and the decreasing numbers it was simply easier to hunt other game.

Pilgrim especially looked forward to the hunting season. It was a time of peace and harmony with nature, and a time that he felt his maker provided a serene and simple explanation of life's full purpose.

Such was his feeling one sun filled morning in October of that same year, when the leaves on the aspen were beginning to turn shades of yellow and red. These were the days that both men loved most.

The previous night they could hear elk bellowing, bugling calls to their harems of cows, contesting their dominance to the lesser bulls. The hunters, discussed their location and planned their strategies for hours. With each bugle heard, they discussed the animals size, location, and dominance with the herd. Also with each bugle, a torrent surge of excitement generated. By the time they went to bed that night, they were so enthusiastic and looked forward to the upcoming events of the next morning's hunt that neither man got much sleep.

Darkness still shrouded the cabin when they sensed it was time to get up and out for the hunt. The dimly lit lantern flickered and a puff of black smoke rose through the lantern's chimney as Buffler tried to adjust it for more light.

Pilgrim rolled from his bunk and slipped his buckskin shirt over his head, then reached for the poker to stir the fireplace ashes. A small blaze ignited, assisting the lantern in illuminating the room. He added a few pieces of wood, and watched as the fire consumed them in flame. He could feel the heat begin to replace the morning chill.

"Should be a good un'," Buffler said. He carried a rather groggy air of enthusiasm.

Pilgrim, still spellbound by the fire and buried in thought heard only the sound of Buffler's voice, not the words.

"Hey, ya danged fool, I'm talkin' ta ya!" shouted Buffler. "Ya still asleep, or jest ain't talkin' this mornin'?"

"Sorry," Pilgrim replied. "Guess I'm a wink or two from bein' rested. Wha'd ya say?"

" I said it was lookin' like a good day to hunt," stressed Buffler.

"Ya, ah'm sure it will be," Pilgrim halfheartedly replied.

They continued to gather up the things they needed for a full-day's hunt. Pilgrim by this time was cognizant and showing the spirited fervor that Buffler expected from his friend.

"Well, let's do it," Buffler beseeched. "Jest as we planned. Ya head on up slope, en' I'll get around ya en come in frum the backside. See ya at the beaver pond 'bout midday."

They walked out the door and immediately headed in opposite directions. Buffler took about twenty paces and paused momentarily. He turned to watch his friend walk out of sight.

Pilgrim was intent on reaching the area that held the elk. He was already preparing his mind and immediately established an alliance with his surroundings. He never turned, or hesitated even for a second. He was quite determined in his quest and his mind fully engaged with his task.

Buffler's early hunt would be in the low area along the creek and around the base of the mountain. His hunt would start at first light; whereas Pilgrim had half a mountain to climb before his hunt would actually begin. The elk were plentiful in both areas, and both men had a knack for working the animals to their own or their partner's advantage.

Buffler leaned against a tree as soon as he reached the creek bank. He paused deliberately to sharpen his senses by keenly watching the sunlight replace the darkness. He watched the woods awaken from its sleep and focused his ears to each new sound of the morning. The time was right.

He felt his hunter's sixth sense take over. He started to take the first step into his stalk, when a commotion broke the natural silence. He heard splashing water in the distance. The sound was moving upstream very fast in his direction, not yet within his sight. Thinking that it might be an elk, Buffler readied his rifle. He caught glimpses through the underbrush, and as it came nearer he saw that it wasn't an elk, it wasn't even an animal. It was a young Indian boy, running scared. As the boy ran in Buffler's direction he caught a glimpse of someone on horseback some distance back and deeper in the forest covering. The boy ran so close to Buffler that with little effort he grabbed him by the arm and immediately muffled his mouth with the other hand. The boy started kicking and squirming; it was all Buffler could do to restrain him. Buffler pulled him tighter and closer as they both slumped against a tree. He pushed his bearded face against the boys ear and kept on shushing him with a constant low toned shhhhh. The boy began to yield to Buffler's strength, but Buffler retained his grasp.

The mounted pursuer was coming nearer and could be heard in the brush on the creek's far side. Buffler gave a short squeeze followed with a soft, nearly inaudible "shhh." The young hostage seemed to comprehend his captor's motivation and completely reposed in Buffler's arms. Buffler could see that the pursuer was a lone soldier dressed in a blue uniform, and, by the way he was searching the surrounding area, had every intention of subduing the boy. Buffler kept his hold on the boy until the soldier disappeared from sight, then ever so slowly loosened his hold on him. The young Indian remained quiet, but jumped to his feet and turned to see his captor, turned savior, for the first time. He seemed to stare right through Buffler's eyes and deep into his mind in search of Buffler's next move. The boys eyes, not even momentarily left the clutching hold they had on his eyes.

"Well, what'a we got here?" Buffler softly inquired. He really didn't say it in a way that he expecting an answer to such an obvious question. "Do ya talk so as I can understand ya, or do ya speak that Injun gibberish?"

The young man did not respond, not even in expression.

"Yer kinda lost out here, ain't ya?" said Buffler. Once again he didn't expect an answer.

"Well, I can't leave ya out here by yerself, and ya done ruined my chances to git that big bull. Guess'n' we might as well go back ta the cabin, git the horses, and go meet Pilgrim as I'd planned, 'afore you showed up."

Buffler motioned the direction he wanted the boy to go. The young Indian boy complied with his wishes and led the two through the thick underbrush. Buffler was awestruck by the boy's quiet movements.

They soon reached the cabin, where Buffler, assuming the boy might bc hungry, went inside and grabbed up a healthy handful of pemmican. He offered it to the boy, who took it in hand, and then walked over to saddle the horse. Buffler didn't look back at the boy as he devoured it.

Buffler mounted the horse and offered a hand to lift the boy to the horses back. The Indian swung on with unassisted ease. They headed back to the creek, but took a trail more direct to the beaver pond than Buffler had first planned.

***

Pilgrim had been nearing the beaver pond with each stalking step of his hunt. He was hunting the land that lay between him and the meeting place. Several hours of daylight had passed, and he was absorbing every enjoyable moment the day had brought him. The sun was shining with such purity and warmth and the colors throughout the mountain side seemed clear. He came upon an elk wallow and detected the pungent mating odors that permeated their meeting place. He saw large spruce trees shredded by the antlers of frustrated bulls.

At that moment he heard the bugling of one elk to left, quickly followed by that of another to his right. Pilgrim was right between them and prepared himself to take advantage of the situation.

He crawled over a large deadfall and buried himself in the middle. He raised his gun and laid it on a heavy branch for support. His experience and knowledge of elk gave him the advantage he needed to bring these two bulls together.

Pilgrim made a short series of musing sounds, much like those of a cow elk. Then he sat quietly in anticipation. The bulls appeared before him almost simultaneously. Without hesitation the bulls locked their antlers in a clashing fervor that Pilgrim had never before witnessed. The bulls pushed and shoved each other with contested strength and tremendous force. The ground was stirred and dusty from battle, and small trees were being broken and trampled from the massive animals as they jostled for position. Pilgrim was so close to the contest between the elk that at times he could have touched them with his gun barrel. He wanted the winner of this bout. He readied his gun and held on the shoulder of the biggest bull. When the skirmish subsided, Pilgrim pulled the trigger and the big bull dropped to ground. The smaller bull stood motionless, watching his adversary writhe in the waning dust. Pilgrim remained motionless for fear the other animal might attack. The remaining bull, after several minutes, accepted his victory and bugled the outcome to all others of his kind. He was proud and seemed to gloat his eminence as he trotted away.

Pilgrim was still shaken by his involvement in this elk battle. His legs were weak with excitement, and his thoughts were jumbled from the commotion. He slowly regained his composure and walked over to the slain giant. His emotions, unlike the other elk, were not of pride and defeat, but feelings of appreciation for its strength, beauty, and source of food that this animal could provide.

Pilgrim had enough time to disembowel the animal before heading to the beaver pond to meet Buffler. He knew that they would have to go back to the cabin later that day to get the pack horses to carry his elk back. It was going to be a long day.

The distance wasn't that far to the beaver pond and he made good time. Pilgrim's spirits were in the clouds, his thoughts about the hunt kept his mind occupied and he arrived before he knew it. In fact, he got there before Buffler did.

Pilgrim lay back on the bank of the pond where the sunlight dappled the ground as it filtered through the tree tops. Moments later he was sound asleep.

Buffler and the Indian boy rode in quietly and unnoticed. Pilgrim was sound asleep. Buffler couldn't pass up such a perfect opportunity to display his true character. He stood the Indian boy directly in front of Pilgrim and motioned to the boy to stay quiet. Buffler backed off a few yards, took his and rifle, and shot off a heavy powder charge, yelling Injuns….Injuns.

Pilgrim's eyes popped open, and they got the size of silver dollars when he saw the Indian boy in front of him. He tried to jump to his feet, but shuffled around for a foothold as he was falling backwards. He stumbled several yards back, and fell butt first, in a pile of fresh horse manure that Buffler's horse appropriately deposited.

Pilgrim saw Buffler standing off to the side laughing so hard that his face was blood red. He looked back at the Indian boy, and he had a grin from ear to ear. Pilgrim was rarely irritated by Buffler's antics, but this one had topped them all….

"Dad blame it, ya danged fool, yer fixin' ta git hurt!" yelled Pilgrim at the both of them. Then he got up, paused a moment, felt his backside, and realized how he must have looked to them.

His frown slowly lifted and turned to laughter too.

"Who's yer friend?" asked Pilgrim, as he tried to lift his embarrassment by changing the subject.

"Found 'im down at the creek runnin' from a soldier," Buffler answered, wiping his nose with his sleeve and trying to keep from laughing.

"I remember this boy from Rock Forehead's camp 'bout three years ago. He and some-a his friends followed me inta the camp," exclaimed Pilgrim. He looked back in the boy's direction.

"Do ya remember me, boy?" he asked. "It's me: Elk Arrow." Pilgrim pounded his fist to his chest in gesture.

The boy responded and mimicked Pilgrim's pronunciation. "Elk Arrow." He nodded and repeated the name, "Elk Arrow."

Pilgrim told Buffler about the elk he had killed, but only the basics. He was saving the details for later that evening back at the cabin after he had had a chance to concoct his spell-binding tale.

"Sure glad ya got a horse, 'twill save lots-a time gittin' that elk back," Pilgrim surmised.

"Kinda planned it thet way," boasted Buffler.

They all went back to the elk and worked diligently to quarter the carcass before nightfall. They tied most of it to the horse. Each of them, including the boy, carried either a hind quarter or a front shoulder.

They arrived at the cabin shortly after dark. They took care of the horses, finished what needed to be done to the meat, and started fixing their well-deserved meal of elk stakes and biscuits. While Buffler was putting the final touches to the meal, Pilgrim prepared a bunk for the boy. They ate ravenously, as Pilgrim told his elk story in great detail. Even the boy seemed to enjoy and understand Pilgrim's dramatic gestures as the story unfolded.

Soon after the food dwindled and the stories turned to talk of the next day's activities, a wearisome calm followed a silent moment. Fatigue had replaced their jocularity and the mood of the camp began to settle. The boy yawned. Pilgrim suggested they get a good night sleep. Moments after turning down the lamp and crawling in their respective bunks the trio slept.

Chapter 10

The next morning the boy awoke first. He stirred the fire to flame with an unburned stick. He sat mesmerized and peered at it scrupulously, as if he were looking for its hidden secrets.

Pilgrim lay in his bunk watching the boy and wondering what thoughts his mind held. Pilgrim remembered very little of the boy's language, and knew just enough to communicate the simple things. The boy's knowledge of the English language was fair in understanding, but came as a difficult task to him when he tried to verbalize it.

"Boy, what's yer name?" Pilgrim asked.

The question startled the boy from his trance. "Quineata," responded the boy. He pounded his clenched fist to his chest as Elk Arrow had done the previous day.

Pilgrim thought for a minute as to what Quineata might have translated to in English. About that time Buffler woke up, rolled over, and farted. He followed it with a huge grin.

Pilgrim told Buffler that he wasn't real sure, but he thought the boy's name meant either Five-Toed Lizard or Little Rooster. Both men chuckled.

Buffler said, "Well, we ought to name him Bad Smell in the Air."

Pilgrim directed his reply to Buffler and said, "That's yer name, ya old fart."

Buffler turned and looked at the boy and said, "Aw, hell, we'll call him Jonas."

The boy picked up on it right away. He pounded his chest and said, "Jonas," and then repeated it once again and looked at Pilgrim for some sign of approval. He then pointed at Pilgrim and said, "Elk Arrow." Then he pointed at Buffler and said, "Ba...Ba. Bad Smell."

Pilgrim laughed and nodded his head.

Buffler looked up with a stern frown and said, "Of all ta dad burn Injuns out ther' I had ta go and find this here smart aleck."

They got up and started in on their routine chores. Buffler went to feed the horses while Pilgrim set Jonas up to scrape the elk hide. Then Pilgrim collected enough firewood to take them through the night. When Pilgrim and Buffler finished their jobs, they met where Jonas was tending to the hide.

"The boy sure knows whut he's doin' ther'," Buffler said.

"Yep, probably been doin' it since he could walk," assured Pilgrim.

When the boy finished they all decided to go to the creek to see if they could catch some trout for their supper. Pilgrim and Buffler spent hours trying to catch the trout on wooden willow poles with some line attached. They carved hooks from elk bones and used worms for bait. Some days they would catch a fish or two, but most of the time they would just sit and talk and enjoy the day.

It didn't take Jonas long to figure out what they were trying to do, and in his youthful exuberance and know how, began building a fish trap. He looked at the creek both upstream and down, and settled on a small hole less than a hundred yards from the position of Pilgrim and Buffler. Jonas started taking rocks to block off the flow above the hole, then positioned more Rocks below the hole, in such a way that the fish entering could not escape.

"Whut's that youngin' doin' now?" inquired Buffler.

"I reckon he's buildin' some kinda fish trap," responded Pilgrim.

When Jonas was satisfied with his efforts, he disappeared momentarily into the willow thicket another fifty yards further downstream and returned with a long willow branch that he continued to whittle on as he approached both men.

Both men found considerable enjoyment just sitting back and watching the boy as he so eagerly and methodically prepared his spear. Once Jonas had a good sharp point and a notch cut near the pointed end, to serve as a barb, he started his stalking vigil at each deep pool he came to. He fished with the same stealth as a great blue heron.

Pilgrim and Buffler admired the boys abilities and could see the deep-seated concentration in the boys face. A few moments passed, and Jonas struck out with uncanny speed and accuracy and lifted a wriggling trout from its domicile. Within a short time, Jonas had enough fish to feed the three of them. He cut a small branch from a nearby alder and laced each fish through the mouth and gills.

Pilgrim motioned for the boy to return. Buffler, with a smile of approval, reached his hand out for Jonas's catch. Jonas yielded to Buffler's request, then sat beside Pilgrim as Buffler headed for the stream bank to clean the fish. Subconsciously, they both watched Buffler through his task, as they started to talk.

Pilgrim was interested in the circumstances that followed his visit to Rock Forehead's village and the events that took place, causing the boys near disaster with the white soldier. The conversation was slow in the beginning. Pilgrim, with the aid of Buffler, was able to glean bits and pieces of the boys story, to make some sense of the Cheyenne's present situation.

At best, they thought Jonas had said that Rock Forehead took half the camp with the soldiers to the new land, and that Lame Horse took the other half with him and escaped the soldiers to the north. Pilgrim nodded his head yes in agreement and knew these things to be true, for he was still there when the decisions were made.

Jonas went on to say that he had gone with Rock Forehead's group, because his family chose to. When they arrived at the new territory, it was an awful place. They were given white-man's clothes, and were sent to white man schools. There was no place to hunt or fish, and his people were forced to give up their ways. No one liked it, but the older people were tired of fighting and gave up. Some of the younger people ran from that place and were to meet at the old camp.

Jonas was the only one to return. He waited at the camp for several weeks for the others to return, but a soldier showed up instead. He took flight. He went on to say that he had planned to wait for the others and lead them north to find Lame Horse's people.

"Well, boy, I'd rightly think yer best chance is with usuns," Buffler said. He looked to Pilgrim for some sign of agreement. Then, with fish in hand motioned for the two of them to follow him back to the cabin.

"These here fish'll taste mighty good with sum' turnips and cornbread, won't they, Pilgrim?" Buffler said with a grin.

Pilgrim gave no reply. Jonas ran downstream to take one last gander at his fish trap, then spun around and ran back to join the others. The three of them split the chores, and in short time had prepared fine meal that afternoon.

Many more joyful moments followed that day, similar to the two previous days. Jonas was a big help, and between the three of them the daily chores were swiftly completed, allowing much more time to hunt, fish, collect herbs, and make useful items.

Signs of winter were closing in with each new day. The nights were getting cold, and the mornings weren't warming as quickly. Ice was forming on the horse troughs every day. It was Jonas's job to break it free, and refill it. The hardest job took the efforts of all three, and that was to get the winter wood supply stacked and ready for the duration of the coming season.

***

That winter came and passed. And even though the winter was relatively easy on them, their bouts with cabin fever coupled with the fact that their supplies were nearly depleted, forced them down the mountain to replenish their supplies much earlier than expected. It was the damp, rainy part of the early spring in 1874. Jonas was looking forward to the trip. He had never before seen a white-man's settlement.

Due primarily to the weather, the trip was made as quickly as possible. Jonas wasn't well received by the town's folk, something that Pilgrim and Buffler hadn't even considered. Buffler picked up a bad cough a couple days out and wasn't feeling much like traveling, and lost all sense of humor once they packed their supplies. They didn't even spend the night.

Jonas was easy to please and enjoyed the new adventure even though the weather put a damper on their activities.

Upon their return, Buffler went straight to his bunk and stayed there for three solid days. His cough continued to worsen and a fever seemed to come and go.

Chapter 11

Buffler remained ill the rest of that spring, the entire summer, and well into the fall season. It was mid-autumn, and periodically he seemed to experience a few good days, but for the most part, his illness hung on. The winter of 1874 was the roughest winter that they had endured. Buffler was too ill to help do anything around the cabin. It was up to Pilgrim and Jonas not only to do all the chores, but to care for Buffler too.

One morning in the early spring of 1875 Pilgrim woke up to find that Buffler had died in his sleep. It was a peaceful way to go, Pilgrim thought. Even though he did his share of sufferin' for nearly a full year, his pain and problems were all gone now. Pilgrim and Jonas buried their friend next to the stream where Buffler first met the boy.

Pilgrim tore a flat board from the side of the cabin, and to the best of his ability, made a marker that was fitting to his friend's memory, and placed it at the head of his grave. Pilgrim gathered up what supplies were left, and packed all the horses. Buffler's personal belongings were packed on his horses as if Buffler himself had performed the task.

Pilgrim took some lamp oil and spread it over the bunks, table and walls and with an ember from the fire place, he lighted a nest of tinder and tossed it on the oil soaked table. The fire quickly spread over the table top and down the legs. Once he was sure that it had taken hold, Pilgrim walked outside, untied his horses and stood next to Jonas as they watched the fire consume the cabin.

Pilgrim stood in complete silence, paying his last respects to his friend, and peacefully saying goodbye to a way of life that he had known and enjoyed for several years. They watched only long enough to satisfy Pilgrim's peace of mind, and with the horses tied in single file, reluctantly turned and walked away. Jonas watched the burning cabin as they passed beyond view, but Pilgrim never looked back.

Pilgrim had no real direction to go, and no plans in mind. He only knew of the many places he didn't want to go to, and that the sanctity of the mountains were the only place he'd ever found peace in his life. He and Jonas spent several months going north, weaving their way up and over the mountains at every other pass.

Several times in their roaming travels, they came across small mining camps and paused days on end to hear the stories the miners had to share, and the occasional company they offered. The only news Pilgrim received about the world surrounding he and Jonas, was from the miners or from the infrequent happenstance encounters with other mountain sojourners such as themselves. Perhaps the most accurate account for the events of the last five years came from an old trusted friend that Pilgrim had known from years past.

Pilgrim had heard from the nearby miner's camp, that an old man by the name of Joshua Bartley lived in a small cabin, along the mountain stream at Crinshaw Pass, less than half a day's ride north. Pilgrim and the boy, after hearing the news, headed straight away to Crinshaw Pass in hopes of seeing Joshua and spending some time with his old friend.

Pilgrim had no trouble locating Bartley's cabin. When he arrived, he saw Bartley working what appeared to be a bear hide. Bartley was so involved in his work that he didn't hear the horses approach. Pilgrim sat quietly for just a moment, as if contemplating what to say, then called out to his friend, "Is that the same dad blame bear ya wuz a skinnin' the last time I seen ya?"

Joshua was shocked by the unexpected voice. He turned to the intruder and took a step forward as he observed him with a great deal of scrutiny through his thick eye glasses.

"Pilgrim," he said, questioning his identity. "Be that you sittin' up ther' on yer horse so high and mighty? How the heck ya been?"

Pilgrim smiled at his old friend, got down from his horse, and greeted him with a double- handed grasp of his forearms.

"I been right healthy I reckon. Yer lookin' good," said Pilgrim.

"Yeah, suppose so, but my rumitiz' bout ta git me down," responded Bartley, and no, this ain't the same bear I wuz a skinnin' some twenty year back, ya danged fool." They both laughed at his seriousness.

"Who's yer friend?" Bartley asked.

"Thet's Jonas," Pilgrim replied. He proudly glanced back at the boy. Don't reckon he's got a last name."

"Pleased to meet ya, youngin'," Bartley said, articulating each word.

"He ain't much fer talking," explained Pilgrim.

Bartley, in true mountain storytelling style, had to continue his account on killing the bear. He added a piece here and a twist there, so that it sounded like a life-threatening confrontation. Pilgrim listened with great enthusiasm. But knowing Bartley as he did, he figured he probably had shot it at a hundred yards or so while it was eating berries.

As so often happens with the mountain people, when they find someone to talk to, they ramble on for days; then once it's all been said, they go off to themselves again and start building new stories for their next encounter. So it was with Pilgrim and Bartley. It seemed that each had a story, one after another.

That evening at supper, Bartley asked, "What ev'r happened ta that friend of yorn, Buffler?"

"He took sick this last year; up an' died bout a month ago. We buried him near the cabin at his favorite spot," said Pilgrim.

"Sorry ta hear that. I always liked thet ole cuss," Bartley sympathetically replied.

From that moment on the hunting, trapping, and stories of hard winters and long dry summers subsided to more somber discussions about the dwindling buffalo herds, gold seekers, and western expansion.

Bartley told Pilgrim that the buffalo were all but wiped out. He explained that the Kiowa, whose life depended on the buffalo and whose religion was based on the buffalo, along with the Comanche and what was left of the Cheyenne, made a futile attempt earlier in the year to drive out the buffalo hunters. "There are more hunters now than there are buffalo, yet President Grant wouldn't sign any regulations to stop the frivolous killing and slaughter of the buffalo. The Kiowa said that the slaughter was so bad that the buffalos' blood ran into the sky. Just fifteen years earlier, one herd alone had over 30,000,000 buffalo." They discussed the fact, and both remembered seeing buffalo in herds that were three miles wide and ten miles long.

"The Indians were driven back, and the herds continue to fall. There are small groups of Indians that will never give up, but only one nation, the Nez Perce, have never signed a treaty with the whites. General Howard was sent to the Clearwater River in Idaho, to find the Nez Perce leader, Chief Joseph. He offered to buy the land from Chief Joseph. The chief told Howard that the earth was the mother to all people, and all he could do was offer to share it with them.

"The Nez Perce are strong in their beliefs and think that it is a disgrace to tell a lie. They are never the people to be the first to break a bargain. Needless to say, that with all the things the whites have done to Indians and the lies they have spoken and broken, Chief Joseph isn't willing to share the land any longer.

"Custer spent the better part of 1873 and 74 gathering up the Cheyenne, Kiowa, Ute, Modock, Shoshone, and Paiute, and placed them on the reservations. The rest of the time he has spent promoting himself to President Grant. He was so proud of his own success for getting so many different Indian nations to the reservations that he called his efforts the Custer Trail.

"President Grant didn't accept Custer's title for his deeds, and for political reasons, he called it the 'Freedom Trail.' The Lakota, on the other hand, called it the, "Thieves Trail," probably the closest thing to the truth.

"When Grant got word of General Howard's failed attempt to buy the Nez Perce and break their spirit, the Washington Government decided it was time to clamp down on the Indians. Not only were they to clamp down on the Nez Perce, but also on the 20,000 Lakota in the Dakota Territory, near the Black Hills. Custer was sent to bring the leaders in, and the word is they have refused to talk."

Pilgrim just shook his head at all this. "What yer tellin' me is that the Indians and the white man finally got a belly full-a each other, don't understand each other, and ain't neither of 'em willin' ta give in ta the other."

"Yep, I guess that 'bout sizes it up," added Bartley.

Pilgrim sat quietly trying his best to absorb the stories that Bartley so eagerly brought him up to date on. Pilgrim settled himself in his chair and fell into an ambiguous stare into the center of the burning embers of the fireplace. His mind was cluttered with the discerning thoughts surrounding the stories as told by Bartley, and his memories of the way things used to be, the untamed frontier, natural by nature and unspoiled by the hands of man.

Bartley quietly got up from his chair and without asking Pilgrim, went to the coffeepot suspended on the pot hanger over the fire and poured two cups of steaming hot brew. He slid one across the table in front of Pilgrim and awaited his reaction. The smell of fresh cup of coffee seemed to stimulate Pilgrim's awareness and he thanked Joshua.

Jonas spent the entire time that Bartley was talking with Pilgrim, looking at the many trinkets that cluttered Bartley's cabin. One object in particular held his attention with extreme fascination. It was a miniature bull elk carved from a piece of elk antler.

Bartley was quite skilled and had an artful eye, as demonstrated by the hundreds of carvings displayed around the room. Bartley watched the boy as he examined each and every piece. He watched the expressions change on the boys face with each new article he saw. He noticed that Jonas kept going back to study the elk now and then.

"You like that trinket, boy?" Bartley gruffly asked and directed a look at Jonas.

Jonas could tell from the change in Bartley's voice that the statement was directed at him, and he thought he had done something wrong. He wasn't really listening, but it didn't matter; he wouldn't have understood it anyway.

Bartley saw right off that he frightened Jonas. He smiled to put him at ease then went to the shelf and took the elk carving and handed it to Jonas. He smiled again, and the boy seemed to understand. Jonas went outside with his new trinket. Moments later he returned with a fleshing tool that he had made and handed it to Joshua. Joshua smiled at the boy, then looked at Pilgrim for a response.

"The boy ain't used ta gittin' somethin' fer nothin'," stated Pilgrim.

Bartley looked at Jonas again and said, "Youngin', you'll never know how bad I need one a' these here scrapin' knives. Why, thet's whut I was a tusslin' with when ya came ridin' in here. Looks ta me it's a good un', too."

Jonas seemed pleased with Bartley's comments and felt that he had offered a fair trade. He looked at the elk again, and again right through to supper time.

Bartley served a bear roast so big that it hardly fit in the pot it was cooked in. That was the first real meal that Pilgrim and Jonas had for some time. A short time after supper, Joshua fixed a bunk for the boy. Jonas wasted no time taking advantage of the comfort and quickly fell asleep as the men continued their conversation. Pilgrim asked Joshua what he thought was going to happen to the Indians.

"Somethin' really big is brewin' further north," Bartley replied. He got up to get a bottle of whiskey from the cabinet and a couple of shot glasses. He hesitated with the details until he finished pouring the glasses brim full. "Don't know fer sure, but hear tell rumors of the Injuns joinin' up with each other."

Pilgrim looked puzzled for a moment before he asked Bartley, "Joinin' up?"

"Yep, all of em, all kinds, all comin' together for one last free fer all with the soldiers, win or lose," explained Bartley.

Both men sat in silence for a few moments, picturing in their mind's eye the bloodbath that might develop and wondering at the outcome of such a skirmish.

"Yep, the Nez Perce, Cheyenne, Arapaho, Gall, Ogallala, Modock, Crow, Sioux, Shoshone, and Lakota, and even some Paiute 're all headed up ta the biggest pow-wow ever," Bartley added.

They both pondered the thought as they sipped their whiskey. "You en' the boy goin' ta stay on fer awhile, Pilgrim? Maybe we can git some trappin' and huntin' in. The youngin' 'ud like thet, ah'm sure," Joshua said in a welcoming tone.

"Got no place we need ta be any time soon," Pilgrim said.

The evening more or less ended on that note, and the two of them retired for the day.

***

Bright and early the next morning, Joshua, rousted both Jonas and Pilgrim from a sound sleep. He was intent on taking the boy on a bear hunt and wanted to waste no time getting started. Pilgrim was up for it, and thought that a good bear hunt might be what he needed to lift his spirits. Bartley looked at Jonas and pointed at one of his many bear-hide rugs and made a growling sound as he held his arms high as an attacking bear would do. He dramatically simulated the act of shooting the bear.

Jonas understood without question what their plans were and scrambled about in his preparations.

Bartley inquired as to the caliber of Pilgrim's rifle, and Pilgrim told him it was a .50 caliber Hawkin.

"May not be enough," the burley bearhunter replied. "Got an extra .54 caliber iffen ya like to try 'er."

"I killed 'em before with this 'ere rifle; no need to change now, don't reckon," Pilgrim replied.

"Sure ya have, but ya ain't never run inta bears as big 'n' mean as they is in these here parts,"Bartley replied jokingly.

"Let's go get the bait," Bartley enthusiastically suggested to his guests. He always kept several areas baited with all kinds of stuff he called his "special concoction." He ran his baited areas as a trapper would his lines, always adding some of the fresh, fowl smelling slop that he had made up the night before. His recipe was hardly ever the same, but consisted of molasses, fish guts, pork grease, chunks of half-rotted meat, and a variety of over ripe, partially smashed berries. He kept his supply in a wooden bucket on the end of a rope, deep in sink hole about a hundred yards from the cabin. He had to, to keep the bears and other varmints out of it until it was ready to use.

"Here, boy; you kin carry this here bait," Bartley ordered, as he handed Jonas the slimy, rope-handled bucket.

Pilgrim and Jonas followed Bartley as he trudged his way on a well beaten path that led them higher on the mountain side.

"Gotta hunt 'em high in the mornin' and low at night," Joshua explained. "They'll wind ya iffen ya don't."

As they approached the first baited area, Bartley motioned for assistants to slow down and be very quiet. He paused, a few steps later, and examined the area with sweeping accuracy. He even lifted his nose to the breeze as if he were trying to smell the presence of a furry beast. He looked at his bait site, then broke the silence.

"Nope, ain't been here!" he exclaimed.

Joshua motioned for the boy to follow him with the bucket, and then proceeded to pour some of the bucket's thick, flowing contents onto the area already stinking from prior baiting.

Without any talking, he led the way further into the bushes. Then the same procedures took place when they reached the second site, then the third. As they were approaching the fourth baited area, Jonas's attention was wandering to other things, and his interest in bear hunting had dissipated. He fell farther and farther behind Pilgrim and Joshua with each step they took.

Pilgrim was consumed with interest as Bartley approached the fourth baited site. He felt a change occur in Joshua's approach and saw an emerging concern fall upon his face. "Bear," he whispered. "I smell him. Where's the boy?" Bartley continued.

Pilgrim turned to see for himself that the boy wasn't there, and cast a worried look in Bartley's direction.

"We'd best be locatin' him real quick, but be quiet," Bartley warned.

Pilgrim backtracked fifty or so yards when he spotted Jonas meandering up the trail, swinging the bucket and lost in the thoughts of another place and time. At that moment a huge grizzly reared to his hind feet only a few yards in front of Jonas. Jonas stopped in his tracks. The bear roared, dropped to all fours and closed in on Jonas. With each step of his awkward hind foot wobble, the fat rippled under his heavy fur. The bear was reaching and waving his front paws for Jonas. Each swat appeared to have a force of vengeful intent.

Pilgrim raised his rifle, and pulled the trigger before his aim had found its mark. He hit the bear in the flank. The bear dropped to all fours, and ran directly at Pilgrim. Pilgrim, pulled his pistol and sent another round at the charging brute. This shot hit the animal in the chest, but did nothing to discourage his fast approach.

Joshua heard all the commotion and ran back to see the charging bear close half the distance between that of Pilgrim and the bear. Bartley reached Pilgrim first and shoved him out of the way, then started flailing his arms and yelling obscenities at the advancing monster. The bear turned into the underbrush, and in an instant there was dead silence.

Pilgrim picked himself up as Bartley retained a watchful eye on the situation. "Is he dead?" Pilgrim asked.

"Don't think so," responded Bartley. "Ain't much worse then a wounded bear."

Jonas was shaking with fear as he moved close to Pilgrim's side. Pilgrim reloaded his rifle and pistol and asked Joshua what they should do.

"Don't rightly know, but I told ya yer rifle weren't big enough," Bartley chastised him.

Pilgrim didn't offer a comeback.

Joshua stood there with a contemplating look about him and after a few passing moments shared his thoughts. "Iffen we wait awhile he may come back, and iffen we go after 'im he's likely goin' ta sneak around us. Iffen he comes in at too close a range, it'll be mighty hard ta get a killin' shot b'fore he gets ya. We could start prayin' he's dead somewhere in them bushes over yonder."

A few moments later Bartley came up with a plan. "Pilgrim, you and the youngin' stay real close together. Don't let me git outta yer sight. I'll follow the critter's blood real slow, one speck at a time. When I motion fer ya ta come on, bring the youngin' all the way to where ah'm a standin', then wait there. Watch our backside, 'specially mine. Oh, one mere thin'; watch mah front side, too," Bartley said in a very serious tone. He dropped his head looking for the first spot of blood. Pilgrim stood vigil with Jonas close at his side, as Bartley slowly trailed the bear's path through the underbrush. Every fifty yards or so, at least before he got out of their sight, he motioned for them to move up to his location. As the blood trail got heavier Bartley's pace quickened.

Bartley paused to tell Pilgrim that he had a good blood trail but had some concern because the bear seemed to be circling its way back. They continued their tracking procedures over and over and found themselves approaching near to the spot where Pilgrim first shot the animal.

Joshua then shouted out, "He's 'ere, died afore he could git back to us."

Pilgrim and the boy ran to see the grizzly. Pilgrim looked at Bartley and said, "Told ya my rifle were enough."

"Yep, ya did at thet, but it took ya two shots to git it done," Joshua quipped back. "'Tain't normally the rifle thet duz the job nohow, but the placement of the ball."

Joshua looked a few yards up the trail and noticed the bucket of bait laying on its side. "Boy, look whut ya went an' done! Ya spilled the bucket of concoction," Bartley said with a smile. Thet bear wern't comin' back fer that bucket, neither. He was comin' back fer you." He grabbed the boy in jest.

"Well, we shur got sum hard work ahead of us," Bartley said. "You'uns go back 'en git the horses, an' I'll git started skinin' 'im."

Their work on the bear lasted throughout the daylight hours. Even with two horses, they had to make two trips. Since Pilgrim killed the bear, it was rightly his to do with as he pleased. He and Bartley talked it over that night, and Pilgrim decided to let Jonas have the hide and claws.

Chapter 12

Pilgrim and Jonas stayed on with Joshua Bartley for several months. Bartley could see in Pilgrim's eyes and in his uneasy actions and almost-nervous state that he was itching for some kind of a change. He seriously doubted if Pilgrim was even aware of his own jitters and uneasiness.

Jonas worked unrelentingly, most every day on his bear-hide projects. He scraped the raw hide, tanned it, cut it in well-planned shapes, and had started hand-stitching the pieces.

Pilgrim's unrest finally got the better of him, and when he finally come up with a plan and a reason for leaving, he spoke to Bartley about it. He felt the need to go north to find out what was happening with the Indian nations.

Bartley warned him not to get to involved and end up losing his topknot. "Don't ya be forgittin' ya ain't no Injun. Ever' Injun left in the whole country's goin'ta be headed thet way, too. Right 'bout now they'z probably not much in the mood ta be talkin' to any white man, includin' you."

Pilgrim listened to Bartley's advice, but his mind was made up. "We'll leave tomorrow at first light," he said.

Jonas saw Pilgrim preparing his belongings, and watched as he started to pack. He sensed they would be leaving. Jonas worked as diligently as he could on his projects, and with great haste. He finished late that night, long after Pilgrim and Joshua had gone to sleep. He then crawled in his bunk for the remaining hours of the night.

Early the next morning Pilgrim's ardent intent was expressed with great exhilaration. He called the boy to a big breakfast that Joshua had toiled over in hours of preparation.

Jonas swiftly concurred to Pilgrim's wishes, and slipped his feet into the new moccasins he had made out of the bear-hide scraps.

"Come on, youngin'; git yer belly full fer yer trip. Yer goin' ta need it," Bartley demanded.

The three of them ate their fill. Pilgrim was anxious to get started and wasted little time after the meal to thank Bartley for his hospitality. Bartley quite understood, and offered to help them with their last-minute preparations.

Jonas pulled several objects from under his bunk and meticulously separated it into two piles. He picked up one pile and laid it at Bartley's feet, the other at Pilgrim's. Bartley's pile of gifts consisted of a pair of mittens and a necklace with five, front bear claws attached. Pilgrim lifted his endowment and found it to be a cold-weather coat garnished with ten bear claws across the forepart. He was impressed with the true quality and detailed workmanship. Pilgrim's glad smile as he slipped the coat over his shoulders, showed all the thanks that was needed and much to the boy's pleasure.

Joshua was overwhelmed by his gift and walked over to his shelf that held all his carvings and reached for a special little gift he could give the youngster in return. He handed the boy a replica of a bear that was standing on its hind legs, just as the monster had once stood before Jonas.

Jonas was thoroughly exhilarated by the gesture, and jested a simulating growl as he so well remembered the bear that day. They all found humor in his expression and busted out in laughter, including Jonas himself.

Pilgrim motioned for Jonas to follow, and as they left the cabin Bartley followed. Their goodbyes were short, after Pilgrim hoisted Jonas to one of Buffler's horses, then mounted his own.

As they rode off, Bartley's last words were, "Keep yer hair on, ya hear?"

Pilgrim waved his arm, assuring Bartley that his words would be heeded.

***

Pilgrim, once he got started on his trip, realized he really had no idea where or why they were going. His unsettled search, for whatever it was that he was looking for, never did provide answers, just a driving desire. It reminded him of the days that he and Buffler roamed the mountains and plains.

Jonas seemed to approve of the direction the two were traveling. Both he and Pilgrim were well aware of the fact that Lame Horse had gone north with his band of followers, and right then finding Lame Horse had merit. Pilgrim could find out what lay in store for the Indian nations, and Jonas would be able to return to his people.

Pilgrim and Jonas traveled for fifteen days and saw no sign of anyone. Their travel was steady, yet considerably less than hurried. On the sixteenth day they happened on a deserted Indian camp. He thought it might be that of the Crow. There appeared to have been nearly fifty lodges, and based on other apparent sign left behind, the Indians had used the site for an extended period of time. There were no signs of battle, compelling their departure. This was obviously a well-planned, well-organized move. Pilgrim could determine from the residuary, weathered sign left by the drag marks of travois, horse tracks, and fire pits, that they left several weeks earlier. He speculated that their travel was in a northwesterly direction.

Pilgrim's perception, if accurate, gave credence to Joshua's bruit pertaining to all the Indian nations rendezvousing somewhere in the northern territories. Pilgrim cast a queried glance at Jonas. The boy acceded to Pilgrim's keen senses, and motioned the direction in which the village had headed. Pilgrim, fully understanding Jonas's gesture, nodded his head in agreement. They followed the trail of the village and thought it would serve not only the safest route to take, but the trail most likely to offer explanations at its end.

Pilgrim had little problem following the telltale signs left by the village now on the move. He let Jonas concentrate his skills on tracking the path of the village, while he focused his attention to anything that appeared out of the ordinary.

Two days' travel and Pilgrim noticed fresher sign that converged with the other trail. The sign indicated that the trail was joined by many others, less than a couple of days prior. It was clearer each step of the way that Bartley's anecdotal tale had increasing merit.

Pilgrim's discernment generated a guarded concern in his awareness of their situation. He felt the dangers of a possible inadvertent confrontation with braves sent out to protect the flanks of the traveling villagers. They were in a potentially dangerous situation and were compelled to pull off the trail for their own protection.

Pilgrim lingered in his commitment to follow, but found his better judgment impaired by his desire to find out what the Indians were up to. He and Jonas paralleled the Indian trail at great distance, and continued in their quest.

Their pursuit was conducted at a much slower pace than that of the entire village. He was bewildered by the thoughts of other groups coming in from either side or worse yet, from the rear. His best judgment, reaffirmed by the contemplation of their options, disclosed the necessity to pull further away from the trail and head due west. Traveling to the west would take them far from any northbound trails and deep into rugged mountain terrain. Travel there would be arduously slow, but much safer.

Twelve days later, Pilgrim and Jonas reached a pass where the trails were heavily worn, showing signs of vast numbers of travelers that had recently passed that way. All markings indicated the movement was from the southeast and continued along the eastern slopes of the Rockies. They appeared to be heading in a northwesterly direction.

Without hesitation or much deliberation, Pilgrim crossed the trail and stayed on their northerly route, holding fast to the protection of the rugged mountains.

Pilgrim and Jonas stayed far enough from the foothills trail to remain undetected by the Indians who traveled there. Every night was a cold camp in order to remain unseen, and their comforts were nonexistent. Jonas spent the waning hours of daylight, making a bow, while Pilgrim contemplated their position and made his decisions as to their next day's travel.

Late one evening, Pilgrim thought he saw the flickering campfires far below their position. He called for Jonas, and he too saw the glimmering light. Pilgrim rested easier that night knowing the Indians exact location.

Pilgrim woke the next morning at the first sign of daylight and was determined to get a closer look at the Indian camp. They remained high in the foot hills and eventually came upon a rocky overlook that offered Pilgrim the distant vantage point he yearned for. They watched, as hundreds of Indians below prepared for their day's journey. There was far too much distance between them to determine who they were.

By the time the sun shone full in the eastern sky, the Indians were on the move and nearly out of sight. Pilgrim breathed a sigh of relief, knowing they were in little danger especially if they held back for a day or two. Pilgrim built a small, smokeless fire using only the driest most brittle branches from the abundant supply of deadfall. He immediately put a pot of water on the hot coals, to brew some coffee that he so strongly desired.

Jonas was putting the finishing touches on the arrows that he had been laboring over for the previous two weeks. He looked deep into Pilgrim's face for some form of facial expression representing approval. Then proceeded to nock an arrow to take a practice shot.

Pilgrim wasn't sure what Jonas was aiming at, but after releasing the string, he could tell by the look on Jonas's face that he must have hit it. Jonas continued to shoot several arrows one after another. Pilgrim was awestruck by the evident skills and coordination that Jonas had demonstrated with the primitive weapon.

Pilgrim heard the repetitive drumming sound of a grouse and paused to determine its location. He looked at Jonas who picked up on it posthaste. Jonas needed little persuasion, and instantly transformed himself into a silent stalker. Jonas was patient in his attempt. He waited for the bird to repeat its wing-flailing mating call, and when it did he moved quickly and silently to close the distance. When Jonas had the bird spotted, his moves were steady yet undetectable.

Pilgrim watched the boy hunt and recalled having witnessed similar skills shown by a friend of many years ago. Those were the hunting skills of Rock Forehead when he sneaked in on, and killed an elk. Pilgrim could see Jonas approach the bird, but couldn't see the grouse from his sitting position. He stood just in time see the wings of the bird start a beating sequence from his drumming log perch, when Jonas let loose an arrow. The bird's feathers provided an explosive spectacle, as Jonas reached for another arrow. He took aim and shot at an approaching hen, temporarily distracted by the strange movements of her mate. Both of Jonas's arrows successfully found their mark, and he hastily retrieved his quarry.

It was apparent to Pilgrim that Jonas was pleased with his hunt, and it showed in the way he approached Pilgrim with tokens of his achievement.

Pilgrim smiled and patted the boy's back. Then he walked over to his packhorse and pulled an iron skillet and some pork grease from the cook pack. Jonas took the hint, and needed no further prodding to perform his remaining duties in preparation for the meal.

Jonas cleaned the birds and saved almost every feather in the process. He carefully pulled the feathers making sure that each was cleanly plucked and free of any fatty tissue. He stuffed them in a little pouch and tied them to the horse he had been riding.

Pilgrim wondered what the boy had in mind for his bag of feathers and knew that Jonas would make something useful from his trophies.

The hot meal along with a couple hot cups of coffee seemed to relax Pilgrim. He lay back and let the warming sun penetrate his body to the depths of his soul, while Jonas's never-ending source of energy allowed him to explore the area around the camp.

Pilgrim's mind relaxed, allowing him to fall into a deep sleep. Several hours later, Jonas's movements around the camp caused

Pilgrim to stir from his nap. When he entirely regained his awareness, the dream that he had experienced became clear in his mind. The vision of great dust clouds consumed hundreds of riders in blue coats. They were lost in the confusion and split up like a frightened herd of antelope. None of the blue coat riders could escape the dust. When the cloud dissipated, the horses were riderless.

This vision of his dream stayed in Pilgrim's thoughts. Recurring depictions of the incident seized his every waking moment with fear that his dream may indeed hold some truth for that which is yet to come.

The following day, Pilgrim and Jonas, headed down to the flat plains at the foothills of an overlook. There they found the overnight camp of the sojourning Indians. The trail was clear, and the plains were open to view in all directions. The two of them followed the trail to the River of the Little Bighorn, where the Indians followed the near bank toward the northeast.

Pilgrim decided to cross the river and trail their course until they either caught up with them or crossed their trail at a river crossing further upstream. They blindly followed the course of the river for four days, being cautious each step of the way.

***

On the fifth day Pilgrim reached an uneasy sense about the their proximity to the Indians and scouted his approach with a watchful eye. They watched as small bands of scouts rode out in all directions. Each group was made up of four to six braves and appeared to be primarily of the Lakota sect. This was a strange sight to Pilgrim for he thought the area was the home of the Crow Nation.

Pilgrim and his young Indian companion worked their way around the Lakota camp without incident, and later found a camp that was Cheyenne.

Jonas boiled with excitement, and tried to explain that they were his people, and that he would be accepted there.

Pilgrim let the boy have one of Buffler's horses; the one that he'd been riding, and go to the camp in hopes of finding Lame Horse.

Several hours passed before Jonas returned, escorted by three other young braves. He motioned to Pilgrim upon his approach that he was to join them. He called him "Elk Arrow" and made him aware that he was to return to the camp with them and that there he would be safe. Pilgrim mounted his horse and rode with his friend, and the other young braves in the direction of the camp.

When they entered the camp twenty or more young Indian boys followed the horses on foot. They reminded him of Jonas when he visited Rock Forehead's camp several years ago. He realized that Jonas was no longer a child and saw him for the first time as a young man and a respected leader among his friends. He saw a strong sense of pride shroud Jonas, when the young man reintroduced him, to those around the primary lodge. It was the lodge of Lame Horse.

Lame Horse wasn't at the camp when Pilgrim arrived, but his camp's people made him feel welcome. The squaws and young girls prepared a place for him around the cook fire and offered him food. Both Jonas and Pilgrim ate their fill. Pilgrim watched as the younger children played in the immediate area. He also watched as a number of young girls gathered around Jonas as he was telling stories with increasing enthusiasm.

Lame Horse rode in camp with four other braves flanking him. He was aware that Elk Arrow had returned with Jonas as soon as he entered the camp. Pilgrim was apprehensive about Lame Horse's return, but felt at ease once he heard Lame Horse greet him. "Elk Arrow, my friend, you have returned to us."

Pilgrim replied, "I, too, am glad ta see my friend." He paused momentarily and continued, "I bring Quinatata back to his people."

"Yes, this I see. Come to my lodge. We have much to talk about," stated Lame Horse. He motioned Pilgrim to lead the way through the entrance to the lodge.

Pilgrim entered the lodge and stepped to the right, the place where visitors were expected to be seated. He waited for Lame Horse to enter, followed by Quinatata. Lame Horse asked them to be seated.

Pilgrim was anxious to find out what was going on with all the Indian movement, but held his tongue for Lame Horse to start the conversation, as is customary in ones own lodge.

"You come far, Elk Arrow," Lame Horse said, opening the talk. "Is it because you return the boy to his own people, or do you come on behalf of your white brother?" Lame Horse's direct line of questioning was much like Pilgrim's own style of conversation.

He responded, "No, my friend, I have no white brothers. My friends 're here, and I worry fer the people and what is ta come to them," responded Pilgrim.

"I, too, worry for the people and what is to come," Lame Horse said. "It will soon be determined."

Lame Horse told Pilgrim that it would be a decision of the Great Spirit, and that his people were spiritual beings on a human journey. He told of the great meeting that was to take place with all the nations. Most of the Indian sects were now represented and preparations were being made for a great Sun Dance.

Lame Horse told of having just met with Sitting Bull of the Lakota. Also represented were Chief Joseph of the Nez Perce, Low Dog of the Gall, Crazy Horse of the Ogallala, and White Bull of the Modock.

"There was much talk about the white soldiers," said Lame Horse. He continued telling that Sitting Bull told of a recent dream he had, where a large dust storm filled the sky like a huge cloud, and with the cloud came soldiers, but the village emerged unharmed.

Pilgrim recalled his dream and thought of the similarities to the events of Sitting Bull's vision.

"There was much talk of a great battle to come, but the time was not then to make that decision," explained Lame Horse.

The talking ended with Chief Joseph's final comment where he said that he was tired of talk that comes to nothing. Lame Horse concluded that the time for final decision would take place at the conclusion of the Sun Dance. "The Sun Dance will begin four days from now," stated Lame Horse. "Tonight we will feast, then I will spend three days and nights in preparation for the ceremony. Go now, the both of you, and help in the preparation of the feast. I must rest."

Pilgrim and Jonas left the chief's lodge and instructed the women to make a feast as Lame Horse had instructed.

Chapter 13

The word of the feast spread through the camp rapidly and everyone took part in the preparations. Even the children had been assigned small tasks. As the sun's great light faded in the western skies, the activities in the center of camp took on a festive nature with light spirited activities and demonstrations of humor and laughter from the older people as they watched the children play their games.

Pilgrim watched the people with great interest. He saw the women as they hustled about making sure that every detail of the meal was in order. A small group of children were being intently scolded by one squaw when their wrestling stirred a dust that was carried in the air over her cook pot.

He closely observed several small groups of braves that were enthralled in serious conversation.

He strongly felt that the small group discussions were conjunct to the same events that Lame Horse had told him of earlier that day. One group seemed to have opposing views that was made apparent by the heated discussion between two braves. Lame Horse emerged from his lodge and looked at the disputatious group who broke off their controversial discussion without delay. Lame Horse chided their activity and the group dispersed.

Darkness fully surrounded the camp, and the flickering camp fires showed on the faces that closely surrounding them. Silhouettes were all that could be seen of distant figures. Some were eating as others danced to the low, rhythmic beat of the drums.

Lame Horse joined Pilgrim and made conversation of things from his childhood. There was no discussion of the things that were to come, and at one point he stopped Pilgrim when he inquired information about the Sun Dance. Pilgrim respected the chief's wishes, withdrew his questions, and proceeded to tell Lame Horse about Jonas's close confrontation with the bear.

Lame Horse was fascinated by Pilgrim's narrative and called for others to hear his tale. The small assembly shared stories for many hours.

One brave came directly to Lame Horse and announced that the sweat lodge was ready. The chief asked Pilgrim to join him in the purification procedures. As the two of them stripped their clothing, Lame Horse explained that there would be no spoken words between them for the next three days during his readiness for the Sun Dance.

The two men entered the lodge naked and silent. The lodge was very hot and took Pilgrim's breath as he entered. The air was thick with steam that surfaced from heated rocks as Lame Horse sprinkled water on them. The lodge flickered from the faint yellow light from the nearby fire that heated the rocks. The pungent smell of smudging sage and smoldering cedar made breathing quite difficult at first, but soon relaxed his breathing, and seemed to calm his inner soul. His mind seemed to be stimulated by the steamy redolence and new clearer thoughts started to materialize.

Lame Horse waved a sprig from a cedar branch gently over the burning ashes of sage, and started to chant a prayer. When he finished, he repeated it, over and over. When Lame Horse felt that his spirit was properly prepared, he wrapped himself in a buffalo robe, left the sanctity of the sweat lodge and headed directly to his own lodge, without a spoken word.

Pilgrim soon followed. He dressed outside the sweat lodge in the light of the dying fire. He had been invited to stay with Quinatata, in his father's, brother's lodge. Pilgrim's body gave way to sleep very quickly, but his soul roamed the plains in a dream. He clearly saw visions of many great Indians, each of which showed great strength. They stood in a great circle and their heads reached the clouds. Many small, soldiers wearing blue, rode on horses the size of ants within the circle of the Indian leaders. The blue color of their coats fell to the ground like rain, and their coats became red.

Pilgrim woke abruptly and looked around the lodge. He heard a stirring of people outside. It was daylight. He exited the lodge in haste to tell Lame Horse of his dream, but remembered that Lame Horse was not to be disturbed during his preparation for the Sun Dance. Pilgrim wondered if he would be invited to the Sun Dance. He was aware that Lame Horse would make that decision unequivocally and that it was not a decision that Pilgrim would have any say. He knew that in the eyes of the other sects, he would probably be considered an enemy. It all depended on Lame Horse's status with the other leaders.

Pilgrim's next three days were filled with anxiety. He was welcome in the camp and it offered him a safe refuge from the inherent dangers that existed elsewhere on the plains. Other sects would see him only as a white man, and any confrontation would mean certain death. He was a prisoner to the safety of the camp. Pilgrim dawdled the time away with Jonas and his cousins. They invited him to join the games that Jonas's age took part in, mostly horse riding skills and tests of strength.

***

The third evening after the feast, Lame Horse appeared outside his lodge, and called for a meeting of the camp's leading braves. He also requested that Pilgrim attend. The request swept through the camp with the speed and silence equal to that of the prairie wind. Braves approached the camp lodge from all directions within moments of hearing the request. Lame Horse entered the lodge first, then the others followed, single file. Pilgrim was the last to enter and took a seat nearest the entryway. There was complete silence as the group of twenty to twenty-five braves settled in their respective seats awaiting the first words from their leader.

Lame Horse opened his presentation with instruction to the others about the Sun Dance. He told them that they would all participate in the four-day ceremony. Pilgrim was hoping that he would be included in that offer, about the time one brave asked Lame Horse if Elk Arrow was allowed to participate. Lame Horse paused, and directed the answer to Pilgrim. "Elk Arrow will be welcome as my guest. He is to go. He is to watch. He can allow his own mind and body to join us, but his talk will not take part in the events."

Lame Horse continued to tell all of them that this was to be a peaceful Sun Dance and that even though many old enemies would be there, they were to respect the ceremony and make it a quest for prayers, answers to prayers, and guidance. At the end of the three days, they were all to return to the camp where their visions could be assessed by the shaman and shared with the tribal council. A decision would be made from those visions, and Lame Horse would then speak in favor of those decisions, in a meeting of the chief's, that would follow two days after the Sun Dance.

"We leave in the morning," concluded Lame Horse.

They all quietly parted, and camp was hushed for the remainder of the night.

Chapter 14

The next morning at the first sign of morning light, before the women and children awoke, Pilgrim was summoned by one of the braves. They quietly gathered by the horses. Twenty-seven braves, Lame Horse, and Pilgrim mounted their horses and rode silently from the camp.

Lame Horse's group passed three other camps on the way to the Sun Dance near Rosebud Creek, and it wasn't until they passed the second camp that Pilgrim realized the magnitude of what was about to take place. His heart pounded in anticipation, and he felt a strong concern for the fact that he was an outsider. He was a white man, and though his heart was with his friends, his appearance kept him separated. He had a fear that increased the closer they got.

The sun had just cleared the horizon when they arrived at the site of the Sun Dance. The double-circled arbor was covered with pine boughs. In the very center of the inner circle, was a single tall cottonwood tree, whose leaves quaked in the mild breeze. There were many colorful strips of brightly colored cloth that were tied to nearly every branch of the tree. Many long leather cords were attached high in the tree draping over the center branch and tied in coils to the trunk. Each of the four directions was represented by a specific color, and each of the four directions was marked at the boundaries of both the inner circle and the outer circle.

Many groups, some larger in number than Lame Horse's group, began to appear. It was apparent from the variety of garments that there were many sects represented.

Pilgrim found that most of them completely ignored his presence, and in some strange way that put him more at ease.

Lame Horse led Pilgrim to the west end of the arbor where the arbor was extended for council lodge in fashion that covered a rather large area. All the leaders were gathering there. He pointed to an area just outside the west lodge under the circular arbor where Pilgrim was to sit. Lame Horse removed his moccasins before he entered the arbor, as did Pilgrim, then he left Pilgrim's side and joined the other leaders at the west arbor lodge.

Pilgrim, watched as three Lakota braves cleansed their bodies with the smoke of burning sage and cedar in a smudging practice. They took their places under the arbor to the left side of Pilgrim, and started the ceremonies with a series of drumbeats and chanting. Many of the Indians joined to form a line, and entered the inner circle one at a time. After they all danced to the four directions, they split up and formed several large circles around the center tree. The chanters were periodically replaced with new chanters as were the drummers. The dancers, would take short breaks and rest in the shade of the west arbor. Their rest was short and seldom taken. They all danced until the sun fell below the western horizon.

It was a time of fasting. No one, including Pilgrim ate food. It was a part of the personal commitment and self denial that brought them their understanding. Some even chose not to drink water.

Several sweat lodges were available to the dancers. Pilgrim helped to keep the fire pits burning that heated the rocks. He heeded Lame Horse's advice and did nothing more than assist others in remedial chores. The first night was spent in spirit awakening tribal groups, denying themselves the self gratifying pleasures of sleep. Pilgrim was invited to enter a lodge. Without participation he listened to their chanting and talk of spirit visions. Pilgrim's spirit joined in their quests through the dark hours of the night.

The next morning at sunrise, the drums called the dancers to the arbor for a repeat of the previous days dancing. The hot summer air held the smoky fragrances of sweet grass, sage, and cedar. At sundown, the dancers once again adjourned to the sweat lodges, then in small groups to the lodges of their choice. Many of the dancers chose to share the night lodges with other sects in search for common visions. The different sects underwent a metamorphic transformation that was found through common bond. They were no longer segregated as they were in the beginning. They all shared a common ground, a similar cause, and the same self denials and personal pains.

The third day started and ended much the same as the first two days, but to Pilgrim, something about the third day seemed different. The dancing, chanted songs and drum beats were different. The prayers were not directed inward. Each of the dancers prayers seemed to be directed outwardly with a semblance of begging with great fervor. A desperation was seen in the faces of all who danced and also in the faces of those who lined the great circle of the arbor. The day was special, a day where all forgot their own needs and prayed for the needs of others. It was a day of healing. The third night, as the two before, was spent in prayer, vision seeking, and self evaluation.

The fourth morning when the sun showed itself at the horizon, the drummers once again called the dancers to the arbor. Pilgrim noticed a certain intensity that wasn't there either of the first two days. The drummers and chanters had an era of urgency in their performances. Dancers often looked too, and reached for the sun. Several dancers paused in prayer at the tree and lay on a buffalo hide while their respective chiefs and shaman cut two side-by-side incisions above each breast through which a bear claw was inserted and thongs tied to each. The thongs were tied to the leather straps that hung from the aspen in the center of the arbor. They continued to dance with the other dancers, and periodically they seemed to draw strength from all who danced, as they pulled with the weight of their bodies against the strap that held them. The chief and the shaman of respective captive dancers would stand before them as a sign for each to find his most inner strength, and with one attempt pull free from his bondage. Dancers that pulled the claws from their chest immediately went to the tree, knelt at the base, and prayed. All successful dancers retired to the west lodge for rest for they had completed their part in the ceremonies.

Another Indian took his place at the tree, with tied thongs around the claws in his chest. Then another and another.

Some of them had incisions made on their shoulder blades, with the claws and thongs attached through strips of their own hide. They were tied to a longer strap that held a buffalo skull. As they danced, they dragged the skull on the ground behind them. At times, the skull would catch on grass clumps but the dancer would continue to pull. Eventually the skull dancers would also pull free of their bondage by tearing their incisions.

All the participants, more than two hundred, were able to tear free from the bonding straps before the sun disappeared, and this was a great sign to the leaders of their people's strength.

The last brave to attempt the dance, was a Lakota brave from Sitting Bull's sect, so given that position in the dance because of his chief's greatness and sponsorship of the ceremonies. The final dancer carried the burden to end. He remained a captive for the entire day representing the self sacrifice of all the sects as one nation in totality.

As the sun completed its journey from east to west and set over the arbor lodge, Sitting Bull and his shaman met first at the tree of prayer and then to the dancers side to request his attempt to release himself. The dancer slowly danced toward the prayer tree allowing slack in the tether. With one great backward lunge he tore free of his bondage and let out a series of ululating yells and the drums and chanting ceased, signifying the end to the Sun Dance. The dancer went to the prayer tree and remained until the crowds around the arbor silently dissipated.

A new attitude was expressed throughout the camp, replacing the solemnity that was present during the entire event. The braves were openly talking and sharing their visions with one another. Food was being prepared all around the camp. Later that night they all slept.

The next morning Lame Horse summoned his people together for their return to their own camp. The braves seemed anxious to share their visions with Lame Horse, but refrained from doing so until the appointed time. They would all have their chance at the meetings that were planned for the following two days, back at the camp. They rode in silence, as Lame Horse proudly led the way.

The first meeting took place at mid-afternoon on the day of their return, and lasted late into the early morning hours of the following day. Each of the twenty-seven braves told of their experiences at the Sun Dance. Each told of his thoughts, the spirits encountered, and visions perceived. Near the end of the first meeting, Lame Horse asked Pilgrim to share his own observations and emotions that were acquired at the Sun Dance.

Pilgrim had waited for this moment for several days, even before the Sun Dance. He first spoke of the Sun Dance, and the visions that appeared to him there. He said that the people showed great strength and that he felt that the spirits of all the sects had joined their powers. He then told of his dream, about the circle of Chief's and the small size of the blue coat soldiers. He told of the blue coats color running from them like rain, and the blue color being replace with that of red. Pilgrim went on to tell of his previous dream where many soldiers disappeared in the great dust cloud.

Lame Horse showed much approval in the words of Pilgrim's dreams. He told them all to go, sleep, and continue to search their hearts for additional guidance provided by the dream world. He told them that he would summon them for a meeting again the following day, and he would tell them what it all meant following consultation with the shaman.

***

None of the twenty-seven braves strayed far from camp the next morning for fear they might miss the summons from Lame Horse. As the day slowly passed each of the twenty-seven braves showed a growing concern. They talked among themselves about Lame Horse's obvious discontent by wasting away the day and that there was much yet to discuss before Lame Horse met with the other leaders.

The western sky started to cast many colors of red to the clouds as the lurid light of the sun grew dim. Lame Horse finally sent out the word to summon the braves. The chief himself asked Pilgrim to attend and walked with him to the camp's meeting lodge. Many of the braves openly showed their disgust with Lame Horse's apparent lackadaisical beckoning, but held their tongues as Pilgrim entered, closely followed by Lame Horse.

Lame Horse sensed the concerns and straightaway disclosed his reasons for making them wait. He said that he had heard all their dreams and visions from the Sun Dance at the previous night's meeting. He used the time to evaluate each man's presentation and interpreted to explain the meaning of the visions. He made them wait to see what they would do with their time, and to see who could demonstrate the most patience. He also said that the meeting was no longer open to discussion. in time he would present them with a decision.

Lame Horse presented his thoughts and visions that were encountered during his daylong search for answers, in a presentation fitting to the great leader. He told the braves that his decisions were based on the dreams and visions that they had actually experienced. He looked directly at each of the braves that made their presentation known.

One by one he explained the interpretation of the visions as agreed with the shaman. After speaking of the twenty-seventh brave's vision, he paused. He summarized his decision by saying, "All your visions represent the same thing. Even the dreams of Elk Arrow see our people to be victorious over the white soldiers. Elk Arrow, you have demonstrated great patience not only at the Sun Dance, but here at camp on this day. This battle is not your battle, but I ask that you ride with me and the other leaders to witness future events, so that you can bear the truth to your people. I will go tomorrow to meet with the other leaders, and I will cast our decision to go to war with the white soldiers. Our decision is made," concluded Lame Horse. He turned and left the lodge.

Pilgrim watched the faces of the twenty-seven braves and was surprised that none of them showed any outward sign of dissension toward Lame Horse's decision or his method of leadership. Each of them silently retreated to their lodges for the night.

***

At first light, three of the braves escorted Lame Horse to the Lakota camp where the meeting of all the leaders took place. Very little talk took place prior to the call for a vote. Each leader was to know how they would represent the wishes of their respective sects, so there was little reason to further discuss their options or second guess the peoples decisions. Each Chief was handed two small stones, as soon as they arrived, one was gray and the other white.

Before the votes were cast, Sitting Bull told the leaders of his recent dream. He said that there were as many soldiers as there were grasshoppers on the plains, but all the white soldiers horses were upside down.

Sitting Bull called for the collection of the stones after he told them that a white stone cast would be the choice of those leaders that supported war. The brave, who collected the stones, dumped the contents of the pouch on the ground in front of them. All the stones in the pouch were white, but one. After the results of the voting were seen by all Sitting Bull told them all to return to their camps and prepare for battle in the ways familiar to the people.

Chapter 15

Lame Horse's camp bustled from the news and preparations were the chores of the day. Not only were the weapons of war made ready, but families were setting their minds for possible losses. Overall, they were a very positive thinking people, and did not dwell on losses before they occurred. All the braves transformed themselves in spirit and took on the look of warriors. They masterfully prepared their minds and practiced their fighting skills. They prepared their spirits with chanted prayers with offerings in the name of the people. They offered the pipe to the four points of the wind and spoke to the Great Spirit, saying things like, "You are there, oh Great One, have pity on us." They had completed their tasks and they were ready.

Seven days after the leaders met, Sitting Bull sent word to all the different sects, that the time had finally come. They were to meet at a place he called Greasy Grass, before daylight the next morning.

Pilgrim was summoned to Lame Horse's lodge soon after the message arrived. "Elk Arrow, are you ready?" Lame Horse calmly asked.

Pilgrim responded, "My prayers are with you."

Lame Horse looked at Pilgrim and said, "Come, my white brother; let's smoke the pipe of friendship."

The camp was especially quiet that night. Coyotes could be heard yipping and howling to each other from within their own territories. The moon gave off abundant light and the stars filled the sky. Pilgrim lay in complete silence as his mind wandered, his ears listened, and his eyes peered through the top of the lodge. He followed the paths of the stars as the hours lapsed one by one. Sleep seemed impossible for him that night as it must have been for the warriors.

"It is time," came the low-toned call of a messenger as he went from lodge to lodge. The message was delivered quickly throughout the camp.

Pilgrim hurriedly grabbed those things that he might need, and joined the others as they prepared their horses. Each of them moved in complete silence, and Pilgrim noticed their war-painted faces and markings on their horses in the light cast by the moon. When all the warriors arrived Lame Horse mounted his horse followed by the others, about one hundred fifty warriors in all. They left the camp at a walk, calmly and silently, but an unspoken excitement reigned over their actions.

Within a two-hour ride from Lame Horse's camp, they met with the other nations at Greasy Grass. According to the count taken, there were some eighteen hundred Indian warriors ready for the confrontation with Custer's soldiers. The scouting accounts of the soldiers' positions were being discussed with the Indian leaders.

General Sheridan had drawn a plan for his troops to be broken in three columns so they could attack the Indians from three different directions. These columns were to be led by Commander Crook, Colonel John Gibbon, and Alfred Terry.

Reno was the commander in charge of two hundred sixty-one soldiers that were to go north then back to the south. The third commanding officer was General George Armstrong Custer. Custer was leading about one hundred forty men, that included his Indian scout by the name of Horn Toad. Horn Toad had told other scouts that Custer bragged to his men that he'd never attacked a band of savages that didn't run.

After the scouts had each given their reports and positions of the blue coats to the Indian leaders, they appointed the positions and strategic duties to the various sects. All the nations readied themselves and waited patiently.

The Modock Chief briefly spoke, telling his warriors that this was a good day to fight and a good day to die.

***

The morning sunrise was red, and cast its color pink to the surrounding clouds. Each of the hundreds of white-soldier tents seemed to share the morning colors with the clouds. As Sheridan looked at the morning sky, he told Custer that the red sky in the morning is generally, a sign of stormy weather later in the day.

Custer seemed unconcerned with Sheridan's weather predictions, as he intently looked into the mirror trimming his mustache. He completely ignored Sheridan's comment.

"It will be a good morning for rounding up the remaining stragglers for the reservations. Don't you think so, George?" Sheridan said. He seemed to be trying in desperation to lure Custer from his mirror. His peers as well as his subordinates often witnessed Custer's display of vanity and ultra ego.

"Actually, General, today I will crush those savages and put an end to their raging terror across this nation," bragged Custer.

The call was made for the soldiers to mount up. Sheridan's troops rode from camp in the company of Reno's soldiers, later to split up. The other soldiers followed to Custer's command. They left the camp to the tune of "The Girl I Left Behind Me," and headed in a westerly direction.

***

Reno's soldiers pulled east of Sheridan's troops, but come midmorning they turned and headed back in a westerly direction. Later that afternoon Sheridan split his three columns, following the plan previously agreed to. He sent them in to surround the small bands of Indians they had finally located.

Colonel John Gibbon circled to the east, keeping out of sight, and using the prairie rises for cover. Alfred Terry took his column of troops to the west, following the same pattern of concealment. Commander Crook lead his forces directly at the fleeing savages. When Commander Crook topped the ridge he saw thirty, to forty Indians holding position and ordered the charge.

The soldiers' attack was quickly turned when the Indians were joined by others in great numbers. By this time the Indian warriors had flanked Terry's soldiers. Colonel Gibbon's column had gone too far to the east and passed the encounter without incident.

Reno's army came in from the east, assuming that Custer would join them from the west. When he realized he was outnumbered four to one, he ordered a retreat, but it was too late. There was no place to go. His men had no cover to take and acted dazed by the increasing numbers of Indians that surrounded them. They watched the massacre unfold around them. Some of the soldiers in great fear never even pulled their guns from their holsters.

Custer, at this time, was several miles to the west, when he saw a great dust cloud from the battle. His troops ran over the ridge, where he witnessed more than a thousand Indians viciously attacking the troops. His soldiers worked on the outer perimeter, and soon found themselves surrounded and greatly out numbered.

***

Pilgrim watched the whole thing take place from the top of the ridge with all the Indian leaders. He was sitting atop his horse next to Lame Horse. The battle from beginning to end seemed to happen in slow motion, but actually ensued in less time than it took a hungry man to eat his meal. He saw the visions come true, not only the visions of others, but his own. He saw the great cloud of dust that consumed the soldiers. He also saw the soldiers' coats turn red, and numerous dead horses motionless and upside down.

Every soldier and every soldier's horse was killed. The ground ran red with blood, as the morning sky had predicted. The Indians continued to cut off the soldiers' arms, legs, and heads. They punched their ears, as if the soldiers had not heard the treaties of the white man. Pilgrim listened intently as each of the Indian leaders gave an account of what had taken place.

Their descriptions were many, but fused by the great victory. White Bull said that it was a glorious battle, and all of them seemed to agree with that. But most of them shared the common belief that this would not be the end. More soldiers, in greater numbers than their own, would eventually come in revenge of this day.

Crazy Horse looked directly at Pilgrim to see if he agreed. Pilgrim, knowing that he was supposed to remain quiet, reluctantly agreed by slowly nodding his head. Crazy Horse asked the council what they were to do now that the battle had been fought and won. Sitting Bull instructed all of the tribes to go back to their own camps. He told them that it was there that they would find the answers to their questions.

Pilgrim followed Lame Horse, as each of the council leaders disengaged their warriors.

A stormy darkness had shrouded the field of death and a rain started to fall. The rain seemed to symbolic of a cleansing, seeking to wash it clean once again. Lame Horse's warriors reported their people's losses in the battle. Very few of his people were killed, and even fewer were wounded. He turned to his warriors, and a quiet, almost sad tone he told them that because of this battle, his people's habits would be changed for seven generations. They were swift to return to camp in the hard rain.

Pilgrim noticed that they all rode proud, but the silence seemed to hold a sad feeling about the group. He wasn't sure whether their moods were enticed by remorse or the loss of their warriors, but he knew that there would be no joyous celebrations upon their return. Camp had already received some word about the battle and were prepared for their return. Each warrior went directly to his own lodge for food and rest. Wailing could be heard throughout the night from the lodges of the warriors that didn't return.

***

The following morning started like most other mornings in the camp prior to the battle. The warriors came from the lodges, one by one, and no longer appeared to be warriors, but the braves they once were. There was much talk of the camp moving north. When Lame Horse appeared before the tribal council later that morning, the decision was final. They would go as far north as needed to escape the white intrusion upon the Cheyenne people. They would search for a land where they could live in peace.

Lame Horse had asked Pilgrim to go with them. Pilgrim knew deep in his heart that there would never be a place of peace for the Cheyenne people, especially after the battle at the Little Bighorn. He never conveyed his true thoughts to Lame Horse, but amiably declined his offer.

They wished each other well and parted ways. The camp prepared to move. Pilgrim also prepared to leave. Before he did, he found Jonas and took him to where the horses were kept. He led both of Buffler's horses to Jonas and handed him the reins. He then mounted his own horse. Jonas looked at Pilgrim, and as best he could, he thanked Pilgrim with a smile. Pilgrim turned to his packhorse and put his hand on the bear coat that Jonas had made for him. He looked at Jonas and returned the smile. For a minute or so, both Pilgrim and Jonas were reminiscing in their own minds about the bear hunt and the days they spent with Bartley. Pilgrim rode south out of the camp watching the Indians as they scrambled around in readiness for their journey. He turned around for a final glance, when he reached the fringe of the camp, and noticed that Jonas was still standing there holding the horses, watching Pilgrim leave. Pilgrim raised his arm, with his rifle in hand, as a final goodbye gesture. He never turned back to see if Jonas had returned the token, but he felt in his heart that he had.

Chapter 16

Pilgrim had nowhere in mind to go. He no longer had a place to go to, nor did he have a reason to go. He wanted desperately to share his knowledge with someone. But who, he had no family and his friends were few. Who would even believe such a yarn? He figured the soldiers would consider him a traitor to his kind, and would probably rather shoot him than listen to his stories.

The only person he knew that would listen to him would be Bartley. Pilgrim headed south on the flat plains, about fifty miles east of the trail Jonas and he had taken when they went north. There wasn't much to fear on the trail; at least that's what he thought.

Most of the Indians were likely to have traveled northeast, north, or further west. It was very unlikely that any of them would travel south into the path of the ever-expanding white army. The army was the first thing that Pilgrim encountered. A large tent camp of soldiers was camped about a hundred miles south of the Little Bighorn river. According to the hundreds of soldiers and horses he saw, they were undoubtedly a support group to Custer's mission.

Only three days had passed since the battle took place, and the visions of what Pilgrim had seen became even clearer after seeing the army post. He had mixed emotions. He didn't agree with the army and hated what they had been doing to the Indians for years. But at the same time he just wanted it all to end. He wasn't sure just how to go about it, but he felt the need to warn them.

The sentry asked Pilgrim to state his business. Pilgrim solemnly asked to see the colonel in charge, and that he had information about Custer's soldiers. The sentinel responded, "You need to talk with

Colonel Nelson Miles," and sent Pilgrim in the direction of the colonel's tent.

The colonel appeared to be restless in nature. He was instructed to wait for Custer's orders, and had heard nothing from his scouts, so he received Pilgrim's first words with jubilant anticipation.

"Sir, you be Colonel Miles?" Pilgrim asked.

"That I am," the colonel said, jumping to his feet.

"I have seen Custer and his soldiers at the Little Bighorn," said Pilgrim.

The colonel's eyes widened with interest and question. "Yes, man, go on."

"They're all dead, sir, all of 'em," said Pilgrim. He paused briefly for the inevitable question that he knew that he wasn't ready to answer.

"That's impossible!" shouted the colonel "How do you know this?"

"Saw it, sir, with mah own eyes," Pilgrim said, knowing that he would have to lie to save himself. "I stumbled onta it...the battlefield, soon after it happened. Not a sign a' life nowheres."

The colonel sat silently in awe, then began to question Pilgrim extensively. The questions were direct and to the point. He wanted to know where he was coming from, where he was going, if he had seen any Indians, and how he managed to evade them.

Pilgrim calmly answered all his questions with simple answers so that he wouldn't be asked for details. At times he told half-truths and when pushed to hard he lied. Pilgrim felt terribly uneasy about getting involved. He wished he hadn't.

There was a thunderous commotion taking place down the corridor from the colonel's tent. Several soldiers on horseback were approaching with three captive braves. The braves' hands were bound in front and their ponies were tied together in a line. The braves held tight to the horse's manes. They each hung their heads low as they rode through the encampment of taunting soldiers. The lead soldier rode up to Colonel Miles and reported what he had seen, and told of the capture of the Indians. Everything that he told the colonel was attestation to Pilgrim's report.

One of the Indians recognized Pilgrim and spit at his feet, in protest to his apparent connection with the soldiers. Pilgrim knew that he had been identified, and worst of all he'd not have a chance to explain.

The colonel was surprised at the Indians insensate display, and asked Pilgrim why the savage had spit at him. Pilgrim's reply was without words. He simply shrugged his shoulders.

Colonel Miles augmented sense of curiosity subsided somewhat when he heard more detailed reports about Custer's confrontation. He asked Pilgrim if he would join him for dinner. The last thing Pilgrim wanted was to stay longer than necessary in the soldier's camp, but now felt an obligation to try to release the captive braves in order to preserve his name with the nations. He knew that his only chance to do so would come after dark, so he accepted the colonel's offer. Pilgrim knew that he would only make his personal matters worse if the army found him to be responsible for the escape of the Indians, and he had to plan it as though they fled on their own.

Pilgrim sat quietly through the meal, which was really no problem, since most of the discussion was between the various ranks about the strategies of war. He later dismissed himself and retired to the tent the colonel provided for his comfort as a guest. He was alone.

Pilgrim waited for the sounds of the camp to subside, and the camp fires to burn low, causing the light to dwindle. He carefully slipped under the back wall of the tent into the darkness that curtained the confines of the camp. He saw two guards about thirty yards from the captives that were talking and smoking their pipes. They never once glanced in the direction of their prisoners.

Pilgrim crawled on his hands and knees to where the Indians were being held. When they noticed his approach, Pilgrim gave them a sign of silence. He cut them free one at a time. Pilgrim moved back through the darkness in the direction of his tent, hoping all the way that their escape wouldn't be noticed until he got settled. He slipped back in the same way that he had left the tent and listened intently for some indication or announcement that the Indians were gone.

He was amazed that nothing had happened for nearly half an hour. He wondered if the Indians had killed the guards or whether the guards noticed but were afraid to declare it for fear of their punishment.

Finally a soldier was heard walking toward the colonel's tent. "Sir, Colonel, sir," the soldier's voice meekly called.

"Yes, what is it, soldier?" said the colonel. His voice clearly indicated dissatisfaction with the interruption.

"It's the Indians, Colonel; they've escaped. Should I send some men after them?" asked the reporting soldier.

Pilgrim heard the colonel exit his tent. He thought he, too, had better make an appearance to give credence to his whereabouts and establish an alibi for himself.

"Should you what?" Colonel Miles asked. "Why, those Indians would have you for breakfast, son. We'll wait till daylight and send a few troops out. This time we won't take the savages alive." The colonel looked at Pilgrim, shook his head and went back in his tent.

Before the first light of day, the bugler sounded reveille, and the camp instantly came to life. Fires were being stirred and soon the aroma of brewing coffee wafted through camp. Pilgrim was up and more than willing to leave right then, but Colonel Miles asked him if he wanted a cup of hot coffee before he left. Pilgrim couldn't turn that down; besides he was obligated to thank the colonel for his hospitality.

Colonel Miles handed Pilgrim a cup of coffee and looked quizzically at Pilgrim as he asked him,
"You ever fight any Indians?"

"Once er twice I s'pose," Pilgrim said. He said it in such a way that he had hoped he wouldn't have to explain the details. He was worried that the colonel suspected something.

"I could use a good scout," said the colonel.

"No, sir, thank ya fer the kind offer, but I'm a trapper and hunter, not a Injun fighter," exclaimed Pilgrim. "Thanks fer the vittles and a place to lay mah head. I best be on mah way," Pilgrim added.

The colonel sent a soldier to fetch Pilgrim's horse as they finished their coffee. Pilgrim listened as the colonel gave the orders to two small, mounted groups of soldiers. One group was to search for the escaped Indians that apparently headed north, and the other was ride one full day west and send word back as to what they might find.

When the soldier returned with his horse Pilgrim mounted and rode in the opposite direction of the soldiers. He decided that from that moment on he wanted no more trysts with the blue coats.

***

Pilgrim traveled about twenty miles that day and reached a small ranchers' town about the time the sun fell behind the mountains. He took his horses to the livery and walked to the clapboard hotel in the center of the community and secured a room for the night.

This was a young, thriving town, and the saloon across from the hotel seemed to be a popular place. Pilgrim decided to find out what was being said about Custer and the Little Big Horn, and if they had even heard about it yet. When he entered, he saw every kind of person imaginable.

There were well-dressed businessmen, miners, cowboys, a couple soldiers, and even a few buck-skinners, but none that he recognized. He walked over to the buck-skinners, thinking that he definitely had more in common with them than anyone else in the place.

"Mind iffen I join ya?" he said. He looked around for one of the three to reply.

"They call me Lizard," the heaviest, burly, white-bearded one spoke out. "This here's Turtle; he's tall'n skinny, but mean as a rattler, an' ever' bit as quick as one, too. Thet ole boy over yonder is Muleskinner; ain't much ya kin say bout him other'n he smells perty bad. Whut's yer name, mister?"

"Zen Bragg, buts most call me Pilgrim," he said.

"Pilgrim...well, Pilgrim, seems like a right fittin' name," Lizard said. He closely observed Pilgrim's actions as he asked Pilgrim where he came from and where he was headed.

"I'm headed back to see a friend a mine by the name of Bartley," Pilgrim told the man.

"'Twould thet be ole Joshua, the Grouch, Bartley?" Turtle asked.

"Well, I think we're talkin' bout the same man," Pilgrim replied. "He is pretty much a grouch most a' the time. I take it ya know 'im."

"Yep, jest came frum ther' bout a week back. Say, ya ain't thet fella he done told me bout, 're ya?" asked Turtle.

"Well, thet depends on whut the fool said!" Pilgrim bellowed out.

"He told me ya wuz with a Injun boy, and ya went north knowin' ya'd probably get yerself scalped," responded Turtle.

"Thet'd be me," admitted Pilgrim.

"Well, tell us'ns what happened. All we heard is thet Custer got whopped som'pin' fierce," stated Lizard.

By this time Pilgrim was feeling pretty comfortable around these men. They all seemed to pretty much accept him, and now he had the news they wanted to hear. Pilgrim was bustin' at the britches to tell someone, and these guys were itching to hear it.

"Well, iffen you'uns were to buy me a whiskey, I s'pose I could bend yer ears awhile," Pilgrim said. He was now proud of the fact he had information that no one else knew.

They not only bought him a drink, they bought him a full bottle. That was an indication that they wanted the full story with all the details.

Pilgrim started with the story of how he first met Lame Horse. All three men seemed to be captivated by his descriptive narration and asked him to continue. He told them everything that had happened; from the time he left with Jonas from Bartley's cabin, right up to Custer's demise. Pilgrim went into particular detail concerning the Sun Dance and why he was chosen to watch the battle take place with the Indian leaders. Pilgrim explained that the Indian's attitudes after the battle were quite refrained and concerned that this would only be the beginning of their end. They were aware that once the word reached the white government that thousands of soldiers would be sent to wipe them out. He told them that most of the Indians fled north, though some fled northeast, and northwest.

Pilgrim went on to tell the complete story of Colonel Miles' soldiers and his overnight stay there, including the release of the Indian captives. His accounts were so clear and descriptive that the men hearing the stories asked very few questions when he had finished.

"So where'd Colonel Miles go after ya seen 'im?" inquired Muleskinner.

"Don't rightly know," answered Pilgrim. "Think he planned ta wait fer more soldiers so's they could chase'm north."

"Well, he better hurry," Lizard replied, "'cause it ain't too fer up ther' to the Canada Territory, and once them Indians reach it, thur as safe as a bird in its nest. I hopes they git plum away."

"Yep, me too," Turtle interjected. 'Tis my opinion thet Custer got's just whut he deserved." Turtle had toned his voice down just a bit so the soldiers at the bar wouldn't hear.

"Mine too," Muleskinner agreed, as he turned to Lizard for confirmation.

Pilgrim was satisfied with their opinions, for they agreed fully with his own. By this time it was getting late, and Pilgrim was beginning to feel the effects from the whiskey. He thanked the three buck skinners for their company and hospitality and excused himself. He returned to his hotel room, and didn't even take the time to pull his moccasins off. He threw himself across the bed, and without delay fell asleep.

Chapter 17

The next morning Pilgrim was disturbed from his sleep by a knock on the door. He rolled over and glanced around the room for the first time. The window was open, and he could hear the sounds of the town below. He sensed that it must be late morning from the air temperature carried by the soft breeze as it entered the room.

Pilgrim's mind cleared with another series of knocks, this time with a bit more fervor. "Mr. Pilgrim, may I speak to you? I am Silas Collinsworth with the Mayoworth Newspaper. Could I ask you a few questions about the Little Bighorn?"

Pilgrim slowly rolled from the bed and wiped the sleep from his eyes and face.

He opened the door to find a nervous little man standing at his door in a finely pressed pin-striped suit and derby hat. "Mr. Pilgrim," the man said in a quavering voice, "I am…"

"Yea, I heard ya the first time. Yer Collinsworth with some newspaper," Pilgrim rudely spouted off.

"Yes, sir, that is correct, and I'd like to ask you a few questions concerning…"

"Heard thet too," interrupted Pilgrim.

"Sir. If I may, I will buy your breakfast if you'll tell me your story," the reporter said. He seemed to be gaining a bit more self confidence.

Pilgrim's stomach growled at that moment and the offer of a free meal was quite appropriate to his needs. The reporter stood quietly awaiting the answer to his offer, as Pilgrim walked over to the pitcher and bowl at the dry sink. He threw some water on his face and wiped it dry using the towel that hung on a rack to one side.

"Yea, I'll tell ya what I seen," answered Pilgrim.

The two men sat through a hearty breakfast, and Pilgrim ate ravenously as he repeated the story that he had told only a few hours earlier to the buck skinners. Pilgrim, holding his thoughts to himself, silently objected to the way the little man with the handlebar mustache kept asking questions. And when he had reached his fill of food, he told the reporter that he had said enough, and excused himself. Pilgrim left the reporter, who continued to work on his notes, and went to the livery for his horses.

***

Pilgrim continued south toward Casper. It was a four-day ride. He reached Casper early in the day, and had planned to stay only long enough to pick up supplies, before heading west toward Bartley's. It was mid morning and town was bustling with people going in every direction. It reminded Pilgrim of ants, moving here and there around an anthill.

He went directly to the Pritchett Mercantile. Pritchett was one of the few goods stores that would still barter a few items. Most of the stores would only deal in currency or gold. Pilgrim entered the mercantile and paid little attention to the people around him, but he could hear the talk around him. Most of the talk was about the reported massacre at the Little Bighorn. Pilgrim went about his business and pretended to be disinterested in their conversations.

Three soldiers walked in about the time one of the patrons mentioned the white man that reported having seen Custer's battle at the Little Bighorn.

"Yea, I read about that," said Pritchett, the store owner. "He surely was a lucky man to have survived that fiasco."

"Ain't nothin' lucky about it," one of the soldiers chided. "When the Army gets hold of him, he'll wish he'd never seen an Indian. He'll be arrested for the traitor that he is."

Pilgrim realized he had made a grave error. There were two sides to every story, and not everyone agreed with his. He wanted to hide, but he remained incognito to those people in the mercantile, and attempted to finish his business.

Pritchett tried to get Pilgrim's opinion on the subject. But, Pilgrim said he really didn't have an opinion, and managed to skirt the issue. He made no barter offers to Pritchett. He paid for his goods in gold to avoid any further attention, and left the store without an incident. Pilgrim packed his goods on his horse and left Casper, headed in the direction of the mountains.

A week later Pilgrim came upon the small town of Lander. This time he was prepared for attitudes of the town's people thinking that he was a traitor, that is, if they knew his true identity. He was curious about what news they had heard, and anything new that might have taken place between the Indians and the soldiers. If he had too, he would lie about whom he was.

Pilgrim tied his horses to the hitching post outside the local café and discretely entered. He tried to remain poised yet appear slightly reclusive to the people as he took a seat. He listened to nearby conversations, and it didn't take long to hear the subject turn to the Little Bighorn. He listened as they detailed the stories they had each heard.

Soon, Pilgrim's name was brought up. The attitudes around this table were quite different from the attitudes expressed at the Mercantile in Casper. Here, they seemed to take his side and speak in his favor; of course there weren't any soldiers around to sway their opinions.

There was some news that Pilgrim overheard that concerned him. It seemed that Colonel John Gibbons was in pursuit of Chief Joseph of the Nez Perce in upper Montana. Many of the Crow that made their home near the Little Bighorn stayed there and were retained by soldiers. Many of the Crow turned enemy to the rest of the Indian nations and were joining the with white armies as guides and trackers. Colonel Miles was searching for the Lakota Chief Sitting Bull. He had taken his search as far north as the Canadian Territory bordering the Montana area.

Pilgrim finished his meal without speaking to anyone and soon left Lander for his two-week journey west to Bartley's cabin. Once he reached the mountains Pilgrim felt the heavy external pressures lift from his inner soul. He was now at ease and felt a rather comfortable feeling of safety knowing that he was back home to a place that he knew. It took him two more days to reach Bartley's.

This time Bartley saw Pilgrim riding toward the cabin and stood out front to greet him. "Well, strike me plum silly; I see ya still got yer hair," Bartley said with a pleased look about him.

"Yep," replied Pilgrim with half a grin. "It's the soldiers thet want a piece a me now."

"Thet's whut I hear tell," Joshua knowingly commented. "C'mon in and tell me bout it, Pilgrim. I got a big pot a stew jest waitin' to be et."

They talked for hours, sharing their stories, and bringing each other up to date on every little detail of their lives from the time that they had last seen each other. Pilgrim asked Joshua if he had seen any Indians in the area since he had left.

"Naw, don't reckon I have," retorted Bartley. "Last Injun I seen wuz thet boy, Jonas. By the way whut ever happened ta him? I kinda took a likin' ta him."

"Got 'im back ta his people. Thet's why Lame Horse took me in," Pilgrim said. "A lotta them young Indian girls wuz mighty glad ta see 'im."

"Whut's yer plans now, Pilgrim?" asked Bartley.

"Don't have none. Kinda thought I might winter out here with ya, iffen ya'd have me," Pilgrim coyly asked.

"Sure can. I got plenty a supplies fer the both of us. Hell, ya danged fool, ya don't need ta ask. Jest pick ya a bunk," offered Bartley. "Maybe we kin git some bear huntin' in this fall."

Pilgrim kind of frowned, and then they both laughed. Pilgrim always admired the way that Bartley lived. He always seemed quite content with what he had and where he was. Joshua always seemed to be aware of what was going on in the world around him, but he hardly ever went anywhere, and never tried to change the inevitable. The news just seemed to come to him. Many of his friends periodically stopped by and filled him in on all the mountain gossip.

Joshua was always quick to give an opinion, but rarely did he ever let anything eat at him. Nothing that ever happened in the outside world ever seemed to affect his lifestyle, nor was he inclined to change because of it.

Pilgrim was ready at this point in his life to live the same way that Bartley did and be satisfied to accept the simple things that life had to offer. Nature could surely be enough to fulfill the basic survival needs of any man. Now was a good time to learn. He planned to glean that demeanor from Bartley over the next several months.

***

The fall season came and they hunted, although Pilgrim left the hunting of bear to Joshua. Pilgrim's hunts were mostly for small game that included grouse and rabbits, and some big game such as elk and mule deer. It was a bountiful season and the men would have little difficulty getting through the winter months. Both men shared the responsibilities of the trap lines once the weather turned cold, and the furs retained a winter luster and were at their peak of fullness.

Both Pilgrim and Joshua delighted in the winter chores and the cold days of winter seemed to have come and gone in short time. The weather soon broke, and signs of spring were abounding. wild flowers were beginning to bloom, trees were budding, and mule deer were fawning. The days were enjoyable.

Pilgrim wasn't particularly in a hurry to leave his friend's company but had decided to go east to the Black Hills area. That area always had a special appeal to him, and Bartley told him that there were still some buffalo in that area. This enticed a deeper interest to his preferred style of hunting.

The day before Pilgrim left, a visitor arrived at Bartley's cabin. It was none other than Turtle. He was one of the buck-skinners that

Pilgrim had first shared his story with. "Thought ya might still be here, Pilgrim," the chagrined visitor remarked.

Bartley was surprised to see that the two knew each other. "C'mon in here, ya dad blame varmint. This calls fer a cel-e-bration," he said.

Pilgrim greeted him and asked about Lizard and Muleskinner.

"Oh, they're okay. They went somewheres East; think it be Missouri. Said they wuz goin' ta take up farmin'. 'Tain't right, I tell ya, jest ain't right fer a mountain man to quit."

Bartley by this time had a new bottle of whiskey poured into three tin cups and offer one to each.

"You got ya a real famous hero here, Bartley," shouted Turtle.

"Hero? Whut the hell ya talkin' 'bout?" questioned Joshua.

"Pilgrim's a real hero. Why he's about the most respected buck-skinner ther' ev'r wuz," Turtle answered.

"Why, all the news sheets frum here ta Washington has made 'im out ta be the greatest buck-skinner ya ev'r heard tell. Why, he's more famous than Custer ev'r hoped ta be. The people 're really takin' his story ta heart, and startin' ta redicule the army fer chasin' the already-beat Injuns.

They even got pictures of 'im drawed on the front pages of ev'r newssheet ya see. Here, Pilgrim; I brung ya one."

Both Pilgrim and Bartley took a look. The drawing really did favor his looks and captured his character quite well. None of them could read, but the picture looked respectful. Pilgrim figured that if the words would have spoken badly of him they would have made him look meaner and distrustful.

"Well, I'll be horn-swaggled, Pilgrim; yer famous," added Joshua.

Pilgrim held his character, and refrained from the gloating prowess that he felt squirming around inside his mind and heart. Pilgrim never uttered a word about the picture or the comments that Turtle had made. He refrained from even the slightest indication of personal pride. The other men found this to be fitting with the character. It was an acceptable and admirable reaction. They did his gloating for him. Pilgrim joined in the conversation when they would talk of other things, but every time they brought up his fame, he was as quiet as a hound dog after a big meal.

The three talked well into the night, and fell asleep long after the whiskey took control.

Turtle asked Pilgrim the next morning if he wanted company for a few days, at least to the eastern foothills. Pilgrim welcomed the companionship as far and as long as he cared to travel with him. Pilgrim and Turtle packed their belongings on their packhorses, said their goodbyes to Bartley and headed east, toward the eastern slopes of the mountains.

Two days of easy riding brought them to the foothills where Turtle decided to turn south, in the direction of Denver. Pilgrim continued in an easterly direction, toward the Black Hills, and made no plans to stop until he got there. He was not rushed and had no specific plans, and he continued at a steady pace. He went around every town in his path, especially Casper. That town had never offered him anything but trouble. It took him twenty-eight days to reach the Black Hills, and he spent another fourteen looking for a place he could call home.

Chapter 18

The fifteenth day after Pilgrim arrived in the Black Hills, he followed a deer along the Aninandak River to the most beautiful and serene area that he had ever encountered. He felt a peacefulness enter his body and knew at that moment that this would be his home. The leaves of the aspen flittered in the light breezes and the sunlight filtered through the spruce and balsas like he had never witnessed before. The rocky cliffs that overlooked the area reached high above the spot he stood. A porcupine waddled through the underbrush only a few yards away and the deer he was following seemed undisturbed by his presence as she browsed the lower bushes.

Pilgrim walked back the river to where he left his horses tied. He led them along a narrow path where the high rock wall joined the rivers edge. That was the only passage to his hideaway. Pilgrim tied his horses close to the area he chose for a cabin site, unloaded the packs from his horse, and unsaddled his other horse. He searched the packs for his axe and proceeded to cut the first logs for his cabin. He downed three trees the first day and cut all the limbs off. He then examined the area and decided that eighteen more logs would clear the spot for his cabin.

He figured that he needed about forty logs in all for the cabin, but didn't want that big of an expanse cleared in the immediate area. He used the horses to drag the logs across the river to build a temporary bridge so that he could get the logs from the other side. He finished out the first day's work by constructing a shelter for his horses from the limbs and boughs of the first trees he cut.

Pilgrim made his camp simple the first night, but took the time to prepare a hot meal and a cup of coffee. The hard, strenuous work exhausted him, and he slept soundly.

The next morning at daylight he was awakened by the gobble of a turkey. Pilgrim recollected that morning with the Indians that stole his horses. The turkey gobbled again. Pilgrim jumped to his feet, grabbed his gun, and as quietly as he could, he moved toward it. The turkey once again gobbled, and Pilgrim's eyes and ears worked together to locate the big bird. He saw it high in spruce about fifty yards off. He raised his gun and waited for the bird's audible call to once again give his location away. The bird sounded, and Pilgrim pulled the trigger. As the smoke rose from his breech and muzzle he could hear the bird falling through the branches of the spruce. He watched as the turkey fell through the bottom limbs and hit the ground with a heavy thud. It has been a long time since Pilgrim had eaten turkey, and the thought of roasted turkey made his mouth water. He cleaned the gobbler and hung it high over his campfire to cook slowly.

While the turkey cooked, he cut several more trees down. He stopped work several times to check on the cooking turkey and periodically turned it. He cut eight trees in all, and removed the limbs from each before the smell of the cooking completely changed his priorities. He gave way to the work and settled in to stuff his famished stomach with the sweet taste of turkey.

Five more days Pilgrim labored with his axe in hand preparing the trees for building. His hands were red and badly blistered from the use of his tools. He spent three days removing four stumps that were in the spot that he wanted his cabin to be. Pilgrim's hands and muscles were so sore that he rested for two days, but used the time to scout the area around his camp.

Two more days were used to cut trees, trim limbs and drag logs. The logs he cut on the far side of the river were spread out far enough that no one would suspect his intentions. After cutting and dragging all the trees from the far side of the river to the cabin site, he spent two days removing drag marks and dismantling his bridge.

The first logs were set in place on the seventeenth day after he started his project. Work was slow, but much less demanding on his body than that of cutting and clearing. Pilgrim notched each log to a perfect fit, then used his horses to pull the logs in place. The work would have been impossible for just one man without the additional strength of the horses. All the logs were put in place three days later, and work on the roof started without delay. Tree branches had already been prepared for rafters and were welcome light work in comparison to all the earlier tasks. Shingling the cabin would consume the most time, compared to the other strenuous jobs, but the work itself was relatively easy. Pilgrim spent many late hours around his campfire splitting shingles from firewood. Making all the shingles took him nearly two weeks of labor-intensive, repetitive effort, but Pilgrim's intense desire to finish, and his endurance allowed the chore to move rather swiftly, at least in his mind. Pilgrim moved into the cabin long before the last shingle was tucked in place.

His next chore would be the construction of the fireplace, and that task would require several items before he could begin. He had to collect rocks, mud, prairie grasses, and blood. The rocks would serve as the primary construction material. The mud, grasses, and blood, would be mixed together to create a mortar to be used between the river rocks. He spent the biggest part of each day collecting these items until he had a sufficient quantity of each.

The riverbed provided him with the rocks, and he used his horses to haul them to the site a few at a time. Fortunately the river wasn't far from his cabin, and when the time came that he needed the mud, he would have an endless supply that could be dredged from the banks along the river. Pilgrim relished the idea of spending at least two days riding several miles out to the prairie where he could easily collect the grasses that were a primary component of the chinking.

During the return from his second trip out for the grasses he came upon the small community of Springville. He stopped there to get a few supplies from the only general store the community had.

The proprietor, Nathan Gantry, had a kind look about him, and Pilgrim's first impression was that of a man that seemed trustworthy. When Pilgrim first walked in the store, Gantry was the only person there. He was dusting and straightening a shelf full of coal oil lamps.

"Hello, stranger," Gantry said with a pleasant smile. "May I help you find something?"

Pilgrim asked about doors and window hinges. Gantry obliged his request, and took him to the back room where the hardware was neatly kept. Gantry never asked a question of Pilgrim, and Pilgrim liked that about him.

Gantry's wife came in the store from the back room and noticed her husband and Pilgrim going through the collection of hinges. She wasted little time in Pilgrim's opinion, demonstrating her authority and exhibiting her personality. "Yer new around here, aren't you?" she demanded. "Do you live in the area?"

Pilgrim tried to maintain a certain degree of pleasantness about him, and restrained himself from saying what he really wanted to. "Yes, ma'am, came frum Colorado," he quietly responded.

That seemed to appease her. She went on about her business, and Pilgrim wondered if she even heard him. "Nathan, we have to get those blankets down from the attic today, Do you hear me, Nathan? Today!" she ordered.

"Yes, dear, I'll get them for you today," replied Mr.Gantry.

Pilgrim picked up two oil lamps and a two-gallon container of coal oil and put them on the counter with ten door hinges that he hand selected. He looked at Gantry and asked him outright if he ever bartered for any goods.

"Well..." Gantry started to respond.

He was interrupted by his wife. "All our merchandise is purchased with either currency or gold!" she blared in a shrieking, irritating tone.

"Now, Mert, if he has something to trade where there is some promise of profit in it for us, we could allow some bartering for goods," retorted Gantry at his wife's order.

"Oh, fiddle-faddle, you and your bartering. That is no way to run a store," she complained.

"Just what might you have for trade?" Gantry asked.

"Nothin' now. Jest askin' so's I kin plan on it fer later visits," replied Pilgrim.

Pilgrim pulled out his gold pouch and proceeded to pour a small amount on the scales.

"Do you mind my asking your name?" inquired Nathan calmly.

Pilgrim momentarily paused, then realized that it would be inevitable they know, and impossible to keep from them over time. "Zen... Zen Bragg," he said.

"Well, I'm pleased to do business with you, Mr. Zen Bragg," Gantry assured Pilgrim.

Pilgrim gathered up his purchases and left the store. He carefully packed his lamps in the fresh prairie grasses that he had collected on his trip in to town. He finished loading his goods and headed back to his cabin.

That night the soft light cast by the lamps helped to add true, warm sense of home to Pilgrim's cabin. He was far from finished, but he was pleased with his accomplishments to that point.

His chimney would require the blood of at least two large animals. He had all the rocks he needed, and the prairie grasses he needed, and would have to get the mud at the time during the actual construction.

Pilgrim rode several miles downstream to the only easy river crossing he knew of, and rode only far enough to find promising deer sign. That is where he tied his horse and started his stalk. In very short time he spotted a large doe. His purpose for the kill was much like that of his Indian friends, where no part of the animal would go unused. At this particular time, he needed the blood from the animal to build his chimney. He wanted to kill the animal quickly and with as little blood loss as possible, and that was going to required a head shot. Pilgrim was quick and accurate with his shot placement, and the deer dropped to the ground immediately. He wasted no time retrieving the animal and hurried back to the camp to bleed it. Much of that day was consumed by the chores of tending to the meat and hide. All of the meat, with the exception of that portion set aside for his evening meal, had to be dried beside the camp fire and demanded nearly constant attention.

The following day he started to build the chimney and fire place. After the second day's work on the chimney, it was necessary to replenish the dwindling blood supply, for he was only half way to completion.

Pilgrim was again successful in an expedient hunt, and this time took a young buck. He bled it and worked the meat and hide just as he'd done a few days prior. Now he had sufficient supplies to finish the chimney.

Three days later, Pilgrim completed his cabin, chimney and all. He was anxious to use his new fireplace, but allowed it to set a couple of days to season, so that the mud wouldn't crack from the heat.

The second evening after the fireplace was finished, he brought his cook fire inside for the first time. It worked well. Pilgrim smiled to himself with pride for the job well done. "This calls fer a cel-e-bration," he said out-loud. Pilgrim shuffled his feet and did a little dance over to the log bench that served as a temporary, makeshift table. He reached for a brand-new bottle of whiskey, popped the cork, and took one large sip of the libation. He sat awkwardly on a large end-piece of a stump and watched the fire burn for hours. He made plans for the next day and several days after that. He was going to make some furniture.

Chapter 19

The summer months were passing, and the first sign of color was beginning to show in the hardwood trees. This was Pilgrim's favorite time of the year. He planned to take a trip to Gantry's store early in the fall season, long before the first signs of winter. Besides, if he got his supplies together before the first snows, there would be the entire fall season of uninterrupted hunting.

Pilgrim gathered up some of his tradable items: two tanned summer deer hides, herb teas and roots, and two antler-handled knives. He thought that though it wasn't much he'd find out once and for all just who was in charge of the store, Mr. Gantry or Mrs. Gantry. Pilgrim really didn't care if the barter went through or not, but what he did hope for was that Mrs. Gantry wouldn't even be there.

It took him a couple of hours to reach Springville, and when he did, things seemed about as quiet as they did the first time he was there. There probably weren't fifty people that were ever in the town at one time. The only thing that kept it going was an occasional stage that stopped with its passengers for an overnight stay, a meal, and a change of horses. Pilgrim just happened to arrive about the same time one of those occasional stages pulled into town. Pilgrim stood at the hitching post and watched as the people on the stage disembarked.

There were two men and three ladies, who were undoubtedly Easterners. They were dressed in their finest attire. They all wore hats: the men in derbies, and all the women wore exquisite broad-brimmed hats that matched the color and material of their long gowns. As they stepped from the stage they each appeared weary from the constant jostling of the coach. They brushed the dust from their clothing and cast disgusted glances about town.

The passengers headed for the café across the street, and one of the ladies, just about the prettiest thing Pilgrim had ever seen, nearly fell when she stumbled in one of the many ruts. She glanced at Pilgrim to see if he had noticed her clumsiness. One of the accompanying gentlemen helped her the rest of the way across.

Pilgrim went into Gantry's store, where the stagecoach drivers had gone. The drivers continued their discussions with Mr. Gantry and paid very little attention to Pilgrim when he entered the room. Mr. Gantry interrupted the stage driver just long enough to say hello to Zen.

The stage driver kept referring to his passengers as the tourists. He explained that they are Eastern tourists presently headed back to Massachusetts. It seems that the army has temporarily stopped any tourism in the National Park in northwestern Wyoming, that happened to be their destination.

Pilgrim had never heard of a National Park in Wyoming, and he wasn't about to ask.

The driver continued to tell Gantry that it all started a couple of months back, just one year after the Little Bighorn, almost to the day. "Eight of Chief Joseph's Nez Perce warriors slipped away to White Bird Canyon and killed some soldiers. Perry, the soldier's leader attacked at the order of General Howard. The reports said that thirty-three soldiers were killed, and only three of the Nez Perce warriors were hurt.

"Then there was the Clearwater River raid where thirteen more soldiers were killed. The Nez Perce went to Bitterroot in Montana looking for allies of the Crow Nation. One report said that there were two hundred Nez Perce, and a reporter for the army reported that there were seven hundred. Don't really matter," the driver added.

"They were at Big Hole, an area in Montana, completely surrounded by mountains. It was there that Colonel John Gibbon tracked the Nez Perce down. He attacked early one morning and cut down about seventy-five of the Nez Perce warriors. The Indian women and children regrouped soon after the initial attack and drove the soldiers from their camp.

"Chief Joseph led the others in his camp to Idaho, then back down to the Yellowstone National Park. That's where they killed some tourists. They say that after Joseph's Indians killed those tourists, that they moved north into Canada with some of their allies of the Crow Nation. They ran north to get away from the white soldiers."

At this point in the driver's story, Gantry excused himself to take care of Pilgrim's needs. "Mr. Bragg, may I assist you in finding something you need?" Gantry asked.

Pilgrim was kind of embarrassed by the attention shown him and felt he had been caught showing an interest in what the coach driver was reporting. "I ain't in any hurry. Besides, I got sumthin' I thought ya might look over fer trade, Bragg said.

"Good, bring them on and I'll have a look see," said Gantry.

Pilgrim left the store for a moment and returned with his trading items. Meanwhile, the driver got Gantry's attention and started in with reports of the Lakota Chief, Sitting Bull. Pilgrim came back in the store about the same time the stage driver mentioned the name of Sitting Bull. He listened to his accounts with great attention this time. He noticed the driver seemed to include him in the conversation by looking at him periodically.

"Last winter the Lakota Chief, Sitting Bull, was at his Smoke Creek Camp near Bear Paw. Bear Paw is in the northern Montana Territory, about forty-miles from the Canada Border. It was there that Colonel Nelson Miles attacked the camp repeatedly. Miles had about six hundred troops that tramped through the Indian camp, at least three times. The soldiers, managed to run the Indians' horses off and they were left helpless to the cold. There were fifty-three soldiers killed during the five day siege. The Indians finally made their way north to Canada where they joined up with Chief Joseph, that is until this spring when Joseph came south to Idaho and Wyoming." The driver hesitated for a moment and looked at Pilgrim, then asked him if they had met somewhere before.

"Don't think so," Pilgrim said.

"Are you sure? You look mighty familiar," replied the stage driver. There was a long pause as the driver observed Pilgrim's face. Pilgrim tried his best to change the subject by his interjecting statement, "They ain't savages, ya know!"

"What do you mean, they aren't savages?" Gantry curiously asked.

"They are a nation of simple people," Pilgrim answered.

"Hey, I know who you are," the driver hollered. "I saw your picture in the newspaper. I thought you looked familiar."

Nathan Gantry showed more surprise to the claim than Pilgrim did. "You know a lot about the tribes, don't you?" remarked the driver. "Mr. Gantry, you're looking at the only white man that survived Custer's last stand at the Little Bighorn."

Pilgrim didn't deny the allegations, and offered no comment.

Gantry looked at Zen. "I seem to recollect something about a mountain man that witnessed the battle, but his name was…"

"Pilgrim!" the driver shouted. "They call him 'Pilgrim.'"

"Is that right, Mr. Bragg? Are you the one that lived with the Indians? I'm sorry, I mean the nations? Are you the one they call 'Pilgrim'?" asked Mr. Gantry.

"S'pose so," Pilgrim said. His tone was rather uncaring at that moment and he no longer cared about the consequences. Pilgrim wasn't sure what to expect. At this point he almost expected ridicule.

Gantry set the tone when he started to ask a few questions about the different tribes and what it was like to live with them. The stage driver also asked his share of the questions. Pilgrim didn't go into to much detail with his answers and he watched their expressions to determine just how far he should go with his explanation.

"What are they like?" inquired Gantry.

"Most like you, Mr. Gantry, jest tryin' ta survive," Pilgrim responded. He demonstrated his confidence in with his answer. "They's a simple people who believe in simple ways. They believe that the Great Father-Spirit is the maker of all things. They believe in

Mother Earth, the giver a' life by her four elements: fire, earth, air, and water." Pilgrim could see that they were totally lost with his explanation, and he hesitated to give a more-detailed account. They stared at him with interest but failed to hear what he was actually saying. Pilgrim changed the subject by pointing at his trading items.

Gantry was quick to take the hint and began to inspect each of the items that Pilgrim had to trade.

"I'll give you seven dollars for the lot," Gantry offered.

Pilgrim felt that for no more than he had, that it was a more-than-fair offer. He accepted that amount without dickering and put the seven dollars toward the purchase of the supplies. Pilgrim took his things and headed for the door.

Neither Gantry nor the stage driver pursued any further discussion about Pilgrim's past, the Indian nations, or the battle at the Bighorn. Pilgrim packed his goods on his pack horse and headed for his home place, leaving his identity in the town that he had hoped would remain a stranger to his past.

Chapter 20

Nathan Gantry and the stagecoach driver continued with discussion that revolved primarily around Pilgrim, and the various accounts of his life with the Indians. The front door of the store opened wide. One of the gentlemen from the stage held the door for the ladies to enter. Their appearance and attitudes seemed to have changed somewhat since their arrival. The ladies had the opportunity to freshen themselves, and the meal they dined on at the café across the street seemed to have tempered their attitudes.

Mrs. Gantry entered from the store from the back room about the same time. She looked at the store full of patrons, and discovered by their appearance that these people were people of class and importance. Mrs. Gantry wasted little time introducing herself to them and boasted of her upper-class upbringing when she was a young girl back East.

Mr. Gantry was repulsed by his wife's forwardness and tried, without success, to restrain her determined attempts to self-serving conversation. He finally broke it off when he looked directly at his wife and said, "Dear, these folks are tired and have come a long way. They don't want to hear about our past."

The youngest lady could see Gantry's irritation and heard it in his voice, but tried to smooth things over by saying that it was quite all right. She added, "I haven't talked to very many people this far west that are as educated and clearly as refined as you and your wife seem to be."

Mrs. Gantry swelled with pride at her comment. "See that, Nathan? This fine young lady wants to talk with someone of her own class."

Nathan, just shook his head and rolled his eyes as the others watched and waited for further comment. Nathan managed to hold his tongue.

As the others continued to look around the store, Mrs. Gantry saw the items laying on the counter that Pilgrim had traded with Gantry. "What on God's green earth is this?" Mert asked.

Nathan, knowing what to expect, calmly and in a low, nearly inaudible tone, replied to her that those were a few items that he traded with Mr. Bragg.

"Mr. Bragg is a worthless vagabond and can't pull his own weight in today's society. He's a filthy old hermit, and has disgusting and uneducated ways," she articulated. It was clear to all that could hear her ranting, that she thought Bragg wasn't a man capable of her self-righteous ways.

Gantry pounded his fist on the counter, "Now hold it right there, Mert. Mr. Bragg is one of the nicest people I've ever encountered. He's honest and has never caused anyone any grief as far as I know."

Realizing that he was making something of an uncomfortable situation for his patrons, he tried to smooth it over by telling the group what he and the stage driver had found out a great deal about Pilgrim's past. He was indeed a man with a respectable past. The stage driver jumped right in on the conversation, and blustered his opinion on what a fine character that Mr. Bragg appeared to be.

Mrs. Gantry listened, but showed little interest and acted as if her opinion could not be swayed about the man, no matter what was said. The Easterners listened with considerable interest. They seemed to find a fascination with Mr. Bragg. His leather buckskins and intrigue associated with his lifestyle especially interested them.

Mrs. Gantry was disturbed by the focus of attention that the group was giving one of her least-favorite customers. She kind of huffed and shook her head after seeing that her efforts to change the subject had been thwarted. She disgustingly turned and pouted off to the back room. No one in the group paid any attention to her little tantrum. They continued to discuss the mountain man.

The young lady of the group was especially captivated by the stories. She asked question after question, most of which couldn't have been answered by either Gantry or the stage driver. She seemed to be more interested in the man, how he lived, and what he thought.

The conversation was devoted to Pilgrim for more than an hour. Long after the others began to talk about other things, the young lady continued to keep the subject of the mountain man alive with her continued questions.

"Will you folks be staying in town for a while?" Gantry asked.

"A couple of days, I suppose. We need to let the horses rest for a while," the stage driver stated. "We've worn them horses down pretty hard the last couple of days."

One of the gentlemen asked Gantry if he and Mrs. Gantry would like to join the group for dinner that evening. Nathan thanked him for the offer and asked what time they would be dining. He told them that he would check with his wife, but assured them that they would be there.

Mrs. Gantry was thrilled by the invitation and couldn't wait for the townspeople to see her in the company of such prominent appearing guests. She chose a silk emerald green gown with white lace trim and a huge bustle. "Nathan, help me get this corset a little tighter," she ordered.

"Goodness, Mert, don't you think you're overdoing it a little bit?" Nathan asked.

"When you're dining in the company of dignitaries, proper attire accounts greatly for their respect. Besides, the first impression is always the most important," she responded.

"I'm sure they already have a first impression that will last them a lifetime," murmured Nathan.

"What did you say, Nathan?" asked Mert.

"I said, I'm sure their impression will last a lifetime," he said.

"That's good dear," she said. She busily continued to fix herself. She primped in the mirror as Nathan looked on. He clearly saw the vanity in her face and felt the chill of her selfish heart.

"Aren't you going to get ready?" Mert asked.

"Yes, dear," he begrudgingly replied.

"Now, I want you to wear this suit. Hurry, hurry; we don't want to be late," she commanded.

Rather than argue, it was often better for Gantry to comply with her wishes. This was definitely one of those times.

Mrs. Gantry was putting on her final touches when Nathan finished dressing. She was wearing white gloves, a large silk hat with a broad rim, and carried a parasol. When he saw her, his face felt flushed with embarrassment.

"Let's go, Nathan; mustn't keep them waiting. Now take my arm so I don't fall," demanded Mrs. Gantry.

Nathan wanted to crawl in a hole. He hoped that no one would see them as they crossed the rutted street to the café', but knew quite well that everyone around would indeed be watching. The town seemed busier than Nathan could ever remember. Everyone seemed to stop and stare as they took their short stroll from the store to the café. Nathan was self conscious of his wife's appearance, and thought to himself that he'd prefer running through a gauntlet than to walk his wife across the street.

As they got to the café a scruffy looking rancher stared at them and stepped out of their way. He mockingly took his hat off and bowed at the waist. Nathan's face turned red.

Mert just looked at the cowhand and remarked, "Well, what are you gawking at? Good heavens, haven't you ever seen respectable people before?" Without even taking a breath, she continued. "Now Nathan, don't you bring up that mountain-man talk. These people have much better things to talk about than some old hermit," she said. Mert's final order came as they entered the café.

Both stage drivers and the four passengers were seated at a large table near the front window of the café. The two gentlemen stood up as the Gantrys approached.

"Good evening, folks," said one of the stage drivers. Both men tilted their hats and politely greeted them.

"Please have a seat," instructed the other man. "I'm Buck," he said. "This here's my shotgun rider, Jasper...Jasper Miss-a-lot."

Everyone chuckled at the last name, realizing that it was a joke and not his real name. That is, everyone but Mert Gantry. "Pleased to meet you, Mr. Missalot," said Mert.

Everyone laughed, leaving Mrs. Gantry with a rather puzzled look on her face. She had absolutely no idea why there was purpose for such humor.

The introductions followed on around the table, and the two gentlemen took it upon themselves to introduce the women. "I am Abbott Forsythe, and this is my wife Elizabeth."

The next gentleman said, "This is my better half, Emma, and my daughter Sarah. My name is Winfred Scarberry."

Nathan started to make the introduction when Mrs. Gantry overrode his soft speech with her shrill voice. "I'm Merty, and this is Nathan. We're the Gantrys. Of course you already know that from the sign on our store."

"Where do you folks hail from?" questioned Mert. She did so even before they could acknowledge the introduction.

"Well," Winfred started to say. Then he looked at Abbott to see who would answer the question. Abbott nodded his head giving the sign for Winfred to continue. "We are all from Boston...Boston, Massachusetts," stated Winfred.

"Oh, oh my, I'm from Boston!" shouted Mert. "I lived there until I was twenty-eight years old. Then I married Nathan, and he brought me to this God-forsaken place. Do you know the Schmidts, Ernest and Mary?" Mert asked Winfred.

"Well, ma'am, Boston has probably grown a lot since you were there. I'm sorry; I don't recall ever having met the Schmidts," replied Mr. Scarberry.

Mrs. Gantry had Mr. Scarberry locked eye to eye in conversation. The others began to talk to the person sitting beside them. Mr. Gantry talked to Buck, while Emma and Sarah were conversing. Elizabeth

Forsythe was whispering in her husband Abbott's ear. Mr. Gantry saw the Forsythes whispering and thought that they were probably discussing Mert's rudeness.

Their dinner arrived, allowing Mr. Scarberry a moment of silence. After being served, Mrs. Gantry continued to talk about Boston's fine dining places, many of which no longer existed, as Mr. Forsythe tried to explain to her. She rambled on to anyone that glanced her way. Near the end of the meal, practicably no one wanted to talk to or acknowledge Mert's presence, especially Nathan.

Nathan asked the two gentlemen what they did for a living.

"Well, Winfred is the owner and editor of the *Boston Gazette,* and I am president of the First Bank of Boston," Abbott said.

Mert started to say something, but this time Nathan drowned her out. Besides, he had the attention of everyone at the table. No one wanted to look her way for fear that they might appear to be seeking a response from her. "Do you all enjoy living in the city?" Nathan asked. He looked toward the Forsythes and the Scarberrys for a response.

The Forsythes both agreed that they loved the city. The Scarberrys hesitated a moment before they answered. Mrs. Scarberry looked at Mr. Gantry and responded, "In all honesty, Winfred and I do like the city and his work is there. But our hearts are in the country. Someday when he retires, we'll find a quiet place out and away. Sarah, on the other hand loves the country. After she saw the mountains, she's talked of nothing else."

Mr. Gantry noticed the beautiful smile that radiated from the young lady's face perfectly and completely framed by her long dark auburn hair. "Sarah," Mr. Gantry said, "just what is it about the mountains that you like?"

Sarah didn't hesitate to respond. "I love their beauty, the peacefulness, and serenity. I like the people that I've met there. They seem to be satisfied with the simple things and seem to be satisfied just to be alive."

"Yes, I suppose so, I never really looked at those things that way." responded Nathan.

"I'd like to meet that gentleman that was in your store today," continued Sarah.

"Which gentleman is that?" asked Mr. Gantry.

"That mountain man," she said.

"Oh yeah, Mr. Bragg," answered Nathan.

"You poor young thing," Mrs. Gantry said. "That's no gentleman; he's a heathen." Then she attempted to change the subject.

Sarah kept asking Mr. Gantry questions about Mr. Bragg. She asked Mr. Gantry if he would introduce her to Mr. Bragg. Nathan told her that he didn't come to town very often and that no one around town even knew where he lived. Mert tried desperately to interrupt any further discussions about Bragg, but Sarah was persistent and inquisitive about him and his lifestyle.

Mrs. Gantry finally jumped up from the table and criticized the topic of discussion. She chided her husband and protested in anger. "If this is the best subject for discussion at the dinner table, I'll just be excusing myself," she blurted.

Both Mr. Forsythe and Mr. Scarberry stood in proper manner, much after the fact, as she marched off through the door of the café. They all watched as she stepped off the wooden walkway and caught the front of her skirt on her shoe. She tumbled forward and lost her balance in the ruts of the street, falling to her hands and knees in the middle of the muddy, rutted street.

Elizabeth was the only onlooker that couldn't hold back audible laughter. The others only did so for the sake of Mr. Gantry's embarrassment. Gantry looked at the others, and back at his wife as she flailed around trying to get to her feet. Then he burst out in laughter. Having broken the ice, they all momentarily joined in the amusement of the situation at Mrs. Gantry's expense.

Sarah was the first to redirect the group's focus of attention by asking her father a most serious question. "Pappa, I've just got to talk to this mountain man. May I stay on long enough to interview him and tell his story? Please, Pappa?" the girl pleaded with her father.

"This is still pretty rough country, Sarah, not the kind of place for a young woman in her twenties," Mr. Scarberry said in a tone loud enough for all to hear. He was looking for the others to agree, but no one, including Mrs. Scarberry, uttered a word.

"Pappa, even you admitted that this trip would give me the opportunity to write a book about the taming of the West, and now that I have a prospective subject to get the information from first hand, how can you say no? Please, don't deny me this opportunity, Pappa," she pleaded.

"Where would you stay? Your Momma and I would worry ourselves silly over you," Winfred said, demonstrating his fatherly concerns. Winfred pondered the idea for a moment and turned to his wife Emma for her thoughts.

"It appears our young girl has grown up, Winfred. I think it would be a good chance for her to see and experience a little more than just one way of life. She's quite capable of taking care of herself," Emma said.

"Me and the Mrs. can see to her safety," offered Nathan Gantry. "We have a spare room that we've been thinking of renting out. That is of course, if she can put up with Mrs. Gantry's ways."

"Oh, please, Pappa," pleaded Sarah.

"Looks like I'm outvoted," said Mr. Scarberry. He patted his daughter's knee and told the stage driver that it looked like there will be one fewer passenger going East.

Sarah smiled at her parents and once again assured them that she would be fine.

***

Two days later the stage was packed and ready to head east. Mr. Scarberry left the front door of the Springville Bank where he had set up a financial account in his daughter's name. He walked across the street and joined the company of his wife and the Forsythes. Sarah was standing there, too.

Mr. And Mrs. Gantry watched from the front steps of their store, as Mr. Scarberry hugged his daughter. Emma then stepped in to say good-by to her daughter as Mr. Scarberry walked over to the Gantry's.

"You take good care of my girl," he said.

"Rest assured, Mr. Scarberry, we will see to it," assured Nathan.

The stage driver asked for everyone to board the coach, and as soon as the last passenger embarked Winfred closed the door. The horses were summoned to action by the slap of the reins and the stage was in motion.

Sarah stood there, silently touched by mixed emotions of both excitement and melancholy. She suddenly felt the realization of her separation as she hesitatingly waved as the stage disappeared at the edge of town.

***

The days went by slowly, and before long winter set in. Sarah spent the days working with the Gantry's in the store. It wasn't long before she'd met most everyone in town. She enjoyed talking with the people and learning about their lives, their families, and lifestyles. But there was one individual that she most wanted to learn about and he had not yet returned.

In late March, the weather broke, and warmer days were to be expected. The fresh air and sunshine drew Sarah to the outside where she could watch and enjoy the flowers on the prairie on the outskirts of town. Each day she would hitch Gantry's buggy to their old horse and make short-distance excursions. Some days she would spend the entire day riding through the open prairie.

Each new day made her more at ease and familiar with the surrounding countryside, and each day she went a little farther from town. Sarah found one area she especially liked, a large boulder in the middle of a prairie meadow, filled with wild lavender with blue and purple blossoms. She thought God had surely designed this special sanctuary for her pleasure, and hers alone. The wild flowers, in their colorful display, filled all the space in every direction from the boulder to the little natural pond that made a perfect watering hole for all kinds of prairie animals to visit. The sun seemed to shine more brightly and warmer at that spot than any where else on the plains. Sarah found comfort in the sun's warmth.

One day she sat atop the boulder and watched two antelope in the distance, cautiously approaching the water hole. They were quite vigilant to their approach and instantly bolted at the horses slightest movement. Sarah stood up to watch the antelope bound away. She held tight to the ends of her shawl and spread her arms above her head like wings, soaking up the warming sunshine.

It was at that very moment that Pilgrim was headed to Springville to replenish his supplies, and the dust from the antelope drew his attention in the direction of the boulder. He saw a silhouetted figure standing on top of a huge boulder and couldn't figure out what it was. All kinds of things went through his mind. The closer he got, the more it appeared to be the form of a person, then the dress made him realized that it was a woman.

What was a woman doing out in the middle of the prairie, standing on top of a boulder, and waving her cape like the wings of a bird? She was facing the opposite direction, with her back to the Pilgrim, and facing the brilliant sun. He approached from behind, slowly and cautiously, because his vision was somewhat obscured by the blaring sun.

Pilgrim sat on his horse at the base of the boulder and watched as she continued to soak in the glorious, enchanting rays of the sun. Sarah, caught in her world of dreams, slowly turned looking skyward. Somewhat startled, she caught a glimpse of the stranger out of the corner of her eye. "Oh, Mr. Bragg, you startled me. I wasn't expecting anyone to be around for miles."

Pilgrim's face must have displayed an inquisitive frown for a split second, for if he heard her right, he thought she called him by name. "Have we met?" he asked.

"Well, not exactly," she responded as she climbed down from her perch.

As soon as Pilgrim saw her face, he remembered having seen her as she stepped so lady like, from the step of the stage coach.

"We've never actually met, but I did see you this last fall when I arrived in Springville on the stage with my parents and their friends," she said.

Pilgrim felt a strange feeling go through his entire body, stirred perhaps by the young lady's natural beauty. He had never seen such a beautiful, delicate looking woman in all his life. "What are you doin' out so fur frum town alone?" he asked. He clearly resonated concern in his voice.

"I come out here quite often, just to be alone for a while." She hesitated for a moment and then continued, "Actually I was hoping to run into you, Mr. Bragg."

Pilgrim didn't quite know how to respond to that and without thinking he said, "Whut on earth would a delicate humming bird such as yourself want with a hound dog like me?"

Sarah blushed at his comment. "Well, Mr. Bragg," she started to say, but Pilgrim interrupted her.

"They call me Pilgrim. My real name is Zen, and you can use whichever name ya feel more comfortable with. And what might I call you?" he asked. Pilgrim was nearly out of breath. He couldn't remember the last time he had spoken so many words at one time. The fact that he was kind of nervous and in the company of a very pretty young lady hadn't helped.

"I'm Sarah, Sarah Scarberry," she said.

"Well, Miss Sarah, pleased to meet ya. You was sayin' something about how you came to be out here," Zen reminded her.

"Yes, I…I am attempting to write a book, sir, a book about the Western people, the mountains, and the stories of the Indian nations. The people in town say that you know more about those subjects than anyone else."

Pilgrim's mind flashed back through some of the key and most memorable moments of his life. He paused intentionally for several moments, and then with honest admittance responded to her comments. "Suppose so."

"Could you help me? Would you tell me what you could so that I may write the truth to all those people who have a genuine interest in hearing the truth and especially those who only hear the exaggerated stories from some of the news articles and storytellers?"

Pilgrim pondered on her questions for several minutes before giving her an answer. Two factors that played strongly in his decision were her captivating beauty and the fact that she actually wanted to write about the truth, something that most people didn't do. "I'll tell ya what you want ta know, Miss Sarah, but you gotta realize that them things yer a writin' 'bout are heartfelt and personal things, stories that really happened and things thet I have seen and done fer real. They's not somethin' I got frum a book nor heard tell of in some stories told."

"But that's what I hope to do, Mr. Bragg.... I'm sorry, I mean Zen. I want the people out East to feel the life of the people and sense the spirit of the mountains without even seeing them. I want them to experience your life through my words. I want people to understand the Indians without ever having seen one. I want them to know them for who they are and what kind of life they live."

"They'll be able ta feel, see, and experience all those things just frum yer words?" asked Pilgrim. He didn't want her to know that he couldn't read.

"Yes, Zen, I hope to make them feel, hear, see, touch, and smell this country out here," she softly said with promise on her face.

Pilgrim could tell by her response that Sarah had a heartfelt sense and a desire, almost an obligation to share it with others. He was practically looking forward to helping her.

Pilgrim and Sarah headed back to Springville together, where he and Sarah spent considerable time sharing stories, stories of the past—not just stories of Pilgrim's past, but stories about Sarah when she was growing up in Boston. Pilgrim loved listening to her talk. Her accent was quite appropriate and added so much to her appearance and femininity.

Three days went by, and each was as enjoyable for Pilgrim as the previous day. He looked forward to meeting with her at the café, and each scheduled visit brought with it a renewed excitement.

Sarah, too enjoyed the time spent with Pilgrim. She saw him as a man of strength and extremely unique in character. She liked his simplicity and felt secure in his company.

Early on the fourth morning, Sarah went to the livery where Pilgrim was staying, and asked if he would take her to see where he lives. Pilgrim thought about it for a while before he gave her a definitive answer. His seclusion was something that was special and he cherished. Taking a visitor, even as special as Sarah, could become the one compromise in his life that may lead to other uninvited guests. He finally decided there would be no harm in doing so, and agreed to take her after he replenished his supplies at Gantry's Store.

Sarah headed down the main street to the telegraph office while Pilgrim got his supplies. She quickly jotted down a message and handed it to Ike, the telegraph operator, who counted the words and figured the total cost to send the message.

"That'll be eighty-five cents, Sarah." Ike told her. He started to send the message as she dug around in her jacket pocket for the money.

Pappa

Am well. Have met with Mr. Bragg. He is an amazing individual. Will send parts of story soon.

Love, Sarah

Sarah handed Ike the exact change, said thank you, and ran excitedly out the door before Ike could say a word.

"That girl surely is in a hurry," mumbled Ike to himself.

Sarah went running into Gantry's about the time Pilgrim settled his account with Mert Gantry.

Of course he had to pay cash. Pilgrim found some humor in the fact that the money he used to pay for his goods came from the trade he made with Mr. Gantry.

"Mrs. Gantry," Sarah said, nearly out of breath, "I'll be gone for a couple of days."

"Where you going, child?" Mert asked.

"Mr. Bragg is going to show me the life of a mountain man," said Sarah, quite innocently and without the slightest hesitation.

"Who? What? Now, I don't know about that, Sarah. I don't think that's such a good idea." Mrs. Gantry worriedly floundered around for something more to say.

"She'll be fine," Pilgrim said. "I'll take good care of her."

"It will be okay, Mrs. Gantry. Besides, I just sent a telegram to my Pappa," Sarah told her.

As they walked toward the door, Pilgrim saw the deer hide displayed on the counter top that he had traded to Mr. Gantry.

"Nice deer hide," commented Zen. He was trying his best to generate a reaction from Mrs. Gantry. He just wanted to hear what kind of response she would come up with. He knew that a simple reference to the hide would surely get her blood to boil.

Her face turned beet red and her anger boiled inside, but she managed to hold her tongue.

Pilgrim packed his supplies on the packhorse and held the reins of the horse, that he rented from the livery for Sarah. They both mounted their horses and headed for Pilgrim's remote cabin, tucked away in the Black Hills. They rode side by side, most of the way, and talked during the entire trip.

Chapter 21

The ride was long in miles, and took well over half a day. But, for Sarah it went fast. Pilgrim didn't seem to notice how fast the time went, and was rather surprised when they arrived at the Aninandak River when they did. They followed the river north for several miles meandering through the foothills. The narrow trail wasn't as easy as the open prairie, and they had to ride single file. Pilgrim led the way to where the mountains rock wall became a part of the river's shoreline.

Pilgrim stopped his horse and dismounted. "Gits a little hard from here, but 'tain't much further," he said. He told Sarah to wait where she was as he carefully led his horses through the rapids waters edge as close as he could to the bluff. He tied both of them to the first tree, once the bank flattened out on the other side of the bluff. Then he returned to where Sarah waited as she was told to do.

"Give me the reins so's I can take you around and ride on through," said Pilgrim.

Sarah handed him the reins and held firm to the saddle horn and squeezed her legs tightly against the pommel of the saddle. When they reached the flats where he tied his horses, he looked up at Sarah.

"Now that wern't so bad, wuz it?" he told her with a gentle smile.

Sarah just pleasantly smiled back as if to assure his comments had been heard. Pilgrim felt her smile surge deep into his heart and he thought then that this woman must be the one thing in his life that must have been missing. He had always thought that he had everything that life had to offer. He was finally made aware by her presence that something had been missing in his life but never once considered that it could be attributed to not having the company of a female share his life. Pilgrim was feeling a special comfort that he had never experienced. He began to realize that he had deep feelings toward Sarah. She made him feel good, weak, confused, but complete every time she was in his company.

Pilgrim thought of her magnificent beauty, her extreme intelligence and book-learned ways. He pondered on the fact that she was frail and only knew the things that city life had to offer. His self-esteem fell quite low when he thought that he had no more to offer her than a buffalo could offer an eagle. He kept his feelings inside, and vowed to keep those feelings to himself. Pilgrim climbed on his horse, and rather coldly motioned for Sarah to follow.

Within a few minutes, Sarah could barely make out a distant structure well concealed in the forest ahead of them. The closer they got, the more her enthusiasm took control. "Is this your home? Is this where you live?" she asked with great excitement.

"This 'ere's it," he modestly replied. "'Tain't much, but it's all I need." His pride was supported by the excitement that her voice expressed.

"It's beautiful," Sarah said with all honestly in her voice.

Pilgrim was humbled by the fact that she liked it. He tied the horses to their hitching post and told her that he'd unsaddle them and put them in the corral later. Sarah couldn't wait for the invitation to go inside. She opened the door and peeked in.

Pilgrim was totally surprised at her reaction to the cabin. "Go on in, and make yerself at home," he said.

They walked in together. Pilgrim opened the window shutters, and started to build a fire to take the chill off.

Sarah stood in one place and looked around, as if to absorb every little detail of the place and the character of the man that had built it. She learned much more about Pilgrim in the few minutes she stood there gazing about, than she had in all the time she'd spent with him in conversation. Perhaps it was the uniqueness of his quaint abode, the simplicity of his lifestyle, or the cleanliness and care shown in the few things that he had, that most appealed to her. Nevertheless, she was exhilarated by, and infatuated with his lifestyle more now than even before.

"Here, warm yerself by this 'ere fire, and I'll see ta the horses," he said. He smiled at her as he walked toward the cabin door.

Sarah was amazed at the homey feeling the cabin offered. The snapping and popping that came from the fireplace gave her warmth that she'd never experienced in her life. She looked at his trophy antlers mounted on the wall, and felt the coarse hair of a Buffalo robe that lay on the bed.

She noticed the craftsmanship involved in the construction of the bed, table and chairs. She noticed every detail of the snowshoes that hung over the door and touched the traps that were hung from a wooden peg in the corner of the room. Leather pouches of all shapes and sizes caught her eye. There was no doubt that each one was hand made. Everything seemed to have a purpose and was put in a special place. Sarah was admiring the bearskin coat that hung over his bed, about the time Pilgrim returned.

"This is a very fine coat," said Sarah.

"A young Indian boy made it for me," Pilgrim replied.

"Oh, please, Zen, tell me about it, please. Don't leave anything out," she pleaded.

Pilgrim once again felt the same special caring feelings that he had felt earlier down by the river. It must have been in the way she said his name. No one ever before had pleaded to him and called his name so graciously and with such a soft voice. "I'll tell ya, Sarah. I'll tell ya everything you want to know, but first I'd better fix us up some grub," he said.

"Grub?" she asked.

At that moment Pilgrim felt embarrassed by his choice of words and wanted desperately to back up to the point just before he said grub. He never before felt obligated to watch his choice of words, and had to remind himself that he was in the presence of a beautiful woman and not just another fellow buck skinner. He never before wanted so badly to meet the approval of someone as badly as he did Sarah's.

"Food," he replied. "You know, supper. Grub is what most of the folks here in the mountains would holler at ya when the night food was ready ta eat." He pondered for a moment at what he said and thought to himself, *Ya danged fool; ya just put yerself deeper in the mud hole than ya was already in.*

"No, please, let me fix dinner while you tell me the story about your coat," Sarah beseeched him.

Pilgrim hesitated to respond right away probably due to the fact that his mind was locked on her use of words. *Dinner. That's the word I should've said.* His face outwardly displayed several mixed expressions, as he was silently conversing with his thoughts.

Sarah waited for a reply, but instead saw Pilgrim's face change and saw the turmoil of emotions that were represented. She thought that she might have been out of line by her offer or maybe she thought she had offended him by something that she had said earlier.

At that same moment Pilgrim's belated response seemed to satisfy the moment for the both of them. "That would be nice," he said. "To fix dinner, that is," he responded rather slowly. He gave forethought to each of the words that he chose from that moment forward. His facial expression accompanying that answer seemed to replace all the others with one that showed satisfaction.

Sarah was somewhat relieved by his response, but remained perplexed as to the cause or meaning behind the display of multiple emotions on his face. She inquired as to where some of the necessities for preparing a full meal were located, and with Pilgrim's occasional assistance, proceeded to prepare a meal. She added just a few feminine touches such as table candles, and proper table settings, in hopes that this meal would be remembered by Pilgrim for a long time to come.

Pilgrim watch her every graceful move as he told her about Bartley, and about finding Jonas. He told her every detail of the bear hunt and the skills that the boy had in making things. His story was so thorough in each and every detail, that Sarah was serving the meal to him about the time he had finished.

They both sat down to the table across from each other. There was a quiet moment to settle at the table when he noticed that she paused and folded her hands together and bowed her head. He sat quietly watching her lips move in silence. When she raised her head their eyes momentarily met. He felt uneasy that she had caught him staring at her.

"'Re you religious?" he asked outright.

"I was raised in a Christian home," she said. "Aren't you a man of religious belief?"

"Don't rightly know much 'bout it," he said.

"Haven't you read the Bible?" Sarah asked.

Pilgrim didn't answer, he didn't want to lie to Sarah, but at the same time he didn't want her to know that he couldn't read. Besides, most of his side of the conversation, at least to this point had already made him feel ignorant.

Sarah felt that there must be a deep-seated reason for his inexplicable silence, and didn't pursue the issue. So, she thought it best to change the subject. "Please tell me more about Jonas," she said, calmly inquiring a response.

Pilgrim was drawn from his silent thought and continued with his story. After a short time had passed, Sarah stopped Pilgrim in the middle of a sentence. "Do you like me?" she asked.

"Of course I like ya," he quickly replied.

"No, Zen, I mean do you like me as a person, or do you like me as a woman?"

Pilgrim was bewildered by her candor. He didn't have the slightest hint as to what he should say or how he should act at that moment. He was well aware of how he felt, but he didn't think that he had said or done anything that might have suggested his interest in her. "Well, I like ya lots," he sheepishly muttered as he looked down at his empty plate.

Sarah jumped up from the table, threw her arms around Pilgrim's neck, and kissed him on the cheek. She knelt down beside his chair and tenderly reached to turn his face to meet her eyes. "I like you too, Mr. Zen Bragg; I like you very much," she said as she pulled him closer to herself and kissed his willing lips.

When their lips met for the first time Pilgrim's whole insides seemed to flutter. He felt a tenderness for this woman that he knew was much more than just liking her. He smiled at her and stared intently into her eyes, and she too felt the passion of his heart. She got to her feet and Pilgrim just sat there deep in thought. "It's gettin' late," he said. "I'll git ya some wood fer the fire. The woodshed's 'bout empty, so I'll be stayin' ther'. You'll be fine in here," he said in a comforting tone. He grabbed a blanket from the table at the head of his bed, and headed for the door.

"Goodnight," she softly spoke.

"Goodnight, Sarah."

Pilgrim tossed and turned all night long. What he was feeling was something that he had never felt in his lifetime. He was in a whole new world of joy. His feelings were so strong for Sarah, he couldn't wait to see her again. He wanted to be with her all the time. Sarah was excited also. She didn't sleep that first night either. She knew that she loved Zen, for who he was and what he stood for. He was the kindest, gentlest man she'd ever met.

The next morning Pilgrim did his chores around the cabin, trying to be somewhat quiet, so as not to wake Sarah. Sarah came to the door and watched as Pilgrim worked around the horses.

He finally noticed her standing in the doorway. "Good morning! Would you care to come in and eat?" Sarah asked.

Pilgrim's heart seemed to skip a beat when he heard her soft and gentle voice. An excitement not unlike that of a child opening a gift on their birthday. He somewhat surprised himself when he replied in an excited tone, "Well, good morning to you, too. Yes, I certainly would."

The two of them shared that day, and three more that followed. They mostly talked doing small chores, talking, and walking along the river. Pilgrim told Sarah on the fourth day that he should probably take her back to town. And though she agreed to go, she made it quite clear that she really didn't want to go back.

As they were leaving the cabin, Sarah asked Pilgrim if he would bring her back sometime.

"I'll bring ya back when the cabin is fit fer a family," he responded.

Sarah looked at Pilgrim in disbelief. "Are you…asking me…"

"I guess I am…askin' ya ta be my woman, that is," he sheepishly said.

She ran back into the cabin as if she had forgotten something, and he never questioned her actions. "I would like that, Zen. I would be the happiest person alive if I were your woman," she said.

They rode back to Springville. When they got there Pilgrim could see Mrs. Gantry sweeping the sidewalk in front of their store. He looked at Sarah and told her that he preferred not to hear Mrs. Gantry's comments.

"I'll be back in bout a month iffen you can make proper arrangements and all," Pilgrim told her as he leaned over for a kiss.

Mrs. Gantry looked up and saw Pilgrim kiss her just before he turned his horse and headed back.

Sarah returned her horse to the livery stable and walked up the street to Gantry's store. As she entered, she heard Mert bending Mr. Gantry's ear about having seen that mountain man kissing her, and as she put it, having his way with her. Mert wasted little time questioning Sarah the second she entered the store. Mr. Gantry tried to calm Mert down without success.

Sarah just looked at the both of them and said, "I'm going to marry Mr. Bragg."

Mert fainted. Sarah looked at Nathan and smiled, then turned around and out the door, headed for the telegraph office.

"Ike, I have a message to send to Boston!" Sarah exclaimed.

"Surely, Miss Sarah. I think I can do that for you."

Sarah wrote her message down and handed it to Ike. Ike read her message and smiled at Sarah. He then started the transmission.

Pappa and Momma,

Am well. Plan to marry Mr. Zen Bragg next month. Please respond.

Love, Sarah

"Ike, would you please send someone to fetch me as soon as you get word back from my Pappa?"

"Surely will, Miss Sarah. This one's on me. Congratulations," Ike said.

"Thanks, Ike," Sarah said as she wheeled around and headed back to Gantry's. When she returned Mr. Gantry was standing over Mert and fanning her with a newspaper.

"What will your father say, Sarah?" Mr. Gantry calmly asked the young lady.

"Don't rightly know," she said. "Guessin' we'll find out pretty soon; I just wired him. Oh, Mr. Gantry, how much would you have to have for those two deer hides?" Sarah asked.

"What would you want with two deer hides?" asked Nathan.

"Never mind that; how much are they?" she asked again.

"How's four dollars sound?"

"Sold!" Sarah shouted. "Oh, Mr. Gantry, how can I get the hair off of them?" Sarah inquired.

"Well, I suppose if you soaked them a couple of days in some water loaded with hardwood ashes, the lye will loosen the hair," explained Nathan.

"Thanks, Mr. Gantry," Sarah said, as she ran out the door with the hides in hand.

A couple of minutes later a young boy came into the store and asked for Sarah. "I think she's around back, Alex. What do you need Sarah for?" asked Gantry.

"Tell her that her father's message has come back," Alex said. He was gawking at the candy in the front of the display case.

"Here, Alex, have a peppermint stick. I'll tell her," Mr. Gantry said. He looked directly at the frowning Mrs. Gantry.

As soon as Sarah was told about the message she ran to the telegraph office to receive the reply.

"Ike, do you…" she said before he interrupted her.

"Sure do, Miss Sarah, right here," he said as he handed her the message.

> *Sarah, both are well. Congratulations dear. Will be there for the wedding.*
>
> *Love Momma and Pappa*

Sarah kissed the telegram and whirled in a complete circle. She reached across the counter, kissed Ike on the cheek, and ran out of the telegraph office.

***

Pilgrim got back to his cabin as the sun was fading in the treetops. When he entered the cabin he found a small Bible on the table and realized that was Sarah's reason for running back into the cabin. He looked at it and held it up to his cheek caressing the memento and already missing her company. Pilgrim worried himself about the fact that he hadn't told Sarah that he couldn't read. He lit the lantern and spent the dark hours of the night planning some needed changes for the cabin.

At first light he grabbed his axe and some rope, tied them on his pack horse, and headed in the taller timber to cut some logs for his addition. His work was intense. Most days started at daylight and didn't stop until sunset. When the addition was completed, he dug a well. When the well was completed he built an outhouse. And when he was nearing the end to his work he realized that the time had been well spent. He had two days left before he was to return to Springville for Sarah, and both of those days were spent resting.

Chapter 22

Sarah's parents arrived only two days before the wedding was scheduled to take place. Sarah got word when the stage would arrive, and anxiously awaited their arrival. "She's as nervous as a jackrabbit in a fox's den," Mr. Gantry told some customers as the stage rolled in out front.

Sarah was greeted with smiles, hugs, and kisses, from both her mother and her father. "Well, young lady, I think you've grown three inches taller," Mr. Scarberry said with glee in his eyes.

"Oh, Pappa," Sarah shyly replied.

"Where's the groom?" Emma asked.

"He'll be here the day after tomorrow," answered Sarah. "Come on, let's get you settled in; then we can spend some time together at the café," insisted Sarah.

"Sounds good to me," conceded Winfred. "I'm famished."

"Oh, Pappa, you're always hungry."

When they got to the café they placed their orders. Emma was eager to hear Sarah's stories about Mr. Bragg, and what led up to their plans to get married. Sarah told her story, leaving not even the slightest detail to reason. Sarah's vivid imagery was quite descriptive, and her parents were intently absorbing her every word.

"Your father and I are so happy for you, dear," Emma said in a comforting tone as she lightly patted Sarah on the shoulder. "We have some news to tell you," Emma continued.

Sarah's heart sank in fear of some bad news, and the expression on Emma's face must have give reason for some concern.

"No, dear, it's nothing bad; it's just that your father sold his newspaper in Boston," said Emma.

"But Pappa, you loved your work. What are you going to do?" asked Sarah.

"Well, Sarah, when we got back home we both found the city to be somewhat confining. Your mother and I discussed it at great length, and we decided to move somewhere out here. I kept one of my printing presses and thought I might find a small town that needed a paper. Of course your being out here and your apparent plans to stay made our decision a lot easier to make," said Mr. Scarberry.

"Oh, that's wonderful!" Sarah shouted. "Are you going to stay in Springville?"

"No," Emma said with a smile. "We haven't really decided, but it won't be to far from here. We would like to find a place on the outskirts of what we consider a medium-sized town. We'll have plenty of time to look around after the wedding."

They shared idle talk through the meal, discussing many things that not only included the wedding plans but prattle that consisted of the most up-to-date information about Boston, a lot of which sounded like gossip.

The women spent the rest of the day, and all of the next, making the final arrangements for Sarah's wedding. Mr. Scarberry spent the better part of his time at Gantry's Store talking primarily about some of the towns around Springville.

***

Pilgrim woke up in a sweating panic on the day of his wedding. His sleep brought on a dream that Sarah wouldn't want to marry him after she found out that he couldn't read. He felt that he hadn't been honest with her, and groped over the guilt of not telling her the truth.

Pilgrim jumped to his feet and hurried around for his trip to Springville. He bathed in the river, and painstakingly trimmed his beard. He put his finest leather trousers on, and slipped a new cotton shirt on that he had never worn before. He looked at his reflection in the window and said out loud, "That's as good as it gits."

Pilgrim glanced around the cabin to make sure that everything was in order for his new bride. The thought of a new bride made his nerves quiver, as he closed the door and headed for his horse. Pilgrim couldn't clearly comprehend the thought of himself married. His surroundings seemed to be blurred by his thoughts of Sarah, the wedding, and the tremendous change that was about to take place in his life. He didn't remember a thing about the ride to town. He was apprehensive and excited at the same time. If you would have asked him what his name was, he'd had to have thought about it before he could have answered the question.

Pilgrim rode into town sitting tall in his saddle. The closer to Gantry's store he got the weaker he became. When he rode up to the hitching post at the front of the store, he climbed down from his horse and felt his knees buckle. It was all he could do to stay on his feet.

Mr. Gantry and Winfred Scarberry stood inside and watched as Pilgrim showed every sign of nervousness. They laughed as he wobbled his way through the front entrance.

"Gettin' married today, Mr. Bragg?" Nathan asked.

The comment made the blood rush from Pilgrim's head, and he nearly yielded to his body's involuntary demand to pass out. Instead he ran into the counter, like a drunk.

"Are you okay, Mr. Bragg?" asked Gantry. "Come over here and sit down."

Pilgrim couldn't respond. He did what he was told, but was totally unaware of his actions. Mr. Gantry and Mr. Scarberry looked at each other and started laughing at Pilgrim's condition. Gantry took some smelling salts from under the counter and held them under Pilgrim's nose. "Here, this ought to help your condition."

Pilgrim immediately responded to the potent smell, and the blood seemed to return to his head with much clearer thoughts.

"So, my daughter has you a bit nervous, does she?" said Scarberry, adding that extra little pressure to Pilgrim's circumstances.

"No, sir, Sarah's not the problem. It's the marryin' that seems to be affecting me," Pilgrim uttered.

Gantry and Scarberry got another chuckle from his unwitting comment. Mr. Gantry went back toward the room where the women were preparing Sarah. He tapped lightly on the door and announced that the groom had arrived.

"You all go get the preacher," Mrs. Gantry ordered, in her typical demanding tone. "We'll be along shortly."

Nathan went back to the store front and repeated Mrs. Gantry's orders to Pilgrim and Mr. Scarberry. They were headed out the door when Mr. Gantry saw Alex. "Alex, I'll get you another peppermint stick if you'll go and fetch the preacher, and just tell him it's time."

Alex didn't hesitate at the offer, and headed down the street toward the parsonage. Pilgrim, Gantry, and Scarberry headed on down the street to the far end of town, where a babbling brook, lined with purple and yellow wild flowers, flowed through a grove of tall oak trees.

Pilgrim listened as the bell at the church tolled the announcement that the wedding was about to take place. Several of the townspeople started to arrive. It wasn't until the preacher came that things quieted down and some sense of formality was established.

The preacher called for Pilgrim to come forward and showed him where to stand. He then announced to the crowd that they would have a word of prayer. Pilgrim felt his knees begin to weaken, but he was able to maintain his strength, and took a deep breath, in order to stave off his nervousness. When the preacher finished the prayer, he looked up at the approaching bride with a smile. Pilgrim could see that the preacher was looking back through the crowd. His curiosity was much stronger than his will, so he slowly turned to see what had caught the preacher's attention.

It was Sarah. She was dressed in a cream-colored buckskin skirt and carried a bouquet of purple and yellow wild flowers. Her hair glimmered in the sunlight. Pilgrim was awed by her beauty as she gracefully walked toward him. When she took her place beside him, she noticed that he looked worried and didn't have the smile she had expected.

She whispered in his ear, "What's wrong?"

"I can't read." He whispered back.

"What?" she said, as if she hadn't heard him the first time.

"I can't read," he repeated. "I thought you might want to know that before you marry me."

"I've known that all along," she assured him. "I love you for being you."

Pilgrim immediately felt lifted from his admission, and his nervousness dissipated. The ceremony continued and moments later ended with a kiss. The preacher introduced the new couple to the crowd as Mr. and Mrs. Zen Bragg. There was a loud cheer from the crowd, and an announcement that the celebration was to be continued at the café.

"Iffen you knew I couldn't read, why'd ya leave me yer Bible?" he asked.

"It was something of mine that would keep me in your thoughts," she responded.

"Yer jest bout the most beautiful thing this here earth has ta offer," he said, with a renewed spirit of the heart.

Sarah kissed him as they made their way through the crowd in the direction of the café. Sarah's father bought her the same horse from the livery that she rode out to Zen's cabin for the first time. Other wedding gifts included blankets, oil lamps, and a cook stove. The dinner celebration lasted late into the evening, and rather than trying to get back to the cabin, they spent the night at the hotel in Springville.

Early the next morning, Pilgrim, Sarah and her parents made plans to take their gifts to the cabin. Mr. and Mrs. Scarberry were going to help deliver the items before they continued the trip further north to a town that sounded promising to their needs.

Pilgrim seriously contemplated how they would manage to get the cook stove around the bluff at the Aninandak River. He knew that the horse and buggy borrowed from the Gantry's would have to stay on the far side of the river passage, for the night. The stove wouldn't be moved from the wagon until he could build a small raft to float across the river.

When they arrived, Pilgrim ferried the ladies, one at a time, through the water's current and around the bluff. Mr. Scarberry chose to wade the river as Pilgrim had done.

Sarah marveled at the changes that Zen had made with her in mind, and showed her appreciation with a hug and a thankful kiss. She looked around as if she were seeing it all for the first time, and began to point specific things out to her mother.

Zen and Mr. Scarberry went to work building a raft that would be used to get the wood cook stove down the river. In short time they were satisfied that the temporary structure would perform its needed task. They dragged the raft to the edge of the river and launched the platform into the frothy flow. Zen held tight to an attached rope as Mr. Scarberry used a long pole to keep it out from the bank. In a couple of hours they had the cook stove loaded and floated the raft back to where they launched it. Carrying it to the cabin took them longer to accomplish than all their previous tasks in total, and required the help of Sarah and her mother.

Mr. Scarberry conversed with the women as Zen cut a hole in he cabin wall and install the stove piping. They all watched as the last pipes were fitted together and the task was completed.

Sarah gathered small pieces of kindling for the preparation of their first meal on the cook stove as Zen announced that the stove was ready to be used. She meticulously placed the kindling under each of the stove plates and used a long thin straw of split wood to light it. Everyone stood around the stove, silently gazing; as if in some kind of trance. Zen watched as the fire built to a popping blaze, then quickly went for the door, breaking the trance for all. Throwing the door open, he swung around to the left, holding tightly to the door jamb and peeked at the protruding stovepipe. The billowing white cloud of smoke rising from top of the stovepipe caused a smile to form on Zen's face: a sign to all that the stove was indeed working properly.

Mrs. Scarberry filled the new lamps with oil, trimmed the wicks, and lighted them from a piece of twisted paper that she ignited from the blaze in the fireplace. The men were standing next to the table, deep in conversation, as Sarah squeezed between them to set the table. Sarah's glance was quite sufficient to each that they were in her way. The men continued in unbroken conversation as they silently stepped in unison toward the fireplace.

Soon, Sarah's small feast was complete, and they all took a seat around the table. Zen had just started to reach for the serving spoon in the potato dish, when Sarah scowled and cleared her throat and asked her Father for a prayer of thanksgiving.

Conversation of many things followed. Not much was said about the past. Most of the discussion was about everyone's plans for the future, including the Scarberrys' plans to find a country home and establish a town newspaper. The meal was an enjoyable time and everyone's future seemed so positive. Several hours passed rather quickly as the conversation continued around the cozy fireplace until the women excused themselves to retire from the day's exhaustive activities.

***

Sarah woke at daybreak. Her stirring to fix breakfast woke her parents, but Zen slept through most of the preparation. The new room addition, where he and Sarah slept, was quiet and comfortable, and for some reason he was exhausted. The smell of Sarah's cooking finally found its way to Zen, and it had been a long time since he experienced the smell of breakfast cooking from his bed. Because of that and his partial dream-state, he was reluctant to get out of bed.

After their morning meal, both Sarah and Zen escorted the Scarberrys back to the horse, where Zen re-hitched their wagon. Neither Sarah nor her parents were fond of long good-byes.

She kissed them both, and Mr. Scarberry shook Zen's hand.

"We'll see you again before long," said Mr. Scarberry, assured them both.

Sarah watched as the wagon followed the trail along the river. Zen noticed Sarah waving at her mother when she turned to see her daughter at a distance.

Zen and Sarah looked at each other, and Sarah remarked that their life together was just beginning. Pilgrim gently squeezed her hand and smiled.

Chapter 23

Their life together was full of happiness and enjoyment for the both of them. Sometime after the first year, Sarah told Zen that she was pregnant. He assured her in his normal soft mannered way that there was plenty of room in their lives and in hearts for a child.

***

The child was a boy that they named Jonas. Zen took great pride in his son. The boy's younger years were spent in the nurturing protection of his mother's caring hands. By the time Jonas was three years old, Sarah started to work with both Zen and the boy, to teach them how to read. Zen spent time with Jonas and taught him how to shoot a gun, tan a hide, and make various things using his hands. When Jonas was eight years old he killed his first turkey, and by the age of ten he was a proficient hunter. Jonas saw the love shared by his parents and accepted it as the way things were meant to be.

Other than a few trips to his grandparents' house in Rapid City, and an occasional trip to Springville with Zen, Jonas's life was secluded. He didn't mind, for he knew of nothing else that his life required.

When he reached the age of fifteen, Jonas reminded Zen of the Indian boy that he once knew. Zen watched the boy work with his hands and make small gifts for his mother and him. Their lives seemed perfect in every way, but even the most perfect life has times of concern, fear, heartbreak, worry, and loss, especially when the lives involve more than just one's self.

Jonas was no exception. When he was four years old he got lost in the woods. His worried mother fretting over the boy's safety remained in the cabin praying for his protection and safe return, while his father frantically searched for him throughout the cold night.

Then there was the time when he was six years old when he stood next to his consoling father as they watched one of their horses take its last breath. Jonas was eight years old when he fell in the river and was carried several miles down the raging waterway as his father desperately ran alongside waiting for the perfect opportunity to pluck his son from the dangerous current.

But the one time that sticks out in his mind as the hardest time of all to get through was when the boy's mother passed away. And the reason I know it was so hard for him and his father to cope with is that I am that boy.

I was fifteen years old when Mom took sick. Dad and I stayed by her side from the onset of her brief illness. One day that she seemed to be feeling a better and appeared to be regaining her strength. She called me to her side, and asked me to reach under her bed and pull out a pouch filled with papers, notes, and newspaper clippings. When I did, she sorted through her cherished notes and found a newspaper clipping with a picture of a man on it, that clearly resembled my father. She handed the yellowed clipping to me and asked me to read it out loud, which I did.

"Mr. Zen Bragg, or as the mountain people call him, Pilgrim, spoke with me recently about the tragedy that befell Colonel George Custer at the Little Bighorn. It seems that Mr. Bragg is the only white man that survived the ordeal, and he was able to do so because he was in the company of the Indian Chief who organized the massacre. Mr. Bragg was reluctant to tell his story for fear that the soldiers would consider him a traitor, but he assured me that fighting between the two groups was not his battle, but was a dispute over the land that belonged to no one. He went on to say that Indians were a part of the land long before the soldiers pushed them from one place to another and squeezed the very life from within their souls. Now I ask, you, reader, is there not some truth in this mountain man's words?"

Mother grasped my hand and said, "Jonas, that's your father. I have more about him in my notes, and I promised him I would write it all down. That I have done, son. My strength and my time left here won't allow me to finish it so others can see what a great person he is. Please write his story and take it to your grandpa in Rapid City; he'll know what to do with it."

I took her notes and spent that whole day and three that followed, looking through each scribbled piece. Before long, I found myself putting the pieces in a systematic sequence and found that the story of my father's life was taking shape.

Mother passed away four days after she handed me that news clipping, and Dad, as strong a man as he was, crumbled at her death. He grieved for days, then weeks, and every time we brought her memory into the conversation, his eyes sweltered with tears and rendered him always leaving him speechless.

Dad and I buried her by her favorite little flower garden that she took so much pride in. He had me make her a headstone that read: "Here lies my wife, mother of my son. May her soul find the same peace that she so caringly shared with us."

I stayed on with Dad until I was nineteen years old. The day came that I finally completed the compilation of mom's notes in the form of a manuscript, and I headed for Rapid City to turn it over to my grandfather, so that he could use his knowledge of the printing business to get it published. I spent two weeks with my grandparents and told them all I could about my mother's life with my father.

I was told of an Indian reservation about a hundred miles northeast of Rapid City, called the Cheyenne River Indian Reservation. My curiosity got the better of me, and I set out to find it. It took me five days of relatively slow travel to find the reservation, and when I arrived, I wasn't received with the greatest respect. I'm not sure what I really expected of these people, and I sure now that they didn't have a clue as to what to expect of me. I was about to turn my futile efforts toward home when I heard the name of Quineata spoken. Quineata was Cheyenne. Could it actually be the same Quineata that my father had known as a child?

I asked if Quineata knew of Elk Arrow. That name, Elk Arrow, they had heard of from the stories that the elders told of the past. Immediately they took an interest in my knowledge of those stories that were once told, and asked to their camp. By that time, most all the Indians spoke fluent English so the difficulty in communication had been removed over the years.

I met with Quineata, who now went by the name of Iron Bear. When I told him who my father was he was pleased. When I told him my name, he sat silently for the longest time. His perspective in retrospect caused a single tear to stream down his cheek.

I stayed at the Red River Reservation for nearly a year at Iron Bear's invitation. The time went so quickly and my departure was difficult. I could see, what it was about the Nation's people that my father admired. And though it was different for the two prior generations, the people there had never lost their spirit and remained to be the same great Nation that my father had spoken of. I returned to Rapid City and picked up a copy of the book that mother had wanted so much for the preservation of my father's lost mountain spirit.

I took the book to my father and he read it over and over. He didn't really see it as the preservation of his life and character, as much as he saw the preservation of his wife's love.

His favorite books for the rest of his life were *Lost Mountain Spirit* and her copy of the Holy Bible.

The Cochin Tribes and Castes

BY

L. K. ANANTHA KRISHNA IYER

IN TWO VOLUMES
VOL. I

GYAN

Published by

GYAN

Gyan Publishing House
5, Ansari Road
Daryaganj, New Delhi-110002
Phone: 011-47034999, 9811692060
E-mail: books@gyanbooks.com

Distribution Network
gyanbooks.com
India, USA, Canada, UK, Australia

ISBN: 978-93-6780-631-9 (Set)
978-93-6780-090-4 (HB)
First Published, 1909

2nd Impression 2024

Printed at: Gyan Press, Delhi.

THE COCHIN TRIBES AND CASTE, VOL. I
Author: L. K. ANANTHA KRISHNA IYER

The
Cochin Tribes and Castes

The
Cochin Tribes and Castes,

VOLUME I.

BY

L. K. ANANTHA KRISHNA IYER, B.A. L.T.,

Superintendent of Ethnography, Cochin State ; Corresponding Member of the Royal Anthropological Institute of Great Britain and Ireland, London; the Bureau of American Ethnology, Washington ; and Corresponding Member of the Anthropological Society, Bombay.

MADRAS:

PUBLISHED FOR THE GOVERNMENT OF COCHIN BY
HIGGINBOTHAM & CO., MOUNT ROAD.
LONDON : LUZAC & CO.

1909.

PREFACE.

Mr. Anantha Krishna Iyer has asked me to write an introductory preface to his volume on the Cochin Tribes and Castes, to which request I willingly consent. Having already read considerable portions of Mr. Iyer's work in its original and unrevised form, I am able to testify to its importance and interest, and to the great desirability of its being read and pondered by students of Ethnology and Sociology in England and the West generally.

It is only in comparatively recent years that the enormous and almost incalculable mass of anthropological materials which India offers to the student, has begun to be systematically utilised. Of course, almost the same might have been stated, not so very long ago, of Europe itself. One could not exactly say of Blumenbach and Prichard and Retzius and Broca and Von Baer that they "were the first that ever burst into that silent sea"; but assuredly a vast field lay open to those great pioneers, a field almost untilled then, but which has since then attracted, I may say, almost innumerable labourers. But India's aspect to the anthropologist is very much the same as that of Europe in the days of those great men. The conquerors and administrators of that wide and manifold country had not time to devote to scientific studies beyond those which offered the speediest returns, such as political and natural history. The Government, whether of the Company or of the Queen, gave no assistance; and the habits and ideas of the people threw great and peculiar difficulties in the way, as indeed they still continue to do. Historians and men of that class, such as Mountstuart Elphinstone, Sir H. Elliot, Dr. T. A. Wise, working in the border-lands of the subject, preserved and accumulated incidentally much material of value to those who would follow them. But Dr. John Short, a Eurasian by the way, was, I think, the first to make systematic observations in physical anthropology; as a pioneer, his methods were unformed, and his achievements but small; still he should not be forgotten.

In our own times, the Government of India have begun to favour and subsidise this work, in taking up which it must be confessed that they lagged behind some of the other European Governments who possess colonies or transmarine possessions. Mr. Risley's Anthropometric Statistics of Bengal and the North-West have begun a new era, and Thurston in Madras and others have done excellent work in similar fields.

Mr. Iyer's labours have been in the main ethnological and sociological, rather than from the physical or somatic side. He has had several great advantages. Thus in the first place, he belongs to India by race and nativity: and had he not been so, it is hardly conceivable that he could have acquired such a vast mass of information on subjects which natives are usually very unwilling to discuss with Europeans. At the same time, he is a fluent and accurate English scholar, able to convey his ideas and observations clearly and unequivocally in that language. In the collection of facts, his official position under the Cochin Government must have been of the greatest service to him. Then, again, Cochin, though limited in extent, is a province affording opportunities to the ethnologist which can hardly be excelled anywhere in India, having a gamut of castes extending from the Brahman and the Nair, among whom features of high Aryan type are common, and whose aspect little else than color discriminates from the upper class European, to the scarcely human wretch who is not, theoretically at least, allowed to crawl within a hundred yards of the Brahman, but who nevertheless, as Mr. Iyer shows, voluntarily circumscribes what little liberty is left to him, by various caste devices and prohibitions. Lastly, the very peculiar forms of matrimony in use among the Nairs, and the prevalence of polyandry among several other castes, complicate the laws of filiation and succession beyond what is generally met with elsewhere, and yield subject-matter for interesting speculations.

With these few remarks, I commend Mr. Anantha Krishna Iyer's volume to the European reader.

John Beddoe

The Chantry,
Bradford-on-Avon.
24th February, 1908.

AUTHOR'S PREFACE.

I was entrusted with the Ethnographical Survey of the Cochin State in 1902, and the work in connection with it had to be done without prejudice to my duties in the Ernakulam College, in which I was an assistant till very lately. My proposal to deal first with the purely Malayali Hindu and animistic castes of the State, was accepted by the Government, and the investigation into the customs and manners of the local hill and jungle tribes and the lowest castes, was made thereupon. The results of these investigations were published from time to time, in the form of a monograph for each tribe or caste, the total number of monographs issued from the Government Press, Ernakulam, being twelve between 1904 and 1906. In July 1907, I was asked by the Diwan to revise these monographs and others then ready for publication in order that they might appear in a single volume with illustrations. The present volume, therefore, is really due to the warm interest taken by the Government of His Highness the Raja and the Diwan whose valuable and eminently suggestive instructions have been carried out by me to the best of my ability in the preparation of this volume.

In regard to the plan and arrangement of the subject-matter, the new volume begins with a preface by John Beddoe, Esq., M.D., LL.D., F.R.S., & F.R.C.P., Past President of the Royal Anthropological Institute of Great Britain and Ireland (1889-91), an introductory chapter by A. H. Keane, Esq., LL.D., F.R.G.S., F.R.A.I., late Vice-President of the Royal Anthropological Institute of Great Britain and Ireland, and then gives a descriptive account of the hill and jungle tribes, and other low castes of the State, in the ascending order of social status. The volume thus deals with all the Malayali and animistic castes, the members of which pollute the high caste-men at various distances, and cannot approach the outer walls of the temples of the higher castes. The photographs of the types of each caste have been taken by me with the exception of a few borrowed from friends.

The higher castes (high and low caste Sudras), Ambalavasies, Elayads, Muthads, Brahmans, Jews, Muhammadans, Christians, and a few other foreign castes of the State, as also the physical anthropology of the inhabitants of the State, will be dealt with in the second and the third volumes respectively.

Investigations on the various tribes and castes herein dealt with were made by myself first hand, but in the handling of such a large number of facts, errors both of omission and commission, can scarcely be avoided. Accuracy in the statement of facts, as far as possible, has all along been my aim, so that the errors, I hope, will be found to be neither numerous nor serious.

I take this opportunity to record my grateful thanks to the late Diwan, M. R. Ry. N. Pattabhirama Rao Garu, B.A., to the present Diwan, A. R. Banerji, Esq., M.A., I.C.S., for his valuable instructions, to John Beddoe, Esq., for his kind preface recommending the perusal of this volume to the European reader, to A. H. Keane, Esq., for the introductory chapter and for much other help received during past years, and to Mrs. Noliny Banerji, M.R.A.S., for the kindness with which she has revised the letterpress of this volume. To Edgar Thurston, Esq., Superintendent of Ethnography, Madras Presidency, to the Rev. Monteith Macphail, M.A., B.D., Professor of History and Economics, Christian College, Madras, to Mr. C. Achyuta Menon B. A., the late Secretary to the Diwan, and to other officials of the State, as also to my friends and correspondents, I express with all sincerity my great sense of indebtedness.

Office of the Ethnographic Survey,
Trichur, 26th October, 1908. L. K. A.

CONTENTS.

—o—

LIST OF ILLUSTRATIONS.

THE COCHIN TRIBES AND CASTES.

INTRODUCTION.

Mr. L. K. Anantha Krishna Iyer, who has invited me to contribute a few introductory remarks to this volume, is already known to European anthropologists as an indefatigable worker in the wide field of Indian ethnology. I had the pleasure of drawing attention to his valuable monographs on the Cochin aborigines in "Man" for March 1907, where I was able to state that this enthusiastic student of primitive peoples had at that time already issued as many as ten special essays bearing an official character and printed at the Government Press, Ernakulam, (1904-06). In its general outline, the series corresponds somewhat to the highly prized "Bulletins" issued by the Madras Government under the superintendence of Mr. Edgar Thurston, and still more closely to those embodied in Mr. H. V. Nanjundayya's "Ethnographical Survey of Mysore" (Bangalore Government Press, 1906-08).

Since his recent appointment as Superintendent of the "Cochin Ethnographical Survey" at Trichur, a town only second in importance to Ernakulam, Mr. Iyer has continued his studies of the local tribes and castes with such zeal and unflagging industry that he has now completed his general survey of all the hill tribes, the multifarious results forming the substance of this richly illustrated volume. It should, however, be explained that this is but a first instalment of the gifted author's comprehensive programme, and it is to be followed in due course by two more volumes, one dealing with the Brahmans, the Nairs, and all the higher castes, the other with the physical anthropology of all the inhabitants of Cochin.

None too soon has this useful work been taken in hand, seeing that Hinduism, a relatively higher phase of culture, is steadily invading the haunts of the jungle peoples and thus gradually effacing many of the most characteristic traits in the life of the childhood of mankind. Such remarks are often made by thoughtful observers, but for the most part pass unheeded because unsupported by actual incidents. It may therefore be well here to specify a few cases in point amongst some of the most primitive groups, such as the Kadars, the Parayans, the Irulans, the Paniyans, and the Pulayans. Reference is made by Mr. Iyer himself to the rapid disappearance of savage usages as seen in the use of tiles and kerosine tins for thatch and foliage; cotton piece-goods and umbrellas for rude local fabrics and sunshades covered with leaves; the substitution of gaudy head dresses for tribal turbans; country jewelry replaced by beads and imitation jewelry from Europe; lucifer matches abolishing fire by friction; bread, beer and spirits instead of the roots, wild berries, and water of the wilderness, and so on. Well may Professor Haddon exclaim "Now is the time to record. An infinitude has been lost to us and a very great deal is now rapidly disappearing. The most interesting materials are becoming lost to us, not only by their disappearance, but by the apathy of those who should delight in recording them before they have become lost to sight and memory."

From all this may at once be seen the inestimable value of the great body of primitive customs and social institutions which Mr. Iyer has rescued from oblivion and here placed at the disposal of ethnical students. Few questions, for instance, are at present more warmly discussed than the relations of magic rites and sorcery to elementary religion, some denying any connection whatsoever, and contending that religion and magic belong to two distinct orders of thought, while others hold with Mr. Sidney Hartland that "religion is saturated with magic," and that it is only in their later development the one becomes separated from the other. Well, a careful study of the data here supplied by Mr. Iyer will, I think, support Mr. Hartland's view, and once for all dispose of this vexed question. He tells us that sickness, death, famine and troubles of all kinds are attributed by the Parayan magicians to the anger of the gods, to whom offerings may not have been given perhaps for want of means. When a woman is under demoniacal influence and makes frantic movements, the Parayan devil-driver and sorcerer mutters some prayers to Parakutty and other deities, ties the sacred thread round the woman's neck, and drinks the toddy supplied for the occasion, whereupon the demon is supposed to leave her. In case of theft, they call in the Parayan wizard, who takes a sword with small bells at the hilt, and prays fervently to his favourite deity, confident that he will help to recover the stolen property and also to punish the thief. Here we have the sorcerer performing the functions of the priest or intercessor in his own person ; in other words, religion and the magic arts are not merely allied and co-operating, but actually interwoven inextricably together not at a late but at a very early phase of religious thought.

Then there is the *oti* cult, a kind of black art practised by these same Parayans, who go through a process of training as in a priestly seminary, and when proficient can make themselves invisible or assume the form of a bull, a cat, or a dog at pleasure. They possess many other miraculous powers, can cause illness or death, and bewitch people, transporting them despite of physical obstacles from one place to another, "and this without their absence being noted by third parties." The student of early beliefs should carefully read the detailed account here given from original sources of the strange functions and misdeeds popularly accredited to these *otiyans,* priests and sorcerers in one. "The records of the criminal courts attest the power and prevalence of this persuasion among the more intelligent and higher classes. The Parayans keep the cult a dead secret, and profess total ignorance owing to the fear of punishment." All this establishes beyond question the unity of the magical and religious lines of thought, which are here clearly seen to be inseparably associated in a single *shamanistic* system, as it may rightly be called. The *otiyans* of Southern India are in fact not perceptibly distinguishable from the Shamans of Siberia and North America.

More important perhaps is the question of the origin and ethnical affinities of these southern aborigines. Without himself advancing any distinct theory on this obscure subject, Mr. Iyer refers to my opinion that "judging from the short stature, low forehead, and the high cheek bones, they belong to the Negrito race, which once formed a substratum throughout the peninsula, though now mainly submerged by the later arrivals of the Kolarians, the Dravidians, and the Aryans." This may, in a very broad way, be taken as representing the views, which I have advanced in several places, but may take the opportunity of here discussing somewhat more fully. In such a discussion, it is obvious that the southern aborigines cannot be treated apart from their remote northern kindred, such as most of the Vindhyan and some even of the Himalayan groups. Though now somewhat isolated, several of the Cochin hill-men had formerly a very wide range, with allied castes and traditions extending throughout Travancore and Mysore northwards to Orissa where the famous temple of Jagannath is closely associated with a low caste Parayan tribe. Traditionally, the warlike Asuras and Daithias (Danavas) who opposed the proto-Aryan invaders of the Panjab, sent expeditions to the Dekhan, where they founded the semi-civilised States of Southern India, and imposed their speech and culture on the aborigines. Hence it is that some of the ruling families in the far south still retain traditions of their northern origin, while "inscriptions assert their descent from Daithia chiefs of the Indus valley" (Dr. Oldham). All the pre-historic movements must in fact be assumed to have set from the north southwards, so that the whole of the Peninsula was occupied during the Stone Ages by successive streams of primitive peoples descending from the Himalayan and Vindhyan slopes to the extremity of the mainland.

Who were these primitive peoples? By popular writers, and even in the last (1901) Census, they are confusedly lumped together as Dravidians, or Munda-Dravidians or Aryo-Dravidians or Indo-Aryans or Scytho-Dravidians, or by other equally unintelligible and misguiding complex terms, and Deniker, amongst others, thinks that he has settled the whole matter by declaring that "the variety of types found in the country is due to the crossing of two indigenous races, Indo-Afghan and Melano-Indian, etc." But surely, groups needing to be thus expressed by compound terms must be assumed to represent still earlier crossings which, however, no attempt is here made to determine. Others go still further in this eliminating process, and Mr. R. P. Chanda proclaims the "essential unity of the Indian race" in which there are no heterogeneous elements (*East and West*: November and December, 1904), and this conclusion seems to be supported by Mr. W. Crooke on anthropometric grounds (*The North-Western Provinces of India*: 1897, *passim*). At least this observer denies the distinction between the Dravidian and Kolarian races, because this distinction depends mainly on the evidence of language and is disproved by anthropometry, which he regards as "the final test." At the same time he thinks it "fairly certain that the Dravidians were of the Negrito type" (page 197).

Then, in their Census Reports, Sir Herbert Risley and his fellow-worker, Mr. E. A. Gait, denounce the time-honoured term *Kolarian* (revived by Sir George Campbell) as "altogether fantastic", and relegate the Kolarians themselves with "the Lost Ten Tribes" to cloudland. Deceived by the remarkably uniform results of his own anthropometric studies, Sir. Herbert claims to have disproved the existence of a distinct Kolarian race, "the so called Kolarians" being simply members of the great Dravidian family, and modern researches have confirmed this view by maintaining a relationship between the Kolarian and the Dravidian languages" (Report page 2789; see also Sir Herbert's *The People of India*: 1908). Thus, as anthropometry claims to prove that there is no distinct *physical Kolarian* type, so philology is called in to prove that there is no distinct *linguistic* Kolarian type, so that Kolarian cannot be a stock language, but must be related to the Dravidian stock language. In the Report the proscribed Kolarian is replaced by Max Müller's *Munda*, this being one of the chief members of the group, and thus is formed the hypothetical Dravido-Munda family, which looms largely in the pages of the Report, where the two component terms are treated as two related branches of one stock language. Such are the main current views, which, although they have received the seal of official authority, are radically wrong; and have in fact once more reduced Indian ethnology to an almost hopeless state of chaos. I therefore propose to introduce some order and method into this wide department of anthropological science, by showing —

(1) that in India there is no fundamental racial unity, the superficial uniformity of physical characters being far less than is commonly supposed, and due not to a fanciful *primordial unity*, but to secular interminglings of several originally distinct ethnical groups superinducing *surface resemblances*:

(2) that the authority of the early Hindu writings claiming racial unity is worthless, their theories being framed mainly in the interest of "the twice-born" and especially of the dominant priestly (Brahmanical) caste:

(3) that, in the present general amalgam, are represented five primary stocks: a submerged *Negrito* probably from Malaysia; *Kolarian*, *Dravidian*, and *Aryan*, who arrived in the order named from beyond the Hindu Kush and the Himalayas; lastly the *Mongol* mainly confined to the Himalayan slopes:

(4) that to the Kolarian, Dravidian, and Aryan ethnical stocks, correspond three distinct linguistic stocks, Kolarian being radically different from Dravidian, and both from Aryan; that there is therefore no "Dravido-Kolarian" or "Dravido-Munda" mother tongue; and that these and the other above mentioned compound terms (Indo-Aryan, Scytho-Dravidian, etc.,) are for the most part meaningless if not actually misguiding. This is a formidable programme which it might take a stout volume to deal with adequately; but it will presently be seen that some

of the points can be disposed of in a few words, while for others *cadet quæstio.*

1 and 2 : Mr. Chanda's essential unity (see above) may be described as a purely *subjective notion,* a pleasant dream at variance with *objective reality.* His contention is that for the proto-Aryans penetrating from the Indus south-eastwards the non-Aryan aborigines were not an alien or independent stock, but a debased Aryan people, and so was still upheld the theory of absolute racial unity in defiance of the actual facts. "But when," he writes, "from the Sudras and the mixed castes we turn our eyes to the third type, the *Vratyas,* we fully perceive how deep-rooted was the ancient Arya's belief in the unity of mankind and how indifferent he was to what is now known as racial difference. Distance in space and use of non-Aryan speech could not shake that belief; even marked differences in physical features, as between himself and the Mongoloid Kiratas and Chinas, counted for nothing. He labelled them *Vratyas* or degenerate ones, and paid a tribute to their independence by calling them the degenerate descendants of one or other of the twice-born castes."

To this it may be replied that it is not a question of what the Vedic Aryas *thought* on racial questions, and if they supposed that the non-Aryan peoples could be transformed even to degraded Aryans by being called Vratyas, it merely shows that the Vedas and still less the later fantastic Puranas cannot be profitably consulted on ethnical matters. No doubt the term Vratya, in the sense of any Brahman, Kshatriya or Vaisya, who has lost caste by neglect of the prescribed rites, is of some antiquity, occurring even in the early Yagur-Veda; but for ethnical purposes it proves no more than do those ridiculous genealogies of many non-Aryan groups which abound in the absolutely worthless Puranas, "ces poèmes mythologiques absurdes," which "consacraient une, trimurti monstrueuse que l' on regarda à tort comme la base de l' indianisme". (Eichhoff). Nor is Manu much more trustworthy, since this shadowy legislator was avowedly the great advocate of Brahman supremacy.

Is it not a matter of common knowledge, faintly disguised by the Code of Manu and by the sham genealogies of the Puranas, that as the early Aryan invaders advanced down the Ganges valley, they everywhere came in contact with fresh indigenous populations, so that despite the Vratya delusion, they were at last fain to draw distinctions based no longer on mere social or functional differences, but on real racial distinctions ?

3 and 4 : Of the five constituent elements here enumerated, the *Aryan* and the *Mongol* may, for the present purpose, be dismissed, the first because not questioned, the second because mainly confined to the southern slopes of the Himalayas, and thus but slightly affecting the great mass of the Indian populations. There remain the *Negrito*, the *Kolarian* and the *Dravidian* which although generally lumped together as "Dravidians" in popular writings and, as we have seen, even in official documents, have nevertheless to be considered separately if we are ever to arrive at a clear understanding of this stupendous "amalgam" of heterogeneous ingredients comprising nearly one-fifth of the "World's Peoples."

The first arrivals were undoubtedly the *Negritos* whom I have called the "submerged element," because they now form the substratum, have nowhere preserved their racial or social independence, have even lost their original Negrito speech, and are now everywhere *merged* in the surrounding Kolarian and Dravidian populations.

Whence came this black element, the presence of which I hope here to place beyond reasonable doubt ? Herr Fehlinger thinks they reached India partly from Africa and partly from Australia (*Naturwiss. Wochenschr.* 1904, iii). But I cannot believe there are two black strains in India. One satisfies all the conditions, and that one can scarcely have come either from Africa which is barred by the Indian Ocean, or from Australia which is shut off by the Eastern Archipelago. Moreover, both Africans and Australians are mostly tall (five feet eight to ten inches), whereas the Dravidians and Kolarians, amongst whom black blood is conspicuous, are nearly all undersized—the Koravas five feet three inches and many Korava women real dwarfs, about four feet nine inches); the Juangs still shorter, under five feet, women four feet eight inches, (Dalton). The inference is that in India the dark autochthons were pigmies apparently allied to the Aetas of the Philippines, and to the Samangs and Sakais still surviving in the Malay Peninsula. From Malaysia these woolly-headed Negritos could easily have moved through Tennasserim and Arakan round the Bay of Bengal to the Himalayan slopes, where they have left traces of their former presence, and whence they gradually spread over the Peninsula most probably in early Palaeolithic times. Their spoor may everywhere be followed from the Negroid flat-faced, curly-haired, Kocch of Assam "with the thick protuberant lips of the Negro" to the swarthy and irregular-featured Nepalese *Hayas*, and thence to the numerous *Santals* of Chota Nagpur "with a cast of countenance almost approaching the Negro type," and to the neighbouring *Bhuniyas* with "coarse Negro-like features and frizzly hair and the diminutive Juang jungle-folk with depressed nasal bone, dilated nostrils, large mouth, very thick lips, and black frizzled hair. The kindred *Dhangars, Khonds* and *Gonds* of the Vindhyan range "show to this day features more closely resembling the *lower Negro type* than any I have met with amongst the tribes of Bengal." Thus speaks Dalton who knew these Vindhyan hill-men well, and who adds that here we still find specimens of the lowest type of humanity; creatures who might justly be regarded as the unimproved descendants of the manufacturers of the stone implements found in the Damodar coal fields. These are the true aborigines, the *Asuras*, from whom a considerable proportion of the black pigment is derived that has darkened the skins of a large section of the [Indian] population."

Equally unmistakable evidences of the underlying Negroid element are presented by the low caste hill-men of the southern uplands. Some years ago Drs. F. Jagor and G. Koerbin collected a great body of anthropological data from over two hundred and fifty of these aborigines representing as many as fifty-four tribes from almost every part of the Madras Presidency. Since then the list has been supplemented by the researches of Mr. E. Thurston, of Mr. Nanjundayya for Mysore and of Mr. Iyer for Cochin. We are now, therefore, in a position to speak with confidence of the general physical characteristics of these jungle peoples, many of whom are so fully described in the present volume that details may be largely dispensed with. It will suffice to say that Negroid contacts and influences are almost everywhere betrayed in the black colour, crisp or frizzly hair, broad nose, thick lips, low stature, very long arms, and other marked Negro traits of these aborigines. Thus, the *Veddas* of Travancore are described as all but black, with hair very black, wavy and crisp, and similar characters are attributed to the *Paniyans* of the Wynaad, the *Kadars* and *Malasers* of Coimbatore and Cochin, the *Kurumbas* and *Irulas* of the Nilghiris, the *Malayalis, Pallis, Shanars*, and *Katumaratis* of the Salem District, the *Vellalas* of Madura and above all to the *Paniyans* " of pronounced Negro features." Here I would ask the reader to study some of the numerous photographs with which Mr. Iyer has enriched this work, all, I believe, taken by himself, and he will find several which also reveal Negroid traits in a very striking manner. Such are the Kadar men, several of the Malayan, and Eravallen women, the Izhuva and Thandapulaya groups.

Now comes the question, how have the present Dravidian and Kolarian low castes acquired these Negroid characters which could not have been brought from beyond the Hindu Kush or the Himalayas, where the indigenous populations have always been either white regular-featured Aryans of Caucasic type or else yellow, lank-haired Mongols? The inference seems obvious that these Dravidians and Kolarians are a blend in diverse proportions of Asiatic intruders with the true black indigenes of the Peninsula. In other words, they acquired their Negroid characters by secular interminglings with the Negrito aborigines.

Now these very interminglings of the three or four fundamental factors lie at the root of all the confusion and complications prevailing throughout the whole field of Indian ethnology. The gradual fusion of the various types has brought about such a *superficial* uniformity amongst the great masses of the settled and urban populations, and even to some extent amongst the outcasts and wild tribes, that the deeper discrepancies are overlooked, the primordial constituent elements obscured and forgotten, and *on anthropometrical grounds* the whole of India is declared by some distinguished ethnologists to be inhabited by a homogeneous race.

Coming now to the Kolarians and Dravidians, we have seen that the former have been banished from the Government Census Reports on the ground that they are indistinguishable from the Dravidians, and that both speak allied forms of the same stock language. It is therefore necessary here to show that the Kolarians are quite a distinct people, and speak dialects belonging to a linguistic family which has no kinship whatever with the Dravidian family.

It may be inferred from the early Hindu records that the Kolarians, who admittedly came from beyond the Himalayas, were the fore-runners of the Dravidas, since in the first broad division between Aryans and non-Aryans the former were classed as *Sud* (*Sudhan*), that is, the "Pure," the latter as *Kol*, the "Impure," literally "Swine," called also *Chuar*, "Brigands," and by other uncomplimentary terms. But it so happened that *Kol* was also a Kolarian word meaning "Man," and was accepted by these natives in this sense, and thus acquired a very wide application. From it was invented a certain eponymous hero, Kola, founder of a powerful State, and his descendants are called *Kols* or *Kolers* to this day and from them India itself was called *Kolaria* (Dalton). Gradually these early inhabitants of the Gangetic plains were either absorbed by the Aryan invaders, or driven southwards to the Vindhyan uplands, where some became Aryanized (the Bhils), and some assimilated to the Dravidians (the Ghonds), while the rest, still numbering over

3,000,000, held aloof from outside influences, retained their tribal usages and primitive religion, and may now be distinguished by their Kolarian speech. That this speech is radically distinct from Dravidian the authors themselves of the Census Report unwittingly admit when they write that Kolarian "exhibits the characteristics of an agglutinating tongue to an extraordinarily complete degree. The only form of speech with which I can compare it in this respect is Turkish. What Professor Max Müller has said about that language applies with equal force to Santali, the typical form of Munda (Kolarian) speech." This alone would suffice to separate Kolarian from Dravidian, since no philologist has ever yet thought of connecting the latter with Turkish.

Then it is added that Kolarian has phonetic sounds unknown to Dravidian, a vigesimal system opposed to a Dravidian decimal, a dual absent in Dravidian, a Dravidian negative voice foreign to Kolarian "the type of which is older than that of Dravidian," and, to crown all, it is stated in a note that "since the above remarks were passed for the press linguistic survey has reached the Munda languages. The comparative examination of these forms of speech will probably show that the Munda and Dravidian languages have not a common origin. The question is however still *sub judice*" (Report, page 278). Not so many years ago, I arrived at the conclusion that Tamil, a typical Dravidian language of which I have some knowledge, has not the remotest connection with Santali, in which suffix is piled upon suffix, often resulting in words of monstrous length such as *dal-ocho-akan-tahen-tac-fin-a-c* from *dal* to strike. The best idea of the enormous number of complex forms which may thus be built upon a single root may be gathered from the fact that the conjugation of this verb *dal* in the third person singular alone occupies nearly a hundred pages in Mr. Skrefsrud's *Santali Grammar*. Of course, there is nothing like this in Tamil, and I have gone into these details at the risk of wearying the reader in order to show once for all how absolutely unrelated are the Kolarian and Dravidian forms of speech. Thus is at the same time established the radical difference of the two races who are all called "Dravidians" in the Census Report.

As the Kolarians entered India most probably from the north or the north-east, so the Dravidians came almost certainly from the north-west where they appear to have left behind them the belated Brahuis of Baluchistan. Beyond the Vindhyan Range they have nearly everywhere absorbed or replaced both the Negrito substratum and the Kolarian indigenes. Hence it is that at present all the natives of the southern uplands—Mysore, Koorg, Cochin, Travancore, etc.,—speak various forms of the Dravidian mother tongue. Here again Mr. Iyer unconsciously supplies some particulars of great ethnical value. Thus we learn that the Nattu Malayans speak a mixed Tamil-Malayan dialect with such a peculiar pronunciation as to be quite unintelligible to the more cultured Dravidians of the plains. In fact their command of articulate speech is so weak that "the defect is made up by *gestures*." The Nayadis also who speak Malayalam pronounce it so badly that strangers "cannot easily comprehend their speech," and the same is true of the Pulayans if not of all the jungle peoples without exception.

All this finds its counterpart amongst the descendants of the plantation Negroes whose mother tongues have for many generations been English, French, Spanish, or Portuguese, yet they still continue to mispronounce or speak those languages barbarously. The phenomenon is explained by the Russian explorer Miklukho Maclay, who rightly attributes the absolute impossibility of our imitating certain utterances in some of the New Guinea languages to "fundamental differences in the anatomical structure of the larynx and the whole muscular system of the organs of speech in the two races" (European and Papuan). But anatomical differences imply racial differences, and thus we again see that the Cochin and other low-caste aborigines now speaking broken Dravidian dialects were not originally Dravidians, but, as above pointed out, a blend in diverse proportion of superimposed Negrito, Kolarian, and Dravidian racial strata.

Referring to the low social status of most of the Cochin natives, Mr. Iyer pays a well-merited tribute to their kindly and even generous treatment by His Highness the present Raja, his Diwan, and in fact all the enlightened officials of this exceedingly well administered autonomous State. Of the Kadar and Malayan clans we read that those "living in the Government forests owe their allegiance to His Highness the Raja who is much interested in their welfare" and that "slavery has now been abolished for many years." If the Pulayans and other low castes do not enjoy the full advantage of their emancipation and in some places still live more or less in the same condition as formerly, it is because they have not yet been able to appreciate the benefits conferred upon them. "They are still obliged to depend upon their masters for maintenance. The extreme conservatism of their masters, and their bigoted adherence to caste, coupled with the primitive customs of the people, and the physical configuration of the soil prevented them from having any intercourse with the outside world and caused their utter degradation. * * * * * * In some places that I visited I found I was regarded with suspicion as it was thought that I was being employed by the Government with a view to loosening the existing bond between the Pulayans and their masters. Nevertheless their condition is slowly changing. They have begun to understand that they are no longer in a state of bondage, and missionaries of various societies do their best to improve their social condition."

I may conclude with an expression of thanks on behalf of all anthropological students, to the Diwan and the other officials of the Cochin State for their active co-operation, support and encouragement of Mr. Krishna Iyer in his ceaseless efforts to unravel the tangled ethnical relations in that region.

A. H. KEANE.

ARAMGAH, 79 BROADHURST GARDENS,
South Hampstead, N. W. London.
12th August, 1908.

A TYPICAL FOREST VIEW. (*Frontispiece.*)

CHAPTER I.

THE KADARS.

Wild inoffensive hill tribes share among themselves the whole of the hilly parts and jungles of the Cochin State. Influenced by all the prejudices of caste, they are divided into two classes, *viz.*, Kàdars and Malayans, who have little intercourse with one another. They are almost similar in character, and this partakes of the rude wildness of their hills, with no savage cruelty of disposition. The Kádars are now chiefly found in the Nelliampathi and Kodasseri hills of the Cochin State, as also in the Anamalai hills of the Coimbatore District. The Kàdars of the Cochin Forests speak a mixture of Tamil and Malayalam, while those of the Anamalai hills speak a kind of Tamil called *Malasir*.[1] They numbered only 310 at the last census, 161 being males and 149 females.

Introduction.

In describing the 'Hindu Type', Dr. Topinard in his well known Anthropology divides the population of the Indian peninsula into three strata, *viz.*, the Black, the Mongolian and the Aryan. The remnants of the first are found in the hills of the Dekkan and Southern India, and their primitive characters, apart from black colour and stature, are difficult to discover. Deniker in the 'Races of Man' mentions the hill tribes of the Anamalai hills (the Malayans, the Kàdars and the Muduvans) and those inhabiting the Cochin and Travancore hills, as belonging to the uncivilized Dravidians. The Anamalai hills of the Coimbatore District of the Madras Presidency form the refuge of a whole series of broken tribes, namely, the wild looking Pulayans, the Muduvans, and the thick-lipped small-bodied Kádars, the lords

Origin and tradition of the tribe.

1. A corrupt Tamil. Census of India, 1901, page 285.

of the hills. "Thrust back by the Aryans from the plains that once were theirs, the aborigines hid themselves in the recesses of the hills like the fossil remains found by geologists in the mountain caves, only these 'specimens' are not dry bones, but a living race of mankind. These hills, almost uninhabited, abound in great monuments (kistavens and dolmens), which the primitive race erected over the graves of the dead."[1] Dr. A. H. Keane, in his recent contribution to the Indian Ethnology in the sumptuous work, 'The Living Races of Mankind,' says, "There is good evidence to show that the first arrivals in India were a black people, most probably Negritos, who made their way from Malayasia round the Bay of Bengal to the Himalayan foot hills, and thence spread over the Peninsula without ever reaching Ceylon. At present there are no distinctly Negrito communities in the land, nor has any clear trace of a distinctly Negrito language yet been discovered. But distinctly Negrito features crop up continually in all the uplands from the Himalayan slopes to Cape Comorin over against Ceylon. The Negritos, in fact, have been absorbed or largely assimilated by the later intruders, and, as of these there are four separate stocks, we call these Negritos the 'submerged fifth.' There is ample evidence for the submergence since they arrived, if not in the early, certainly in the Tertiary period many thousands of years ago." He also adds that many primitive tribes are found in the plateau of the Dekkan and in the uplands of the Southern India, and are in close contact with the Kolerians, while others passed into Ceylon in remote times where they are probably true aborigines. To the primitive groups above referred to belong Malayans, Kàdars, Ullàdans, Eravàllens, Paniyans and many other tribes, who, though speaking the Dravidian dialects, are not full-blooded Dravidas; but represent different Negrito, Kolerian, Dravidian and Aryan blends. They have kept themselves aloof from contact with the Aryan intruders, and have therefore preserved the Negroid strain and other primitive

1. Sir William Wilson Hunter's Indian Empire, pages 92 and 93.

THE KADAR HUTS.

non-Aryan characters.[1] They were never conquered and hence belonged to no caste. They are on that account even to this day animists in religion. Above all, says Ratzel in his History of Mankind, crossing in all directions and variety in degrees of decadence is responsible for the multiplicity of primitive races.

Habitations.

The idea of defence seems to have been the first motive for the grouping of huts into villages called *pathics*, which are situated either on the skirts of hills or on the way up them. The choice of a village site is much influenced by the vicinity of a water supply. Generally their villages, which are seldom permanent, are to be found on the banks of a stream, or on an open glade in a dense forest. Each village or *pathy* consists of from ten to fifteen or twenty huts, which are usually built of bamboo, and rarely of timber. The walls and roofs are of the same material. The doors form sliding panels of bamboo work (*thazhuthal* or split bamboo). The roofs are skilfully thatched with leaves of teak, Punna, Calophyllum Inophyllum, or grass, whichever of these is easily available to them in the neighbourhood of their *pathies*. A part of the floor inside the hut is slightly raised, and on this they sleep. A kind of coarse grass mat which they themselves weave of *kora* (Cyperus juncifolius) serves as bed. If the floor be damp, the mat is spread on *thazhuthal*. These sleeping places are in some localities constructed somewhat at an elevation from the ground to keep off dampness, leeches, and blue bottle flies, which flourish in moist climates during the rainy months and to ward off the attacks of wild beasts. Sometimes stages are constructed for the same purpose. A fire place occupies a corner of the huts.

With habitations are naturally connected furniture, and methods of heating and lighting. Their furniture consists of a few coarse mats, some *thazhuthal* and a few pieces of wooden planks. For heating purposes, fire is always preserved in a

1. The Living Races of Mankind, pages 258 and 259.

portion of the hut. The long and difficult method of producing it compels them to preserve it as one of their precious things. Almost everywhere women are in charge of it. Deniker says, that among the Australians the women who let the fire go out are punished very severely, and that the Papuans of New Guinea prefer to go several leagues in search of fire to a neighbouring tribe than to light another. The preparation of 'new fire' among a great number of tribes, especially in America and Oceania, is celebrated with festivals and religious ceremonies. The Malayans and the Kàdars produce fire by striking a piece of flint with a piece of steel. The sparks of fire produced by percussion are made to fall on a kind of pith which is like cotton and which is placed near it. This method, says Deniker, is practised by few backward Fugeans, Eskimo and Aleuts.[1] The vessels in domestic use consist of a few earthen pots for cooking and the rest are all made of bamboo. They keep water in a large hollow bamboo block (*kambhom*), a yard or two in length, the nodes and internodes of which are bored an inch or two in diameter to hold a large quantity of water in the space between them. Whenever they go to a distant part of the forest, where they may have to stay for a day or two, they take this vessel full of water. It is wonderful to see the ingenuity of these people whose wants are few and whose life is very simple. They take advantage of every resource open to them in the neighbourhood of their *pathics*. With the bamboos of the forest, the leaves of trees, and the bark of certain creepers used as ropes, they build, in a very short time, comfortable huts with their bill hooks. Their requirements are, in fact, satisfied with the materials available in the vicinity of their abodes.

Marriage customs.

Marriages among the Kàdars are arranged by the contracting parties themselves, for girls are married only after they are grown up. The rule of exogamy holds to a certain extent, for a man may not marry a girl related to him on the male side. Thus he may not

1. Deniker, The Races of Man, page 158.

marry a paternal uncle's daughter, or paternal grand-uncle's daughter and so on. Further, as a rule, marriage between persons descended in a direct line from the same parents is forbidden, if the relationship can be traced, but to some extent the custom prevails among them of a man's marrying the daughter of his maternal uncle. When a girl comes of age she is lodged in a separate hut for seven days. On the morning of the seventh day she bathes, and becomes free from pollution. The day is one of festivity to the tribesmen of the neighbourhood. Their belief in pollution is so strong that if a polluted woman bathes in a stream, none will touch or take water down from the stream for fear of being tainted by it. A Kadar who enters into conjugal relations with a young woman of the tribe gives no bride's-price, but gives presents of cloths to her parents, uncles, brothers and sisters. The betrothal is cemented by an exchange of betel-leaves and areca nuts between the parents of the engaged couple; and during the period of engagement, the young man's parents give meals of rice and other things to the bride elect. There is no formal ceremony performed for the wedding. On the day appointed the bridegroom goes to the hut of the bride elect escorted by friends and relations, who are given cordial welcome and seated on mats. The bride and bridegroom stand face to face on a decorated pandal which is erected in front of the bride's hut, while men and women dance separately to the music of drum and pipe. The bridegroom's mother ties the *tali* (marriage badge) of gold or silver round the bride's neck, and her father puts a turban on the head of the bridegroom. The little fingers of the right hands of the contracting parties are linked together as a token of their union and they walk in procession round the pandal. Then sitting on a mat of Kádar manufacture, they exchange betel. Soon after, the bride accompanies the bridegroom to his hut, where a similar feast is indulged in for two days by the relations and friends on both sides.

In some places the following marriage custom is also in vogue. Any one who wishes to marry goes out of his own village and lives there for a whole year during which he chooses a suitable girl for his wife. At the end of the year he returns to his own village, and obtains permission from the villagers to effect the contemplated union. He then comes to the village of the bride elect and gives her as dowry the amount he has saved, and also gives presents of cloths to her parents, brothers, sisters and maternal uncle. On the day chosen for the wedding, a *tali* of gold or a ring attached to a thread is tied round the neck of the bride. After the usual marriage feast, the married couple go to the groom's hut, where his friends and relations are treated to a dinner. After a few weeks, a new hut is erected where they reside and maintain themselves by the wages of their own labour. The marriage customs above described are precisely similar to those prevailing among the African Bushmen. Among them a young man, when of age, looks out for a wife, not by way of purchase, but by sending presents through kinsfolk. Acceptance means consent. Marriage is ratified by a carouse and by presents to the relations of the bride. Marriage once contracted, women in all civilized countries are no longer free. From this moment, either the husband, the family on the father's side, the mother's side or the clan see strictly to the observance of the marriage rules which are in vogue, and punish every slip on the part of the woman who was free before marriage. As a rule Kàdar girls are modest and childlike in their behaviour, and when married they make good wives and become models of constancy. It is said that a young couple will sometimes pass several nights after their nuptials without exchanging a word, and to such an extent do they carry their bashfulness that they avoid looking at each other. In fact their behaviour would lead one to believe that some serious quarrel had arisen.

Pregnancy and childbirth.

Pregnancy is indicated by a change in costume. The main cloth worn round the loins is removed and tied above the breast, and the second cloth is, as usual, thrown diagonally above the left shoulder and below the right arm-pit. No ceremony is performed for a Kádar woman before the birth of a child; but if she is believed to be under demoniacal influences, the headman of the tribe, *Valia Muppan*, is informed. He then sends for a devil driver, who, by his magic sets her free from it. During childbirth, the woman assumes a sitting posture leaning on a support. Professional midwives are unknown, and she is attended by an old woman, generally her mother. Soon after a child is born both the mother and the baby are bathed in warm water, and, for two or three weeks, she takes a medicine which is a decoction of anise, ginger, pepper, mustard, calamus and asafœtida, which are all well fried and boiled in water, a small portion of which is taken both in the morning and evening, boiled rice and meat fried in cocoanut oil being her usual diet. She returns to the main hut after she becomes free from pollution, which lasts for ten days, and mingles with the rest of her family. Children are nourished by their mothers for six or seven months and are afterwards put on a diet of boiled rice and *kanji*. For three months after the birth of the child the woman is said to be unclean.

Naming ceremony.

It is generally performed on the day when the mother is free from pollution, but may sometimes be postponed to any date either previous to the termination of confinement or during the sixth month, when the father, who sprinkles a little water on the child three times, calls out the name as many times loudly as to be audible to those present. A small feast is indulged in on the occasion by the members of the family and the Muppan (headman), who is also invited. Among some people the name given is not borne through life, and owing to the fear of spirits the Dyaks change their names to deceive them, but the custom of changing names is not found to prevail among these hill-men. Though the naming of the child is often associated with the ceremonial cleaning, there is no real connection between the two rites beyond their coming at the same early time of life. The names in common use among men are Velandi, Kunju, Kittu Pilla, Malli, Chelamban, Chownden, Alakku Pilla and Moyali Muppan, while the common names for women are Karuppayi, Ramayi, Vellayammal, Ponnayi, Nelli and Karumbi. Some of these names are borrowed from the low caste-men of the plains with whom they associate in the forests during the working season.

The ear-boring and the nose-boring for a girl are usually done on the occasion of naming, but may sometimes be postponed to any convenient date. Invariably the Muppan performs the boring; but if he cannot do it, the father of the child or any other male member of the village undertakes it. A lamp is lighted and placed before the child, and the blessing of the ancestors is invoked before the operation is commenced.

It varies from a short period to throughout their whole life.

Duration of conjugal union.

Frequently the husband discards his wife, when she ceases to please him, and she then returns to her parents. Sometimes divorce is hedged round with certain formalities of established custom. Marriage can be dissolved for incompatibility of temper, and disobedience on the part of the wife without appeal to any higher authority than a council of elders, who hear arguments on both sides and pronounce judgment upon the evidence. The council has absolute control over them. In the event of any disobedience or immoral conduct on their part, they would be expelled from their community which would mean being turned out of the jungle to obtain a living in the best way he or she could. In a case like this she finds her refuge among the very low caste-men of the plains.

Polygamy and Polyandry.

Polygamy is indulged in with a view to increase the numerical strength of their tribe. In the code of polygamous etiquette, the first wife takes precedence over the others and each has her cooking utensils. The more wives a man has, the richer and more esteemed is he. It is said that polygamy is diffused all over the world either in the form in which it is found among Mahomadans, Australians and American Indians or in its modified form lawful concubinage, all over the east, and that women among them are considered very much as slaves from whom pleasure and labour may be obtained. A somewhat similar view is held by these hill-men among whom polyandry is unknown. In this connection it is interesting to note, that the chastity of the Kadar women is highly commendable, and that the regard shown to the marital tie is so great, that one wonders how this happens among a people among whom ceremonial marriage is more or less unknown. Widows are never allowed to marry, but may live in a state of concubinage.

Family life.

It is said that in many of the aboriginal tribes in India, the family is hardly yet formed, and that it is yet in the process of formation, but among the Cochin hill tribes this state has long passed. The evolution of the family is in a sufficiently advanced stage, and it is always the paternal personality that predominates. The father dictates to his children the rules which govern their conduct and establish the moral precepts which have been handed down to them by their forefathers. The mothers warn their daughters to be obedient to their husbands and endeavour to please them. The father lives with his wife and children in a hut of his own construction, supporting them until they are grown up. He also gets them married when they are of age. The sons, when married, live with their wives along with their parents, contributing their share of maintenance, or in separate huts of their own making. In certain months of the year the males are busy in the collection of the forest produce, when they have enough to eat by their sale proceeds; while in other months they have to live on the edible fruits and roots of the forests in their neighbourhood. Sometimes when they roam over the forests in search of them and when they cannot return home, they erect flimsy sheds thatched with plantain leaves wherein they stay for the night, protecting themselves against wild beasts by keeping fire around them. Their women also collect, with their digging spud, the roots of many plants which serve as food. They cook the family meals, tend the children, bring water from the stream close by, keep the huts in order, and accompany their husbands for some outdoor work. They are treated with affection and allowed a certain amount of freedom. Children are brought up without any education whatever. At the age of six or seven they are taken to the jungles in the daily peregrination of their parents, and are shown the different methods of collecting the minor forest produce. Any deviation from the beaten track traced out by their ancestors whom they adore is repugnant to them. A philanthropic missionary of the State, who wished to educate these people and their children and to proselytise them opened a school, but had to give it up for want of proper attendance.

Inheritance and Tribal organization.

Among the Kàdars the son succeeds to the property of his father, but in the case of Muppans the eldest nephew succeeds them. As has been said, twenty or thirty huts form a *pathy*. The members of the *pathy* are under the control of a headman, called *muppan*, who is, with their consent, appointed by His Highness the Raja. The *muppan* is given a stick with a silver head at one end. It is the symbol of his authority. He presides at the marriage, funeral and other ceremonies, and decides all tribal disputes, and visits all delinquents with corporal punishment, whenever necessary. They are averse to all kinds of innovations, and no innovations can be adopted without the consent of the *muppans*. The *muppans'* wives go by the name of *muppathies*, and their position among the Kádar women corresponds to that of their husbands among them.

Religion.

The religion of the Kâdars is a rude animism. All kinds of sickness and other calamities are believed to be the work of the demons whom it is necessary to propitiate. They are a god-fearing set of people, and are the particular worshippers of Kali. On the occasion of the offering to Kali, a number of virgin girls are asked to bathe preliminary to the preparation of the offering, which consists of rice and some vegetables cooked in honey and made into a sweet pudding. The rice for this preparation is unhusked by these girls. The offering is considered to be sacred and is partaken by all men, women, and children assembled there, and then. Ayyappan is another deity whom they worship, and whose aid they beseech in all their enterprises. They also worship their dead ancestors, whose blessings and aid are invoked in times of illness and other calamities in their families, and also before the commencement of all auspicious undertakings. Malavázhi (ruler of hills) is another vague sylvan deity whom they worship. They believe that it is this deity who protects them against the attacks of wild beasts in the forests. It is for him that they rigidly observe all kinds of pollution, the negligence of which will rouse his indignation when they may be exposed to all kinds of danger from the wild beasts of the forests.

The following account of animism professed by the Kádars is taken from the Imperial Census Report.[1] Special interest attaches to the religion of the Kàdars as representing a comparatively early stage in the process of conversion to Brahmanism which the aboriginal races of Bengal are undergoing. The real working religion of the tribe is pure animism of the ty p which still survives comparatively untouched by Hindu influences among the Santals, Mundas and Orans of Chota Nagpur. Like these, Kádars believe themselves to be encompassed about

1. Page 407.

by a host of invisible powers, some of whom are thought to be their ancestors, while others seem to embody nothing more definite than the vague sense of the mysterious, uncanny with which the hills, streams and the lonely forests inspire the savage magination. Of these shadowy forms, no images are made, nor are they conceived of as wearing any bodily shape. A roughly moulded lump of clay in an open glade, a queer shaped stone bedaubed with vermilion—this is all the visible presentiment that does duty for all. Their names are legion and their attributes are barely known. But so much is certain that to neglect their worship brings disaster to the offender, death or disorder to the household, murrain among the cattle and blight on his crops. In order to avert these ills, but so far as I can gather without the hope of any benefit from gods, who are active only to do evil, the Kádar sacrifices pigs, fowls, goats, and pigeons, and offers ghee, molasses, and heads of Indian corn in the sacred groves in which his deities are supposed to dwell. The priest is a man of the tribe who combines the sacred functions with those of the barber to the Kádars of the villages of the neighbourhood. The offerings are eaten by the worshippers. For all this, the Kádars, if questioned about their religion, will reply that they are Hindus and will talk vaguely about their Hindu gods (Parameswar, Vishnu) as if they live in the very odour of orthodoxy, instead of being in fact wholly outside the sphere of the Brahmanical system. To talk about the Hindu gods is usually the first step towards that insensible adoption of the externals of Hinduism which takes the place of formal and open conversion which sterner and less adoptive creeds demand. The next step is to set up Brahmans, whose influence, furthered by a variety of social forces, gradually disposes of the tribal gods and transforms them into orthodox shapes, and gives them places in the regular pantheon, as local manifestations of this or that well known principle, and relegates them to a decent and inoffensive obscurity as household or village deities. Last of all, if the tribe is an influential one, it gives itself brevet rank like the Rajaputs.

The Kádar have their dead buried. As soon as a man dies, his body is washed by his son, if he has one, and in the case of a woman, the duty is perform-by her daughter. The women begin to cry in loud chorus, and then the men speedily join in, when they all weep together, eulogising his good deeds till, through sheer exhaustion, they are compelled to desist. If the parties stop weeping, they soon get up a funeral dance, in which the members of the family take part. A band of music, drum and pipe, plays wild tunes outside the hut, without accompanying the funeral party to the grave. Covered over with a piece of new cloth, the body is placed over a bamboo bier, which is carried to the graveyard far away from the village with rice thrown over it as it leaves the hut. The grave is dug from four to five feet deep and after the corpse is laid in it on a mat with the head towards the south it is filled in with earth. No stone nor any monument is erected to indicate the spot. Sometimes a big stone is placed near the head of the corpse, and the water, as being the last portion that the deceased is given to drink, is poured on the stone. Any ornaments or trinkets that the deceased had at the time of death are buried with the body and removed on the date of expiry of the pollution. The place of interment is, after that, never more visited. The burial grounds are, as a rule, never visited by them for fear of ghosts which may haunt their houses and torment their children. They observe the pollution for ten days, and on the morning of the tenth day they become free from it by a plunge bath. That day is one of estivity to their friends and relations. At the end of the year, they hold a memorial festival in which their relations and neighbours are invited to a feast with drinks and dances. "Menhir, cromlech, dolmen and stone circle", says Ratzel, "are found in the Khassia hills and in those of Coimbatore. Similar ones are also found in the hills of the Cochin State. The burning of bodies never takes place in the neighbourhood of them. The dolmens may perhaps serve as sacrificial tables, while the numerous single-stone pillars may make one think

Disposal of the dead.

of stone worship. Stone circles and stone pillars are here associated with graves. Most of the dolmen-like stone structures contain earthenware vessels of fine workmanship and remains of iron."[1]

Occupation.

The primary occupation of the Kàdar and other jungle tribes is the collection of forest produce. The following are the chief minor products of the hills :—

1. Kadugu, mustard (Sinapis nigra).
2. Màkani kizhangu: the root of Cynanchum is a favourite pickle with the people though it smells exactly like bugs.
3. Inji, wild ginger (Amomum zingiber).
4. Manchal, wild turmeric (Curcuma longa).
5. Mattipal, (Aliyanthus malabarica) the juice of a tree which concretes into gum used generally as an incense.
6. Kunkilium, the resin of a tree (Chloroxylon dupada) which is a kind of frankincense.
7. Shikkay, (the fruit of Mimosa saponifera), used as soap by the natives to wash the oil out of the hair.
8. Lavanga patta, the bark of Laurus cassia.
9. Cardamoms.
10. Myrobalans and wild pepper.
11. Thanikka, the fruit of Terminalia bellerica.
12. Poovakuru, the fruit of Cacalia rotundifolia.
13. Thena, Panicum italicum.
14. Mezhuku, Beeswax.
15. Nellikka, the fruit of Phyllanthus emblica.
16. Paruthi, Gossypium herbaceum.
17. Thippili, Long pepper.
18. Pathiri, Bignonia suaveolens.
19. Vella Elengi, Mimusops elengi.
20. Kanjirakuru the fruit of Nux vomica.
21. Lemon grass.

1. Ratzel's History of Mankind. Vol. II.

The minor forest produce is the property of the Government, the collection of which is let on contract for a certain sum of money to contractors who with the aid of Kàdars and Malayans have it collected and sold in the markets. The contractors supply them with rice, salt, sometimes chillies, tobacco, and opium, and give them money to purchase other necessary articles such as cloth, etc. The hill-men are quite independent during the summer months, when they are solely engaged in the collection of the forest produce. They have now plenty to eat. The total income derived from minor produce is about Rs. 3,000, a year.

It has been said, that, but for the Kàdars and the elephants, the Cochin forests would have been useless. Both are the denizens of the hills and forests, and, when properly utilized, they are invaluable help to those who wish to extract the priceless treasures of the forests. But for the elephants none could lift a log, and if it were not for the Kàdars, none dare move an inch in the forests. During the forest working season these men are employed by the forest contractors for collecting minor forest produce. They are peculiarly expert in tree climbing, which is almost an instinct with them; and whatever the height or girth of a tree, in some cases trees grow to a height of 100 or 150 feet and a girth over twenty feet they climb to the top, like black monkeys. Honey gathering is a favourite occupation with them, which they invariably do after nightfall with a torch under the cover of darkness, to avoid the sting of bees. When the trees are quite straight and without branches, the ascent is facilitated by means of small wooden pegs driven into the trees, which serve as so many foot rests. The quantity of honey collected by the jungle tribes is very great and is the product of four distinct species of bees. The larger portion is collected by a middle sized bee which makes its nest in the hollow stems of old trees. The nest is attacked fearlessly by the honey-hunters, who profess to be proof against the stings by means of secret charms, but we can vouch for the fact that the charm necessary for it is a moderate amount of fortitude, for the tree-bees do not attack in combined swarms as do the rock-bees, and therefore the stings received are not numerous, neither is the pain caused so very severe as to affect the thick skin of the natives. The only trouble in collecting this is the enlarging of the hole by which the bees enter their nests. The rock-bee, the honey (*Malanten*) of which is of a superior quality is a large bee that builds its nest in the cavities of rocks and on the edges of appalling precipices. It is a most fearful adversary, so much so that the native bee collectors dare not attack it in the day time. If they are attacked by an intruder, they begin a united persistent attack and, as their stings are severe, it is almost impossible to escape from the attack, and it is most dangerous to go near them. The natives take the combs at night and the mode of procedure evinces a cool daring which one would never expect in such a cowardly race. He makes a chain of rings of rattan or bamboo and this chain over 100 feet in length is lowered from the top of the precipice until it reaches a point where the bees' nests are. This being done, a dark windy night is chosen and the honey-hunter either alone or accompanied by his wife, brother or son, when it is pitch-dark, descends this loosely hanging ladder with a firebrand, and keeping away the bees by means of his torch, he collects the honey and thus secures the prize. To look at one of these ladders as it hangs over the face of some fearful cliff and to imagine the scene is to make one's flesh creep. For the feat of daring he feels amply rewarded if a rupee is given. The bees appear to be sluggishly stupid on dark nights and hence the rationale of this method of procedure. There is another honey producing bee found in the hills which makes its nest on the bare trunk of the bush; the comb is generally in the shape of, and about the size of, a goose's egg, and so pure and delicate and clean is the wax that the whole comb may be eaten, just as it is found, wax and all. There is also a fourth kind of bee which builds its nest on the branches of trees, some of which are of great height. Acuteness of the senses, bodily toughness, defiant audacity to the point of contempt of death together with an insinuating cunning and a great knowledge of Nature are the characteristics of the wild tribes, to which the Kàdars are no exceptions. They do the ordinary cooly labour of cutting timber and of constructing rest houses and get wages of from five to seven annas per day. The wages they receive for the extraction of forest produce depend upon the quantity and quality of the produce they bring. *Onam* presents in the shape of rice, cloths, coats, turbans, caps, ear-rings, rings, tobacco, opium, salt, oil and cocoanuts are freely distributed by the Forest Department every year. They are very busy in the collection of wax and honey in the months of March and April and cardamoms in July and August.

The Kàdars presume to know everything about the forest. The people of each locality or village are well acquainted with the tract considered particularly their own, and resent encroachments on their precincts. They trace as if by instinct the devious paths of the forests and decide almost with unerring certainty on the number and variety of animals that may have traversed them. They know the animals by their foot-prints and find out their whereabouts probably by the peculiar and wonderful development of their olfactory nerves. It is wonderful to see them track a wounded animal, and nothing escapes their eyes. They hurry along very quickly, hold a brief board of speechless enquiry on a fugitive foam flake, investigate a down trodden blade of grass and wax silently eloquent over a single hair. When a Kàdar or a Malayan has gone to a forest a long way off from his *pathy*, he goes on cutting twigs and leaves, so that his wife or son may trace the way to bring him food. Their services are availed of by *shikaries* in tracking and beating game. Sir William Crookes, the great Indian Ethnologist, says, "One thing the jungle dweller does acquire by this course of life is a marvellous insight into Nature and her secrets. His eyesight or power of hearing is wonderful. He sees or hears a tiger creeping down a ravine long before sportsmen will. Everything in the forest has a meaning for him, the grunt of the monkey as the tiger comes beneath his tree, the hoarse alarm bark of the stag. From the way the vultures hover in the air, he will tell whether the tiger has finished his meal or is still tearing the carcase. Every displaced pebble denotes to him a foot-mark, a broken grass stalk will tell him something." They are better trackers and drivers of game than hunters, and often accompany European and other *shikaries* in their hunting expeditions. They sometimes hunt tigers, bisons and bears, by shooting them from a safe position at a distance. Deer and wild hogs are caught in snares and beaten to death. They divide themselves into two parties one of which is engaged in driving the game, while the other either aims at them or catches the smaller animals in snares. To catch fish during the summer months, they dam the mountain streams and poison the water, when they die and float. They are famous snake charmers, and assert that they possess the knowledge of some tree, the green leaf of which taken internally and applied externally to any part affected with venom is an infallible cure.

They help the Government and private landlords in the elephant catching operations. The elephants are very destructive, and they attack the lonely traveller often with fatal results. They are often a dreadful nuisance to the farmers who live near forests, and who have by their own industry, prevented large areas of land from being thrown out of cultivation. On strong and high trees stages are constructed, to which the guards and trackers fly to take refuge when attacked by a solitary tusker who takes vengeance upon them for helping sportsmen to destroy them. The elephants are sometimes caught in pits, a large number of which (about fifteen feet in depth and from fourteen to eighteen feet in diameter at the mouth) are dug by the side of a stream or other water reservoir which they frequent during the summer months, especially during nights. These pits do not

THE KADARS AS TRACKERS IN THE FORESTS.

have the same width at the bottom. The mouths of the pits are covered with pieces of split bamboos, boughs and earth, with dry leaves over them and they are never placed on a track where the huge beast may suspect a trap. A tree may be found by the side of a path, against which an elephant will probably stop to rub his body, and there, in the ecstasy of friction, he may for a moment, be off his guard, when the destructive pit yawns before him. It is generally the young ones that are caught. As soon as it is known that an elephant has fallen into a pit, the forest authorities are informed. The Kàdars or Malayans in the neighbourhood cut huge branches of trees and place them across the mouth, so that he may not escape. Tame elephants are brought up, who speak to him, and try to make him feel at home in this uncomfortable situation, and gradually the pit is filled up till his fore-legs are supported, the leaves and tender branches being held up to him as food. Strong ropes are passed round his neck, when he holds up his trunk. He comes out of the pit and walks out between his tame companions who chastise him if he gives trouble. His hind legs are hobbled and to the hobbles are tied ropes (*vakka*) which again are fastened round trees, so that at every rush he makes, he is pulled up with a painful jerk. He is also pulled in front with a rope held by a tame elephant. Finally he is, with the aid of a large number of Kàdars or Malayans and his tame companions, led off to a strong shed built of the teak of his native forest, where he is pestered, punished and beaten by tame elephants and elephant keepers, till at last he becomes fit for use as a timber carrier, road-maker and beast of burden, and if docile and well favoured, he may live to carry the sacred idol and swell and adorn the religious processions in the temple festivals of the State. Sometimes the elephant dies in the pit or in captivity. It is said that an elephant which had once been caught and had escaped, would never move in the forest without testing the ground before it with a large branch of a tree held in his trunk.

The jungle tribes are everywhere presumed to serve the

Forest Department, within whose jurisdiction they live. They are given certain presents and concessions which are denied to the inhabitants of the plains. This has been in vogue in the State for a long time. Frequent contact of these forest people with the merchants of the plains and the high wages which they receive from the coffee planters who employ them on their estates have tended a great deal to estrange them from their relationship with the Government. Their relation with the Government is that of servants. They have to lead the way to Government officials to the different tracts of the forests, to attend to the elephant-capturing operations, namely, the covering of pits, to watch whether elephants have fallen, and if so, to announce the fall to the Forest officials, to water and feed the elephants in pits till they are *kralled*, and also to construct *madoms* for the Government, whenever necessary. They get an *edangazhi* ($\frac{1}{5}$ of a Madras measure) of rice for covering and watching the pits; while for tracking and constructing *madoms*, they are given three annas worth of rice and six pies per day. The number of Malayans to watch the pits is determined by the number of pits within a certain area of the village. For feeding the elephants in pits a Kadar or Malayan gets three annas worth of rice and three pies per day. On the *kralling* day there is a general distribution of rice among the young and old members both male and female. The Malayans of the village at the time offer, at the cost of Government, sacrifices which consist of boiled rice, cocoanut and toddy to propitiate their family deities (the spirits of the departed), Chathan (Sastha) and Puliamballly Namburi Achan, who is believed by them to have been the greatest of magicians.

The Kádar women weave a kind of coarse grass mat and a strong rattan basket.

Weapons.

The Kadars are provided with only two rude weapons, namely, a bill hook and a digging spud, and they work wonders with them. With the former they build comfortable houses, make bridges with canes and branches, rafts out of bamboos, a carving knife out of *etah*, a comb out of bamboo and a match from dry wood, and with the latter they dig the ground in search of wild roots. The former is also a weapon of defence, and after all they are not, in the least, costly, though they are used for so many purposes.

Their relation with the ruler of the State.

The Kàdars are supposed to be the vassals of the ruler of the State. To him they are attached by the strongest ties of personal affection and regard. Whenever His Highness the Raja tours in the forests they follow him, carry him from place to place in *manjals* or palanquins, carry *samans* and in fact do everything for him. His Highness in return is much attached to them, feeds them, gives them cloths, ornaments, combs and looking glasses. Above all he treats them with great affection, using always kind words to them. It is said that these peculiar people could never be frightened into doing anything, and that when any harsh words are used, they simply move away from one place to another. One forest to them is as good as another, and they get their few wants supplied either here or there. They are quite simple, unsophisticated, and utter aliens to vice and trickery. They are plain and straightforward in their dealings, never tell a lie, and never deceive one another. Work they never shirk, and, being sturdy and strong, they are fit for any kind of physical exertion or endurance. In the carrying of loads and weights they are very enduring and have a great capacity for rapidly recruiting. Altogether they are a quiet and submissive race, obeying the slightest expression of a wish and very grateful for any assistance or attention.

Social status.

These hill-men are called the *chandalas* of the forests (Ḳàttu Neechanmar). The touch of the Malayans pollutes the Kádars and *vice versa*. When asked as to their social position each affirms his superiority to the other. The Kádars consider the bison as an unclean beast and never touch its body. In the same way they consider the elephant's dung also. Wild elephants are held in veneration, but the tamed ones are believed to have lost the divine element in them. Short tailed black monkeys are hunted and put to death, because they are considered to be a sort of curse to the forests. They eat at the hands of all castes except Parayan, Pulayan and Ulládan.

Dietary of the tribe.

The following roots of plants form the chief articles of food for the Kàdars. They are generally eaten in the form of curry:—

1. Nootta kizhangu (root)—Dioscora pentaphylla.
2. Thali do Corypha umbraculifera.
3. Nara do Atalantia monophylla.
4. Chandana do Pterocarpus santalinus.
5. Chel do Scirpus articulatus.
6. Kannira do Strychnos colubrina.
7. Chaval do The fruit-like sprout of Artocarpus.
8. Vettila do Piper betel.

They rarely go in for animal food. On occasions they indulge in animal food chiefly fish but on no account would they touch bison, though it is to be had in abundance. The abhorrence of bison's flesh on the part of these people is similar to that of pork on the part of the Mahomadans. It is purely sentimental, but there is not a single Kàdar man or woman who would touch bison's flesh. Rice is a luxury with them and the occasions on which they eat it are very rare. It is noteworthy that these people are not unacquainted with intoxicants, opium and toddy being their chief favourites. They take opium in small quantities and like it very much, but toddy is liked even more, and both men and women freely indulge in it.

Appearance, physical and general characteristics.

The colour of the Kadar skin is generally dark, varying from it to lighter shades of complexion according to locality. The members of the tribe residing in localities frequented by the low caste-men of the plains appear to be the descendants of cross breeding, while those in the very interior whereto the men of the plains have very little access, possess the genuine features of the tribe. They are short in stature, the average height of the men and women being 157·7 and 143 centimetres respectively. Their noses are flat and somewhat depressed and the nasal index of the males and females is 89·8 and 88 respectively. Both men and women have long dark wavy hair well parted on the crown of the head and smoothed with cocoanut oil and tied into a knot behind. The parting of the hair and the fashion of tying the knot coupled with their shyness, give the former an effiminate appearance. Some have long curling hair also. They are of strong build and robust in shoulder and thigh, their arms very long, and like the Paniyans, they are deep chested, which is well adapted to mountaineering. They have great powers of endurance and carry heavy loads on their backs. The frequently nomadic habits of these people in search of edible fruits and roots for food, and water, cause their women also to carry their utensils on their back often with a child on the top of their household goods. The babies, on the backs of their mothers, are often huddled up in a dirty cloth with the ends slung over the shoulders and held in the hands over the chest. It is said that they afford a typical example of happiness without culture. "Unspoiled by education the advancing wave of which has not engulfed them, they still retain many of their primitive customs and manners."[1] Thus they do not belie their ancestry. For the most part they are light hearted and easy tempered. They prove very communicative when once their shyness is overcome. While naturally frank and far more truthful than the people of the plains, they have been, of late, contracting some pilfering propensities which are manifested in the simplest and most maladroit manner. Few people in fact, in the plains enjoy a happier life, than the residents on these hills, who are accustomed to a hardy outdoor

1. Madras Museum Bulletin, Vol. II, page 133.

life and are capable of appreciating to the full the enjoyment of an 'apathetic rest' as perfect bliss. Isolated from the outer world, they depend upon their labour for all their necessaries and most of the luxuries of life. They are, in fact, blissfully contented with their life as it is, completely absorbed with their devotion to the hill life and their sylvan deities who are believed ever to watch over their welfare. Altogether they appear to be a quiet and submissive tribe, obeying the slightest expression of a wish and grateful for any assistance or attention.

Dress and ornaments.

The males like other classes of hill-men are scantily clad, wearing plain loin cloths and somewhat similar ones round the necks. Some of the Nelliampathi Kádars, who were brought to me for examination appeared so neatly dressed in *vaisties* of English manufacture round the loins, with similar small ones tied as turbans, that they looked like Tamil Chetties on the plains. Some of them wear ear-rings made of brass. Women wear a *podava*, eight yards long, half of which is tied round the loins, while the other half serves to cover the upper part of the body. Some put on a red mark of vermilion on the forehead, and have cadjan rolls in the dilated lobe of each ear, which on important occasions, are substituted by gilt *thódas*. A few of them are seen wearing brass nose-rings, while some wear also necklets of glass and brass beads with imitation Venetian sequins, steel and brass bangles on the right upper arm and fore-arm and *metties* (brass rings round the second toe of the right foot). On the whole they appear to be so well dressed that they look like Chetti women, though short and dark.

The most interesting custom prevailing among the Kádars, and never found in any other caste-men, is that of chipping all or some of the incisor teeth, both upper and lower, into the form of sharp pointed, but not serrated cone. The operation is performed with a chisel or bill hook and file by the members of the tribe skilled thereat, on boys at the age of

A KADAR GROUP.

eighteen and girls at the age of ten or thereabouts. The girl to be operated on lies down and places her head against a female friend who holds her head firmly. A third woman takes a sharpened bill hook and chips away the teeth till they are shaded to a point, the girl operated on, writhing and groaning with the pain. After the operation she looks dazed and in a few hours the face begins to swell. Swelling and pain last for a day or two accompanied by severe headache. The custom of deforming the teeth is not confined to Southern India, but is found prevailing among different tribes in Africa and Australia, where the practice is, in general, confined to the chipping of the incisor teeth. Westermark in his History of Human Marriage, says, that when the age of puberty is drawing near, in several parts of Africa and Australia, they knock out some teeth knowing that they would otherwise run the risk of being rejected on account of ugliness. In the Malaya Peninsula, the practice of filing the teeth and blackening is a necessary prelude to marriage. Further, Darwin, in his Descent of Man, writes, that the natives of the Upper Nile knock out the four front teeth, saying that they do not wish to resemble brutes. Some tribes, says Dr. Livingstone, knock out the two incisors, because they give the face a hideous appearance. The following lines are taken from the Madras Journal of Literature and Science. "These little dwarfish people file their front teeth in points to facilitate their eating the hardest roots. There is some nerve shown in this and we may look with wonder and respect upon the exiled lords of the ancient land when we see that, rather than serve those who usurped the country, they chose to live, where the food was beyond their natural powers and could be eaten only by such a preparation of their teeth. It is possible, that in the absence of better arms, they reckoned upon these pointed teeth as weapons, in case their conquerors should follow them to their mountain home."

Games.

The Kàdars are fond of music and singing. Sometimes they form a ring by joining hands and advance in step towards the centre and again retire while circling round and round. When wearied with dancing they sing. Some eight of them formed a party at my desire and danced, singing some Tamil tunes. They frequently come to the plains, take part in the village festivals, attend dramas, at which low caste-men are actors and return to their wild abodes quite drunk. It is delightful to hear the hearty shrieks of laughter of the rude curly haired children wholly illiterate and happy in their ignorance as they are found dancing in the evening, and indulging in their primitive amusements.

Conclusion.

"It has been said that the more remote and unknown the caste, race or tribe, the more valuable is the evidence afforded by the study of its institutions from the probability of their being less mixed with those of European origin. Tribes which only a few years ago were living in a wild state, clad in a cool and simple garb of forest leaves and buried away in the depths of jungles, have now come under the domesticating and sometimes detrimental influence of contact with Europeans, with a resulting modification of their conditions of life, morality and even language." The Paniyans of Wynad, the Irulans on the slopes of the Nilgiris, the hill tribes of the Cochin Forests now work regularly for daily wages on the Planters' estates. The rapid disappearance of the savages at the present time, and the rapidity with which they are being reduced to the standard of European manners and those of high caste-men, render it necessary to correct the sources of error as soon as possible. "The employment of tiles and kerosine tins in lieu of primitive thatch, the import of cotton piece goods and umbrellas instead of country made goods and umbrellas covered with leaves, the decline of national costume, the substitution of caps of gaudy hue and pith turbans for national turbans, the replacement of peasant jewelry made by indigenous manufacture by beads and imitation jewelry made in Europe, the use of lucifer matches by 'aboriginal' tribes who formerly made fire by friction, the supply of new forms of food and of beer and spirits in the bazaars, the administration of justice instead of that distributed by the old village panchayets, the attempts of the low castes to elevate themselves by the adoption of the customs and manners of the higher castes, the spread of western education, religious teaching and conversion to Christianity by European missionaries—these and many other factors are the causes of a radical change in the ethnographic conditions of the country." In the words of Professor A. C. Haddon of Cambridge, "Now is the time to record. An infinitude has been lost to us and a very great deal is now rapidly disappearing. The most interesting materials are becoming lost to us, not only by their disappearance, but by the apathy of those who should delight in recording them before they have become lost to sight and memory."

CHAPTER II.

THE MALAYANS.

I. THE NATTU MALAYANS.
II. THE KONGA MALAYANS.

Introduction.

The Malayans are another jungle tribe inhabiting the Cochin forests. They are divided into two sub-tribes, *viz.*, (1) the Nàttu (native) Malayans, who are probably the original inhabitants of the hills, and (2) the Konga Malayans or Malasar, who appear to have immigrated from the forests of the Coimbatore District and settled in the State forests. These two sub-tribes widely differ in their customs and manners. The word 'Malayans' means hill-men. The name is apparently derived from *mala*, a hill, and *kaira*, to go up, for their present designation seems to be an abbreviation of *malakaira* or *malaira*. This is not quite correct. The high caste people affirm that they and the Kàdars are identical races, and that the only distinction is that the Malayans live on the western side of the ghauts, *i. e.*, on the Malabar side, while the Kàdars live on the eastern or Coimbatore side. The Malayans are quite different in character from the slave-like Pulayans. They partake rather of the character of the aborigines and of the Hindus of the plains, though they are as much below the latter socially, as they are elevated above them topographically. They are also called Kàttu Neechanmar (aborigines of the forests) and are found in the Machàd, Pálapilli, and Paravattani forests of the Cochin State. The two sub-tribes are separately treated, and the Nàttu Malayans claim our first attention. They speak a language which is a mixture of Tamil and Malayalam with a somewhat curious pronunciation. Conversing among themselves, they are perfectly unintelligible to the people of the plains. This however arises only from the dissonant sound conveyed by their harsh and abrupt utterance. Among these people, language does not constitute the only means by which they communicate their ideas. Their command of language is poor, the defect of which is made up by gestures. Whenever an officer or a member of a higher caste puts them a question, they invariably say "yes", with a nodding of the head, believing that a negative answer might displease him. A lateral shaking and raising of the head signifies a denial.

I. THE NATTU MALAYANS.

Origin and tradition of the tribe.

On questioning the Nàttu Malayans as to their origin, they said that they considered themselves to be the descendants of Siva and Parvathi, who, in the disguise of male and female hunters went to grant the boon of a divine arrow (Pasupatha missile) to Arjuna who was doing penance in the forest. Some believe that the women are the descendants of Surpanakha, the sister of the giant Ravana, whose breasts were cut off by Lakshmana, the brother of Rama, during their exile in the forests. This story was given by the Malayans of the Pálapilli forests. Some among them say that they were, at a remote period, Nairs, and were brought to a state of degradation by the reprehensible conduct of their womenkind, who were outcasted owing to their illicit intercourse with low caste-men of the plains. They call themselves Mala Nairs (hill Nairs) whose marriage, funeral, and other customs are similar to those of the Nairs. Whatever be the truth of the former assertion, the story points to their having been the earliest inhabitants of the forests.

Habitations.

The habitations of the Malayans are similar to those of the Kàdars which are merely flimsy huts roofed with bamboos and leaves. In some forests their huts are of a peculiar pattern. They are raised on clumps of bamboos, which are all cut about the middle to the same height so as to produce an even surface high up from the ground. This surface is then converted into a sort of flooring by spreading planks closely all over it, and over the planks a thick layer of mud is beaten down and rendered firm. Then other planks are fixed perpendicularly to the four sides of the flooring in closely set order so as to serve as walls. Over these latter is put a roofing of planks, and openings are made in them, thus making a stronghold against the devastations of wild animals. Entrance to this dwelling is facilitated by means of a ladder made by cutting away the knots from a single bamboo outside the clump and leaving only the root ends of these knots to serve as stairs or steps to ascend or descend by. The Malayans keep in their huts all the year round a number of very strong bows and arrows, the latter with slightly spread out and sharpened iron ends, some of which are kept always in their furnaces to keep them red-hot and ready to be shot at any wild animals that may approach them. It is said that South Indian hill tribes have dwelling places on trees, and the hill-men of Cochin are no exception. Very often huts are constructed on trees, a security against tigers and elephants, their fellow occupants of the woods, with whom they share or dispute possession.

The Malayans are somewhat migratory and necessity often leads them to the inhabited parts, where no inducement can persuade them to remain permanently. In their rambling tours they often carry a staff or pike, a knife stuck in the girdle, and sometimes bows and arrows. A basket hung from the shoulders contains some few necessary utensils. They are followed by their dogs and the women loaded with the younger children and other impedimenta of their family. They wander from place to place as caprice or convenience may dictate. They have, of late, commenced to live in permanent huts in some localities in the forests.

Tribes are divided into clans. The Malayans, though living in clans, know little of that union and attachment that belong to such an association. Each clan has its petty chief (*muppan*),

THE NATTU MALAYANS IN SEARCH OF EDIBLE ROOTS.

and the clans living in the Government forests owe their allegiance to His Highness the Raja who is much interested in their welfare, while those residing in the Chittur forests serve under local landlords. Caprice alone leads them to transfer their fealty from one landlord to another. The following are the names of some of the clans among the Náttu Malayans:—

1. Katathukar
2. Thonykkar
3. Pokkenkar
4. Eranattukar
5. Ayambakkar
6. Nellakkar
7. Chakkenkar
8. Kootenkar
9. Kunnikkar

Our enquiries lead us to conclude that some bear the names of the places in the forests which they occupy. Some are named after persons who have distinguished themselves in former times. In the latter case the connection with the original founders is preserved by keeping their images in stone in their huts and worshipping them in times of danger. Before a young man goes to marry, he propitiates the ancestral image by offerings.

Marriage customs.

Among the Náttu Malayans the marriage of girls is celebrated after the tenth year. The girls have no voice in the choice of their husbands. The parents are solely responsible and there is no match making ceremony. When a young man has to be married, his parents look out for a girl, and when she is selected, her parents are consulted. In the event of their approval, the bridegroom's mother ties a thread dyed with turmeric round the neck of the girl which signifies that the girl is betrothed and no other young man may have a claim upon her. An auspicious day is chosen on which the bridegroom's party go to the bride's hut, where they are well entertained. The wedding garment is given to the bride, and they depart with the bride, who is then accompanied by her parents and friends, to the bridegroom's hut where a similar entertainment is held, after which they hand over the girl and depart. The two entertainments are necessary for the termination of the wedding. Marriage is indissoluble except when the woman goes wrong and when such an event happens, the people of the village assemble, the woman is well flogged and returned to her parents. The husband never receives her back, but any other person who is so inclined may marry her. A girl who has reached the age of puberty as a virgin is considered impure, and no person will take her for a wife. A man may have two wives, but a woman cannot have two husbands. Widows are allowed to marry any member of the tribe except a relative of the deceased or a member of the same village. No special dress is worn by a widow to denote any symptom of mourning.

Pregnancy and childbirth.

No ceremony is performed for a woman who is about to become a mother. A separate hut is erected for her delivery and her mother or some old woman acts the part of nurse. The period of pollution is for fifteen days, during which the woman is under special treatment, and her usual food is *chama* (Panicum miliaceum) *kanji*. She moves with the rest of the family only after the period of pollution is over.

The child is named either on the twenty-eighth day or during the third month, when it is also fed with rice. The ear-boring also takes place on the same day. The names in common use among men are Raman, Ayyappan, Velayudhan, Harichandran, among women, Kochi, Mati, and Lakshmi. These appellations appear to have been recent adoptions from the high caste-men with whom they associate in the forests during the working season.

Inheritance and Tribal organization.

Among the Nâttu Malayans, the nephews succeed to the property of their maternal uncles. Any member of the tribe who wishes to provide for his wife and children must do so with the consent of his nephews. They are very poor and leave little or nothing for others to inherit. Nevertheless they take pride in making the above statements. In every village consisting of twenty or thirty huts the Malayans have a headman whose duty it is to direct his fellow-men in all kinds of work for the Government in the forest, for which they receive wages. He presides over all ceremonies, and settles all disputes with a council of old men, and punishes the delinquents with fine or excommunication. The Panikkan is a title given to the headman of the tribe, who with his followers work for the Government in the elephant catching operations, for which they used to get four rupees and a rupee worth of paddy, but of late, this custom has been discontinued. The State now avails itself of their services only when necessary and they are paid wages for their work. They recognise no laws, and find no occasion to resort to them. Disputes and quarrels among them, when not settled by themselves, are mediated by the Forest Department, whose decisions are willingly accepted. They believe in magic, sorcery, and witchcraft, and have vague ideas of omens. The sound of a lizard, or the meeting of a man or cow, makes them desist from a journey, as it predicts some approaching calamity.

Religion.

The religion of the Malayans of the Palapilli and other forests consists of the worship of Veerabhadran and Bhadrakali, both of whom are represented by a collection of stones under a tree or in a small shed. During the forty-one days of the *Mandalam* (first Vrischikam to the tenth Dhanu, *i. e.*, 15th November to the 25th December), one of the Malayans in every *pathy* bathes early in the morning and places on the floor a lamp with a cotton thread, believing it to be Veerabhadran, and performs *puja* to him. He does not go hunting during the period, and strictly abstains from animal food. On the last day, offerings of sheep, fowls, etc., are made to him, and the festival is closed by a feast to the villagers.

Mallan is another demoniacal deity whom they worship. Once a year in April, the sacrifice above referred to is offered, but if they neglect to do this, they believe that he sends elephants and tigers to destroy them and their huts.

Bhadrakali is worshipped in the same way. The auspicious days of these people are *Makaram* and *Karkadaka sankranthis*,[1] *Vishu*,[2] *Onam*,[3] and *Mandalam*. When questioned as to their ideas of gods, they say that they are like men themselves, but invisible, yet all powerful. In the offering of sacrifices they take special care to have them served on separate leaves, lest they should quarrel with one another and do harm to the worshippers. This belief is common to all low caste-men of the plains. Their stones or idols are not taken as mere symbols or portraits of deities, but they mostly imagine that the deities dwell or rather are embodied in them, so that the stones themselves are regarded as real gods, capable of giving health and prosperity to mankind. Further, they hold them in fear and pious reverence and believe that their favour can be sought by sacrifice alone. The Malayans have a strong belief in the existence of spirits, who are intimately associated with human beings and act in a way as their guardian angels. Each man believes that he himself and his neighbour have many spirits at their command, and therefore, if one offends another, his bodily health may suffer or he may even lose his life as a punishment through the influence of the spirits of the injured man. If, for example, a quantity of beeswax be perceived on a tree by a Malayan, he first examines the bark to see, if one of his tribe has seen it before him and left his mark there. Should one have done so, nothing will induce him to touch it for fear of consequences which might ensue from his offended neighbour's spirit. They do not believe that their spirits have power over white races. They do not treat the sick, but pray to the gods for their recovery in the belief that all kinds of illness are sent by them as a punishment for their failure to make them due offerings.

1. The first of Makaram (January-February) and Karkadakam (July-August).
2. The first of Medom (April-May).
3. The national festival in Malabar in Chingam (August-September).

In the Ottunad forests of the Mukundapuram Taluk is found a ruinous temple dedicated to a goddess. The idol has been displaced from its original position and is now covered with brushwood. The name Ottunad signifies that in this temple *vcdas* were recited, and that a large number of Brahmans were fed. There is a grinding stone here on which is inscribed in Malayalam 'അമ്പത പറ ജീരകം' (fifty *paras* of cumin seed) which enables us to understand what grand feasts were held for the Brahmans. The cumin seed forms only a very small item even in grand feasts, and this bears testimony to the fact that they were celebrated in former times to entertain a large multitude of Brahmans. In Elikkode also there is a temple dedicated to Ganapathi, and the image, which is of a good workmanship, is placed in its proper position on a sacred pedestal in perfectly good order. Several other similar ones are also placed near it. Wells and their foundations are also found in the neighbourhood. In several places (Paruthipara, Chakkiparamba hill) of the forests there are *muniyaras* (small stone edifices), in which sages are said to have done penance in by-gone days. These *muniyaras* consist of three upright granite slabs which serve as walls on three sides. The height is hardly enough for one man to enter in by creeping and to remain in a sitting posture. It is reported that, when one of them was excavated, a trident, a lamp and a hookha were found in it. There are three such *muniyaras* of circular shape in Paruthipara, a place two miles off from Parakadavu. It is believed that numerous Nambudiri *illams* and Sudra houses existed in these parts which must have been deserted some three hundred years back; for, inscriptions prior to this period are seen in Vattezhuthu (the old Mappila or Tamil alphabet) and Kolezhuthu characters, while inscriptions now seen are in Malayalam characters.

Occupation.

The primary occupation of the Malayans as of the other hill tribes is the collection of forest produce. The Malayans like the Kàdars are under the protection and control of the Forest Department, and are bound to serve it whenever they are called upon to do so. In return, they are given lands for cultivation free of tax, presents for the *Onam* festivities, bamboos, brushwood for the construction of their huts, and similar gifts and concessions which are not allowed to the inhabitants of the plains. The forests around a village are, by the villagers themselves, divided for the collection of the minor forest produce, and any encroachment of a member of the tribe upon the division allotted to another is never met with on the belief that the offended man will bring about the complete ruin of the offender through the intervention of his ancestors. They are expert trackers and are very clever at setting traps and snares to catch hares, deer, and other wild beasts. They catch fish by damming streams in the hot weather and throwing into the water some leaf or root which stupifies them. They have, of late, commenced to clear small portions of the forest near their huts to cultivate paddy, and some among them possess a few bullocks and buffaloes for ploughing, in addition to their few agricultural implements.

Malaya women like the Kádar women weave a coarse kind of grass mat out of *kora* (Cyperus juncifolius). Fine long fibres are made out of the grass and arranged side by side in order, and a fine thread of their own making is passed through them with the help of an iron pointer provided with a long wooden handle. The mat though coarse is sufficiently soft, and the sides are not folded and stitched.

Food.

The greater part of their food consists of wild yams (Dioscorea) when they have nothing to give to the trader for rice. They take *kanji* prepared from *chama* (Panicum miliaceum), *kora*, and *kambu* (Holcus spicatus). This is consumed in the morning before they go to work and the same *kanji* with roots boiled and salted forms their evening meal. During the working season, they live upon rice, paddy, salt and other products supplied to them by the contractors, while at other times they depend upon the wild roots of the forests. Sometimes they make a

A NATTU MALAYAN GROUP.

delicious preparation out of bamboo seed. They fill a hollow bamboo, two feet in length and four or five inches in diameter with the seed above referred to, and pour in honey and then close the mouth of the bamboo air tight. This is then coated with a layer of earth and placed in a bright red-hot fire, sufficient time being allowed for the grain to be well boiled in the honey. The bamboo splits, when quite red-hot, and in the inside is seen a cylindrical soft and sweet mass, which forms their dainty meal with which they welcome high caste-men, who happen to stay in their midst for a night. This they consume with a deep draught of water. They eat the remains of carcases left by tigers, as also the flesh of deer, bison, and goat but abstain from touching the flesh of the cow, wolf, elephant, and tiger.

Social status.

The Nàttu Malayans possess a social superiority over the Tamil Malayans, who are not allowed to approach them within a certain distance. They observe a kind of pollution towards their Konga brethren. There is neither intermarriage nor interdining between them. They eat at the hands of the Brahmans, Nairs, and Izhuvans, but abstain from taking the food of Pulayans, Parayans, and other low caste-men.

Physical and mental characteristics of the tribe, dress and ornaments.

The Nàttu Malayans are either dark or dark brown in colour, short in stature, and have a kind of triangular face pointing to the chin. They appear to be strong and healthy and have great powers of endurance. They are gentle, submissive, trustworthy and contented, clinging to their old wild habits. They generally wear an ordinary loin cloth; but ten or twelve of them out of the twenty persons who were seen in the Palapilli forests were wearing good *mundus* (four cubits by two cubits and a half), and had flannel shirts with an upper cloth on the shoulders over the shirts which is an instance of the influence of modern civilization upon these primitive people. Some had knives stuck in their girdles, and axes with wooden handles on their shoulders. The hair on the head which is black and oily is well parted in the middle and tied in a knot behind. Some had ear-rings. Their head-man, whose name is Harichandran, wore the silver bangle given him by His Highness the Raja, to denote the symbol of rank and superiority over his fellow tribesmen. Even persons over fifty are not grey haired. Their women are short in stature, either dark or dark brown in complexion, and have long thick tufts of hair of a wavy nature which are not allowed to grow wild. The ear lobes of all of them are bored and sufficiently dilated to contain either lead discs or rolled palm leaf discs. The daughter of the head-man was found to wear a gilt *thoda*. Some wear nose-rings. A necklace of brass and glass beads forms their chief ornament for the neck. Some wear brass, iron, and bell metal bangles and brass rings. Two of them were seen with a bell metal ring *(metti)* for the second toe of each foot. Their dress consists of a white cloth of four or five yards folded twice and worn round to cover the breast. Some have an upper cloth. This method of dressing prevails among the Toda women whose costume is thicker and broader. Some of them appear to be as handsome as Nair women. A stranger who first sees them would hardly believe them to be women of the jungle tribe. The purity of the tribe, we are informed, is being outraged.

II. THE KONGA MALAYANS.

The tribal origin.

The Konga (Tamil) Malayans, living in the Chittur Taluk of the State form a small sub-tribe of hill-men, and appear to have been immigrants from the hills of the Coimbatore District. They have no traditions of their origin, but seem to be allied to the hill-men of the North Arcot and Salem Districts. Very probably they are the descendants of the inhabitants of the plains whose ancestors were driven to the hills at a remote period. They speak Tamil,

Marriage customs.

A Konga Malayan must not take his wife from his own sept, but he may marry within his mother's sept, and the union of first cousins is generally permitted. When a man wishes to marry his son to any girl of the village, he speaks to her parents, while the parties are very young. The father of the girl gives her to the first suitor. Should the boy die before the ceremony takes place, the poor girl finds it difficult to get a husband. The boy's father, when the proper time arrives, gives a dinner to all his relations, with two *fanams* to the girl for a new dress and one *fanam* (four annas seven pies) worth of spirituous liquor to the guests. The girl is delivered over to the boy and the marriage is considered valid. In some places the following custom is observed. The bride's price is five rupees, which is given to the bride's parents, when the negotiations for the wedding are made. The auspicious day is chosen, and the bridegroom with his parents, relations and friends goes to the hut of the bride, where they are well entertained. The wedding garment is given to the bride, and a string dyed yellow, to which a brass ring is attached, is tied round the neck of the girl. The guests are treated to a dinner. The wedding is then practically over and the bride is taken to the hut of the bridegroom. Soon after the marriage, the couple reside in a separate hut newly erected, and maintain themselves by their own work. The elder sons of the family generally build separate huts for themselves after marriage, and the parents continue to live with the younger sons, but the elder sons contribute to their support, when they are no longer able to work.

Among the Konga Malayans, the women after childbirth are under no special treatment. The naming ceremony takes place generally in the third month. No special day is chosen. On any day they choose, the husband and wife bathe and dress in their new garments, and sit side by side with their child on a rice pan. A member of the tribe, *pujari* (priest), acts the part of a *velichapad* (oracle), and in his hysterical moment gives a name to the child. A few cocoanuts, plantains, and four annas are given him for his services. The names in common use among males are Mallan Muppan, Karuppan Muppan, Thamman, Chatayan, Velli, Pidari, and Karumala Muppan, while those among females are Kali, Arasi, Malli, Kathi, Mayal, Chettichi and Nayithi. These are the names of the demoniacal gods whom they adore.

Inheritance and tribal organization.

Among the Konga Malayans the son inherits the property of his father. In every village consisting of twenty or thirty huts, they have a head-man called *Muppan*, whose duty it is to direct his fellow men to different kinds of work on the lands of their landlords. He has to hear all complaints from his tribesmen and redress their grievances, settle all disputes, preside at marriage and funeral ceremonies and has in fact to do everything connected with the well-being of the tribe. He is subordinate to an agent or manager (*Manigar*) of the landlord, and the latter is, in the northern part of the State, a Tamil Sudra or a Nair, who is responsible to his master for the proper conduct of the *Muppan* and his followers. In the event of any of these men running away from the land of his landlord, he and the *Muppan* have to bring them back. Any theft or adultery committed by a member of the tribe has to be enquired into by them, and the punishment in serious cases is inflicted in consultation with the landlord.

Religion.

The Konga Malayans are animists, but, owing to their contact with the low caste-men of the plains, and their attendance during the village festivals, they have been slowly imbibing the higher forms of worship. Investigations were made in two localities, namely, Chittur and Kollenkode forests. The names of the gods and the account of the worship in these forests are given below.

1. Karumala Muppan.
2. Mallambara Andan.
3. Nayithi Athal.
4. Manakkadamma.
5. Paliyamma.
6. Kali.

The first and the second are evidently their local demoniacal gods, named after the rocks on which they are supposed to reside, and are regarded as the tutelary deities. The next four are the different names of Kali, and have no separate shrines, but are represented by a few stones, or rather a collection of stones, surrounded by a mud wall under a thatched roof. In some *pathies* (villages) these stones are to be found located under a tree, and one of the Malayans acts as a *pujari* (priest); he makes oracular responses by becoming a *velichapad* (oracle), whose words are believed to be divine, and are accepted as if directly emanating from their gods by inspiration. The Malayans of the Kollenkode forests worship Bhagavathi, Nagaswami, and Muniyappan. Bhagavathi is represented by a rude stone placed beneath a tree. On the first Friday in Makaram (December-January), they propitiate her by breaking sixty-two cocoanuts before her. Two days before the performance of the *puja*, the people of the village go to the shrine and fast, spending day and night in songs and wild dancing. On the morning of the festival day they bathe and stand in pious reverence before the deity. Offerings of sheep, boiled rice dyed yellow, cocoanuts, and plantain fruits are given in honour of the goddess. The deity Nagaswami is Subramania, and is borrowed from the worship of the higher castes. He is worshipped with offerings of milk, plantain fruits, and cocoanuts. Muniyappan is evidently a demoniacal god, and is believed to be gratified only with the sacrifice of a sheep, a fowl, and boiled rice.

Funeral ceremonies.

When a Konga Malayan dies, his son or nephew goes to his landlord and gets four or eight annas with which he purchases toddy. Those present there drink it, and dance round in honour of the deceased. They then weep and keep the body until the tribesmen from various *pathies* assemble and dance again. After an hour or two a few of them take the corpse on a bamboo bier. The tribesmen accompany the bier and leave it half the way to the burial place and return home. A grave is dug for the burial of the dead body which is placed in it, and the grave is then filled in with earth and stones. They observe pollution for three days and on the fourth morning, relatives and friends are invited to a feast at which toddy is freely used. They never perform the *sradha*, but once a year, on an auspicious day, they give offerings to the spirit of the departed, while others invite their tribesmen to a grand feast.

Occupation.

In the Chittur and Walayar forests, the Konga Malayans live as hired agricultural labourers and wood cutters. They cultivate *chama, kora*, and other grains in the lands of their masters, giving a portion of the produce to the landlords as rent, and keeping the rest for themselves. Though living in a state of bondage under their landlords they are somewhat addicted to stealing, burglary and robbery. It is said that they do not belong, properly speaking, to the hill tribes.

Their appearance and mode of life.

In stature the Konga Malayans are as tall as the Nàttu Malayans, and are somewhat taller than the Kadars. They are dark in colour without exception, and have a tendency to the flat nose and thick lips of the Kadars. Their foreheads and the general shape of their heads are not of a fine mould. Their clothing consists of a *vaisti* worn round the loins and tucked in between the legs, and they have also an upper garment. Some put on a *kambli* (blanket) folded on their shoulders. They wear dirty cloths and appear to be altogether an uncleanly set of people not taking a bath even once a week. Living in malarial localities, they are subject to malaria, and do not seem to be strong and healthy. Their women are lean and dark in colour. Brass and rolled palm-leaf discs form their ear ornaments, and they wear a necklace of brass beads for the neck and a bell metal ring (*metti*) round the second toe of each foot. Their tufts of hair on the head are not made smooth with oil. When they have an oil bath, they use clay and cow-dung to remove the oily matter. They dress somewhat like the Kadar women, and do not appear to be cheerful like their sisters of the other forests, but are timid and poverty-stricken.

THE KONGA MALAYANS.

CHAPTER III.

THE ERAVALLENS, THE NAYADIS AND THE ULLADANS.

I. THE ERAVALLENS.

The origin and tradition of the tribe.

The Eravallens, also called Villu Vedans (hunters using bows and arrows), form a wild inoffensive jungle tribe found in the Chittur Taluk of the Cochin State. Though some speak Malayalam, yet their language is Tamil. They are very poor and there are no titles among them, the elderly members of the tribe being addressed as *Muthans* (elderly men) and *Pattans* (grand-fathers). They are a rude timid primitive people like the other jungle tribes of the State and have no knowledge of their origin, but under the civilizing influence of their masters their status has somewhat improved. They live in villages called *pathies*, situated in the forests of the State. Their huts are similar to those of the Malayans, but their habits are less migratory than those of the Malayans and Kadars.

Dress and personal adornment.

Both men and women are better clad than the Malayans, Pulayans, and other low castes. The males wear *vaisties* (cloths with a coloured border three yards in length), one end of which hangs loose, while the other is tucked in between the legs. They have a shoulder cloth, either hanging loosely over their shoulders, or sometimes tied to their turbans. They allow their hair to grow long like that of women, but do not, for want of means, anoint it with oil. They grow moustaches and wear round the neck a necklace of small white beads to distinguish them from the Malayans, who are always afraid of them. Some wear brass and finger rings. The women dress like the Kadar and Konga Malaya women. Their ear ornaments are made of a long palmyra leaf, rolled into a disc, and the ear lobes are sufficiently dilated to contain them. It is said that they take an oil bath once a week.

Marriage customs.

Among the Eravállens a young man is never allowed to marry unless he is able to support a wife, and in this they set an excellent example to the members of the higher castes. An Eravallen who wishes to see his son married, visits the parents of a girl with his brother-in-law and a few relatives, who make the proposal. If the proposal is agreed to, the wedding-day is fixed, and all the preliminary arrangements are made at the hut of the bride, where the relatives assembled are treated to dinner. The bride's price is only a rupee. The parents of the bride and bridegroom visit their respective landlords with a few packets of betel-leaves, nuts, and tobacco, and inform them of their marriage proposal. The landlords give a few rupees worth of paddy to defray a portion of the wedding expenses. They celebrate their weddings on Mondays. On a Monday previous to the wedding ceremony, the sister of the bridegroom with a few of her relations and friends goes to the bride's hut and presents her parents with the bride's money, and a brass ring for the bride. On the Monday chosen for the wedding, the same company with a few more go there and dress the girl in the new garment brought by them. They are treated to a grand dinner as on the previous occasion. They then return with the bride to the hut of the bridegroom, where also the parties assembled are twice entertained. On the Monday after this, the bridegroom and the bride are taken to the bride's hut, where they stay for a week and then return to the bridegroom's hut. The marriage is now formally over, and the expenses connected therewith come to about thirty rupees. The *tali* tying is dispensed with as among the Izhuvans of the Chittur Taluk. The bridegroom gets nothing as a present during the wedding, but this is reserved for the *Karkadaka sankranthi*, when he is invited by his father-in-law to a sumptuous dinner, and is given two *vaistics* and a turban. Henceforward, the married couple live in a separate hut and support themselves by their own labour.

If a girl is married before she attains puberty, she stays with her parents till she comes of age, and joins her husband only after puberty. A girl who comes of age is lodged in a separate hut (*muttuchala*), erected at a distance of a furlong from the main hut. Only a few girl friends are allowed to be in company with her during the period of her seclusion, which is generally seven days, during which food is served to her at a distance, when she comes to take it. No grown up member approaches her for fear of pollution. She bathes on the morning of the seventh day, and is then allowed to enter the hut. The day is one of festivity to her relations and friends. Subsequent menstrual periods are for three days, and the bathing for the removal of pollution takes place on the fourth day. If a girl is married before she attains her puberty, her husband contributes something for the expenses of the ceremony. A young woman going wrong with a man of the caste used in former times to be put to death, but is now turned out of caste. Instances of the kind are, it is said, extremely rare.

No ceremony is performed for a pregnant woman during the fifth or seventh month like the *Pumsavanam* [1] and *Seemantham* among Brahmans, or the *Pulikudi* [3] of other castes. If she dreams of dogs, cats, or wild animals coming to threaten her, it is believed that she is possessed of demons. Then a devil driver from this or some other caste is invited to treat her. He draws a hideous figure (*kalam*) on the floor with powdered rice, turmeric, and charcoal, and the woman is seated in front of it. He sings and beats his small drum or mutters his *mantram*. A lamp is lighted and frankincense is also burned, then a *kaibali* [4]

1. A domestic ceremony on the mother's perceiving the signs of conception.
2. Parting the hair on the head.
3. A ceremony observed by women in the fourth, sixth or the eighth month of their first pregnancy.
4. An offering in the hand for the demon.

is waved round her face. The woman is worked up to a hysterical state and makes frantic movements. Boiled rice, beaten rice (*avil*), plantains, cocoanuts, and fowls are offered to the demon. If he is quite satisfied, he may leave her, or offer the conditions on which he will leave her. If she remains silent and unmoved all the time, then it is supposed that no demon resides in her body. Very often a *yanthram* or charm is made on a piece of cadjan leaf which is rolled up, attached to a thread and worn round the neck of the woman.

The customs connected with pregnancy and childbirth are similar to those of the Malayans, but the period of pollution is for seven days. The women bathes on the eighth day and is removed to another hut close to the main hut, but is regarded as being under pollution for five months. Her diet during this period is simple, and she is strictly forbidden to take meat. The only medicine administered to her during the period is a mixture of pepper, dried ginger, and palm sugar mixed with toddy. She comes back to the main hut after purifying herself by a bath at the end of the five months, and the day on which she returns is one of festivity.

The child is named only after two years, when they are satisfied as to its health and the likelihood of its enjoying a long life. A male child is named after its grand-father and a female after its grand-mother. The names in use for men are Kannan (Krishnan), Otukan, Kothandan, Kecharan and Attukaran, while their women are called Kanni (feminine of Kannan), Keyi (Kaikeyi), Otuka and Ramayi. The use of Hindu divine names is a recent innovation, being imitated from the names of the members of the higher castes, with whom they frequently come in contact.

In the matter of widow marriage these primitive people teach the higher castes a valuable lesson. Among them a widow may re-marry, but may marry only a widower. It is called *Mundakettuka* (marrying a widow). When they both have children by their first marriage, the widower must make a solemn promise to his tribesmen that he will treat and support all the children impartially. The present of a brass ring and cloth is essential, but the ceremony is not a grand one.

A man can divorce his wife, if he is not satisfied with her, but the divorced wife can mate only with a widower. Such cases, it is said, are very rare among them. Polygamy and polyandry are absolutely unknown.

As regards inheritance, the son succeeds to the property of his father. They have no tribal assembly, and disputes seldom occur among them.

Religion.

In religion the Eravallens are pure animists. They believe that the forests and hills are full of demons disposed to do them harm. Many of these demons are supposed to live in trees and are believed to rule wild beasts also. They also believe in certain local demons that are supposed to reside in rocks, trees, or peaks, and to have influence over particular families or villages. The offerings made to them are intended apparently rather to mitigate their hunger than with the idea of obtaining benefits for the worshippers. In no case are wicked actions performed in their honour, such conduct being regarded as insulting to them. Their gods are Kali, Muni, Kannimar (seven maidens), and Karuppa Rayan. Kali is adored to obtain her protection for themselves and their families while living in the forest. Muni is worshipped for the protection of their cattle and in order to have a good harvest. Kannimar and Karuppa Rayan are their family deities, who watch over their welfare. Offerings of boiled rice, plantains, cocoanuts, and beaten rice are given to propitiate them. Kali and Muni are worshipped in the forests and the others in their huts. Offerings are also made to Kali and Muni both when they plough and sow and when they reap. They are propitiated because they are supposed to protect their corn from destruction by wild beasts. Certain days are regarded as luckier than others for particular actions. Thus Mondays are looked upon as lucky for marriages and for sowing the fields, Wednesdays for building, and Fridays for reaping. They propitiate their sylvan deities both before the construction and the occupation of their dwellings.

The Eravallens have their dead buried and they observe the pollution for five days. On the morning of the sixth day, the chief mourner, who may be the son or younger brother of the deceased, is shaved, then he bathes, and offers to the spirit of the departed boiled rice, plantains, fowls, and parched rice. A feast is also given to the tribesmen who are assembled once a year at the harvest season, the time of the year when food is most abundant. They also worship the spirits of their departed ancestors with offerings. Brothers perform the ceremony of the deceased in the absence of a son. Five days' pollution is also observed for the death of children.

Occupation.

Their chief occupation is agriculture. They plough dry lands for the cultivation of *chama* (Panicum miliaceum), *cholam* (Sorghum vulgare), dholl (Cajanus Indicus) and gingili seeds. Ploughing and sowing begin in the middle of May and harvesting begins in November. During these months they are wholly occupied with agriculture. During the other months of the year, gardening, fencing, and thatching are their chief occupations. They are skillful hunters. Owing to their familiarity and acquaintance with the forests, they can point out places frequented by wild beasts, which they recognise by smell, either to warn travellers against danger or to guide sportsmen to the game. When they go on a hunting expedition ten or fifteen of them form a party, and they are armed with knives, bows and arrows. Some of them beat up the game which is driven to a particular spot, where it is caught in a large net already spread, when it is either shot with arrows or beaten to death. The animals hunted are hares, porcupines and wild hogs. The game is always equally divided. They are good marksmen and are skillful enough to be able to shoot birds while flying.

THE ERAVALLENS.

Food.

The food of the Eravallens consists chiefly of *kanji* made either of *chama* or *cholam* with a mixture of tamarind, salt, and chillies. It is prepared during the night and is taken the next morning. The same food is again prepared for the midday meal, with a vegetable curry consisting of dholl, horse-gram, etc., and other vegetables grown in the garden of their masters, which they have to watch. They eat the flesh of sheep, fowls, pigs, hares, quails, doves, and even of toads. They eat from the hand of Brahmans, Nairs, Kammalans, and Izhuvans, but refuse to take anything cooked by Mannans, Panans, Parayans, and Cherumans. They bathe when touched by Chakkiliyans, Parayans, and Cherumans. On the other hand, they recognise their social inferiority to the Brahmans and Nairs, and stand at a distance from them to avoid polluting them.

Their present condition.

Eravallens do not live as small independent communities, but are mostly attached to farmers, under whom they work for the daily wages of three annas worth of paddy. During the *Kathira* (the harvest festival) in the village temple of their landlords, when sheaves of corn are brought in, every male member gets from his landlord two *vaisties*, and every woman a *potava*. During the *Onam* and *Vishu* festivals, eight annas worth of paddy, two cocoanuts, a small quantity of gingili and cocoanut oil are also given. The landlords partly defray their marriage and funeral expenses by a grant of a few rupees worth of paddy, some salt, and chillies. Sometimes they agree to work for twenty *valloms* [1] a year. Sometimes to improve their condition, they borrow some money from their landlords and purchase a bullock, or a buffalo or two, to cultivate a plot of ground, after clearing a portion of the forest belonging to their masters. They raise some crops and save something to pay off the debt. Should they be so unfortunate as to fail in the undertaking, they willingly mortgage themselves

1. A large corn measure.

to their masters or to some other person for the wages above mentioned, and wait for some favourable opportunity to pay off the debt. Women never surrender themselves to work in a state of bondage, but are independent day labourers. The Eravallens are certified by their masters to be always truthful, honest, and faithful, and they never, like the Pulayans of the northern parts of the State, ungratefully run away from their employers.

——:o:——

II. THE NAYADIS.

Tribal origin.

The author of 'Jàthinirnayam', a Malayalam work which deals with the description of castes in Malabar says that the Parayans, Pulayans, Nayadis, and Ulladans form the *chandalas* of the plains (Nàttu Neechanmar), their social position being determined by the order in which they are mentioned. From this it would appear that the Nayadis are superior in status to the Ulladans, who however deny it. They live in the rural and jungly tracts of South Malabar, and in the northern parts of the Cochin State, and their huts are similar to those of the Ulladans. They are, as the name implies, skillful hunters. They speak Malayalam, but so badly mispronounce words that those not familiar with them cannot easily comprehend their speech. They are fond of the long sound of O.

Marriage customs.

Marriage is endogamous, and is generally performed after, but sometimes also before, puberty. It is never determined by courtship, and it is the parents who arrange the match.

A suitable young woman is sought for in the matrimonial market, and the conjugal contract is made by the parents of the young man, whose conduct the woman's parents are satisfied with. The bride's price is only a rupee. The day for the ceremony is chosen, when the bridegroom, dressed in a small neat loin cloth and a skull cap made of the bark of areca palm, with his parents, sisters, relatives, and friends, arrives at the hut of the bride at the appointed time, taking with him a necklace of glass beads and two pieces of cloth (*kacha*) for the bride, who is bathed and dressed in her new wedding garments. There is no *tali* tying. A small feast is held for the guests assembled, and the provisions for it are a few months' savings of paddy, or rice obtained as wages or charity from the high caste-men of the village. From that day they live together as man and wife. Next morning the guests depart. The bridegroom goes to his hut with the bride, and generally nobody from her hut accompanies them. But if she weeps at the time of departure, she is consoled by her parents who assure her that she will be well fed and clothed in her husband's hut, and that she will in future live in comfort. A similar feast is held in the hut of the bridegroom. After a week's stay there they are invited to the bride's hut, where also they reside for a few days, and then return to the bridegroom's hut.

Amongst the Nayadis widows can re-marry, but without any formal ceremony. The brothers of the deceased do not as a rule form any conjugal union with the widows left by the latter. Polygamy and polyandry are unknown among them.

If the husband does not approve of his wife's conduct, she is taken to her parent's hut. Divorce is soon effected, and he gets back half her purchase money. The wife who finds it difficult to get on with her husband goes back to her hut, and returns her purchase money. The grown up children live with the father, while the younger ones, if any, reside with the mother, who is free to marry again. When the children desire to see their mother, they are sent to her and she keeps them for a day or two. Adultery is regarded with abhorrence, and it is believed that those who are guilty of it are liable to be attacked either by wild beasts or demons. Conjugal fidelity prevails, if it is not absolutely the rule, amongst them.

Pregnancy and childbirth.

When a woman is pregnant, she craves for the flesh of a monkey or a jungle squirrel during the sixth month. During the seventh month they perform a ceremony of exorcism *(ozhinnukalayuka)* which relieves her from demoniacal influences, if any. Abortion and other kinds of illness are all attributed to the malignant influences of evil spirits whom they always fear, and to ward off such calamities they tie round their necks a magic thread, invoking the aid and support of their hill deities as also the spirits of their ancestors.

They put up a separate small hut for delivery, where the woman retires for labour, when her mother, mother-in-law or sister, her friends or relatives attend her for the time being. The mother's diet after childbirth is merely boiled rice, and she goes to no work for another seven months. The pollution is for ten days during which the husband avoids seeing her. The naming ceremony takes place on the twenty-eighth day. The child is named after its grand-father, if it is a male, and after its grand-mother, if it is a female. The names in common use among men are Chankaran, Karappan, Ayyappan, Chakkan, and among women, Kali, Neeli, Kurumba, Mundi.

Inheritance and tribal organization.

Among the Nayadis, the son succeeds to the property of his father, which consists generally of his hut and a few utensils.

Magic.

Whenever these people labour under any calamity or disease, they consult their astrologer, a Parayan, who is also their magician or sorcerer, as to the means of relief. He cleverly manages to elicit the true facts and circumstances, and then takes a handful of paddy and divides it into groups of four, three, or two grains. According to the group he gets, he makes certain predictions, which he could have made without all this trouble, or which they could have reached for themselves on calm deliberation. He attributes the calamity to the anger of their gods, to whom offerings may not have been given in time perhaps for want of means. When a woman is under demoniacal influence and makes frantic movements, the Parayan, their devil driver and sorcerer, is invited and is furnished with a thread and some toddy. Muttering some prayers to Parakutty and other deities, he ties the thread round the woman's neck, and drinks the toddy supplied for the occasion. Then the demon is supposed to leave her. It is thus that these poor people are duped. As a safeguard against snake bite they wear a brass ring on one of their toes, and say that it has been a successful cure in many such cases. While engaged in catching rats from their holes, they wear round their wrists snake-shaped metallic rings as a preventive against rat bite.

Religion.

The Nayadis are animists, and they believe in the existence of certain demoniacal gods, namely, Mallan, Malavàzhi, and Parakutty, who are supposed to live in the hills and forests, watching over their welfare and protecting them against the attacks of wild beasts, any negligence or indifference on their part to propitiate them by offerings, being punishable by their appearance in dreams either thrashing them, or immersing them in water. All accidents are attributed to their disfavour, and even rain and thunder are supposed to be caused by them. Parakutty is the demon who aids them in their hunting excursions, brings them the game, and protects them against the attacks of wild animals. When they fail to get the expected game, they go to the length of abusing him for his ingratitude, and for betraying the trust they have reposed in him. Stones are sometimes seen located on a raised ground beneath a tree representing the images of Parakutty and their other favourite demons for whom a sheep or a fowl is killed, and the blood is let fall on them. A *puja* is performed by their priest during the night once a year, especially when they have some savings, with the offerings of boiled rice, toddy and husk, when the people stand at a distance, being forbidden to look at what is being done. He claps his hands when it is over, and they approach and offer their prayers in praise of them. "O Malla, Malavazhi! O Parakutty! O Father! O Mother! We have given you these offerings, which we have with difficulty obtained from *Thampurakkal* (members of the higher castes) as alms. May you accept them and protect us and our children against wild beasts, as we wander through the forests." After this, they partake of the offerings and return home. Living in forests and far remote from the members of the higher castes, these poor people have very few or no opportunities of knowing anything about the higher forms of Hinduism.

Funeral customs.

Generally the Nayadis have their burial grounds, and either burn the dead or bury them. When a person of their caste dies, the pollution lasts for ten days. On the tenth day, they collect a small quantity of rice, some grass, water in a cocoanut shell, an entire plantain leaf, and a lighted wick. The agnates all assemble and go to a river or water reservoir close by to bathe. A sand heap, or a figure made of earth to represent the deceased, is made and the plantain leaf with the articles above referred to is placed near it. The eldest son begins the ceremony by standing before the leaf with his face towards the east; he pours the water twelve times, when the others respectfully prostrate themselves before it, leaving the rice to be eaten by the crows. They return home, and the *enangan* purifies them by sprinkling on each member a little of the mixture of the water mixed with cow-dung, when they are supposed to be free from pollution. Those assembled are sumptuously fed. The eldest son performs the *deeksha* ceremony (allowing the hair to grow) for a year, and abstains from eating meat during this period. He performs the ceremony of *sradha* at the end of the year, when he terminates his *deeksha*. On the *Karkadaka sankranthi* or some other auspicious day he zealously makes offerings to his ancestors with the implicit belief that the prosperity of his family depends upon their blessings.

Occupation.

The Nayadis as a class are averse to manual labour. They collect honey, bees' wax and resin (*mattipasa*) from the *mattipal* tree (Aliyanthus malabarica) which they sell for a few copper coins, with which they purchase their few articles of daily consumption, such as salt, chillies, dried fish, tobacco, and toddy. They make a kind of rope from malanar plants and the bark of *kayul* trees. They make slings of fibres with which they shoot birds. During the *Onam* and *Vishu* festivals, the Nayadis offer four ropes to every Namburi *illam* and two to every Nair house near their village; in return for which they get some paddy and a few copper coins and a piece of cloth. They are sometimes employed in ploughing, sowing, weeding, transplanting, and even reaping in the forest cultivation, for which they get a few annas worth of paddy. They have to watch the fields at night against the attacks of wild beasts. They collect *incha* (bark of Acacia Intsia) which is soaked in water, and the fibre is used as soap.

Whenever there is a grand feast in a *thara* (village) or any locality, they stand far away from the public road, leaving there a piece of their ragged cloth and howling for charity from the passers-by. By a wise arrangement of the old local chieftains, a *desam* (village) is assigned to each Nayadi wherein he enjoys certain privileges, and no members of his caste from another village may encroach upon his rights. On birthdays, anniversaries and other festive occasions in well-to-do neighbouring houses, the Nayadis have their share of curry and rice. When they have no work, they go out and stand at a distance from each house in the *thara*, howling with their stentorian voices for charity. The inmates of some of them take a handful of rice, salt, chillies, tamarind, oil, mustard, cocoanut, and a few pice in a vessel and move them round the head of a child or adult supposed to be under the influence of a demon or the potency of the evil eye, and hand them over to the Nayadi, who is then asked to curse (*prakuka*). The peculiar feature about a Nayadi's curse is that it always has an effect the opposite of what it purports, and hence when a Nayadi is asked to curse, he complies by invoking misery and evil upon the person who has given him alms. The terms used by him for such invocations are *attupo*[1], *mutinjupo*[2], *adimondupo*[3], etc. He does so gladly and returns home. When a person is suffering from any severe disease and is on the verge of death, a coarse black blanket (*kambli*) is bought, at the four corners of which sesamum or gingili seeds, mustard, turmeric, and cocoanuts are tied up, and it is passed three times over the patient. It is then given to a Nayadi together with an umbrella, a stick, and a cucumber. It is called *Kaladanom*, which is an offering to Yama, the god of death, who has to be propitiated in order that the calamity may be averted. The disease is supposed to be transferred to the Nayadi who has accepted it. Receiving this, he prays for the long life and prosperity of the patient. He then returns home and places the gifts before his Mallan, Malavazhi, and Parakutty, with the prayer that the disease may not be transferred to himself.[4]

These miserable specimens of humanity pass their days howling for charity under the midday sun in summer and in rain during the monsoon months, and they have also to watch the crops of their landlords at night. "This tribe," says Buchanan, "as long as they continue to be in Malabar, will be useless to others, and will exercise no influence in the country. They should be removed bodily to some place where they would be compelled to work for their sustenance." They were at one time skillful hunters and excellent shots. They used to accompany the Nairs in their hunting excursions as beaters. They themselves sometimes go out hunting and catch toads, tortoises, deer, and other animals with the help of dogs, and beat them to death. Their weapons are slings, knives, axes, and swords. Those who live in the forests of a landlord render him some agricultural service, for which they receive small wages in kind for their subsistence. Others who live in the Sirkar forests get better wages.

1 and 2. To perish. 3. To be a slave. 4. This is done generally on Saturdays.

THE NAYADIS GOING FOR ALMS.

Food.

Their chief food is *kanji* and boiled rice, which they prepare early in the morning, and as soon as this is taken they go either to work or to seek alms. Should they get anything during the day, they have their evening meal; otherwise they have to starve for the night. Anything that remains out of the morning meal is given to the children during the day. They consume the roots of the nux vomica. The roots are cut into thin slices, which are boiled with salt to form a vegetable curry. Among the vegetables are included tubers of yams (Dioscorea) and colocasia, mangoes, jackfruits, and pumpkins. Sometimes they take the remains of meals prepared the previous night, which are generally *kanji* or rice boiled in water. They consume the flesh of monkeys, goats, wild squirrels, deer, rats, doves, quails, fowls, paddy birds, tortoises, and crocodiles. They never eat the flesh of dogs, land-crabs, shell-fish, beef, vermin, snakes, lizards, or jackals.

Social status.

It has already been said that they are the *chandalas* of the plains, and as such they cannot approach the habitations and the members of other castes. With much difficulty they cross public roads. They pollute a Brahman by approaching him within a distance of three hundred feet, and he has to bathe, renew his sacred thread, and take *panchagavyam*.[1] Whenever they have to pass by a field, they always announce their approach by their persistent clamour, so that others may not be polluted. They are the lowest of castes, but do not partake of the preparations of the Pulayans and Parayans. Some are becoming converts to Christianity, and take a great interest in the study and utterance of Christian prayers and songs. Others become converts to Mahomadanism, and maintain themselves by alms from Moslems. These are called Thoppiyitta (cap-wearing) Nayadis.

Personal appearance.

In some places they have tufts of hair on the top of their heads, while in others, they appear clean shaven. They wear a small dirty loin cloth extending

1. The five gifts of the cow, *viz.*, milk, curds, butter, urine, and dung.

above the knees, and are seldom seen with a second one. They wear ear-rings of brass, and also wear charms round the arms or loins to cure diseases or protect themselves from the attack of demons. The women are dark in colour, and lean and stunted in growth. They wear a dirty loin cloth (*kacha*) which is twice folded, and are seldom seen with an upper cloth. The lobes of the ears are dilated to contain wooden plugs which serve as *thodas* or ear-rings. Round the neck are several strings of beads with shells and pendants, which are not removed after the death of their husbands. Virgins do not wear any ornaments in particular. Men and women are often seen standing at a distance with dishevelled hair and jaded looks, and appear to be as timid as some of the animals of the forest that they live among. Their condition is one of misery and they seem to make no efforts to better themselves. On the whole they are a truthful people and not given to stealing.

III. THE ULLADANS.

The Ulladans belong to the lowest caste among the purely Malayali Hindu and animistic castes of the Cochin State. The word 'Ulladan' is said to be derived from the words *ull*, meaning 'within,' and *otunnu*, meaning 'runs,' and thus signifies one who runs away into the forest at the sight of the approach of a member of any of the higher castes. The word also means one that lives in the interior. Classed as they are among the jungle tribes, they form at present the lowest class of slaves attached to the soil, and are called the *chandalas*[1] of the plains. Dr. A. H. Keane says that they form a member of the primitive groups of Southern India, representing the Negrito and Dravidian blend. They are very few in number, for they numbered only 439 at the last census, 211 being males and 228 females. The language they speak is Malayalam, and these people

---

1. Members of the lowest caste.

are all illiterate. They are found in Irinjalakuda, Pallipuram, Edakochi, Kumbalom, Ezhuvinna, Neendakara, Manacheri, and Chellanam, and for the most they are not migratory in their habits, but remain in one place. The tribe is divided into four endogamous septs, known by the names Ulladan, Cherappan, Thalippan, and Nayadis. There is no interdining nor intermarrying between these different septs, and popularly the Ulladans and Nayadis are regarded as separate tribes. The Thalippans act as barbers, and perform the priestly functions at the funeral ceremonies of the members of the tribe.

Habitation.

Their huts are situated in the forests of the plains by the side of paddy flats, or in cocoanut gardens far remote from the habitations of the members of most of the higher castes, for only the Syrian Christians are found in their neighbourhood. These huts are erected on short bamboo posts, the roofs and the four sides of which are covered with plaited cocoanut leaves. A bamboo framework with the same leaves serves the purpose of a door. The floor of the huts is neither raised nor beaten down, and differs very little from the sandy ground outside them. A few plaited cocoanut leaves and a coarse mat of their own weaving form their only furniture, and serve as beds for them at night. Their vessels in domestic use consist of a few earthen pots for cooking and holding water, and a few earthen dishes from which they drink water and take their food. Some large pieces of the bark of the areca palm containing salt, chillies, etc., were also found on the floor inside the hut. They have no store-room; what little they seem to possess as food and clothing is placed in small baskets suspended from the framework of the roof by means of wooden hooks. Their huts appear to be used merely as temporary shelters which they occupy at night; for, during the day the Ulladans live in the open air. A corner of the hut is used as the fire-place, but cooking is done outside the huts during the summer months. All the members of the family sleep together in the same hut, but in some cases a newly married couple put up a small separate hut for themselves.

Marriage customs.

Adult marriage is the rule among the Ulladans. There is generally no age limit for the marriage of a girl, nor is there any social penalty if it is put off for an indefinite time. Like the Izhuvans, the Ulladans who live around Ernakulam usually celebrate the *tali* tying ceremony for their girls after their fifth year; but if the ceremony is put off or not performed, the girl's parents are not liable to any punishment. The person who ties the *tali* is generally the girl's cousin or any young man of her tribe in the neighbourhood, and he may become the girl's husband if he can give her a piece of cloth (*muri*). In the localities where the *tali* tying ceremony is performed for a girl in her childhood, the ceremony is dispensed with on the occasion of her marriage. As a rule Ulladans do not marry their relatives, though they can give no reason for their not doing so; but in places, *e. g.*, Ernakulam and Kumbalom, a young Ulladan sometimes marries the daughter of his maternal uncle. Marriage is purely a civil contract, and is usually arranged by the parents or agents of the contracting parties. Divorce also is a simple matter and is easily effected. If a husband does not like his wife on the score of infidelity or other misconduct, he has merely to take her back to her parents and give her into their charge, while a woman who wishes a separation from her husband, simply goes back to her parents. No stigma attaches to the divorced parties, and both are free to marry again. Widows also are at liberty to marry any member of the tribe, except the deceased husband's brother. In connection with such a re-marriage very few ceremonies are performed. The children by the first husband remain with their mother till they are old enough to shift for themselves. An Ulladan may have more than one wife, but no woman may have more than one husband. When the man has more than one wife, they, as a rule, live in the same hut, but often, to prevent jealousy and misunderstandings, he provides them with separate huts. Sexual licence before marriage is neither recognised nor tolerated. Should an unmarried girl become pregnant and the fact be known, her secret lover is summoned by the tribesmen, who compel him to take her to wife, as otherwise they are placed under a ban. Eventually they may be driven to the necessity of becoming converts to Christianity.

When a young man wishes to marry, his father and maternal uncle speak to the parents of the girl whom they wish to choose. In the event of their willingness, the parents and other relatives on both sides meet together at the hut of the bride elect to make the preliminary negotiations for the wedding, after which the bridegroom's party is entertained there. The bride's price, which is generally half a rupee, but may rise up to five rupees, is paid at the time. The number of guests to attend the wedding is also determined. The bride's parents and uncle then go to the hut of the bridegroom elect, where they are treated to a dinner of which toddy forms an important item. On the day appointed for the wedding, the bridegroom goes to the hut of the bride elect escorted by his friends and relatives who are all sumptuously fed. The bridegroom's sister garlands the bride, and the bridegroom ties the *tali* (a brass ring attached to a thread) round the neck of the bride. The next morning the bride is led to the hut of the bridegroom, where also a feast is given to her relatives who accompany them. After staying there for a week, the married couple go to the hut of the bride, where they stay for a few days. Then the bridegroom takes the bride to his own hut. Now the marriage is formally over. A week or two after the wedding, the consummation takes place in the bridegroom's hut without any formal ceremony. The following marriage custom prevails among the Ulladans of Travancore. The ceremony is simple, and is employed by some of the low tribes at certain times, although not practised by the Ulladans of Cochin. A small round building is made of leaves, and inside this the bride is ensconced. All the eligible young men of the village then assemble and form a ring round the hut. At a short distance sits the girl's father or nearest male relative with tom tom in his hands, and a few more musical instruments complete the scene. Presently music begins, and a chant, sung by the father, may be translated as follows:—

Take the stick my sweetest daughter,
Now take the stick my dearest love,
Should you not capture the husband you wish for,
Remember it is fate decides whom you shall have.

The young men, each armed with a bamboo, begin dancing round the hut into which each of them thrusts his stick. This continues for an hour, when the owner of whichever bamboo she seizes becomes the fortunate husband of the concealed bride. A feast then follows, and the ceremony is complete. The newly married couple live separately in a new hut which does not cost much to erect. The Ulladans hold strict views as to the chastity of both married and unmarried women, and there is nothing like free love among them. The women do not go out to work like the Pulaya women. The husbands provide for the wife and children, while the wives cook and minister to the wants of children. Some Ullada women whom I talked to near Ernakulam told me that they would not lower themselves by going to work, as they are the descendants of the chiefs of the forest.

Pregnancy and childbirth.

Owing to the poverty of the Ulladans, a woman who is about to become a mother is not subjected to any special treatment, and all misadventures connected with the birth of children are ascribed to the anger of their gods. Shortly before the birth of the child, a ceremony known as *Pulikudi* is performed. A sour mixture is administered to the woman by her maternal uncle, and the day is observed as one of festivity for friends and relatives. For the birth of the child a separate hut is erected, and the woman is attended by an old woman, generally her mother. As soon as the child is born, both the mother and the child are bathed in warm water, and for three weeks a small doze of *pettu marunnu* (delivery medicine), a medicine used also by the Izhuvans, is administered every morning and evening to the mother, while her diet for a fortnight consists of boiled rice and vegetable curry. The period of pollution varies, being eleven days in some places, and sixteen in others. When that is over, the woman is allowed to come to the verandah of her hut, and after a further period of two weeks, she may after a bath enter the hut and mingle with the rest of the family. Children are nursed by their mothers for six or seven months, after which they are put on a diet of boiled rice or *kanji*. The naming ceremony usually takes place on the twenty-eighth day after birth, but in some cases it is deferred till the sixth month, when the naming and the weaning take place together. An important ceremony for girls, which is also the occasion for a feast, is that of ear-boring. It takes place during the fifth or sixth year, and is performed by a grown up woman, generally the aunt of the girl whose ears are to be bored. The holes then made in the ears are gradually dilated till they become of the desired size.

Inheritance and tribal organization.

The Ulladans are so poor that the question of inheritance is but of little importance among them. If a man dies, leaving any property, whatever, in some cases, it goes to his sister's son, and in other cases to his own son. All relationship is reckoned through the female side, and a child takes the name of its mother's family.

The tribal assembly consists of the elderly members of the tribe. There is a head-man who is called *Muppan*, and he has an assistant who is known as *Ponamban*. The head-man has to preside at all marriage and funeral ceremonies, and to decide all disputes connected with the tribe. The tribal assembly meets chiefly to deal with cases of immorality, and the guilty parties are summoned before the assembly. The head-man who presides over the assembly inquires into the matter, and in the event of the accused parties confessing their guilt, they are taken before His Highness the Raja, who is informed of the circumstances. The male culprit is sometimes beaten or fined, and the woman is given some water or the milk of a green cocoanut, and this is supposed to set her free from all sin. When a fine is imposed, it is sometimes spent on the purchase of toddy which is shared among the tribesmen present. The head-man gets a few *puthans* (one *puthan* is equal to ten pies) for his trouble.

Religion.

In religion the Ulladans are pure animists or demon worshippers. All cases of sickness and other calamities are attributed to the malignant influence of demons, whom it is necessary to propitiate. They adore the following deities, *viz.*, Kappiri, Theekutty, and Chathan, all of whom are represented by a few stones placed under a thatched roof called *kottil.* Offerings of rice flour, sheep, fowls, toddy, rice, cocoanuts, and plantains are given on Fridays in the month of Kanni (September-October). One of the tribesmen who acts as a *velichapad* (oracle), speaks to the others as if by inspiration, and also casts out demons who are supposed to reside in the bodies of women. When he resumes his former self, he takes half the offerings to himself, allowing the other half for distribution among the by-standers. They also worship the spirits of the departed members of their families who, they believe, appear to them in dreams, and ask them for whatever they want. They also believe that in the event of their neglecting to give what is asked, these spirits will cause serious calamities to the family.

Funeral ceremonies.

The Ulladans generally bury their dead in special places called *chotala,* but some of them bury the corpse a few yards away from their huts. They observe the pollution for fifteen days, and on the morning of the sixteenth the Thalippan comes, cleans the hut and its surroundings, and sprinkles cow-dung mixed with water on the members of the family as they return from bathing, in order that they may be freed from pollution. They entertain their tribesmen that day. It is a custom among the Ulladans, Pulayans, and other low classes that, when they are invited to a feast, they bring with them some rice, curry stuffs, toddy, or a few annas to meet the expenses of the feast. Very often the above articles are obtained as a gift from the charitably disposed members of the higher castes. At the end of the year a similar feast is given to the tribesmen. Among the Ulladans, the nephew is the chief mourner, for, as has been mentioned, the nephew usually succeeds to the property of a dead uncle, and he proves his right of ownership by acting as chief mourner.

Occupation.

The Ulladans on the sea coast make boats and cut timber. Their brethren in the interior are ignorant of boat-making, but collect some of the minor forest produce and sell it to contractors. They gather honey formed on bushes, small trees, or sometimes on the ground. But the honey collected by them is so small in quantity, that they get only a few annas in exchange for it. During the agricultural season they engage in every kind of agricultural work, such as ploughing, sowing, transplanting, reaping, and fencing. They also herd the cattle of the farmers, and get for their labour a few annas worth of paddy. For most months in the year they are in a half starving condition, and therefore resort to eating every kind of wild root and animal they can get hold of. They are often seen thrusting a long stick into the holes wherein rats may be found and move it so violently as to kill them there or force them to come out, when they catch and kill them. They are eaten boiled with salt and they catch and eat tortoises also. Sometimes they pursue the latter in tanks or attack them in their holes and kill them there. Very often in rural parts both men and women are found with poles ready to be thrust into any holes there may be by the side of fences or where bamboos grow luxuriantly. They also catch crocodiles by placing the carcase of a fowl, sheep, or some other animal on the bank of a canal or by the side of a tank, where crocodiles are to be found. Into it is thrust a pointed piece of iron fastened to a strong cord. When the crocodile comes out of the water to eat the bait, or tries to carry it off, the piece of iron becomes firmly fixed in its mouth, and it is unable to get away, upon which the Ulladans, who are watching, approach and kill it with their clubs and knives. They catch fish with baits and by poisoning the water. They are also said to be adepts at spearing, by a skillful stroke of their knives, any fish they may find swimming near the surface. They are trackers of game rather than hunters, and very often accompany Syrian Christians and Mahomadans who go hunting to provide themselves with meat of all kinds for their wedding feasts. The Ulladans are engaged only to beat up the game. For this service they are given their meals while the wedding feast lasts, in addition to three annas worth of paddy for each beater. When nothing is obtained in hunting they have to be satisfied with only one day's meal, in addition to the three annas worth of paddy. They are armed with clubs and seldom take dogs with them, fearing that these may drive away the game. When any animal is killed in hunting, the right side of the back goes to the Government. It is given to the Forest officer who auctions it, and the money obtained is sent to the Taluk treasury. The left side of the back is claimed by the member of the party who has killed it. He also gets the head and the tongue. The head-man among the Ulladans also gets a share, and the remainder of the carcase is equally divided among the members who have formed the party. Should any dispute arise regarding the division of the game, the man who shot the animal is entrusted with the settlement of the dispute and his decisions are final. In cases where the hunting party is organised by the Moplahs, the Ulladans get wages and meals for their trouble. They are forbidden to hunt in places where elephant pits are dug.

Food.

The Ulladans, as has been indicated, live upon a mixed diet. Early in the morning before they go to work, they take some *kanji* prepared during the previous night. About midday they drink *kanji* freshly prepared with salt and chillies, but if they do not possess this, they eat the roots of plants obtained from the forests. At night they eat boiled rice with a preparation of the flesh of the rats, tortoises, fish, or crocodiles procured during the day. In addition to the animals above referred to, they eat also the flesh of the sheep, deer, and fowls, but abstain from eating the flesh of the cows, bisons, snakes, and crows.

THE ULLADANS.

Social status.

As regards their social status, the Ulladans, like the Nayadis, are the *chandalas* of the plains. Their approach, to within a distance of sixty-four feet, pollutes the Brahmans and all higher castes including the Sudras (Nairs). Some of these castes (Ulladans, Nayadis, Pulayans, and Parayans) pollute one another by touch or approach. Hence the Ulladans cannot walk along the public roads, or come to the bazaars, nor can they approach the precincts of any town or locality where the members of higher castes reside. They eat the food of all castes above them, except that of the Pulayans and the Parayans, who profess to be polluted by these poor people. It is curious to note that the Ullada women consider it degrading to go for work like the Pulaya women. They say that their husbands have to provide for them.

Appearance.

In personal appearance the Ulladans are short and dark. They have dark eyes of all shadès, long and narrow faces, straight noses, and lips of medium size. Their heads are rather short and broad, and are covered with black woolly hair, which is not well parted nor softened with oil, but is allowed to grow wild and tied into a knot on the top. Their clothing is very scanty. The men wear round the loins a small piece of cloth which is usually much the worse for wear. Their women wear a thread round the loins, and a strip of cloth connected with it is worn for decency's sake. This kind of cloth is found to be in use among the Pulaya women also. The women have their ears bored and dilated, but not even discs of palm leaves are inserted in the holes. Some wear a necklace of glass beads, while others wear only a black thread. Altogether the Ulladans are miserably poor, and their dirty habits make their presence unpleasant. The higher castes, however, who know their disabilities and their starving condition, often take pity on them and give them presents of rice, oil, salt, and chillies.

CHAPTER IV.

THE PARAYANS.

The Parayans belong to a very low caste of the agrestic serfs of Cochin next to the Pulayans. They numbered 8,841 at the last census, 4,646 being males, 4,195 females, and formed 1·60 per cent of the Hindu population of the State. They speak a kind of vulgar Malayalam, and the words are so badly mispronounced that a high caste-man can hardly make them out.

Origin and tradition of the caste.

The word "Parayan" is derived from "*para*," a drum. The Parayans delight in drum-beating, and are generally called on to act as drummers at funerals, marriages, and village festivals of Tamil Sudras. Some say that they are of the drummer caste, and have obtained the name from the instrument. This does not seem to be quite correct, for it is in the highest degree improbable, that a large community should owe its name to an occasional occupation. They have been exclusively, from a remote period, the agricultural labourers of the Tamil Districts, and there have been also, among them, weavers, leather workers, cobblers, and weavers of grass mats. Dr. Gustav Oppert states that Pallans, Pallis, and Parayans were men of the hill country, though some deny that they are so, for they appear in no way connected with the hills, nor do they now possess any trace of the worship of the hill deities. Further, in very old Tamil works, the word "Pulayan" is used to denote those who are now called Parayans. Mr. Francis, in his Census Report for 1901, shows by an inscription that the Parayans were known as such during the eleventh century.

The word "Parayan" also means an outcast from every caste. The Parayan calls himself to this day "the elder Brahman", claiming in this manner precedence over the Brahman.

The Brahmans on the other hand ascribe the origin of the Parayans and other low castes to the connection of Brahman women with low caste-men, or to the curse which sages like Viswamithra were so fond of uttering against their flesh and blood, or against any one who was unfortunate enough to cross them in their desires. The legend of the curse of Viswamithra against Vasishta, his famous puranic rival, is very interesting, as it describes the origin of some wild tribes like the Sabaras and Pulindas of the puranas.

According to another puranic legend, Vasishta was the son of Urvasi and the husband of a Chandala woman of the Chakkili (shoe-maker) caste, who was in fact Arundhati, reborn as a Chandali. She bore him one hundred sons, ninety-six of whom disobeyed their father, and were on that account accursed to the Panchama (fifth) caste, while the four others remained Brahmans. They are regarded as the representatives of the ancient Dravidian population. It is said that they do not represent a strictly ethnological subdivision.

Though the Parayans and Pulayans occupy a low and despicable position in the places where they live, they have preserved and still cherish the memory of their former greatness, and regard themselves as the original owners of the soil. There are instances to show that they were at one time in a flourishing state, and they possessed privileges which they could not have gained from the Brahmans. At Melkotta and in the Aiyengar Vaishnava temple at Bailur, the Holeyas or Canarese Parayans have the right of entering the temple three days in the year, specially set apart for them, and in the great Saiva festival at Tiruvallur of the Tanjore District, the head-man of the Parayans is mounted on the elephant with the god and carries his *chouri* (yak-tail, fly fan). At Sreeperumbuthur in the Chingleput District they possess a similar privilege for having sheltered an image of the incarnation of Vishnu during a Mussalman raid. Even now, a Parayan annually becomes the husband of Egathál, the tutelary deity of the George Town in Madras, and actually ties the *tali* or marriage badge round the neck of the image. They are also allowed to take part in pulling the cars of the idols along with the Brahmans in the car festivals at Conjeevaram, Kumbakonam, and Sreevilliputhur. Their touch is not believed to defile the rope or the car. Many among them have become famous as poets and saints. Thiruvallavar Nayanar, the author of Kural and his so called sister the famous poetess Avvai, the Vaishnavar Alwar, were the most famous of them. The great Saivite saint Nanda is well-known to the Hindus of all castes. Even now, there is a general belief in some of the Tamil Districts that the Parayans know the village boundaries better than any one else. It is said that they are wonderfully expert in marking out where boundaries should run even when the Government demarcation stones are concealed by the overgrowth of prickly pear or have been removed. Mr. H A. Stuart records a custom "which prevails in some parts of making a Parayan walk the boundaries of a field with a pot of water on his head when there is any dispute about their exact position.[1]" He thinks that the only satisfactory explanation of this is that the connection of Parayans with the soil is of much longer standing than that of other castes.

From the foregoing facts it may be supposed that the Parayans may, very probably, have been the very early settlers in the land, and the representatives of the ancient Dravidian population, and that they must have been brought to this state of degradation by the conquest of some civilised race.

In the Cochin State, the Parayans are found almost everywhere in the rural parts, and are probably the descendants of those of the Tamil Districts, who must have immigrated to these parts in remote times. A large number of them originally migrated to the hilly parts, while some have settled in the plains. The two sets of people have different modes of living. As regards diet, the hill-men live upon the wild roots of plants, while

1. Census of India, Vol. XIII, Madras, Page 245.

those on the plains eat carrion, even that of cows. The former made use of the barks of trees and skins of animals for their garments, and the latter resorted to cotton cloths (*mundus*). Now all wear pieces of cotton cloth and live in poor huts. Like the great men among the Parayans of the Tamil Districts in ancient times, there were, in Kerala also, some remarkable men, the life and career of two of whom described below, may not be without interest.

There lived in ancient times in the kingdom of Avanthy (Malwa) a hermit named Vyagrapàtha, a disciple of Pathanjali, the famous Hindu grammarian. He was, for some fault or other, cursed by his preceptor (*guru*), and transformed into a ghost (Bramharakshas), with the condition that he could resume his former self in the event of his teaching a young man the whole of the science of grammar. As a ghost he had the ill luck to live on a tree for a long time, looking out for a proper disciple. He used to put the question പചധാതോഃ ക്ത്വാന്തം കിം രൂപം (what is the past participle of the root *pachu*?) to every one who came to take shelter under the tree, and trouble those who could not answer it. A young Brahman named Chandragupta, with the eager desire to learn the subject under a *guru* (preceptor), was travelling from place to place to find out a suitable teacher, but could not get one competent to teach him. With much anxiety and disappointment, he chanced to stand underneath the tree, when, to his astonishment, the question was put to him. Well pleased at the correct answer given by the young man, the ghost asked him who he was and whither he was going. The Brahman mentioned the object of his mission. The ghost at last got the opportunity of teaching the young man and found in Chandragupta a zealous disciple, who, with the potency of a medicine given him by the preceptor, which deprived him of sleep and hunger, studied the subject day and night and admirably mastered it in a short time from the top of the tree to which he was taken. The *guru*, blessing him with a warning not to wade through water, recovered his former self and got his salvation. With a view to test the warning of his preceptor, Chandragupta determined to cross the river Chupŕa, requesting the maidens of all castes who were bathing there to help him, should any calamity befall him in water on his way. He was drowned, but was saved by a Sudra girl among them. Recovering his consciousness, he thanked her for her favour, and, with a view to reward her, he asked her what she wanted. The maiden desired to be his wife. Chandragupta could not but condescend to take her as wife, but could do so only after his union with the maidens of the three higher castes. Entering into wedlock with a Brahman, a Kshatriya, and a Vaisya maiden, he wedded the Sudra girl and lived a happy conjugal life. He had, by the Brahman wife, the famous Vararuchi, the great astrologer; by the Kshatriya wife, the renowned Vikramaditya; by the Sudra wife, Bhartrihari. He eventually became an ascetic by the name of Govindaswamy and breathed his last.

Vararuchi became the king of Avanthy and ruled till Vikramaditya came of age, when he abdicated in his favour. Once when he was taking rest under an *aswastha* tree (Ficus religiosa), invoking the support of the deity living therein, he overheard a conversation between two Gandharvas on the tree, that he would marry a Paraya girl, at whose birth one of them attended for some offerings. He felt sorry for it, and averted it by requesting the king to have her enclosed in a box and floated down the river with a nail stuck into her head. The box was however taken possession of by a Brahman who was bathing in its lower course. He opened it and found a beautiful girl whom he considered a divine gift and looked upon her as his own daughter. She grew to be a beautiful maiden. One day the pious Brahman was looking out for a guest to mess with him and saw Vararuchi passing by, whom he invited. He said he would accept the invitation only on condition that he would arrange to prepare eighteen curries and give him what remained after feeding a hundred Brahmans. The Brahman host was quite embarrassed at the impracticable demand of his guest, but the maiden, who was close by, consoled him by the promise that she would satisfy the guest's requirements, and wished him to bathe and be ready to dine with him. She took out a long leaf and placed thereon a ginger preparation which corresponded to eighteen curries. A little of boiled rice (*havis*) also out of that used as offerings for his *Vaiswadeva* ceremony, was placed along with it. This corresponded to the food offered to a hundred deities in the performance of the ceremony. Seeing this, the guest was very much pleased, and he gladly dined with the host. Knowing all this to be the work of the maiden, he eagerly desired to have her as his wife, to which the Brahman readily consented. Vararuchi wedded her and lived a happy married life. One day, while conversing about their past life he chanced to see the nail stuck into her head and knew her to be the girl whom he had caused to be floated down the stream. Consoling himself that he could not avoid the sad irony of fate, he resolved to go on pilgrimage with his wife, travelling from place to place, bathing in various rivers and worshipping the deities in many temples. At last he came to Kerala, where he had, by her, twelve sons, all of whom except one were left on the roadside and taken care of by members of different castes. They were all remarkable for their wisdom and believed to be *avatar* (incarnation) of Vishnu, and performed many miracles, the stories of which are well-known among all classes of people in Malabar. Pâkkanar, the great Parayan, was one of them.

Once when a few Brahmans resolved to go to Benares, they saw Pakkanar, who dissuaded them by saying that the journey to the sacred city was not productive of salvation. Knowing them bent upon going to the city, and with a desire to prove to them the fruitlessness of their journey, he plucked a lotus flower from a stagnant pool close to his hut, and gave it to them with the instruction to have it delivered over to a hand that would rise from the Ganges, when they should say that it was meant for the goddess Ganga from Pakkanar.

They did as directed and conveyed this miracle after their return home. Pakkanar led them to the pool again and said "Please return the lotus flower, O Ganga, I sent to thee". It soon came into the hand of Pakkanar. He thus proved to demonstration the fruitlessness of their journey. The holy Ganges water exists here just as much as it exists in the largest river. Another story which is equally interesting is the following.

Pakkanar earned his livelihood by the sale of his wicker work, which he did every day. One day he could not sell his baskets and rice pan, and as he had to go starving, his neighbouring landlord, who knew this, gave him some milk which was all what he could spare. He took it thankfully and told the master to think of him whenever he was in danger. The landlord had a daughter married to a young man, and while living with him, she was about to die of snake-bite; but the father remembered the words of Pakkanar who was thought of as directed. He came running and cured her of the snake-bite. Pakkanar's hut, with another small one, containing his image worshipped by the members of the family, is still to be seen at Trithala, a place six miles west of Pattambi Railway Station.

Another story in connection with one of his brothers may not be without interest. He was called Narayana Branthan. He pretended to be a lunatic all his life and took special delight in rolling huge stones up a neighbouring hill and leaving them there, so that they easily rolled down with great force, when he would clap his hands and laugh merrily. Though a son of a learned and pious Brahman, he mingled freely with the members of all castes and had no scruples to dine with them. A Nambudiri requested him to choose an auspicious day for the performance of his son's *Upanayanam* (ceremony for wearing the sacred thread). He told him that twelve o'clock on the new moon night in Karkadakam (July-August) would be the most auspicious time, and that he would be present there then. This was disappointing to the Brahman, for no day could be more inauspicious for the performance of this ceremony. The day approached and the lunatic was there as promised. The most lucky time was drawing near. The members of the family as well as those assembled there asked him as to the propriety of the time for the celebration of the ceremony. He called out the boy's father to the court-yard, and asked him to look up to the sky, when he saw, to his great astonishment, the Heavens brilliantly illuminated and the God Bramha changing his holy thread. They were immensely pleased and the boy was soon invested with the holy thread. Such were the miracles performed by Pakkanar and his brothers.

Marriage customs.

Marriage among kinsfolk is rigorously prohibited. Union between a man and a woman of the same family within four degrees on the mother's side or within six degrees on the father's side is not permissible. A young man may marry the daughter of his maternal uncle and no member of the caste can mate with a woman descended from his mother's younger or elder sister. Girls are married before and after puberty, generally between twelve and sixteen years of age. The custom of early marriage has obtained in this caste from a remote period. The boys and girls have no voice in the matter, and the parents are solely responsible for it. Marriage is also called *Penkoda* for the performance of which Mondays are generally chosen, while Sundays are considered to be inauspicious. The offer for the marriage of a girl comes from the bridegroom's family. A rupee in advance and two cloths are given to the parents of the bride elect on the day of settlement On the day previous to the celebration, the bridegroom and his party arrive at the hut of the bride where they are entertained with *kanji* and toddy. The next day, at the lucky moment, the *tali*, which is a copper or a brass ring attached to a thread, is tied round the neck of the girl, who is purified by a bath, neatly dressed, and well adorned. This is followed by a feast in which toddy is an indispensable item, but meat is excluded. The feast being over, they play on their musical instruments, a pipe and a drum, which lasts for an hour or two during the day and is continued throughout the night. The ceremony and the feast last for two days in the hut of the bride after which the bridegroom and his party return to his hut with the bride, where also the bride's party are similarly entertained. In some places, the expenses are shared by the bridegroom's parents.

A Parayan may marry more than one woman; but these half starved people are generally content with one wife. Polyandry is, at present, unknown, because it is censured and counted as criminal. Widow marriage is freely allowed. A widow is, with the consent of her parents, at liberty to marry anybody but must remain a widow for the year after the death of her husband. If she has children and does not desire to marry, she remains in the family of her husband, where she and her young ones are properly looked after. A young widow who unites herself with another has her children supported by him, but in no case is she allowed to marry her brother-in-law. A Parayan, on the other hand, may marry his deceased wife's sister. The ceremonies connected with such a marriage are just the same as those detailed above, but not on so grand a scale. He has no claim to any property which his wife may have acquired from her former husband. Generally the wives have no personal property and are simply the chattels of their husbands. They do not solely depend upon their husbands for maintenance, but work for wages by themselves. The provisions for sons or daughters depend upon their will and earning. If the husband does not like his wife, he is at liberty to divorce her, for divorce is very easy with them; and the customs connected therewith are similar to those prevailing among the Ulladans.

Pregnancy and childbirth.

When a married young woman is pregnant, she is taken to her parent's hut during the seventh or the eighth month, during which no ceremony is performed. The woman after childbirth is secluded for two weeks in a temporary hut erected at a short distance from the main hut. During the time of her seclusion she is debarred from touching vessels and provisions, and has to be fed by another person. Her usual diet is *kanji* in the morning and boiled rice at night. The only medicine which is administered to her during the period, is a mixture of coriander seeds, and *uluva* (Trigonella foenum græc) prepared by bruising and boiling in water and mixed with *kanji*. On the tenth day some male member of the family goes to his Brahman or Nair landlord from whom he gets some water and milk, which is sprinkled on her and her baby. She can now come to the verandah of her hut and be there for five days, after which by a bath in cold water and further purification, she can enter the hut and mingle freely with others. The temporary hut is burned and reduced to ashes. The husband defrays the expenses for the first fifteen days, and the parents till the twenty-eighth day, when she rejoins her husband. There is a feast in his house for the relations and others that are invited. The naming ceremony falls on that date.

They follow the Marumakkathayam [1] law of inheritance. They have a kind of caste assembly. The senior members of the caste meet on important occasions such as when adultery is committed or when an unmarried woman becomes pregnant or when caste rules are outraged. Their deliberations are serious and their decisions final.

Inheritance and caste assembly.

The Parayans of Malabar and Cochin are remarkable for their black magic, the secrets of which they never let out even under fear of death. In rural parts, they are consulted in all matters relating to theft, demoniacal influence, and the killing of enemies, for all of which they are amply rewarded. Whenever anything is stolen in a family, a Paraya magician is, by preference, sought after, and informed of the occurrence. Giving hopes of recovery, the wily Parayan receives from his client half a rupee worth of paddy and a few annas with which he purchases some plantain fruits, a cocoanut or two, some toddy, camphor, frankincense, and rice flour. He bathes and goes to his favourite deity Parakutty (a debased form of Vishnu called also Kutty Chathan or little Sastha, which is represented by a stone placed in front of his hut). Camphor and frankincense are burned, and the offerings above referred to are made. Armed with a sword provided with small bells at the hilt, he prays to him, rattling an iron instrument and sometimes sings to invoke the deity until the voice almost fails. He is then confident that the Parakutty will help him in the recovery of the stolen property by threat or injury to the person who has stolen it. He thinks that his god is highly gratified and sometimes the property is found or secretly replaced in the house of the owner. Should he fail to get it, the Paraya magician is again informed of the fact, when he prays in a more indignant and abusive form and he thinks that his object is sure to be gained this time. His prayers are mild if the stolen property alone has to be obtained, but if the thief has to be punished, his prayers are redoubled and supposed to

Magic.

1. Succession through nephews.

be readily granted. The thief becomes mad and blood passes through his nose and mouth. The treatment of the haunted man for recovery in such cases is attended with serious difficulties, because the deity, having once done the harm to the victim, may or may not help him in undoing it. In the imagination of the ignorant Parayan, the deity appears to possess the propensity to do mischief, and he has to be again gratified and won over by a second dose of bribery in the shape of prayers and offerings. It is the belief of these simple people and of the members of other castes living within the village that all kinds of illness are caused by the grave provocation of the deities to whom their accustomed or vowed offerings may not have been given. When a person is ill or under the influence of any demon, an astrologer and then a magician named by the former are often consulted. The latter takes a cadjan leaf or a small copper or silver sheet, draws thereon a cabalastic figure, and mutters a *mantram.* He rolls it and ties it to a thread to be worn either round the neck in the case of a woman or round the loins in the case of a man. The person with this charm is supposed to be set free from his illness or from the demoniacal influences, if any.

Oti cult.

Oti cult is the cult of breaking human body by magic. It is the name given to a kind of black art practised by the Parayans who, when proficient in it, can render themselves invisible, or assume the form of a bull, a cat, or a dog as they like. They are supposed to be able to entice pregnant women from their houses at midnight to destroy the fœtus in the womb, and substitute for it other substances, to bring sickness and death upon others, and so to bewitch people as to transport them despite of physical obstacles from one place to another, and this without their absence being noted by third parties. Vengeance and fear have led to horrible reprisals for fancied injuries. A Parayan who wishes to practise the cult, goes to a *guru* (preceptor) and falls at his feet, humbly requesting that he may be admitted into the mysteries of the art. The preceptor first tries to dissuade him, but the disciple persists in the desire to learn it, when he is tried by various tests as to his fitness. He follows his preceptor to the forest and lonely places at midnight. The latter suddenly makes himself invisible and soon appears before him in the form of a terrible bull, a ferocious dog, or an elephant, when the novice should remain bold, calm, and collected. He is also required to pass a night or two in a forest which, according to his firm belief, is full of strange beings or elementals howling horribly. He should remain unmoved. By these and other trials, he is tested as to his fitness. Having passed through these ordeals, his *guru* is pleased to initiate him into the brotherhood by the performance of a *puja* on an auspicious day to his favourite Neeli, called also Kallatikode Neeli, through whose aid he works his black art. Flesh and liquor are consumed and the disciple is taught how to prepare the potent medicines (*pilla thilam* and *angola thilam*) for the working of his cult.

The chief ingredient in the preparation of the *pilla thilam* (infant oil) is the fœtus, six or seven months old, of a young woman in her first pregnancy. She should belong to a caste other than his own. He sets out at midnight from his hut to the house of the woman he has selected, round which he walks several times, shaking a cocoanut shell *gurusi* (a compound of water, lime, and turmeric) muttering some *mantram* to invoke the aid of his deity. He also draws a *yanthram* (cabalastic figure) on the earth, taking special care to observe the omens as he starts. Should they be unfavourable, he puts it off for another favourable opportunity. By the potency of his cult the woman is made to come out, and even if the door of the room in which she sleeps, be under lock and key, she knocks her head against it, until she finds her way out. She thus comes out and yields herself to the influence of the Paraya magician, who leads her to a retired spot either in the compound or elsewhere in the neighbourhood, strips her naked, and asks her to lie flat. She does so and a *chora kindi* [1] is placed close to the

1. A vessel made of Curcurbita lagenaria.

vagina. The womb expands and fœtus comes out in a moment. A few leaves of some plant are placed, and the womb contracts. Sometimes they fill the womb with some rubbish when the woman instantly dies. Care is taken that the fœtus does not touch the ground, lest his purpose be defeated and the efficacy of the medicine completely lost. It is cut to pieces, dried and afterwards exposed to the smoke above a fire-place. It is then placed in a vessel, provided with a hole or two, below which there is another vessel. The two together are placed in a larger vessel filled with water and heated by a bright fire. The heat must be so intense as to affect the fœtus, from which a kind of liquid drops and collects in the second vessel in an hour and a half. He then takes a human skull and reduces it to fine powder, which is mixed with a portion of the liquid (*thilam* or oil). A mark on the forehead is made of this mixture and the oil is rubbed on certain parts of the body and he drinks a measure of cow-dung water. He then thinks that he can assume the figure of any animal he likes, and believes that he can successfully achieve his object in view, which is generally to murder or maim a person hated by the *otiyan* or his whilom patron.

The other medicine is extracted from a tree called *angola* (Alangium hexapetalum). A curious st ry is mentioned in connection with the particular fruit of this tree which bears a very large number during the fructifying season, among which one is believed to possess life and motion. It is also believed that this fruit can descend and return to its position during dark nights. The possession of this can be attained by the aid of Chàthan or Káppiri, a demon, or by an expert waiting down the tree during dark nights, when it must be caught in its attempts to ascend the tree to return to its position. When it is obtained, the extraction of the oil from it involves precisely the same operations as that for extracting the infant oil, and this must be done in seven hours, after it is caught hold of. A mark made of this oil on the forehead, will enable the possessor to achieve his desires and to transform himself into any animal he likes.

When a person has an enemy whom he wishes to kill, a Paraya magician who practises the cult is sought for, and he is remunerated to his satisfaction. With his consent, the name of the enemy is given. Identifying his residence, the Parayan either himself alone, or with the aid of another, like himself, sets out on a dark midnight, offering his prayers to the deity to help him in the perpetration of the deed. He goes drunk. In the event of the omens being unfavourable, he postpones it for another occasion. Any person accidently meeting him is at once dispatched with a blow. Should the omens be favourable, he gladly goes on his errand and, with the aid of his medicine and the potency of his *mantrams*, causes the victim to come out, when he becomes so stupified, that the magician puts him to death either with a hard blow on his head or by suffocating him to death with two sticks pressed on his neck. This reminds one of the Thugs' strangulation.[1]

People generally believe that an *otiyan* can transform himself into a dog, a cat, an elephant, or a white bull at his will and pleasure, while going to carry out his purpose; but as a matter of fact he is in his human form. It is an illusion or the chimera of the imagination of the people to believe him to be such and such an animal. Similar beliefs are also current among the savage races of other countries. Among the Bushmen, "Sorcerers assume the forms of beasts and jackals". Near Loanda, Livingstone found "A chief may metamorphose himself into a lion, kill any animal he chooses, and resume his proper form." Among the Mayas of Central America, "Sorcerers could transform themselves into dogs, pigs, and other animals." These people still believe in the truth of their transformations, but there are some who totally deny them. They walk with a heavy club making some wild cries in imitation of those wild animals, which lead men to suspect that they appear in their guise, but they are easily made out. For, they

1. I am indebted to a Paraya magician at Shoranur for this information.

are wild and singularly horrible, both human and inhuman at the same time. Their acts during night are nullified by the magicians of higher cults.

This cult has been practised by the Parayans some twenty years ago, to a very large extent, in the rural parts of the northern division of the State, and in the Taluks of Palghat and Valluvanad, and even now, it has not quite died out. The cases of extracting the fœtus and of putting persons to death by *oti*, are not now heard of, owing to the fear of Government officials, landlords, and others in whose lands they live, and who will punish them, should such atrocities be committed in their midst. The records of criminal courts attest the power and prevalence of this persuasion among the more intelligent and higher classes. The Parayans keep the cult a dead secret, and profess total ignorance owing to the fear of punishment.

The following story, told by a respectable pensioned officer and landlord of the State, will not be out of place in connection with this account. A village Nair official of the Valluvanad Taluk, who had two fine bullocks, was asked by a Moplah for the disposal of one of them at any price. The Nair was unwilling to part with him. The former thereupon engaged some of his own men to rob him of the bull, but could not get a suitable opportunity, for the cowshed was under lock and key. One day, the village officer was away from home and was expected rather late at night. Availing themselves of this opportunity, the robbers stood outside the gate, some being engaged in opening the cowshed to remove the bullock. They saw a Parayan and his wife, walking several times round the house, and practising the cult. The Parayan did not see the robbers who were, from the shed witnessing all that they were doing, a young woman coming out and lying on the ground. He would have done his work, if they had remained quiet, but they soon caught hold of him and had him tied to a tree, calling out the owner of the house to come out. The owner of the house, suspecting them to be robbers, did not first respond to their call, but afterwards came out and saw what had taken place. The Parayan and his wife were thrashed, and the robbers gladly rewarded with the bullock they desired. This strange story is avowed to be true.

Religion.

The Parayans of the Tamil Districts adore Siva and Vishnu, and their chief goddess is Athàl who represents Párvathi, and Pidàri, who, in her evil inclinations, is called Káli. Different personifications of Káli and

Párvathi are variously named. They enjoy even now many privileges. In Mysore, a Holeya is a priest for every village goddess. The great Vaishnava reformer Sri Ramanuja Chariar has given them the privilege of entering temples for three days in the year; because they showed him the image of Chelva Pillai, who is an incarnation of Vishnu. The origin of the famous temple of Jagannath is closely connected with a low caste Parayan. There had also been other pious devotees among them.

In Malabar, Cochin, and Travancore, no curious vestiges of their ancient greatness are seen as among their brethren of the Tamil Districts. In respect of religious worship, there are however some points of similarity. They have no temples of their own, though they worship Siva and Káli, whose names they often utter in pious reverence. The following story [1] is told in connection with the origin of their adoration.

In Tretayuga (the second age) a Parayan, named Samvara, and his wife, Puliny were living in a forest. One day they chanced to come across a dilapidated temple, and, while searching there, they came by a *Siralinga* (stone cylinder or image of Siva). They kept and adored it as sacred, gave daily offerings of flesh, smeared it with ashes from the burial ground, and used to partake of the offerings On a certain day, the Paraya devotee could not get the ashes, and he therefore consulted his wife as to what should be done. A lucky idea, but a very sad one, flashed across her mind. She readily offered herself to have her body burned to ashes for the *puja* that day, and persisted that the daily *puja* should not, on any account, be missed. With much grief and reluctance, the husband perpetrated the deed, and performed the *puja*. But after this, he got up and, as was his wont, called out his wife to give her as usual a portion of the *prasadom* (offerings) thinking that she was alive and forgetting for a moment what he had done, when to his utter amazement, he saw her in flesh and blood receiving it. Henceforward, they worshipped the deity very fervently and piously. Highly pleased with them, Siva appeared in person, gave them absolution, and vanished.

Some among the Parayans remember stories of Samvara and Pákkanar, and feel proud that they were born in their midst, and obtained salvation as pious devotees.

Parakutty and Châthan are their minor gods, to whom offerings are made as by the members of other castes. The very

1. Skanda Puranom, Bramhothara *khandom*: Puliny's salvation.

THE PARAYANS DEVIL DANCE.

filthy members of the present generation worship Káli or Bhagavathi. In every village in the rural parts, there are small Bhagavathi temples, to the deity of which they are devoutly attached and who look to their aid in times of illness such as fever, small-pox, cholera, and the like, and also in times of personal calamities. Kodungallur Bhagavathi is their guardian deity. They take part in the festivals (*vela*) connected with the shrine. A few days before the festival a piece of cloth is given to their *velichapad* (oracle), who dresses himself in it, wears round his neck a piece of red cloth, a peculiar dress round his loins, and a few small bells (*chelamba*) tied to a string, round his leg. He is also provided with a suitable covering for the head. With a few others of his caste, one with a basket on his head for paddy, two others with drums, and one with a pipe, he goes to every Nair house and gets one or two measures of paddy and continues to do so for seven days. With this they defray the expenses on behalf of the deity during the festival. On that day their *velichapad* and twenty or thirty others go to a shed put up at a distance from the *kavu* (temple) and delight themselves by dancing and singing to the accompaniment of drum and flute, in honour of the goddess. Some of them put on the guise of ghosts and dance towards the deity, to whom it is supposed to give great pleasure. Thus dead drunk they spend day and night, and on the next morning they depart. The members of the musical party are given three measures of rice for their work before they return home. The festival is called *Vela* and the collection of paddy is known as *Para*.

On the first of every month they perform a ceremony known as *Kalasam* on behalf of the spirits of the departed. They get ready, fish, meat (fried), toddy, rice, parched grain, plantain fruits, cocoanuts, and *pappadam*[1], and place them on a long leaf in front of a lighted lamp. They stand near in a prayerful attitude for a short time and say, "Ye, dead ancestors, come and take these which we have procured for you with much difficulty; and

1. A thin, crisp cake of *uzhunnu* (Phaseolus radiatus).

protect us." It also happens, that one among them works himself into a convulsive fit to act the part of a *velichapad* and speaks to them as if by inspiration. They have no temples, but have what they call *daivappura* (a small thatched shed containing a few stones in it) in front of their huts. Every one is a priest who is fit to perform the *Kalasam*.

On the ninth day of asterism (*Ayiliam*) in the latter part of September or in the beginning of October, the Parayans bring, near a Bhagavathi temple, fine strong he-buffaloes well adorned with garlands of flowers and small bells round their necks. The buffaloes are given a sufficient quantity of toddy with which the Parayans also are dead drunk. These animals belonging to different owners are made to run in competition on the maidan round the temple, when they are irritated and made wild by the peculiar hoarse noise of drum-beating, their loud songs, and cries of the by-standers. This continues for two, three, or four hours in the afternoon of that day. A large number of the Parayans and people of other castes gather round the race-ground to witness the race. It is intended to obtain the favour and good will of the goddess Bhagavathi, and to keep the he-buffaloes strong and healthy. This is a national festival in Malabar known as *Pothu ottal* (Buffalo race).

Funeral customs.

When a grown up member of their caste breathes his last the usual lamentation follows. Relatives and other caste-men assemble, and carry the dead body on a bier to the burial ground, which is either in his own compound or outside, in the neighbourhood. A grave is dug, the floor made smooth, and the body covered with a mat is placed in it. A little rice is put into the grave as food for the spirit of the departed, and it is then filled in with layers of earth. Those assembled return home after bathing, and the chief mourner is either his son or nephew who is in charge of the ceremonies. The pollution lasts for sixteen days, and the ceremonies connected therewith, are precisely the same as those of the Pulayans which shall be described hereafter.

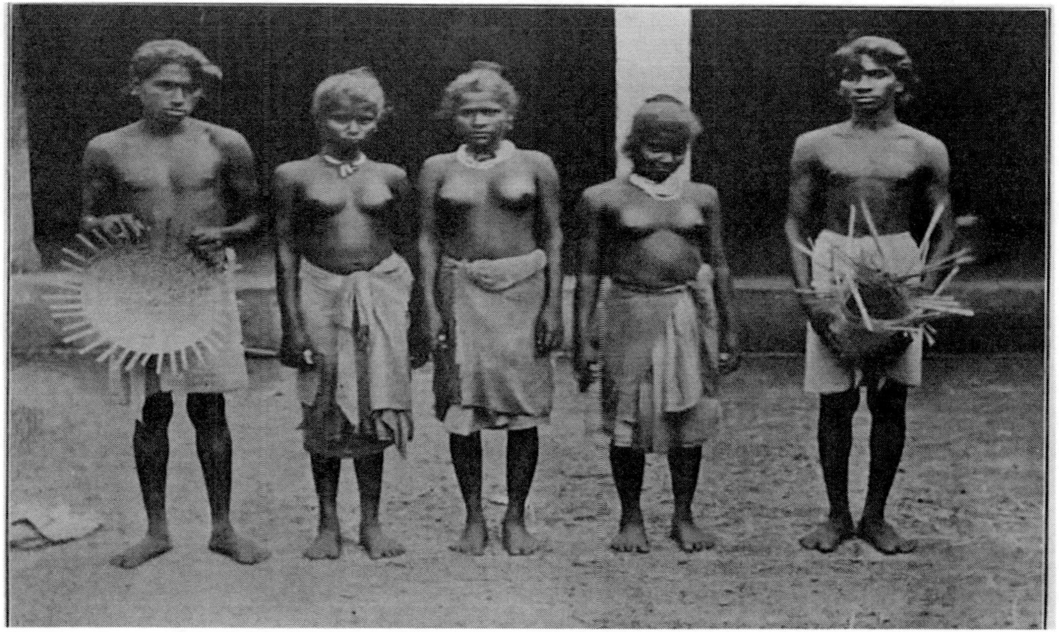

THE PARAYANS' WICKER WORK.

Parayans follow their old occupation, namely, the manufacture of wicker-work (baskets), bamboo mats, and umbrellas. They also engage themselves in every kind of agricultural work, and their wages range from one and a half to two annas worth of paddy. They plough the ground, but do not use the buffaloes, which are regarded as unclean. They bathe at the mere touch of them, but have no objection to using bullocks. They skin animals and reserve the hides for themselves. It is said that, with few exceptions, all their women are basket-makers, netters, and weavers. The men supply them with bamboos, and sometimes take part in the work. The tools of the basket-maker are of the simplest character, those necessary for the harvesting of the material and those used in the manufacture. Fine splints of bamboo are made by the males and the women weave them. In making baskets, the woman starts from the centre of the bottom, coiling and warping the splints as she proceeds with the split pieces, so as to bind it to the preceding turn, drawing her splints between the spirals. When the splint is exhausted, the end is tucked in behind the spiral and another one started in the same manner but so carefully joined as to escape detection. In the northern parts of the State, this industry is carried on by the Kavaras. They supply the local wants, and the bamboo mats are largely sent for sale beyond the State. Merchants give some advance to the Parayans for the making of bamboo mats.

Occupation.

The Parayans are treated as the lowest of low castes, and yet they do not eat at the hands of Ulladans, Nayadis, and Pulayans, who are regarded as inferior to them. As they are complete outcasts, their presence carries pollution to the members of higher castes within about half a furlong. They cannot walk through the public roads nor in the vicinity of houses occupied by the higher castes. Even at the police station where they were examined, they stood at such a long distance, that they could not distinctly

Social status.

be heard. They cannot draw water from the wells belonging to other castes from whom they live far remote, but can freely do so from the wells of Mahomadans, Christians or Pulayans. They are their own barber and washerman. They take part in the festivals of Bhagavathi temples in rural parts, but have to stand far away from them and cannot, on any account, approach the temple walls. Pulayans consider themselves superior to the Parayans. Strictly orthodox Pulayans have to bathe five times, and let blood flow in order to be purified from pollution if they touch a Parayan.

Appearance.

The Parayans are either very dark brown or blackish in complexion. Their hair is black, and noses short and flat or slightly concave with somewhat wide nostrils. There eyes are large, round, and black. They appear to be stronger than the Pulayans and very rarely bathe or wash their bodies. A cloth purchased at harvest time, is worn till it falls to fine pieces. Their dress, food, and dwelling are all alike uncleanly.

Conclusion.

In rural parts, Parayans' huts may be seen far away on hill side, and the inmates appear so cowardly that, at the sight of the approach of a member of some higher caste, they run away to the forest close by. On the other hand they are much dreaded on account of their witchcraft. It is said, that, at times, they kidnap the children of the Nairs and hide them in the forest, to bring them up as their own. Many, now-a-days, become converts to Christianity, and under Christian influence and teaching, they are rendered more sensible and acceptable to their employers.

THE PARAYA WOMEN.

CHAPTER V.

THE PULAYANS.

The Pulayans of Cochin form an important class of the agrestic serfs, both in point of number and as forming a typical representative of a tribe. They are, in the northern parts of the State, called the Cherumans. They are wholly illiterate and speak a kind of low Malayalam largely mixed up with Tamil words and terminations. It is very probable, that they are the descendants of the original inhabitants of Kerala who must have been Tamil-speaking, for the earliest form of the Malayalam language is Kodum Tamil (the oldest form of Tamil). Dr. A. H. Keane remarks, that the fact that these and other low tribes speaking Dravidian Malayalam is very curious, and that it finds its analogue in the broken English of the Negroes of North America and elsewhere. He thinks that they had a language which is now forgotten. When they speak of bodily members such as an eye or ear to a superior, they prefix to it the epithet 'old' and say 'old eye' or 'old ear'. They call their children 'calves,' their silver 'copper,' and their paddy 'chaff'. When addressing one, they begin by saying, 'Your slave has got permission'. The Nairs they call *thampurans* (lords).

Traditions of the caste.

The question of their origin is still undecided. The word 'Pulayan' is derived from '*pula*' which means pollution. If the word '*pula*' may be regarded as another form of '*palla*', the Pallans of the Tamil Districts and the Pulayans of Cochin, Travancore, and Malabar are identical tribes, who have been, from a remote period, subject to the same kind of treatment from their masters. The name 'Cherumans' or 'Cheramakkal' is said to signify 'the sons of the soil,' but some say it means *cheriamakkal* (little children), as Parasurama is said to have directed their being cared for and treated as such,

It is said that Malabar constituted the ancient Chera kingdom. In the name Cheranad or the country (*nad*) of the Cheras given to the district lying along the coast, and inland south-east of Calicut, we still find that the ancient name is preserved. Chernad, part of the Ernad Taluk and the neighbourhood of it, appear to have been the most thickly populated parts of the country. Ernad, Valluvanad, and Ponnani are the three Taluks of Malabar from which converts to Islam have been drawn from the slave population, which must have been denser in these Taluks than elsewhere. There is therefore something to be said in favour of the view that the Pulayans or Cherumans were the aborigines of Malabar. According to one tradition they are supposed to be descendants of the aborigines conquered by the Chola kings who preferred slavery to freedom and starvation in the jungles. The native tradition assigns their creation to Parasurama who is said to have given them to the Brahmans to till the soil. They are regarded, by some, as the descendants of the Dravidian immigrants and, by others, as the descendants of the old Turanean race that peopled India before the Aryan invasion. Like Africa, India has received influxes of population from other parts of the world, but the dark peoples are now merged in the fairer invaders. Dr. A. H. Keane also is of the same opinion, and adds, that, judging from the short stature, low forehead, and the high cheek bones, they belong to the Negrito race, which once formed a substratum throughout the peninsula, though now mainly submerged by the later arrivals of the Kolerians, Dravidians, and the Aryans. From traditions current among the Pulayans themselves, it would appear, that once upon a time they had dominions over several parts of the country. A person called Aikkara Yajaman whose ancestors were Pulaya kings, is still held in considerable respect by the Pulayans of north Travancore and duly acknowledged as their chieftain, and lord, while the name Aikkaranad still remains to suggest that there is some truth in the ancient tale. In Trivandrum on the banks of the Velli lake is a hill called Pulayanar Kotta (fort), where it is believed that a

Pulaya king once ruled. The Pulayans round Trivandrum, assert even to this day, that in former times, a Pulaya king ruled and had his castle not far from the present capital of Travancore.

As a Parayan found at Melkota the image of Chelva Pillai, as a Savara was originally in possession of the sacred stone which became the idol in the temple of Jagannath, so also is the worship of Padmanabha in Trivandrum, intimately connected with a Pulayan. Once, the story goes, a Pulakalli (Pulaya woman) who was living with her husband in the *Ananthan kadu* (jungle) suddenly heard the cry of a baby. She rushed to the spot, and saw to her surprise a child lying on the ground, protected by a cobra. She had pity on it and nursed it like her own. The appearance of the snake intimated to her the divine origin of the infant. This proved to be true, for the child was an incarnation of Vishnu. As soon as the Raja of Travancore heard of the wonderful event, he built a shrine on the spot where the baby had been found and dedicated it to Padmanabha.

There is also another story regarding the origin of these people. The Pulayans got, as a boon from the god Siva, along with a spade and an axe, the right to clear forests, to cultivate lands, and to own them. When other people came and took possession of their lands, they were advised to work under them. That they were the original inhabitants of the land is proved by certain rights they have possessed from time immemorial in the Bhagavathi temples in the villages they live in.

Regarding the origin of the Thanda Pulayans, one of the sub-tribes among the Pulayans of the southern parts of the State, the following account is given. The name 'Thanda Pulayan' is given to them because of the *thanda* garment worn by their females. *Thanda* is a water-plant (Isolepis articulata Nees), the leaves of which are cut into lengths of two feet woven at one end and tied round their waist, in such a manner that the strings unwoven hang loosely round the loins up to the knees. In regard to the origin of this kind of dress, there is a curious story that a certain high caste-man who owned lands in the localities inhabited by these people, chanced to sow seeds and plant vegetables. He was surprised to find that his work was useless, for he found that everything he did, disappeared in a mysterious manner. Not a trace of what he sowed or planted was to be seen the next day. With a view to clear the mystery, he kept a close watch at night, when he saw coming out of a hole, certain human beings quite naked. They were pursued, when a man and a woman were caught. Impressed with the sense of shame at their wretched condition, he threw his upper garment to the male. Having nothing to give to the other, he plucked and threw a few *thanda* leaves on her to dress herself with. They are also called Kuzhi Pulayans, because they were found emerging from a pit (*kuzhi*).

In Travancore, the Pulayans are said to have been divided into the eastern and western clans. The eastern Pulayans were the slaves of Duryodhana, while those of the west were attached to the Pandus. These formed the two rival parties in the war of the Mahabharata. The defeat of Duryodhana is the cause of their degradation. Some attempts were made to trace the origin of this story, but nobody could enlighten me on the subject.

Predial slavery.

By far the greater part of the labour in the field was and is even now performed by the Cherumans or Pulayans in Malabar, Cochin, and Travancore. These people were the absolute property of the *thampurans* or lords, and were employed in any kind of labour which their masters pleased. They were not attached to the soil, but might be sold or transferred in any manner that their masters thought fit; only a wife could not be sold separately. Children were separated from their parents, and brothers from their sisters. The slaves were of different castes, namely, Pulayans or Cherumans, Eralans, and Parayans, and the differences in the marriage customs of these castes caused considerable variations in the

THE THANDAPULAYA WOMEN.

rights of masters to the children of their slaves, as these rights depended upon the caste to which they belonged. The master was bound to give the slave a certain allowance of provisions. A man or woman able to work received two to three annas worth of paddy daily. Children and old persons unable to work were given half this pittance, while no allowance whatever was given for infants. This was totally inadequate to support them, but the slaves on each estate used to get one twenty-first part of the gross paddy crop in order to encourage them to be careful and industrious. A male slave received seven cubits of cloth—sufficient for two *mundus*—and a woman fourteen cubits—sufficient for two *muris*.

Condition of the slaves in former times.

Slavery was common in former times throughout the western coast and the prejudices of the high caste people rendered the degradation of the slaves complete. They were in many places attached to the soil, and their market value was not much above that of the cattle united with them in the same bondage, while they were far below them in the estimation in which they were held. Though a slavery deserving commiseration, it was by no means the most rigid form of that wretched state. They were regarded with capricious indifference by their masters, who were either Brahmans, Nairs or Native Christians, who, though they were divided in caste, agreed in oppression. Personal chastisement was not often inflicted, yet they experienced little sympathy in sickness, when they were left to nature. They were also dismissed to poverty, and in age abandoned. Manumission was rarely practised nor indeed even desired. They never possessed property of any kind. Their freedom could only be productive of starvation or a change of servitude which occurred, when they were presented to a temple in compliance with some superstitious vow.

In very early times the murder of a slave was scarcely considered a crime. The deed of transfer generally contained the clause, "You may sell or kill him or her." They had no ideas beyond their occupation, and were never guilty of any violence to their masters, to whom they were absolutely obedient from the sluggish apathy of their character, which rendered them ever mindful of their own lot. Being themselves born slaves, their children also were born slaves, and every landlord had a number of them. In cases of indigence, a Pulaya uncle and mother might sell a child for about fourteen or seventeen rupees, and if a higher price had been given, it would have been of no use to them, as the proprietor would have taken the surplus. The eldest son was the property of the owner, but the mother had also the right of redeeming the first child for four rupees and a half whether the possessor liked it or not.

The subsistence of the slaves.

The Pulayans were employed only in agriculture and their labours were repaid in grain, their wages being three measures of paddy for a man, two for a woman, and one for a child. This was all they had to live upon, and even this was not regularly paid, being reduced to half on days they did not work, and withheld entirely if they showed any symptoms of refractoriness. Harvest to them was a period of comparative plenty, but their meagre, squalid appearance often betrayed the insufficiency of their diet to which both sexes were equally doomed. A large number of slaves belonged to the Government to which they were escheated along with other property on the extinction of their owners' families, and they were partly employed on Government lands and partly rented to ryots. These poor creatures, as forming a peculiar and numerous caste, were granted certain privileges which secured their maintenance, so that none might perish from want. Their masters no doubt were bound to give them food, but in Malabar, the Pulayans had the right of building, planting, and doing all agricultural work, and for that, they received wages in paddy. The estates on which they worked might belong to their masters or to some one else. If their master were not in need of out-door labour, they might seek it elsewhere, but they had to take care to be ready to appear before him at his summons, and if they failed to appear, they were punished.

In ancient times slaves were held by different kinds of tenure. There were, says Francis Buchanan, three modes of transferring the usufruct slaves. The first was by *jenm* or sale, where the full value of the slave was given, and the property was entirely transferred to a new master who was, in some measure, bound by his interest to attend to the welfare of his slave. A young man with his wife used to be sold for seventy or hundred rupees. Four or five children, two of whom were beginning to work, would make the family worth one hundred and forty or one hundred and seventy rupees. The second manner of transferring the labour of slaves was by *kanom* or mortgage. The proprietor by this received a loan of money, generally two-thirds of the value of the slaves, and a small quantity of paddy to show that his right over them still existed. He might either resume his property, *i. e.*, the slaves, whenever he pleased to repay the money borrowed without the payment of any interest. In the case of any of the slaves dying, the *kanom* holder was bound to supply another of equal value. The lender of the money maintained them and had their labour for the interest of his money and for their support. The third method of transferring or employing slaves was letting them out for *pattom* or rent. In this case, for an annual sum, the master lent them to another man who commanded their labour and supported them. The annual *pattom* or rent was two rupees and a quarter, and half as much for a woman. The last two tenures, says Buchanan, were abominable; for the person who exacted the labour and furnished the subsistence of the slave, was directly interested in increasing the former and diminishing the latter as much as possible. In fact the slaves were severely treated, and their diminutive stature and squalid appearance certified to the want of adequate nourishment. Five families of slaves numbering twenty-five persons of all ages are, it may be mentioned, adequate for the cultivation of twelve and a half acres of rice land.

Abolition of slavery.

Theoretically serfdom in Malabar was abolished about sixty years ago. Mr. Logan gives the following account of the abolition of slavery in his Manual of

Malabar:—The question of slavery and the slave trade attracted the early attention of the Honourable Company's Government. In the year 1792, the year in which British rule commenced, a proclamation was issued against dealing in slaves. A person offering a slave for sale was considered to be a thief. Both the dealer and the purchaser were severely dealt with. Fishermen and Moplahs conveying slaves were severely flogged and fined at the rate of ten rupees for each slave, and the vessels used in trade were confiscated. This proclamation was directed against the prevalent practice of robbers carrying off by force the children of the most useful inhabitants, the Tiyyans, and their cultivators. This practice was kept alive by the facility with which the slaves could be sold on the coast to the agents of vessels, engaged in the trade, sailing from the French settlement at Mahe and the Dutch settlement at Cochin. These ships in general, carried the slaves to the French islands. In 1819 the Principal Collector wrote a report on the condition of the Cherumans, and received orders, that the practice of selling slaves for arrears of revenue be immediately discontinued. In 1836, the Government ordered a remission in the Collector's accounts of Rs. 927—13—0 which was the annual revenue from the slaves on the Government lands in Malabar. In 1841, Mr. E. B. Thomas, the Judge at Calicut, wrote in strong terms, a letter to Sadir Adalat in which he pointed out that women in some Taluks fetched high prices in order to breed slaves; that the average cost of a young male under ten years was about Rs. 3—8—0, of a female somewhat less; that an infant ten months in age was sold in a court auction for Rs. 1—10—6; and that, in a recent suit, the right to twenty slaves was the sole matter for litigation and was disposed of on its merits. In a further letter he pointed out that the slaves had increased in numbers. The Government of India passed Act V of 1843 of which the provisions were widely published throughout Malabar. "Any person claiming a slave as *jenm, kanom* or *panayam,* the right of such claim will not be investigated into at any one of the public offices or courts." In 1852, and again in 1855, the fact that traffic in slaves still continued, was brought to the notice of the Government, but no measures for the emancipation of the Cherumans were deemed to be necessary. The penalties for slave dealing contained in the Penal Code which came into force on 1st January, 1862 were the final blow to slavery in India, especially in Malabar. [1]

In the Cochin State also, the same kind of slavery and slave dealing as was prevailing in Malabar, had been long in existence. A copy of the proclamation dealing with the abolition of slavery and the slave trade was communicated to His Highness the then Raja of the State. It was published in the same year, declaring it a serious offence to buy and sell slaves in the State, to thrash and confine them for petty faults. It also put a stop to the sale of slaves for court decrees and arrears of rent, and gave freedom to the Pulaya slaves residing and working in the Government lands.

The present condition of the slaves.

Though emancipated the Pulayans were for a long time, and are even now in many localities, more or less in the same condition as formerly, and have been unable to appreciate the benefits conferred upon them. They are still obliged to depend upon their masters for maintenance. The extreme conservatism of their masters and their bigotted adherence to caste, coupled with the primitive customs of the people, and the physical configuration of the soil prevented them from having any intercourse with the outside world and caused their utter degradation. Their name is still connected with everything revolting, and they are shunned as if infected with plague. The high caste-men view their presence with a mixture of alarm and indignation and even towns and markets would be considered to be defiled by their approach. The old men amongst the Pulayans still say, that they were better off in the days previous to their emancipation, for they were then well fed, married, and looked

1. Logan's Manual of Malabar, pages 148 to 151.

after by their masters, while they are now left to a great extent to shift for themselves. Though slavery has now been abolished for many years, the name slave, *valliyal*, (a person receiving *valli*, the allowance of paddy given to a slave) still survives, and there is bondage real though not nominal. There are *jenmies* (landlords) and farmers in the State owning twenty, thirty, and even more than a hundred Pulayans who work under them and are satisfied with the two or two and a half measures of paddy doled out to them as wages for their hard work in the fields during the day and for watching the crops at night. Now-a-days, their masters are afraid of their running away, but do nothing to improve their condition, and their wages are still at the rates above referred to. In some places that I visited, I found I was regarded with suspicion, as it was thought, that I was being employed by the Government, with a view to loosening the existing bond between the Pulayans and their masters. Nevertheless their condition is slowly changing. They have begun to understand that they are no longer in a state of bondage under their masters. Some go to plantations in the Wynaad or to work in the Kolar gold mines, where they get high wages for their work, and missionaries of various societies do their best to improve their social condition.

Internal structure of the caste.

There are numerous classes or subdivisions among the Pulayans, and though all are regarded as degraded by the higher castes, they are as punctilious as to the shades of difference between them and as to questions of social precedence, as are their more fortunate masters, the Nairs. The total number of subdivisions in Malabar according to the last census statistics is thirty-seven, of which the most important were Kanakka Cherumans, Pula Cherumans, Eralans, Koodans, and Rolans. In the northern parts of the Cochin State, especially in the Chittur Taluk, the following sub-tribes which are merely endogamous septs are found in the order of social precedence in which it is stated: Eralans or Era Cherumans, so called because of their being permitted to come as far as the eaves (*era*) of the Izhuva houses. Konga Cherumans, Koodans, Kanakka Cherumans, and Pula Cherumans or Pasu Pulayans. In the southern parts of the State, the Pulayans are divided into several classes, namely, Kulamary or Valluva Pulayans, Vettuvans or Vettuva Pulayans, and Thanda Pulayans. There are quite different divisions in Travancore. The fact is that in rural parts they form a kind of isolated community consisting of one or two sub-tribes, each professing its superiority to the other with no intermarriage nor interdining, and professing total ignorance of their brethren in other localities. Hence a proper classification in the order of social precedence becomes difficult, each sub-tribe claiming superiority to the other. Each sub-tribe is further subdivided into *illams* or *koottams* (family groups) which are ascertained during marriage negotiations so as to avoid connections being formed between the members of the same family group. The following are the names of some of them obtained from the Pulayans around Cochin: Thandelathu Koottam, Moothanam Koottam, Nambiyar Koottam, Thachili Koottam, Pulikunnethu Koottam, Paruthi Koottam, Kochanam Koottam, Mannathu Koottam, and Naringana Koottam. These names are either the house names of their masters or those of the masters whose slaves their ancestors may have been in former times. Invariably the Koottams go after the names of their masters.

Habitations.

Their habitations, which are generally called *madams*, are put up on the banks of fields, or nestle under trees along their borders, so that they may watch the crops after the toils of the day are over. They are so situated as to be far out of the way of polluting high caste people. The Pulayans were discouraged from erecting better accommodation under the idea, that, if they were more comfortable they would be less disposed to move as cultivation required. Their huts are similar to those of the poorest among other low castes. The floor is slightly raised and is generally damp during the rainy months. The roof which is thatched either with palmyra or plaited cocoanut leaves, is supported on four or six bamboo or wooden posts, with the sides covered with bamboo mats, palmyra leaves, plaited cocoanut leaves or reeds. In some parts huts with mud walls and thatched roofs are also seen. There is only a single room and the door is low and made of a single palm leaf or reeds. Sometimes a small low opening serves the purpose of the door. The fire-place is in one corner of the hut, and cooking is done inside the hut in the rainy months and outside during summer. These huts are deficient in ventilation and the air is always more or less foul. In the Chittur and Palghat Taluks, the huts of the Kanakka Cherumans are made of mud walls, with wooden doors and roofs thatched with palmyra leaves. They are provided with verandahs either in front or on all sides, and are situated in small compounds (*parambas*) in the midst of paddy fields. Their furniture consists only of a few mats, and their utensils of a few pots for cooking and for keeping water, and a few dishes for holding food. In addition to these, I found in the huts examined, a wooden mortar and a few pestles for pounding rice, several pans, a few fish baskets, a few cocoanut shells for keeping salt and other things, a few baskets, some big and small, (in one of which their dirty cloths were kept), some mats of their own making, and a vessel for containing toddy. These form the total property of a Pulayan and seem to satisfy all his requirements.

Puberty customs.

When a Pulaya girl comes of age, she is lodged in a separate hut for seven days, during which food is served to her at a distance, and she is forbidden to go out and play with her friends. On the morning of the first day, a song called *malapattu* is sung for an hour by a Parayan to the accompaniment of drum and pipe, for which he gets seven annas worth of paddy and his assistants get three annas each. As soon as this is over, seven cocoanuts are broken, and the water is poured over the head of the girl, and the broken halves are distributed among the five *vallons* and the seven girls who are invited to take part in the performance of the ceremony, besides the caste-men of the *kara* (village). On the morning of the seventh day, the *vallons* of the *kara* and the caste-men are again invited, when the latter bring with them some rice, vegetables, and toddy to defray the expenses of the feast. Some more water is also poured on the girl's head at the time and each of the *vallons* is paid a measure of rice. At dawn, the chief host, the mother of the girl gives oil to the seven Pulaya maidens and to her daughter for an oil bath, when they go to a neighbouring tank or stream to bathe and return home. The girl is then neatly dressed and adorned in her best. Her face is painted yellow and marked with spots of various colours. She stands before a few Parayans, who play on their flute and drum to cast out the demons, if any, from her body. The girl leaps with frantic movements if she is possessed with them, in which case, the Parayans transfer them to a tree close by, driving a nail into the trunk after due offerings. If she is not possessed with them, she remains unmoved, and the Parayans bring the music to a close. The girl is again bathed with her companions who are all treated to a dinner, and the ceremony comes to an end with a feast to the caste-men. The ceremony described above is performed by the Valluva Pulayans in the southern parts, near and around the suburbs of Cochin, but is unknown among other sub-tribes elsewhere. It is a belief among these and other people that girls and women during the menses are under the malign influence of demons which are cast out by ceremonial offerings.

Marriage customs.

Among the Pulayans marriage is endogamous so far as the sub-tribe is concerned. It is, however, strictly prohibited among the members of the same *koottam* (clan). In the Chittur and Palghat Taluks the members of the same village do not generally marry, for they believe that their ancestors may have been the slaves of some local landlord, and may have descended from the same parents, though their relationship may be forgotten. In many places a young man marries the daughter of his maternal uncle.

The marriage customs of the Pulayans are different in different places. In more than half a dozen places where my notes have been taken, they vary with the subdivisions of the caste. In the southern part of the State the Pulaya girls are married before they are grown up, while in other places, this custom is not followed. Where it is followed, and near and around Cochin the custom is universal, it is considered a great disgrace for a girl to remain unmarried. In some cases if a girl is too poor to be married, the caste-men of her *kara* or village raise a subscription and marry her to one of themselves. In some subdivisions the relations of girls, who fail to obtain husbands for them, lose all their rights over them, and in former times such girls were handed over to the head-men (*vallons*) who either married them to their own sons or sold them to slave-masters.

The marriage customs of the Pulayans, as has been said, vary in different places as their subdivisions. When a Pulayan wishes to marry, he applies to his master who is bound to defray his expenses. He gives two rupees to the bride's master, one rupee seven annas to her mother, four and a half annas worth of cloth to the bride, seven annas worth of cloth to the bridegroom, and about three rupees for the marriage feast. In all the expenses may come to about ten rupees. The ceremony consists in putting a brass ring on the bride's finger, which is followed by a feast to friends and relations of the *kara* (village) who are invited. The wife accompanies the bridegroom on the following day. If the husband becomes tired of his wife, he may, with her consent, give her to any other person who will pay the expenses incurred at the marriage. In some cases the husband and wife serve different masters, and the women of this class are given in usufruct, scarcely ever in complete possession. The eldest male child belongs to the master of the father; the rest of the family remain with the mother, while young, but being the property of the owner revert to him when of an age to be useful. She also follows in the event of her becoming a widow.

In some places a man brings a woman to his master and says that he wishes to keep her as his wife. She receives her allowance of rice, but she may leave her husband when she likes, and is not particular in changing one spouse for another. The husband's master by the old law maintains his wife and children until they are able to work, when the eldest son becomes his property and the other children the property of the mother's master.

In other places the marriage ceremonies of the Era Cherumans are more formal. The bridegroom's party goes to the bride's hut and presents rice and betel-leaf to the head of the family, and then asks for the bride. Consent is indicated by the bride's brother placing some rice and cloth in the midst of the assembly and throwing rice on the head-man of the caste who is present. On the appointed day the bridegroom goes to the hut with two companions and presents the girl with cloth and three rupees two annas. From that day he is regarded as her husband, but the girl cannot be taken to the hut until the ceremony called *Mangalam* is performed. The bridegroom's party goes in procession to the bride's hut where a feast awaits them. The man presents sweetmeats to the girl's brother. Then the caste priest recites the names and the family history of the two persons and the names of their masters and deities. They are seated in a pandal before a lamp and a heap of rice, when one of the assembly gets up and delivers a speech on the duties of married life, touching upon the evils of theft, cheating, adultery, and the like. Rice is thrown on the heads of the couple and the man prostrates himself at the feet of the elders. The next day they proceed to the husband's hut, and rice is again thrown on their heads. Then the party assembled makes presents to the pair, a part of which goes to the priest and a part to the master of the husband.

Among the Konga Cherumans, a young man who wishes to marry sends his sister to tie the *tali* and bring her to his family. The custom is borrowed from the Izhuvans of the same Taluk.

In the Oorakam Proverthy of the Trichur Taluk, where my notes were taken, I find that the marriage prevalent among the Pulayans of that locality and the neighbouring parts is a rude form of *sambandham* (free will union), the form of marriage which prevails among the Nairs, whose serfs a large majority of them are. A young woman's husband is called a *sambandhakaran*, and he comes to her hut with his wages after the day's work and stays there for the night. Both may serve under different masters. A somewhat similar custom prevails among the Pula Cherumans of the Trichur Taluk. The connection is called *merungu kooduka* which means to tame or to associate with the girl. A young man who wishes to marry goes to the parents of the young woman and asks their consent to associate with their daughter. If they approve, he goes to her at night as often as he likes. The woman seldom comes to stay in the husband's hut and only with the permission of the *thamar* (landlord).

The Kanakka Cherumans in the northern parts of the State have the following form of marriage. The preliminary arrangements for the wedding are made in the bride's hut in the presence of her parents, relations, and the caste-men of the village. The auspicious day for the wedding is fixed, and a sum of one rupee seven annas is paid as the bride's price. Those assembled are treated to a dinner. A similar entertainment is also held at the bridegroom's hut to the parents of the bride, her uncle, and others who come to see the bridegroom. On the morning of the day fixed for the wedding, the bridegroom and his party go to the bride's hut where they are welcomed and seated on mats in a small pandal put up for the occasion. A *muri* (a piece of cloth), a *thoda* (ear disc), and two small *mundus* (pieces of cloth) are the marriage presents to the bride elect. A vessel full of paddy, a lighted lamp, and a cocoanut are placed on a conspicuous part in the booth, to which the bride is taken and seated by the side of the bridegroom. With prayers to their gods for the blessings on the couple, the bridegroom ties the *tali* round the neck of the bride. The ceremony is soon closed with a grand feast to the guests and others invited to attend the wedding. Toddy is an indispensable item of the feast. During the night they amuse themselves by dancing a kind of wild dance in which both men and women joyfully take part. The next day the bridegroom goes to his own hut along with his wife and his party. The guests are entertained in his hut. After a week, two persons from the bride's hut come to invite the bridegroom and the bride to the hut of the latter, where the bridegroom stays for a few days, and returns home. The marriage is now practically over and he goes to the bride's hut as often as he likes. Before the bridegroom enters the pandal, the bride has to go seven times round the pandal with seven virgins also before her. By a strange custom the bride's mother does not approach the bridegroom, lest it may cause ceremonial pollution.

The marriage customs of the Valluva Pulayans in the southern parts of the State especially in the Cochin-Kanayanur Taluk are more formal and interesting. The average age of a young man for marriage is between fifteen and twenty, while that of a girl is between ten and twelve. Before a young Pulayan thinks of marriage, he has to contract a formal and voluntary friendship with another young Pulayan of the same age and locality. If he is not socially inclined, his father selects one for him from a Pulaya family of the same or higher status, but not of the same *illam*. If the two parents agree among themselves, they meet in the hut of either of them with a view to solemnising it. They fix a day for the ceremony and invite their *vallon* and the caste-men of the village. The guests are treated to a feast in the usual Pulaya fashion. The chief guest and the host eat together from the same dish. After the feast, the father of the boy who has to obtain a friend for his son enquires of the *vallon* and those assembled there, whether he may be permitted to buy friendship by the payment of money. They give their permission and the boy's father gives the money to the father of the selected friend. The two boys then clasp hands and they are never to quarrel. The new friend from that date, becomes a member of the boy's family. He comes in and goes out of their hut as he likes. There is no ceremony performed in it, nor anything done without consulting him. He is thus an inseparable factor in all ceremonies especially in marriage.

The first observance in marriage consists in seeing the girl. The bridegroom elect, his friend, father, and maternal uncle go to the bride's hut to see whether they are satisfied with the girl. If the wedding is not to take place at an early date, the bridegroom's parents have to keep up their claim on the bride elect, by sending presents to her guardians. The presents, generally sweetmeats, are taken to her hut by the bridegroom and his friend, who are well fed by the mother of the girl and are given a few necessaries, when they take leave of her the next morning. The next observance is the marriage negotiation, which consists in giving the bride's price and choosing an auspicious day in consultation with the local astrologer (Kaniyan). On the evening previous to the wedding, the friends and relations of the bridegroom are treated to a feast in his hut. Next day at dawn, the bridegroom and his friend purified by a bath, and each neatly dressed in a white cloth with a handkerchief tied over it, and with a knife stuck into their girdles, go to the hut of the bride elect, accompanied by a party of friends. They are all well received and seated on mats spread on the floor. Upon a mat specially made by the bride's mother are placed three measures of rice, some particles of gold, a brass plate, a plank with a white and red cover on it. The bridegroom, after making seven rounds around the pandal, stands on the plank and the bride soon follows making three rounds, when four women hold a canopy of cloth over her head and seven virgins go in front of her. The bride then stands beside her man and then they face each other. The girl's guardian puts on the wedding necklace, a gold bead on a string. Musical tunes are played, and prayers are offered up to the sun to bless the necklace which is tied round the neck of the girl. The bridegroom's friend standing behind tightens the knot already made. The religious part of the ceremony is now over, and the bridegroom and the bride are taken inside the hut, and food is served to them in the same leaf. Next the guests are fed, and then they begin the *poli* or subscription. A piece of silk or any red cloth is spread on the floor or a brass plate is placed before the husband. The guests assembled put in a few annas and take leave of the chief host as they depart. The bride is soon taken to the bridegroom's hut, and her parents visit her the next day and get a consideration in return. On the fourth day the bridegroom and the bride bathe and worship the local deity, and on the seventh day they again return to the bride's hut, when the *tali* is formally removed from the neck of the girl who is bedecked with brass beads round her neck, rings in her ears, and armlets. The next morning, the mother-in-law presents her son-in-law and his friend with a few necessaries of life and sends them home with her daughter.

At a wedding among the Cherumans of Malabar, when the wedding party sets out they form a large gang of people, and at intervals, the men set to at stick play, the women singing in chorus to encourage them. Let us see—let us see—the stick play (*vaditallu*), Oh Cherumar! At their weddings men and women mingle indiscriminately in dancing. On the arrival of the bride at the bridegroom's hut, she is expected to weep loudly and deplore her fate; and, on entering, she must tread on a pestle placed across the threshold. The custom prevails among the Pula Cherumans and is dying out.

In the northern parts of the State, there is a relic of the primitive custom, namely, that a young woman before marriage mates with one or two paramours with the connivance of her parents. Eventually one of them marries her, but this illicit union ceases at once after marriage.

Thanda marriage.

The Thanda Pulaya girls are married either before or after they come of age, but there is another ceremony performed for every girl during her seventh or eighth year. This is called the *Thanda kalyanam* or *Thanda* marriage. It consists in having the girl dressed, in an auspicious hour, usually at twelve o'clock on the day appointed, with a leafy garment made of the *thanda* plant by a woman, generally a relative, or, in her absence, one that is selected for the purpose. The relations and friends are invited and entertained with rice, curry, toddy, and fish obtained from the back-water. The ceremony comes to an end after meals. Before this ceremony, the girl is devoid of any dress except the tender bark of an areca plant to prevent exposure. The *thanda* garment can be worn only after the performance of this ceremony.

Among the Thanda Pulayans, the wedding presents to the girl consist of a piece of cloth and a marriage badge (*tali*) made of conch shell. The price of the girl, which is usually six and a quarter to ten and a half rupees, is given by the parents of the bridegroom before the performance of the ceremony. Of this amount, one rupee ten and a half annas goes to the brother of the bride's father; similar sums are given to the bride's maternal uncle and *thamar* or the landlord, while the balance is received by the parents of the bride. The *tali* is tied round the girl's neck at the auspicious hour usually at twelve o'clock, after which the guests assembled are sumptuously fed with rice, curry, fish, and toddy The girl is then taken to her landlord who gives one rupee worth of paddy and all the cocoanuts of the tree on which she happens to lean. The marriage is over by the evening, when the bride is taken to the hut of the bridegroom. At the time of departure, the bride's uncle, catching hold of her hand, gives her in charge of the bridegroom's uncle. Usually nobody accompanies the girl to her husband's hut at the time.

Polygamy and polyandry are almost unknown, but the former is common among the Thanda Pulayans. The Kanakka Cherumans of Palghat consider it a disgrace to have two wives located either in the same or different huts. Men who have two wives are not admitted into their society. A Thanda Pulayan may take two or three wives all married in the usual fashion.

A woman, after the death of her husband, may marry anybody she likes, except her brother-in-law. If she marries again, the children, if any, go with the mother to the new husband; and, if sufficiently grown up, they stay in the mother's family, and live by their own labour. A woman who does not like her husband may leave him after returning the money spent on her marriage, while a man who wishes to relinquish his wife, is not entitled to any portion of the money spent. In the former case the money is generally provided by the new husband.

Pregnancy and childbirth.

During the seventh month of pregnancy of a young woman, the ceremony of *Pulikudi* or tamarind juice drinking is performed for her, similar to that performed for the young women of other castes. This is also an occasion for finding out whether or not she is possessed, and, if she is, of casting out the devils that are in her. The wife is brought back to the hut of her own family. The devil-driver erects a tentlike structure, and covers it with plantain bark and leaves of the cocoanut tree. The flower of an areca palm is fixed at the apex. A cocoanut palm flower is cut out and covered with a piece of cloth, the cut part being exposed. The woman is seated in front of the tentlike structure with the flower in her lap, which symbolizes the yet unborn child. The water of a green cocoanut in spoons made of the leaf of the jack tree is poured over the cut end by those assembled, namely, the *vallon*, the guardian, the brothers, and sisters present. The devil-driver then breaks open the flower, and, by looking at the fruits, predicts the sex of the child to be born. If there are fruits at the end nearest the stem, the child will live, and if the number of fruits is even, there will be twins. There will be a death if any fruit is not well formed. The devil-driver repeats an incantation whereby he invokes the aid of Kàli who is believed to be present in the tent. He fans the woman with the flower, and she throws up rice and a flower on it. He repeats another incantation, which is a prayer to Kali, to cast out the devil from her body. This magical ceremony is called *Garbha-bali* (pregnancy offering).

The structure, with the offering, is taken up and placed in a corner of the compound reserved for gods. The devotee then goes through the remaining forms of the ceremony. She pours into twenty-one leaf spoons placed in front of the tent, a mixture of cow's milk, water of the tender cocoanut, flowers, and turmeric powder. Then she walks round the tent seven times, and with a palm flower sprinkles the same mixture on it. Next she throws a handful of rice and paddy, after revolving each handful of rice round her head; and then she covers the offering with a piece of cloth. She now returns and her husband puts into her mouth seven globules of prepared tamarind which is believed to have a medicinal effect. The devil-driver now rubs her body with Phlomis petals and paddy, and thereby finds out whether she is possessed or not, and if she is, the devil is driven out with the usual offerings. The devil-driver gets, for his services, twelve measures and a half of paddy and two pieces of cloth. Similar customs also prevail among other castes. The husband should not, during this period, get shaved.

When a young woman is about to give birth to a child, she is lodged in a small hut near her dwelling, and is attended by her mother and a few elderly women of the family. After the child is born, the mother and the baby are bathed. She is purified by a bath on the seventh day. The woman who has acted as midwife draws on the ground seven lines at an interval of two feet from one another, and spreads over them aloe leaves torn to shreads. Then, with burning sticks in her hand, the mother with the baby goes seven times over the leaves backwards and forwards, and the mother is purified. For these seven days the father should not eat anything made of rice. He manages to live on toddy, fruit, and other things. It is customary during these days for the friends of the woman to visit the hut where she is and see the baby and the mother. The mother and the baby remain in the lodge for sixteen days, when she is purified by a bath so as to be free from pollution, after which she goes to the main hut. Her *enangathy* sweeps the hut and compound, and sprinkles water mixed with cow-dung on her body, as she returns after the bath. In some places the barks of *athi* (Ficus Racemosa) and *ithi* (Ficus Indica) are well beaten and bruised and mixed with water. Some milk is also added to this mixture and this is sprinkled both inside and outside the hut. Only after this do they think that the hut and the compound are purified. Among the Cherumans of Palghat, the period of pollution lasts for ten days. The expenses connected with this are defrayed by the husband. The woman is under no special treatment after delivery. Her body is rubbed with oil and turmeric which are washed off by a bath in warm water. The husband also bathes to cleanse himself from pollution. The mother eats the usual food, rice, and fish or fowl, and for two months, she takes a ball of an acid pulp of the fruit of Garcina roxburgha and black pepper ground, both morning and evening. To the new born child, water of a green cocoanut is given either on the third or the fourth day, to supply the deficiency in mother's milk. The child is bathed in warm water and after ten days it is rubbed with oil and turmeric which are soon removed. The limbs are shaken, the nose gently pulled out, and the child is nursed for two years.

The naming ceremony falls on the twenty-eighth day after birth. The day is one of festivity to friends and relations. The names in common use among men are, Kurumban, Cháthan, Thevan, Anjanan, Thuluvan, Maniyan, Vallon, Vithon, Kochen, Oonniyalan, Payinkili, Charalan, Mathakili, Izhuvathi, Kurali, while those among women are Kurumba, Punala, Mayithanam, Azhaki, Kunjala, Thiruma, Pazhukka, Thenankili, Cherukoti, Cherunila, Oma, Puna, and Anathara.

The ceremony of ear-boring takes place during the sixth or seventh year of a boy or girl. The *vallon*, who is invited, bores the ears with a sharp needle. The wound is healed by applying cocoanut oil, and the hole is gradually widened by inserting cork, a wooden plug, or a roll of palm leaves. The caste-men of the village are invited to be present and fed. The landlord gives the parents of the child a rupee worth of paddy and this, together with what the guests bring, goes to defray the expenses of the ceremony. After the meal, they go with drum-beating to the house of the *thamar* (landlord) and present him with beaten rice which is distributed among his servants. The ear-borer gets, for his services, eight annas worth of paddy, a cocoanut, a vessel of rice, and four annas. The hair of the child is cut when it begins to walk.

Adultery and divorce.

A woman found to be going wrong with a Parayan is outcasted, and she becomes a convert to Christianity or Mahomadanism. If it takes place within the caste, she is well thrashed and prevented from resorting to the bad practice. In certain cases when the illicit connection becomes public, the caste-men of the village meet with their *vallon* (head-man), and conduct a regular enquiry into the matter and pronounce verdict upon evidence. If a young woman becomes pregnant before marriage, her lover, should he be a Pulayan, is compelled to marry her, as otherwise she is placed under a ban. If both are married, the lover is well thrashed and fined. The woman is taken before a *thandan* (an Izhuva head-man) who, after enquiry, gives her the water of a green cocoanut which she is asked to drink, when she is believed to be freed from the sin. Her husband may take her back again as wife or she is at liberty to marry another. The *thandan* gets a few annas, betel-leaves, nuts, and tobacco. Both the woman's father and the lover are fined, and the fine is spent in the purchase of toddy which is indulged in by those present there at the time. Inclinations to such wicked purposes are said to be rare among these half starving people; nevertheless, instances of boys and girls of very handsome appearance were met with by me in the course of my investigations, which are the products of clandestine intercourse with the members of other castes. There is a curious custom current among the Thanda Pulayans, that, when one of them is thrashed with a *thanda* garment, he is so much disgraced in the eyes of his fellow-men that he is not admitted into their society.

CHAPTER VI.

THE PULAYANS

(Continued).

Inheritance.

Both systems of inheritance, namely, succession through the son and that through the nephew, are found amongst the Pulayans. When questioned as to which custom they follow, they invariably answer the latter, while at the same time they say that they look after their sons and daughters properly. The truth is that they have no property to bequeath, but merely subsist on the wages of their work. In many cases they follow the custom of their Nair landlords. The Kanakka Cherumans of Palghat follow the system of inheritance through sons.

Tribal assembly.

The Pulayans have a tribal assembly which consists of the elderly members of the caste, who meet on all important occasions affecting the welfare of the caste. They have their *vallon* or *valiyavan* (great man) who presides at their marriage, funeral, and other ceremonies, and decides all disputes among the Pulayans with the aid of the caste-men of the village. He is entitled to a fee for all his services, as also to the following privileges, namely, an umbrella of palm leaves slightly concave with a long handle, the bracelet of honour, the box for keeping betel-leaves and a long ear-ring made of gold. As the president of the elders, he is the supreme judge and law-giver or the expounder of the tribal custom, and his verdict is binding in all cases of theft, adultery, and the like. As has been already said, his presence and sanction are necessary for all marriage and funeral ceremonies. In fact he is responsible for the good behaviour of his people. The other functionaries are the Kuruppan and the Vadikkaran. Kuruppan is a corrupt form of *Kurippan,* which means one who makes notes or writes. He is the officer who is next in dignity to the *vallon*, and helps the *vallon* in the exercise of his authority. In the trial of offences, he takes the chief part in sifting evidence, and declares the facts of the case. The Vadikkaran is the constable who brings the parties to the suit, keeps order, and inflicts punishment on the offender.

In the Palghat Taluk of south Malabar, it is said that the Cherumans in former times used to hold grand meetings for cases of theft, adultery, divorce, etc., at *Kannati kutti vattal.*[1] These assemblies consisted of the members of their caste in the localities between the Valayar forests and Karimpuzha (in the Valluvanad Taluk), and in those between the northern and southern hills. It is also said that their deliberations used to last for several days together, and that this was their tribal court. In the event of any body's committing a crime, the punishment inflicted on him was a fine of a few rupees or sometimes a sound thrashing. To prove his innocence, an accused man had to swear, "കണ്ണാടി സ്വരൂപം ആണെ ഞാൻ ചെയ്തിട്ടില്ല." [By Kannati *swaroopam* (assembly) I have not done it]. This assembly was held so sacred that no Cheruman, who had committed a crime, would swear falsely by it. As time went on, they found it difficult to meet and so left off assembling together. At present, for all similar cases, they invite the head-men and the elderly members of several villages to come together for deliberation and decision. For all cases of adultery a fine of eighteen rupees or thirty-three rupees four annas, was imposed upon the parents of the woman and her lover. Such a woman was allowed to marry one or two years after the birth of the child.

Religion.

The Pulayans are pure animists, but are slowly adopting the higher forms of worship. Their gods are Parakutty, Karinkutty, Cháthan, and the spirits of

1. Beneath a large banyan tree at Kannati near Palghat.

their ancestors. Offerings to these gods are given on *Karkadakam* and *Makara sankranthis, Onam, Vishu* and other auspicious days, when one of the Pulayans present turns a *velichapad* and speaks to the assembly as if by inspiration. They are also devout worshippers of Kàli or Bhagavathi, whose aid is invoked in all times of danger and illness, and they take part in the village festivals celebrated in honour of her. Kodungallur Bhagavathi is their guardian deity, and she is rudely represented by an image or stone on a raised piece of ground in the open air. Very probably, Kàli has been identified with the village goddess of the Dravidians, who watches over the welfare of the inhabitants of the villages in rural parts. The Pulayans also believe that spirits exercise an influence over the members of their families, and, therefore, regular offerings are given to them every year on *Sankranthi* days. Their priest is one of their own caste-men, and at the beginning of the new year, he offers to the goddess fowls, fruits, and toddy.

The chief festivals in which the Pulayans take part, are—(1) *Pooram Vela*. This, which may be described as the Saturnalia of Malabar, is an important festival held in the village Bhagavathi temples. It is a festival in which the members of all castes below Brahmans take part, and it is held either in Kumbhom (February-March), or in Meenom (March-April). The Cherumans of the northern parts as well as the Pulayans of the southern parts of the State, attend the festival, and join the procession after a sumptuous meal and toddy drinking according to their custom. Toy horses are made and attached to long bamboo poles, and these are carried by the people to the neighbourhood of the temple. As they go, they leap and dance to the accompaniment of pipe and drum. One among them who acts as a *velichapad* (devil-dancer) goes in front of them, and after a good deal of dancing and loud praying in honour of the deity, they return home.

(2) *Vittu iduka*. This festival, which consists in bringing paddy seeds to the temple of the village goddess Bhagavathi, is

an important one and is celebrated on the day of *Bharani*, the second lunar day in Kumbhom (February-March). Standing at a distance assigned to them by the village authorities, where they offer prayers to Kàli, they put the paddy grains, which they have brought, on a bamboo mat, spread in front of them, after which they return home.

In the Chittur Taluk of the State, there is a festival called *Kathiru*, celebrated in honour of the village goddess in the month of Vrischikam (November-December). A special feature of these festivals is the presence, at the temple of the village goddess, of a large number of domelike structures made of bamboo and plantain stems, richly ornamented and hung with flowers, leaves, and ears of corn. These structures called *sarakoodams*, and small globular packets of palmyra leaves (*kathirkoodus*) containing handfuls of paddy rolled up in straw, are fixed on a pair of parallel bamboo poles, and carried by the Pulayans, who, with pipe and drum, start in procession from the various farms surrounding the village, early enough to reach the temple about dusk in the evening, when they all merge into one great concourse of people, shouting and dancing, and setting off fireworks as they advance. The former are arranged in beautiful rows in front of the village goddess, when Bengal lights are lighted, and fireworks again exhibited. The latter are thrown away among the crowds of spectators all along the route, and also on arrival at the temple. The spectators, both young and old, scramble to obtain as many of the packets of corn as possible and carry them home. They are then hung in front of the houses, for it is believed that their presence will help to promote the prosperity of the family, until the festival comes round again next year. The greater the number of trophies obtained for a family by its members, the greater, it is believed, will be the prosperity of the family. The crowds then disperse. At night the Pulayans and other serfs who have accompanied the procession to the temple are, in the majority of cases, fed by their respective masters at their houses, and then all go back to the farms. The festival is one of the very few occasions on which Pulayans and other agrestic serfs, who are supposed to impart, so to speak, a long distance atmospheric pollution, and consequently may not approach the habitations of high caste Hindus, are freely allowed to enter villages and worship in the village temples which generally occupy the central positions in those villages.

(3) *Mandalam vilakku.* This is a forty-one days festival held in Bhagavathi temples lasting from the first of Vrischikam (November-December), to the tenth of Dhanu (December-January). During it the temples are brightly illuminated both inside and outside at night. There is much music and drum-beating at night, and offerings of cooked peas or Bengal gram and cakes are made to the goddess, after which they are distributed among those present. The forty-first day, the day on which the festival terminates, is one of grand celebration, when all castemen attend the temple. The Cherumans, Malayans, and Eravallens attend the festival in Chittur. They also attend the *Konga Pada* festival there. In rural parts of the State, a kind of puppet show performance (*Olapava koothu*) is acted by Kosavans (Potters) and Tamil Chetties, in honour of the village deity to which they contribute their share of subscription. They also attend the cock festival of Cranganore and offer sacrifices of fowls there.

Funeral customs.

When a Pulayan is dead, the caste-men in the neighbourhood are informed. An offering is made to the Kodungallur Bhagavathi who is believed to watch over their welfare, and is regarded as their ancestral deity. The relatives, one by one, bring a new piece of cloth, with rice and paddy, which are intended to be thrown over the dead, tied in the four corners of the cloth. The cloth is placed over the corpse and they cry aloud three times beating their breasts after which they retire. The corpse is then bathed, dressed, and placed on a bier. A few Parayans are invited to beat drums and to play on their musical instruments—a performance which is continued for an hour or two. After this, a few bits of plantain leaves with rice flour and paddy are placed near the corpse to serve as food for the spirit of the dead. The bier is carried to the graveyard by six bearers, three on each side. The grave is dug, and after the body covered with a piece of cloth has been lowered into it, it is filled in with earth. Twenty-one small bits of leaves are placed over the grave above the spot where the mouth of the dead man would be, with a double-branched twig fixed to the centre. A cocoanut is cut open, and its water is allowed to flow in the direction of the twig which represents the dead man's mouth. Such of the members of the family as could not give him *kanji* or boiled rice before death, now give it to him. The six bearers prostrate themselves before the corpse, three on each side of the grave. The priest then puts on the grave a ripe cocoanut and a tender one for the spirit of the dead man to eat and drink. Then all go home and indulge in toddy and *aval* (beaten rice). The priest gets twelve measures of rice, the grave diggers twelve annas, the *vallon* two annas, and the bearers each an anna. The son or the nephew is the chief mourner, who erects a mound of earth on the south side of the hut and uses it as a place of worship. For seven days, both morning and evening, he prostrates himself before it and sprinkles the water of a tender cocoanut on it, and on the eighth evening, his friends, relatives, the *vallon*, and the devil-driver assemble together. The devil-driver turns round and blows his conch, finds out the position of the ghost and whether it has taken up its abode in the mound or is kept under restraint by some deity. Should the latter be the case, the ceremony of deliverance has to be performed, after which the spirit is set up as a household deity. The chief mourner bathes early in the morning and offers a rice ball offering (*pinda bali*) to the departed spirit. This he continues for fifteen days, and on the morning of the sixteenth, the members of the family bathe to be free from pollution, and their *enangan* cleans the hut and the compound by sweeping and by sprinkling

A PULAYAN AND HIS WIFE GOING FOR FIELD WORK.

water mixed with cow-dung. He also sprinkles the same water on the members of the family as they return after their bath. The chief mourner gets shaved, bathes, and returns to the hut. Some boiled rice, paddy, and pieces of cocoanut are placed on a plantain leaf, and he, with the members of his family, calls on the spirit of the dead to take them. Then they all bathe again and return home. The caste-men who have assembled there by invitation are sumptuously fed. The chief mourner observes the *deeksha* (allowing the hair to grow as a sign of mourning), and after the expiry of the year a similar feast is given to the caste-men.

Occupation.

The Pulayans are by occupation agricultural labourers, and take part in every kind of agricultural work, such as fencing, ploughing, manuring, sowing, weeding, transplanting, reaping, pumping out water and putting up embankments for *kole* cultivation, thatching farm-houses, and watching the gardens of their masters. The cultivation of paddy is the occupation to which they devote most attention, and the grain is not defiled though it is the product of their labour. Men, women, and children are always seen working together in their masters' paddy fields which must be guarded during night against the trespass of cattle and the depredations of robbers or wild animals. They keep awake during night, shouting aloud or singing in a dull monotonous tone or beating drum to ward off the approach of cattle or wild beasts. It is astonishing to see these people sinking in water, four or five feet in depth, for the whole day without any fear of disease, to take from the back-water heavy slabs of solidified mud by means of sharp stakes, for the purpose of putting up embankments. When once they put up, they begin the pumping out of water from the field day and night by means of water-wheels trodden by six, seven, or more men. Given a quantity of toddy every now and then, they can work for any length of time. During the rainy months they live from hand to mouth, while during the harvest they are able to save something, and it is then that they devise the means of spending what they save. It is also then that they can afford to lie ill and to call for the assistance of the devil-driver, to hold social feasts and dances, to celebrate marriages, to go to law over women's quarrels, and to give offerings to their gods. Thus, all their savings are soon squandered. During the summer months, they are in some places engaged in agriculture, while in other localities they go to the forests to bring firewood or thorn bushes for their masters. In all kinds of work, except during harvest, their wages are at the rate already described. Sometimes when expressed by want or hunger, they steal the cocoanuts, areca nuts, or paddy belonging to their masters, and when they are about to be caught, they run away to distant places to work under some other landlord. If they are caught in the meanwhile, they are well thrashed. Some are found working in the houses of Syrian Christians, where Pulaya women act as sweepers, cooks, and as rice-pounders. The hard work is only from six to eight months when they get, for their wages, two annas worth of paddy, which they take to the nearest shop called *mattupeedika* (exchange shop), where they purchase salt, chillies etc., for a portion of the paddy. The other portion is boiled and dried to get the rice out of it. It is then that they often prepare the *kanji* for the night's meal. It is often very late in the evening that they get their wages. Some of the Pulayans work in plantations where their wages are higher. Pulaya women are sometimes seen kneeling in water to gather in their basket any grains that may have been left in the fields after harvest. They catch fish from the back-waters, and make baskets and coarse mats for sale.

There are some curious customs connected with harvest prevalent amongst the Pulayans of the southern parts of the State. Before reaping, the Pulaya head-man asks his master whether he may begin to reap. Permission having been granted, he faces to the east and puts the sickle to the stalks. The first stalks he reserves for the gods of his master, and the second for those of his caste-men. Before threshing, the same head-man takes a few stalks of corn from the sheaf intended for their gods, and sprinkles toddy on them. Another Pulayan does the same thing for the various reapers, and says, as he does so, "Come threshing corn, increase." This is called "filling the threshing floor," and each man threshes his own sheaves. When the threshing is over, the head-man puts his master's sheaf in the centre of the floor and his own at a short distance outside in order that the two sets of gods may look on with favour. The head-man is privileged to measure the corn sitting with his two assistants, saying, "Come paddy, increase," as he counts. He has a peculiar method of counting. The first measure he calls "Good paddy," the second, "Bad paddy," the third, "Good paddy," and so on alternately, the odd numbers being called "good paddy," and the even "bad paddy," until he has counted ten. The eleventh is the share of the reaper. He takes a handful of it and places it in a basket, half of which falls to him, to his assistants, and to the watchman, while the other half is given away in charity to the poor men that come to the threshing place.

In the northern parts of the State, before reaping is begun, offerings of goats, fowls, and cocoanuts are made to Mallan and Muni. The Cheruma head-man faces east and applies his sickle to the stalks, reserving the first stalk for the deities above mentioned. The corn is threshed and measured by one of them, and, as he does so, he says *labham* (profit) for one, *chetham* (loss) for two, and so on alternately up to ten. The eleventh becomes the share of the reapers who thus get one-tenth of the total quantity of corn threshed. The poor people that attend the spot at the time are also given a handful of the grain.

After reaping, the members of the castes named below receive a small portion of the corn and straw for the services rendered by them to the farmers in the course of the months during which cultivation has been carried on. A large heap, sufficient to produce a few measures of paddy is given to each of the following:—(1) The Carpenters, for making and repairing ploughs, etc. (2) The Blacksmiths, for making sickles, knives, and other tools. (3) The Parayans, for lifting and placing the loads of straw on the heads of the Cherumans who have to carry them to the farm-yard. (4) The Mannan or Washerman, for keeping birds, insects, etc., away from the fields by magic. (5) The Vilkurup, for treating the Cherumans when they are ill and for shampooing them when wanted. (6) The Kaniyan or Astrologer, for informing them of the auspicious times for ploughing, sowing, transplanting, and reaping, and also of the time for giving rice, vegetables, oil, etc., to the Cherumans during the *Onam* festival. A small portion of the field near the rest-hut of the Pulaya watchman is left unreaped, the crop on which gives the watchman about ten annas worth of paddy. The Cherumans who are engaged in reaping get two heaps of corn each for every field. For measuring the corn from the farm-yard, a Cheruman gets an anna of paddy in addition to his daily wages. One rupee eight annas worth of paddy are also set apart for the local village deity. During the month of Karkadakam, the masters of the Cherumans give every Cheruman, a fowl, some oil, garlic, mustard, anise seeds, pepper, and turmeric. They prepare a decoction of seeds and boil the flesh of the fowl in it, and on this they feast for three days, during which they are allowed to take rest. Three days' wages are also given in advance. This more nourishing diet and the rest are intended to give them strength.

Social status.

As regards social status, Pulayans eat at the hands of all caste-men above them, but abstain from eating the food prepared by the Velakkathalavans (barbers), Mannàns (washermen), Pànans, Vettuvans, Parayans, Nayadis, Ulladans, Malayans, and Kadars. The Pulayans in the southern parts of the State have to stand at a distance of ninety feet from Brahmans and sixty-four feet from Nairs, and at shorter distances from the lower castes according to their position in the social scale. They are polluted by Pula Cherumans, Parayans, Nayadis, and Ulladans. The Kanakka Cherumans of the Chittur Taluk pollute Era Cherumans and Konga Cherumans by touch and by approach within a distance of seven or eight feet, and are themselves polluted by Pula Cherumans, Parayans, and Vettuvans, who have to stand at some distance from them. Pulayans and Vettuvans bathe when they approach one another, for, as regards their status, there is a point of dispute as to who are superior to the other. Pulayans live far away from the vicinity of the high caste-men, and cannot approach within a hundred and twenty feet of the outer wall of the temples of the high castes. They are denied admission to the markets, and must stand at a distance to make their purchases or sales. They are a debased ignorant race, and appear almost as timid as hares at the approach of human beings. A European can scarcely succeed in coming near them, as their eyes and ears are always on the watch for strangers, and they rush away at their approach, in spite of every attempt to stop them. They rarely go along the public roads, but if they do, they keep looking about to see if any person of a higher caste is near, and if there is, they dare not proceed. When on or near a road, they shout to give notice or warning of their approach, as their presence within a certain distance causes pollution to the people of the superior castes. When defiled by the touch of a Nayadi, a Cheruman has to bathe in seven tanks and let a few drops of blood flow out from one of his fingers. A Brahman who enters into the compound of a Pulayan, has to change his holy thread, and take *panchagavyam* so as to be purified from pollution. In this connection it is curious to note that Malayans who have sometimes been said to be inferior in status to Pulayans are above them; for, a Malayan considers himself to be defiled by the touch, or by approach within a certain distance, of a Pulayan, and bathes to be free from pollution. Further a Malayan stands at a less distance from the high caste-men than the Pulayans or the Cherumans do. The Valluva Pulayan of the

Trichur Taluk fasts for three days living on toddy and green cocoanuts, if he happens to touch a cow that has recently calved. He has also to fast for three days after his wife has had a child.

Food.

Rice, vegetables, fish, and any quantity of toddy form their chief articles of food. Early in the morning they drink the remains of the *kanji* or rice-water prepared during the previous night, but those who live in the southern parts of the State are said not to do this. They take two meals a day and at them partake of fish and toddy whenever they can procure them. When the rice is half boiled, fish and vegetables are put in, and the mixture thus made is eaten. Sometimes when a Pulayan keeps watch in the fields at night, his wife catches some fish, gathers some vegetables, and gives him rice and curry in the field. If she fails to catch fish, she takes the boiled rice, salt, and chillies, and on her way to him, she catches a fish or two, which she puts inside the pot, and the Pulayan eats the mixture with relish. The husband eats the food from the rice basket, and the wife from the pot. It is the privilege of the wife to eat the remains of what the husband has eaten. It often happens that they have nothing to eat on days on which they do no work, and though they work hard, they often suffer from want of food. Like all slaves they form evil habits of stealing, sensuality, drunkenness, and vice which produce or increase suffering. Their lot is a hard one. In rural parts, very early in the morning, they may be seen going with a pot or leaf-basket to their masters' houses for the remains of food and instructions for the day's work. They are kept toiling all day manuring, planting, weeding, and transplanting with the sun or rain beating upon their naked heads and often with their feet in the mire or water several feet deep. In the evening after their hard work, when they return to their huts hungry or fatigued, they have to prepare their food which consists of rice with some pepper and salt or perhaps some curry, and before their meal is prepared, it is about ten o'clock or sometimes even later. They hunt for crabs, tiny fish, snails in the fields, the eggs of red ants, or winged white ants, or anything else

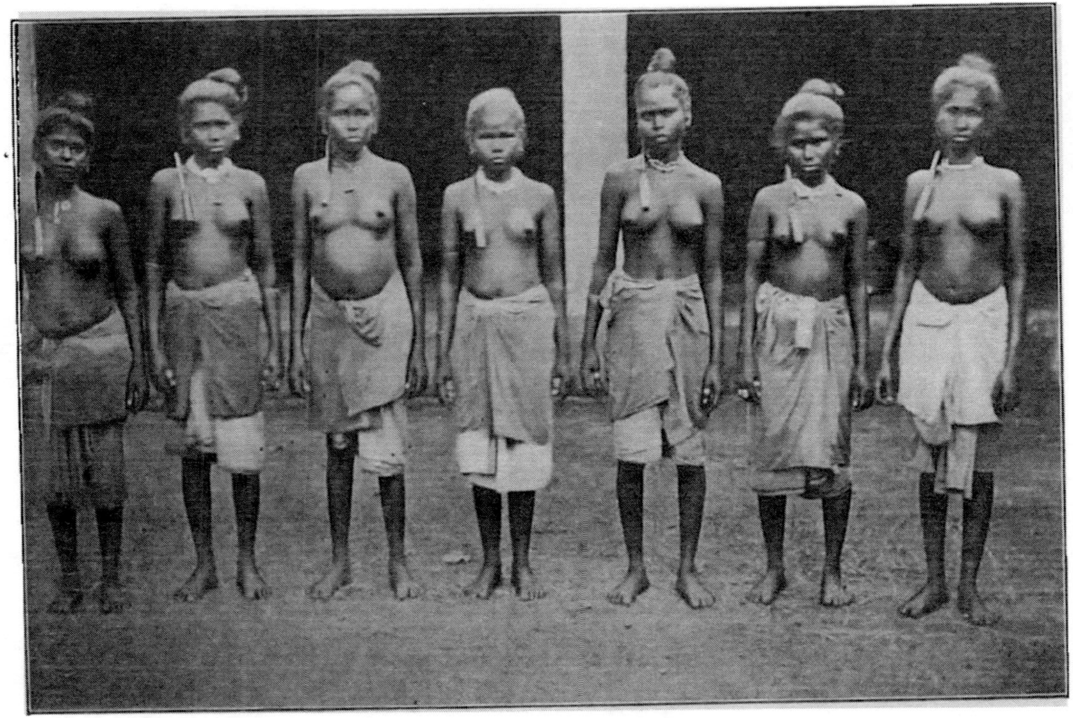

A GROUP OF PULAYA WOMEN.

they can get. They abstain from eating beef, and therefore rank above the Parayans. The Pula Cherumans, on the contrary, kill cows when they can afford to do so, and eat the beef and sell the hide. Instances of cow killing by the Parayans and Pula Cherumans are frequent in rural parts.

Dress and personal adornment.

As regards dress, the men wear round the loins *mundus* which seldom extend below the knees and are worn until they fall to pieces. They wear a similar dirty cloth on their shoulders. Kanakka Cherumans in the northern parts, and Pulayans in the southern parts, shave their heads clean, while the Era Cherumans, Konga Cherumans, and Pula Cherumans grow a tuft of hair on the top of their heads. They are seldom seen with any ornaments on. Women wear a *kacha*, a piece of cloth seven cubits in length, round the loins, and seldom cover their breasts. They wear a black thread round the loins to which is attached a strip of cloth. The hair on the head is neither well parted nor oiled, but is merely tied into a knot pointing upward and slightly inclined to the back of the head. The ear holes are sufficiently dilated to contain wooden plugs, by the side of which there is another small hole containing ten to fifteen small iron rings. These latter are seen among the Pulaya women of Chalakudi and not in other localities. A necklace of glass beads of European manufacture, long enough to go several times, is worn round the neck. Brass armlets, sometimes more than a dozen in number, are worn round each arm, and sometimes they are so numerous as to extend as far as the elbow.

Games.

The Pulayans are fond of music and dancing, their musical instruments being the pipe and the drum. Their dances and games appear to be connected in some way with their religious observances. Their favourite dance is the *Kole kali* or club dance. A party of ten or twelve men, provided with two sticks, each a yard in length, stand in a circle, and move round, striking at the sticks and keeping time with their feet and singing at the same time. The circle is alternately widened and narrowed. It is an exciting game. The *Vatta kali* is another kind of wild dance. This also requires a party of ten or twelve men, and sometimes young women also join them. The party move in a circle, clapping their hands while they sing a kind of rude song. Another of their performances is called the *Thattinmel kali* which is intended to propitiate the goddess Bhagavathi. Four wooden poles are firmly stuck into the ground, two of which are connected by two horizontal pieces of wood, over which planks are arranged. A party of Pulayans dance on the top of this to the music of their pipe and drum. This is generally erected in front of the Bhagavathi temple, and the dancing takes place immediately after the harvest. They have also a circular dance performed on the occasion of marriage celebrations by women.

Missionary work.

Much missionary work is being carried on among the Pulayans. The following information has been obtained through my correspondence with the Christian Societies in the State. In the Archdiocese of Verapoly, a few hundreds of cases of conversion of the Pulayans to Christianity take place every year, and the converts are given secular primary instruction. Their moral and religious instruction is attended to in a special manner. The Reverend A. E. David, of the Church Mission Society of Trichur, says:—"We have been working among the Pulayans for the last thirty-five years in and around Trichur. There are two hundreds of Pulaya converts in two places, and they have been very much raised from their low state of degradation—their mode of living, their manners and position they now occupy, are vastly superior to what their fellow-men enjoy. Many of their men, women, and children are taught reading and writing, and their girls needle-work also. One boy and girl have passed the Lower Secondary Examination, and this is the highest standard they have reached in education. There are some boys in the Upper Primary classes reading English. A school for them was started in a rural part, which went on well for some time, but was abolished owing to the opposition of the masters of the Pulayans. In the Kunnamkulam Pastorate, there are, I hear, twelve families of Pulaya converts consisting of thirteen men, eighteen women, and twenty-five children, making a total of fifty-six persons in all." The Reverend P. J. Joshua says that as soon as a Pulayan becomes a convert, he is allowed unreservedly to mingle with the other Christians, who give him free entrance into their houses, and in this respect they are more liberal and less superstitious than those in Cochin and Travancore. In the latter State, they have separate churches, but their attendance in other churches is freely allowed. The Pulaya converts are more decent and less uncleanly in their habits than other Pulayans. Their children are admitted into the schools and some of them are learning English and the vernacular. They are poor and maintain themselves by cooly work, but have shown their aptitude for other kinds of work as well. One of them is a teacher, another a farmer on a small scale, a third a coppersmith, and a fourth is a maistry with a small number of coolies under him. The reverend gentleman says that, if opportunities are given them of improving their talents, they will be a benefit to their down-trodden community and to the mission societies that are ever doing their best to improve their condition.

Vital statistics.

The Pulayans with the various sub-tribes numbered at the last census 59,840; 28,814 being males and 31,026 females. The latter exceeded the former by 2,212. They form about 75 per cent. of the agrestic serfs and 11 per cent. of the Hindu population of the State. It is said that, if men or any other kind of animals were invariably mated early, and if their offspring were always reared with care, their numbers would increase in a geometrical ratio, and that in no large number of generations they would occupy every habitable space. As a matter of fact, the number of inhabitants of most countries remains fairly stationary, for there are certain influences which neutralize the tendency to increase. I made an investigation into the vital statistics of twenty Pulaya families in different parts of the State. Of the fifty women belonging to these families, I found that two had no children and that the other forty-eight had had 258 children. Of these children, seventy had died. Of the living children, eighty-one were males, and one hundred and seven females. The proportion of male to female children is thus as two to three. Fever, small-pox, dysentery, diarrhœa are the prevailing causes of mortality. There are few unmarried Pulayans and very few of the married women have no children. The child-bearing age which is between fifteen and twenty-five ends between the forty-fifth and fiftieth years. No diet is adopted nor any practice followed by Pulaya women to check fertility. They welcome the birth of children as God's gift, and fecundity is esteemed as conducive to increasing the numerical strength of the caste. Comparing the population of the census return of 1891, (51,251) with that of 1901, the latter shows an increase of 8,589. The Pulaya population has thus been increasing in spite of the numerous instances of conversion to Christianity.

Appearance.

The external appearance of these serfs varies very much. They are sometimes remarkable for an extreme darkness of complexion, and their black colour, which cannot be the effect of exposure, approaches that of an African; but they are invariably stamped with the Hindu features and they do not bear the appearance of being a distinct race. The bark (spathe) of the areca palm furnishes, in some places, the whole of their clothing which, at best, never exceeds a bit of cloth merely sufficient for the purposes of decency. Their hair is allowed to grow wild and forms an immense matted and filthy mass. The Era Cherumans and Konga Cherumans are fairer in complexion than the Pulayans and Cherumans with their sub-tribes. The Cherumans of the northern parts of the State and the Pulayans of the southern parts are either of short or medium stature. Their complexion is invariably dark, and only rarely dark-brown or reddish brown,

Conclusion.

The Pulayans are very quarrelsome among themselves, but always unite to oppose the members of other castes when disputes arise with them. Closely connected with their masters, as they are, they do not appear to be equally affectionate and faithful to them. This is perhaps owing to their being overworked and underfed by their masters. They ought to be better housed, better clothed, and better fed. If attempts are not made for the improvement of their present condition, they will be in course of time lost to the Hindu community, as many of them have become and are becoming converts to Mahomadanism and Christianity.

CHAPTER VII.

THE VETTUVANS, THE KOODANS, AND THE KANAKKANS.

—:o:—

I. THE VETTUVANS.

The Vettuvans, also called Vettuva Pulayans, form the lowest sub-tribe among the agrestic serfs of the State, and are found in Manakodi, Oorakam, Peringottukara Proverthy, Karumbala, Valanchamudi, Azhikode and Kaipamangalam. They numbered 6,349 at the last census, 3,099 being males and 3,250 females.

The names 'Vedan' and 'Vettuvan' appear to be derived from the same root meaning hunter. There is a caste with the same name in the Districts of Selam, Coimbatore, and Madura. They are said to be the descendants of Vedars (hunters), who served as soldiers under Kongu kings. Tradition says that Kongu kings invited Vettuvans from the Chola and Pandya countries to assist them against the Keralas. They now call themselves Vettuva Vellalans. In Malabar and Cochin they are the degraded caste of agricultural serfs, *shikaries*, and collectors of forest produce in the jungles. Whether the members of the caste are the descendants of the people in the Tamil Districts, it is not possible to say.

There are no subdivisions in the caste. It is said there are two endogamous divisions in Malabar called *Kuti* and *Peringala* which do not exist in the State. They are endogamous as regards the caste and exogamous as regards the clan (*taravad*). Some of them are named Mantra Taravad, Puthu Taravad, Mala Taravad, and Chakkandi Taravad.

THE VETTUVANS.

Marriage customs.

Marriage within the clan (*taravad*) is prohibited, but is permissible between the members of two *taravads*. They do not observe the custom of a young man marrying the daughter of his maternal uncle. Girls are married rarely before, but generally after, puberty. The average marriageable age of a girl is between twelve and fifteen, while that of a boy is between sixteen and twenty. The offer of betrothal always comes from the boy's family. When a match is approved of by the parents of the bride and bridegroom, the necessary negotiations and settlement of the day for the wedding are made at the hut of the former in the presence of the *enangans* (middle-men) and relatives on both sides. The bride's money is four rupees and four annas, out of which one rupee six annas and six pies is paid on the spot, and the number of guests from the bridegroom's side to attend the wedding is also fixed. On the morning of the lucky day chosen for the wedding, the bridegroom, purified by a bath, and dressed in a neat piece of cloth with a second one hanging loosely on his shoulders, and a suitable covering for his head, goes to the hut of the bride, accompanied by his parents, uncles, relations, and friends, who are welcomed and seated on mats in a decorated pandal put up for the time being in front of it. At the lucky moment, the bride, who is slightly veiled, is taken to the pandal and seated in front of the bridegroom, who ties the *tali* round her neck. After this the guests are treated to a dinner of rice, toddy, etc., and then served with betel-leaves and nuts. On the same evening or the next morning the bridegroom with the bride returns home, where also a similar entertainment takes place. At the time of his departure, he has to pay his bride's maternal uncle and her sister each four annas and a half, and to her paternal uncle and her sister two annas and a quarter and betel-leaves. This is called *kaimatakkuka*, and is probably the survival of an old custom of the bridegroom's paying something to each member of the bride's family as a reward for permitting her to accompany him. The expenses of the bride's parents in connection with the wedding are almost self-supporting; for, the sum of money is raised by subscription either in coin or in kind received from the castemen who are invited. The bridegroom's parents have also to spend a similar sum.

The Vettuvans are generally monogamists; but some have two wives. The junior wife who is selected either by the first wife or sister has always to obey and respect the senior wife. They reside in one and the same hut; but in the event of any quarrelling, they are either located separately or one of them is turned out. A woman cannot have more than one husband, but a widow may marry her brother-in-law or anybody she likes.

When an unmarried woman becomes pregnant, her parents, as soon as they become aware of the fact, inform their local headman, Kanakkan or Kuruppan, who convenes a meeting of the elderly members of the community, for the purpose of summoning the secret lover and prosecuting the necessary enquiries. In the event of the confession of the charge, he is asked to marry her. The matter does not end there. They go to the local Thandan (head-man among the Izhuvans), and relate to him the incident who, thereupon, gives him water in a vessel (*kindi vellom*). She is asked to drink this as well as water mixed with cowdung, and is then made to let flow a few drops of blood from her body. After this he says '*dosham theernnu*' (free from guilt). Should the lover however be unwilling to marry her, he is thrashed and placed under a ban. In case of their being related to each other, they are both turned out of caste, and the woman who is freed from the guilt may marry again. The Thandan and their head-man get, for their privileges, four annas out of the fine imposed upon them, four packets of betel-leaves, eight areca nuts, and three tobacco leaves. The balance which then remains is spent on toddy and beaten rice for the assembled. It is curious to note that a wife is punished for adultery, while the husband is allowed to go free. The reason is simple, as Diderot says, the tyranny of man has converted the possession of woman into property. Divorce is easy with them, and a man can repudiate his wife on the score of some serious misconduct, in which case he can leave her in charge of her parents and get back the purchase money. The man who next mates with her will pay him. The wife also, on some dislike or other, may separate herself from her husband, and the children, if young, will follow the mother, while grown up children remain with the father.

Inheritance and village organization.

Among the Vettuvans, the son succeeds to the property of his father. They have even now the rudiments of the caste assembly. The village head-man is called the *Kuruppan* or *Kanakkan* who has a subordinate called *Kaikkaran*. He has the power to call on and preside over a meeting, to enquire into the breaches of caste rules, such as theft, adultery, and the like, and to punish offenders in accordance with the opinion of the majority. The decisions are enforced on pain of loss of caste, fine, and even thrashing. The head-man has always a share of the fine and the balance is spent on toddy. They believe in magic, sorcery, and witchcraft. Pànan or Parayan is their magician or sorcerer and devil-driver.

Religion.

The Vettuvans profess the lower forms of Hinduism. Their chief gods are Chevva, Chàthan, Karinkutty, Parakutty, Káppiri, Kandakaranan, and also Namburi Thampuran. They give regular offerings to them, lest the gods should become angry and cause serious calamities to the members of their families. Images of gods are made of bell-metal and worshipped in their huts. The deceased ancestors are also worshipped as gods, to whom are given different kinds of offerings, in which toddy forms an indispensable item.

In Oorakam and its neighbourhood, where the notes were taken, information was obtained, that there was no tree-tapping and that toddy brought to them for sale was largely adulterated with water and very costly. Their gods were very angry, for they were not satisfied with it. They caused fever, deafness, and the like. The blind faith in their gods is such, that they cannot dispense with the offerings of toddy. They worship Kàli also. Kumbhom Bharani, an important festival celebrated in honour of the goddess in the Cranganore temple is observed by them. On the morning of this day, tunes are played, and special songs called *Thottampattu* are sung in honour of her. Sacrifices are offered to the deity very early, and a *puja* is also performed for the sword, anklets, and bells, which are all placed in front of the deity, and songs are again sung, when one of them turns a *velichapad* and speaks as if by inspiration. Wearing the above ornaments, they go to a temple in front of which, and on a mat, they empty out a large quantity of paddy, and again play and sing.

Funeral ceremonies.

The funeral ceremonies of Vettuvans are somewhat elaborate. When a member of the caste breathes his last, his relations, friends, and other castemen of the *kara* (village) are all informed of the event. They attend and take part in the obsequies. The dead body is bathed and dressed in a new piece of cloth. Some gold rubbed on a stone in water is poured into his mouth by his sons and daughters. *Karuvanguka* or *guruthwom vanguka* is an important ceremony performed by his sons and daughters. It consists in taking sixteen small bits of plantain leaves with some rice on each and placing it on the forehead, neck, chest, loins, thighs, hands, legs, feet, etc., and washing the last two and collecting the water, which is taken by the members junior to him in the family. After this, the dead body is placed on the bier, which is carried by four persons to the grave. The nearest relatives of the family, four in number, called *Bhedakkars*, with a *mundu* tied round their heads, walk in front of the procession. The grave to contain the dead body is dug and a new cloth is spread to place the corpse on it. It is soon filled in with layers of earth and stones to keep off dogs and jackals from disturbing the dead body. All those who have accompanied the chief mourner bathe and return home, while the members of the family fast for the night. The eldest son who is the chief mourner bathes early morning, offers the *pindabali* (rice ball offering) to the spirit of the departed, which is continued for fifteen days. On the seventh day the chief mourner and the *enangan* go to the graveyard and level the part slightly raised. A piece of stone kept near the foot is taken and placed on a leaf. Some toddy, arrack, and water of the green cocoanut are poured over it as offerings. By some magic the spirit is supposed to be living in it. It is brought home and kept outside the hut in a cocoanut shell, containing oil mixed with turmeric, until the pollution is over. The pollution is for fifteen days, and on the night of the fifteenth they fast. On the morning of the sixteenth all the caste-men of the *kara* (village), who are invited, bring with them rice, curry stuffs, and toddy. Anointing themselves with oil, they all go to bathe after which the *enangan* sprinkles water mixed with cow-dung to show that they are freed from pollution. The stone is also purified by a dip in water and then brought home. The members assembled are fed and they depart. The chief mourner who has to perform the *deeksha* does not shave for a year, bathes in the early morning, and offers the *bali* before going for work. This he continues for a year, at the end of which he gets himself shaved and celebrates a feast called *Masom* in honour of the departed. The stone representing the image of the departed is placed on a seat in a conspicuous part of the hut. An image made of wood or copper sometimes takes its place. It is thenceforward worshipped and believed to watch over the welfare of the family. Regular offerings are given to it on *Karkadakam* and *Thulam sankranthis*, *Onam*, *Vishu*, and on the festival day of the local temple. For those who have no sons or nephews, the relatives perform the ceremony. It is a disgrace and dishonour to the whole community to allow a dead body of their caste to be buried by a Mahomadan or Christian. Should he have none behind him, the caste-men will, by a subscription, give him an honourable burial.

They eat at the hands of Brahmans, Sudras, Kammalans, and Izhuvans, but never anything prepared by a Velan, Pànan, Velakkathalavan (barber), Kanakkan, and Koodan. The castes below them in status are Pulayan, Nayadi, and Ulladan. They consider themselves superior to Pulayans, and are careful not to be polluted by them. When they approach one another they feel themselves polluted. A Vettuvan who is polluted by a Nayadi or an Ulladan fasts for seven days, subsisting on water, tender cocoanuts, and toddy. On the eighth day he bathes and takes his regular meals, lest they believe that their gods become angry and disappear. As *chandalas* of the plains, any distance less than sixty-four feet will pollute the higher castes. They stand at a distance of twenty-four feet from the Kammalans, while Nayadis and Ulladans stand far from them. Owing to their disabilities and low wages, many turn either Christians or Mahomadans, and work for wages of two and a half to three annas worth of paddy a day.

Social status.

——:o:——

II. THE KOODANS.

In the order of social precedence, the Koodans come next to the Kanakkans, and they form a small minority among the agricultural labourers found in the northern parts of the State. especially in the Talapilli Taluk. At the last census they were returned as numbering ninety-nine,—fifty being males and forty-nine females. They live in huts similar to those of the other classes of Pulayans. They speak Malayalam and are wholly illiterate.

As among other classes of agrestic serfs, marriage does not exist among them. With persons who are connected with one another, all matrimonial alliances are avoided, neither do they adopt the custom of mating with the daughters of maternal uncles which obtains in some places. Girls are married generally after

Marriage customs.

. THE KOODANS.

puberty, rarely before it. The terms 'marriage', 'wife', and husband' cannot be strictly applied to their conjugal relations, as they resort to *sambandham* (a free will union) like the Nairs. A Koodan can enter into a *sambandham* with a woman either of his own or of the Pulaya caste. He has to bathe before he returns to his hut, if he should stay with a woman of the latter caste for the previous night. This proves that he belongs to a caste superior to that of the Pulayans, and the union resembles that of a Brahman with a Sudra woman. Should a woman of the Koodan caste mate with a Pulayan, she is at once turned out of caste. A Koodan who wishes to enter into a *sambandham* with a woman of his own or of the Pulaya caste goes to her hut with one or two of his relations or friends to recommend him to the parents of the woman to permit him to enter into conjugal relations with their daughter or form *kudikooduka*. With their permission, either expressed or implied, they become a kind of husband and wife and in most cases the will of the man and the woman is sufficient for the union, which is attended with no ceremony nor any expense. The services of a middle-man, and the ceremony of match-making are all dispensed with. The husband has nothing to give his wife except the paddy which he gets as wages, when he goes to her, so as to save her the trouble of feeding him then. Working for a master from morning till night, watching his fields at night, and hardly getting two annas worth of paddy to maintain himself, he has no saving by which to purchase a cloth or an ornament for his beloved. The woman generally stays with her parents in her hut, and very often her lover comes to her with his wages after the day's hard work and stays with her for the night. Should she wish to accompany him to his hut, she does so with her wages in the evening. If a woman who has no open lover becomes pregnant, her fault is condoned when she mentions her lover's name. They are then allowed to continue their existing relation. Virginity is no condition whatever for the formation of any conjugal union. This holds between a man and a woman so long as they like each other. When they fall out for some reason or other, they separate and are at liberty to form new unions.

The Koodans are monogamists, and their women are not polyandrous. Adultery is no social sin with them, nor is it regarded with abhorrence, for divorce is very easy. Widows may re-marry and may even associate with their brothers-in-law.

Inheritance and tribal organization.

The Koodans follow the Marumakkathayam law of inheritance though, in fact, they have no property to inherit except sometimes a sheep or a few fowls. The children are the members of the mother's family. They have no tribal meeting, but all disputes, cases of theft, and other offences, are settled by their masters, whose decisions are final. Culprits are thrashed, but not fined. They believe in magic and sorcery. Mannàns and Mahomadan Moplahs are sometimes consulted, and these dupe them.

Religion.

They profess the lower forms of Hinduism, and worship the local village deity (Kàli), and the spirits of their ancestors, whom they represent by means of stones placed on a raised floor under a tree, and to whom boiled rice, parched grain, husk, toddy, plantain fruits, and cocoanuts are offered on the *Vishu* and *Onam* festivals and on *Karkadakam, Thulam* and *Makara sankranthis.* Care is always taken to have the offerings served separately on leaves, lest the beings reverenced should quarrel with one another and do them harm. Should illness such as cholera, small-pox, or fever break out in a family, some fowls with an anna or two, are offered to the goddess Bhagavathi in the temple close by, as she is believed to be able to save them from the impending calamity.

Occupation and their social condition.

The Koodans are agricultural labourers and take part in every kind of work connected with agriculture, such as turning the soil, ploughing, sowing, manuring, weeding, transplanting, and the like; as soon as the monsoon is over, they work in gardens, turning the soil, watering, and fencing. Thus they work all the year round as directed by their masters. They are landless day labourers working under a landlord or farmer, from early morning till sunset with the exception of an hour or two at midday, for a small pittance of ten pies worth of paddy during the months of June, July, and August, and one anna eight pies during the other months of the year. They get for the *Onam* and *Visha* festivals six annas worth of paddy, some salt, cocoanut oil, and chillies. On the day of the village festival they are given presents of cloth by their masters, as also toddy, arrack, and the other articles above referred to. They dress themselves in their best, and are treated to a sumptuous dinner. With shouts of joy they attend and take part in the village festival. When they fall ill, they are properly looked after by their masters, both on account of their good feelings towards them and also of the loss of work they may have to sustain, should they be laid up for a long time. Whenever a landlord or farmer has more men than he can afford to supply with work and wages, he generally lends their services to another on a *pattom* (rent) of one rupee eight annas worth of paddy a year for a male, and one rupee two annas for a female. The new master gives them work and wages, and sends them back when their services are no longer wanted. Should a Koodan run away from his master, he is brought back either by threats or by mild words; should these fail, there is no remedy to force him back. In spite of the abolition of slavery some sixty years ago, they are in a state of nominal bondage. In fact they live in small huts with insufficient food and with nothing but a small *mundu* to dress themselves with, plodding on from day to day with no hope of improving their condition.

Social status.

As to status, they eat and drink at the hands of all castes except Parayan, Pulayan, Ulladan, and Nayadi, and no other caste eats with them. In some parts of the State, they approach the houses of Izhuvans, but they have to keep themselves at a distance of forty-eight feet from all the high caste Hindus. They are polluted by Pulayans, Nayadis, and Ulladans, who have to stand at some distance from them. They may take water from the wells of Moplahs. They are their own barbers and washermen, and may approach the temples of their village goddess Káli on some special days, while at other times they have to stand far away.

—:o:—

III. THE KANAKKANS.

Tradition of the caste.

The Kanakkans who are returned at the last census as 5,917 include 2,974 males and 2,943 females, and are found in Trichur and the southern Taluks of the State. They form one of the important tribes among the agrestic serfs of the State. Though formerly a cultivating caste, many are now engaged in boating, fishing, and other kinds of labour, and are, perhaps for this reason, superior to the rest of the agricultural classes. They speak Malayalam and are wholly illiterate. Their habits are settled, and their huts are similar to those of the poor Izhuvans.

The meaning of the word 'Kanakkans' (accountants), as applied to them and the Pulayans, does not throw any light on their origin. They belong to the slave castes, and are even now attached to some landlords in the State. In the Taluks of Trichur, Mukundapuram, and Cranganore, where information was obtained about them, it is reported that they are the *atiyars* (slaves) of Chittur Manakkal Namburipad at Perumanom near Trichur, and they owe him a kind of allegiance even now. With a view to ascertain the truth of this, I went to the Namburi landlord, who told me that the members of the caste, not only from almost all parts of the State, but also from the British Taluks of Ponnani, Chowghat and even from Calicut, come to him with a *thirumulkazhcha*, that is, a few annas in token of their allegiance. This fact was also confirmed by a *Kanakkanar* (head-man) at Cranganore, who told me that he and his caste-men were the slaves of the same landlord, though on disputes connected with the caste, they abide by the decision of the local Raja. In the event of any illness or calamity in the family of a Kanakkan, an astrologer (Kaniyan), who is often consulted as to the cause and remedy, sometimes reminds the members of their negligence regarding their allegiance to the landlord, and suggests the advisability of paying respects to him (*Nambikooru*) with a few annas. On the eighth day of asterism (*Pooyam*) in Makaram (January-February), these people from various parts of the State present themselves in a body, with a few annas each to owe their allegiance to him. My informant also mentions the following story. "One of his ancestors chanced to pay his respects to one of the rulers of the State when the residence of the royal family was in Cochin. On arriving near the town, the boat capsized in a storm, but was luckily saved by the bravery of a few rowers of this caste. The Raja, who witnessed the incident from a window of his palace, admired their valour and desired to enlist some Kanakkans into his service."

There are four endogamous divisions among them, namely, Patunna Kanakkan, the members of which used to work in salt pans, Vettuva Kanakkan, Chavala Kanakkan, and Paràttu Kanakkan. Each of these sub-castes is further subdivided into certain clans (*kiriyams*) which are exogamous. Some of them are named Vengatti Kiriyam, Pátu Kiriyam, Chera Kiriyam, Payingini Kiriyam, and Vattekàttu Kiriyam.

Marriage customs.

Members of the same clan (*kiriyam*) may not intermarry. All the men and women thereof are regarded as brothers and sisters, and as such are bound to respect each other. This custom appears to be a true survival of a very ancient organization of exogamic clans with maternal filiation. Among the lowest races of primitive society, marriage within the clan or sub-tribe is regarded as a crime and sin, and is visited with severe punishment. Whoever forms such illegal connection is outlawed and tracked through the wood like game and put to death, and the children born of such social incest are exterminated. It is on this principle that the marriage of a half-sister or of a step-mother is prohibited. This is probably a relic of the custom above referred to among the very low castes. A young man may marry the daughter of his maternal uncle, but this is not permissible in some places.

Both infant and adult marriages take place, and may be celebrated by Patunna Kanakkans at any time between the tenth and the thirteenth year of a girl, while the Vettuva Kanakkans may celebrate it only after girls attain their puberty. It is never determined by courtship, and the parents are solely responsible for all such matrimonial alliances. Boys are married between sixteen and twenty years of age. As soon as a young man is sufficiently old, his parents look out for a girl as wife, and when she is chosen, the negotiations leading to marriage, are opened by the father of the bridegroom, who, along with his brother-in-law and his *enangan*, goes to the hut of the bride elect, where, in the midst of relations and friends previously assembled, the formal arrangements are made, and a portion of the bride's money is also paid. The auspicious day for the wedding is settled, and the number of guests to be invited is also fixed. There is an entertainment for those that are assembled. A similar one is also held at the hut of the bridegroom elect. These people are too poor to consult the local Kaniyan (astrologer); but if it be discovered that they were born on the day of the same constellation, the match is at once rejected. The *Kanakkanar* (headman) must be duly informed and invited to the wedding.

On the lucky day chosen for the celebration of the marriage, the bridegroom neatly dressed, and with a knife and stylus,—probably to symbolise that he can read and write—sets out from his hut, accompanied by his relatives and other men of the village, to go to the hut of the bride, where they are welcomed and seated on mats in a pandal put up for the occasion. The bride, partially veiled, is taken to the pandal and seated along with the bridegroom, to both of whom a sweet preparation of milk, sugar, and a few pieces of plantain fruits, is given to establish the fact that they have become husband and wife. There is no *tali* tying then. The guests assembled are treated to a sumptuous dinner. As they take leave of the host, each of them pays a few annas to meet the expenses of the ceremony. The bridegroom, with the bride and those who have accompanied him, then returns to his hut, where also the same ceremonies are gone through, and the guests well fed. The bridegroom and the bride are seated together and the sweet preparation is given, after which the parents and the maternal uncle of the former, touching the heads of both, say 'my son', 'my daughter', 'my nephew', 'my niece', meaning that the bride has become a member of their family along with her husband. They throw some rice on the heads of the couple in token of their blessings. After this, the couple live together as husband and wife.

In some places marriage is performed by proxy. As there is no *tali* tying, the bridegroom's sister or somebody else goes to take the bride to his hut. Her price is only one rupee and two annas. A young Vettuva Kanakkan, however, cannot marry by proxy, nor can the *tali* tying ceremony be dispensed with in his case; but the ceremonies connected with the marriage are similar to those already described.

The customs connected with pregnancy, childbirth, and naming are just the same as those described in my account of the Pulayans. The names in common use among males, are Manikkan, Ettikoran, Ettisankaran, and Velu, and among females, Ettuli, Káli, Kotha, Valli, and Neeli. Children are often called by pet names. Grown up men use a surname, which is generally the name of their father. Very often their house name also is attached to this.

Neither polygamy nor polyandry prevails among the Kanakkans. A man may marry his sister-in-law after the death of his wife, so also may a woman enter into conjugal relations with her brother-in-law; or she can, with the consent of her parents, marry anybody she likes. Grown up children live with their paternal uncles. The formalities connected with the marriage are the same as those detailed above, but the marriage is never celebrated on a grand scale. The instances connected with adultery and other misconduct are dealt with as among the Vettuvans. If a woman has abandoned herself to the wishes of a member of the lower caste, she is put out of caste, and becomes a Christian or Mahomadan.

Inheritance and tribal assembly.

Among the Kanakkans the sons succeed to the property of their fathers. The institution of the tribal enquiry exists among them in a rudimentary form. The head-man who is called the *Kanakkanar* presides over the meeting of the caste-men on occasions of marriage, death, and caste disputes. His privileges are embodied in a *Theettooram* (Royal order) given to a member of the caste. A translation of it is given here. "He may preside at the marriage, funeral, and other ceremonies of his caste-men and obtain a small fee as remuneration for his service. He may use a stick, a stylus, and a knife lined with gold. He may wear a white coat, turban, ear-rings, and use an umbrella. He may also construct a shed with six posts for marriage ceremonies. He has to pay a tax of ten annas to the Sirkar." All minor offences, such as petty thefts and quarrels, are dealt with by the head-man and the punishments inflicted by him. Chittur Manakkal Namburipad in the Talapilli Taluk, the Cranganore Raja in the Cranganore Taluk, and His Highness the Maharaja exercise absolute powers in the settlement of disputes connected with this and other castes.

Magic, sorcery, and witchcraft are believed in; but persons who know and practise the art are very rare among them. They go to a Pánan, Velan, or Parayan whenever they require his services.

THE KANAKKA BOATMEN.

Religion.

In matters of religious worship, the Kanakkans follow the higher castes. They profess Hinduism and worship Siva, Vishnu, Ganapathi, and Subramania. Mookkan, Chàthan, Kandakaranan, and the spirits of their ancestors are also adored. Cháthan cannot be worshipped in Cranganore, for he is opposed to the local deity. Wooden or brass images of their ancestors are kept in their huts, to whom regular sacrifices are offered on *Karkadakam, Thulam,* and *Makara sankranthis.* In their compounds is often seen a raised floor beneath a tree, on which are placed a few stones representing the images of the demons whom they greatly fear and respect, and to whom sacrifices are offered on leaves separately. Vettuva Kanakkans do homage to Kàppiri and Veerabhadran also.

Occupation.

At present their chief occupations are net-fishing in summer in the back-waters, lumbering, boating, pumping out water from paddy fields by water-wheels, and all kinds of agricultural labour. At one time they were solely engaged in the manufacture of salt from the back-waters in the State. Women occupy themselves in coir making and agricultural labour. The Vettuva Kanakkans are engaged in cocoanut cultivation and making lime out of shells. They are very skillful in climbing cocoanut trees to pluck cocoanuts. They gather bamboo and do ploughing and agricultural labour.

The lumbering operations referred to above include not only cutting timber but floating it down the flooded rivers in the rainy season. Large bamboo rafts are made, on each side of which blocks of timber are provided with holes, through which a piece of wood or bamboo is passed transversely and is firmly tied by strong ropes to the bamboo rafts. The whole is then floated on water and rowed to Cochin and other localities on the river or back-water side. In the felling and floating of timber, men's wages range from five to six annas a day, and in agricultural labour, men get two to three annas worth of paddy, while women get three-fourths of this pittance. The implements in common use among the Kanakkans are boat, paddle, net, rudder, knife, sickle, and axe.

Social status.

They accept food prepared by the members of the higher castes as also of Kammalans, Izhuvans, and of Moplahs; but they have strong objections to eating at the hands of Veluthedan (washerman), Velakkathalavan (barber), Pànan, Velan, and Kaniyan. The touch of the Kanakkans pollute Izhuvans, but Pulayans, Ulladans, and Nayadis have to stand far away from them. They have to keep themselves at a distance of forty-eight feet from the high caste Hindus and pollute Kammalans and Vàlans within a short distance. They cannot approach the temples of the higher castes; but, in the rural parts, they take part in the temple festivals. In Cranganore, they can come as far as *kozhikkallu*, a stone outside the temple at a short distance from it, on which fowls are offered by the low caste people.

CHAPTER VIII.

THE PULLUVANS.

Name and tradition of the caste.

The name 'Pulluvan' is fancifully derived from *pullu*, a hawk. The reason is that the Pulluvan is clever in remedying the disorders, which pregnant women and babies suffer from the supposed evil influence of these birds. They are a set of herbalists, and the following tradition is current among them. When the great Khandava forest was in conflagration, the snakes therein were all destroyed in the flames, but a large five hooded serpent, half burnt and half scalded, flew in the agony of death, and chanced to fall down in a part of what is called Kuttanad. Local men point out the sites of modern Alleppy. Two women who were at the time on their way to take water from a well close by, were requested by the serpent to pour seven pots of water on his body, probably to mitigate the pains of his burning sensation, and also to turn the pot sidewise for him to get in. His request was complied with, and the serpent got in, but would not go out in spite of their repeated entreaties. He then desired one of them to take him home and have him located in a room on the western part of the house; she refused to do so, being afraid of the serpent, when she was advised to cover the mouth of the pot with a piece of cloth, and she did as desired. The room in which he was located was ordered to be closed for a week. Her husband, who was ignorant of the fact, tried to open the door, but could not do so, except by exerting the utmost strength. He entered the room and found to his surprise an ant-hill, with a passage for the snake to go out. He disturbed his residence, when the snake came out and bit him and he died instantly. His wife burst into loud lamentations and found that she could not maintain herself in future. The serpent nevertheless consoled her, and devised a plan by which she could support herself without difficulty. It was that she should go to every house and say '*dhana visham* (give me alms and be saved from snake poison),' and that on hearing this, the inmates of the house would give her alms, by which she was enabled to maintain herself. Thus the snakes were causing annoyances in the houses of people, which, when known, were remedied by the entertainment of these people. Hence when a Pulluvan and Pulluvathi (Pulluvan's wife) go for alms to a house with their *pulluvakudam* (a pot which serves as a friction drum), they are asked to sing, and are then given alms.

Puberty customs.

Amongst them when a girl attains her maturity, she is not located in a separate building put up for the time being, but is allowed to remain in a separate room. On the seventh morning, she is anointed by seven young women who give offerings to the demons if she is possessed of them, and then bathed. The offerings consist of the bark of a plantain tree made in the form of a triangle, on which small bits of tender cocoanut leaves and lighted candles are fixed. This is waved round her face several times, and floated away on the water as she bathes. This is believed to have the power of relieving the girl from the influence of demons. She is taken home after her bath, and her friends and relations are invited and fed according to the means of her parents. In the event of her marriage taking place before puberty, she would be going to the hut of her husband and staying there for a few days every now and then. If she attains her maturity during her stay there, the parents of the girl attend the ceremony in the bridegroom's hut, and pay nine annas for the expense. This custom is in vogue among the Izhuvans also.

Marriage customs.

A Pulluvan may marry the daughter of his maternal uncle. In certain parts of the Valluvanad Taluk, marriage is allowed between the members of the same family. In Palghat, members of the caste in the same village intermarry, and have peculiar prejudices against contracting matrimonial alliances among the caste-men of different localities.

Both infant and adult marriages take place among the Pulluvans. The first is the *Thalikettukalyanom* (*tali* tying ceremony) which, as among the Nairs and the Izhuvans, is performed during the seventh, ninth, eleventh, or thirteenth year of a girl. In some places, some who are too poor to perform it conveniently put it off.

The caste-men are very poor, and as such their ceremonies connected with the *Thalikettukalyanom* are very simple. An auspicious day is chosen for the performance of the ceremony, when the father of the girl invites his nephew or some relation of his, in the absence of whom, any other boy of twelve or thirteen years of age, who is asked to pass the *tali* (conjugal collar) round the neck of the girl. The pseudo bridegroom, after the conclusion of the ceremony, stays in the hut of the bride for four days, and on the fourth morning, they bathe and go to the nearest temple to worship the deities. They both take their meals, after which comes the divorce from this fictitious connection. This is called *acharamkodukkal.* The bridegroom receives the present of a *mundu* and a few annas for this ephemeral union, and is no longer the husband of the girl. It is the father of the girl that provides her with the *tali* and the cloth on the ceremonial day. The parents are not subject to any penalty if this is either put off or not performed. Many fail to celebrate it.

It is not the duty of the father to find out a suitable bridegroom for his daughter. The bride is selected for a young man by his parents. As in all other castes, the parents of the boys and girls arrange marriages with absolute authority and without consulting the parties interested. The preliminaries are shortly debated and settled between them in the presence of an *enangan* on each side, who acts the part of a middle-man. The *tali* and the wedding dress are brought by the parents of the bridegroom. On the day fixed, at the auspicious hour, the bridegroom, purifying himself by a bath and neatly dressed, arrives with his relations and friends at the booth prepared for the occasion, and there they are well received. The bride, dressed in new garments, is taken to the pandal, and the *tali* tying ceremony is performed. Then follows the feast, after which they chew betel. Each of the guests puts on a metal plate a few annas varying from four to eight, as he takes leave of the host. This is called the *poli* or subscription, which is intended to defray the expenses of the ceremony. The bridegroom with his bride departs to his own hut soon after. Usually a member from the hut of the bride accompanies the girl. The newly married couple stays there for three days, after which they are invited back to the hut of the bride. Thenceforward they live together as husband and wife.

Among the Pulluvans, a man cannot have more than one wife, nor can a woman allow herself to conjugal servitude to more than one. Should her husband die, she can join in the bonds of wedlock with any of his younger brothers.

Pregnancy and childbirth.

When a woman is pregnant, a ceremony, called *Puliyoonu*, is performed in her husband's hut during the seventh month, after which she is allowed to accompany her parents. When she takes leave of her mother-in-law, she obtains from her as present, a *kacha*, called *enathuni* (a piece of cloth), and a plate to be used at meals. Delivery takes place in her own house. The news of a male or a female issue is carried to the house of her husband by her *enangan*, who receives four annas seven pies for his services. In Palghat, the sisters of the bridegroom or other women related to him present the woman in confinement with two pieces of cloth on the seventh day for wearing after pollution, which lasts for fifteen days though she bathes on the seventh day. On the sixteenth morning she again bathes and the *enangan's* wife sprinkles water mixed with cow-dung to cleanse her from pollution and gets eight annas for her services. There is also a feast that day.

Adultery and divorce.

A Pulluvan can repudiate his wife for adultery, sterility, immodesty, disobedience or loquacity. He must in that case leave her in charge of her parents, explaining to them the circumstances under which he has been forced to do so They may also separate by mutual agreement, the children sometimes following the mother and sometimes the father. Though the man has always the right of repudiation or divorce, very often, the reciprocal right also exists. There is a curious custom to be noticed in this connection. Should the parents have no objection to their daughters being divorced, they give the husband a piece of cloth. The custom is called *murikodukkuka*, which means that the cloth he has given is returned, and that the divorce has been effected. Should he have children, it is not at once allowed.

It is said that in former times they had legitimate or illicit intercourse with their sisters. I enquired about this in half a dozen places, and was assured that the custom does not exist at present. When they are questioned on this, they emphatically deny it. In the event of a like incident in another caste, the members thereof contemptuously ask, "Is he a Pulluvan?" This bears testimony to the fact, that this open or clandestine connection must have sometime or other existed among them.

Inheritance and caste assembly.

They follow the Makkathayam law of inheritance. They have nothing worth calling property except perhaps their small thatched huts with a few earthen vessels, and they are destined to live upon the charity of others. There is therefore nothing to be said with regard to the question of inheritance. They have their caste assemblies (*parishas*), which adjudicate upon adultery, theft, and like offences. The members, called *parishakkar*, are the principal ones of the thirty-one families, who settle disputes and decide on the fine or other punishment to be inflicted.

Magic and sorcery.

Pulluvans fully believe in magic and sorcery. Every kind of sickness is attributed to the influence of some demon, the remedy for which lies very much in the power of a magician or a sorcerer. In some cases the village astrologer is consulted, who, with his calculations, may rightly divine the cause of the illness. Among these people an astrologer can easily draw his conclusions from the particulars of the circumstances explained to him. He soon suggests that the disease or the calamity may have been due to the provocation of their family or other gods, to whom sacrifices or offerings may not have been given in time. Under such circumstances a *velichapad* or an oracle, who may be one of their own family, or somebody not connected with it is consulted. Bathing and dressing himself in a new piece of cloth, he enters on the scene with a sword in hand and his legs girt with small bells, and stands in front of the deity in pious contemplation. After a short time, he advances with short steps, and rolling his eyes, he makes a few frantic cuts on his forehead. He is already in convulsive shiver, and works himself up to a state of inspiration, and in this state, he utters certain disjointed sentences which are believed to be the words of their gods. Believing them to be the means of remedy or relieving themselves from the besetting calamities, they reverentially bow before the *velichapad* and act as commanded by him.

When women, pregnant or otherwise, or even children walk alone during midday, they are supposed to be possessed of any or all of the following demons, *viz.*, Yakshi, Gandharvan, Káppiri, which are treated as beings of adoration, but not worshipped regularily. Fever, want of milk in a woman's breast, and bloodlessness are all ascribed to the malicious influence of these demons. Under such circumstances, the woman frequently falls in convulsive fits. A magician is sent for, and he, by his *mantrams* and magic songs, controls and gratifies the demons with suitable offerings, and then commands them to depart by oath and to extort a promise that they would never again enter her body. In some cases, when the demons are so obstinate in making their demands in regard to offerings as not to leave her, a wooden figure or image is made and the tuft of a woman's hair is tied round its head. The figure is fixed to a tree, and nails are driven through the neck and breast, when the demons are supposed to have left her. If men or children are under the influence of these demons, mere sacrifices will satisfy the purpose. In this connection it must be said that there are magicians among all the castes in Malabar. The lower the caste, the greater is the belief in the potency of their influence.

A man, who wishes to have the demon brought under his control, must bathe early morning for forty-one days, cook for himself, and be under a kind of religious vow. He should have no association with his wife during the period and be free from pollution of any kind. Every night after ten o' clock, he should bathe in a tank or river and stand stark naked in water up to his loins, offering his prayers to the deity, whom he wishes to get under his control. The substance of his prayers is this: "I offer thee my prayers, so that thou mayest bless me with what I want." Thus, with his mind fully centred on the deity, he should mutter them 101, 1,001, 10,001 times during the period. Should he continue to do so for forty-one days, with firm resolution, in spite of all obstacles and intimidation from them, the deity would be pleased to grant him the boon. He would even present himself in person whenever he is thought of. To achieve this, it would be better for him to have a training and guidance from a *guru* (preceptor) in which case, he should proceed to act with permission. If the directions given to him are not properly followed, the results of his labour are supposed to drive him mad.

Religion.

With no education and association with higher castes, they profess the lower forms of Hinduism, worshipping the deities of the Brahmanic temples from a distance. They have also crude ideas of religion and believe in spirits of all sorts and sizes. They adore the following deities, namely, Velayudhan, Ayyappan, Rahu, Muni, and the demons, Cháthan, Mookkan, Kandakaranan, Karinkutty, Theekutty,

Parakkutty, Kappiri, and Kalladimuttan. All these deities are never located in any compound; but a few stones representing some of them are often seen beneath a tree, on a floor slightly raised. Rahu is worshipped on Sundays, Tuesdays, and Fridays before they go for alms. Muni is a well intentioned deity, to whom they contribute once a year offerings of boiled rice, parched rice, plantains, and cocoanuts, which are distributed among those present on the occasion. The offerings to Mookkan, Karinkutty, and other demoniacal gods are generally given according to the means at the disposal of those who do the *pujas*, and very often they perform the *pujas* at night. A *padmam* (floral diagram) is drawn on the floor with nine divisions marked by rice flour, on each of which are placed pieces of green cocoanut leaves and some cotton wicks dipped in cocoanut oil and lighted. Camphor and frankincense are burned to add to the solemnity of the occasion. Besides sheep and fowls, parched rice, boiled beans, jaggery, husk, earthen cake, toddy, and plantains are offered. If sheep has to be sacrificed, boiled rice is offered at twelve o'clock. The sheep is brought in front and water is sprinkled on its head before it is killed. If the sheep shakes its head, so as to be free from water, it is a good omen.

On all new moon days, and on *Karkadakam* and *Thulam sankranthis*, offerings are given to the souls of the departed. They consist of mutton, fowls, toddy, and other preparations, which are served on a large plantain leaf. They prostrate themselves before them and offer prayers by saying, " Ye dead ancestors, we offer what we can afford. May ye take them and be pleased to protect us." On the night previous to the new moon, the man, who has to give offerings, bathes and cooks for himself, and on the new moon day he bathes and offers rice balls to the spirits of the departed. Any slight dereliction or even indifference in regard to the sacrificial service is attended with great domestic calamities. The Pulluvans fully believe, that so long as they approach them by their worship and offerings, their desires are gratified. They court their favour at

THE PULLUVANS WITH MUSICAL INSTRUMENTS.

times by promising more sacrifices, if they will help them either in the achievement of their object or in the destruction of their enemies. Sometimes they do their *pujas* on a large scale, praying for defence against their enemies when they try to harm them, and at other times they pray in secret. They also consult *velichapads* as to the results of their undertaking. They resort to a curious method of calculating, beforehand, the result of a project in which they are engaged, by piously placing before their gods two bouquets of flowers, one red and the other white, and having one of them taken by a child with his eyes closed. The white one predicts happy results, and the other quite the reverse.

Occupation.

Their original occupation is to go for alms to the houses of the members of other castes, especially the Nairs, Izhuvans, and Kammalans. When a Pulluvan goes for it, he takes his *pulluvakudam*, and a woman (either his wife or somebody else) accompanies him. They also preside at the ceremony of *Pambin thullal*. A pandal supported by four poles driven to the ground is put up for the purpose, and the tops of these poles are connected with a network of strings, over which a silk or a red cloth is spread to form a temporary canopy. This pandal is well decorated, and the floor below the pandal is slightly raised and smoothed. A hideous figure of the size of a big serpent is drawn with rice flour, turmeric (Curcuma longa), *kuvva* (Curcuma augustifolia), powdered charcoal, and another kind of green powder. These five powders are essential, for their colours are visible on the necks of serpents. Some rice is scattered on the floor and on the sides, and ripe and green cocoanuts are placed on a small quantity of rice and paddy on each side. A *puja* for Ganapathi is performed to see that the whole ceremony terminates well. A good deal of frankincense is burned, and a lamp is placed on a plate to add to the purity, sanctity, and solemnity of the occasion. The members of the house come round the decorated pandal as a token of reverence and take their seats close by. It often happens that the members of several neighbouring families take part in the ceremony.

The women, from whom devils have to be cast out, bathe and take their seats on the western side, each with a flower pod of the areca palm. The Pulluvan, with his wife or daughter begins his shrill musical tunes (on serpents), vocal and instrumental, alternately. As they sing, the young female members, already sanctified by bath and seated there, appear to be influenced by the modulation of the tunes and the smell of the perfumes. They gradually move their heads in a circle, which soon quickens, and the long locks of hair are soon let loose. These movements appear to keep time with the Pulluvan's music. In their unconscious state, they beat upon the floor and wipe off the figure drawn, and the anthers all fall to the ground. As soon as this is done, they go to a serpent grove close by, where there may be a few stone-images of serpents before which they prostrate themselves. They now recover their consciousness, and take milk, water of the green cocoanut, and plantain fruits, and fast for the night; then the Pulluvan terminates his songs, and the ceremony is over. This is also called *kalam kottal.* They are not able to maintain themselves and their families by the hereditary profession of their caste, and therefore go for all kinds of day-labour, *viz.*, sowing, ploughing, reaping, fencing, cutting timber, and get the daily wages of four to five annas either in kind or coin. There are neither landlords, tenure-holders nor occupancy ryots among them. They are mere landless day-labourers living in the huts of their own build on the waste lands of some landlord, for which they pay a nominal ground rent.

Social status.

They have no objection to take anything prepared by the Brahmans, Nairs, Kammalans, and Izhuvans, but will never eat anything prepared by Mannans and Kaniyans. In point of pollution, they are more like Izhuvans. They pollute carpenters and Izhuvans by touch, but are polluted by Cherumans, Pulayans, Parayans, Ulládans, and others. Their approach to within thirty feet pollutes Brahmans, Kshatriyas, and Sudras.

CHAPTER IX.

THE VELANS.

—:o:—

The Velans of Cochin, like the Pánans, are a caste of devil-dancers, sorcerers, and quack doctors, and are, in the northern parts of the State, called Perumannans [1] or Mannáns (washermen). They numbered 8,239 in the last census, 4,009 being males, 4,230 females. The Velans and the Mannáns differ slightly in their customs and manners, and in some places they neither interdine nor intermarry, while in others they interdine but do not intermarry.

There are no sub-castes [2] among the Velans, who, in Ernakulam, Cochin, and other places, are said to belong to the following eight *illams* (endogamous septs), namely, Pàla Illam Attipalli Illam, Thàmarasseri Illam, Panankat Illam, and Thali Illam. Similar *illam* division exists among the Perumannans of the Trichur Taluk. They are Thachampalli Illam, Eramangalath Illam, Cherusseri Illam, and Purathikàd Illam. In the same Taluk, the name of the place in which they live is also prefixed to their names. The Perumannans of the Chittur Taluk have no knowledge of this *illam* division existing among

1. My informant, a Perumannan at Trichur, told me that their caste-men south of the Karuvannur bridge, about ten miles south of Trichur, are called Velans, and that they neither interdine nor intermarry, because they give *mattu* (a washed cloth) to carpenters to be free from pollution. The Mannans who give the *mattu* to Izhuvans do not give it to Kammalans who are superior to them in social status. I am not furnished with any satisfactory explanation for the observance of this custom.

2. In the Trichur Taluk, the Mannans are said to belong to the following four subdivisions, namely,

(1) Perumannans—washermen for Brahmans, Nairs, and Izhuvans.
(2) Thachan Mannans—washermen for Kammalans.
(3) Theenda Mannans—washermen for the fishing castes.
(4) Punnekkadan.

them. These subdivisions which are not found in other places do not appear to be real exogamous divisions. Similar divisions are also noticed among the Pànans.

Origin of the caste. The following ingenious story is given me regarding the origin of the Velans and Mannàns. Once when god Parameswara and his wife Parvathi were amusing themselves, the latter chanced to make an elephant with earth which was accidentally trodden upon by the former, whence arose a man who stood bowing before them. He was called the Mannàn, because he came out of *man* (earth), and to him was assigned his present occupation. This tradition is referred to in the songs which they sing on the fourth day of a girl's first menses, when she takes a ceremonial bath to be free from pollution.

Habitations. The Velans are found all over the southern parts of the State like their brethren in the northern parts, and the former live in thatched huts in cocoanut gardens, while the Mannáns occupy similar dwellings in small compounds either of their own or of some landlords whose tenants they may be. They are very poor and have no furniture of any kind except a few coarse mats, on which they sleep, and one or two wooden planks to sit on. Their utensils are earthen, but a few enamelled dishes and tumblers were seen in some of the huts examined by me.

Puberty customs. When a girl attains her puberty she is at once bathed and located in a room of the hut. The period of her seclusion is four days, during which she is in a state of pollution. On the morning of the fourth day, she is seated in a pandal put up in front of the hut, and made to hold in her hand a leafy vessel filled with rice, a few annas, and a lighted wick, when a few of their caste-men sing songs connected with puberty till as late as one or two o'clock, and then the girl is bathed. After this, the caste-men and women, who are invited, are feasted along with the girl, who is neatly dressed and adorned in her best. Again the girl takes her seat in the pandal and the tunes begin, and are continued till seven or eight next morning, when the ceremony comes to an end. The songsters are remunerated with one rupee eight annas worth of paddy, twenty-eight cocoanuts, thirteen annas and four pies, and two pieces of cloth. The songs are in some families postponed to the sixteenth day of the girl's marriage. Very poor people dispense with them altogether.

The translation of one of the songs is given here. "One day a girl and her friends were playing merrily on the banks of a river, when one of them noticed some blood on her dress. They took her home, and her parents believed it to have been caused by some wound, but on enquiry knew that their daughter was in her menses. The daughter asked her mother as to what she did with the cloth she wore during her menses, when she was told that she bathed and came home, leaving it on a branch of a mango tree. On further enquiry she knew that goddess Ganga purified herself by a bath, leaving her cloth in the river: that goddess Earth buried it in earth: and that Panchali returned home after a bath, leaving her dress on one of the branches of a banyan tree. Unwilling to lose her dress, the girl went to the god Parameswara and implored his aid to get somebody to have her cloth washed, when, muttering a *mantram*, he sprinkled some water, a few drops of which went up and became stars, and from a few more which fell on the leaves of a banyan tree, there came out a man, to whom was assigned the task of washing the cloths of the women in their courses, wearing which alone, the women are purified by a bath."

Marriage customs.

Among the Velans of the south and the Mannàns of the north, girls are married sometimes when they are grown up, and sometimes when they are still infants. As amongst the Panans and Vilkurups, the *tali* tying ceremony for girls of nine, eleven, or twelve years of age is indispensable, the neglect of this ceremony being punishable by excommunication. The formalities connected with it are the same as those described in my account of other castes.

Both infant and adult marriages are allowed and practised. When a young man of the Velan caste has attained the marriageable age, his father and maternal uncle select a suitable girl as wife, after proper examination into the agreement of their horoscopes. The preliminaries are arranged in the hut of the girl, and a portion of the bride's price (four rupees and a quarter) is also paid at the time. The auspicious day for the wedding is fixed, and the number of guests that should attend it is also determined. The wedding is celebrated in the girl's hut, in front of which a shed is put up. The ceremony generally takes place during the night. A few hours before it, the bridegroom and his party arrive at the bride's hut, where they are welcomed and seated on mats spread on the floor in the pandal. At the auspicious hour, when the relatives on both sides and the caste-men are assembled, the bridegroom's *enangan* hands over a metal plate containing the wedding suit, the bride's price, and a few packets of betel-leaves and nuts to the bride's *enangan*, who takes everything except the cloth to be given to the bride's mother and returns the plate. The bridegroom's sister dresses the bride in the new cloth, and takes her to the pandal to seat her along with the bridegroom and to serve one or two spoonfuls of milk and a few pieces of plantain fruits, when the bride is formally declared to be the wife of the young man and a member of his family, which is the binding portion of the ceremony. The guests assembled are treated to a feast, after which they are served with betel-leaves, nuts, and tobacco. The rest of the night is spent in merry song and dancing. The next morning the bride's party is treated to a rice *kanji* at eight o' clock, and to a sumptuous meal at twelve o' clock, after which they return to the bridegroom's hut accompanied by the bride, her parents, and relations, all of whom receive a similar welcome. The formalities are gone through here also, and the bride's party is feasted. On the fourth morning, the married couple bathe and dress themselves neatly to worship the deity in the local temple. After dinner, they go to the bride's hut, where they spend a week or two, after which the bridegroom returns to his own hut with his wife. The marriage is formally over. It is now that the bride receives a few ornaments, a metal dish for use at meals, a lamp, and a few metallic utensils which vary according to the circumstances of her parents. Thenceforward, the husband and wife live with the parents of the former in their family. The marriage expenses in the bride's family amount to about fifty or sixty rupees, while for the bridegroom, they come to a little less. The chief item of expenditure in both the families is the feeding.

Among the Mannáns of the northern parts of the State, the following marriage customs are found to prevail. The bridegroom's father, his maternal uncle, *enangan*, and the third man or middle-man conjointly select the girl after ascertaining the agreement of horoscopes. The preliminaries are arranged as before, and the day for the wedding is also determined. Just at the auspicious moment on the wedding day, when the relatives on both sides and the caste-men are assembled in the shed in front of the bride's hut, the bridegroom's father takes up a metal plate containing the wedding dress, the bride's price (three rupees six annas), and a few packets of betel-leaves, nuts, and tobacco, and gives it to the bride's parents, after first repeating sentences of which the following is the substance. " A lighted lamp is placed in the shed. Four mats are spread round it in the direction of east, west, north, and south. A metallic plate containing some rice, flowers, and betel-leaves is placed in front of the lamp, and the elderly members of the caste and the relatives on both sides are assembled. According to the traditional custom of the caste, the young man's father, maternal uncle, *enangan*, and the third or middle-man conjointly selected the girl after satisfying themselves as to the due agreement of horoscopes and ascertaining the *illams* and *kiriyams* on both sides. They have negotiated for the girl, and settled the day on which the marriage is to take place. In token of this, they have eaten with the bride's family. The claims of the girl for two pieces of cloth for *Onam*, nine annas for *Thiruwathira* (a festival in Dhanu, *i. e.*, December-January) and *Vishu* (first of Medam *i. e.*, about the twelfth of April) are satisfied, and she has been taken by the young man to the village festival. They have now come for the celebration of the wedding. There have been times when he has heard of twenty-eight rupees eight annas as the price of the bride, and has seen fourteen rupees six annas as the price of the same, but it is now six rupees. It thus varies, and may be increased or diminished according to the will, pleasure, and means of the parties. With one rupee two annas as the price of the bride and two rupees four annas for ornaments, and with the packets of betel-leaves, nuts, and the wedding dress in a metal plate, 'May I, ye elderly members, give it to the girl's parents?' " "Shall I," answers the girl's father, "accept it?" Receiving it, the father gives it to his brother-in-law who gives it to the *enangan* and he takes everything in it except the wedding suit, which he hands over to the bridegroom's *enangan*. The latter gives it to the bridegroom's sister, to have the bride dressed in it. The other portions of the ceremony are the same as those described above.

In Palghat and the Chittur Taluk of the State, a short declaration is made to the following effect. "According to the customary traditions of the caste, when a young man of one locality comes to take a girl of another locality and takes her as wife, 'Ye, elderly members assembled here, may these four bundles of betel-leaves, four measures of rice, two pieces of cloth (wedding suit), and two rupees thirteen annas, be given to the bride's parents?' " "Shall these be accepted?" says the bride's *enangan*. When the bride accompanies the bridegroom to his hut, another formal statement is made, of which the following is the general tenor. "Thrash thou mayest, but not with a stick. Thou mayest not accuse her of bad conduct. Thou mayest not cut off her ears, breast, nose, and tufts of hair. Thou mayest not take her to a tank (to bathe) or a temple (for swearing). Thou mayest keep and protect her as long as thou wantest. When thou dost not want her, give her maintenance, and take back the children, for they are thine own."

As has been said, the day on which the wedding takes place, is spent in songs sung by some of their caste-men. These songs, which are puranic, refer to the marriage of Sita, wife of Ráma, hero of Ramayana, of Subhadra, wife of Arjuna, and of Panchali, wife of the Pandavas, and are not without fun and humour.

Polygamy and polyandry.

Polygamy is not prohibited, but it is rarely practised by the Velans and Mannàns. They are very poor, and find it difficult to support a single wife and her children. Barrenness, bodily defect or incurable disease, or want of additional hands for work, may sometimes induce them to take more than one wife. Polyandry does not prevail among the Velans, but is common among the Mannáns of the northern parts of the State. The formalities connected with it are the same as those described in my account of the other polyandrous castes.

Widow marriage.

A Velan woman who loses her husband may marry another man of her caste, if she likes, a year after her husband's death. Her children, if sufficiently young, reside with her, until they are grown up, when, they are left in the family of their father. The formalities of the wedding consist in the husband's giving two pieces of cloth to the woman who wishes to enter into wedlock with him. After this, she forfeits all claims on the property of her former husband. Young widows sometimes marry in this manner, but grown up women with children seldom think of a second marriage. Among the Mannàns, on the other hand, a widow may marry any one of her brothers-in-law.

Adultery and divorce.

A woman committing adultery with a member of her own caste is well thrashed with a view to deter her from a repetition of the crime. A woman who disposes of herself to a member of a lower caste is outcasted. Both among the Velans and Mannàns, divorce is an easy affair, for a man, who does not like his wife, has only to take her to her hut and give her in charge of her parents, informing them of the circumstances which have induced him to adopt such a course. A woman, who does not like her husband, may relinquish him and join her parents. In both the cases, the woman divorced is at liberty to marry again.

Pregnancy and childbirth.

When a woman is pregnant, the ceremony of *Pulikudi* (drinking of tamarind juice) is performed for her during the ninth month in the hut of her husband. The juice is extracted from tamarind (Tamarindus Indica), *kodapuli* (Garcinia cambogia), *nerinjampuli* (Hibiscus), and the leaves of *ambazhampuli* (Spondias). A large branch of an *ambazhampuli* (Spondias) is stuck to the ground in the central court-yard, near which the pregnant woman is seated. The husband gives three small spoonfuls of the juice to his wife, and then seven times with her *cheruthali* (an ornament for the neck) dipped in the juice. Among the Mannàns, the woman's brother gives it three times to her. Should her sister-in-law give it in a small vessel, she has a claim for two pieces of cloth. After this, a quarter measure of gingelly oil is poured upon her head to be rubbed all over her body, and she soon bathes using Acacia Intsia as soap. Her relatives and the caste-men that are invited are sumptuously fed. In the meantime, some of them crack jokes by asking the pregnant woman to promise her baby (son or daughter), in marriage to theirs, when grown up. They all bless her for a safe delivery, and a healthy child. After her dinner, her parents take her home.

A woman who is about to become a mother is lodged in a separate room for her delivery, attended by her mother and one or two grown up women who act as midwives. As soon as delivery takes place, both the mother and the baby are bathed in warm water. The period of pollution is for fifteen days. For the first three days, she is given a dose of dried ginger mixed with palmyra jaggery, and for the next three days a mixture of garlic and jaggery. Her diet during the first three days is rice *kanji* with small scrapings of cocoanuts, which help the formation of the mother's milk to feed the baby. For the next three days, the juice of *kodapuli* (Garcinia cambogia), boiled with mustard, cumin seeds, and *kodal wrukki* (Achyranthes aspera), and also of the leaves of *muringa* (Hyperanthera moringa), is given, after which for a few more days, a dose of the flesh of fowl mixed with mustard, cumin seeds and *ulura* (Trigonella foenum græc) boiled in gingelly oil is taken. She bathes in water boiled with medicinal herbs on the fourth, seventh, ninth, eleventh, and the sixteenth days. On the morning of the sixteenth day her *enangathy* (*enangan's* wife), cleans her room with water mixed with cow-dung and sweeps the compound. Wearing a *mattu* (washed cloth) brought by a washerwoman, she bathes to be free from pollution. She may now enter the hut and mingle with the rest of the family. She is under a mild medical treatment for one or two months to regain her former health. The expenses connected with the delivery are defrayed by her husband.

The ceremony of naming takes place either on the twenty-eighth day or the sixth month; in the latter case feeding also takes place along with it. The occasion is one of festivity to their friends and relations. The ceremony of ear-boring for a male baby falls during the sixth month, and for a girl during the fifth or sixth year.

Inheritance and caste assembly.

Among Velans and Mannàns, the sons inherit the property of their fathers. They are poor, and have little to inherit. They have their caste assemblies, which consist of the elderly members who meet on all occasions affecting the welfare of the caste-men, and their decisions are final.

Magic and sorcery.

Velans and Mannàns practise magic and sorcery. As has been said, all diseases that flesh is heir to, are, in the opinion of these people, caused by the malignant demons, and these men profess to cure, with the aid of their *mantrams* and amulets, people suffering from maladies. The muttering of a certain *mantram* and the throwing of *bhasmam* (holy ashes), in propitiation of the small-pox demon, are believed to effect a radical cure on persons suffering from small-pox and diseases of a similar nature. Approximate translations are here offered of this *mantram* and others.

1. "Om, O, thou, Pallyamma! mother with tusk-like teeth, that in demoniacal form, appearest on the burning ground, called *omkara*, with burning piles flaming around, with one breast on one of thy shoulders and playing with the other as with a ball, with thy tongue stretched out and wound round thy head, with grass, beans, and pepper in thy left hand, with gingelly seeds and *chama* grains in thy right hand, that scatterest and sowest broadcast the seeds of small-pox and allied pox; O! let the seeds that thou hast sown, and those that thou hast not sown, dry up inside and get charred outside. Be thou as if intoxicated with joy! Be thou as if intoxicated with joy! Protect thou, Protect thou!"

The small-pox demon is in the Tamil districts called Mariyamma, who is the village goddess (*Grama Devatha*). The legend is that she was expelled from Heaven on account of her haughtiness, and she is more feared for causing, in her anger, plague, small-pox, and other calamities, than beloved for removing them. Her aid is often solicited for protection from the attack of demon. In Malabar, Cochin, and Travancore, she is known as Kàli or Bhagavathi, and festivals are held in honour of her.

2. Malign influence of birds on children.—"O, thou, round eyed short Karinkali[1] with big ears, born from the third incessantly burning eye of Siva! come, come, and be in my possession." If the above *mantram* be muttered sixteen times, and *bhasmam* thrown over the body of a child, the operator breathing violently the while, a radical cure will be effected. If the *mantram* be muttered into a vessel of water the same number of times, and the child bathed in it, the cure will be equally effective.

1. Cheriakarinkali=Dark coloured young goddess, Kali. Her ears are very large. In the war with Darika (an *asura* or demon), it is said that her ears were so large as to conceal a large number of elephants.

3. "O, thou, swine faced mother! that catchest hold of my enemy, coming charging me by the neck, with thy tusks thrust into his body; draggest him on the ground and standest slowly, chewing and eating, thrusting once and thrusting thy tusks, rubbing again, and wearing down his body, chewing once more and again; thou, mother that controllest 4448 demons presiding over all kinds of maladies, seventy-two Bhairavans, eighteen kinds of epileptic fits (*korkas*)[1], twelve kinds of Muyalis, and all other kinds of illness, as also twelve Kandakaranans (demons with bell-shaped ear), be under my possession, so long as I serve thee." This *mantram*, when repeated sixteen times with *bhasmam* (holy ashes) thrown on the body of a patient, is a cure for all kinds of fits and fever.

4. "O, Bhadrakali, that hast drunk the full cup! O, thou, that holdest the sword of royalty in thy right hand, and that half sittest on a high seat! place under control, as I am piously uttering the *mantrams* to serve thee, all demons, namely, Yakshi, Gandharvan, Poomalagandharvan, Chutali, Neerali, Nilankari, Chuzhali, and many others, who cause all kinds of illness that flesh is heir to. O, holy mother, Bhadrakali! I vow by my preceptor."

5. For devil-driving.—"O, thou, Karinkutty [2] (black dwarf) of Vedapuram in Vellanad, that pluckest the fruits of the right hand branch of strichnos nux vomica, and keepest toddy in its shell, drinking the blood of black domestic fowl, drumming and keeping time on the rind of the fruit, filling and blowing thy pipe or horn through the nose! O, thou, primeval black dwarf! so long as I utter thy proper *mantrams*, I beg thee to cause such demons as would not dance to dance and others to jump and drive them out. O, thou, Karinkutty! come, come, and enable me to succeed in my attempts."

1. *Korka* is a kind of fever. Its symptoms are ague, change of bodily colour to darkness, trembling as with fear, bodily distortion, and flow of saliva.

2. Karinkutty is an incarnation of Vishnu in his *tamas* (dark moments).

6. "O, thou goddess with face, O, thou with face like that of a bear, and thou, a hunter! I utter thy *mantrams* and meditate upon thee, and, therefore, request thee to tread upon my enemies, burst open their bodies to drink their blood and yawn to take complete rest; drive out such demons as cause convulsions of the body both from within and without, and all kinds of fever. Scatter them as dust. I swear by thee and my preceptor *Swaha*.[1]"

7. Potency of evil eye.—"Salutation to thee, O, God! Even as the Moon wanes in its brightness at the sight of the Sun, even as the bird *chakora* (crow-pheasant) disappears at the sight of the Moon even as the great Vasuki (king of serpents) vanishes at the sight of *chakora*, even as the poison vanishes from his head, so may the potency of his evil eye, with thy aid, vanish." The muttering of this *mantram* with *bhasmam* thrown over the body of a patient is an effective cure for the potency of the evil eye.

8. *Mantram* to cause delay in the occurrence of menses. —"Salutation to thee, O, Mars, the son of the goddess Earth!" If this *mantram* be muttered on a thread dyed yellow with turmeric, and if the thread be placed on both the palms joined together, and if the number of days for which the occurrence of the menses should be delayed be thought of, the postponement would be caused by wearing it either round the neck or the loins. The thread with a ring attached to it and worn round the neck is equally effective. In the belief of these people, it may be postponed even to a few months.

9. *Mantram* preventing cows from milking.—"Om, *koss* (a mystic word of destructive import)! dry up the liquid (water); kindly present me with thy gracious aspect. O, thou with the great sword in thy hands, the great trident! dry up the cow's udder even as a tiger. I swear by thee and my preceptor."

1. *Swaha* is mystic syllable uttered by the sorcerer when he throws ashes, etc., on the patient or otherwise employs or propitiates his goddess. It is a Sanskrit word for sacrifice.

10. *Mantram* causing cows to give milk.—"Even as the swelling on the holy feet of Mahadeva due to the bite of a crocodile, has subsided and gone down, so go down; I swear by my preceptor."

11. *Mantram* to remove thorn thrust into the sole of the foot.—"When Parameswara and Parvathi started on their hunting expedition, a thorn entered the feet of her ladyship. It was doubted to be the thorn of a bamboo or an ant or a nux vomica. Even so, may this poison cease to hurt, O, Lord! I swear by my preceptor."

12. "Take the head of a dog and burn it, and plant on it a *vellakuthi* plant (sap wood). Burn camphor, frankincense and adore it. Then pluck the root. Then mix it with the milk of a dog and the bones of a cat. A mark of the mixture on the forehead can enable a person to assume the figure of any animal he thinks of."

13. "Before a stick of the *malankara* plant, worship with a lighted wick and incense. Then chant the Sakti *mantram* 101 times, and then mutter the *mantram* to give life at the bottom. Watch carefully which way the stick inclines. Proceed to the south of the stick, and pluck the whiskers of a live tiger and make with them a ball of the *veerali* silk, and string it with silk and enclose it within the ear. Stand on the palms of the hand to attain the disguise of a tiger, and with the stick in hand, think of a cat, white bull, or any other animal. Then you will, in the eyes of others, appear as such."

14. "Take the nest of a crow from a margosa tree, and bury it in the cremation ground. Then take and throw it in the house of your enemy. The house will soon take fire."

15. "Take the ashes of the burial ground on which an ass has been rolling on a Sunday or a Saturday, and keep it in the house of your enemy. The members of the family will soon quit the house or a severe illness will attack them."

Religion.

The Velans and Mannáns are animists, and worship a set of demoniacal gods, namely, Chàndan, Mundian, Kandakaranan, Karinkutty, and Chàthan, all of whom are separately represented by stones which are located underneath a tree in the corners of their compounds; and offerings of sheep, fowls, plantain fruits, cocoanuts, parched rice, and beaten rice are made to them on the tenth of Dhanu (last week of December), on a Tuesday in Makaram (January-February), and on Kumbhom Bharani (second asterism in March-April). They also adore the goddess Bhagavathi and the spirits of their departed ancestors, who are believed to exercise their influence in the families of these people for everything good or bad. Sometimes when they go to Cranganore to worship the goddess there, they visit the senior male members of the local Nair, Kammalan, and Izhuvan families to take leave of them, when they are given a few annas with which they purchase fowls, etc., to be given as offerings to the goddess. Wooden or metallic images, representing the spirits of their departed ancestors, are located in a room of their huts and worshipped with offerings on new moon and *sankranthi* nights.

Funeral customs.

The Velans and Mannàns either bury or burn the dead. The sons are the chief mourners who perform the funeral rites, and the nephews and brothers, if any, take part in them. Their priests are known as Kurups, who preside at the ceremonies. The pollution lasts for sixteen days, and on the morning of the sixteenth day, the hut of the dead man or woman is well swept and cleaned by sprinkling water mixed with cow-dung. The members of the family dressed in the *mattu* (a washed cloth worn before bathing) brought by the washerman, bathe to be free from pollution. The caste-men including their friends and relations are invited and feasted. A similar funeral feast is also held at the end of the year.

A VELANS' DANCE.

Occupation.

The chief occupation of the Velans and Mannàns is the giving of *mattu* to Brahmans, Kshatriyas, Antharalajathis, Nairs, Kammalans, and Izhuvans for wearing before going to bathe on the day on which they are freed from pollution. A girl or grown up woman in her courses on the morning of the fourth day, a woman in confinement on the fifth, ninth, eleventh, and sixteenth days, and all the members of a family under birth and death pollutions on the sixteenth day, have to use it. They bathe wearing the washed cloth, and return it as soon as the bath is over. It may either belong to the washerman or have been previously given to him by the members of the family. He gets an anna or a measure of paddy for his service to the woman in the menses, and six annas for birth and death pollutions. The Velans give the *mattu* to all caste-men above mentioned, while the Mannàns refuse to give it to the Kammàlans, and thereby profess themselves to be superior in status to them. They wash cloths to dress the idols in some of the high caste temples. As has been said, they wash cloth for the caste-men above referred to, and their washing consists in first plunging the dirty cloths in water mixed with cow-dung and beating them on a stone by the side of a tank, canal, or river, and again immersing them in water mixed with wood ashes or *charamannu*, after which they are exposed to steam for a few hours and again beaten on the stone, slightly moistening in water now and then, until they appear to be quite clean. They are then dried in the sun, and again moistened with a solution of starch and indigo, when they are exposed to the air to dry. When dry, they are well folded and beaten with a heavy club, so as to be like those ironed. The remuneration for washing varies from three to six pies per cloth. The Velans of Cranganore and Cochin-Kanayanur Taluks ascend cocoanut trees to pluck cocoanuts, and get about eight to ten annas for every hundred trees they go up. They make umbrellas. Some among them practise magic and sorcery, and some are quack doctors who treat sickly children. Some are now engaged in agricultural operations, while a few others make beds, pillows, and coats. There are also a few of them in every village who are songsters and whose services are availed of on certain ceremonial occasions, namely, on the bathing day of a girl in her first menses, on the wedding night, and also when religious ceremonies are performed and sacrifices to their gods offered. Some are experts in drum-beating and are invited by low caste-men of the rural parts. The Mannans also follow the same occupations.

Social status.

The Velans and Mannàns eat at the hands of all caste-men above them, namely, Brahmans, Kshatriyas Nairs, and Izhuvans. The former take the food of Kammalans, while the latter abstain from doing so. They do not eat the food prepared by Kaniyans, Panans, Vilkurups, and all caste-men of equal or inferior status. They have to stand at a distance of twenty-four feet from the Brahmans, and are, polluted by the touch of the caste-men above mentioned. They have their own barbers and are themselves their washermen. They stand far away from the outer wall of the temples of high caste-men, and are not allowed to take water from the wells of high caste Sudras, nor are they allowed to live in their midst.

CHAPTER X.

THE PANANS.

The Panans are a caste of people who claim an equal social status with the Kaniyans, because of their knowledge of magic, sorcery, and devil driving. They numbered 2,781 according to the last Cochin Census Report, 1,403 being males, and 1,378 females. It is sometimes said that the Panans and Kaniyans form a division of the Izhuva caste, but according to the results of my investigations, they are distinct communities without interdining. They are also called Koravans in the south.

Traditions of the caste.

In the Madras Census Report of 1891, it is said that the Panans are, in some places, called Malayans and that they may be descendants of that hill tribe who have settled in the plains. The Panans who, as a matter of fact, know nothing of their origin, give as the traditional account of their origin a distorted version of the tradition as to the origin of the Izhuvans which is found in the Mackenzie Manuscripts and is mentioned by me in my account dealing with that caste. The story in the Panan version is as follows: One day a washerman of Cheraman Perumal chanced to wash his dress very clean; on being asked by the Perumal as to the cause of it, the washerman said, that it was due to the suggestion of a handsome carpenter girl, who saw him while washing. The Perumal, pleased with the girl, desired her to be married to his washerman. The parents of the girl were duly consulted and they could not refuse the offer as it came from their own ruler but the carpenters resented it, for if the proposal were accepted and the marriage celebrated, it might not only place the members of her family under a ban, but would also bring on dishonour to the caste-men. To avert the contemplated union, they resorted to the following device.

A pandal was erected and tastefully decorated. Just at the auspicious hour, when the bridegroom and his party were properly seated on mats in the pandal, the carpenters brought a puppet exactly resembling the bride, and placed it by his side, when, suddenly, by a clever artifice the carpenters caused the building to tumble down, and thereby killed all those who were in it. They immediately left the Perumal's country and took refuge in the island of Ceylon. The ruler thereupon was much embarrassed both because of the disaster to the washerman and by the flight of the carpenters, for he had none in his country to build houses. A few Panans were sent for and they brought the carpenters back. On their return, they were given some fruit of the palmyra palm which they ate. They sowed the seeds in their own places and these afterwards grew into large fruit-bearing palms. The Panans possessed the privilege of keeping these trees as their own, but subsequently made them over to Izhuvans, who, in memory of this, give even to-day two dishes of food to the Panans on all ceremonial occasions in their houses. The Panans have been called *Nettaris* by the Izhuvans because of their having originally planted these trees.

There are no sub-castes among the Panans. The caste is endogamous; but the caste-men belong to different *kiriyams*. The names of some of the Kiriyams in the Palghat Taluk are Puthana Kiriyam, Mangat Kiriyam, Chera Kiriyam, Kanaya Kiriyam, Pandiyam Pulli Kiriyam, Kaniyathi Kiriyam, Valayanthatta Kiriyam, Kallu Kiriyam, Karutha Kiriyam, and Ariri Kiriyam.

Habitations.

The Panans are found in small numbers in all the rural parts of the State. Every village consists of a few families, the members of which live by their labour in their own and in the adjacent villages. They live in small thatched huts, similar to those of Kaniyans, and other allied caste-men. Usually each hut is situated in a small separate compound, but sometimes several small huts are built near one another in one compound, with a small one wherein their gods are located. Their huts are provided with verandahs.

Marriage customs.

Marriage is endogamous with regard to the caste, and exogamous in respect of the *kiriyams*. A young man may marry the daughter of his maternal uncle. Marriage is permissible as in other castes both before and after puberty. The *tali* tying ceremony for girls below twelve years of age is indispensable, and the neglect of this ceremony is punishable by excommunication. The real marriage is a kind of *sambandham*, such as prevails among the Nairs, and is similar to that of the Kaniyans and other allied caste-men. The bridegroom's sister gives the wedding dress to the bride and seats her alongside of the bridegroom. A sweet preparation made of milk, sugar, and pieces of plantains is given to the couple, and it is this ceremony which unites them as husband and wife. After regular feasts in their own fashion, the bridegroom and his party along with the bride and her relatives go to the bridegroom's house, and there they are well entertained. The same sweet preparation is given to both of them. In cases where the formal marriage ceremony is postponed after the negotiations between the bridegroom's and bride's parties have been completed in the presence of their respective middlemen (*enangans*) and the bride's price has been given, the bridegroom is at liberty to go to the bride's house and live with her—a fact which shows that it is considered that the young woman is his, as soon as the price is paid. The caste-men are poor, and several brothers may enter into wedlock with one young woman. The ceremonies connected with it are the same as those of the Kaniyans and the Izhuvans of the northern parts of the State. Polygamy does not prevail among them; but a widow may marry her brother-in-law. The customs connected with divorce are similar to those prevailing in other castes.

Inheritance.

Among the Panans, the sons inherit the property of their fathers; as a matter of fact they are poor and have very little to bequeath.

Titles are practically unknown among them; but a Panan who was brought to me for examination at Trichur told me that one of his ancestors got the title of *Panikkan*, and that he had the privilege of wearing a gold ear-ring, of carrying a walking-stick with a silver head at one end, and of using a knife provided with a stile. *Kapradan* also is a title given to the head-man in the Palghat Taluk, and he is also endowed with certain privileges as will be seen from my account of their funeral ceremonies. When a *Kapradan* dies, his son inherits the title on condition of his presenting an umbrella to the Palghat Raja.

Magic and sorcery.

There are magicians and sorcerers among them, who sometimes, at the request even of the high caste-men, practise the black art. Some of the Panans like the Parayans engage in magical rites of a repulsive character, in order to become possessor of a powerful "medicine," the possession of which is believed to have the power of obtaining anything he wishes. They also believe in the existence of a demoniacal hierarchy. Changili Karuppan, Pechi, Oodara Karuppan, Káli, Chotala Karuppan, Chotala Bhadrakali, Yakshi, Gandharvan, and Hanuman are the names of the chief demons whom they profess to control with the aid of *mantrams* and offerings. They also believe that they can both send one or more of these demons into the bodies of men, and that they can cast them out when persons are possessed of them. They profess to cure all kinds of diseases in children with the aid of magic and medicines; and all caste-men believe that harm or even death may be caused to men with the aid of these sorcerers. In such cases an astrologer is consulted, and according to his calculations, the aid of a magician is sought for.

When a person is suffering from what are believed to be demoniacal attacks, he is relieved by the performance of the following ceremony called *Pathalahomam*. A pit about six feet in length, three feet in depth, and a foot or two in breadth is dug. A Panan covered with a new piece of cloth is made to lie in the pit which is filled in with earth, a small hole being left for him to breathe. Over the middle of his body the earth is raised and made level. A sacred fire (*homam*) is made over this with the branches of a jack tree. Near it a large square is drawn with sixty-four small divisions, in each of which a small leaf with some paddy, rice, and flowers and lighted candles is placed. Gingelly seeds, mustard seeds, grains of *chama* (Panicum miliaceum), horse-gram, eight fragrant things, the skin of snakes, the dung of the elephant, the milk of the *pala* tree, twigs of the banyan tree, *dharba* grass, *nila narakam* (Naregamia alata) oil, and ghee are put into it, until it burns bright. The sick man is brought in front of it, and then the sorcerer authoritatively asks him—or rather the demon residing in his body—to take these things. The sorcerer puts the above mentioned substances into the fire, muttering his prayers all the while, invoking the favour of Veerabhadran or Kanda-karanan. The significance of the prayers is this: "O Kanda-karana, the King of the Devas, I have no body, that is, my body is getting weaker and weaker and I am possessed of some demon which is killing me. Kindly help me and give me strength." This done, another operation is begun. A fowl is buried, a small portion of the earth above it is raised and made level. The figure of a man is drawn by the side of it. Three *homams* (sacred fires) are raised, one at the head, one at the middle, and one at the foot. The above mentioned grains and substances are put into fire. A large square with sixty-four smaller squares in it is drawn, in each of which a leaf with grains of paddy, rice, and flowers is placed. Another *mantram* in praise of the deities already mentioned is uttered, and a song is sung at the time. After finishing this, a small structure in the form of a temple is made, and a small plantain tree is placed by the side of it. A *padmam* (floral diagram) is drawn and a *puja* is performed for the Paradevatha, the queen of demons. The sorcerer makes offerings of toddy, beaten rice, plantains, and cocoanuts, when he soon turns an oracle and, as one inspired, tells them what the deity wishes, and gives them information as regards the departure of the demons from his body. It is now believed that the patient is free from all demoniacal attacks. The buried man is exhumed and allowed to go home.

In the Palghat Taluk, the following act of sorcery is practised, which is believed to relieve persons from demoniacal attacks and from disease. If, in the house of any caste-men, it is suspected that some malign influence is being exercised by demons, a Panan is sent for, who comes in the evening with his colleagues. A *homam* or sacred fire is lit with the branches of the trees above mentioned, into which are thrown six kinds of grains, as well as oil and ghee. Whilst this is being done, Kallatikode Neeli, the presiding archdemon, is propitiated with songs and offerings. The next part of the ceremony consists in bringing a bier, and placing a Panan on it and a measure of rice at his head. He is, as is done in the case of a dead body, covered with a piece of new cloth, and a small plantain tree is placed between the thighs. At his head, a sheep, and at his legs, a fowl is killed. He pretends gradually to recover consciousness. In this state he is taken outside the compound. The Panan lying on the bier evidently pretends to be dead as if killed by the attack of some demon. The propitiation with songs and offerings is intended to gratify the demons. This is an instance of of sympathetic magic.

Oti cult.

Some among the Panans practise the *oti* cult like the Parayans. A Panan who is an adept in the black art, bathes early in the morning, dresses in a cloth unwashed, and performs the *puja* to his deity, after which he goes in search of a *kotuveli* plant (Plumbago Ceylanica). When he has found it, he goes round it three times every day, and continues to do so for ninety days, prostrating himself every day before it, and on the last night which must be a new moon night, at midnight, he performs the *puja* to the plant, burning camphor and frankincense, and, after three times going round it, prostrates himself before it. He then thrusts three small candles on it, and advances twenty paces in front of it. With his mouth closed and without any fear, he plucks the root and buries it in the ashes on the cremation ground, after which he pours the water of seven green cocoanuts on it. He then goes round it twenty-one times, muttering all the while certain *mantrams*. This being over, he plunges himself in water and stands erect until it extends to his mouth. He takes a mouthful of water which he empties on the spot, and takes the plant with the root out, which he believes to be possessing peculiar virtues. When it is taken to the closed door of a house, it has the power to entice a pregnant woman and cause her to come out, when the fœtus is removed. It is all secretly done at midnight. The head, hands, and legs are cut off, the trunk is taken to a dark coloured rock, on which it is cut into nine pieces, which are all burned until they are blackened. At this stage one piece boils, and it is placed in a new earthen pot into which is added the water of nine green cocoanuts. The pot is removed to the burial ground, where the Panan performs a *puja*, in honour of his favourite deity. He fixes two poles deep in the earth at a distance of thirty feet from each other. The two poles are connected by a strong wire from which is suspended the pot to be heated and boiled. Seven fire-places are made beneath the wire, over the middle of which is the pot. The branches of the following trees, namely, bamboo, *katalati* (Achyranthes aspera), *oonga* (Bauhinia variegata), cocoanut palm, jack tree, and *pavatta* (Pavetta Indica), are used in forming a bright fire. The mixture in the pot is soon boiled, and becomes oily, at which stage it is passed through a fine cloth. The oil is preserved, and a mark made with this on the forehead enables the possessor to realize anything that is thought of. The sorcerer must be in a state of vow for twenty-one days, and live on a diet of *chama kanji*. The deity whose aid is necessary is also propitiated with offerings.

One of the ceremonies the Panans perform is called *Thukil onarthuka* (waking from sleep). In the month of Karkadakam (July-August), a Panan with his wife, provided with a drum and cymbals (*kuzhithalam*), goes to the houses of Brahmans and Nairs after midnight and sings sacred songs. During the first week, they sing standing underneath a banyan tree near the western gate of the Trichur temple. From the temple authorities they get five measures of paddy, half a measure of rice, some gingelly oil, and a cocoanut. For their services in other houses, they get a similar remuneration. This is intended to drive evil spirits, if any, away from houses.

Another of their festivals is known as *Panan kali*. The traditional account of its institution is the following. Once when a Panan and his wife went to a forest to bring bamboos for the manufacture of umbrellas, they missed their way and the night approached, when they could not return. They soon became afraid because of the varieties of noise heard by them in the forest. They collected some pieces of dry bamboo and leaves of trees, which they burned. In the presence of the light thus obtained, the woman caught hold of a creeper hanging from a tree, and danced in honour of Bhagavathi, when the husband of the woman sang songs in praise of the goddess. The day dawned at last and they found their way home in safety. In memory of this incident the Panans organize a party for a regular play. There should be two female actors and ten male actors for the play, which is acted all through the night.

Religion.

Like every great intellectual and moral manifestation, the religious feeling in any caste is the expression of the mental condition peculiar to that caste. The Kaniyans and the Panikkans are a somewhat learned caste; and their astrology and divination lead them to the worship of higher deities. The Panans, on the other hand, resort to the practice of the black art; and their religion consists in an all-pervading demonology. Their chief gods are Mookkan, Chathan, Kappiri, Malankorathi, and Kali. *Pujas* are performed to them on the first of Medam (April-May), Karkadakam (July-August), at the Desara, and on a Tuesday in Makaram (January-February). These deities are represented by stones placed under a tree. They are washed with water on the aforesaid days, and offerings of sheep, fowls, as also *malar* (parched rice), plantains, cocoanuts, and boiled rice are made to them. Their belief is, that those deities are ever prone to do harm to them, and should therefore be propitiated with offerings. The Panans also worship the spirits of their ancestors who pass for their household gods and

THE PANANS' DEVIL DANCE.

whose help they seek in all times of danger. They fast on new moon nights, and on the eleventh night after full or new moon.

Funeral customs.

The dead bodies of Panans are generally buried, but those of the old and somewhat well-to-do men and women are burned. The chief mourner is the son, or in the absence of a son, one of his brothers, if any, takes the place. The pollution is for fifteen days. The caste-men being very poor, the rice-ball offering is made only on the last day. In Palghat when the *Kapradan* dies, the Raja is informed and he sends to the chief mourner a sword, a shield, a spear, a few small guns with some gunpowder for a few discharges, a silver bangle, and a few necklaces. As the dead body is taken to the burial ground, the chief mourner, his son, wearing the ornaments follows it. In front of it go a few persons armed with the weapons above referred to. Three discharges are fired, (1) when the dead body is removed from his house, (2) when it is placed on the ground, and (3) when it is burned. The chief mourner returns home after a bath along with the rest of the family. During the period of pollution, the chief mourner bathes early in the morning and propitiates the spirit of the departed with rice-ball offerings (*pinda bali*). On the sixteenth morning, he and the rest of the family bathe to free themselves from pollution, and entertain the caste-men to a feast that day. The next day he pays his respects to the Raja with an umbrella of his own making, when the Raja bestows upon him the title of *Kapradan*. He observes the *deeksha* (a vow by which he does not shave) for a year, at the end of which he gives a similar feast to his caste-men.

Occupation.

The Panan is the barber of the polluting castes above the Cherumans. By profession he is an umbrella-maker, but curiously enough, he cannot make the whole of an umbrella. He may make the frame work, but the covering of it must be the work of the females of his caste. If he has no female relatives of his own capable of finishing the umbrellas he makes, he must secure the services of other females in the neighbourhood. The covering is of palmyra leaves,

The price of an ordinary umbrella varies from three to eight annas. They are more serviceable than those of European manufacture. Panans also engage in all kinds of agricultural work and earn from three to four annas a day. In villages they build mud walls and get about the same wages. Their women act as midwives.

Social status.

As regards social position, they eat at the hands of the Brahmans, Nairs, Kammalans, and Izhuvans, and abstain from taking the food of all caste-men below them. They have to stand at a distance of thirty-two feet from the Brahmans. Panans and Kaniyans pollute one another if they touch, and both bathe should they happen to do so. They are their own barbers and washermen. They live in the vicinity of the Izhuvans, but cannot live in the Nair *tharas,* nor can they take water from the wells of the Kammalans. They cannot approach the outer walls of the Brahman temples, neither are they allowed to enter the Brahman streets in Palghat.

CHAPTER X

(Continued).

THE VILKURUPS.

Vilkurups are so called because their occupation in former times was to train low caste young men to athletic feats and arms, and to make bows and arrows. They numbered 1,407 in the last Census of the Cochin State, 704 being males and 703 females. In the last Madras Census Report the people of this caste are said to be the same with Tol-Kollans (leather workers); but in the Cochin State they are found to be different communities without intermarriage and interdining. The caste-men are generally illiterate and speak Malayalam. There are no sub-castes in the caste, but the caste-men are said to belong to the following four *kiriyams* (houses or families), namely, Mangat Kiriyam, Veluthiri Kiriyam, Nedumbara Kiriyam, and Ayni Kiriyam.

The name of the caste.

The Vilkurups are very poor, and they live in small thatched huts, situated in shady compounds. Sometimes a few families in different huts reside in the same compound. They are found in small numbers in the villages of the rural parts throughout the State.

Habitations.

As in other castes, marriage is never permissible between the members of the same *kiriyams;* but there is no objection to a young man marrying the daughter of his maternal uncle. Girls are married both before and after puberty. The *tali* tying ceremony for girls is performed before they attain puberty or maturity, and the omission of this ceremony would place them and their parents under a ban. It is always the maternal uncles that provide them with the *tali* (marriage badge) and the dress (two pieces of cloth) for the

Marriage customs.

ceremony. Should a girl be married by the man who ties the *tali*, they are given at his own expense. The real marriage for the young women of this caste is a kind of *sambandham* (free will union), such as prevails among the Kaniyans and Panans. It is celebrated only a few months after the preliminary negotiations; for, in the meanwhile, the bride elect has a claim for two pieces of cloth during *Onam* and nine annas during *Thiruvathira* (a festival in December) and *Vishu*, from the bridegroom. If these presents, however, are paid in advance, the ceremony may be performed all at once. If, for some reason or other, the formal weddings have to be put off, the bridegroom's father and uncle go along with him to the bride's hut, pay the bride's price, one rupee, six annas and six pies to her mother, and ask her to give him a plank to sit on and a mat to lie on whenever he comes. To this she gives consent, and from that day the bridegroom has the privilege of living in his wife's hut until the formal ceremony is performed. He may continue to do so until she is about to become a mother, but cannot take her to his own hut. A man may marry two sisters and live with them in the same hut, if they get on amicably; but if they do not get on well together, they may be lodged separately at his own expense. Such instances, however, are not very common. Fraternal polyandry exists among these people and the ceremonies connected with it are the same as in other polyandrous castes. The children born of this union are the sons of all of them, and without any distinction they call all the brothers, fathers. The caste-men feel ashamed of the existence of such a custom and, when questioned about it, they invariably answer either that the custom is no longer in vogue or that it is to be found only in other localities. Adultery is blamed and punished as an outrage upon property. When committed with a member of the caste, the woman is well thrashed so as to prevent the recurrence of the crime; but, if she is found guilty of adultery with a member of a lower caste, she is soon outcasted. Divorce is optional and is purely an individual action. If a husband wishes to repudiate his wife, he is not bound to allege any reason; he simply loses the price he has paid.

Among the Vilkurups the succession to property is in the male line. They have their caste assemblies, consisting of the elderly members of the village who meet on all important occasions concerning the welfare of the caste-men.

Inheritance and caste assembly.

The Vilkurups are animists and their chief deities are Chàthan, Karinkutty, Kandakaranan, Veerabhadran, and Bhagavathi, who are represented by a few stones located either in a small hut or underneath a tree in their compounds. They are propitiated with offerings of sheep, fowls, bread, plantains, cocoanuts, boiled rice, and parched rice during the months of Karkadakam (July-August), Kanni (Desara), *Mandalam* (December), and on a Tuesday in Makaram (January-February). Sometimes Velans are invited to sing in praise of these deities, for which they get a few annas and a portion of the offerings. They also adore the spirits of their ancestors to whom offerings are made generally on new moon nights.

Religion.

Their dead bodies are generally buried, but those of old persons are sometimes burned. The son is the chief mourner and performs the ceremonies. The pollution lasts for fifteen days. On the sixteenth day the members of the family bathe to be free from it; and the caste-men are invited to a grand feast on that day, as well as on the last day of the year

Funeral customs.

In former times, as has been said, the occupations of the caste were the training of the low caste-men to all kinds of athletic feats, and to the use of sticks for defending themselves in fighting and of bows and arrows, and they also engaged in shampooing and in pial-school teaching. In these days of civilization their services are no longer required for those purposes, owing to the disappearance of the martial spirit of the people for want of opportunities; and they occupy themselves now with shampooing, umbrella-making, polishing and painting walking-sticks, quarrying laterite stones for building purposes, and agriculture. Necessity compels them to engage

Occupation.

in more than one occupation in order that they may work and get wages all through the year. In Nair families during *tali* tying ceremonies, and also during the *Onam* festival, the village Vilkurup has to bring a bow and a few arrows, and for this he gets a few annas, besides a measure of rice, some curry-stuffs, and oil on the latter occasion. Thus he is an indispensable factor in the ancient village organization. For all kinds of dislocation in the body, and in case of nervous debility, they are called in for shampooing. The patient is made to lie on a plank; a mixture of three oils, namely, gingelly oil, castor oil, and the oil extracted from the nut of the Rubia manjista, boiled with medicinal herbs and well cooled, is poured over the patient's body, which is then well shampooed. He is subsequently bathed in warm water in which have been boiled certain medicinal herbs. This process is continued for a week or two.

Social status.

As regards social status, the Vilkurups eat at the hands of Brahmans, Nairs, Kammalans, and Izhuvans and abstain from eating the food of Barbers, washermen, Kaniyans, Panans, Pulluvans, and all caste-men below them. They stand at a distance of thirty-two feet from the Brahmans and the Nairs; and the Pulayans and Parayans have to stand far away from them. They live in localities occupied by the Izhuvans. They cannot approach the Brahman temples and have to stand far away from the outer wall. They are their own barbers and washermen.

—— o ——

CHAPTER XI.

THE KANIYANS.

——:o:——

The name of the caste.

The people known as the Kaniyans form a small but important caste among the indigenous population of the Cochin State. According to the Rev: H. Gundert, they are a tribe of astrologers and umbrella-makers, who are of low social status and are forced to stand thirty-six steps away from the Brahmans. They are, in the northern parts of the State, called Kalari Panikkans, on account of their having been in charge of *kalaris* (gymnastic or military schools), and these profess to be socially superior to their brethren of the south. Nevertheless the two classes of people are called in common Ganikans, Panikkans, Kurups, and Asans. Some consider that the name 'Kaniyan' is another form of *kana—ajan* or *asan* which means a teacher of athletic feats or arts of war. The Kalari Panikkans derive the word from "*kow vandhia kana ajan,*" that is, they are respected by men and women, because they let the families of low caste-men know the auspicious moments for performing all ceremonies and because of their being teachers of fencing and other arts of war. The words 'Panikkan' and 'Kurup' once meant a fencing-master or teacher. They are now titles among the Nairs, Izhuvans, and Kaniyans. Asan is a village teacher, and Ganikan means a calculator or astrologer.

Traditional origin.

Regarding the origin of the Kaniyans, various legends are current. Once, says one of these legends, when the god Subramania, son of Siva, and his friend were learning astrology, they knew that the sound of a lizard close by foreboded some evil to the mother of Subramania. The friend practised some magical rite which averted the evil. The mother, who had been in a state of unconsciousness, suddenly woke up as if from slumber, and asked the son '*kani-ar*' meaning who it was that she looked at, to which the son replied that she was looking at a Kaniyan (astrologer). The Kaniyans still believe that the umbrella, the stick, the holy ashes, and the purse of cowries, which form the paraphernalia of a Kaniyan now-a-days, were given to them by Subramania.

The following is another tradition regarding the origin of the caste. In ancient times, it is said, that Panans, Velans, and Kaniyans were practising magic, probably an inheritance of their ancestors, but that astrology as a profession was practised exclusively by the Brahmans. Thalakkaleth Bhattathiripad was the most renowned of the astrologers of the time. He had a son whose horoscope he cast, and from it he concluded that his son would live long. Unfortunately he proved to be mistaken, for his son soon died. Unable to find out the error in his calculation and prediction, he took the horoscope to an equally famous astrologer of the Chola kingdom, who, aware of the case of his advent, directed him to adore some deity that might aid him in the working out of his predictions. Accordingly he came to the Trichur temple where, as directed, he spent some days in devotion to the deity. Thereafter he worked wonders in astrology, and became so well known in Malabar, Cochin, and Travancore, that he commanded the respect and admiration of the rulers. They invited him to cast horoscopes and make predictions, and for doing so he was liberally rewarded. One day a Brahman, hearing that his *guru* at Benares was seriously ill, consulted the Bhattathiripad as to whether and how he would be able to see him before his death. The Brahman astrologer directed him to go to the southern side of the Trichur temple, where he would see two persons coming towards him, who might gratify his desire to see his preceptor. These persons were really the servants of Yama (the god of death). They asked him to touch them and he at once found himself at the side of his teacher. The Brahman was asked, who had directed him to them, and on his telling them that it was the renowned Brahman astrologer, they cursed him saying that he would become an outcast. This fate came as no surprise to the astrologer, for he had already perceived from an evil

THE BURIAL PLACE OF THE BRAHMAN ASTROLOGER, THALAKALATH BHATTATHIRIPAD.

conjunction of the planets, that disgrace and danger were impending. To try to avoid the sad fate which he foresaw, he left his home and friends, and set out on a boating excursion in a river close by Pazhur, a place eighteen miles distant east of Ernakulam. The night was dark and it was midnight when he reached the middle of the stream. A severe storm accompanied by rain had come on, and the river was in flood. He was swept off to an unknown region and he scrambled ashore in torrents of rain and in darkness. Seeing a light in a house near where he had landed, he made for it in an exhausted condition. On reaching it, he lay down on the verandah at the gate of the house, musing on the untoward events of the night and on his affectionate family whom he had left. The hut belonged to the family of a Kaniyan, who, as it happened, had had a quarrel with his wife that day and had left his hut. Anxiously expecting her husband's return, the wife opened the door about midnight, and seeing a man lying on the verandah, mistook him for her husband and admitted him to the house. The man was so rapt in his thoughts of his home that he fancied that he was at home and it was not till he woke up from slumber that he realized that he was in the hut of a Kaniyan. On calculating the precise time, he saw that the prediction, that he would become an outcast, had been fulfilled. He accepted the degradation and lived the rest of his days with the Kaniya woman as his wife. She bore him several sons whom, in due course, he educated in the lore of his profession, and, by his influence, obtained for them an important place in the Hindu social system as astrologers (Ganikans). He translated several works on astrology into the vernacular for the benefit of the Sudras. It is said that, according to his instructions, his body after his death, was placed in a coffin and buried in the courtyard of the house. The spot is still shown and an elevated platform is constructed with a thatched roof over it. A lighted lamp is placed at all times on the platform, and in front of it astrological calculations and predictions are made, for, it is believed that those who made such calculations there will have the aid of the spirit of their dead Brahman ancestor, who was so learned in the science, that he could tell of events long past and predict even future births. As an instance of the last, the following incident may be given. Once the great Brahman ascetic, Vilwamangalath Swamiyar was suffering severely from pains in the stomach, when he prayed to the divine Krishna for relief. Finding no remedy, he turned to a Brahman friend, a Yogi, who gave him some *bhasmam* (holy ashes), which he took and which relieved him of the pains. He mentioned the fact to his beloved god Krishna who, by the pious adoration of the ascetic, appeared before him, when he said he would have three births in the world instead of one which was destined for him. Being very anxious to know what these births would be, he consulted the Bhattathiripad, who said that he would be born first as a *chera* (ratsnake, Coryphodon), second as an ox, and third as a *tulsi* plant (holy basil, Ocymum sanctum), and that he would be along with him in these births. With great pleasure he returned home. It is also said that the astrologer himself was born as an ox, and was in this form afterwards supported by the members of his family. The incident is said to have taken place at Pazhur, and the members of the family are called Pazhur Kaniyans. They are well known throughout Malabar, Cochin, and Travancore for their predictions in astrology, and all classes of people even now resort to them for aid in predictions.

Curiously enough, the Kalari Panikkans in the northern parts of the State have a different account of the origin of the caste. Once, they say, a sage and astrologer, named Ganikan, was making predictions to a Sudra regarding his future destiny. As this was done by him when in an uncleanly state, he was cursed by the *Saptharishis* (the seven sages). The Panikkans who are reputed to be his descendants are ordained to be teachers and astrologers of all caste-men below Brahmans.

The old village organization.

According to the old village organization in Malabar, Cochin, and Travancore, every *thara* or *kara* (village) consisted of all caste-men below Brahmans, especially the Nairs of all classes, more or less living in

THE KANIYANS' KALARI.

a community, as also Kammalans, Izhuvans, Panans, Mannans, and other castes of more or less equal status, living farther apart. For every such village in the northern parts of the State, there was also a Kalari Panikkan with a *kalari* (gymnastic or military school) where the young men of the village, chiefly the Nairs, were trained to all kinds of athletic feats and to arms. The institution of the *kalaris* has now disappeared, though the buildings remain in some places, and the Panikkans are now mainly astrologers and village teachers. In this connection it is interesting to note how these people became masters of *kalaris*. According to their own statement, Parasurama, the great coloniser of Kerala established *kalaris* throughout the kingdom and appointed them as the masters to train Sudra young men in all kinds of feats (one thousand and eight in number) for the protection of the country against foreign invaders. These feats are called *adavoos*, and the trained young men *adavil janangal*, two hundred of whom formed a regiment. The Nairs who then formed the fighting race of Malabar, Cochin, and Travancore were mostly trained by the Panikkans. In memory of this, the Kalari Panikkans of the northern parts of the State and of south Malabar profess even now a preceptorship to the Nairs, and the Nairs show them some respect by being present at their marriages and other ceremonies, as will be described in the following pages. The Panikkans say that the Nairs obtained their *kalaris* from them. There can be no doubt that throughout these States, the Nair Panikkans, Kurups as well as the Kaniyans, were masters of *kalaris* in former times. I have no information as to who were originally in charge of them. I am inclined to believe that, during former times, there were these gymnastic schools for every caste in the rural parts, where the young men of the caste were trained to arms and all kinds of feats. But when these people ceased to be warlike, the *kalaris* became things of the past, and astrology and the teaching of children of the village became the occupation of the Kaniyans. The Kaniyans of the south had no *kalaris*, and their occupation had long been confined to casting horoscopes, making predictions, and also to teaching children. The old village organization is even now preserved to a certain extent. The Kalari Panikkans and the Kaniyans have in a large measure superseded the Brahmans in the profession of astrology, a fact easily accounted for by the store which is set upon their services as diviners of future events. This has enabled them to occupy a place of importance in every village, and their services are still considered to be of great importance in all matters.

The functions of a Kaniyan in a thara.

It would indeed be difficult to mention a single important occasion in every day life when the Kaniyan is not at hand as a guiding spirit, foretelling lucky days and lucky hours, casting horoscopes, explaining the causes of calamities, prescribing remedies for untoward events, and physicking sick persons. Seeds cannot be sown, nor trees planted, unless the Kaniyan has been consulted beforehand. He is even asked to consult his *sastras* to find lucky days and moments for setting out on a journey, commencing an enterprise, giving a loan, executing a deed, or shaving the head. On all such important occasions as births, naming children, shaving the heads of boys for the first time, marriages, beginning the alphabet, the Kaniyan is, of course, indispensable. His work in short, mixes him up with the greatest as with the most trivial of the domestic events of the people, and his influence and position are correspondingly great. The astrologer's finding is as solemnly regarded with all due reverence as the oracle of God himself with the justice of which every one ought to be satisfied, and the poorer classes follow his advice unhesitatingly. The astrologer is busy throughout the year. During the period of harvest he has to collect paddy from every farmer for his services in connection with agriculture, and in the season of marriages he has to cast the horoscopes of those between whom a marriage is being arranged, and examine whether they agree before the marriage negotiations are completed. His most lucrative business is the casting of horoscopes of persons that come to him, recording the events of a man's life from

THE KANIYANS' PRAYERS BEFORE PREDICTION.

birth to death, pointing out dangerous periods of life, prescribing rules and ceremonies to be observed by individuals for the purpose of propitiating the gods and planets, and so averting the calamities of dangerous times. He also names favourable times for the commencement of all undertakings, and the science of astrology sets forth in considerable detail the person's disposition and mental qualities as affected by the position of planets in the zodiac at the moment of birth. All this is a work of labour and of time. There are few members of respectable families who are not provided with horoscopes, and nobody grudges to pay a few rupees or sometimes as much as ten or twelve rupees for a horoscope according to the position and reputation of the astrologer.

Two things are essential to an astrologer, namely, a bag of cowries and an almanac. When any one comes to consult him, he quietly sits down, facing the sun, on a plank seat or mat, murmuring some *mantrams* or sacred verses, opens his bag of cowries, and pours them on the floor. With his right hand he moves them slowly round and round, solemnly reciting a stanza or two in praise of the god Subramania, of his *guru* or teacher, and of his favourite deity, invoking their help. He then stops and explains what he has been doing, at the same time taking a handful of cowries from the heap and placing them on one side. In front is a diagram consisting of twelve compartments drawn with a piece of soapstone on the floor. Before commencing operations with the diagram, he selects three or five of the cowries from the top of the heap, and places them in a line on the right hand side. These represent Ganapathi (the belly god, the remover of all obstacles), the Sun, the planet Jupiter, Saraswati (the goddess of speech), and his *guru*. To all of these the astrologer makes due obeisance, touching his ears and the ground three times with both hands. The cowries are next arranged in the compartments by the astrologer who quotes meanwhile the authority on which he makes such moves. Finally, he explains the results and ends with again worshipping the deified cowries which he had placed to witness the operations.

Internal structure of the caste.

In the Madras Census Report of 1891, it is said that seven subdivisions of the Kaniyans have been returned, but the Census Commissioner doubts the existence of any true subdivisions. In the Cochin State also, no true subdivision exists, but there is some difference in the social status between the Kaniyans of the southern and the Kalari Panikkans of the northern parts of the State. The latter, as has been mentioned, profess a kind of superiority in status to the former on the following grounds, namely, that the former have no *kalaris* which, as I have mentioned now, imply preceptorship to the Nairs, who take part in their ceremonies and receive their blessings. It is also said by the latter, that the occupation of the former was once that of umbrella-making and that astrology as a profession has been recently adopted by them. There is at present neither intermarriage nor interdining between them. The Kaniyans pollute the Kalari Panikkans by touch. My own investigations lead me to believe that they are one and the same people, the difference in the social status being probably due to the absence of association owing to distance and local environments.

There are six *gotrams* or *illams* (endogamous septs) among the Kalari Panikkans, the names of which with their vernacular equivalents are as follow :—

Gotrams.		*Vernacular names.*
1. Viswamitra gotram		Apra
2. Parasara	do	Manga
3. Kasyapa	do	Poovam
4. Vasishta	do	Kundi
5. Bhrigu	do	Mathsiam
6. Marichi	do	Chaitanyam

Of the above six *gotrams*, the first four are, in the opinion of these people, superior to the last two, who are believed to be the descendants of Kalari Panikkans by the women of castes lower in status to them. The members of the first four septs neither dine with those of the last two, nor marry their girls. The Kaniyans of the southern parts of the State are said to belong to the following six endogamous septs, namely, Pambar Illam, Thachar Illam, Kutapana Graham, Thandula Graham, Kuruvila Graham, and Chowlamangalath Illam, the origin and significance of which they are unable to say. The names of some of them are derived from their house names.

Habitations.

The houses of the Kalari Panikkans in the northern parts of the State are similar to those of the poorer classes of Izhuvans. They vary from twenty-five to forty feet in length, and from fifteen to twenty-five feet in breadth. The walls are made either of clay, laterite, stones, or bricks, and the roofs, which are all of bamboo frame-work, are thatched either with palmyra or plaited cocoanut leaves. These houses are provided with somewhat substantial doors and a few old fashioned windows, the latter of which do not admit sufficient light and air. There is a row of three or four rooms, in front of which is a narrow passage. One or two rooms at one end are used as the sleeping apartments; the middle one, which is completely dark in broad day-light, is the store-room of the family. The room at the other end is the kitchen, and there is no separate dining room, the narrow passage close to it being used for the purpose. There are verandahs on one or two sides. Either connected with, or a little detached from, the main buildings are their *kalaris* in which are located their gods. The houses are situated in neat shady compounds, consisting of a few mango, cocoanut, jack, and other trees, growing thereon, with a small gate-house opposite to the main building. Such a gate-house serving as an anteroom is peculiar to the houses here as in Travancore and Malabar. In times gone by, the permission to build a gate-house was a rare privilege, but with the change in the old order of things, the restriction upon building gate-houses has, like many others of its kind, ceased to exist. A separate name is given to every house and its compound. The houses are kept sufficiently neat, and the surroundings are well swept every morning. The houses of the Kaniyans in the south are not strongly built. They are thatched buildings; the walls are made of bamboo frame-work and the rooms are generally partitioned with the same materials.

Their furniture consists of a few small mats and wooden planks, on which they seat their visitors, a rudely made wooden cot, and a few coarse mats and pillows stuffed with rice husk. Their utensils for daily use are small earthen dishes, in which food is served, and some larger ones for holding water, a few bell-metal or enamel dishes for taking food, some bell-metal vessels and enamel tumblers for drinking water, and a few wooden spoons or cocoanut shells provided with thin bamboo handles.

Marriage customs.

There is no intermarriage between the members of the same *gotram* or *illam*, while it is permissible between those of different *illams*. A young man may marry the daughter of his maternal uncle. Girls among the Kaniyans and Kalari Panikkans are married sometimes when they are grown up, sometimes when they are still infants. Amongst the Nairs, the *Thalikettukalyanam* (*tali* tying ceremony) is performed before their girls are eleven or twelve years of age. A young man, either the cousin of the girl or an adult in a family of equal status in the same or the adjacent village, is chosen to tie the *tali* after it has been seen that there is due agreement between the horoscopes of the parties. A few days before the ceremony, the necessary preparations are made. A pandal is put up in front of the girl's house and well decorated. A small stool covered with a piece of white cloth is placed in a conspicuous part of the pandal, near which are also placed a small metallic mirror, a cane, and a cadjan manuscript. On the day of the ceremony, Ganapathi is worshipped and offerings of cocoanuts, plantain fruits, and parched rice are made in order that the ceremony may come to a successful conclusion. The goddess Saraswathi is next adored with similar offerings. The girl, who has to fast on the three previous nights, bathes in the morning, and is neatly dressed and adorned in her best. The pseudo bridegroom is decked out for the occasion in valuable ornaments, conspicuous among which is the combined style and knife (to show that he can read and write) thrust into his girdle and highly embellished with silver and gold work. When he sets out on his wedding journey, he is accompanied by a party of Nairs, who escort him firing guns, blowing horns, and beating tom toms as the procession advances to the house of the bride, and the same proceeding is followed, when the bridegroom returns home with the bride. As soon as the party arrives at the gate, a vessel of *guruthi* (water mixed with lime and turmeric) is waved round the face of the bridegroom, who is also garlanded, and the guests are welcomed. The girl's brother washes the feet of the bridegroom and leads him to a seat already prepared for him. One of the bride's female relatives, generally her aunt, plays a conspicuous part in the ceremony. She seats the bride on a plantain leaf covered over with seven and a half measures of rice. The bride is either led or carried by her uncle with her eyes closed, two betel-leaves being held firmly pressed by her against her eyelids. The *tali* and the cloth are provided for her by the *kalari* head-man. The *tali* is tied round the neck of the girl by the *enangathy* (the wife of the *enangan* or kinsman), while the bride is seated on the rice with her back to the bridegroom. The bridegroom knots the string at the back of the bride's neck at the precise moment, when the astrologers present declare, "The moment is come and it greets you with offers of beauty, long life, wealth, sweet wedlock, posterity, and happiness." "Seize thou the occasion," say the bystanders, "and marry the bride, and prosperity will attend thee." The wedding guests here break in with a solemn chorus of "Aha—aha." The *tali* string is thereupon promptly tied by the bridegroom, when a portion of the Ramayana is read. The *enangathy* then seats the bride beside the bridegroom and joins their hands. The rice on which the bride was seated becomes the astrologer's fee with eight annas added to it in money. The *enangathy* then feeds the youthful pair with sweets, and makes various little jokes at the bridegroom's expense. While doing this, she comes behind the pair with rice on both hands, and sprinkles it over their heads with prayers and good wishes, and this is done in turn by all the relations beginning with the parents. The wedding ceremony concludes with the pair making obeisance to their elders.

The guests assembled are treated to a grand dinner. Among the Palghat Kalari Panikkans, the *kalari* deity, Kannika Parameswari is adored and offerings are made to her before dinner to invoke her blessings on the married couple. The festivities last for four days, and on the morning of the fourth, the bride and bridegroom bathe and worship the deity in the local temple, and after a sumptuous meal, the latter severs his connection with his wife, and takes leave of her, receiving two pieces of cloth and a few annas for this ephemeral union. The girl is at liberty to take any other man as husband afterwards. If the bridegroom above referred to wishes to take her as wife, he may do so. In that case, on the third day after the *tali* tying ceremony the party adjourns to the bridegroom's house, where the bride's party and other guests assembled are treated to grand feasts according to their custom, and on the fifth day the party disperses. Among the Kalari Panikkans, the Nairs of the *thara* or village meet together a week or two before the celebration of the marriage and subscribe for the expenses of the wedding, and they also take part in the celebrations.

Among the Kaniyans of the south as well as the Panikkans of the north, early betrothals by parents are very common, and even when these are not the rule, it is still the parents who make the choice of husband or wife for their children, and a young woman is never allowed to choose a husband for herself. When a young man has arrived at a marriageable age, his parents ask him if he looks with favour upon any particular girl of their acquaintance. Upon his replying in the affirmative, they select a girl after the horoscopes have been properly cast and examined and it is found that they are in agreement. It is not etiquette for the youth or his parents themselves to make the first move. Generally the *enangan* acts as the intermediary and he diplomatically sounds the parents of the girl as to their willingness to accept the youth as their son-in-law. Sometimes the father and the uncle of the youth visit the parents of the girl. If the girl's parents consider the match desirable, they signify their consent and fix a day for formally talking over the matter. On the appointed day, the father and the uncle of the youth, along with a few of their relations and friends, go to the house of the girl, where also are assembled the friends and relations of the girl's parents. There is a formal talk about the matter and the *illams* of the two families are ascertained. The guests are treated to a feast. On that occasion the youth's *enangan* mentions the *illam* and parentage of the bridegroom elect, and asks the *enangan* of the bride elect whether her parents are willing to have the proposed matrimonial alliance. The latter answers in the affirmative in the presence of those assembled. The formal arrangement is now made, and they all partake of the meal, after which they chew betel and take leave of their host. This ceremony is called *Jathakam vanguka* (getting the horoscope). The next ceremony is *Veedu kazhcha* (seeing the house of the bridegroom), *i. e.*, they fix a day for a visit to the bridegroom. The party of the bride elect is treated to a similar feast. The relatives and kinsmen of both parties make preparations for the ceremony on an auspicious day already fixed.

On the evening previous to the celebration of the wedding which is really a *sambandham* (the customary nuptial union of man and woman), the bridegroom and his party arrive at the house of the bride, where they are welcomed and treated to a grand supper. The wedding dress, which the bridegroom has brought, is given to the bride, who is neatly dressed and adorned in her best. The night is spent in dancing on the part of the women and in songs and in various games on the part of the men. The next morning at nine o'clock, the guests are treated to *kanji*, and at twelve o'clock to a sumptuous meal. The bridegroom and the bride are then seated side by side, and a sweet preparation made of milk, sugar, and pieces of plantains is given to them by their parents, uncles, and the *enangans* with their wives. This is essential and the partaking of this food is the ceremony which unites them as husband and wife. The bridegroom and his party return home, accompanied by the bride, her parents, and relations, and there the bride's party is well entertained during the night as well as on the next day. Just before the feast, the bridegroom's mother gives the bridegroom and the bride the sweet preparation already referred to. Among the Panikkans of the northern parts, the bridegroom and the bride are taken to the *kalari*, and there the *kalari muppan* (the Nair head-man) and others address the bride in the presence of the assembled multitude as the Panikkathi (Panikkan's wife) of the village *kalari*, signifying thereby that the married couple have become husband and wife in the family of the Panikkan of that *kalari*. After dinner, the bride's party takes leave of the bridegroom's parents, the guests, as they depart, paying a few annas each towards the expense of the feast.

There are certain curious customs observed by the Nairs, Kalari Panikkans, and other low caste-men, both before and after the *tali* tying ceremony of a girl. They are performed to learn beforehand the welfare and destiny of the bride and bridegroom as well as of those with whom they are intimately connected. Among the Kalari Panikkans and the Kaniyans, the parents of the bride send a messenger with a measure of rice, one or two cocoanuts, and a few packets of betel-leaves, to formally invite their *enangan* for the performance of the *Ashtamangallyam* [1] ceremony before the *tali* tying. This *enangan*, being himself an astrologer, makes various predictions, which he bases on the appearance of the messenger, his dress, gait, and manner of talking. These predictions have reference to the termination and future results, happy or otherwise, of the ceremony. The *enangan* then lays his finger along his nose and blows down. He notes through which nostril the air passes and predicts accordingly. The Malayalam verse in accordance with which the predictions are made may be translated as follows:—"If the

1. Eight auspicious things, namely, rice, paddy, tender leaves of cocoanut trees, an arrow, a looking glass, a well washed cloth, burning fire, and a small wooden case called "cheppu" made in a particular fashion.

messenger is on the side of the expired air passing through one of the nostrils of the *enangan*, prosperity, happiness, and long life shall attend the bride and bridegroom ; if on the opposite side, the reverse will happen." The *enangan* then takes twelve betel-leaves, and, on looking at their appearance, makes predictions for the same purpose according to the following scheme. This mode of predicting is called *Thamboola prasnam* (astrological predictions based on looking at betel-leaves).

No.	Order.	Appearance.	Prediction.
1	First betel-leaf.	Good (without defect)	Fame and good health to the bride.
		Bad and defective	Sickness.
2	Second do	Bad	Sickness and misfortune to bride's parents and others in the family, weakness in speech, defect in the right eye, loss of wealth.
		Good	Freedom from the misfortunes above referred to.
3	Third do	Good	Courage, strength to brothers, and help from them, sickness in the left ear.
		Bad	Loss of brothers, animosity of brothers against the elders.
4	Fourth do	Good	Good health to mother, uncle and relatives, and possession of a good house.
		Bad	Ill health to mother, uncle and relatives, and loss of house.
5	Fifth do	Good	Keen intelligence, wisdom, strength, enjoyment of the results of virtuous deeds done in previous births, and the possession of sons.
		Bad	Dullness, ignorance, and loss of sons.
6	Sixth do	Good	Deceit, theft, destruction by enemies, bodily ailments, and death.
		Bad	Partial freedom from the above.
7	Seventh do	Good	Marriage, enjoyment of worldly pleasures, recovery of lost wealth, and affection.
		Bad	Freedom from the above.
8	Eighth do	Good	Loss of everything, loss of fame and house, servitude, serious misfortune.
		Bad	Partial freedom from the above.
9	Ninth do	Good	Happiness, charity, kindness, inclination to do virtuous deeds, penance, respect to father, possession of sons, good nature, and teachership.
		Bad	Non-attainment of the above.
10	Tenth do	Good	Building of temple, house, helping the poor, and success in all attempts and deeds.
11	Eleventh do	Good	Attainment of everything desired, possession of sons, gain of wealth, commanding obedience from all.
12	Twelfth do	Good	Sin, expenditure, being an outcast, and loss of title.

When the *enangan* arrives at the gate of the bride's house a lamp is brought in front of him, and looking at its flame, he makes predictions according to the following scheme:—

No.	Nature of the flame.	Prediction.
1	Steady flame	Happiness and enjoyment.
2	Movement and burning of the flame straight up	Long life.
3	Making noise while burning	Sickness.
4	Bending of the flame	Short life.
5	Extinction of the flame	Death.

On the fourth day, when the bridegroom and the bride return home after worshipping the deities in the local temple, they are seated on planks, side by side, and a pot of water is placed in front of them. In this pot are put twelve packets which the bride is directed to take out and to give one after another to persons named at the time. The packet which each person receives is supposed to predict something beneficial or otherwise.

No.	Packet.	The person receiving it.	Prediction.
1	Packet of gold	Bride	Wealth and happiness.
2	do silver	Any one in the assembly	Increase of corn.
3	do copper	Enangan	Misfortune.
4	do iron	Father	Death.
5	do salt	Mother	Attainment of everything good.
6	do pepper	Bridegroom	do
7	do paddy	Maternal uncle	Increase of corn.
8	do rice	Master of the ceremony	do
9	do sandal wood	Middleman	Virtue.
10	do holy ashes	Enangathy	Blessings of Siva.

Puberty customs.

When a girl reaches puberty, she is bathed and dressed in a cloth dyed yellow with turmeric. She is lodged in a room of the house for the period of her seclusion, which is generally four days, during which only her girl friends associate with her. On the fourth day, she and her friends have an oil bath in a stream or tank close by. A triangular figure made of the bark of a plantain tree, with lighted candles and pieces of tender leaves of a cocoanut tree thrust on the three sides, on which is sprinkled the blood of a fowl just killed, is waved round the head of the girl as she plunges into the water. As they return home after the bath, they are escorted by a few Nairs provided with swords and guns, and there is the music of drum and pipe. The girl is seated in a conspicuous part of the house, when a woman waves round her face, a vessel containing water mixed with turmeric powder and lime, which is believed to free her from the power of the evil-eye or any demoniacal influence. Another woman of the family throws pieces of bread to the four corners of the house to invoke the blessings of the deities presiding over the cardinal points. The women of the caste who are invited are then feasted, after which the men are fed. This is followed by a circular dance of the women. A woman of the washerman caste is also engaged to be present to sing at the time. She has also to give a newly washed cloth to the girl to wear after her bath in order to be free from pollution. If a girl is married before puberty, and if, during her stay in the house of her husband, she attains puberty, the expenses connected with the ceremony and the feast on the last day are defrayed by his parents, while her parents contribute only a portion.

A woman in menses was and is even now a thing of abhorrence in the eyes of all people, from the belief that she imparted misfortune to the opposite sex in many ways. For instance, among the savage tribes, it is a belief, that if she stepped in a sheath of arrows, the arrows would be rendered useless to the owner thereafter, and may even become the cause of his death. If she passed in front of a hunter carrying a bow, the weapon would never shoot straight again. The father or husband of a woman in menses would never think of going hunting himself, nor would other hunters allow him to accompany them. No luck would attend him himself, and he would bring misfortune upon others also. Among the Hindus, no man can set out on a journey nor can any ceremony be performed in his house, when his wife is in menses. Hence it is that they are kept in a state of seclusion, lying in a penitential mood, which is supposed to be rewarded by long life and continual good health in after years. It is believed by all the Hindus that, on the very day on which a woman's menstrual course begins, she assumes the character of a *chandalini* [1], on the second day she becomes a sinful woman, on the third day her impurity amounts to that of a corrupted woman, and on the fourth day she becomes an anchorite, and becomes pure when she has performed her ablutions. On the first day of her menstrual epoch, a woman is not to be approached with sexual intent. A man who goes to his wife that day cuts his life short; the second day, a man enjoying his wife should imbibe a great sin; on the third day, a man must not approach her, for so doing, she would turn a harlot.

On the appearance of the menses, a woman, being impure, should seem to slip abashed into the inner apartment, and be unseen by anybody. She should cover her body with a single piece of cloth, look on herself as being in a very mean and pitiable condition becoming her state, and remain silent with her head bent down, in spirit dejected, her whole aspect prone to the ground, and eyes and hands inexpressive of any motion. She should eat such food as boiled rice in earthen pot during night only, sleep on the ground in a calm state of mind, and so pass the first three days. On the fourth day, the sun having risen, she should perform her ablution and when afterwards she has put on her water washed vesture, she is restored to purity.

During the first three days of the menstruation, a woman should avoid taking her food from metal or broken earthen dishes, should abjure drinking, eating meat of any kind, wearing wreaths of flowers and ornaments, sleeping during the day, chewing betels, and cleaning the teeth with dentifrice or any kind of tooth-powder. She should take her food from a concave

1. A woman who is outcasted or a low caste woman.

pot made of baked clay, and drink water by holding the liquid in the hold formed by both the palms of her hands. She should abjure foods derived from the milk of the cow and the milk itself, should not blacken the borders of her eyes with collyrium, should not lie in a scented or high bed, should not touch fire, and should not weep. She should neither anoint her body with oil nor bathe. She should not leave her own country to go to distant lands, walk on common paths, cross the track of animals, milk cows, walk by the side of flowering plants, nor observe the celestial bodies. To state briefly, a woman in her menses should give up every kind of luxury. Hindu astrologers predict the results of the married life and the future career of girls by observing phenomena connected with their pubescence. As an account of it is of some anthropological importance, it is given below.

No.	I. Appearance of the first menses	Results of married life.
	(1) in the different months.	
1	Medam (April-May)	Unhappiness or misery to the husband.
2	Edavam (May-June)	Increase of cows.
3	Mithunam (June-July)	Happy conjugal life.
4	Karkadakam (July-August)	Tendency to prostitution. Affection to the members of the family.
5	Chingam (August-September)	Many children.
6	Kanni (September-October)	Evil disposition.
7	Thulam (October-November)	Possession of a son. Widowhood.
8	Vrischikam (Nov.-December)	Tendency to malign others.
9	Dhanu (December-January)	Handsome children.
10	Makaram (January-February)	Intention to be virtuous.
11	Kumbham (February-March)	Wealth. Affection to family.
12	Meenam (March-April)	Possession of children. Happiness.
	(2) in the different days of the week.	
1	Sunday	Illness. Family ruin.
2	Monday	Chastity. Long life.
3	Tuesday	Poverty. Loss of chastity.
4	Wednesday	Possession of children, fortune, and prosperity.
5	Thursday	Felicity, increase of wealth and wealthy husband.
6	Friday	Beauty, affection to husband, and mother to many sons.
7	Saturday	Misery, ruin, and barrenness.

No.	I. Appearance of the first menses			Results of married life.
	(3) in the different days after the full or new moon.			
1	Pradhama (first day after the full or new moon)			Short life, slightly happy.
2	Dwithiya (second		do)	Barrenness.
3	Thrithiya (third		do)	do
4	Chathurthi (fourth		do)	Premature death of the woman.
5	Panchami (fifth		do)	Disposition to quarrel.
6	Shashti (sixth		do)	Tendency to prostitute.
7	Sapthami (seventh		do)	Mother to one child.
8	Ashtami (eighth		do)	Termagant.
9	Navami (ninth		do)	Sorrow and misfortune.
10	Desami (tenth		do)	Possession of children.
11	Ekadesi (eleventh		do)	Neatness and beauty.
12	Dwadesi (twelfth		do)	Maligning propensity.
13	Thrayodesi (thirteenth		do)	Barrenness.
14	Chathurdesi (fourteenth		do)	Tendency to prostitute, poverty.
15	Full moon			Piety and good fortune.
16	New moon			Poverty and premature old age.
	(4) in the different days of the lunar asterism.			
1	Aswathi	1st	constellation	Happiness.
2	Bharani	2nd	do	Vagrancy.
3	Karthika	3rd	do	Poverty.
4	Rohini	4th	do	Sons.
5	Makiram	5th	do	Beauty.
6	Ardra	6th	do	Chastity.
7	Punartham	7th	do	Love to husband.
8	Pooyam	8th	do	Hypocrisy.
9	Ayilyam	9th	do	Loss of children.
10	Makam	10th	do	Abortion.
11	Pooram	11th	do	Increase of wealth and property.
12	Uthram	12th	do	Support to relatives.
13	Astham	13th	do	Chastity.
14	Chithira	14th	do	Many children.
15	Swathi	15th	do	Beauty.
16	Visakham	16th	do	Love to husband.
17	Anusham	17th	do	Divorce.
18	Ketta	18th	do	Sons
19	Moolam	19th	do	Sorrow.
20	Pooradam	20th	do	Wealth.
21	Uthradam	21st	do	Happiness.
22	Thiruvonam	22nd	do	Sons.
23	Avittam	23rd	do	Long and happy married life.
24	Chathayam	24th	do	Possession of good husband.
25	Poorattathi	25th	do	Happiness.
26	Uthrattathi	26th	do	Wealth and prosperity.
27	Revathi	27th	do	Misery.

No.	I. Appearance of the first menses	Results of married life.
	Another method.	
1	Twelve Nakshatrams from Uthradam	Best.
2	Ardra and the six following	Good.
3	The remaining	Widowhood.
	(5) in the different lagnams (the risings of a sign).	
1	Medam	Poverty.
2	Edavam	Few children.
3	Mithunam	Loss of husband.
4	Karkadakam	Many children.
5	Chingam	Separation from husband.
6	Kanni	Chastity.
7	Thulam	Wealth.
8	Vrischikam	Adultery.
9	Dhanu	Model life.
10	Makaram	Want of modesty.
11	Kumbham	Wealth.
12	Meenam	Children.
	(6) on the seventh house from birth sign.	
1	Sun	Widowhood.
2	Moon	Many children.
3	Mars	Red complexion.
4	Mercury	Barrenness.
5	Jupiter	Unhappiness.
6	Venus	Loss of house.
7	Saturn	Illness.
8	Rahu	Widowhood.
9	Kethu	Object of hatred.
	(7) during the conjunction of the different planets in the rasi (a sign of the zodiac) or lagnam.	
1	Sun	Widowhood.
2	Moon	A female ascetic.
3	Mars	Death.
4	Mercury	Barrenness.
5	Jupiter	Piety to God.
6	Venus	Barrenness.
7	Saturn	Prostitution.
8	Rahu	do
9	Kethu	Easily accessible.

No.	II. First observation of the menses by—	Results of married life.
1	a girl	Sorrow.
2	a virgin	Virtue.
3	a widow	Widowhood.
4	a sickly woman	Illness.
5	a dancing woman	Enjoyment.
6	a married woman wit h oil in her hand	Long married life.
7	a man	Sorrow.
8	a maid servant	Poverty.
	III. Indications from the cloth worn at the time.	
1	Red cloth	Virtue.
2	White cloth	Anger.
3	Black cloth	Fame.
	IV. Nature of blood drops.	
1	Round red drops	Wealth.
2	Square do	Destruction of enemies.
3	Crescent do	Long life.
4	Lengthy do	Sorrow.
5	Oval do	Riches.
6	Cluster of do	Sons or children.

When, on a girl attaining her puberty, her parents consult an astrologer as to her destiny, the latter ascertains the number of *ghatikas* [1] at the time of the first appearance of the menses, and then deducts three from it. To this remainder are added the day's *thithi* (a day after the full or new moon) and *vara* (day of the week). The number thus got is divided by twelve, and the remainder known. If it be two, four, seven, nine, ten, or twelve, the astrologer predicts misery, while three, five, six, eight, or eleven, indicate virtue. If, for example, a girl attains puberty on the twenty-fifth Vrischikam 1079 at two o' clock, the day being Wednesday and the *thithi Chathurdesi* (fourteenth day of the moon) the number of *ghatikas* is first determined which is twenty. From this, three is deducted. This remainder with the *thithi* and the day amounts to thirty-five which, divided by twelve, leaves the remainder eleven. This predicts virtue.

1. Periods of twenty-four minutes each.

No.	Ghatikas	Prediction.
1	Dawn	Virtue or happiness.
2	Between dawn and midday	Pilgrimage.
3	Midday	Sons.
4	Between midday and evening	Thievish propensities.
5	Evening	Many children.
6	Sunset	Harlot.
7	Fore-night	Long life.
8	Midnight	Widowhood.
9	After midnight	Sickness.
10	Twilight	Unhappiness.

No.	I. Months	Means suggesting the remedies for the evils above referred to.
1	Medam (March-April)	Wearing of a red cloth by the wife and presenting it to a married woman with a pot of water.
2	Karkadakam (July-August)	Gift of fruits to a pious Brahman.
3	Thulam (October-November)	Present of a red cloth with a few measures of rice tied to one end, and also of a *tali* and *kunkumam* (red powder vermilion) to a married woman.
4	Vrischikam (Nov:–December)	Gift of a metal lamp lighted with ghee to a Siva temple.
	II. Days of the week	
1	Sunday	Gift of wheat.
2	Tuesday	Same as I (3) above.
3	Saturday	Gift of a bronze vessel full of oil and another with milk to a married woman. The girl should be made to see her face in the oil.
	III. Days of the moon	
1	Pradhama	Worship in a Siva temple and gift of gingelly seeds.
2	Chathurthi	Gift of a lamp to a Siva temple.
3	Shashti	Gift of a gold image of a cow to a pious and learned Brahman
4	Ashtami	Sugar water to be distributed to children.
5	Dwadesi	Same as the above.
6	Chathurdesi	Going round a banyan tree eight times and feeding three women.
7	Full moon	Gift of a pumpkin (Cucurbita maxima) with some money to a Brahman.
8	New moon	Same as the above.

No.	IV. Days of constellation		Means of remedy.
1	Bharani, the 2nd constellation		Twigs of *vanhi* tree should be used to light the sacred fire, and the woman should go round it twenty-seven times.
2	Karthika, the 3rd	do	Seventy-two lamps fed with ghee should be placed in a temple dedicated to Subramania, and the young woman should be asked to go 227 times round the temple. Twenty-seven Brahmans should also be fed.
3	Thiruvathira, the 6th	do	A married woman and her children should be fed after their bath. The gift of a cloth also to the former.
4	Ayilyam, the 9th	do	Gift of fruits to children and worship of Siva.
5	Makam, the 10th	do	Worship of the village deity.
6	Pooram, the 11th	do	Worship of family deities.
7	Astham, the 13th	do	An image made of *kusa* grass should be cremated, and with the ashes thereof a mark should be made on her face daily. 1008 leaves of the *vilwa* tree, and 108 lotus flowers must be used in the performance of a *puja* to Siva. Some Brahmans also should be fed.
8	Chithira, the 14th	do	Performance of a *puja* with lotus flowers and the feeding of Brahmans.
9	Visakham, the 16th	do	Gift of cloths to Brahmans, going round a banyan tree 108 times, and the worship of the family deity.
10	Pooradam, the 20th	do	Worship in a Vishnu temple, lighting a ghee lamp with cotton wick, gift of pumpkin (Cucurbita maxima) with a few annas to a Brahman.
11	Poorattathi, the 25th	do	Sugar in water to children, pansupari to women.

The marriage expenses in a poor Kaniyan's family amount to fifty rupees and in well-to-do families vary from one hundred to two hundred rupees. The expenses among the Kalari Panikkans are met by a joint contribution of the inhabitants of the village, who meet together at the *kalari*, a few weeks before the celebration of the wedding, to subscribe the amount. The bridegrooms among them have to give *kachas* (pieces of cloth for women) to their mothers-in-law, sisters, and to their mothers. This custom does not prevail among the Kaniyans of the south.

CHAPTER XII.

THE KANIYANS

(Continued).

—:o:—

Among the Kaniyans as well as the Panikkans, polyandry largely prevails. If a young woman is intended to be the wife of several brothers, the eldest brother goes to the bride's house and gives her a cloth and takes her home the next day along with her parents and relations who are all well entertained. The young woman and the brothers are seated together, and a sweet preparation is given to them which signifies that she has become the common wife of all. The *kalari muppan*, the Nair head-man of the village, also declares them to be all married to her. The guests then depart, and the bridegroom (the eldest brother) and the bride are invited to what they call *virunnu-oon* (sumptuous meal) in the house of the latter, where they stay for a few days. The bridegroom returns home with the bride. The other brothers, one after another, are similarly entertained along with the bride in her house. Verses are recited on the occasion of the departure of the bride from her house with the bridegroom. These verses invoke blessings on the marriage and give the husband advice as to how he should treat his wife.

Polyandry and polygamy.

The Kaniyans explain their custom of practising polyandry by saying that their caste-men are very poor, and cannot afford the expenses of the large families that there might be, if the brothers married different women and had separate families. The brothers cannot afford to live together for a long time, for they very often go from place to place to earn their livelihood by astrology. Each brother is at home only for a few days in each month, and hence practically the woman may have only one husband at a time. If several of them happen to be at home together for a few weeks, each in turn associates with the woman in accordance with the directions given by their mother. Further, there is only one *kalari* in a village in charge of a Panikkan, who has to support his family consisting of several members with the small income he obtains for the services he renders to the inhabitants of the village belonging to it. A division in the family by individual marriages would not lead to any additional increase of income from that village, nor could the superfluous members of the family go and settle in another village; for that would mean encroaching upon the rights of another Panikkan already established there. The custom of fraternal polyandry has also, they say, a religious sanction [1] in support of it; but it is only a survival of the primitive one. The prevalence of this custom is, in my opinion, due to purely economic grounds; it is however rapidly disappearing before the onward march of western civilization. Children born of this union are regarded as the sons of all the brothers, and these are all addressed as father.

Polygamy is almost unknown, and as the women are generally polyandrous widows are rare. Should a woman have a single husband she may, after his death, marry either his brother, any member of her husband's family, or anybody else she likes. The taking of the sweet preparations already referred to is the binding portion of the ceremony. In the event of her marrying another man, she relinquishes all claims upon the property of her deceased husband. A woman committing adultery with a member of her caste may ultimately marry him; but she is outcasted if she is found to mate with one of another low caste. Such instances, they say, are very rare. A man may divorce his wife on the score of the absence of mutual affection, sickness, or want of chastity on the part of the wife. He has, in that case, to return all that belongs to her, when he gets back a thread from the cloth she wears, which signifies that he has

1. Panchali was the common wife of the five brothers, Yudhishtira, Arjuna, Bhima, Nakula, and Sahadeva.

received all that he has given for the wedding. A woman who does not like her husband may, in the presence of an *enangan*, declare her unwillingness to stay with him and may go back to her parents. In the case of several brothers marrying a woman, if any disunion arises between one of the husbands and the wife, both are at liberty to make a conjugal separation.

Pregnancy and childbirth.

When a young woman is about to become a mother, the ceremony of *Pulikudi* is performed for her during the seventh or ninth month of her pregnancy. It consists in taking a mixture of the juices from five different kinds of leaves, in which are placed three small balls of rice. The mixture is taken in a small spoon, made of gold weighing five *fanams*, shaped like a jack tree leaf. This is followed by a feast to her friends and relations, after which she is taken to the house.

At the birth of a child, the woman is confined to a separate room, and is there attended by her mother and a few women of experience. Soon after the child is born, the mother and her baby are bathed in warm water. The period of pollution is for fifteen days and during that time she is under a special kind of treatment. Garlic, *pavattu* (Pavetta Indica), palmyra jaggery, and *pettu marunnu* (delivery medicine) are all dried and finely powdered, and the mixture is taken in gingelly oil. The period of seclusion is for fifty-six days. Before the expiry of this period the juice of *kodapuli* is extracted and well boiled, and is taken for six days. The woman bathes in hot water containing medicinal herbs for the first fifteen days, after which she bathes on alternate days.

The naming ceremony falls in the sixth month. The child, if a boy, is called after his grand-father or one of his ancestors. If it is a girl, the name is taken either from her father's or mother's side. The names in common use among men are Gopalan, Madhavan, Velan, Chami, Chathu, Kittu, Unni, Perakunni, Ravunni, Appukuttan, Prabhakaran, Kumaran, and Krishnan, and among women, Lakshmi, Kunji, Karthyayani,

Madhavi, Paru, Chinnu, Ammini, Ammu, and Janaki. They also use pet names, such as, Kuttan, Chinnu, Appu, Bhanunni, and Kunji Manu. The term '*nakshatram* (star),' is abusively applied to an individual among the Panikkans. The ceremonies connected with the tonsure, ear-boring, and beginning the alphabet, are similar to those that I shall describe in my account of the Izhuvans.

Inheritance and caste assembly.

Among the Kaniyans and Kalari Panikkans, the succession to property is through the son. They have, as in other castes, their caste assembly which consists of the elderly men not of one village, but of several adjacent villages. They are invited to meet when important cases involving caste disputes crop up. The caste-men invite also the Nair gentlemen of the village for the meeting which is held at their village *kalari*. The deliberation lasts for several days and then the decision arrived at by the assembly is given effect to. Delinquents are either fined or compelled to give a dinner to the caste-men at the village *kalari*. Any fine imposed upon the culprits goes to the *kalari*. The culprits are also made to swear before a lighted lamp placed on a plank in front of the deity in the *kalari*.

Astrological predictions.

As has been said, the Panikkans and Kaniyans are astrologers and as such they believe in astrological predictions which they also expound to all high caste-men who go to consult them on the following particulars:—

Travelling.— The following eight points are considered before a person sets out on a journey, and no day predicting evil consequences is chosen for the purpose. They are:— (1) *Varasoolam* (an inauspicious week day), (2) *Nakshatram* (a lunar asterism), (3) *Thithi* (a lunar day), (4) *Rasi* (a sign of the zodiac), (5) *Yogini* (a naked deity armed with an impaling stake and endowed with superhuman powers), (6) *Panchakam* (consisting of five), (7) *Gandantham* (a perilous time), and (8) *Yogam* (connection as of stars). Detailed information concerning these points is given below:—

(1) *Varasoolam.*— Mondays and Saturdays are inauspicious for journeys towards the east, Tuesdays and Wednesdays towards the north, Thursdays towards the south, and Fridays and Sundays towards the west.

(2) *Nakshatram.*— The following lunar asterisms, namely, Aswathi, Pushyam, Punarvasu, Astham, Anusham, Thiruvonam, Moolam, Avittam, and Revathi are favourable to the undertaking of any journey, as they are attended with a speedy accomplishment of the purpose in view, while Bharani, Ardra, Ayilyam, Makam, Pooradam, Poorattathi, and Ketta are very inauspicious. Persons leaving their houses on these days are not likely to return alive, nor do seeds sown on these days produce a good harvest.

(3) *Thithi.*—

No.	Lunar days	Prediction.
1	First day of the moon	Loss or failure.
2	Second do	Success.
3	Third do	do
4	Fourth do	Quarrel.
5	Fifth do	do
6	Sixth do	Riches.
7	Seventh do	Fear from enemies or robbers.
8	Eighth do	Felicity of relations.
9	Ninth do	Failure.
10	Tenth do	do
11	Eleventh do	First 18 hours good. Next 6 hours bad.
12	Twelfth do	Good
13	Thirteenth do	Success.
14	Fourteenth do	do
15	Full moon	Bad.
16	New moon	Complete failure in the forenoon and success in the afternoon.

(4) *Rasi.*—

No.	Rasi (sign of the zodiac)	Prediction.
1	Medam	Loss of life.
2	Edavam	Happiness.
3	Mithunam	Loss of life.
4	Karkadakam	Kingship.
5	Chingam	Success.
6	Kanni	Fever.
7	Thulam	Success.
8	Vrischikam	Very inauspicious.
9	Dhanu	Victory over enemies.
10	Makaram	Imprisonment
11	Kumbham	Thrashing on the road.
12	Meenam	Rain combined with success.

(5) *Yogini.*— The *thithies, i. e.*, ten lunar days, beginning from Pradhama (first lunar day) have each a *yogini* directed towards the east, north, south-east, south-west, south, west, north-west, north-east, sky, and earth respectively. It is again repeated for the next ten days and thirdly for the last ten. Travelling towards the *yogini* or the left side of it is believed to be fatal, while that towards the rear and right side is very auspicious.

(6) *Panchakam.*—*Thithi* (lunar day), *nakshatram* (lunar asterism), *day*, *rasi*, and *lagnam* must be written separately in five positions. Fifteen is added to the first number, twelve to the second, ten to the third, eight to the fourth and four to the fifth. Each sum is then divided by nine. If the remainder be five, it is called *roga panchakam* for the first, *agni panchakam* for the second, *raja panchakam* for the third, *chora panchakam* for the fourth, and *mrithyu panchakam* for the fifth. If there be no remainder it is called *nishpanchakam*. The remainder five in each of the numbers above referred to, predicts illness, fear of fire, court business, fear of shedding blood, and death respectively, which are all avoided except the third, and the last with no remainder is preferred.

(7) *Gandantham.*—The first six hours of Aswathi, Makam, and Moolam, and the last six hours of Ayilyam, Ketta, and

Revathi are *gandanthams* or perilous times, and are therefore unfavourable for the undertaking of any journey. One born at such a time causes the ruin of the families on the father's as well as on the mother's side. Should he however live long, he will attain the status of a ruler.

Shaving.—Certain days of the week are inauspicious for shaving, when they come in conjunction with certain phases of the moon and certain prescribed asterisms, nor can shaving be done on the eve of anniversaries, on days of nativity as well as those after them in the same month, at night, during the period of one's wife's pregnancy, after meals, on religious days, on Fridays, during the first quarter of Kumbham, the first half of Dhanu, the first twenty-one days of Karkadakam, and the whole of Kanni, on the first, third, fifth, and seventh days after the days of nativity, on a particular sign of the zodiac, and on days when the sacred thread has been renewed. All the other days, chiefly the tenth, twelfth, and thirtieth of every month are favourable. It is said that fortune favours those who submit to the process once in fifteen days, and to allow more than thirty days to elapse is to court disease. A temporary exception might be made in favour of emergent calls, such as, royal commands, headache, consecration, the close of *yagas* (sacrifices), religious observances and ceremonies, and marriages, when shaving is compulsory, in which case these rules need not be observed. If the shaving takes place on a wrong day, then a proper day must be chosen soon after the former, and the same ceremony gone through over again.

Oil bath.—This should not be taken on certain asterisms and phases of the moon, on birthdays, or on the days of passage of any sign of the zodiac from one position to another. It may be taken on Saturday, Monday, and Wednesday. The young, the old, and the invalid, however, are not bound by these rules, and may take it every day, provided the oil is boiled with flower, linear grass, excrements of cows, and earth in it, on Sunday, Friday, Thursday, and Tuesday respectively.

Monetary transactions.—The following lunar asterisms, namely, Karthika, Uthram, Moolam, Makam, Chithira, and Revathi are unfavourable to all monetary transactions; for the money lent on these days may not be returned, and further they may give rise to the loss of the remaining wealth of the parties. All other days besides those above mentioned are believed to be good.

Vishu.

On the morning of *Vishu*, the first of Medom (April-May), the members of all higher castes bathe early, and neatly dressed, worship the village and family deities. With a desire to determine the prosperity or otherwise of a Nair family for the year, the senior member thereof takes a cocoanut, and after the necessary *pujas* and prayers, rolls it on the even floor in a conspicuous part of the house, specially purified, by cow-dung mixed with water. The direction of movement and the position at rest, are noted, and on them the following scheme of predictions is based:—

No.	Direction of movement	Prediction.
1	East	Good health, success, good harvest, increase of cattle, dainty meals.
2	South-east	Quarreling, ill health, wounds all over the body, failure of crops.
3	South	Loss of life.
4	South-west	Illness, failure of crops, death of relatives.
5	West	Abundant crops, gain of wealth.
6	North-west	Uneasiness of mind, quarreling with wife, fear of thieves, fear from wound.
7	North	Gain of wealth, happiness, presents from kings, good health, abundant crops.
8	North-east	Failure in undertaking, loss in agriculture.
9	Top and bottom	Fear of death and enemies.

Omens.

The Kaniyans, like the members of other castes, believe in omens. Any business, which they may have on hand, will be determined to their satisfaction, if they should, on starting, see a couple of Brahmans, a married woman, a single Sudra, such birds as crows, pigeons, etc., beasts, such as deer, etc., moving from left to right, dogs and jackals moving inversely, wild goose, cock, ruddy goose, peacock seen singly or in couples, either at right or at left, the rainbow seen on the right or left side, butter-milk, raw juice, flower, ghee, red cotton juice, metallic mug, *karuka* grass (Agrostis linearis), Rajas, respectable men, white cloth, white horse, flag-staff, turban, triumphal arch, burning fire, good eatables or drink, carts with men in, elephants, cows with their young ones, bulls with ropes tied to their necks, palanquin, or hear bell ringing, peacock and Indian crane warbling sweetly, bellowing of oxen, auspicious words, harmonious human voice, or such sounds as are made by birds or beasts, sounds of harps, flutes, timbrels, tabors, and other musical instruments, sounds of hymns, or if gentle breeze happen around at the time of journey. The following, on the other hand, prognosticate bad omens, namely, the sight of men deprived of any of their limbs, such as the lame, the blind, etc., broken vessels, a man in sorrow, a barber, a widow, the hearing of words expressive of sorrow, burning destroying, the alarming cry of "alas, alas," loud screams, the sight of serpent, cat, or monkey passing across the road, vociferous beasts or birds, jackals, dogs, kites crying loud from the eastern side, a buffalo, a donkey, a temple bull, black grains, salt, liquor, dirty faggots, any horrible figures, vehicles carried with legs upwards, dishes and cups with mouth downwards, broom-stick, ashes, oil, winnow, and hatchet.

The following predictions are made from the first appearance of the waxing of the moon after new moon :—

No.	First appearance	Prediction.
1	On Sunday	Happiness.
2	On Monday	Dishonour.
3	On Tuesday	Death.
4	On Wednesday	Fear.
5	On Thursday	Wealth.
6	On Friday	Female enjoyment.
7	On Saturday	Sickness.
8	Through the clouds	Fear from enemies.
9	Through water by reflection	Misery.
10	Through trees	Loss of wealth.

The following predictions are made from the falling of lizards :—

No.	I. Place of falling	Prediction.
	(1) In the case of a man.	
1	On the head and lock of hair	Health.
2	,, left cheek	Sight of friends.
3	,, right cheek	Gain of friendship.
4	,, knot of hair	Illness.
5	,, end of the knot of hair	Destruction.
6	,, head	Death.
7	,, forehead	Gain of wealth.
8	,, eyebrows	Loss of wealth.
9	,, middle of eyebrows	Gain of wealth.
10	,, right eye	Good or happy sign.
11	,, left eye	Confinement.
12	,, mouth	Sumptuous meal.
13	,, nose	Happiness.
14	,, end of the nose	Sorrow.
15	,, right ear	Gain of wealth.
16	,, left ear	Sorrow.
17	,, region of the cheek	Sumptuous meal.
18	,, lower lip	Gain of wealth.
19	,, upper lip	Quarrelling.
20	,, lip and the chin	Death.
21	,, chin	Fear of kings.
22	,, neck	Advent of relatives.
23	,, back of the neck	Fear of enemies.
24	,, right shoulder	Success.
25	,, left shoulder	Defeat.
26	,, hand	Loss of wealth.
27	,, wrist	Gain of jewels.
28	,, back of the palm	Loss of wealth.
29	,, fingers	Advent of friends.
30	,, middle of the hand	Health.
31	,, back	False news.
32	,, ribs	Sight of friends.
33	,, abdomen	Gain of wealth.
34	,, chest	Increase of happiness.
35	,, breast	Happiness.
36	,, arm-pits	Enjoyment with women.
37	,, left hand	Sorrow.
38	,, right hand	Fame.
39	,, palm	Quarrelling with wife.
40	,, wrist	Loss of wealth.
41	,, nails	do
42	,, back of the palm fingers	Decoration.
43	,, nails	Destruction.
44	,, middle of the palm	Gain of wealth.
45	,, loins	Neat dress.
46	,, nipple	Success, fame
47	,, lower region of the abdomen	Illness.
48	,, private part	Death.

No.	I. Place of falling	Prediction.
49	On the thighs	Loss of dress.
50	,, loins, posteriors	Loss of fame.
51	,, anus	Illness.
52	,, knees	Confinement.
53	,, region below the knees	Death of women.
	(2) *In the case of a woman.*	
54	On the head	Happiness.
55	,, top of the head	Death.
56	,, tuft of hair	Illness.
57	,, knot (top)	Death.
58	,, nape of the neck	Daily quarrelling.
59	,, forehead	Loss of wealth.
60	,, right cheek	Widowhood.
61	,, left cheek	Sight of friends.
62	,, right ear	Longevity.
63	,, left ear	Acquisition of ornaments.
64	,, right eye	Sight of friends.
65	,, nose	Illness.
66	,, upper lip	Quarrelling.
67	,, lower lip	Gain of wealth.
68	,, two lips when closed together	Destruction.
69	,, lip and the chin	Quarrelling.
70	,, mouth	Sumptuous meal.
71	,, neck	Decoration.
72	,, arm-pits	Health and wealth.
73	,, back	Separation from friends.
74	,, ribs	Sight of distant relatives.
75	,, shoulders	Health.
76	Below the shoulder	Acquisition of jewels set with precious stones.
77	On the right palm	Loss of wealth.
78	,, left palm	Gain in everything.
79	,, right wrist	Sorrow, loss of wealth.
80	,, left wrist	Decoration of the body.
81	,, middle of the hand	Great happiness.
82	,, back of the finger	Acquisition of jewels.
83	,, nails	Death.
84	,, breast	Great sorrow.
85	,, neck	Health and happiness.
86	,, abdomen	Sons.
87	,, abdomen of a virgin	Marriage.
88	,, nipple	Fame, intelligence.
89	,, private part	Death.
90	,, loins	Costly dress.
91	,, anus	Illness.
92	,, thighs	Sons or daughters.
93	,, knees	Confinement.
94	,, below the knees	Loss of wealth.
95	,, chin bone	Death.
96	,, right leg (foot)	Exile.
97	,, left ,,	Death of enemies.
98	,, fingers of the feet	Possession of sons or wealth.
99	,, ankle	Journey to a distant place.

No.	I. Place of falling	Prediction.
100	On the upper part of the foot	Death.
101	,, big toes	Happiness.
102	,, nails	Loss of cows and servants.
103	,, forepart of the foot	Loss of enemies.
104	,, bed while lying	Misfortune.
105	,, seat while sitting	Both good and evil sign.
106	,, vessel with a portion of the cooked food	Friendship with relatives.
	(3) In the case of a lizard falling	
107	on any part of the body of a man while setting out on a journey	The good or bad result affects the enemy.
108	on the plate while eating	Food must be rejected.
109	,, empty plate	Illness, sorrow.
110	,, fire while cooking	Death of wife.
111	in the temple	Death of the king's wife.
112	in the midst of an assembly	Death of the presiding officer.
113	when the owner of the house and two others are conversing	Death to the better of them.
114	on a lamp while burning	Destruction to the house. The house must be vacated for three months.
115	on the dress or ornaments	Quarrelling or loss of fame.
116	,, weapon of a warrior	Fighting with his enemies, the death of the latter.
117	,, vehicle	Journey to a distant place.
	(4) In the case of—	
118	two lizards falling while quarrelling	Less sorrow and happiness.
	II Lunar day on which the lizard falls	
1	First day of the waxing or waning of the moon	Great influence.
2	Second ,,	Becoming a king.
3	Third ,,	Great gain.
4	Fourth ,,	Illness.
5	Fifth ,,	Acquisition of wealth.
6	Sixth ,,	do
7	Seventh ,,	do
8	Eighth ,,	Death.
9	Ninth ,,	do
10	Tenth ,,	do
11	Eleventh ,,	Possession of sons, wealth.
12	Twelfth ,,	Wealth.
13	Thirteenth ,,	Loss in any enterprise.
14	Fourteenth ,,	Loss of wealth.
15	Full moon	Loss or death of relations or wealth.
16	New moon	do

No.	III. Day of the week on which the lizard falls	Prediction.
1	Monday	
2	Wednesday	Acquisition of wealth.
3	Thursday	
4	Friday	
5	Sunday	
6	Tuesday	Loss of wealth.
7	Saturday	
	IV. Day of constellation on which the lizard falls	
1	Aswathi, first constellation	Longevity, strength.
2	Bharani, second do	Illness.
3	Karthika, third do	Loss of wealth.
4	Rohini, fourth do	Gain of wealth.
5	Makiram, fifth do	do
6	Ardra, sixth do	Death.
7	Punartham, seventh do	Gain of wealth.
8	Pooyam, eighth do	do
9	Avilyam, ninth do	Death.
10	Makam, tenth do	Marriage.
11	Pooram, eleventh do	Sickness.
12	Uthram, twelfth do	Happiness.
13	Astham, thirteenth do	do
14	Chithira, fourteenth do	do
15	Swathi, fifteenth do	do
16	Visakham, sixteenth do	Loss of wealth.
17	Anusham, seventeenth do	Attainment of kingdom.
18	Ketta, eighteenth do	Destruction.
19	Moolam, nineteenth do	Health.
20	Pooradam, twentieth do	Death.
21	Uthradam, twenty-first do	Marriage.
22	Thiruvonam, twenty-second do	Attainment of kingdom.
23	Avittam, twenty-third do	Loss of wealth.
24	Chathayam, twenty-fourth do	Happiness.
25	Poorattathi, twenty-fifth do	do
26	Uthrattathi, twenty-sixth do	do
27	Revathi, twenty-seventh do	Attainment of kingdom.
	V. Lagnam (the rising of a sign) on which the lizard falls	
1	Medam	Gain of wealth.
2	Edavam	do
3	Mithunam	Daughter.
4	Karkadakam	Increase of wealth.
5	Chingam	Possession of sons.
6	Kanni	Loss of wealth.
7	Thulam	Dress.
8	Vrischikam	do
9	Dhanu	Gain of wealth.
10	Makaram	do

No.	V. Lagnam (the rising of a sign) on which the lizard falls	Prediction.
11	Kumbham	Ruin.
12	Meenam	Increase of sorrow.
	VI. Direction of movement of the lizard after falling on the body	
1	Moving eastward	Acquisition of anything desired.
2	,, south-east	Fear of fire.
3	,, southward	Death.
4	,, south-west	Quarrelling.
5	,, westward	Gain of wealth.
6	,, north-east	Illness.
7	,, northward	Fame.
8	,, north-west	Acquisition of anything desired.
	VII. Direction of sound of the lizard	
1	From above, east, north, west.	Attainment of everything desired.
2	,, south-east	Acquisition of wealth.
3	,, north-west	Journey to another country.
4	,, south-west	Sorrow.
5	,, north-east	Unbearable grief.
6	,, south	Death.

A person, on whom a lizard has fallen, should at once bathe with his dress, take a dose of *panchagavyam*, and look at his face in a vessel full of ghee. He should also make an image of gold, dress it in a red cloth, and, after the necessary *pujas*, give it to a Brahman proficient in the Vedas. He should also light the holy fire, *Mrithyumjayahomam*[1].

Religion.

Both the Kalari Panikkans and the Kaniyans are generally worshippers of Siva, but they are not disinclined to engage in the worship of Vishnu also. It is said that their *kalaris* are forty-two feet long, and contain the images of forty-two deities. The following are the most important of them, namely, Subramania, Sastha, Ganapathi, Veerabhadran, Narasimham, Ashtabhairavas, Hanuman, and Bhadrakali. Some of their *kalaris*, which were seen by me in the

1. A sacrificial fire resorted to in great danger to avert death.

THE KANIYANS' TEMPLE.

various parts of the State, contain stone and old metal images of these gods. Every night a lamp is lighted in front of them for their worship. During the *Mandalam* (forty-one days from the first of Vrischikam to the tenth of Dhanu, *i. e.*, fifteenth November to the twenty-fifth December), the senior member of the Panikkan's family bathes early morning, and performs his *pujas* to all of them, making offerings of boiled rice, plantains, and cocoanuts. On the forty-first day, *i. e.*, the last day of the *Mandalam*, a grand *puja* is performed individually to every one of the deities in the *kalari* and this lasts for twenty-four hours from sunrise to sunrise, when offerings of boiled rice, parched rice (*malar*), sheep, and fowls are also given. This is the grand *puja* and is performed once in the course of the year. Besides this, some of their deities are worshipped for special objects. For instance, Subramania is adored for the sake of astrology, Sastha for wealth and offspring. They are also the worshippers of Sakthi in any one of her following manifestations, namely, Bala, Thripura, Mathangi, Ambika, Durga, and Bhadrakali, the object of their worship being to obtain her blessing so as to secure accuracy in their astrological predictions. Further, every member of the caste who is proficient in astrology daily offers, after an early bath, his prayers to the seven planets. Among the minor deities whom they worship are also Mallan, Mundian, Muni, and Ayutha Vadukan, the first three of which they worship for the prosperity of their cattle, and the last for their success in the training of young men in athletic feats. These deities are represented by stones placed at the root of some shady trees in their compounds. They also worship the spirits of their ancestors, on the new moon nights in Karkadakam (July-August), Thulam (October-November), and Makaram (December-January). The Kalari Panikkans celebrate a kind of feast for the spirits of their female ancestors. This is generally done a few days before the celebration of a wedding in their houses, and is probably intended to obtain their blessings for the happy married life of the bride. This corresponds to the performance of *Sumangalya prarthana* (the feast for the spirits of departed virgins and married women) performed by Brahmans in their families.

At times when small-pox, cholera, and other pestilential diseases prevail in a village, special *pujas* are offered to Marriyamma (the small-pox demon) and Bhadrakali, who are believed to preside over all kinds of disease and who should therefore be propitiated. On these occasions their priest turns a *velichapad*, and speaks to the village men as if by inspiration, telling them when and how the maladies will subside. On a Tuesday and Friday in the month of Medam (April-May) these deities are adored with offerings. Among animals, cows, serpents, elephants, and Brahmini kites, and among trees, the *arayal* (Ficus religiosa), the margosa (Gentiana chirayita), the *nelli* (Phyllanthus Emblica, and the *pala* (Echites scholaris) are also venerated. Every Monday (*Somavaram*), *Ekadesi* (the eleventh day after the waxing or waning of the moon), *Pradosham* (the thirteenth day after the full or new moon), and *Shashti* (the sixth day) is looked upon as auspicious. They fast on the nights of these days.

It is understood that all ill luck, misfortune, calamity, and sickness are due to the provocation of certain deities who should be propitiated with offerings. These astrologers are supposed to be able to tell us what deities presiding over our destinies are malevolent, and how they should be worshipped and satisfied with offerings. When persons are sick or in trouble, a Kaniyan or Panikkan is sent for and consulted, and he performs certain ceremonies with magical squares of twelve divisions. When he discovers what spirit is the cause of the evil, he states how it may be satisfied with offerings. Some of them profess to be magicians and to possess *mantrams* with which they cast out devils.

Funeral customs.

When a Kalari Panikkan or a Kaniyan is at the point of death, his sons, nephews, or relations who may be beside him either recite the divine names of Rama, Krishna, or Siva, or read aloud certain portions of the

Ramayana in order that his soul may pass to heaven. When he is dead, his relations and friends and the Nairs of the village are informed. The village head-man *(kalari muppan)* provides the chief mourner with a measure of rice, a few cocoanuts, some paddy, and a new cloth to cover the dead body. The corpse is washed and dressed in the new cloth. *Bhasmam* (holy ashes) and sandal paste are rubbed over the forehead, chest, and both hands, and water mixed with rice flour and turmeric powder are sprinkled all round it The dead body is placed on a long plantain leaf and a piece of cocoanut is placed on its breast. The body is then placed on a bamboo bier which is carried to the southern corner of the compound. In Palghat, Chittur, and other places, families do not allow their compounds to be used for the funeral rites of the dead, but special grounds not far from their habitations are assigned to the members of each caste. The dead body is placed on the ground in the burning-ground, and the junior members of the family go round several times and prostrate themselves before it. It is then placed on a pile of fire-wood cut from the branches of a mango tree. Over the corpse are piled pieces of fire-wood, and the fire is applied to the pile by the son, who is the chief mourner. As soon as it burns well, the members of the family sprinkle water on it, and the chief mourner, after going round it several times, breaks the pot near the head of the dead man. Those of the caste-men, who are in the burning-ground with the chief mourner, return home after a bath. The members of the family also bathe and return home. The chief mourner plants a tender branch of a cocoanut tree in the court-yard of his house, and pours water round it every morning after his bath with offerings of rice balls (*pinda bali*) in honour of the departed spirit that is believed to be very thirsty and hungry. This he continues for seven days, and on the seventh day he removes it, planting a similar one by the side of a stream or a tank close by. From that day to the fourteenth, he bathes early, pours water round it, and offers rice balls to the departed spirit. On the morning of the fourteenth day, the chief mourner and the members of the family bathe at six o'clock, and dress themselves in cloths freshly brought by the washerman. The former then offers the sacrifice of *pinda*, after which they again bathe, returning the dress to the same washerman. On the fifteenth day, the house is well cleaned by the *enangathy* (*enangan's* wife), who sweeps the compound, sprinkles over it water mixed with cow-dung and makes it pure by the water (*punyaham*) given by the Brahmans after the recital of a *mantram*. Then all have an oil bath, and on the night of that day, the caste-men are treated to a grant feast, after which the ceremony is over. From that day for six months or a year, the chief mourner bathes early in the morning, cooks his food, gives the same offerings to the departed spirit, and is in the condition of one who has taken a religious vow. He observes the *deeksha* (a kind of vow without shaving) for six months or a year, after which he gives a similar feast to the caste-men of the village.

In the event of a member of the caste dying without a son, his nephew or brother who is the chief mourner performs the ceremony for him. If a person die an unnatural death by committing suicide or otherwise, the ceremonies above described are performed during the first fifteen days, by the chief mourner, who may be either his son or nephew or brother, and he goes to a sacred place where he offers the rice balls, and then spends some money on entertaining a few Brahmans in memory of him. They also make images of their ancestors, which they locate in one of their rooms and propitiate with offerings. They believe that the spirits of good men abide with God, while those of wicked men become *pisachas* (ghosts), who cause much trouble, and some of whom are believed to be so obstinate that they are propitiated with sacrifices in holy places, such as Benares or Rameswaram, where due ceremonies also have to be performed.

Occupation.

As has been said, the chief occupation of the Kalari Panikkans in former times was to train Nair young men and others to all kinds of athletic sports and to arms. Some curious old weapons of war covered with rust were seen by me in their *kalaris*, but they would not part with them. After Nairs and other caste-men ceased to be soldiers, their occupation was chiefly confined to the training of young men in athletic sports and in dramatic performances, in addition to their profession of astrology. Gradually the former was less cared for, and astrology became their chief occupation and it is by it that they are in these days earning their livelihood. The *kalaris* have become things of the past, but the belief in astrology among all castes of people leads them to resort to their aid and to consult them in times of illness and difficulties, and no ceremony is performed by the Sudras without the Kaniyans being consulted. They get a few annas for their services in all ceremonies performed by the Nairs and low caste-men of the village, as also for their predictions in astrology. They have also to inform the farmers of the auspicious moments for ploughing, sowing, transplanting, and reaping, and also of the time for the distribution of rice, vegetables, and oil to the Cherumans for the *Onam* and *Vishu* festivals. For these services, every farmer during the harvest gives them a bundle or two of his crop, sufficient to fetch them a few measures of paddy. In spite of the numerous sources of income from the villages in which they live, they appear to be poor. Some of their houses which I had the opportunity of seeing are small and in a dilapidated state. Their *kalaris*, once much frequented by the Nairs and other caste-men of the village, show no signs of their former greatness, as they are left uncared for, for want of funds. It is said, that the Kaniyans were originally umbrella-makers and that they afterwards adopted the profession of astrology. Every village in the southern parts of the State has a Kaniyan, whose duties are precisely similar to those of the Panikkans. Some are magicians and physicians also.

Status of the caste.

As already stated, the Kalari Panikkans and Kaniyans are, though learned, of low status and form a distinct division more or less on a level with the Izhuvans. If one of them approaches within thirty-six feet of a Brahman and twenty-four feet of a Nair, he pollutes them, but on marriage occasions a Nair gives a gift (*dakshina*) of a few annas and betel-leaves to the astrologer standing close beside him and yet there is no pollution. The Malayalam proverb, പണിക്കർക്കു പണത്തൊടം അശുദ്ധം (on marriage occasions the Nairs give *dakshina* almost touching the hand) reminds us of this fact. They eat at the hands of Brahmans, Nairs, and Tamil Chetties, but do not eat the food prepared by the Barbers, Washermen, Izhuvans, Kammalans, Panans, and Velans, whom they consider as below them in the social scale. They have their own barbers and washermen. They may approach the outer wall of the Brahman temples.

Dress and ornaments.

The men wear *mundus* round the loins and a similar garment on their shoulders. They wear gold ear-rings and rings for the fingers. As regards colour, they are found in all shades of complexion. They shave their bodies clean, leaving an oval or round patch of hair on the top of their head. Their women wear an ordinary loin cloth, but the tattoo form of dressing like that of the Nair women is also not uncommon amongst them. They also use a small *mundu* to cover their breasts when they go out, and have of late begun to wear petticoats. They are generally cleanly in their habits, but appear to be prematurely old owing perhaps either to an insufficient diet or to polyandrous habits. The hair on the head is well parted and oiled, and is sometimes tied into a knot behind, but more commonly it is straight up, sometimes inclined to the left side.

Games.

The Kalari Panikkans were, as has been said, formerly the teachers of all games to the Sudras and low caste-men. These games were very popular, but have now fallen mostly into disuse. There are still a few

A KANIYAN GRCUP.

among the Panikkans, here and there, fit to teach young men various feats, some of which are the following:—

(1) *Pitichu kali.*—Two persons play on their drums (*chendas*), while a third person well dressed in a *kacha*, with a turban on his head, and provided with a sword and shield, performs various feats in harmony with the drum beating. It is a kind of sword dance.

(2) *Parishathalam kali.*—A large pandal is erected in front of the house where the performance is to take place, and a few boys below sixteen, who have been previously trained in it by their *asan* (teacher) are brought there, well dressed. The performance takes place during the night, *chenda*, *maddalam*, *chengala*, and *elathalam* (circular bell-metal plates slightly concave in the middle) being the instruments used in it. After the performance, the boys present themselves before their *asan* and remunerate him with whatever they can afford. Parties are used to be organized to give this performance on all auspicious occasions in rural districts.

(3) *Kolati.*—This is an amusing diversion in which sticks play a prominent part. Around a lighted lamp, a number of persons stand in a circle, each with a stick, a foot in length and as thick as a thumb, in each hand. They begin to sing first in slow and gradually in rapid measure. The time measure is marked by each hitting his neighbour's sticks with his on both sides. Much dexterity and precision are required, as also experience in combined action and movements, lest the amateur should be hit by his neighbours as the measure is accelerated. There is only one refrain for every song so that it becomes monotonous after some time, but expert singers manage sometimes to vary it. The songs are invariably in praise of God or man.

Conclusion.

According to the Cochin Census Report of 1901, the Kaniyans, including the Kalari Panikkans, number 2,547, 1,272 being males, and 1,275 females. It has been asserted sometimes that the Kaniyans, including the Kalari Panikkans, are merely divisions of the Izhuva tribe, and that they are agricultural in pursuits; but they form a distinctly separate community and agriculture is not their occupation. They are poor and less worldly than Panans, Velans, Vilkurups, Pulluvans, and Paravans, and they are frank, honest, truthful, and God-fearing.

CHAPTER XIII.

THE FISHING CASTES.

—:o:—

THE fishing castes of Cochin, which, though nominally include the four sub-castes, namely, Valan, Arayan or Katalarayan, Mukkuvan, and Marakkan, really consist of the first two, the members of the last two being mostly sojourners from the sea-coasts of Malabar and Travancore adjoining the State. Though merely sub-castes, the caste-men thereof profess to belong to four distinct castes, widely differing from one another in customs and manners. In all, they numbered 11,683, 6,110 being males and 5,573 females, forming 21 per cent. of the Hindu, and 1·4 per cent. of the total population of the State. They chiefly occupy the shores of the back-waters and the sea, and are an important community pursuing the traditional occupation of fishing and boat service. In the following pages are described the customs and manners of the people of each of the sub-castes, and those of the Valans are first treated.

—:o:—

I. THE VALANS.

Origin and tradition of the caste.

The word 'Valan' is derived from '*vala*', which means fish in a tank; some consider the word to be another form of '*valayan*,' which signifies a person who throws a net for fishing. According to the tradition and current belief of these people, they were brought to Kerala by Parasurama for plying boats and conveying passengers across the rivers and back-waters on the Western Coast. Another tradition is that the Valans were also Arayans, and they became a separate caste, only after one of the Perumals had selected some of their families for boat service, and conferred on them special privileges. The descendants of these families were called the Valans, whose social elevation above the former, with whom there is neither intermarriage nor interdining, appears to have been due to their long and frequent contact with the high caste-men living in the vicinity of rivers and back-waters. They even now pride themselves, that their caste is one of remote antiquity, and that Vedavyasa, the author of the Puranas, and Guha, who rendered the boat service to the divine Rama, his Sita, and his brother Lakshmana, across the Ganges in the course of their exile to the forest, were among the caste-men.

Subdivisions of the caste.

There is no subdivision in the caste; but the caste-men are said to belong to the four exogamous divisions or *illams* (houses of Namburies), namely, Alayakad, Ennalu, Vaisyakiriyam, and Vazhapally, which correspond to the *gotrams* of the Brahmans or to four clans, the members of each of which are perhaps descended from a common ancestor. According to traditions current among them, they were once attached to the four Namburi *illams* above mentioned for services of some kind, and were even the descendants of the members of the *illams*, but were doomed to the present state of degradation on account of some misconduct. Evidently, the above story is cooked up to elevate themselves in social status, and I am inclined to believe that they must have been the *atiyars* (slaves) of the four aforesaid Brahman families, owing a kind of allegiance (*nambikooru*) like the Kanakkans to the Chittur Manakkal Namburipad at Perumanom of the Trichur Taluk. Even now these Brahman families are held in great respect by the Valans, who, when afflicted with family calamities, visit the respective *illams* with presents of a few packets of betel-leaves and a few annas to receive the blessings of their Brahman masters, which, according to their belief, may tend to avert them.

Habitations.

The low sandy tract of land on each side of the back-water which forms littoral slip, is the abode of these low caste fishermen, in the neighbourhood of

A VALAN MARRIAGE GROUP.

which, no high caste-man will choose his residence. In some places, more especially south of Cranganore, their houses are dotted along the banks of the back-water, often nearly hidden by cocoanut trees, while at intervals the white picturesque fronts of numerous Roman Catholic and Romo-Syrian churches are perceived. These houses are in fact mere flimsy huts, a few of which occupied by the members of several families may be seen huddled together in the same compound abounding in the growth of cocoanut trees, with space hardly enough to dry their fish and nets. In the majority of cases, the compounds belong to *jenmies* (landlords) who lease them out either rent free or on nominal rent, and who are often so kind as to allow them some cocoanuts for their consumption, and leaves sufficient to thatch their houses. About ten per cent. of their houses are built of wood and stones, while a large majority of them are made of mud or bamboo frame-work, and hardly spaceous enough to accommodate the members who own them. During the summer months, cooking is done outside the houses, and very few take rest inside them after hard work, for even during hot days, their compounds are shady and breezy enough, when they may be seen basking in the sun after midnight toil, or drying the nets or the fish. Their utensils are few, consisting of earthen vessels and enamel dishes, and their furniture a few wooden planks and coarse mats to serve as beds.

Marriage customs.

The girls of the Valans are married both before and after puberty; but the *Thalikettukalyanam* (*tali* tying ceremony) for girls is indispensable before they come of age, as otherwise they and their parents are put out of caste. Both for the *tali* tying ceremony and for the real marriage, the bride and the bridegroom must be of different *illams* or *gotrams*. In regard to the former, as soon as an auspicious day is fixed, the girl's party visits the *Aravan* with a present of six annas and eight pies and a few packets of betel-leaves, when he gives his permission, and issues an order to the *Ponamban*, his subordinate of the *kadavu* (village) to see that the ceremony is properly conducted. The *Ponamban*, the bridegroom, and his party go to the house of the bride. At the appointed hour, the *Ponambans* and the caste-men of the two *kadavus* assemble, after depositing six annas and eight pies in recognition of the presence of the *Aravan*, and the *tali* is handed over by the priest to the bridegroom, who ties it round the neck of the bride in the midst of the joyous shouts of the multitude assembled on the occasion. The ceremony always takes place at night, and the festivities generally last for two days. From this, it must be understood, that the *tali* tier is not necessarily the husband of the girl, but is merely the pseudo bridegroom or pseudo husband, who is sent away with two pieces of cloth and a few annas at the termination of the ceremony. Should he, however, wish to have her as wife, he should, at his own expense, provide her with a *tali*, a wedding dress, and a few rupees as the price of the bride. Generally it is the maternal uncle of the bride, that provides her with the first two items at the time of the ceremony.

The actual marriage is more ceremonial in its nature. The maternal uncle or the father of a young Valan, who wishes to marry, first visits the girl, and if he approves of the match for his nephew or son, the *illam* is ascertained and the astrologer consulted to assure themselves that the] horoscopes agree. If astrology does not stand in the way, they forthwith proceed to the girl's house, where they are well entertained. The bride's parents and relatives return the visit to the bridegroom's house, where they are likewise treated to a feast. The two parties then propose a day for the formal declaration of the proposed union. On that day a Valan from the bridegroom's village, seven to nine elders, and the *Ponamban* who is in charge of the bride, go to her house, and in the presence of the assembled multitude, a member from each party deposits on a plank, four annas and a few betel-leaves in token of *enangu mattam* or exchange of co-caste-men from each party for the due fulfilment of the contract thus publicly entered into. Then they fix the date of marriage, and retire from the bride's house. On the appointed day, the bridegroom's party proceeds to the bride's house with two pieces of cloth, a rupee or a rupee and a half, rice, some packets of betel-leaves, etc. The bride is already dressed and adorned in her best, and one piece of cloth, rice, and money are paid to the girl's mother, as the price of the bride. After the usual feasts, the bridal party returns to the bridegroom's house, which is entered at an auspicious hour. They are received at the gate with a lamp and a vessel of water, a small quantity of which is sprinkled on the married couple. They are soon welcomed in by the seniors of the house, and are seated together, when sweets are given, and the bride formally declared to be a member of the bridegroom's family. The ceremony closes with the usual feasts, and the expenses connected therewith are the same on both sides.

A man may marry more than one woman; but no woman may enter into conjugal relations with more than one man. A widow may, with the consent of her parents, enter into wedlock with any member of her caste except her brothers-in-law, in which case her children by the first husband will be looked after by the members of his family. Divorce is effected by either party making an application to the *Aravan*, who has to be presented with from twelve annas to six rupees and a half according to the means of the applicant, when the *Aravan* in token of dissolution, issues a letter to the members of the particular village to which the applicant belongs, and on the declaration of the same, he or she has to pay to his or her village caste-men four annas.

Puberty customs.

When a Valan girl comes of age, she is lodged in a room of the house, and is under pollution for four days. She is bathed on the fourth day, when the caste-men and the women of the neighbourhood, along with the relatives and friends are treated to a sumptuous dinner. There is also, among them, a curious custom, called *theralikka, i. e.,* causing the girl to attain maturity, which is merely placing her under seclusion in a separate room, and proclaiming that she has come of age. Under such circumstances, the caste-women of the neighbourhood along with the washer-woman (Velathi) assemble in the house of the girl, when the latter pours a small quantity of gingelly oil on her head and rubs her body with turmeric powder, after which she is proclaimed to have attained puberty. She is bathed and lodged in a separate room as before; and the four days' pollution as also the festivity are observed as already referred to. The custom has long been in existence, but is now being abandoned by a large majority of their community, because it is found to be absurd and meaningless and also detrimental to the future health of the girls. The origin of this, which prevails in other castes as well, is probably due to the attempts on the part of girls' parents to promote the marital relations between the sexes, when they are liable to be relieved of their responsibilities of support.

Inheritance and tribal organization.

In respect of inheritance, the Valans follow a system which partakes of the character of succession from father to son and from maternal uncle to nephew. Among them, the self acquired property is generally divided equally between his brothers and sons, while the ancestral property, if any, goes to the brothers. Here it may be observed, that the great majority of these people are mere day-labourers, and that each man has a small house of his own which, as already stated, is not often roomy enough to accommodate all the members of the family, and that his property consists of a few tools, implements, or other equipments of his profession. His brother does not often go to fight over a share of these, but allows his brother's sons to enjoy them. Grown up sons generally separate when they marry, and keep their own house, so that the latter system of inheritance, as practised by them, does not carry with it, some of its main characteristic features.

They have, as among other caste-men, their tribal organization, and their head-man, *Aravan* or *Aravar*, is appointed by *Theettooram* or writ issued by His Highness the Raja, and the head-man appoints other social heads, called *Ponambans*, one, two, or three of whom are stationed at each *desam* (village) or *kadavu* (landing-place).

The Valans are expert rowers, and possess the special privilege of rowing from Thripunathura the boat of His Highness the Raja for his installation in the Cochin palace, when the *Aravan* with sword in hand, has to stand in front of him in the boat. Further, on the occasion of any journey of His Highness the Raja through the back-waters or on occasions of State functions, such as the visit of the British Resident, the Governor, or other similar dignitaries, the head-man has to lead the way as an escort in a snake-boat, as it is called, plied with paddles, and to supply the requisite number of men for rowing the boats of these high officials and their retinue or other members of their establishments. He has also to see that, during their stay at the Residency, they are furnished with the necessary fish food, for all of which the men are endowed with the privilege of fishing in certain assigned portions of the back-waters free of tax. They are now deprived of these privileges, and are given wages for the services rendered to the State, which levies a tax on fishing.

Before the development of the Government authority, and the establishment of administrative departments, the *Aravans* wielded great influence and authority as they still do to a very limited extent, not only in matters social, but also in civil and criminal disputes arising from the members of the community. For all social functions matrimonial, funeral, etc., their permission has to be obtained and paid for. The members of the community have to visit their head-man with presents of betel-leaves, money, and sometimes rice and paddy. The head-man generally directs the proper conduct of all ceremonies by writs issued to the *Ponambans* under him. The *Ponambans* also are entitled to small perquisites on ceremonial occasions. Thus the *Aravan* is an important and indispensable factor in the Valan community, and his appointment, though not virtually hereditary, passes at his death to the next qualified senior member of his family, who may be his brother, son, or nephew, but even this rule has been violated by the appointment of a person from a different family. The *Aravan* has the honour of receiving from His Highness the Raja presents of cloth (two *pavu mundus*) during the *Onam* festival, six annas and eight pies on the *Athachamayam* day, and a similar sum for the *Vishu*. At his death, the ruler of the State sends a piece of silk cloth, a piece of sandal-wood, and about ten rupees for defraying the expenses of his funeral ceremonies.

Religion.

The Valans profess Hinduism, and the mode of worship does not divide them into sects. Siva, Vishnu, and the heroes of the Hindu puranas are all worshipped with equal reverence. Like other caste-men, they entertain special reverence for Bhagavathi, who is propitiated with offerings of rice flour, toddy, green cocoanuts, plantain fruits, and fowls on Tuesdays and Fridays. A grand festival, called Kumbhom Bharani (cock festival), is held in the middle of March, when the Nairs and low caste-men offer up cocks to Bhagavathi beseeching immunity from diseases during the succeeding year. In fact, people from all parts of Malabar, Cochin, and Travancore attend the festival, and the whole country near the lines of marching rings with shouts of "*nada nada* (walk, walk, or march)" of the pilgrims to Cranganore, her holy residence. In their passage up to the shrine, the cry of "*nada nada*" is varied by terms of unmeasured abuse at this goddess. The abusive language, it is believed, is acceptable to her and, on arrival at the shrine they desecrate it in every conceivable manner on the belief that this too is acceptable. They throw stones and filth, howling volleys of opprobrium at her shrine. The chief of the Arayan caste, Koolimuttath Arayan has the privilege of being the first to be present on the occasion. The image in the temple is said to have been recently introduced. There is a door in the temple which is apparently of stone, but fixed in half opened position. A tradition is attached to this, and is believed in by the Hindus and Christians, which asserts that St. Thomas and Bhagavathi held a discussion at Palliport about the respective merits of the Christian and Hindu religions. Arguments became warm, and Bhagavathi, considering it best to cease further discussions, decamped, and jumping across the Cranganore river, made straight for the pagoda. St. Thomas, not to be outdone, rapidly gave chase, and just as the deity got inside the door, the saint reached its outside and, setting his foot between it and the door-post, prevented its closure: there they both stood until the door turned to stone.

Another important festival usually held at Cranganore is the *Makara vilakku*, which falls on the first Makaram (about the fifteenth January), during the night of which there is a good deal of illumination both in and round the temple. A procession of ten or twelve elephants all fully decorated, goes round it several times accompanied by drum beating and the tunes of instrumental music, which are attended by a large number of people.

Chourimala Iyyappan or Sastha, a sylvan deity, whose abode is Chourimala (a hill in Travancore) is another of their favourite deities. Besides these, they worship some demi-gods, or demons, Kallachan Muri and Kochu Mallan, who are ever disposed to do them harm, and who are therefore propitiated with offerings of fowls. They have a patron, who is also worshipped at Cranganore, and the spirits of their dead ancestors are held in great veneration by these people, who propitiate them with offerings on the new moon and *Sankranthi* days of Karkadakam, Thulam, and Makaram.

The most important festivals which are observed by these people in common with other high caste-men are *Mandalam vilakku*, *Sivarathri*, *Vishu*, *Onam*, and *Desara*, a short account of the first two of which is given below.

Mandalam vilakku.—This festival takes place during the last seven days of the *Mandalam* (first Vrischikam to the tenth

Dhanu, *i. e.*, from the 15th November to the 25th December). During this festival, the Valans enjoy themselves in music and drum beating during the day, the jarring sound of the latter of which is simply unbearable. During nights, some of them developing themselves into a kind of hysterical fits, profess themselves to be oracles, with the demons like Gandharva, Yakshi, or Bhagavathi, dwelling in their bodies, in their incorporeal forms, and publicly come forward, to whom consultations are made as to future events. Their advice is respectfully and thankfully received and acted upon. Sacrifices of sheep, fowls, green cocoanuts, and plantain fruits are offered to the demons, believed to be residing within, and are afterwards liberally distributed among the caste-men and others present there at the time.

Sivarathri.—This festival comes on the last day of Magha. The whole day and night are dedicated to the worship of Siva, and the Valans, like all other high caste-men, go to Alvai, bathe in the river, and keep themselves awake during the night, reading Siva Purana and reciting his names. Early morning the next day, they bathe and make rice ball offerings to the spirits of the departed ancestors and return home.

The Valans observe the Hindu fasts and festivals, like the high caste Sudras. They have no temples of their own, but on all important occasions worship the deities of the temples of the higher castes by standing at a long distance from the outer walls of the sacred edifices. On important religious occasions, Embrans are invited to perform the *Kalasam* ceremony, for which they are liberally rewarded, and the latter do not lose their caste status on that account, nor are they under any social disability. From a comparison of the religious study of the Valans with that of the allied caste-men, it may be safely said, that they, like the rest, were animists, but, owing to the influence of the high caste-men and their frequent contact with them, they are rapidly imbibing the higher forms of worship. The caste-men are becoming more and more literate, which helps the study of the religious works; and there are some among them, who compose

THE VALAN WOMEN ROWING A BOAT.

Vanchipattu (songs sung while rowing boats) with plots from their puranic study. Thus they are more God-fearing than, and morally superior to, their allied caste-men.

Funeral customs.

The Valans either burn or bury their dead bodies. The chief mourner is either the son or the nephew, who performs the funeral ceremonies as directed by their priest (*Cheethayyan*) who lives on the sea-coast, and attends wearing a new cloth, a sacred thread (*Poonanul*), and a turban. The ceremony is begun either on the second, fifth, or the seventh day, when the chief mourner, bathing early in the morning, offers the *pinda bali* (rice ball offering) to the spirit of the deceased, which is continued for the first thirteen days, and on the morning of the thirteenth day, the nearest relatives get shaved. On the fifteenth day, the caste-men of the locality, his friends and relatives are treated to a grand dinner, and on the sixteenth day, another offering (*mana pindam*) is made to the spirit of the departed, and thrown into the back-water close by. Every day during the ceremony, a vessel full of rice is given to the priest, who, for his services, gets ten rupees also. If the funeral ceremonies are not properly performed for a man who is dead, his ghost is believed to haunt the house, when an astrologer is consulted, and his advice invariably followed. What is called *Samhara homam* (sacred fire) is kept up, and an image of the man in silver or gold is made and purified by the recital of holy *mantrams*. Another purificatory ceremony is also performed, after which the image is handed over to a priest in the temple close by, with a rupee or two. This being over, the funeral rites are performed in honour of the dead.

Occupation.

As has been said, fishing is the chief occupation of the Valans, who confine themselves to the rivers and back-waters, which besides extending north and south, send off numerous branches and many subdivisions, that are shallow in some places, especially in the northern portion of the Chetwye branch; but those between Cranganore and Cochin, are at all times, navigable. The fish that inhabit the enormous expanse of the back-water, and those that live in rivers, tanks, and other inland waters locally known as *chals*, *kappus*, and *kayals* as also those that abound in the sea, afford much interest and occupation to the various classes of people. They give constant employment to the fishermen, supply the people with food, the shop-keepers with salted provisions and oil extracted from them, and the naturalist with the variety and interest in the numerous families composing the tribes. The number and variety of forms which exist, the beauty of some species, the extraordinary habits of others, says Francis Day, render fish one of the most interesting divisions of the animal kingdom, perhaps enhanced by the difficulty in ascertaining the individual peculiarities.

The fishing implements are very primitive and the modes of fishing, says the same author, vary according to the seasons of the year, and may be divided into those employed in the deep sea along the coast, and in the rivers and back-waters. These again may be subdivided into several different methods, a short description of some of which may be found to be interesting. In the wide inland rivers, fishermen employ cast nets in the following manner. Each man is in a boat, which is propelled by a boy with a bamboo. The fisherman has a cast net and a small cocoanut shell, which he throws into the river, about twenty yards in front of the boat; it comes down with a splash and is said to be done to scare away crocodiles. As the boat approaches the place where the cocoanut shell was thrown, the man casts his net around the spot. This method is only for obtaining small fish, and as many as fifteen boats are to be seen thus employed in one place, one following the other in rapid succession, some trying in the centre, and others on the side of the river.

Fishing in small boats appears at times a dangerous occupation, the small canoe only steadied by the paddle of one man seated in it, looks as if it must be swamped every minute. Very large fish are sometimes caught in this way.

Fishing with a bait continues all day long in Cochin during the rainy months, when work is at a stand-still, and five or six persons may be seen at each jetty busily engaged in this occupation. Large numbers of the bagrus tribe are thus captured. Should one hooked be too large for the fisherman to manage, the man in the next boat comes to his assistance, and demands a quarter of the fish for his trouble. This is carried all through the year, and the size of some of the bagri thus caught is enormous.

Fish are shot in various ways, by a Chittagong bamboo, which is a hollow tube, down which the arrow is propelled by the marksman's mouth. This mode is sometimes remunerative, and is followed by persons who sneak along the shore of sluggish streams, or of the back-water; sometimes they climb up trees, and there await a good shot, or the sportsman quietly seats himself near some narrow channel that passes from one wide piece of water into another, and watches for his prey. Some of the fishermen shoot with bows and arrows, and some others with cross bows, the iron arrow or bolt of which is attached by the line to the bow to prevent its being lost. Netting fish, catching them with hooks, or shooting them with arrows are not the only means employed for catching fish. Bamboo labyrinths, bamboo baskets, and even bare hands are called into use. Fishermen sometimes walk about in the muds and, when they feel a fish move, endeavour to cover it with the larger end of the basket, which is forced down some distance into the mud, and the hand is then passed downwards through the upper extremity, and the fish taken out. There is also another plan of catching them by the hand, which is by having two lines to which white cocoanut leaves are attached, and tied to the fisherman's two great toes from which they diverge, the other end of which being held by another man a good way off, and some distance apart. When these lines are taken, the fish become frightened, and, strange as it may appear, cluster for protection around the man's feet, who is able to stoop down, and catch them with his hands by watching his opportunity.

A good many fish, especially eels and crabs, are captured in bamboo labyrinths, which are common along the back-water, and are made of split bamboos, passing perpendicularly out of the water, and leading to a large baited chamber. A dead cat is often employed as a bait for crabs, a string being attached to its body, and after it has been in the water for some time, it is pulled up with the crustacea adherent to it. Fish are obtained from the inland rivers by poisoning them, and this can be done only when the water is low. A dam is put up across a certain portion, and the poison placed within it. It generally consists of Coculus Indicus pounded with rice, croton oil seeds, etc. The fish thus caught are sent away for sale or dried when sold.

The most common method employed for fishing in the back-waters is by attaching a funnel shaped net of small meshes made of twist cotton (varying from twenty to twenty-five feet in length) to two stakes planted at a distance of eight to ten feet, and these stakes are scattered throughout the length and breadth of the back-waters. The fish that enter into the nets at flood tide are unable to return to the sea, and numbers of very large ones, especially prawns, are captured in this way. These are also caught by the *chengadam* method, *i. e.*, by fishing with two boats with an iron chain hanging from a pole stretched across them. When the boats are dragged along the water, the frightened prawns jump into them, which are in a slanting position. This species of fish is abundant in the back-water between October and March and in the sea after the monsoons.

Sometimes Valans catch crocodiles. A number of sharp iron needles, each one or two inches in length, is tied across each other at right angles, and thrust into a mass of rotten flesh attached to a long rope. The mass is then thrown

THE CONICAL FISHING NET.

into canals or places in the back-waters which are frequented by crocodiles. When one comes to eat the meat, the needles become stuck to the mouth, when a few fishermen approach him with spears and aim at the sides, but never on the backs. They are also caught in nets.

In the town of British Cochin, at the mouth of the Periyar river or the opening of the big back-water system into sea, and within a distance of half a mile on the Cochin and Vypeen banks, where there are about eighty of these nets, one comes across the largest and several are met with as one proceeds up the back-waters. Outside, however, a radius of ten miles from Cochin, they are rarities (except at Palliport), and they are practically unknown in the country north of Palliport. The nets with their wooden work, viewed from a distance, have the appearance of masts of sailing ships, and in the harbour of Cochin, the one might be mistaken by the foreigners for the other; a closer scrutiny however easily discloses the curious net. Briefly, it consists of (1) a jetty or bridge of wood and bamboos with one end ordinarily existing on the land, and the other end on the main pillars in the sea or back-waters with, of course, intermediate pillars between, on which the body of the bridge is supported, (2) an axle turning on holes bored near the top of each of the two end pillars, (3) two wooden isosceles triangles or sheers placed at right angles to each other with the axle as the common base and along a wooden pole connecting the apexes and holding the triangles in position, (4) two angular or semicircular wooden poles, called yards, of equal size (ordinarily four equal poles tied together) crossing each other at right angles or so as to form equal angles, suspended at the middle by a string from the apex of the triangles on the sea side, (5) a four cornered net attached at the four corners to the four ends of the angular or semicircular poles above referred to, the net being rather baggy and tapering to a point or ball as the centre is approached, (6) a loose rope from the tapering point or ball of the net tied on to one of the sides of the triangle on the sea side, and (7) a ballast of stones suspended by ropes from the apex of the triangle on the land side, as well as one or two long ropes hanging from the same apex. The angular or semicircular wooden poles referred to in (4), and the cornered net have often to withstand heavy currents, and ropes from the yard-arms run up to the land side to prevent their being washed away. Ordinarily only three ropes are used, two on the flow side and one on the other. Thus the Chinese net proper is complete with these arrangements, and the only other thing that may be referred to as an inseparable adjunct to it is the landing bag for taking the fish out of the net. This bag is a net attached to a pole, and is practically of the same pattern as that used by English boys and girls in catching butter-flies.

The length of the triangles, as also of the bridge, is generally between thirty and thirty-two feet, and the net about sixteen feet square, the whole cost of net equipment being about fifty-five rupees. The net has to be renewed every year at a cost of fifteen rupees, but the wood-work lasts long and needs only occasional repairs. Sometimes the whole frame including the bridge stands far out and wholly in water, when, in place of land, an artificial platform is constructed. The platform and the land are connected together by a single line of bamboo tied on poles planted in the water, and the line serves as a bridge from the land to the platform. The number of men required to work the net at a time is neither more than three nor less than two, who stand on the land side of the platform often in a shed constructed to protect themselves from the rays of the sun, and raise or lower the ropes hanging from the apex of the triangular frame-work on the land side, correspondingly raising or lowering the other similar frame-work with its yard and the big nets (the latter going up and down like buckets), and when they find that they have a good catch of fish, one of them rushes along the bridge, pulls up the rope attached to the ball of the net, and scoops out the contents by means of the landing bag. They work according to tides,

THE CHINESE FISHING NETS.

for between five and six hours, both day and night during spring. During the months of June, July, and August, there is no work at night, and the catch is very poor, while during the favourable season, the value of the catch of a single night would vary between five and fifteen rupees, an occasional bumper catch going up even to twenty rupees. Prawns form the main catch at night and fishes at day.

The nets are owned ordinarily by the owners of the adjacent land, who even claim, that no one can put up any nets on the water, adjoining their land without their consent or payment of rent, which generally varies between eight and eighteen rupees, according to the ignorance of the net owners, and latterly, the British Government also has been levying a tax of three rupees per net, crediting the receipts to land revenue miscellaneous. The rule with regard to the proceeds of the catch is that the owner who works with the assistance of the coolies shares equally with them, if the value of the catch is over four *puthans* or three annas and four pies, and nothing if the cost of the same is less. In partnership working, the share depends upon the articles of agreement.

The origin of these nets is rather obscure in spite of the term "Chinese nets" suggesting it, but it is known that, from a reliable authority, it is not found in China, nor for that matter in any other country except in Cochin, but a small portable hand net is seen in several parts of the world, namely, on the Euphrates, in Calcutta, Surat, and China also. It consists of a small pole with a string at the end, two cross yards suspended therefrom, and a square net attached to the yard-arms. It is worked by one hand with as much facility as any fishing rod, and is, when the work is finished, slung over the shoulder and easily carried about. Such a net does not differ from that used to catch butter-flies, and is very possibly evolved therefrom with the mechanism of the local picotta (*thulam* or *etham*) with its stone weight or ballast added to it. It should be mentioned, in this connection, that, of old, the authorship of all mechanical contrivances was ascribed in Malabar to China first, as it is now ascribed to *Seema* or England, and no inference could therefore be drawn about the source of an article which went under the name of China or *Seema*, except that it was not of native origin, and the most curious fact, in this connection, about the net, is that every part of it is known even in Malayalam by the Portuguese word, and some of the verbs themselves connected with the actions taken are also Portuguese with the Malayalam endings. A list of the Portuguese words in use with their meanings is given below.

(1) Ponthi = Bridge.

(2) Capsanti = Axle.

(3) Catrica or Catric = Triangles.

(4) Boras = Yards.

(5) Prolsa = The portion of the net ending in a ball.

(6) Ballaston = Stone weight.

(7) Esthain = Platform.

(8) Corda = Ropes.

(9) Odar = Braces or ropes connecting the yard-arms with the land.

(10) Borda = Borders of the net.

(11) Stucco = Pillars.

If the current is strong, and working impossible, they say in Malayalam, that the net won't *parur* or *parikkilla* (be successfully used). The above facts lead me to conclude, that the Chinese net is an invention of the Portuguese, Eurasian, or Popus (fishermen having European names, dressing like Europeans, and also speaking Portuguese), unless it is presumed, that the make of the net has latterly deteriorated. This method of fishing is continued all through the monsoon (excepting on very stormy days), and this affords excellent criterion of the tribes and species to be found in the rainy months, and renders Cochin the best place along the West Coast for making observations on this subject. A plan somewhat similar to this is employed on a small scale for catching crabs. A net, three feet square, is supported at the four corners by two small sticks fastened crosswise; attached to the centre of these sticks, where they cross, is a string to pull it by or let it down, and a piece of meat is tied to the middle of the net inside. This is let down from a wharf, left under water for a few minutes, and then pulled up again, and crabs coming to feed the meat are thus caught.[1]

Fishing with a line is seldom attempted in the deep sea except for sharks, rays, and other large fish. The hooks employed are of two kinds, the roughest, although perhaps the strongest, being of native manufacture, and the others named China hooks are of English make. The hook is fastened to a kind of fibre called *thumbu*, said to be derived from the sea weed, but more probably one of the species of palms. For a very large fish a brass wire is attached to the hook, and on one of these two substances, the lead for sinking the bait is placed. The lines are either hemp, cotton, or the fibre of Talipot palm (Caryota urens) which is obtained by maceration. But, although very strong, these lines are very apt to snap when suddenly bent.

Fish caught are taken with the net itself into the boat from the fishing places, and as the net is drawn out of water, it is usually washed as well. The whole work is generally done by boys, who go in pairs in small boats to the stake site, where the net had been tied some hours previously just as the tide began to run out. They are quickly rowed back to the shore, where the scene is lively and interesting with the women folk that crowd the landing place with baskets that would hold one to two maunds of fish. The tail ends of the net are then united, and the fish caught is emptied into the baskets, which, when full, are carried by the women, and so swung several times in water as to wash them completely, after which they

1. I am indebted to M. R. Ry. P. Narayana Menon, Avl., B. A., Deputy Collector of Mangalore for the account of the Chinese nets.

are taken home on their heads. The night catches are kept in baskets till the next morning, when they are spread out in the sun either on mats or on the ground. In the event of any larger fish being caught, they are taken inland and hawked about in the neighbourhood or sold in the bazaars or badly salted, dried, and kept for sale in the weekly markets or to be taken to hilly tracts. The prawns and other small species are dried in the sun and bundled up in mats or gathered and put into baskets for sale or handed over to middle-men on a small profit. Some fish, says Francis Day, are eaten fresh, some are preferred salted, and others are used in the arts, manufactures, or in medicine. It is prepared in a variety of ways. During the hot weather, large numbers of the species of mackerel are daily landed at Vypeen, where the daily salting process is carried on by the natives or by persons who come over from Ceylon for that purpose, and to assist in the capture. The first process consists in a coolly making one cut with a sharp knife along the backbone from head to tail, and then a second down its ventral surface exposing its intestines. It is then thrown over to a woman, who, having removed its inside, tosses it with two handles into a basket, which when half full is carried by two men to the sea-shore, where the fish are washed without being removed, and when clean, they are thrown on some leaves, and the salting begins. Women and children put some black salt into each cut, and throw the fish in a boat beside them on the shore in which there is brine. There they remain for a few hours, and are afterwards spread out in the open air, where they are dried and packed in square bundles of 1,000 each, and usually sold for export to Colombo. The salt fish is also in great request among the coolies employed as agricultural labourers in other parts of the Presidency, and the carriages which bring down coffee from the inland hilly tracts reconvey a large amount of this. Prawns are cured either by drying them in the sun or by boiling and drying them afterwards. If boiled, the shells are separated by heating, and the inner stuff which gets broken into the shape of peas, is packed separately either in bags or in mats, as is generally the case, when it is intended for the Burma market. It is largely used for local consumption also. The above process is done partly by fishermen and partly by middle-men, who, in that case, buy up the catch immediately after it is landed. The business, I hear, is a lucrative one, and a candy of 600 lbs is worth locally about Rs. 120.

Fish as a manufactured commodity.

Fish oil is largely extracted from the immense shoals of sardines (Sardinella Neohowii), which are found off Malabar and Ceylon, where, owing to the ignorance of the people, they have been used to manure cocoanut trees and paddy lands or to feed pigs and poultry, besides their being to a small extent an article of food. The process of extraction of the fish oil consists in ripening the fish, placing them in large vessels containing water, and then heating them. The whole mass is well stirred from time to time, and cold water is added to allow the oily matter to come up to the surface, which at this time has no offensive smell. When the oil has come up to the surface, it is skimmed off into buckets with spoons, and then allowed to stand for a night and day, after which it is boiled afresh, and skimmed from time to time, till all the scum has been taken off, and the oil is quite ready for use. There is also another plan which is mostly carried out in a boat which is divided into two by a perforated iron compartment, the fish being left to decompose in water on one side, and the oil floating through the partition to the other where it is skimmed off. The fish oil is as useful as other animal oils, and its export, which was at one time unrecognized, has been, and is still, increasing. Isinglass or fish maw is prepared from the swimming bladder of a species of siluroid, one of the sub-group *ari* or cat-fish, which is called *yeta* by the natives, and which grows from two to two and a half inches in length. The maws are roughly circular bladders, extracted from the fish and dried in the sun. They also form an article of export.

Fisheries thus give employment to a large number of people, along the coast and back-water either in capturing the spoil, in preparing them for the market or in their carriage to distant places, as well as to the numerous trades to which they are of a greater or less importance. In all civilized countries the fishing industry is recognized to be a necessary complement of the agricultural industry, and fish supplements the food supply of the poorer classes who are engaged in agricultural pursuits. In inland parts the slave castes derive their nutriment from those which they catch early in the morning and late in the evening when not engaged in agricultural labour. In former times, each fisherman had to pay a yearly tax upon the net he used in the State of Travancore, and those, who lived in the town of Cochin or under the Dutch protection, had to bring eight pounds weight of fish daily to the senior official; while in the Portuguese territory, besides their taxes, none of the produce could be taken to the market, until the clergy were first served with what they required. At one time, there was no tax upon fishermen or on the implements of trade either in the British territory or in the Native State of Cochin, but from the entries in the old revenue accounts prior to 993 M. E., it is seen that there were four sources of income to the State, under fisheries, namely, tax on fishing nets, rent on fishing stakes, rent on fishery farming in inland waters, and small imposts on each basket of fish carried from the sea-shore to the Narakkal *kadavu*. Under the old system, Her Highness the Amma Raja used to grant *Theettoorams* (Royal writs) to men of different castes and creeds in the State to enjoy special privileges, regarding fisheries in the back-waters of Cochin and Kanayanur Taluks.

Legends about fish.

At Edathra Kavu, nearly eight miles north-east of Chalakudy, is a temple dedicated to Bhagavathi situated at the river's bank where the fish receive a supply of food every week, and it is believed that whoever kills any, will certainly die within the year. There is a tradition that a Portuguese priest ridiculed this idle legend, and started in a boat with the intention of catching some after having vainly attempted to obtain the assistance of the

THE VALAN WOMEN SELLING FISH.

boat-man. He fired his gun at one of the fish with fatal effect, and it instantly sank. He then directed his servant to dive down and bring up the game; but as he declined, the priest soon went down himself, where, according to the native account, he found a lot of demons, who however vanished, when he made the sign of the cross. He then seized his prey, but hardly had he touched the planks of the boat to get in when it miraculously disappeared. The priest then returned home, and died in two days.

A fish is an emblem of Vishnu, in commemoration of his first incarnation, who, in this form, is said to have rescued the Vedas from the waters of the flood, and for this reason, it has become an object of adoration by pious Hindus. It is also one of the symbols of the kings of Madura (ancient Pandia), whose standard was called *Meen koda* or Fish Standard, which proved them to be Vaishnavite Hindus. The fish is also found on Buddhist seals. The kings of Pandia received tribute from the Rajas of Travancore, and many copper coins with the figure of fish on them are found in that State, and even so far north as Cochin, although it would be a puzzle to an ichthyologist to decide to which family they belong.[1] To this day, the Rajputs are said to have a fish carried before their most illustrious chieftains, when setting out on important expeditions. Even witchcraft claims its share in the finny tribes, and the fortunate possessor of the tail of a ray with its spine intact is believed to be safe from the effects of spells and charms as well as able to face the evil-eye with impunity.

Appearance and dress.

The Valans present a marked and distinct approximation to the physiognomy of the high caste-men, and many show a more decided tendency to obesity. There is a mildness in the expression of their countenance, which at once banishes the idea of their belonging to a low caste. They are found in all shades of complexion, and keep the upper part of the body naked, when they are

1. Land of the Perumals, page 493.

seen to advantage. The hair on the head is plentiful, wavy, and glossy like that of a Nair, with a round patch of hair, smoothed with cocoanut or gingelly oil, growing a little to the back from the forehead. The remaining part of the head, face, as well as the whole body are periodically shaven. The Valan women (Valathies) are also found in all shades of colour, and many are as handsome as the Nair ladies, and their tufts of hair, which are sufficiently long and kept smooth with the oils above referred to, are drawn tight and left slanting on the top of the head bordering on the left ear. Their dress is quite simple, and they wear a simple loin cloth with a small piece of cloth hanging loosely either over the shoulders or round the necks. Women's dress is equally simple, and their loin cloth is eight or nine cubits in length, which is generally folded before wearing. They also leave their bosom uncovered; but, changes for the better decency are taking place as in other higher castes, and the young women wear petticoats of gaudy hue provided with fanciful buttons, on public and ceremonial occasions. They also adopt the tattoo form of dressing like the Nair women. Clothing amongst children is totally disregarded and some mothers, who are very particular, tie round their loins, a string and a small piece of cloth, a plantain leaf or the leaf of an areca palm attached to it for decency's sake. Generally they are seen naked, or nudity is the prevailing fashion among the children of the low castes everywhere in the State ; but as they grow older, a slight advance is made in the clothing department, and there is never a superfluity of drapery for want of means.

Jewelry.

Valans do not lag behind other caste-men in the profuse use of ornaments. The males wear gold ear-rings, and rings for the fingers. The ears of girls, both in this and other castes, undergo heavy punishments, and when children are a year old, or even less, their ears are pierced and a small quil, a piece of cotton thread, or a bit of wood is inserted into the hole. The wound is gradually healed by the

THE VALAN WOMEN.

constant application of cocoanut oil; and as the irritation subsides, a bit of lead is substituted, and subsequently when this has enlarged the hole, a piece of plantain, cocoanut, or palmyra leaf is rolled up and put in: this is gradually increased in size until the entire lobe is expanded into a circular hole, capable of containing a large round plug, often with or more than, an inch in diameter. The appearance of two such ones, with circular flattened or slightly convex tops, in front of each ear, is believed to enhance a woman's beauty. The enormous orifice is probably intended to enable her to wear gold ornaments on her wedding day. They are not worn before marriage, and are afterwards taken out to be used on grand occasions. Wooden plugs are used by the poor women, while the rich wear gilt or gold ones. In some instances, they are worn constantly until the birth of a child. The rings adorn the fingers and toes, the fore-arms are covered with bangles as are also the legs, while gold necklaces of various kinds are worn round their necks.

Games.

Both men and women are a merry set of people, and have various games. The former dance in various forms to the accompaniment of vocal and instrumental music, while the latter sing and dance like the Nair women. Besides these, they play foot ball, chess, dice, and cards, and sometimes amuse themselves in personal combats. The following is a description of some of their games.

Foot ball match.—This is different in detail from the corresponding European one. A small stick is planted at a prominent spot, and the strong young men divide themselves into two hostile parties and open the match. One party stands at the post, while the other stands a little away from it. The ball, which is made of coir rope, is propelled by the palm of the hand towards the rival party, who furiously scrambles for it, vying with each other to catch and stop it on its onward career. This done, one of the members takes it in, and aiming at the post, throws the ball in its directions. If the ball hits the post or if any one member of the hostile rank catches the ball in its progress up through the air, but not when it touches the ground, then the particular player's turn is over. Then another man takes up the turn and continues it, and when all the members of one party have each his turn, the rival section begins the play exactly in the same manner and under the same rules as the previous section.

Attakalam.—This is really a boyish pastime though grown up men also take part in it. A large circle is drawn on a plain sandy floor, and members are selected for each of the two sections from amongst the assemblage, one of which is placed in a collective body inside the circle, while the other should stand around the outside. The latter can then try with, of course, as little injury to themselves as possible to strike at, and bring out, the former who are inside, each by each. In the interval between one outsider getting inside and touching the body of any one amongst the inside group, the latter are allowed to beat and worry the antagonist; but the moment he touches the person of the inside man, he gets complete immunity from violence at the hands of the rest of the inside batch, and the person who is caught, is at liberty to strike him and struggle to prevent his being driven out. If he gets turned out, then he is no more to remain inside, and when the whole of the inside are thus driven out, the first batch has finished its turn, and is then followed up by the other batch, and if anybody is left inside, and he cannot be driven out, his party is successful. Sometimes presents are given to the winners when their play is appreciated.

Chuvattu kali (dancing on the ground).—This is an exciting game played by a party of Valans standing in a circle. The movements of the feet and the fingers perfectly harmonize with the songs peculiarly fitted to each dancing, and the circle is alternately narrowed and widened.

Kole kali (stick dance).—This also is an exciting game in which sixteen members take part, each having two sticks, two feet in length. Both men and women take part in this.

A VALAN DANCE.

Kaikotti kali.—This is a game played by the males, as also by young women. A number of young women, joining together in a circular row at a pre-arranged spot, begin dancing. The songs are many and varied, and some of them are isolated ones composed in pure Malayalam, touching some specialised topic, while there are more dignified ones extracted from the dramatic literature of the country. Standing on the ground in a ring without touching each other, one member thereof opens the ball by reciting a couplet from one of these songs, after which she is caught up by the rest of the party in equally profuse strains. Then she sings the next couplet, which is followed up by the rest of the party collectively, and so on until the whole song is similarly ended. Thus the whole atmosphere of many a household is filled with vociferous yet dull melody of charming voices of lady singers adding to the jollity and attractiveness of the occasion all around.

Uzhinhal.—It is a game of grown up girls. A long bamboo piece is taken and split from the root to the end of it, leaving the other end untouched. Then two holes are bored, one at the end of each of the two parts into which the bamboo is split. Now another piece of the same material about a yard in length is divided along the grain into two equal parts. One of these is taken, and its both ends are cut into equal points, which are thrust into the poles of the long bamboo pieces, spoken of before. This is securely nailed and strongly attached between the split portions of the long bamboo, which is then hung perpendicularly by means of a very light strong rope to a strong horizontal branch of a neighbouring tree. Then the player sits on the piece attached between the split portions which are firmly held by her two hands. The whole bamboo mechanism is propelled by some one from behind, and the girls or young women derive a good deal of pleasure in swinging forwards and backwards. The game is resorted to on the occasion of the *Thiruvathira* festival in Dhanu (December-January).

Theatrical entertainments.—They have very few of the kind, which are of the most primitive type. They have been, of late, imitating the *Katha kali* of the higher castes, which are called *Attam kalis* (plays involving dancing to the accompaniment of vocal and instrumental music). Their musical instruments chiefly consist of (1) *maddalam*, sounded by means of the fingers of the hand, (2) *chenda*, sounded with drum sticks and (3) *elathalam*, which consists of two thick circular metal pieces with a protrusion in the middle, provided with holes through which strong cords are passed. These instruments and drums are so beaten as to produce ringing rhythmic sound fitting in with the music of the singers.

Food.

The food of the people is as varied as the castes and creeds, and a Valan generally begins the day by having a pound or two of pounded rice boiled in two or three pints of water, to which some ghee is added, if he can afford it. This preparation is called *kanji*, which forms the morning meal of himself and his family and is drunk with the aid of some pickles. He then chews some betel-leaves, nuts, and tobacco, and goes for his work, and at twelve or one, he expects his wife to have prepared his breakfast, but some continue without anything until three or four in the afternoon. The meal consists of boiled rice, which is made more palatable by the addition of some fish either curried or fried in cocoanut oil. If they can afford it, some curry or other preparation, made of vegetables, herbs, fruits, and other pungent articles, is placed in another vessel or a plantain leaf, and with this they moisten the rice from time to time. The man never touches his food with his left hand, for it is considered to be impure. The rice ready for eating is heaped up into a mound with a depression on the top, in the centre of which is an amalgamation of various other articles. He opens his mouth, and throws the food in the form of little balls, and when thirsty, drinks hot water or ginger water, taking care that the receptable containing water does not touch the lips at all. Having finished his meal, he goes outside the door and water is poured from a brass vessel over his hands to be cleaned. The wife cooks the meals and serves them, but cannot eat in the presence of, or at the same time as, her lord and master, except on the day of her marriage, such being considered as both indecent and disrespectful. The evening meal, which is also of the same nature, is between seven and eight or between eight and nine at night. There are many articles available for human food, and a Valan best knows, what he wants. Sometimes, when he has nothing to eat, he resorts to the oil cake (the refuse of the cocoanut after the oil has been expressed), which is usually given to cattle and poultry. The fruit of the jack, banana, brinjals, and other vegetables, the roots of the sweet potato and other plants give some of the greatest delicacies. Animal food is also abundantly resorted to. Fish of every species, which they catch, is consumed, and mutton and fowls form their chief dietary. They avoid squirrels, lizards, foxes, and all reptorial ones. Their great luxury is toddy without which they cannot get on. Their hard work in fishing and boat rowing demands it, and a Valan can go on with his work for hours together with the drinking of toddy at an interval of several hours. Nothing, but a pot of toddy or a promise of it on reaching the shore, can induce him to row his canoe against adverse winds and currents. Notwithstanding the fact, that the native in India is held up as a model to sobriety and good health from abstemious living, it must be said, that the Valans and other low caste-men are not free from the prevalent vice of drunkenness, and it is believed that more than half their earnings is squandered in this vice.

Social status.

The rules respecting the distances maintained between persons of various castes and their subdivisions were and are even now very strict in these parts. The members of the fishing castes come in the order of social precedence below the Izhuvans, and have to stand at a distance of thirty-six feet from Brahmans, Kshatriyas, and high caste Sudras, so as not to pollute them. They eat the food and drink the water of the high caste-men above mentioned, but totally abstain from taking the food of the caste-men below them. They have their own barber and washerman, and have also their priests, who belong to a caste or rather sub-caste below them. While passing through public roads, they have continually to call out from a distance, to be heard by persons of the higher castes in order that the latter may not be polluted. They have to stand at a certain distance from the outer wall of high caste temples, when they go to worship the deities therein. These fishermen, who entertain serious objections on religious grounds to take the food of the caste-men below them, are perfectly willing to partake of the food of the native Christians and Mahomadans, who are outside the pale of the Hindu castes.

—0:0—

THE KATALARAYANS.

CHAPTER XIV.

THE FISHING CASTES

(Continued).

11. THE KATALARAYANS.

——:o:——

The Katalarayans (sea Arayans), otherwise called Katakkoties, are a tribe of people lower in status to the Valans, and live along the coast from Cranganore to Cochin, rarely going inland. They were of great service to the Portuguese and the Dutch in their palmy days, acting as boat-men in transhipping their commodities, and supplying them with fish. They were, in former times, considered as an inferior race, and, as such, precluded from travelling along the public roads, and consequently obliged to keep to the sea-coast. They numbered 4,081 at the last census, 2,141 being males, and 1,940 females.

Among their own community, they distinguish themselves by four distinct appellations, which are Sankhan, Bharathan, Amukkuvan, and Mukkuvan. Of these, the Arayans or the Katalarayans belong to the first group, and the Valans to the second. Amukkuvans are a sub-caste of the Katalarayans, doing priestly functions to the members of both the groups. All these groups are Prathilomajas. The caste-men belong to the four *illams* or groups (endogamous septs), namely, Kattotillam, Karotillam, Chempotillam, and Ponnotillam, the origin and significance of which are not quite clear.

Marriage customs. As in other castes, marriage between the members of the same sept is strictly prohibited, while that between those of different septs is pèrmissible. The girls of the Katalarayans are married both before and after puberty. The *tali* tying ceremony, which is compulsory in the case of Valan girls before they are of age, is conveniently put off, and takes place along with the real marriage, the preliminary negotiations and settlements of which are substantially the same as those prevailing among the Valans. The auspicious hour for marriage is between three and eight in the morning, and on the evening previous to this, the bridegroom and his party arrive at the house of the bride, where they are welcomed and treated to a grand feast, after which, the guests along with the bridegroom and the bride, seated somewhat apart, in a pandal tastefully decorated and brightly illuminated, are entertained with songs of the Velan (washerman) and his wife, alluding to the marriage of Sita (wife of Rama) or Parvathi (wife of Siva), with the belief that they may bring about a happy conjugal union. These are continued until sunrise, when the priest hands over the marriage badge to the bridegroom, who ties it round the neck of the bride. The songs are again continued for an hour or two, after which *poli* begins, *i. e.*, the guests who have assembled contribute a rupee, eight annas, or four annas according to their means, the collection of which goes for the remuneration of the priest, the songsters, and the drummers. The guests are again sumptuously entertained at twelve o' clock, after which the bridegroom and his party return with the bride to his house. At the time of departure or nearly an hour before it, the bridegroom ties a few rupees or a sovereign to a corner of the cloth covering her body, probably to induce her to accompany him. Just then, the bride's price which is 101 *puthans* or five rupees, four annas, and two pies is paid to her parents in satisfaction of their having disposed of her; and this custom refers to the ancient system of marriage by purchase. The bridal party is similarly entertained in the bridegroom's house, where also, at an auspicious hour, the married couple are seated together, and served with a few pieces of plantain fruits and some milk, when the bride is formally declared to be a member of the husband's family.

If a girl attains her maturity after her marriage, she is secluded for a period of eleven days. She bathes on the first, fourth, seventh, and the eleventh days, and on the last day the caste-men and women are entertained with a grand feast, the expenses connected therewith being met by the husband.

The Katalarayans have rarely more than one wife, and no woman can have more than one husband. A widow may, a year after the death of her husband, enter into conjugal relations with any member of the caste, except her brother-in-law. The customs connected with divorce are the same as those prevailing among the Valans.

Inheritance and tribal organization.

Among the Arayans, the succession is in the male line, that is, the sons succeed to the property of their father. These sea fishermen have their head-men (*Aravans*), whose duties to the caste-men are the same as those of the head-men of the Valans; but they are not without special privileges. When the senior male or female member of the ruling family dies, the former *Aravan* has the special privilege of being the first successor to the masnad with his *thirumulkazhcha* (nuzzer), which consists of a small quantity of salt packed in a plantain leaf with rope and a Venetian ducat or other gold coin. During the period of mourning, visits of condolence from durbar officials and *sthanies* or noblemen are received only after the *Aravan's* visit. When the Bhagavathi temple of Cranganore is defiled during the cock festival in Meenam (March-April), Koolimutteth Aravan has the special privilege of entering the temple in preference to other caste-men.

Religion.

The Katalarayans profess Hinduism, and their modes of worship and other religious observances are the same as those of the Valans.

Funeral customs.

The sea fishermen either burn or bury their dead. The period of pollution is for eleven days, and the agnates are freed from it by a bath on the eleventh day. On the twelfth day, the caste-men of the village including the relatives and friends are treated to a grand feast.

The son, who is the chief mourner, observes the *deeksha* (a vow by which he does not shave) for a year, at the expiry of which he gets shaved. He performs the *sradha* every year in honour of the dead.

Occupation.

The Katalarayans, as has been said, are sea fishermen, and their modes of fishing are as follow. Their nets are generally made of cotton thread, and when large wall nets are employed, they are generally the joint property of several persons. Meshes of three sizes are used, according to the class or rather the power of the fish it is intended to capture. One share which is a distinct piece of netting and usually belongs to one person is about five yards square; and a wall net sometimes consists of about forty of these pieces fastened together. These wall nets are employed for catching large fish and also shoals of small ones. The larger ropes are inevitable and made of coir. The mackerel net is generally a single wall net, about one hundred yards long, by eighteen feet deep, floated by hollow cocoanut shells weighted below with stones. When a shoal of mackerel is perceived, a heavy stone is fixed to one end of the net which is thrown into the sea, and the boat to which the other end of the net is attached is rowed quickly round the shoal. The same kind of net, about half a mile in length, is sometimes used; when shoals of fish come near the shore, one end is kept there, and the other carried round them, and thus enclosed, they are dragged to land. When round nets are employed, two boats are required. In the centre of the net is a long funnel, otherwise it is much the same as that used in catching mackerel. The funnel is first thrown into the sea, and then the two boats, to each of which one end of the net is attached, are rowed rapidly through the shoals. Cast nets are also used from the shore by a number of fishermen who station themselves either in the early morning or in the afternoon along the coast from fifty to hundred yards apart. They keep a careful watch on the water, and on perceiving a fish rise sufficiently near the land, rush down, and attempt to throw their nets over it. Trolling from the shore at the river's mouth is carried on only in the morning or evening during the winter months of the year, when the sea is smooth. The line is from eighty to hundred yards in length, and held wound round the left hand, the hook is fastened to the line by a brass wire, and the bait is a live fish. The fisherman, after giving an impetus by twirling round and round his head, throws it with great precision fifty to sixty yards. A man is always close by with a cast net, catching baits which he sells for one quarter of an anna each. The mode of fishing is very exciting, but is very uncertain in its results, and therefore usually carried on by coolies before their day's work has begun or after its termination.

During some months of the year, their boats leave for the deep sea fishing at four o' clock in the afternoon, and having remained all night in the open sea, may be seen returning with heir captures at about seven o' clock the following morning, when purchasers meet them as they land. At other times, they leave at day-break, and return at about four in the afternoon to sell their cargo on coming to shore, either in lots or as a whole. Should the weather appear stormy, no boats go out to sea, and fishing with nets, except in the river or back-water, is unknown; consequently the loss of fishing vessels with all hands on board is of very rare occurrence.

Formerly, on the death of a prince of Malabar, all fishing was temporarily prohibited, and only renewed after three days, when the spirit of the departed was supposed to have had time enough to choose its abode without molestation, and this rule is still in force.

Social status.

As has been said, the Katalarayans were, in former times, obliged to keep to the sea-coast, and were, owing to their social degradation, precluded from travelling along the public roads. This disability was, during the days of the Portuguese supremacy in these parts, taken advantage of by the Romish missionaries, who turned their attention to the conversion of these poor sea fishermen, a large majority of whom, at present, acknowledge the Roman Catholic religion, and are thus elevated in the social scale. Relapsing into heathenism, they became out casts, between whom and the Katalarayans, there is neither intermarriage nor interdining. These disabilities have long ago vanished, and they enjoy the privilege of walking through public roads as other caste-men, but have to keep to the same distance as the Valans, to the Brahmans, Kshatriyas, and high caste Sudras, whose food and water they have no objection to take. They are still in a backward state, and very few of them are literate. In physical appearance they appear to be strong and healthy, and their women who are distinguished from Valathies (Valan women) are also handsome.

III. THE MUKKUVANS.

The Mukkuvans are the sea fishermen of the Malabar coast, a small number of whom lives along the shores of the Cochin State. They were returned as 1,436 at the census of 1,891 while they were only thirty in number in 1,901. It is said that the Valans and the Arayans are the indigenous elements in the State, and that the small number of Mukkuvans and Marakkans must be regarded as sojourners from the coasts of Malabar and Travancore adjoining the State. The variation in the figures of the Mukkuvans is partly due to an error in the popular language, which does not often take note of the nice distinctions of these sub-castes, and partly due to the vague use of the names 'Mukkuvans' and 'Katalarayans', as being easily interchangeable. The Katalarayans of the State somewhat correspond with the Mukkuvans in spite of the local variations in their customs and manners. The word 'Mukkuvan' is connected with the Canarese '*Moger*;' both the words come from the same root which means 'to dive'. According to a tradition, Mukkuvans and Tiyyans are said to be immigrants from Ceylon.

A MUKKUVAN GROUP.

Internal structure of the caste.

The Mukkuvans, that live along the coast from Cranganore to Cannanore, belong to the same four *illams* as the Katalarayans, while those, that inhabit the coast from Chavakkad as far as Cranganore, belong to three *illams*, and there is, strictly speaking, no intermarriage nor interdining between the two sets of people. Nevertheless, a member of any one of the four *illams* can dine with one of the three *illams* and take a woman as concubine, while one of the latter cannot take his meals in the house of one of the former without cleaning the vessels used by him, nor can he marry a woman without her loss of caste. This leads to the conclusion that the members of the four *illams* are superior in status to those of the three. Further, the word '*illam*' which means a Namburi house is applied to this and other inferior castes; and so far as my enquiries show, the Mukkuva *illams* do not bear the names of any of the Namburi houses, now known to exist or to have existed.

Marriage customs.

Marriage of girls among the Mukkuvans may take place either before or after puberty, and is allowed, as among the Valans and Arayans, between the members of different groups or *illams*; in other words, it is exogamous, so far as the *illams* are concerned. Further, marriage customs differ in different places, for instance, in Cochin, Ponnani, Chavakkad, and other places the caste-men are not very particular about the *tali* tying ceremony, and the *tali* is generally tied by the maternal aunt of the girl or some senior woman in the family. A girl who comes of age is under seclusion for four days, and on the morning of the fourth day, a woman of the washerman caste sings certain songs, after which the girl is bathed, and the caste-men and women that are invited are sumptuously fed.

The customs connected with the preliminary negotiations leading to the marriage of a young Mukkuvan are the same as those referred to in the account of the Valans and Arayans. On the auspicious day chosen for the celebration of the wedding, a feast is held in the house of the bridegroom for his friends and relatives who form the marriage procession, making a somewhat noisy progress to the house of the bride, where the whole party is entertained. After supper, the bridegroom is introduced to the bride, who is dressed and adorned in her best; and to a corner of the cloth covering her body, he ties two or three rupees, and leaves her with a few betel-leaves, nuts, and tobacco for his companions and himself to chew. The rest of the night is spent in music and dancing. At twelve o' clock the next day, the guests are again treated to a grand feast, after which, the bridegroom returns to his house with the bride, making a gift of six rupees to the bride's father, four rupees to her mother, three rupees for meals, and a rupee for distribution among the grown up men assembled there at the time. These gifts vary in different places, and the customs also vary slightly. The bride's price is ten rupees and a half, and at the time of departure, the bridegroom places a rupee on the lighted lamp in the shed and takes leave of his father-in-law with the present of a rupee. The bride accompanies the bridegroom's sister, who adorns and dresses her with the new cloths and ornaments brought by her. On the arrival of the bridal party at the bridegroom's house, similar entertainments are given to the guests, and the married couple are seated together, when an egg and a cocoanut are waved round their faces, and some sweets also given thereafter. The bride is then formally declared to be a member of the family, after which the marriage is over.

As already stated, the marriage customs of the Mukkuvans of Ponnani, Chavakkad, and other places bordering on the State slightly differ from those detailed above, but somewhat correspond with those of the Izhuvans of those parts as well as elsewhere. On the morning of the wedding day, the bride is anointed with oil and decked with leafy ornaments, and then bathed. In fact, all the ceremonies performed for girls on the bathing day of their first menses are strictly followed. A few hours before the lucky time, the bridegroom, neatly dressed and well adorned, arrives at the house of the bride, accompanied by his party, who are welcomed and well entertained. The bridegroom is seated on a conspicuous seat made for the occasion in the marriage booth put up in front of the main building, and the floor of the booth is covered with mats or white cloths and blankets brought by the *kavuthian* for the assembled guests to sit on. At the auspicious hour, the bride's sister-in-law dresses her in the cloths brought by her and also adorns her with gold ornaments of her own and with those borrowed for the occasion. She is soon led to the booth, where the washerman (Velan) and his wife entertain those assembled therein with their usual wedding song, and in the midst of joyous shouts and the tunes of vocal and instrumental music, the bridegroom, receiving the conjugal collar from the priest, ties it round her neck. The married couple are then taken to the main building, where they sup together, and the rest of the night is spent in music and dancing. After a similar feast the next day at twelve o'clock, the bridegroom returns home, accompanied by the bridal party and his followers. The entire party is well entertained, and the bridegroom and the bride are served with the usual sweets, and the latter is formally declared to be a member of the family. The marriage is then said to be over.

The marriage customs obtaining among the Mukkuvans of North Malabar may afford some interest to those who pursue the study of comparative ethnography, and are as described below. The marriage consists of two ceremonies, namely, (1) *Thalikettukalyanam* (*tali* tying ceremony, known also as *Pandal kalyanam*, marriage ceremony in the shed, or *Vettila kalyanam* betel-leaf ceremony) and (2) nuptials. The performance of the former ceremony is compulsory for girls before puberty, as the negligence of it will place her and others in the family under a ban. When the *tali* tying ceremony has to be performed for a girl, an auspicious day is chosen with the consent of the local head-man and his assistant who must be invited, and for whose presence a sum of two annas is paid. Two or three days before this, a male member as well as two women of the family invite the caste-men and women of the village with a present of half a packet of betel-leaves and five nuts to each member, and the caste head-man, whose presence is indispensable, with a full packet and two nuts. The girl fasts during the previous night, and is seated on a plank without touching the floor. On the morning of the auspicious day, she is bathed by seven women with seven vessels of water, after which she is neatly dressed and brought to the pandal put up in front of the house. If the husband for the girl has been already decided on, the *tali* is tied either by his sister or by some grown up woman of his family, as otherwise the same function devolves on the paternal aunt. Then the usual feast follows with a liberal distribution of betel-leaves, nuts, and tobacco to the guests assembled.

As regards the real marriage (nuptials), there are three different forms now in vogue among these sea fishermen, with ceremonies or formalities more or less alike, each having different degrees of importance and permanence, but varying chiefly in the amount of the bride's price; and these are (1) *Mangalam*, (2) *Veettil kalyanam* (joining the house), and (3) *Udukkan kodukkal* (giving cloths). A man, who has a wife by the first form of marriage, cannot have one more of the same form or another by the second form, but may have one in the third form, which corresponds with a kind of concubinage. Similarly, a man, having a wife in the second form, may not have one more in the same form, but may keep a concubine of the third class, while a fisherman, having one of the third kind, may enter into conjugal union with one in the first or second kind. Further, a woman married to a man by *Mangalam* lives with her husband in his family, and is maintained by him during his life-time, and in the event of his death, she and her children may be entitled to maintenance for a year. A wife of the second class under similar circumstances may be looked after for six months. A man may have more than one wife, but a woman cannot have more than one husband. Further, a woman after the death of her husband is allowed to marry; but, if she were married in the first form, she has to be in a state of mourning for a year, while widows, according to the second and third forms of marriage, are in mourning for six and three months respectively, during which they should confine themselves mostly to their rooms. Again, on the contrary, on the death of the wife of the first class, the husband must shut himself up for three days, and both the father and the son must observe *deeksha* for a year. In the case of the demise of the wife of the third class, only the son goes into mourning.

Pregnancy and childbirth.

Among the Mukkuvans, when the first pregnancy of a wife is announced, a ceremony known as *Pulikudi* (drinking of the tamarind juice) is performed for her, when fourteen or twenty-one women of the village bring bread and sweet meat. They are all treated to a feast, after which the woman in the family goes to her house, where also the same ceremony is performed during the ninth month. These women, as other caste-women, are exposed to magic, witchcraft, and diabolical agencies, and all careful precautions are taken to guard her from evil; and promises of offerings are made to Káli or Bhagavathi, and to the sainted dead of the family if they vouchsafe an easy delivery. Thorny branches of the bel tree (Aegle Marmelos) are hung at the door of the room of her delivery, and also scared away by the smoke from an old shoe which is burnt for the purpose. The woman sits on her heels during accouchement, and is supported by her female relatives. She is attended by a woman of her caste for fifteen days which is the period of her impurity. When it is announced that the child is a boy, a cocoanut is broken as a sign of thanksgiving to the deity (Bhagavathi), who saved her. After the cord is cut, both the mother and the baby are bathed in warm water, and a mixture of sugar and honey is dropped on its tongue. A little of gold is also sometimes rubbed in the mixture. In South Malabar and Cochin, the birth of a son is announced by three loud shouts to convey their rejoicing, and the birth of a daughter by three hard blows on the floor outside the room of her confinement. The woman and her baby are again bathed on the third day. For the first three days, her diet consists of some bread, coffee, and rice gruel, and for the next ten days, boiled rice and some curry. A few doses of *pettu marunnu* (delivery medicine) and a few small cupfuls of some vegetable decoction (*nadi kashayam* and *marma kashayam*) are also given for the improvement of her general health. The wife of the local *kavuthiyan* (barber and priest) attends on her on the morning of the sixteenth day, cleans her room and its surroundings with water mixed with cow-dung and bathes her to be purified. On the twenty-eighth day, the boy or girl is invested by the aunt with a thread containing some small pieces of gold shaped into a kind of ornament. It is a ceremonial day, on which there is a feast to those who are invited. Feeding and naming take place together on the sixth month. The wife joins the husband after a period of ninety days, at the expiry of which the woman's sister-in-law comes to take her with a few pieces of cloth for her dress. The ceremony of ear-boring takes place during the fifth or sixth year. In former times, the local *asan* (teacher) used to bore the ears, and was rewarded with a few rupees for his services. Any member of the family may now do it, and the day is one of festivity to his friends and relations, and this constitutes the initiation.

There are no special ceremonies in connection with twins, but they are considered inauspicious. If, during the pregnancy of a woman, an eclipse happen to occur, she is made to sit quiet while it lasts, with a stone pestle in her hand, and is not made to touch or move any cutting instrument.

Divorce.

Divorce is settled by caste Panchayets, and either party may apply for a divorce, when a Panchayet is held, and whoever loses the suit is fined. In North Malabar, a man who wants to divorce his wife must pay Rs. 85—2—0, and a woman who applies for a judicial separation from her husband has to pay Rs. 112—2—0. In South Malabar, payment in either case is Rs. 90—4—0. Of the payment thus made, only a third goes to the party concerned, one-third goes to the local temple, and the remaining third is shared by the head-man and the Panchayet. This refers to the first form of marriage already described. In the case of a marriage of the second class, payment is only three rupees and three rupees and a half, and this is divided equally between the temple and the members of the Panchayet. If either party be dissatisfied with the decision of the Panchayet of his village, he or she can, at his or her own expense, convene a Panchayet of another village, and its decision is final.

Inheritance and caste assembly.

As regards inheritance, succession is in the male line in Cochin and South Malabar, and in the female line in North Malabar. In the latter case, neither wives nor children have any right to the father's property, which has not been alienated in their favour during his life-time.

The Mukkuvans have their caste assemblies which meet on all important occasions connected with the welfare of the caste, and are presided over by their caste head-man called the *Aravan*, whose powers over the caste-men are absolute and whose appointment is hereditary. He has a subordinate, called *Ponamban* in Cochin and *Kadavan* in Malabar. His duties consist in executing the business committed to his charge by the former, whose sources of income from the families of the caste-men are multifarious. The *Aravan* gets (1) nine annas at the time of fixing an auspicious hour for the *tali* tying and nuptial ceremonies, (2) four annas and six pies before he is invited for the above ceremonies, (3) one rupee and two annas for giving permission to put up a pandal during marriage, (4) the same amount as present from the bridegroom at the time of the departure with the bride, (5) a fair share of the sum deposited by the person applying for divorce, and (6) a few rupees in all funeral ceremonies.

Religion.

The religion of the Mukkuvans is that of the orthodox low caste Hindu, Vishnu and Siva being worshipped with equal reverence. Among the minor gods, Subramania and Sastha appear to be most in favour. Kodungallur Bhagavathi is their guardian deity. They are also the Sakthi worshippers. Ancestors are worshipped with offerings on new moon days and *Sankranthis*.

Funeral customs.

The dead bodies of the Mukkuvans are both burned and buried. When a member of the caste breathes his last, the fishermen of the village, when informed, suspend their work that day and attend the funeral. The corpse is placed on a bier brought by the barber, with the head towards the south, and it is then dressed in new cloths and decked with ornaments. Four persons, appointed to carry the bier, bathe in the sea, and take the dead body to the grave. Four old women engage in loud lamentations. A few pieces of the cloths on the dead body are torn out and preserved by the son and those who have to perform funeral obsequies. The bearers and the near relatives of the deceased then bathe in the sea, and place the body in the grave. A small piece of gold, a little water, and some flowers are placed in the nose, and all present drop water in the mouth of the corpse placed in the grave, which is soon covered up. The son or the nephew, who performs the funeral ceremonies, goes round the grave three times with a pot of water on his head, and then throws rice and flowers on the grave. After the interment, all return to the house and worship a lamp lit by a barber woman. The next of kin is then taken to the sea-shore by the barber, and there oblations of water are given to the deceased. Until the fourteenth day, the barber woman sprinkles water on the agnates, and on this day, the barber makes an image of the deceased with rice, which the relatives one and all worship. The barber next gives them rice and tamarind which they eat. He is then paid four rupees by the wife or husband of the deceased as the case may be. The head-men also are paid their fees. Rice and cocoanuts are then distributed to all the houses of the village, and the son performs the last funeral ceremony at the grave. That night, the agnates all go in procession to the shore, and the funeral cakes and a piece of hair of the son are thrown into the sea. There is a feast on that day as well as on the following day. On the fifteenth day, the barber, after the feast, distributes sandal and jaggery to the people assembled on the occasion, and these leave the house without touching the eaves. If the deceased man has a wife of the first class, her *tali* is broken by the barber woman and put into the grave. A cloth is thrown on her head, and a pot of water poured over it. She is in mourning for a year, and during this period, her relatives visit her. On the death of such a wife, if the husband be alive, three pots of water are thrown on his head, and he is confined to his house in a state of mourning for three days. The caste priest is the barber, who is called *kavuthiyan*.

Occupation.

The Mukkuvans are sea fishermen, and as such, fishing has long been, and is even now, the chief occupation of a large majority of the population. There are also some among them, who are cultivators, physicians, teachers, merchants, and contractors in boat service at the harbours, while a small minority holds appointments in the public service in the British parts.

Social status.

In former times, they occupied a low state in the estimation of the high caste-men, and were precluded from passing along the public roads. Being obliged to keep to the coast, and unable to bear the social disabilities, many became Christians, and converts to Islam (*Puislams* or *puthia* Islams or new Islams), and were thus elevated in the social scale. All *Puislams* follow the occupation of fishing, and in every family there is a rule, that one child at least shall become a Mussalman. In the northernmost Taluk of Malabar, there is a custom that Mukkuva females, during their periods, cannot remain in the house, but must occupy the house of a Moplah, which shows that the two castes live on very close terms. The restrictions above referred to have not been removed, and they have to stand at a distance of thirty-two feet from the Brahmans, Kshatriyas, and high caste Sudras, whose food and water they have no objection to take and drink. They profess to be on a level with the Kammalans and Izhuvans, between whom and them there is no pollution by touch. They do not eat the food of Panan and Mannan (washerman). They have their own barber and washerman. They adore the deities in the Brahmanic temples by standing at a distance from the outer wall. During the cock festival in the Bhagavathi temple of Cranganore, these people are allowed to worship the deity in preference to the Izhuvans, and the Raja allows vessels to be given to the caste-men, who come from distant places; these privileges are refused to other caste-men.

——0:0——

CHAPTER XV.

THE IZHUVANS.

——:o:——

Izhuvans, also called Illavans, are a wide spread tribe of people inhabiting Malabar, Cochin, and Travancore. Known as they are under different names with more or less variations in their customs and manners, they form one and the same caste. In North Malabar as far as Calicut, they are known as Tiyyans, and in Cochin and Travancore, as Chovans or Izhuvans. They are believed to be closely allied to the Tamil speaking Shannars of the Tinnavelly District and to the Billavas of South Canara. Numerically, they occupy a high position in the population of the State. They numbered 1,84,504 at the last census, 91,524 being males and 92,980 females, and formed 33·2 per cent. of the Hindu population, out-numbering the Sudra population by 11·7 per cent. The caste is, on the whole, literate, and ranked as the third among the literates, the native Christians and the Nairs being the first and the second respectively. Among the Izhuvans, 62·51 per cent. of the males, and 9·54 of the females can read and write.

Origin and tradition of the caste.

The etymology of the words 'Izhuvan' and 'Tiyyan', goes to show that they were probably immigrants from Ceylon. The word 'Tiyyan' is another form of '*dweepan*', which means an islander, while 'Izhuvan' signifies one that belongs to *Izham*, which is an old name for Ceylon. It is said that the Izhuvans and Tiyyans are the descendants of the Shannar colonists from Ceylon, and that, in their migrations to Malabar, they brought with them the cocoanut and palmyra palms, the cultivation of which is even now their chief occupation.[1] The word 'Chovan' is a corruption of '*sevakan*' or workman, and shows the position held by these

1. Mackenzie manuscripts.

men in the country of their adoption. Some 130 years ago, they were largely employed as soldiers along with the Nairs by the old rulers of Travancore, the chief of whom was the Raja of Ambalapuzha and Purakad. Even so late as during the reign of Maharaja Rama Varma, who died in 973 M. E., a large number of Chovans were employed as soldiers in Travancore. So also had the Tiyyans of North Malabar formed a military class in former times, and there was a Tiyya regiment of a thousand soldiers at Tellicherry with men of their own caste, who held high and responsible posts, and also distinguished themselves by the most conspicuous gallantry and fidelity. The survival of their former greatness is still kept by the costumes of the bridegroom and his friends on their marriage occasions, namely, a pointed helmet on the head, the *kacha* cloth worn round the waist, a knife stuck in the girdle, and drawn swords and shields in the hands of the bridegroom and his two friends. The sword and shield dance were the indispensable accompaniments until lately, all denoting a warlike career. There are also other traditions in regard to the origin and early history of the caste, which are described below.

In the Mackenzie manuscripts, there is a story that seven Gandharva women had seven sons, from whom the Izhuvans are said to have descended. It is said that the Shannars of the Tinnavelly District, and not the Illavans, are the descendants of the Gandharva women.

There is another story that a Pandyan princess of Kshatriya family known as Ali married Narasimha, a Kshatriya Raja of the Carnatic. The married couple migrated to Ceylon, where they remained sovereigns of the country under the title of Izha Perumal. That line became extinct and their relations and adherents returned to their old country, where they have since remained. Many of the Shannars have, of late, put forward a claim to be considered Kshatriyas. This is, of course, says Mr. H. A. Stuart, absurd, as there is no such thing as Dravidian Kshatriyas.

In a Tamil puranic work, there is the mention of the name of a king Illa of Ceylon, who went to Chidambaram, where a religious discussion took place between the Buddhist priests and the Saivite devotee Manickiavachakar in the presence of king Illa and Chola and that finally king Illa was converted to the Saivite faith. His descendants are known as the 'Illavans,' and Mr. H. A. Stuart defines the word to mean natives of Ceylon. It is also said that the Illa kings, like the Kodamba kings of Mysore, must have belonged to the toddy drawing class.

Mr. H. A. Stuart writes in the Census Report of 1891 as follows:—

"It is by no means certain that Shannars were not at one time a warlike tribe, for we find traces of a military occupation of the several primitive tribes among several toddy drawing castes of the south. Toddy drawing is the special occupation of the several primitive tribes spread over the south-west of India, bearing different names in various parts. They were employed by former rulers as foot-soldiers and body-guards, being noted for their fidelity."

"The toddy drawing sect was closely connected with the kingdom of Vijayanagar. It would seem probable that they were at one time in the service of Vijayanagar kings and formed an important element in the fighting forces of the Hindu kingdoms of the south."

In the time of Cheraman Perumal, a woman of the washerman caste was washing her cloth in water mixed with ashes. She wanted somebody to aid her in holding the other end, but seeing nobody, she called a young daughter of an Asari (carpenter), who was alone in the house. The child did as requested, not knowing that it was an infringement of the rules of her caste. One day, the washerwoman made bold to enter the house of the carpenter, who demanded angrily how she dared to cross his threshold, when the woman scornfully answered that she belonged to the same caste as he, since his daughter had helped to hold her cloth. The carpenter, who felt much provoked by this insolent reply and the disgrace which it had brought upon him, killed her on the spot. Upon this, her husband and friends complained to the Perumal, who took up their cause and threatened the carpenters, whereupon the latter combined together, left the country of the Perumal, and took refuge in the island of Ceylon, where they were welcomed by the king of Candy. The Perumal felt embarrassed at their departure, and requested the king of the island to send him some of the carpenters, for he had none in his own dominions who could build a house. He also promised to do them no harm, and yet they would have no confidence in him; but at last they consented to go back on condition that the king of Candy would send four Chovans and their wives to protect them and to witness the Perumal's attitude towards them. The king granted their request on the understanding that, in all wedding, funeral, and other ceremonies, they would promise to pay the Izhuvans (Chovans) three measures of rice as a tribute for their protection. This privilege of the Chovans is still kept up, and from these four Chovans, the Izhuvans are said to have descended.[1] The Tiyyans of North Malabar claim their descent from an outcasted Namburi woman. It is said that they had a chief named Mannanar, a Tiyya baron.

Internal structure of the caste.

There are several subdivisions or sub-castes among them, but broadly speaking, three sub-castes, namely, Tiyya Chone (Chovan), Pandy Chone, and Velakandi Chone, are found in Cochin, and two, namely, Nadi Chone and Pachilli Chone are found in Travancore.[2] According to the late Cochin Census Report, there are only three subdivisions, namely, (1) Pandy Izhuvans, (2) Malayalam Izhuvans, and (3) Tiyyans of North Malabar. They are also divided into *illams* and *kiriyams* (family groups), which resemble the Brahmanic *gotrams*. This may be traced even among the Pulayans and Mukkuvans. Mutil, Chothi, Mayyanat, and Matambi are some

1. Mackenzie manuscripts.

2. These divisions are fast dying out.

of their *illams*. Mr. E. K. Krishnan, the retired Sub-Judge, says, that the Tiyyans of North Malabar belong to eight *illams* and thirty-two *kiriyams*, and even now they call themselves eight *illakkars*. The eight *illams* referred to, are Nellikka, Pullanni, Vangeri, Kozhikalan, Patayanguti, Manankuti, Thenankuti, and Velakkamkuti. Kozhikalan, he says, is superior to the rest. The real significance of this division is not clear.

Habitations.

Their habits are settled, and they are found in all parts of the State. The poorer classes of people live in huts with mud walls and thatched roofs, with a room or two and a verandah either in front or all around, while the richer people have their houses like those of the Nairs. Both when the foundation of the house is laid and when the construction is completed, *pujas* are performed by the head-man of the carpenters. A few days before occupation, a grand *puja* is performed, and sacrifices of goats, fowls, etc., are given to lower orders of the demons, who are supposed to have been dwelling in the wood with which the house was constructed. Cocoanuts are broken inside and outside the house to propitiate the demons, whose names are frequently repeated at the time. This ceremony is performed by all classes of Hindus before occupation, and refers to the survival of the tree worship, as some trees are believed to be the residence or rather the material frame of the spirits of the woods.[1] Cutting them would provoke the spirits that reside in them, which should therefore be propitiated. No Hindu, even to this day, will dare to cut down a tree like *aswastham* (Ficus religiosa), which, when cut down under necessity, is offered to a temple to be used as fuel. The ceremony next in importance to that detailed above, is the *Kudi*

1. In the rural parts of the Coimbatore District, the custom of giving notice to the spirits or demons residing in a tamarind tree, to vacate it, before it is cut down, still prevails. The wording of the notice runs thus: "Take notice, ye spirits or demons residing in the tree, that you are required to vacate it before such and such a date, as it is resolved to cut it down." This is written on the trunk of the tree, a few days before it is meant to be cut down. There are also certain *mantrams* uttered in the ceremony of *sradh*, giving notice to the demons, if any, residing in the house to vacate it for the reception of *pitres*.

pokal (occupying the house), which is performed by Kammalans. *Pal kachal* (boiling milk) is also another important ceremony performed by the members of the caste. The caste-men are invited, and a milk preparation made in the house is tasted by some and consumed by others, which is tantamount to the taking of meals in the newly constructed house. The carpenters, masons, brick-layers, and others, who have taken part in the construction of the house, are given some presents of cloth, a few rupees, and a bangle commensurate with their skilfulness and status. With prayers to God to enable the occupants of the house to live a long happy life and with blessings on them, they take leave of the master of the house after a sumptuous meal. The caste-men are also similarly entertained. This is called *Thachoda*.

Prohibitions of intermarriage.

In former times, intermarriages among the Izhuvans were permissible between members of the same locality, the violation of which was visited with social excommunication of the parties concerned with their families. There is also an old custom observed both by the Nairs and Tiyyans of North Malabar, which is, that a woman, who crosses the Kora river, is supposed to lose her caste; and the orthodox belief is, that it is not competent for her to marry a man of South Malabar; while, in South Malabar, on the contrary, alliance with a male or female of North Malabar is considered preferable, on the ground that the Tiyyans profess to belong to a distinct caste, superior in social status to the Izhuvans. There has been, of late, a tendency to violate the custom above referred to, but the instances are not as many as might be expected from the influence of education. As in higher castes, social status also influences the parties in matrimonial alliances, and a man in respectable position and affluent circumstances marries his daughter to a young man whose parents are also in like circumstances. In marital relations, wealth goes after its kind. The best form of marriage, among all castes below Brahmans, is where a young man marries the daughter of his maternal uncle, over whom he has a preferential claim. In some places, a man may marry his deceased brother's wife, but the custom, I hear, is dying out. Speaking broadly, marriage is exogamous as regards the *illam* or *kiriyam*, which corresponds to a *gotram*.

"It is said that women are not, as a rule, liable to any social excommunication, if they live with Europeans, and the consequence is, that there has been a large admixture of European blood, and the caste itself has been materially raised in social scale; and in appearance, they are as handsome as the Europeans. It may be said in a general way, that, to a European eye, the best favoured men and women found in the district are the inhabitants of Kadathanad, Iruvulnad, and Kottayam, a large majority of whom belongs to the Tiyya community."[1] It is true that there is an elevation both physically and mentally in the progeny of such a parentage; but, on actual enquiries about this, it is known that this union is looked upon with disfavour and contempt by the respectable members among the caste-men and by the orthodox community, that such women and children with their families are under a ban, and that respectable Tiyya gentlemen, who have married the daughters of European parentage are not, even now, allowed to enjoy the privileges of the caste. There are, I hear, several such instances in Tellicherry and Cannanore, and women of respectable families do not enter into conjugal relations with Europeans.

Puberty customs.

As soon as a girl is known as having attained puberty, the women of the neighbourhood, chiefly friends and relations are invited. A kind of loud noise called *kurava* is made with the object of publicly announcing the glad tidings. The girl is bathed and dressed, after which she is lodged in a separate room, care being taken not to allow anybody except her girl friends to mingle freely with her for fear of pollution. On the fourth day, the female friends and relations who are invited take her accompanied with the noise above referred to, to the nearest tank to bathe her, after which she wears the *mattu kacha* brought by the washerwoman. She is again lodged in

1. Logan's Manual of Malabar, page 143.

the room. The caste-women are invited and entertained with *pan supari*. On the seventh day, the same formalities are again gone through as on the fourth day, and the guests are invited to a luncheon. On the fifteenth day, a pandal is put up in front of the house and tastefully decorated, and the caste-women and others are again invited. A washerwoman, who is also invited, entertains the guests assembled with her songs, chiefly puranic, referring to the marriage of Subhadra, Sita, or some deity, and to the happy conjugal life which they enjoyed. There is also what is called *Ammana attam*. This consists of three hollow balls made either of wood or of bell-metal, containing some pebbles. The balls are thrown up and caught at regular intervals, so as to keep time to the tunes sung at the time. The woman, who is an expert, is looking up with her attention wholly directed to the height to which the balls go and the way in which they should be caught during their descent and again thrown up. This is a very interesting game. The whole night is merrily spent, and on the sixteenth morning, after a few ceremonies, the girl, in the presence of the guests assembled, is led to touch the cooking utensils in the kitchen, mortar, pestle, etc., most probably intended to initiate her into the domestic duties of a woman in the family. The guests assembled are there treated to a feast. In the case of poor people, there is a free distribution of *pan supari* instead of feeding. For all her subsequent menses she has to bathe on the fourth day. The washerwoman's *mattu kacha* is indispensable, as, without it, she is not freed from pollution. Her room also has to be swept and cow-dunged and the water in which she bathes is also mixed with it; for it is believed to have a purifying influence. In North Malabar, all the ceremonies above referred to are not attended to. The girl stays in a separate room during her menses, and on the fourth day she bathes. The services of a washerwoman are availed of, and a grand entertainment is given to those invited on the fourth day. The subsequent menstrual period is only for three days, and the bathing takes place on the morning of the fourth day. Should a girl be married before

AN IZHUVA BRIDE AND HER PARTY.

puberty and she attain it during her stay with her husband, the expenses connected with it are defrayed by the parents of her husband. The bride's parents attend the ceremony, and pay nine annas and two pies.

Marriage customs.

The girls among the Izhuvans of Cochin and the Tiyyans of North Malabar are married both before and after they come of age, and the *Thalikettu-kalyanam* (*tali* tying ceremony) for them is compulsory before they are nine or ten years of age, the omission or negligence of which will place them and their parents under a ban. Nevertheless, in some places, the ceremony is put off until the girls attain their maturity. In every family this takes place once in ten or eleven years, and to save unnecessary expenditure all the girls therein are made to undergo the ceremony at the same time. On an auspicious day, the members and relatives of the family assemble together and send for the local Kaniyan (astrologer) to examine the girl's date of birth, and the position of the planets, and to have them compared with those of the boy, generally of his nephew or another young man, whom they choose as pseudo bridegroom. If the horoscopes of the boy and the girl agree, the astrologer expatiates on the merits of the coincidence on a piece of cadjan leaf, which he gives to the girl's parents or *karanavan* (senior male member), who hands it over to the boy's parents or *karanavan*. If the parties agree, an auspicious day is chosen for the performance of the ceremony. If they disagree, some other boy is chosen, and the horoscopes are again cast. The due examination of the horoscopes and the information of the coincidence to the parties concerned, form what is called *Charthu pidi*. At an auspicious hour, the village carpenter chooses a site for the erection of a pandal, and plants a pole amidst the merry shouting of those assembled there. Two or three days before the date of marriage, the father and the near relatives of the bride proceed to her house with an astrologer for the ceremony of *Ashtamangallyam*, which is performed in the presence of the *Thandan* (head-man) and his assistant, the *Ponamban*. The bride is made to go round it several times. A pot with a quantity of water and paddy in it is placed over a fire-place, and the paddy is boiled and dried for the preparation of beaten rice to be used for the ceremony. The girl is made to remain in a state of vow, and subjected to a sparing vegetable diet. On the day previous to the performance of the ceremony, there is the *Kalathi* or taking the girl out to worship the Sun. A woman of the caste, called Izhuvathy, provided with a lighted lamp, a vessel of water, some parched rice, called *malar*, some plantain fruits, and a cocoanut, seats the girl on a plank in the decorated pandal with the above articles in front, and performs the ceremony of *Shadangozhikkal*, when songs are sung by the caste-women assembled there by invitation. The girl, smeared with oil and decked out with ornaments made of the cocoanut leaves, for the head, ears, hands, loins, and legs, is taken to a tank close by, by a company of maidens amidst the sounds of vocal and instrumental music. There also certain ceremonies are gone through, and the girl is bathed and taken home in procession. She is neatly dressed and adorned in her best, and the parties assembled are treated to a feast called *Athazham oottu*. After this, the girl is seated on a plank covered with a piece of white cloth. The whole night is merrily spent by the young and grown up women with a variety of puranic songs. The next morning, the girl is made to stand on a dais erected on the eastern side of the pandal, where again she has to pass through certain ceremonies amidst loud drum beating and merry tunes of vocal and instrumental music. The girl is then made to go round the seat three times and directed to worship the Sun again. This being over, she is allowed to go and sit comfortably inside the house. A stool, covered with a piece of silk cloth, is placed there, and on this there is a casket, a looking glass, and a sword.

Along with relations and friends, and amidst the noise of *chenda*, drum beating, shouts, and instrumental music, the bridegroom, well adorned and neatly dressed, riding on a horse or an elephant, if he is rich, or sitting on shoulders of a man, if he is poor, comes to the house of the bride. On his entering the gate or at a little distance from it, some of the inmates of the house with their relations and friends, provided with lamps, a metal plate, and a band of music, meet the party of the bridegroom and lead them to the pavilion, where again they perform a kind of ceremony, after which the bride and bridegroom are taken to their assigned seats by their respective fathers-in-law. In the case of a number of girls who have to undergo the *tali* tying ceremony, the eldest sits on the decorated platform, while the others sit on wooden planks, having their heads covered with white or red cloths. The bride has some betel-leaf rolled to fill up the holes between her fingers, in order that she may completely cover her face. She is made to come round him, and is at last seated on the dais prepared for her, while the bridegroom is asked to stand behind her. The *tali* or the marriage badge, tied to a thread dyed yellow with turmeric, is handed over to the bridegroom, who, with the permission of the guardian as well as those assembled there, ties it at an auspicious hour, when drum beating and musical tunes are on their full swing. He then takes his seat on the right side of the bride. A pot of water is placed in front of him with a few mango leaves and a silver coin. The women, who are invited, sprinkle a few drops of water one after another, putting ten or twenty pies into the pot. This is called *Vechuthali*. The males also contribute something at the time. This is followed by the *poli* and the presentation of cloth, and soon after, by a grand feast to the wedding party. The bride and the bridegroom are taken inside the house. The next two days are days of festivity to the bridegroom's party, who is entertained with music and dramatic performances during night. The fourth and the last day, called *Nalam kuli* (bathing on the fourth day), is also one of great festivity and ceremony. As soon as this is over, the bridegroom and the bride are dressed and adorned in their best, and they go to the nearest temple to worship the deities. The marriage ceremony is now over. The bridegroom remains in the house of the bride for a few more days, after which the marriage badge is taken off. The vicarious husband, if he may be so called, receiving two *mundus* (pieces of cloth) and a rupee or two, is allowed to depart in peace. All the ceremonies performed and all the formalities gone through do not practically bind the bridegroom to the bride. Should he however wish to have her as wife, it is incumbent on him to bring the *tali* and the *manthrakodi*, when he becomes her husband.

Among the Tiyyans of North Malabar, the customs connected with the *tali* tying ceremony vary to some extent. A day is appointed in consultation with the astrologer, and for four days previous to this, the girl is bathed every morning and dressed in the cloths of the washerwoman (Velathi). She is confined to a room, and a maid-servant is in attendance. She may not touch anybody during these days. On the fifth day, the village goldsmith brings the *tali*, and the girl is taken in procession by her uncle's wife, to the public tank where she bathes. The girl's brother plants an arrow on one side of the tank, before the girl gets into the water, and a ceremony is observed with the object of driving away the evil spirits, if any, from it. After the bath, the girl is taken in procession to the central room of the house, and the barber throws rice on her head. She is taken veiled to the marriage booth, and some water of the green cocoanut is sprinkled on her head. The *tali* is tied round her neck, either by the maternal or paternal aunt or by the would-be mother-in-law, if the husband for her has been already selected. In South Malabar, this ceremony is dispensed with, but the *tali* is tied either by the bridegroom or his sister during the marriage, and the *Thandan* plays an important part in the ceremony as usual.

Among all castes below Brahmans, the proposal for marriage always comes from the side of the bridegroom. When a young man has to be married, his father and maternal uncle go in search of a suitable girl. When she is rightly chosen, they open the subject with her parents, who give their consent after being satisfied with the would-be bridegroom. Horoscopes are then examined, and if they agree, visits are exchanged by the relatives of the two parties in ratification of the proposal.

A day is then fixed, and information given to the girl's family. The two parties visit the village head-man (*Thandan*) with the customary dues of eight annas and betel-leaf to get his permission for the union. He issues a letter to the ***Ponamban*** under him to see that the ceremony is properly conducted. The latter gets a small fee of three annas and eight pies and betel-leaf. On the day appointed for the celebration of the wedding, the bridegroom and his party proceed in procession to the bride's house, with shouts, five kinds of drum beating, and with a grand display of swords and athletic sports. The bride's mother, the *Thandan's* wife, and a few of the female friends, stand at the entrance of the pavilion ready to welcome the bridegroom and his party. The male members of the house welcome those who have accompanied him with the sprinkling of rose-water, and seat them all on mats spread on the floor with a free distribution of *pan supari*. The fathers or the *karanavans* (senior members) of the bride and bridegroom, with the permission of the assembly, stand east to west with the approval of the elders assembled there; and the former receives the bride's price from the latter along with the wedding garments and eight annas. Then there is a grand feast for the guests assembled. A lamp is lighted and placed in the pavilion in front of the assembly, when the bride's maternal uncle, taking her to the door, makes a declaration to the bridegroom with the permission of the members assembled there. The following is the substance of the declaration:—"I offer thee this girl, and thou mayest protect and punish her when necessary. Thou mayest send her back, when thou dost not wish to have her as wife." This statement is made, when the parties follow the succession through females, and where the succession is through males, the following declaration is made:—" I offer thee this girl, so that thou mayest protect and punish her when necessary. It is further incumbent upon thee to have her children as heirs to thy property as well as to that of thy *taravad* (family)." As soon as this is said, she is handed over to the bridegroom. The lighted lamp represents the god of fire (*Agni*) to witness the solemnity of the occasion. Soon after, the party disperses and goes with the bride to the bridegroom's house, where a similar welcome is made, and a grand entertainment given. The bride is seated on the left side of the bridegroom, when rice and flower are thrown on the married couple, and blessings for their long and happy conjugal life showered on them. This custom prevails among the Izhuvans in Cochin.

In some of the Taluks of South Malabar, the following marriage customs are in vogue. In marital relations, the Izhuvans differ but little from the Nairs, but with them the real marriage ceremony is much more formal. At the betrothal ceremony, which is managed by two relatives and by a *Thandan* (head-man or priest) on each side, the bridegroom's party tenders payment of one rupee and two annas, apparently for the food they have partaken, and then five and a quarter rupees and two new pieces of cloth, as a sign of the conclusion of the bargain. At the end of this part of the proceedings, the groom's *Thandan* gives to the bride's *Thandan* two betel-leaves with certain remarks, of which the following is the tenor : "We shall be coming for the marriage with a party of so many on such and such a date," to which the bride's *Thandan* replies, "If you satisfy our claims with, say, ten and a half rupees in cash, and six pieces of new cloth, we shall hand over the girl to you."

Before the wedding day, the bridegroom goes and visits all his friends and relations, accompanied by five women, all well clad and bedecked. If he accepts food in any house, it is a sign that the inmates are invited to the wedding.

The bridegroom, with his relations and friends, sets out to the bride's house on the wedding day, on observing a favourable omen. He is accompanied by two other youths, dressed exactly like himself, and others of his male relations and friends armed with swords and targets playing in front of him. On arrival at the wedding pavilion, the bride's *Thandan* wisely collects the swords and keeps them in his own charge. The three youths, dressed exactly alike, sit together and have rice strewn over them in common. The bridegroom's sister brings in the bride and seats her behind the bridegroom; the other female relatives stand behind, and the bride's mother is conspicuous in a special red cloth thrown over her shoulders. If the bride has not already had her *tali* tied, the groom now puts it round her neck, and her sister ties it at the auspicious moment pronounced by the astrologer present for that purpose. After this, the bride moves back to her seat behind the groom, and his sister then asks permission of the assembly to pay the bride's price (*kanam*). The bride's mother also seeks permission in similar fashion, to receive at her hands the cloths and ten and a half rupees in cash. The groom and his two friends are then served with food, etc., which they, in dumb show, pretend to take, and at the conclusion of this, they rise up and march straight home with the bride, who must be held by the groom's sister all the while.

As they step out of the wedding pavilion, they are met by the *machun* or uncle's son, who prevents the groom from taking possession of her, on the score of his better claim to wed her. He is supposed to contest him for the hand of the young woman, and his two friends pretend to help him in the fray. The *machun* is at last prevailed upon to let her depart along with the husband on receipt of nine annas. On reaching the bridegroom's house, the bride and groom must enter the door, placing their right feet simultaneously on the door step. The feast is kept up at the groom's house for two days, and for two more days at the bride's, the parties assisting each other, and also making presents to the couple.

In North Malabar, the wedding, which is called *Mangalam*, takes place generally only after the man is about twenty years of age; but, if an old parent or grand parent wishes to see their child married, the rite may be celebrated earlier. Marriages are arranged by parents or agents. On an appointed day, the two parties to the contract assemble in the bride's house, and before the assembly, the agent of the bridegroom announces that, with the consent of the elders, the head-men, and relatives, such and such a man of such and such a *kiriyam* (clan) enters into conjugal relations with such and such a woman of such and such a *kiriyam*, and hands over the bride's price, which is called *parya panam* (bride's price) and amounts to two rupees and twelve annas. This is received by the woman's father or uncle, who replies with suitable words of the above import. Then a feast follows at the expense of the bridegroom. On the day appointed for the ceremony, the bridegroom goes with his friends and relations, taking cloths for the bride, and on reaching the bride's house, these cloths are placed in the central room. There is the usual feast, and then the relatives make presents of money which are duly recorded, in order that the family may make similar presents at the marriage ceremonies of the donors. The persons present, male and female, are then counted and twice the number of *vellies* (one *velli* is equal to three annas and four pies) is tied up in a piece of cloth with rice and taken to the central room, where the couple are seated, and there, after the elders have thrown rice on the couple, it is handed over as purchase money or *kanam* to the bride's father or uncle. The bridegroom's sister then escorts the bride in procession to his house, where also grand feasts are held to the bride's party, who is properly welcomed.

In the Taluks of Palghat and Chittur, where the Makkathayam law of inheritance prevails, the marriage customs are simpler and somewhat different. Girls are married in infancy if suitable husbands are procurable; otherwise, only the *tali* tying ceremony is resorted to. The marriage is called *Vittukettu* here, which lasts for four days. The young man who ties the *tali* is the nephew of the girl's father, one of his relations, or one in the neighbourhood. This vicarious husband stays in the bride's house only for four days, and on the fourth morning he and his pseudo wife worship the deities in the temple close by. The divorce takes place by the removal of the marriage badge, and the husband takes leave of the girl's parents, receiving two pieces of cloth and four or eight annas for the ephemeral union. This is analogous to the custom prevailing among the Nairs.

On the day on which negotiations leading to marriage are made, the parties perform a ceremony called *Kainana* (moistening the hand). When the caste-men including the friends and relations of both sides are assembled in the house of the bride for the settlement of the marriage, they are treated to a feast, of which meat forms an important item. Just when meals are prepared and served on leaves and when the members are properly seated, the bridegroom's *enangan* asks the members if he may begin to partake of the meals. The term used for this permission is, "*Kainanakkattay* (let me moisten the hand by eating, on behalf of, or in honour of, the girl, intended as wife for the son of such and such a man)." The bride's *enangan* says there is no objection. It is only then, that the others partake of the meal. If the betrothal takes place after puberty, the following statement is made by the groom's *enangan*: "May I moisten my hand and eat." The bride's *enangan* says there is no objection.

On the day fixed for the wedding, the bridegroom's sister, accompanied by a few of her female friends and relations, goes to the house of the bride, dresses her in the new garments brought to her, and ties the conjugal collar round her neck on behalf of her brother. The guests are treated to a sumptuous dinner, after which the bride accompanies her sister-in-law to the house of her husband, where she stays for a day or two. She is then taken back to her house, and after a few days' stay, she rejoins her husband. Ornaments according to the means of her parents are given at the time.

In ancient times when migrations after migrations from the land of their birth (Ceylon) had taken place, the king of the island was reluctant to allow any further efflux. Nevertheless, many people resolved to leave their native country, when the sovereign thought it prudent to extort an oath from them that they would not marry and settle in the land to which they were going. In obedience to this oath of their ancestors, the Izhuvans of Palghat and Chittur do not themselves marry, but allow their sisters to do so for them.

There is also another strange custom prevailing there. In marriage and funeral festivities, the members invited divide themselves into groups of four, and sit round the large plantain leaves in which the boiled rice, curry, etc., are served for dinner.

In the northern part of the State, especially in the Talapilly Taluk, and in the Valluvanad Taluk of South Malabar, there is a peculiar form of marriage prevailing among the Izhuvans, who are called Thandans. In a family in which there are four or five brothers living together, the eldest of them marries an adult woman, who, by a simple ceremony, becomes the wife of all. The bridegroom, with his sister and others, goes to the house of the bride elect, where they are well received. The sister or some other relation of the bridegroom hands over to the *enangan* or to the uncle of the bride, a plate containing the wedding garment and a sum of Re. 1—10—0 or Rs. 5—4—0 as the price of the bride, reciting certain verses, the approximate translation of which is as follows:—"I, with the plate in hand, make obeisance to the good old men assembled in the shed. I invoke your blessings for the unobstructed celebration of the marriage which has to be solemnized in your presence, in obedience to the time honoured custom of our ancestors. The relations of the bride, her *enangan* and her caste-men are there. The lamp in the shed is trimmed to produce a bright light. The *enangan* unites the groom's father and the bride's uncle. Placing a few packets of betel-leaves and nuts in a metal plate, the two parties mention their *gotrams* (clans). The bride's price together with the wedding garment is placed therein. I may be excused for any fault, committed by me in my request before the assembly." Receiving the plate, the bride's *enangan* gives a reply, which may be translated thus:—"Thrash thou mayest, but not with a stick. Thou mayest not accuse her of bad conduct. Thou mayest not cut off her ears, breasts, and tuft of hair. Thou mayest not take her to a tank or a *kavu* (temple belonging to high caste-men). Thou mayest keep and protect her as long as thou wishest. When thou wishest to relinquish her, thou art at liberty to leave her here, and we shall accept her even if she may have ten children, provided that you will satisfy their claims for maintenance thereafter." The bride and bridegroom are then seated on a mat, and given some milk, plantain fruits, and sugar. This completes the union. The guests are entertained at a dinner, after which the bridegroom returns home with the bride. At this stage, the bride is the wife only of the eldest brother. If she is however intended as the wife of his brothers, the sweet preparation is served to them and the bride, either in the hut of the bridegroom by their mother, or in that of the bride by their mother-in-law. Thenceforward, she becomes the common wife of all. It is the custom even now for four or five brothers to marry a young woman. They follow the conduct of the Pandavas. Should this union be proved to be unpleasant or inconvenient, one of them marries again and keeps her either himself or allows her to be the wife of others also. The sons or daughters are the common property of all of them.

There are two theories in respect of the prevalence of polyandry in Malabar in ancient times. It might be that the Namburi Brahmans had introduced it on economic grounds to serve their own purpose, or that the Nairs might have brought it with them when they settled in Malabar or adopted it from the aborigines.

There are various influences at work among the Nairs and Tiyyans, which help on social evolution in favour of an organized system of marriage. The following may be mentioned amongst them :—(1) The gifts from husbands and fathers to wives and children. (2) The general practice in North Malabar and elsewhere to some extent for the wife to live with her husband, not only when the latter has self acquired property, but also with the permission of his *karanavan* when he has no such property. (3) The imitation of this custom in South Malabar also. (4) The growing practice of forming matrimonial alliances at a distance, instead of, in the vicinity, as was the case prior to the introduction of railways, and the increased facilities of communication. (5) The uniform and rigorous administration of justice in British courts which prevents men from taking law into their own hands. (6) The exigencies of official life. (7) The steadily increasing influence of western education and culture.

Pregnancy and childbirth.

When a woman is pregnant, she takes no prescribed diet, but avoids rice and hot meals as much as possible. During the fifth or the ninth month, a ceremony called *Pulikudi* is performed. On the day previous to the ceremony, small branches of the tamarind tree, tied together by a thread, are brought and planted on the ground in front of the court-yard or near the main entrance, when the pregnant woman stands in front of them and then goes seven times round them. What is called *Kalam thullal* is played during the night to relieve the woman from any demoniacal influence she may be subject to. Next morning also, she comes round it seven times, and the preparation of tamarind juice is poured into her mouth by the husband. This is called *Pumsavanam*. The husband's *deeksha* is now over.

The Izhuvans, who are much given to devil charming or devil driving, resort to a ceremony, called *Theyyattam*, a corrupt form of *Deva attam* (playing at gods), which takes place in the fifth month of pregnancy of a woman. A leafy arbor is constructed, and in front of it, the terrible figure of Chamundi, the queen of the demons, made of rice flour, turmeric, and charcoal powders, is drawn; a party of not less than eighteen washermen is organized to represent the demons. On being invoked, these demons go to the stage in pairs, dance, caper, jump, roar, fight, and drench each other with saffron water. By their capers and exercises, they gradually work themselves up to a state of frenzy, until they are possessed of the devil. At this juncture, fowl and animals are thrown to them to appease their fury. These they attack and kill and tear, as a tiger does his prey. After half an hour the convulsions cease, the demon declares its pleasure, and much fatigued, retires to give place to others. The whole night is spent with much tom-tom, noise, and shouting. This takes place in the northern parts of the State.

A woman about to be confined is put in a separate room for her delivery and is attended by a midwife. If the infant delivered is male, one of the women present makes a *kurava* cry; if female, she strikes the earth with the midrib of a cocoanut leaf to remove the fear of demons. The infant is washed, and a ceremony called *Thottureka* is performed. A little palm sugar and some onion are mixed in water and a few drops of this are left at the baby's mouth by some female relative or friend whose virtues it may acquire. Some give the water of a green cocoanut; while others rub a little gold on a stone, which is then washed with water, and given to the baby.

The parents note the exact time of birth, by observing the length of the shadow during the day or the positions of stars during the night, and the horoscope is cast. The house is now regarded as polluted, and the husband goes somewhere else to eat. The pollution is called *valaima*. On the seventh day, the room of her confinement is swept and cleaned with cow-dung by the Velathi (washerwoman). On the fifth, seventh, and ninth days, her female friends visit her and keep her room tidy. On the ninth or the eleventh day, the mother with her baby is laid on a bed or a mat, after removing the one she has been already using. This is called *Padukkamattal* (change of bedding). In some places, the pollution lasts for fifteen days, when the woman and her baby are bathed, and she purifies herself by taking *Panchagavyam*. This is called *Pathinanchamkadavu* or *Nishkramanam*. The ceremony of *Jathakarmam* removes the baby of all uncleanliness, but the mother in confinement does not become pure.

As soon as the delivery is over, the mother is given a mixture of the juice of ginger and honey. For the first three days, she takes another medicine, which consists of nutmegs, cardamoms, *vayambu* (Acorus Calamus), *kachol* (Curcuma Zerumbet), and garlic, all well dried or otherwise warmed, and reduced to fine powder, which is mixed with the juice of *poothumba* (Decaneurum molle) and *karithumba* (Nepeta Malabarica). On the fourth day, she is given a mild purgative, which consists of a small dose of cocoanut oil, prepared by boiling the milk extracted from its pulp together with garlic, which is an indispensable element in all such medicines. For the next ten days, she takes a medicine called *pettu marunnu* (delivery medicine), which consists, among other things, of pepper, garlic, aloes, cloves, cardamoms, cinnamon, coriander seeds, and anise. All these are powdered and mixed with gingelly oil, and a pretty large dose is taken twice every day before meals. It is also mixed with the liquid, out of which coarse palmyra sugar is manufactured. The cocoanut oil preparation is also used as a healing ointment. In some cases, a medicine is prepared in arrack and given to the woman in confinement. The treatment during the next twelve days, *i. e.*, from the sixteenth to the twenty-eighth consists in her taking the *dhanwanthara* or *nadi kashayam* (vegetable decoctions). After the twenty-eighth day, she takes some medicine that contributes to the general recruitment of her health.

As regards diet, she is forbidden to take anything but mere boiled rice and pepper water for the first fifteen days. Then she is given a mixture of anise and garden cress early morning, and after an hour, a cup of *kanji* till the twenty-eighth day. At noon, she takes the usual food above referred to. After the twenty-eighth day, the restrictions are less rigid, and she takes such meals as will tend to improve her body.

For the first three days after delivery, she washes her body below the neck in warm water. Then for twelve days from the third to the fifteenth, she bathes in water, boiled with the leaves and barks of medicinal herbs, namely, *poothumba* (Decaneurum molle), *karithumba* (Nepeta Malabarica), *karinotta* (Samadera Indica), and the bark of *poovarasu* (Hibiscus populneus) and containing a small bag of *kunthurukkam* (Boswellia thurifera), husk, and bits of cocoanut shells. The water is well boiled in a large vessel during the night and slowly allowed to cool for the morning bath. Generally, the lying-in-woman rubs her body with a prepared oil, before she bathes in the water described above;

After the sixteenth till the twenty-eighth day, she bathes daily in warm water, but has oil bath every day or every other day. After the twenty-eighth, the woman in confinement bathes as often as she finds it necessary for the improvement of her bodily health. Thus the woman is subjected to treatment for three months. Women in well to do families avoid this by resorting to the treatment of a qualified medical man.

Naming customs.

In ancient times, the Namburies, who formed the landed aristocracy in Malabar, Cochin, and Travancore, and who held the Sudras in a state of subjection, were consulted in all matters affecting their interests, and their advice was gladly accepted by them. Whenever a child was born among the Sudras, they intimate the fact to the Namburi landlords who, according to the Malayalam proverb, "the word of the Namburi is the gospel of the Nair," gave a clumsy name to it. The names thus given closely corresponded with *bhuthas* (demons), *prethas* (souls of the dead), and *pisachas* (ghosts). Some of the names given to the males are Chathan, Konthan, Muttan, Thari, Kori, Makki, while those given to the females are Koli, Kooli, Ooli, Achi, Nachi, and Elochi. The Namburies, who had monopolized all the learning in Kerala, had their pride subdued by the famous Malayalam poet, Thunjeth Ramanujan, who made the sacred books public by his free translation of many of them into Malayalam. Since then, divine names were freely given to the Sudras. The names now in common use among men are Krishnan, Govindan, Mukundan, and among women, Kartyayini, Narayani, Madhavi, Lakshmi, Devaki, and Janaki. The naming ceremony takes place either on the twenty-eighth day or on an auspicious day during the sixth month, when the baby, if male, is named after its grandfather or some grown up male member, and if female, after its grand-mother. The day is one of festivity to their friends and relations.

Some of the other ceremonies performed for children are *Annaprasanam*, *Chowla* (tonsure), ear-boring, and *Vidyarambham*. The name '*Annaprasanam*' suggests the idea of feeding the child with rice for the first time. For this, an auspicious hour is fixed by an astrologer, and on this occasion, friends and relations are entertained. Parents, who are too poor to perform the ceremony, take the child to the nearest temple, where they feed it with boiled rice and curry given as offerings to the deity. *Chowla* is a ceremonial occasion, at which the head of the child is got shaved for the first time on an auspicious day fixed by an astrologer. As soon as the shaving is over, the child is bathed for being purified from the defilement caused by the touch of the barbar. The ceremony ends with a feast. Ear-boring is another occasion for a ceremony and a feast. The *Vidyarambham* ceremony (learning the alphabet) is performed during the fifth year, at which the child is initiated into the mysteries of the alphabet and taught to write on sand. The preceptor is given a few annas for his services.

Adultery and divorce.

Adultery is very rare among the Izhuvans, as it is regarded with abhorrence. Mr. Logan, in the District Manual of Malabar, says, that female chastity in Malabar is as good as elsewhere, though marriage is not a legal institution, and that nowhere else, it is more jealously guarded and its breach more savagely avenged. The system of enforced privacy in the case of women and their early home training lend weight to Mr. Logan's remark in Malabar. The remark is equally true in the Cochin State.

Divorce is called *Aacharam kodukkal,* which is allowed either by mutual consent or at the will of the spouse, in the following cases, namely, want of mutual affection between husband and wife, want of chastity on the part of the wife, faithlessness on the part of the husband, impotency, barrenness, levity of conduct, insanity, and other like causes. In all such cases, the important elderly members must meet together and give their verdict. If the husband divorces his wife, he should take her to her house and leave her in charge of her parents. He gets back half his bride's money or has sometimes to forfeit the whole. If the wife does not like the husband, she goes back to her house, and the husband gets back his dues. The woman divorced can marry again, but the wedding is not performed on a grand scale. The children are left with the father among those who follow the law of succession through males, and in the mother's family among the followers of the law of succession through females.

Polygamy and polyandry.

A man has liberty to marry more than one woman, nevertheless the practice is seldom resorted to. Polyandry prevails among the Thandans of the Talapilly Taluk of the State as well as in the Valluvanad and Ernad Taluks of South Malabar. It is similar to the fraternal polyandry prevailing in Tibet.

——:o:——

CHAPTER XVI.

THE IZHUVANS

(Continued).

—— :o:——

Inheritance.

The Izhuvans of North Malabar, southern parts of the Cochin State, and Travancore as far as Quilon follow the succession through females, while in South Malabar and in the northern parts of the State, the law of succession through males prevails; but in Travancore, south of Quilon, a combination of the above two systems prevails, in which the wife and children of an Izhuvan inherit not less than one-half of his self acquisition. It is said that they are not governed by the Hindu law pure and simple. Their usages with regard to divorce, remarriage, and inheritance are not entirely in accordance with the Hindu law, though the succession of sons obtains amongst them. A community following the *makkathayam* law (law of succession through males) must not be taken to be necessarily governed by the Hindu law of inheritance in all its incidents. It has been decided that the rule of impartibility applies to the Tiyyans irrespective of the rule of succession obtaining among them. The self acquired property of a Tiyyan devolves at his death on the *taravad*. A brother is held entitled to the management of the property. The Tiyyans of North Malabar follow the *marumakkathayam* law (law of succession through females) and are governed by the rules and usages of an ordinary Malabar *taravad*. A system of mixed inheritance has also been recognized among them. The issues of parents governed by different systems of law are entitled to their father's property in accordance with the rules of *makkathayam* and to the property of the mother's *taravad* in accordance with the law of *marumakkathayam*. In Chathunni *v.* Sankaran (8 M 238), the parties to which were the Tiyyans of North Malabar, it was held by the Madras High Court, that, where a woman belonging to a Malabar *taravad*, governed by the *marumakkathayam* law, has issues by a man who is governed by *makkathayam* law, such issues are *prima facie* entitled to the father's property in accordance with the *makkathayam* law, and to the property of the mother's *taravad* in accordance with the *marumakkathayam* law. It is said that the self acquired property of a man is divided equally between his wife and children on the one hand and his nephews on the other. But in Rarichan *v*. Perichi (15 M 281) the Judges (Collins C. J. and Parker J.) held that a custom had been made out under which, in South Malabar, or at all events, in the Calicut Taluk, in an undivided Tiyya *taravad*, the self acquired property of one of the members passed on his death to his brother in preference to his widow. In another case (19 M 1), where the brothers were divided and had no community of interest, it was held (by Parker and Subramania Iyer J. J.) that on the death of a member of a *marumakkathayam taravad*, his widow and daughter were entitled to his self acquisition in preference to his father's brothers. It is also held that, among the Calicut *makkathayam* Tiyyans, the widow of a deceased owner was a preferential heir to his mother. Among them, no compulsory partition could be effected at the will of one member of the *taravad* (17 M 184). In Velu *v*. Chamu (22 M 297), which was a suit for partition among persons belonging to the Izhuva caste in Palghat, it was urged that the ordinary Hindu law relating to partibility of property had no application to Izhuvans. Nevertheless, the right to partition has been tacitly assumed and upheld by the decisions of the Madras High Court. The custom also is in support of the view as adduced in evidence by a respectable Tiyya gentleman of Calicut in O. S. No. 583 of 1899 on the file of the Additional Munsiff of Calicut, which came up before the High Court (S. A. 518 of 1901).

Among the *makkathayam* Tiyyans of South Malabar and the Cochin State, there is no difference in customary law. The female members of the family get no share in partition, but are only entitled to maintenance out of the income of the family property. Among males, partition is allowed, and the females cease to have any interest in the family of their birth, when they marry and assume the family name of their husbands. At the time of partition, it is usual to make provision for the maintenance and marriage expenses of the unmarried sisters. If possible, the family house is, in partition, generally allotted to the youngest brother or his representatives. If a co-sharer dies without issues or with daughters only, his share passes by survivorship to the remaining co-parceners. The system of allotting a share called *pitri-bhaga* does not prevail, so that, if a man had two sons by one wife and three sons by another wife, the property would be divided into five equal shares, one of which goes to each of them. It is also said that compulsory partition in a family, in the absence of a *karar*, can be enforced among the Izhuvans of South Malabar. If the father has no widows nor sons left behind him, his property goes to his daughter and not to his divided brothers. When, in an undivided family, a male member acquires any property through his self-exertion, and dies without leaving a will, then the property must descend to his *taravad*. The widow has a right to such property, but its management rests with the males of the *taravad*. In such a case, neither the daughter given away in marriage nor her children can have any right to the property of her father. Women cannot enforce partition, but they have a right to claim maintenance and to reside in their family house. Among the Izhuvans of Cochin and Travancore, the following methods of partition are also sanctioned by custom:—(1) The ancestral property goes to the nephew; from Quilon to Trivandrum, the sons and nephews get equal shares of the *karanavan's* self acquired property. (2) The dowry of a woman, obtained either from her father or from her *karanavan*, remains unaffected in the partition of a *taravad* property. (3) A woman, who is either barren or has lost her children, having self acquired property along with that of her husband, is entitled to a fair portion, if partition is effected after the death of her husband. (4) If any property acquired either in the name of a man, of his wife or of both, the woman with no children is entitled to half the portion after the death of her husband. (5) A man, who has married a woman and has children by her, should give her a portion of his earnings in the event of his divorcing her. (6) If the junior male and female members, while living with their parents, acquire property, it shall be their own, and cannot be included in the partition of their family property or in that of their parents.

Tribal organization.

In former times, the Izhuvans, in certain parts of the State, had a council of thirty-one and sixty-one elderly men of their caste to settle all disputes, connected with the caste, and their decisions were always final. In the Chittur Taluk of the State and the adjoining Palghat Taluk of South Malabar, the caste-men used to meet under a *Pandalil Ilippa*, a shed under the *ilippa* tree, *i. e.*, Bassia latifolia, in Thenkurussi village, near Palghat, for the purpose above referred to. Gradually, as population increased, members from all the villages found it inconvenient to attend, and it was therefore arranged for each village to have its own assembly of elders. Besides these councils, the caste-men in certain localities used to appoint four of their own men to settle all disputes, preside at all ceremonies, summon their caste-men, and convene meetings for the settlement of all important matters relating to the welfare of the caste. In the southern parts of the State, only one man is appointed by the ruler of the State, for specified localities, and he is called the *Thandan* (head-man of the caste in his village), whose privileges consist in wearing a gold knife and style, walking before a Nair with a cloth on his head, riding on a palanquin or a horse, carrying a silk umbrella, and having a brass lamp borne before him, for each of which he pays separately a tax to the Government. Any person, using these privileges unauthorized, lays himself open to a penalty. His local deputies, who are *Ponambans* or *Veettukarans*, are appointed by him, and besides them, there are elected men, two, four, or six for each village or a number of villages, known as *Kaikkars* or managers, and their business is to make preliminary enquiries about social disputes and convene meetings before the *Thandan* for the arbitration and settlement of all such disputes. These are but relics of the ancient village communities. On occasions, such as a public durbar, a State procession, etc., intimation is given to the head-man, who sends for the necessary caste-men to put up festoons and to sweep the roads. In Travancore and North Malabar, the head-men of the caste are known by the names of *Panikkans* and *Tharakaranavans* (the senior men or head-men of the villages), whose social functions and status are substantially the same as those detailed above. Thus, in the Cochin State the name '*Thandan*' is given to the head-man of the caste, while in the adjoining Taluks of Palghat and Valluvanad it is referred to a sub-caste, the members of which observe the custom of polyandry.

Magic, sorcery, and witchcraft.

The Izhuvans, like other classes of people, believe in magic, sorcery, and witchcraft. When a house or its compound is haunted by a demon, doing harm to the residents therein, or when a woman is possessed by the same being, a Kaniyan (astrologer), who is often consulted, mentions, by his calculations, the name of the demon, and suggests the means of relief, which in both cases is sought for by the aid of a magician or devil-driver. In the former case, *mantrams* (magic formulæ) are uttered and written on thin sheets of copper, lead, or on cadjan leaves which are buried in the four corners of the house or compound. Sometimes sacrificial fires (*homams*) in honour of the deity, Ganapathi, are also offered to get relief from it. In some cases, the demom can be located in trees. A devil driver, with the aid of his *mantrams*, makes it reside in a pot which is buried underneath a large stone by the side of a river or a large stream. A woman who is possessed of a demon can be relieved from it by any one of the following methods, namely, (1) by causing it to appear in the person who makes some involuntary movements, and making it depart by offerings, (2) by growing sacrificial fires, or (3) by transferring it to some other body. The first of the methods above referred to is described here. The magician, who is invited to cast out the devil, is furnished with every thing he requires for the performance of the ceremony. He chooses a spot either in the house, or outside it in the court-yard, and purifies it with water mixed cow-dung. This spot is scattered over with burned ashes, over which a *yantram* (cabalastic figure) is drawn and the several portions of it are coloured yellow, green, red, black, and white with powders. He writes on each portion a letter of the *Gayatri* which he mutters at the same time. He also puts on it some rice and flower. Over this, he places a piece of cloth, three betel-leaves, and an areca nut. On a small pandal close to it are placed a few pieces of small plantain leaves with rice and flower on them. A few drops of water are also sprinkled thereon and he mutters the *mantram* ജലഗന്ധ പുഷ്പധൂപദീപംയനമഃ (salutation with water, frankincense, flower, aromatic vapour, and light). A few flowers and some sandal are thrown over the *yantram*. Frankincense is burned and a light is waved in front of it. A lighted lamp is burned at the side of it. The woman possessed of demon is bathed and dressed in a new garment and allowed to take her seat on a plantain leaf with her face towards the east. Muttering the *Gayatri mantram* and throwing some holy ashes (*bhasmam*) on her head, he gives her some rice and flower to wave round her head three times and directs her to put them on the figure with a prayer that she may be relieved from the demoniacal possession. With pious meditations on the deity and his *guru*, he again mutters certain *mantrams*.

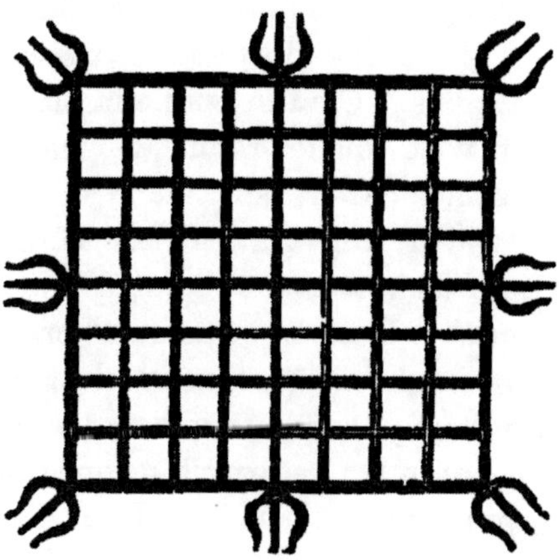

A Yantram.

The woman holds a flower of the areca palm. The magician's disciples at the time sing songs, keeping time either with beating on a bell-metal or with a tabor, and the woman puts rice and flower on the figure. The substance of this and other songs sung at the time is as follows :—"As the Devas were oppressed by the Asuras, and as they were not able to perform their daily religious rites, they requested the aid of Siva and began to praise him. From his third and sparkling eye came Kali in her terrible aspects. Clad in silk and black skin, with anklets round her feet, with snakes round her neck, and armed with many weapons in her hands, she stood at the gate of the giant Darika and called him for battle. Many hard contests were fought. His head was at last severed from his body and thrown on the ground. His body was burst open by his own sword and the blood which he drank was received in his shield, and his intestines completely eaten. His bones were broken to pieces. As Kali was joyfully returning after the victory, Siva thought that he would be smashed by her. He appeared to her in the form of a bright fire. The goddess stood amazed. May my salutation be to such a deity."

"Salutation by me to Narayana, Bhagavathi, Ganapathi, Subramania, Parabramham, the tutelary deity, the preceptor, Siva, and the great sages, who are all represented by the symbolic letters of *Hari sri ga na pa tha ye na mah.*"

At this stage, the woman possessed of demon becomes excited at the musical tunes and utterance of the *mantrams.* The demon is supposed to make its appearance in her body, which is thrown in convulsive movements. The frenzied demoniac seems to be tossed and shaken in, ever pained and wrenched as though some living creature were tearing or twisting her from within, till she becomes subdued by the exorcist. The devil-driver, pretending to have the power to control the demon, askes her the name of the demon living in her body. If she remains silent, he beats her with a cane, believing that his thrashing may affect the demon and not the woman.

Sometimes he catches hold of her hair and ties a knot, muttering a *mantram*. This done, the demon speaks through her, and promises to leave her for ever on receipt of the offerings. At once, the magician brings a lamp and makes it swear thus :—"By me, by Kali, by thee, by Markandeya, I depart from this body." This said, the woman lies prostrate in a swoon. The magician utters the *Jeeva prathishta mantram*, and sprinkles some water on her, and the woman recovers her consciousness. The following is the substance of this *mantram*:—"O! Markandeya, may thy *mantram* be effectual in bringing her back to life and help her in the complete relief from the possession of the demons." The magician next performs what is called *Gurusikodukkuka* (giving water with lime and turmeric dissolved in it). Small pieces of plantain leaves, each two inches in breadth, are placed on a *chakram* (magical figure) with sixty-four divisions made of the bark of the plantain tree. Over the bark at regular intervals are stuck pieces of cocoanut leaves and lighted torches. The magician takes it in his hand, singing songs in praise of Kali, and places it on the ground. He then takes a few vessels filled with rice flour, toddy, and arrack, and the *gurusi* mixed with the blood of a fowl or two, which are intended as offerings for the demons. The following is the substance of the song, sung on the occasion:—"I am here giving the origin of the cock and the hen. When the great giant Mahishasura requested Brahma for a boon, and was returning home, the sword of Kali, touching the body of the giant, caused the blood to fall on the ground in two drops, which turned into a cock and hen. The flap on his face and lips were as red as red-hot charcoal, and the eyes as convex as the belly. O Kali, mayest thou come and drink the blood of the hen held in my left hand and killed with the sword in my right hand, as it came running joyfully."

The *chakram* is then taken either to a spot where several roads meet, or to the side of a river or a canal at three in the morning, and placed there. The *gurusi* is poured on the ground. A big torch is lighted and the rice flour scattered on the ground. He then extinguishes the light and returns home.

Sometimes the above *mantrams* are dispensed with. The figures of demons are drawn, and the songs in praise of Kali sung for devil driving. All kinds of disease are believed to be caused by spirits of deceased ancestors. They are cured by the performance of elaborate ceremonies and offerings to propitiate them. Charms are also worn to ward off their attacks. These people believe in oracular manifestations.

Religion.

Izhuvans profess Hinduism, and as some say, they are more the worshippers of Siva than of Vishnu. They are also animists to some extent. They worship Kali, who is in fact the tutelary deity in every part of Malabar, Cochin, and Travancore, as in other parts of India. It is said that the great Parasurama had established one hundred and eight Durga temples for the protection of the people against demons. There are some famous ancient temples in the State, at Cranganore, Pazhayannur, Cochin, and Chottanikara. The goddess is called Aghora Sakthi (the queen of demons), and in her fierce and cruel aspects, she protects the people against the demons. She is represented as wearing on her head a fiery snake encircled by serpents. Siva's signs are also marked on her forehead. Lion's fangs protrude from her mouth and she possesses ten hands, two of which are clasped together and two empty, while three on the right side carry a rope, a parrot, and a spear, and three on the left side, a drum with a snake, fire, and trident respectively. Kodungallur Bhagavathi is the customary cultus of the caste, and is zealously adored by the Izhuvans, with the offerings of fowls. The chief festival in the temple is the cock festival, a detailed account of which is given in page 238 of this volume.

The Izhuvans had formerly few or no temples of their own. In many parts of the interior can often be seen a kind of pyramidal pillars or stones with their faces towards the cardinal points and often in the vicinity of a tamarind tree (Tamarindus Indica). In front of them is a slightly elevated flat surface made of earth, on which the offerings to their gods are given. A small pandal is also put up on festive occasions. Bloody sacrifices and devil dancings are the essential items of the ceremonies of these demon worshippers, and the persons who officiate at such ceremonies are the *velichapads*, rotators of demons, either of their own caste or the Nairs. The animals to be sacrificed on such occasions are smeared with turmeric and adorned with flowers. The head is severed at one blow and is held up over the altar so that the blood may fall on it. The sacrificed animal is distributed to those present there, who cook and eat it, and in some cases the *velichapad* drinks its blood. During the ceremony, he appears like one possessed, and jumps and rushes through the fire, and strikes his forehead with sharp instruments until he is covered with blood. This kind of animistic worship is gradually going down in many parts of Cochin and Travancore, where the people, owing to their gradual enlightenment, advancement in education, and the influence of Brimhasri Narayana Guruswamy, a learned and pious *sanyasi*, have begun to introduce higher forms of worship. Temples for the worship of Siva, Subramania, and Ganapathi have been erected, and images consecrated according to the Vedic *mantram* and the dictates of the *guru* mentioned above. The temple at Srinarayanapuram near Thannir Mukkam has the image consecrated by the former method, while the images of other temples in Cochin and Travancore are by the latter. *Pujas* are performed seven times in some and three in others every day, according to the Brahmanic rules. The festivals in honour of these deities last for seven days in some temples, and for three in others. The priests are from their own caste trained under Brahmans, and they have to wear the holy thread and maintain celibacy. In other temples, the festivals are precisely similar to those taking place in Brahmanic temples. Reforms in this direction are introduced by their learned and pious devotee.

Ganapathi is a homely village god of all Hindu castes of people. Prayers are offered to him for overcoming hindrances and difficulties, whether in performing religious acts, writing books, building houses, making journeys, or undertaking anything. He is therefore the typical embodiment of success in life with its usual accompaniments of good living, prosperity, and peace. He is believed to be the chief of Siva's host of spirits, and he controls malignant spirits, who are ever plotting evil and causing hindrances and difficulties.

Subramania is called the god of war and commands the army of angels against the evil demons, who try to overcome and enslave the gods. In Malabar, where his cultus largely prevails, he is worshipped by those who wish to be relieved from evil spirits, and by women who desire to obtain handsome sons. The worship of Ganapathi and Subramania appears to be a mere offshoot of Saivam.

Veerabhadra is regarded as an *avatar* of Vishnu, who according to Vishnupurana comes from the mouth of Siva, to spoil the sacrifices of Daksha. He is described as a divine being with a thousand heads, a thousand eyes, a thousand feet, wielding a thousand clubs, a thousand shafts, holding the shell, the disks, the mace, and bearing a blazing bow and battle-axe.

Iyyappan or Sastha is believed to be the supreme God and highest ruler among the non-Aryan aborigines in Southern India. He is rightly called Sastha (ruler) or Iyyappan (respectable father) and the chief of the *bhutas* or ghosts, whom he restrains from inflicting harm on human beings. He is in this respect identified with Siva, who is called *Bhuthesa or Bhuthanadha*, the chief of the ghosts. Worshipped as he is by all castes of people in Southern India, especially, in Malabar, Cochin, and Travancore, he is more revered and feared by the low castes in rural parts. He is often represented as mounting on an elephant or on a horse. He rides with sword in hand over hills and dales to clear the country of all obnoxious spirits. Followed by his retinue during midnight, he goes for hunting, armed with swords and surrounded by torch-bearers. Any one who meets the hunting party on the road is sure to meet certain death. When not riding, he is supposed to be in a sitting posture as a red-skinned man. On his head he wears a crown, on his forehead are painted the three lines of *vibhuthi* (holy ashes), and on his tuft-like locks hang strings of pearls which adorn also his ears and neck. Ornaments cover his arms, hands, feet as well as waist. As an emblem of his royal authority, he carries a sceptre in his hand, and a girdle encircles his waist and left leg. He wears no clothing on the upper part of his body, but covers his loins with a gay coloured cloth.

There lived in ancient times a demon, named Bhasmasura, who by his severe penance gained the favour of Iswara, and got from him a boon that, whatever he touched with his hand should be turned to ashes. Receiving this, he wished to test it on Siva himself, who ran away and concealed himself in the flower of a plant growing in a tank. He thence prayed to Vishnu to rescue him, who thereupon appeared to the demon in the form of a *mohini* (damsel). At the sight of her, his passions overpowered him, and he lost control of his senses; the virgin consented to yield to his wishes, if he would rub oil on his head and bathe in the water of the tank close by. The demon did so and was reduced to ashes, as his hand touched his head. Siva then left his hiding place, and saw Vishnu in the form of a handsome virgin. Seeing her thus, his passions became uncontrollable. The result of this union of Hari and Hara was the birth of Sastha. The above story appears to be the invention of the Brahman priesthood to destroy the old idea of non-Aryan gods which still influences the masses.

There is hardly any place in the rural parts of Malabar, Cochin, and Travancore, which does not possess a small temple (with or without roof) or shrine beneath a shady tree or by the side of a brook, dedicated to the worship of Sastha. As people, especially, the Sudras and the lower castes, were largely agricultural, and fond of hunting, and as they had to live and work in forests, they began the propitiation of this deity for protection against demons and all kinds of illness. He thus became the favoured deity of the Sudras. Brahmans also must have borrowed the worship of this god from them. There are special *mantrams*, to be used in the worship of this deity, and Wednesdays and Saturdays are auspicious for the adoration of this chief and ruler of the demons. During the last ten days of the *Mandalam*, a festival in honour of him is celebrated. In some parts of the country, when children are afflicted with maladies, parents make to him offerings of rice boiled in milk and sugar (*payasam*), fruits, etc. There are temples for this deity where *pujas* are performed and daily offerings given by the Sudras, who never offer animal sacrifices. Their special songs called *Sasthapattu* (songs in honour of Sastha) are sung to propitiate him in order to avert any pestilential disease, prevailing in the villages, to prevent failure of monsoons, and to keep off evil demons. In fulfilment of certain vows, Sudras go to Chourimala, a hill in Travancore, to adore him and make offerings to him, as he is supposed to reside there.

After recovery from illness or to commemorate any piece of good fortune (acquisition of wealth or the birth of a son) in a Sudra family, the members thereof celebrate a festival in honour of Iyyappan by inviting a band of Sudra songsters well versed in the songs in praise of him. A small structure in the form of a temple is made in a conspicuous part of the house, and a small stool with an image thereon, is placed in the temple. The figure of Iyyappan is also drawn on the floor, *pujas* are performed, and offerings of rice boiled in milk, sugar, plantains, fruits, etc., are made to him. The song lasts for the whole night and is accompanied by tabor beating. One of them turns a *velichapad* at the end, and dances or walks up and down in an excited manner amid the noisy music, while an attendant sings songs describing the deeds of demons. He finally succumbs in a frenzied fit and gives out oracular responses to any enquiries addressed to him. Most of the by-standers consult him as to their wants and destinies.

Some of the minor demons whom the caste-men worship are Kuttichathan, Parakutty, Karinkutty, Muni, Mundian, and Kandakaranan. These are believed to be either the debased aspects of Sastha or the subordinate demons under him. The unbridled malignity of these demons ever excites the fear of the people of the lower castes to such a degree that they, the descendants of the non-Aryan aborigines, always seek their protection by doing pious worship and by making offerings to them. These demons take possession of the bodies of living men, produce unpleasant affections of all kinds or even death, cause other misfortunes in their families, or impel them to frantic movements in which all devils delight. They are believed to assume the form of any animal they choose. Hence, every village has its own peculiar demon or demons to whose attacks they believe themselves to be exposed. It is on this belief that small temples and shrines are erected for them in rural parts, which are often frequented for worship, and where festivals are celebrated every year. It is also probable that these places of worship have been in existence long antecedent to the introduction of the Aryan faith.

Sakthi worship.

In the simplest acceptation of the term, it is the worship of a power or force personified as a goddess with a view to possess supernatural powers for the achievement of anything desired through her help. Devibhagavatham contains a description of Sakthi. She is neither man, woman, nor eunuch. At the time of the destruction of the world, she is perception, intelligence, firmness, remembrance, prosperity, faithfulness, pity, beauty, hunger, tranquillity, idleness, old age, strength, and weakness. What is she not? What is there without her? She is represented to be the first being from whom an entire mythological system emanates. She stands at helm. The goddess Mahadevi of the Sakthi hierarchy is the person from whom even Bramha, Vishnu, and Siva are evolved, and they absorb all her functions. She is a duplicate of Siva, her husband. Just as Siva is at one time white (*swetha sukla*) both in complexion and in character, and at another black (*kala*), so his female nature also becomes one half white (*gauri*) and the other black (*kala*). In her mild nature, she evolves herself into Uma, Gauri, and Parvathi, and in her fierce nature into Kali, Durga, Chandi, and Chamundi. In Harivamsa of Mahabharatha, and other poems, Sakthi, the female energy, shows herself in many prayers and heroes, and has many names.

Even from a very remote period, the Dravidians of India appear to have worshipped the mother earth, the representative of female energy, as the principal deity. This worship was accepted by the Aryans, and bears testimony to the fact that, throughout India, the *Grama devathas* of the Dravidians were transformed into *Kshethra devathas* of the Aryans. This worship is mentioned even in the puranas, but the *thantrams* contain the prescriptions and rituals, which are sometimes called the fifth Veda. They belong to a very remote period, and are highly esteemed by the Brahmans.

The Sakthi worshippers are divided into two main sects, namely, right handed worshippers, chiefly the Saivites, and left handed worshippers or the Vaishnavites. The former make the puranas the real Veda, and are devoted either to Siva or Vishnu in their double nature as male or female. Rice mixed with sugar and milk, plantains, fruits, and parched rice (*malar*) are presented as *nivedya* or offerings to the deity. The left handed worshippers, on the other hand, base their worship and ceremonial on *thantrams*, other ceremonials, and bloody sacrifices. The former do not indulge in obscene display, and enforce the observance of all or some of the five things, *viz.*, *makara* (fish), *madia* (liquor), *mamsa* (meat), *mudra* (mystical intertwinning of the fingers), and *maithuna* (sexual intercourse). The former are regarded as pure as the Vedas, while the latter are deemed low and fit only for the Sudras. Nevertheless such sacrifices are made by the Brahmans also. *Thantrams* are considered as Vedas by the latter sect.

A man who wishes to perform the puja must be initiated by a *guru* (preceptor), who teaches him certain mystics. The ceremony should not be performed unless the moon, planets, and stars are favourable. The *pujas* of the Sakthi worshipper should take place in secret and with closed doors in accordance with the *thantric* precepts. It is further said, that Vedas, Sastras, and Puranas are likened to a common woman open to all, while the mystical rite of a Sakthi worshipper is likened to a high born secluded woman. In order to realize the object of devotion, a Saktha has recourse to *mantrams*, which must be carefully repeated in order to become efficient. Men and women assemble to worship the goddess in proper style. The male devotees are called *Bhairavans* and the female *Nayikas*. Sakthi is represented by a naked woman and the above mentioned *makaras* are observed. The ceremony is in the holy circle *Sreechakra*, and is celebrated to ensure *sayujia* or identification with the supreme spirit. In one of the *thantrams* laid down in connection with the worship, Siva, addressing his wife, says, "All men have my form. Any one who makes any distinction of caste is a foolish soul." There is also another method of propitiating the deity. A mystical diagram, called a *yanthram*, generally inverted triangles or combinations of triangular figures, is drawn on a copper plate, which is supposed to possess occult or mystical powers. This is placed on a lotus diagram, the *bigas* belonging to the goddess being inscribed on each side of the petals. The holy *Sreechakra* is also drawn in the diagram, and *pujas* are performed as before. The offerings to be presented may be of either kind. Sakthas worship their deity in preference to any other to obtain in this world supernatural powers and in the next final beatitude, and though the

A Yantram.

devotee is indulging in grossest carnal passions, his mind is absorbed in the supreme deity.

In Malabar, as in other parts of India, there are Sakthi worshippers among the Brahmans and Sudras, carrying on this cult very secretly. They resort to one of these methods, and Brahmans or members of their own caste officiate at such ceremonies with the offerings already described. There are also five other methods of propitiating the deity in order to acquire superhuman powers, *viz.*, *Mantras*, *Bijas*, *Kavachas*, *Nyasas*, and *Mudras*. An account of it is given below.

The Sakthi *puja* is performed generally during night in accordance with the *thantric* precepts. The performer of the *puja* gets up early in the morning and meditates on his *guru* (preceptor) for his blessings on the success of the *puja*. He bathes and performs *achamanu* (rinsing the mouth with water), facing eastward, and repeats certain *mantrams*, after which he rubs the prescribed parts of the body with *vibhuthi* (holy ashes). With pious reverence, he enters the room set apart for the worship, accompanied by his wife, who is called *Sakthi*, and his assistant, *Parikarmi*. Two lighted lamps are placed in a conspicuous part of the room. He performs his *namaskaram* to the deity, and taking his seat on a tiger or deer skin, adores the *Ashta dik palakas* (the gods of the eight points). Considering himself to be the *Virat*, he repeats various *mantrams* all favourable to the propitiation of the goddess. He keeps in front of him a vessel containing water, a conch shell with water inside, and some sandal paste. He then performs the *manasapuja* (worship of the mind or soul) and repeats the sacred *mantrams* connected with the worship. The Sakthas resort to the five methods of propitiation of the goddess above referred to, with a view to acquire superhuman powers. A wooden seat made according to the prescribed rules of worship is made ready, well washed, and purified with holy water (*theertham*). The sandal paste is spread upon it, on which is drawn the holy circle *Sreechakram*. It is supposed to represent the orb of the earth, nine triangles being drawn within the circle to denote the nine continents. In the centre is the drawing of a mouth which is supposed to represent the female energy (Sakthi), presiding over the circle. *Bijaksharas* are also written on it. Before the grand Sakthi *puja* is begun, Ganapathi and Sankaracharya *guru* are worshipped, and offerings of cocoanuts, plantains, etc., are made to them. Washing his hands and cleaning a part of the floor of the room, the Saktha now prepares for the grand worship of Sakthi. Several vessels filled with toddy and meat (cooked), and all covered with betel-leaves, are placed in front of him. He performs the *puja* with the long recital of *mantrams* and epithets in praise of Sakthi, putting flowers on the circle. This lasts for more than two hours, after which the offerings above referred to are given. The Saktha gives his wife, and *Parikarmi*, his assistant, who attend and take part in the worship, *theertham* (holy water) and *prasadam* (leavings of offerings). All of them partake of the offerings which are distributed among the inmates of the family. The *puja* takes seven or eight hours for its completion. The essential part of the Saktha ceremony consists in the taking of meat and liquor. The Sakthas believe that true knowledge can be acquired only by taking spirituous liquor. It is, they believe, productive of salvation, learning, power, wealth, destruction of enemies, curing of diseases, and removal of sin.

Ancestor worship.

Ancestor worship is one of the great branches of the religion of mankind, and prevails among all castes in Malabar. The dead ancestor is supposed to become a deified spirit after the performance of funeral rites, and to protect the members of the family. In times of sickness and other calamities, their aid is invoked by offerings. People of the lower castes still attribute all sufferings to their provocation. Neglect to perform the regular rites is supposed to leave the departed spirit in the condition of a *pisacha* or foul wandering spirit, disposed to revenge for its misery by a variety of malignant acts on the members of the family. It is also believed that the orders of the demons were formerly human souls, to which proper funeral rites had not been given after burial, and hence they are supposed to wreak vengeance on the living. The spirits of men or women, who die of cholera, small-pox, child-birth, or who die by committing suicide, wreak vengeance on the living and cause misfortunes (*Pretha badha*) to their families, and those spirits are always looked upon with fear. Due performance of rites enjoined by *sastras* will make them harmless *pitres*, which have to progress through various other stages before they are finally admitted into Heaven. Hence it is that people of all Hindu castes perform elaborate funeral ceremonies, make gifts, flock to Gaya, Haridwar, and other sacred places to offer *pindas* (rice ball offerings) to the souls of the departed; for, the efficacy of the service conducted in those places is supposed to help them to attain final bliss more easily. The Izhuvans perform the *sradha*, which they call the giving of offerings to the departed spirits of their ancestors. In every house a room containing a few images of their ancestors is set apart for such religious purposes. Once every year, they perform the *sradha* at which boiled rice, plantain fruits, cocoanuts, and parched rice (*malar*), are served on a plantain leaf with a lamp lighted in front of it, and they pray, " May ye, ancestors, take this and protect us. " Saying this, they close the room and all come out, with the belief that the spirits would come and take them. After some time, they open the door and distribute the offerings among the inmates of the house. Similar offerings are also given on *Karkadakam*, *Thula*, and *Makara sankranthis*, and on new moon days. It is for this purpose that every Hindu prays for a son by blood or adoption, who shall give him the due sacrifices after death. " May there be born in our family, " the manes are supposed to say, " a man to offer us on the thirteenth day of the moon, rice boiled in milk, honey, and ghee. " One who thus gives to the deceased ancestors offerings preceded and followed by sacrifices to the greater deities, is rewarded by merit and happiness.

Serpent worship.

In the south-west corner of the compound about the house of every Nair, Izhuvan, or member of the other castes in Malabar, Cochin, and Travançore, there is a serpent grove, and the serpents exercise an evil influence, if their shrines are not properly respected. These shrines are called *Chittrakoodam, Nagakotta*, or *Vishathan kavu.* Carved granite stones representing the figures of hooded serpents are seen in every serpent grove in the compounds of people of almost every Hindu caste in the States above referred to. Leprosy, itch, barrenness in women, death of children, frequent appearance of snakes in gardens, and all other calamities are believed to be brought about by, and set down to, the anger of the serpents. Therefore, every snake shrine is worshipped, and *pujas* are performed with offerings of milk, eggs, and boiled rice in the month of Kumbham on *Ayiliam* day. In the event of any calamity in a family, an astrologer, who is consulted generally attributes it to the anger of the serpents and the only remedy that is suggested is the formation of a serpent shrine with elaborate ceremonies and sacrifices to obtain their good will and pleasure.

The earliest civilization of Southern India is ascribed to the Dravidians, who, as many authorities consider, came from Northern India. They are supposed to have been displaced by the Aryans and it is also believed that colonies were established by them in South India long before the Aryans came to India. Inscriptions of the tenth and eleventh centuries show that the ruling chiefs of the kingdoms in South India belonged to the Naga race, and held the serpent banner, and that a part of Canara was called the territory of the Naga people. Further, the earliest settlements in Ceylon were founded by these people. Though they had settled in the south, they never abandoned their possessions in the north of India. From these and other facts, it is concluded, that the Dravidians belonged to the Naga race. The population of these colonies consisted mainly of the aborigines, who adopted their customs, religion, and, to a great extent, the language of the Dravidians. At a later period, the worship of the Brahmanical deities was also introduced, though much of the old religion and mode of life was retained. The worship of the hooded serpent is general among the Dravidians of South India. Rudely sculptured images are found underneath almost every tree. In Malabar, Cochin, and Travancore, they are, even to this day, worshipped in *kavus* or serpent groves which, like those in the villages of the Punjab, are left untouched by axe or spade. A *Naga kavu*, near Travancore, is the property of a family, whose ancestors were among the Nagas, spared from the burning of the Khandava forest in Punjab by Arjuna. Every male of this family, even to this day, is called Vasuki, the deified hero of the Naga people of Northern India. Divine honours are paid to the Naga demi-gods as ancestors, and among these ancestors of the Dravidians are the Naga Rajas, who are also worshipped as ancestors by their descendants in North India. Offerings of milk, flour, and fruits given to the serpents even now are not the usual food of serpents but are the food of human beings. The burning of a cobra and providing it with a winding sheet after its death resembles the funeral ceremonies of men. The worship may be a kind of ancestor worship. Further, the Dravidians are divided into Cheras, Cholas, and Pandyas. 'Cheras' is the Dravidian equivalent for 'Naga', *Chera-mandala* means *Naga-mandala* or *Naga-dweepa* and not Naga country. This points to the Asura origin of the Dravidians of the south. There still exists a set of people over the valley of the Ganges, who are called Cheras or Seoris, claiming their descent from the serpent gods, and who appear to have been ousted by the Mahomadans. These people might be the kinsmen of the Cheras, on account of the similarity in the social customs. There are also many tribes in the Beas valley and other adjacent localities, who worship hooded serpents and profess to belong to the old solar race. Thus, the serpent worship is not peculiar to Malabar, but prevailed more or less in many parts of India in ancient times.

Hook-swinging.

The custom of swinging as a religious or rather a magical rite was practised not only in India, but in all parts of the world, by people in a low state of civilization to ensure good harvest, to secure a good catch of fish, to drive away rain, and to be expiated for suicide by hanging.

There are two kinds of hook-swinging, *viz.*, *Garuda thookkam* (Brahmini kite-swinging) and *Thony thookkam* (boat-swinging), and the ceremony is performed in fulfillment of a vow to obtain some favour of the deity Kali, before whose presence this is performed. The performer of the ceremony should bathe early in the morning and be in a state of preparation either for a year or for forty-one days by worshipping the deity Bhagavathi. He must strictly abstain himself from meat, all kinds of intoxicating liquors, and from association with women. During the morning hours, the performer dresses himself in a garment tucked into the waistband, rubs his body with oil, and is shampooed particularly on the back; a portion of the flesh in the middle is stretched for the insertion of a hook. He is also taught by his instructor to perform various feats, called *payitta*. This he continues till the festival, when he has to swing in fulfillment of the vow.

For kite-swinging, a kind of car resting on two axles provided with four wheels is used. On it, there is a horizontal beam resting on two vertical supports. A strong rope tied to a ring attached to the beam is connected with the hook which passes through the flesh on the back. Over the beam there is a small roof which is tastefully decorated, and the inside of which is spacious enough for two or three persons to swing at a time. There is a different arrangement in some places; instead of the beam and the supports, there is a small pole, on which rests a horizontal beam provided with a metallic ring at one end. The beam acts as a lever so that one end of it can be either raised or lowered so as to give some rest to the swinger. The rope tied to the ring is connected with the hook and the waistband. For boat-swinging the same kind of vehicle without wheels is in use. For kite-swinging, the performer has his face painted green, and he has to put on artificial lips and wings similar to those of a kite. He wears long locks of hair like those of an actor in a *Kadha kali* and the feats are in harmony with the tunes of the musical instrument. As he swings, the car is moved three, five, seven, nine, or eleven times round the temples. In boat-swinging he has to put on the same kind of dress, except the lips and the wings, and there is the covered car without the wheels. It is carried round the temple with the swinger performing his feats on it to the accompaniment of music, as above mentioned.

Pillayeduthu thookkam is a kind of swinging with a child by the swinger in fulfillment of a vow. The child, that has to be swung, is taken to the temple by his parents, who pay to the temple authorities, thirty-four *chakrams*[1] in Travancore and sixty-four *puthans*[2] in Cochin. The child is then handed over to the swinger who carries the child as he swings. These performances are sometimes made at the expense of the temple, but more generally of persons who make the outlay in fulfillment of a vow. In the latter case, it costs as much as one hundred and fifty rupees for the kite-swinger, but only thirty rupees for the boat-swinger. During the festival they are fed in the temple, owing to their being in a state of vow.

It is the Nairs, Kammalans (carpenters, blacksmiths, etc.), Kuruppans, and Izhuvans who perform the swinging in fulfillment of a vow. In the fight between the goddess Kali and the demon Darika, the latter was completely defeated, and the former, biting him on the back, drank his blood to gratify her feeling of animosity. Hook-swinging symbolises this incident, and the blood-shed caused by the insertion of the hook through the flesh is intended as an offering to the goddess.

Funeral customs.

The poor among the Izhuvans bury their dead, while the rich burn them. When an aged person breathes his last, his caste-men in the neighbourhood are sent for, and the relatives, both men and women, visit the dead body, which is washed and dressed neat, and the forehead, breast, and hands thereof are marked with sandal paste. The floor near the outer door is cleaned with cow-dung, and the corpse is laid thereon with the thumbs and toes tied

1. A *chakram* is a Travancore coin worth seven pies.
2. A *puthan* is a Cochin coin worth ten pies.

together and head towards the south. In some places, the *Thandan* (head-man), who is invited, constructs a shed of cocoanut palm leaves in the yard, wherein the dead body is placed; and the barber, who is the priest, presiding over the ceremony, takes some paddy, beats it free from husk, mixes with it some scraped cocoanut, and keeps the mixture in a cup, when the sons or nephews, along with the relatives of the deceased, put a small pinch of the mixture into its mouth, and burst out in loud lamentations. The corpse is then covered with a new piece of cloth, and the members of the family, who have to take part in the funeral rites, also dress themselves in new garments. The dead body is removed to the eastern side of the main entrance and slightly to the southern side called *pattara sthanam*, where also certain ceremonies are gone through. It is then placed on a bamboo bier and taken to the southern side of the compound which serves as the cremation ground, where it is either buried or burned. In the former case, water is poured over the ground for five days, and Panans keep watch for five nights during which drums are sounded to scare away evil spirits that are supposed to haunt the grave. The son or the nephew who is the chief mourner performs some ceremonies there, and all the agnates go round the grave three times as a mark of respect, when their priest, *i. e.*, the barber, breaks the pot of water over it. Then they all bathe and return home and fast for the night. From the next morning to the fifteenth, the chief mourner bathes early morning and offers the funeral cakes to the spirit of the departed. The ceremony of *Sanchayana* (the collection of the bones) falls on the fifth day, when the bones are preserved to be deposited in a tank, river, or sea, at their convenience. Pollution lasts for ten days in the case of those who follow the inheritance in the male line, and fifteen days among those in the female line, at the expiry of which *pula kuli* (bathing to be free from pollution) takes place. On the night previous to this they all fast, and, on the eleventh or the sixteenth morning, the members of the family under pollution, rubbing gingelly oil over their bodies, bathe with the removal of oily matter, when the priest sprinkles water mixed with cow-dung, which along with the Velan's *mattu* purifies them from pollution. After this some ceremonies are performed and offerings made to the spirit of the departed. The bones already preserved are placed in a metal plate and carried by the chief mourner, who is accompanied by the other members of his family, to a river or sea where they are deposited. Then they all return home after bath, and those that are assembled are sumptuously entertained. The other duties of the chief mourner to the departed spirit are the same as those described on the funeral customs of other castes. There is a custom among the Izhuvans in the northern parts of the State that, when they have to observe death pollution, and have no means to meet the expenses connected with it, they put off the observance of it to some convenient time, by preserving a piece of cloth which they wear, in a pot, kept in a corner of the house. It is believed that they are free from it, so long as the polluted cloth is in the pot. When they can afford to observe it, they remove the cloth.

As has been already mentioned, the priest, who is also the barber, and his wife play an important part in all the ceremonies performed by the caste-men, and they are well rewarded for their services. The tradition is that, when the Izhuvans first came to Kerala, Cheraman Perumal appointed a Brahman to preside over all their ceremonies which brought on a social degradation. Thus, he and his descendants were called *Izhuvathies, Izhuva Vadhiars* or Izhuva priests, known also as *Vathies, Komarattans, Aduthones* (persons closely connected) *Kurups,* and *Panikkans.* They are now a separate sub-caste following their inheritance in the male line. Whenever they have to perform marriage, funeral, or other ceremonies, they inform the important members of the Izhuva community who, with the members of the caste, contribute to the expenses connected therewith, take part in them, and see to everything being properly done.

THE IZHUVANS WITH TODDY DRAWING POTS.

CHAPTER XVII.

THE IZHUVANS

(Continued).

—:o:—

Occupation.

The hereditary occupations of the community, as a whole, have been, from early times, the rearing and cultivation of the cocoanut and palmyra palms, toddy drawing, and arrack distilling. They also manufacture coarse sugar (jaggery) from toddy in the following manner.

When the spadix or flowering branch is half shot, and the spathe or covering of the flowers has not opened, the Izhuvan cuts off its point and binds the stump round with a leaf and beats the remaining part of the spadix with a small stick. For fifteen days this operation is repeated, a thin slice being removed daily. The stump then begins to bleed, and a pot is placed under it to receive the juice which is the *kallu* or toddy. Afterwards, a thin slice is daily taken from the stump, which is then secured by a ligature, but after it has begun to bleed, the beating is stopped. The juice is removed once a day. If it be intended for drinking, nothing is put into the pot, and it will keep for three days. On the fourth day it becomes sour, and what has not been sold to drink, while fermenting, is distilled into arrack. The liquor is distilled without addition and the spirit is not rectified. In the pot intended to receive the juice, that is to be boiled into jaggery, a little quicklime is put to prevent fermentation, and the juice boiled on the day on which it is taken from the tree.

It is said that agriculture is the chief occupation of half the population of the State. The implements of husbandry are of the most primitive kind, and the knowledge of the principles of cultivation and manure is mostly empirical. There is an old Malayalam poem in manuscript which is a translation of a Sanskrit work on agriculture, called Kerala Kalpam, believed to have been compiled by the great Parasurama for the benefit of the Arya Brahmans, by whom he colonised Kerala. Children of the agricultural classes in rural parts, especially in the northern parts of the State, are taught this poem in pyal schools, while in southern parts, it is almost unknown. The methods of cultivation now in vogue among the agricultural classes are mostly in accordance with the precepts laid down in this work, a short account of which may be found to be useful and interesting.

The following story is told to account for the heavy rain in Kerala. In days of yore, there was, at one time, no rain in the kingdoms of Chera, Chola, and Pandya, and all living beings were dying of starvation. The kings of the three kingdoms could not find means to mitigate the sufferings of their subjects. They consulted with one another and resolved to do penance to the god of rain. Temporarily leaving the administration of affairs in the hands of the ministers, they went to the forest, did penance to Indra, the god of rain, who, at the intercession of the great gods, took pity on them and blessed each of them with rain for four months in the year. Well pleased, they returned to their kingdoms, but soon became discontented, because the first had not enough of rain, while the other two had too much of it. They again went to the god of rain and conveyed to him their grievances, whereupon he directed the kings of Chola and Pandya to give two months' rain to the king of Chera. All the three rulers now felt quite satisfied. The king of Chera thus got eight months' rain for his kingdom, while the other two were satisfied with two months' rain in their own kingdoms. Their days of birth, namely, *Thiruvathira* (the sixth asterism) in Mithunam (June-July), *Swathi* (Arcturus) in Thulam (October-November), and *Moolam* (the nineteenth asterism) in Kumbham (February-March) are worthy of remembrance. For, on these auspicious days commence the monsoons, namely, the south-west monsoon in Malabar, the north-east monsoon or *Thula varsham* in the kingdom of Chola, and the rainy season in the kingdom of Pandya. What are called ambrosial showers of rain are said to fall on these kingdoms during the two weeks beginning from the aforesaid dates. It is the belief of all castes among the Hindus even now that seeds of plants sown on these days will produce a rich harvest. These periods are called *Nattu velas* (the best time for planting) in the respective kingdoms and held sacred by the people of these countries.

The unit of measurement of the quantity of rain falling upon earth is called a *para*, which is the measurement of the Devas and consists of the quantity of rain falling upon land sixty *yojanas* or 600 miles in length and a hundred *yojanas* or 1,000 miles in breadth. There are some verses, an approximate translation of which is given below, which show how a forecast can be made as to the quantity of rain that may be had, and the result of the harvest, by the occurrence of *Vishu*, the 1st of Medam (April-May), on the different week days.

If *Vishu* (first of Medam) falls upon a Saturday, there will fall one *para* of rain in Kerala, and poor harvest and poverty among people will be the consequence. If it comes on a Sunday or Tuesday, there will be two *paras* of rain, and the crops will be somewhat good. If on a Monday, three *paras* of rain will fall, and the harvest will be rich and the crops abundant. If on a Thursday, four *paras* of rain will fall, and the crops will be abundant, and harvest so rich that no sign of any famine in the land nor poverty among the people will be seen.

The following six asterisms (lunar days), *viz.*, Rohini, Punartham, Pooyam, Astham, Uthram, and Moolam, the three *karanoms* (constellations of the lunar fortnight), *viz.*, Simhakaranom, Pulikaranom, and Anakaranom, and Mithunam, Karkadakam, Chingam, Makaram and Meenam *rasees* are auspicious for sowing. A statement showing the inauspicious times for sowing is given below:—

No.	Time	Meaning	Explanation or other remarks
1	Night ..		Poor harvest.
2	Gulikakalam ..	Time of the son of Saturn	Full details are given below.
3	Kanni, Vrischikam, and Dhanu rasees ..		Do
4	Gandantham ..	A perilous time	Vide page 214.
5	Vishanadika ..	Poisonous period	Four Indian hours in each *nakshathram* (star) that presides over the day.
6	Panthanal ..		The second, seventh, and twelfth days after the waxing and waning of the moon. A house thatched on these days will take fire.
7	Shashti ..		The sixth day after the waxing and waning of the moon.
8	Veliyerakkam ..	Low tide	
9	Pannikaranom, Pasukaranom and Kazhuthakaranom ..		A *karanom* is the eleventh constellation of the lunar fortnight
10	Rasees (aspected by evil planets) ..		
11	Latam and Argalam .. (Inauspicious days)		
12	Vaidhrathayogam ..	Inauspicious time	Sun and moon standing in the same *ayanam* and like declension.
13	Days of eclipse ..		
14	Adhimasom ..		Thirteenth lunar month occurring every fourth year.
15	When Jupiter aspects Venus and *vice versa* ..		
16	Saturdays and Sundays		

A day is, according to the Hindu astrology, divided into twelve *rasees* (signs of the zodiac), each of which has a certain number of *ghatikas* (periods of twenty-four minutes each). The number of *ghatikas* set apart for each *rasi* is given below:–

No.	Name of the *rasi*	Corresponding English name	Number of *ghatikas*	Remarks
1	Medam ..	Aries	4¼	
2	Edavam ..	Taurus	4¾	
3	Mithunam ..	Gemini	5¼	
4	Karkadakam ..	Cancer	5½	
5	Chingam ..	Leo	5¼	
6	Kanni ..	Virgo	5	The crops raised by seeds sown in this *rasi* will be removed by robbers.
7	Thulam ..	Libra	5	The crops obtained from seeds sown in these two *rasees* will be destroyed.
8	Vrischikam ..	Scorpio	5¼	
9	Dhanu ..	Sagittarius	5½	
10	Makaram ..	Capricornus	5¼	
11	Kumbham ..	Aquarius	4¾	
12	Meenam ..	Pisces	4¼	
	Total		60	

The following are the *gulikakalams* for the week days:—

No.	Days of the week	Day		Night	
		Ghatika	Time	Ghatika	Time
1	Sunday	26th	4-24 P. M.	10th	10 P. M.
2	Monday	22nd	2-48 P. M.	6th	8-24 P. M.
3	Tuesday	18th	1-12 P. M.	2nd	6-48 P. M.
4	Wednesday	14th	11-36 A. M.	26th	4-24 A. M.
5	Thursday	10th	9-24 A. M.	22nd	2-48 A. M
6	Friday	6th	8-24 A. M.	18th	1-24 A. M.
7	Saturday	2nd	6-48 A. M.	14th	11-36 A. M.

The lands which should not be taken up for sowing are those overgrown with phlomis, *chengana* (a kind of grass), bamboos, and thorny plants. Hard stony grounds and tracts frequented by wild beasts are also avoided. On the contrary, lands with a mixture of sand and earth, those drained by springs from the hill-sides (*malaneer*) as well as those manured by river-silt and sewage impurities can be well taken up for cultivation. The lands taken up for cultivation should be well fenced and manured with leaves, dung of cattle, and ashes. The banks between fields should be sufficiently strong, and grass should not be allowed to grow on them, as it may draw the manure off the fields. When ploughing, the plough must penetrate deep into the ground to turn the layers of earth. The bullocks must never be thrashed, but must be cheerfully led and enticed by songs. The ground for sowing seeds and transplanting must be ploughed not less than six times. A bullock and a buffalo must not be yoked together.

Men with no piety to god, no respect for their *guru* (preceptor) and Brahmans, no frugal habits, no farm-house, no straw to provide for bullocks in Kanni (September-October), no adequate wages to be given to workmen, and those who are dull, sleepy, and addicted to drinking, and who do not keep a proper account of income and expenditure, nor provide themselves with a sufficient storage of grain for the wages of workmen under them, nor maintain themselves in Karkadakam (July-August), nor have the necessary implements of husbandry, namely, crow-bar, hatchet, sword, axe, spade, and various kinds of wickerwork, are quite unfit to be cultivators. The bullocks to be used for ploughing and other agricultural purposes should be white with black or red spots, active, small, and fair, like ponies, have thick nose, raised head, bent and small horns, long tail, and no decaying teeth, pass soft dung, eat its food quickly, and have the hind part round and fat, and the backbone nearly straight and raised. Those which have long hoofs, small tails, bent backbones, thick and heavy horns, marks of leprosy, decaying teeth, no horns, and the hind legs touching each other while walking, should be rejected. Buffaloes should be dark coloured with round bodies. The cattle shed must have its floor paved with wooden planks,

THE IZHUVA CULTIVATORS.

well cleaned, and partitioned. The dung must be removed to a distance as its smell is very offensive to them.

All lands in the State may broadly be divided into wet lands and *parambas*. Of the former, those situated on the margin of the back-waters are generally embanked for paddy cultivation, and they afford much scope for reclamations and improvements. As these lands are submerged under salt water, their cultivation is taken up only after the showers of rain diminish the brackishness of the water. The soil is clayish and brackish, and ploughing is out of question. The cultivation is carried on in the simplest way possible. The fields are dug up into square or rectangular plots, each a square yard or two in area, and sprouted seeds are sown over these plots and covered over with the same soil; in a few days, they take root and grow into luxurious plants. In other fields, sowing begins in May, a few weeks before the monsoon. There are some fields, which give two and three crops, but the salt water fields give only one crop. A good harvest depends upon the timely showers of rain, as the plants are otherwise scorched by the sun, making the water more brackish. Leaves, cattle-dung, and ashes are the chief kinds of manure.

Paddy cultivation in the State is generally of three kinds, namely, dry seed cultivation, sprouted cultivation, and transplanted paddy cultivation.

Dry seed cultivation.—For this kind of cultivation, the fields, after the preceding crop has been cut in Vrischikam (November-December) and Dhanu (December-January), are ploughed. The ploughings are continued several times till Medam (April-May), and some ashes are sprinkled every now and then on the fields. After a few showers of rain in Medam, the seeds are sown broadcast. Some farmers plough in the seed, while others cover it with a hoe. The ashes are again thrown on the field. The weeds (*kala* or that which has to be removed or lost) are removed a month after the seeds have been sown. The banks are repaired, and the water is confined on the field. Weeds are again removed in July. The harvest falls in the latter part of Kanni or Thulam. This method of cultivation is applied to a single crop of *kazhama*, *ariyan*, and *ariviri* (varieties of paddy), and the harvest is in Vrischikam. Should a double crop be raised, the sowing takes place in Medam and the harvest in Karkadakam and Chingam. The second crop is begun in two weeks' time.

Sprouted cultivation.—The fields for this are ploughed a dozen times, and are always kept full of water, except when the plough is at work. The field is drained, until the water does not stand deeper than a hand's breadth. At each ploughing, some leaves of any bush or weed, that can be procured, are put into the mud, which is smoothed by dragging over it, a plank yoked to two oxen. The water is drained off by two or three channels formed with a hoe, and the prepared seed is sown. As the corn grows more and more, water is allowed to rest on the field. The kinds of paddy thus cultivated are fifteen in number and require from three to six months for their growth. This cultivation is resorted to in fields on which dry seeds can be sown.

Transplanted paddy cultivation.—The manner of ploughing and manuring is the same as in the case of sprouted seed and performed in the same season. If the ground be clean, the seedlings are transplanted immediately from the fields in which they are raised into those in which they may be reared into maturity. When they are planted, the fields contain three inches depth of water, which gradually increases as the plant grows. Good farmers plough the ground over twelve times in advance.

The auspicious time at which seeds are sown for dry seed cultivation is during the *Bharani* and the *Karthika Nattu velas* *i. e.*, from the fourteenth Medam to the tenth Edavam. The time for the sprouted cultivation is during the *Makiram Nattu vela* which begins from the twenty-third Edavam and lasts till the seventh Mithunam. The transplanted cultivation begins during *Thiruvathira Nattu vela*, *i. e.*, seventh Mithunam to the twenty-first.

Punja cultivation.—Sowing is in Kumbham and the harvest about the end of Medam and the beginning of Edavam.

Kole cultivation.—This kind of cultivation is peculiar to Cochin, Travancore, and Malabar. It means the cultivation of paddy in fresh water lakes after draining away the water. The whole of the Trichur lake is cultivated in this way. The beds are partitioned and temporarily bunded into plots of varying extent, and the water is pumped out before sowing. It is a speculative undertaking, for, if the bunds put up give way owing to some mishap or if the monsoon sets in very early, there is danger of the whole crop being submerged and lost. In normal seasons the outturn is good, and a good *kole* harvest saves the State from the effects of a bad harvest in other fields. There has been of late an improvement in the methods of draining the lakes, as steam-engine is used instead of the primitive water-wheels. The sowing begins in Makaram and the harvest in Medam or Edavam.

Modan cultivation.—The dry lands are well ploughed and the sowing takes place in Medam and the harvest in Chingam.

Cocoanut cultivation.—The seeds must be ripe and fully developed cocoanuts, obtained from cocoanut trees, which have been yielding good and big ones during the previous twelve years. They should not, while plucking, be allowed to fall on the ground. The nuts should be sown by the side of turmeric plants. When they sprout and grow into tender plants, they should be planted during *Thiruvathira Nattu vela* in soil, which must be a mixture of mud and sand, found near the banks of rivers, where the tide flows, and near inlets from the sea, by which the whole coast is very much intersected. They are planted in *parambas* or gardens. Holes are dug throughout for the reception of young palms, and the pits are generally three feet square and three feet in depth. In the bottom of each pit, a small hole is made to receive the young plant, together with some ashes and salt. A little earth is then put round the roots, and the young tree gets a little water. For the first three weeks, it must be watered three times a day; afterwards, once in two days, and once every month a little ash must be put into each pit until the tree is three years old. During the *Nattu vela,* a trench, two feet deep, is dug round the young tree to gather water near it during the rainy season, after which the whole garden is ploughed, and the trenches levelled. Every young tree is allowed to have one basketful of ashes. Before the rains, the trenches are renewed as before, and filled up at the end of the monsoon.

When the trees begin to flower for the first time, a trial is made by cutting a flowering branch to ascertain whether they will be fit for producing nuts or palm-wine. If the cut bleed, they are fit for the latter purpose. In that case, they are let to the Izhuvans, who extract the juice and distill it into arrack. In a good soil, the tree yields juice all the year round, but in poor soil it exhausts in six months. The trees which yield very numerous nuts often grow to a considerable size. In favourable soil, they produce twelve bunches in a year. Ordinary trees give only six bunches.

When the position of Jupiter at the time of sowing is in the first, fourth, seventh, and tenth *rasees* called also as *kendras,* the trees will have a luxuriant growth bearing bunches of large cocoanuts. Mondays, Wednesdays, Thursdays, and Fridays are also auspicious. *Rasees* aspected by benefics, namely, Jupiter Venus, and well associated Mercury, are also favourable for planting. Full Moon, Mercury, and Venus aspecting the seventh *rasi,* and Jupiter aspecting the fifth, seventh, and ninth *rasees,* are also favourable. These planets aspect one another at an angle of 180 degrees.

Cultivation of areca palm.—The seeds of the areca palm must be ripe and full grown. They should be sown on good soil and must be carefully tended till they sprout and become young plants, when they should be planted in soil replete with moisture.

Paramba (high land) cultivation.—In the arable parts of the high lands or *parambas* the following crops are cultivated, namely, *modan* or hill rice, *ellu* or gingelly seeds, *uzhunnu* or Phaseolus radiatus, *karim payaru* or Dolichus catjang, and *chama* or Panicum miliaceum. This kind of land is in general cultivated once in two years only, and requires a year's fallow to recover its strength, but in places near villages where it receives manure or is much frequented by men and cattle, it gives a crop every year. Whatever crops are to be raised, the long grass and bushes growing on this ground are always cut down by the roots, and burned before the first ploughing. for the ashes serve as a necessary manure.

Cultivation of gingelly seeds or sesamum.—These are of two kinds, namely, *cheria* (small) *ellu* and *valia* (large) *ellu*, and are sown separately. They are cultivated at the same season, in the same manner, and in the same kind of soil. In Karkadakam (July-August), the small bushes growing on the soil must be cut, dried, and burned to ashes which may serve as manure. In Chingam (August-September), after seven days' fine weather, the seeds are sown, and covered with the plough. Too much rain is unfavourable. Four weeks after the south-west rain cease, north-east monsoon ought to begin. Should this happen, there will be a good crop.

The seeds sown on Tuesday will cause death to the farmer, and crops will be destroyed, if sown on Friday. Saturday is equally inauspicious. Wednesday is good. Small gingelly seeds, if sown on *Pooram Nattu vela*, will produce a rich harvest. *Makam Nattu vela* is equally good for large seeds even on laterite soil. *Ayilyam Nattu vela* is also favourable.

Cultivation of pulses.—All the pulses like *uzhunnu, payaru*, etc., are cultivated in the same manner as *ellu*. The field is ploughed once in Makaram, and the seeds sown immediately afterwards, and covered with a cross ploughing. In Chingam they ripen without further trouble. The seeds for the cultivation of the pulse should be sown in *Bharani Nattu vela*. The seeds for *cheru modan* are sown in *Rohini Nattu vela*. The forest must, about the same time, be cleared for the cultivation of *uzhunnu* and *payaru* seeds which should be sown on *parambas* overgrown with *thakara* (Indigofera hirsuta).

The cultivation of *chama* is also begun at the same time. For *chama* (Panicum miliaceum), the field is ploughed five times in Medam. After a shower of rain, it is harrowed with a rake drawn by oxen, then the seed is sown and covered with another harrowing. It is ripe in Karkadakam.

In such parts of the high lands as are manured sufficiently to enable there to produce annually a crop of grain, a rotation has been introduced, the first year *chama*, the second year *uzhunnu*, and the third year *payaru*. Another rotation is alternate crops of sesamum and *chama*. The pulses and sesamum can never be shown in the same field.

In jungly tracts, the Izhuvans cut timber, saw wood, and collect fire-wood. Many are engaged in weaving, oil pressing, boat building, boating and coir making. Some are employed as cooks and servants under Europeans. There are also among them, a few merchants, physicians, teachers, astrologers, and magicians. As population increases, they resort to various occupations to which they easily gain access.

The Izhuvans have recently organized a registered association called *Sree Narayana Paripalini Yogam* of over 600 members, working for the religious, social, and industrial advancement of the members of the caste in Malabar, Cochin, and Travancore. The association has been working for two years, and has opened an exhibition in January, 1905, at Quilon in Travancore. The principal agricultural products raised and exhibited by them were paddy, pepper, tapioca, betel-leaves, areca nut, pulses, and yarns. Among the manufactures were textile fabrics, sugar, toddy, liquor, and coir. Some good specimens of ivory and cocoanut shell carving were also among the exhibits. Though the exhibition was not a complete success, yet they have done their best.

Social status. The status of the Izhuvans in former times seems to have been very low. In their manuscript memoirs of Travancore and Cochin, Ward and Conner say that they were treated with contempt by the members of the higher castes, and were owned in a kind of servitude, mitigated to be sure, when contrasted with the predial slaves. They also add that during late years the caste has been raised in some measure from the low state of degradation in which they were held, and that the repeal of poll-tax, from which the lowest poverty could not exempt the abrogation of the *oozhium* (forced labour) and many vexatious restraints, might have taught them their own rights and given them confidence to claim liberty. Francis Day, in his 'Land of the Perumals', says that if a Chogan or Izhuvan dare to pollute a Nair by approaching nearer than the prescribed distance, he was at liberty to cut him down. They are a people, says he, despised by the higher castes, such as the Brahmans and the Nairs, who, whenever they required money, invariably looked to these classes, whence to obtain it. Always destitute of literature, both sacred and profane, they were not solicitous for education. Fearful of losing money, they often buried their savings. Suspicious of not obtaining justice from the laws of the realm, they often resorted to ordeals. Even at present, they have recourse to the decision of the Panchayets or umpires chosen with the consent of both parties. They were not permitted to enter within a native court of justice as they might pollute the judges, who were members of the higher castes. The Nairs were their paid advocates in these courts of justice. All these restrictions and the customs above referred to, with the exception of the question of pollution, have vanished. Their approach within thirty-six feet pollutes Brahmans, Kshatriyas, and high castes Sudras. In Pharoah's Gazetteer it is said that, in North Malabar, they may approach within five feet, and generally actual contact only is considered to cause pollution. So far as my information goes, this does not appear to be correct. They cannot approach Brahman houses or temples, nor can they pass through Brahman villages in Palghat. No member of any higher caste eats with them. They eat at the hands of all castes above them, but strictly abstain from taking the food of Kammalans, Valans, Arayans, and the members of other low castes. They live in *tharas* (villages) of their own and are not allowed to take water from the wells of high caste-men. They have their washerman and barber. The Tiyyans of North Malabar are more advanced than their brethren in the States of Cochin and Travancore, and are not rising to the level of high caste-men, who look upon them with jealousy. It is disappointing to see that their children are not admitted into the Zamorin's College, Calicut, though as Christian converts, they are welcome. Such restrictions do not exist in the orthodox States of Cochin and Travancore.

Dress.

The males and females were not formerly permitted to wear an upper garment above the waist. These and other restrictions were in force throughout Malabar till the beginning of the century, and in Travancore till 1859. In Cochin it is somewhat observed even now. Even in the British territory, where this restriction does not exist, they manifest no desire to dress decently. The males wear round their loins a *mundu* of four cubits in length and two cubits and half to three cubits in breadth. When they go out, they wear a second also. In North Malabar, they wear a turban, generally a coloured handkerchief. The well to do people and the school-going young men in North Malabar wear coats and caps, boots and trousers. The officers dress themselves in European fashion. Usually they have an oval patch of hair on the top of their head tied into a knot like the Nairs, but many crop their hair like the native Christians and shave their faces clean. The males wear ear-rings and rings made of gold or set with rubies.

Women of the richer class wear round their loins a piece of white cloth, three yards in length, a yard and a quarter in breadth either with or without a coloured or laced border, tucked in at the ends. A small laced cloth is also put on to cover their breasts. Young women wear petticoats also. Women of the middle and poorer classes wear round their loins a *kacha* (a piece of cloth four yards in length and a yard and a quarter in breadth), folded twice. It is only when they go out that they wear a second cloth. In Palghat and the Chittur Taluk of the State, the women wear a dark coloured cloth (*kanki*) with no

THE IZHUVA WOMEN.

second cloth, even when they are seen on public roads. They wear their hair smooth, and keep the knot on the right side or sometimes straight up, which does in a way distinguish them from the Nair women.

Conclusion.

Judging from the physical appearance, the Izhuvans, both males and females, are generally so neat and handsome that it is not easily possible to distinguish them from the Nairs. It is still more so in North Malabar. The women can be easily made out from the following characteristics. The tattoo form of dressing does not prevail among them. The ornaments of the Izhuva women differ from those of Nair women. They are on the whole as handsome as the Nair women and are very industrious.

As a class, the caste-men are very industrious, and though they are not generally opulent, there are men of wealth and influence among them. In North Malabar they have been appreciating the benefits of English education, and a large number of children of the well to do people is receiving higher education. Many have gained high University honours and are employed in all departments of the public service. In this respect, their brethren in the States of Cochin and Travancore lag behind them. Owing partly to the poverty of the people, and partly to their disabilities, very few have been taking advantage of the instructions given them in State high schools. Admission to the public service has been recently thrown open to them. In point of education, they cannot compare favourably either with the Nairs or with their brethren in North Malabar. The caste is now striving to come up in the social scale.

CHAPTER XVIII.

THE KAMMALANS.

Internal structure of the caste.

The Kammalans, who are also called *Nanku parisha* or *Panchalans*, are the artisan classes, living in all the villages and towns of the State. They are, strictly speaking, one caste, the members of which are divided into six occupational groups or sub-castes, namely, (1) Marasaris or workers in wood (carpenters), (2) Kallasaris (stone-masons), (3) Kollans (blacksmiths), (4) Moosaris (bell-metal workers), (5) Thattans (goldsmiths), and (6) Tolkollans (leather workers). The Marasaris are again subdivided into Thachans (wood-cutters), Avens, Poozhi Asaris, Ettila Parisha, Ircha Thachans (sawers of wood), and Kolli Vetties. The Kollans are also subdivided into Palisa Kollans, Katachi Kollans, and Theepori Kollans. The Kallasaris and Moosaris have each a subdivision, namely, Silpi Asaris (image makers) and Chembu Kotties (copper workers). The minor subdivisions are based chiefly on occupation, and are mere endogamous septs, the members of which, with the exception of the Silpi Asaris, are inferior in social status to those of the main divisions. This affords evidence to the fact how caste formation is based on occupation. In the Tamil and Telugu districts, these occupations are interchangeable, but in Cochin and Malabar, they are pursued by the members of the respective sub-castes, any deviation from which will entail the disapprobation of the community and eventually lead to excommunication. The total number of Kammalans in the State is 29,809; of these, 15,533 are Marasaris, 6,407 Kollans, 2,328 Kallasaris, 888 Moosaris, 3,554 Thattans and 1,099 Tolkollans. They form 3·6 per cent. of the total population, and are chiefly a rural people, 93·6 per cent. of them being found outside of the towns.

The Kammalans believe themselves to have sprung up from Viswakarma, the divine architect; and claiming this divine parentage, they profess their superiority to the Brahmans who are the descendants of the mortal *rishies* (sages). They now call themselves "*Viswa Brahmans*" to emphasize their exalted pedigree. This claim of the community in the Tamil districts has led to riots and cases in the law courts, and was as vehemently asserted as ever at the last census; and though anything which might tend to revive the bad blood to which it has led is to be depreciated, it seems necessary to shortly set out a few of the obstacles to the recognition of their superiority to the rest of the community which the Kammalans do not appear to have yet surmounted.

Traditional origin.

The Kammalans base their claims upon three things, *viz.*, (1) decisions in the courts of justice, (2) some instances in the Vedas, and (3) certain passages from *Moolasthanam* and *Silpisastram* and other similar works on architecture. The decisions in the law courts merely state, that the Kammalans may be allowed to perform such rites as they choose without molestation. As to the Vedas, it is not the Kammalans who quote scripture, but these writings were composed long before the present caste system originated, so that the chance passages or sentences are of little weight in the controversy.

There can be no doubt that the Kammalans' claim is comparatively of recent origin. The inscriptions of 1013 A. D. show that at that time they had to live outside the villages in hamlets of their own, like the Parayans and other low castes. A later one, since translated (S. I. Incriptions, Vol. III, Part I, page 47), gives an order of one of the Chola kings, that they should be permitted to blow conches, beat drums at their weddings and funerals, to wear sandals, to plaster houses, and to show by implication that the above privileges were never previously conceded to them.

It is not difficult to account for the low position held by the Kammalans, for it must be remembered that in early times the military castes of India, as elsewhere, looked down upon all engaged in labour, whether skilled or otherwise. With the decline of military power, however, it was natural that a useful caste like the Kammalans should gradually improve in its position; and the reaction from this long oppression has led them to make exaggerated claims described above, which are ridiculed by every other caste, high or low[1].

The Kammalans of Cochin and Malabar do not advance any such pretensions to be Brahmans, as those above mentioned, but merely take a lower position of a polluting caste below the Sudras. They are, I believe, the very early immigrants from the Tamil districts, and the early epigraphical records point to the existence of five classes of Kammalans in Malabar in the beginning of the ninth century. The following tradition also is current in respect of their origin and early settlement in the land of Kerala. Once, when the Perumal compelled a carpenter girl to marry a young man of the washerman caste, the carpenters in a body opposed it, and eventually left the land of the Perumal, who soon became embarrassed at their absence, as he had none in the land to build houses. Though invited by the subsequent Perumals, they refused to return from the land of their exile, Ceylon (a nursery ground of artisans, cultivators, and servants in those early days). The king of the island was requested to send some of them in charge of the islanders, and the request was complied with; and the practice exists, even to this day, of the Kammalans receiving, at their marriages, presents from the Izhuvans, and even dining with them.

Puberty customs.

When a Kammalan girl comes of age, she is at once bathed, which is called *Kandukuli*, (bathing at the sight of the menses), and she is kept under seclusion for fifteen days, during which a few girls are allowed to be in her company to amuse her. She is given rich and nourishing meals and sweet meats, but meat is strictly forbidden. The members of all the subdivisions are invited on the first and the fourth day, and betel-leaves and nuts are freely distributed. The girl is bathed on the fourth, seventh, eleventh, and the

1. Madras Census Report, 1891.

sixteenth days. On the morning of the last aforesaid day, they are again invited to a sumptuous feast. The girl, being smeared with gingelly oil, is taken by the caste-women and the girl friends to the nearest tank or river for a bath, and they all return home in procession. The members assembled are treated to a grand dinner. The girl is then allowed to enter the kitchen, touch the utensils, and mingle with the inmates of the house. The village washerwoman entertains them with her songs during the night. Their caste priest, the *Kurup*, cleans the room and the surroundings on the morning of the sixteenth day and purifies them by sprinkling water mixed with cow-dung. A girl, that is married before puberty, stays with her parents until she attains the age of womanhood. There is no special ceremony for the nuptials; but an auspicious day is chosen for it, when the bride's parents are invited to attend. Adult marriage is the rule, infant marriage an exception.

Marriage customs.

The girls of the Kammalans are married both before and after they come of age. There is no harm if a woman is unmarried, but all young women generally enter into conjugal relations within a few years after they arrive at the period of womanhood. In no case is sexual licence allowed or tolerated before marriage; should, however, any such case occur, the girls and her parents are placed under a ban. They do not generally intermarry among the various subdivisions, although there is no objection for doing so, but they interdine freely. There is also no objection to exchange daughters in marriage between the members of two families of each subdivision. Males often marry before they are twenty years of age. As in other castes, a young man may marry the daughter of his maternal uncle.

The two forms of marriage, *viz.*, the *tali* tying and the *podamuri* or *sambandham* are in vogue among the Kammalans, as among the Nairs and the Izhuvans, the former of which is compulsory and takes place before girls come of age. The omission or negligence of this ceremony will place a girl and her parents under excommunication. The latter is celebrated in a few years after she attains the period of womanhood. The ceremonies connected with both are the same as those prevailing among the Nairs and the Izhuvans. The bride's price is eleven annas, one rupee and five annas, two rupees, and three rupees and three annas, varying according to the circumstances of the bridegroom and his parents. There is a peculiar custom that, on the night of the last day of the *tali* tying ceremony at three o'clock, the bridegroom and his party, standing at the entrance of the room in which the bride and her party remain, sing a series of love songs which are appropriately answered by the bride's party in the same strain, and these last till day-break, when the party that wins is liberally rewarded with sweet meats. The songs from the groom's party convey the uncontrollable passion for the bride, while those from the bride's party express the reluctance to yield to his wishes, on the score of his previous bad conduct. These songs transcend the bounds of decency, and a translation of which is therefore out of place. When the *podamuri* or *sambandham* is performed for a young woman, she is, so to speak, adopted into his family. The giving of the sweet preparation, and formally calling her as a member of his family are the binding portions of the ceremony. If the *tali* tier of a girl wishes to keep her as a wife, he has the preference to anybody else, and to none else may she be given without his consent. Polygamy, though allowable, is seldom practised, and polyandry in the fraternal or adelphic form prevails among them as among the poor people of the other allied castes. They quote, for their authority, the instance of the five Pandavides, who had a wife in common, which by no means prevented each brother from trying his luck elsewhere, and contracting marriage on his own account; but all the wives they brought had to accept the supremacy of the great incomparable Krishna Draupadi. A Kammalan, while observing the simplest and most general form of this polyandry, rarely enters into conjugal relations with a woman of his caste without formally repudiating his connection with the common wife. In this form the husbands are the brothers, the wife lives in their house, and the children are their children who inherit the property. The formalities connected with this form of marriage are the same as those described in my account of the Izhuvans. This custom, which prevails in other parts of India, notably in Ceylon, is fast dying out among these and other caste-men, owing to the influence of western civilization. A widow may marry her brother-in-law or anybody she chooses; in the latter case, she forfeits all her rights over the property of the deceased husband and the children left by him. Divorce also is very easy, either party being at liberty to separate from the other, and the woman divorced may marry again. This, however, is done by the decision of the majority of the elderly caste-men assembled for the purpose.

Inheritance and caste assembly.

Among the Kammalans, the law of succession to property is in the male line, that is, from father to son. Women have no share in the family property; but, in the event of any partition being effected in a family, the unmarried daughters have each a share, and none at all when they marry.

The Kammalans have their caste assemblies which consist of the elderly members of all the subdivisions living in the village; and they meet on all occasions affecting the welfare of the community. All caste disputes are settled by them, and the culprits are generally fined, and, in extreme cases, put out of caste. In the absence of their assembly being represented by the local members of all the subdivisions, their meeting is informal. There are some, among them, to whom *Theettoorams* (Royal writs) have been given, allowing them certain privileges, but there are no head-men as among other castes.

Magic, sorcery, and witchcraft.

Kammalans believe in magic, sorcery, and witchcraft, and there are, among them, persons, who practise black art to entice a young woman for the sake of a man and *vice versa*. A woman, who eats a fruit or a piece of bread on which some *mantram* is muttered, becomes obedient to the will of the giver. A piece of cadjan leaf, copper, iron, or gold leaf on which a *yantram* or cabalastic figure is drawn and rolled, and the *mantram* muttered thereon, is sometimes buried beneath the steps on which a woman may tread, when she becomes subservient to the will of the doer. Another kind of performance which they often resort to is to make a figure, with wood or wax, of a man or woman who has to be victimized, and burn a bright fire (*homam*) with the twigs of nux vomica dipped in ghee. Pepper and chillies are thrown into the fire and the *mantrams* muttered. The victim's body will have a burning sensation, and if the wooden or waxen figure is thrown into the fire, the victim may die. These are instances of sympathetic magic. There is also another method by which the same result is arrived at. An image of wood or wax in the likeness of a man or woman is placed in a pot which contains *guruthi* (water mixed with lime and turmeric). With the recital of the necessary *mantram*, it is placed over the fire, and, as it boils, the person is seriously injured, and he instantly dies. They believe in devil driving, and the methods and formalities are similar to those described in my account of the Izhuvans. They have faith in astrology and have their horoscopes cast, when quite young, and consult an astrologer in times of sickness and misfortunes. His predictions are based on the planetary positions at the time of occurrence, when remedies suggested by him are at once resorted to. This practice is in common with the other caste-men. In times of cholera or small-pox raging in a village, the *velichapad* of the Bhagavathi temple in his hysterical moments (when the spirit of the deity is within) announces to the manager of the temple and others of the village, the anger or displeasure of the village deity and directs them as to the methods to be adopted for her propitiation with offerings. The local men levy a contribution from the caste-men of the village to celebrate a grand feast in honour of her, which is believed to relieve them from the calamity. The same method of propitiation is also adopted in the event of a similar occurrence in a family.

THE ASARIS (CARPENTERS) IN THE WORKSHOP.

Religion.

In religion, the Kammalans have the same forms of worship as the Nairs and the Izhuvans. All Hindu holy-days are observed by them with equal reverence. They have temples of their own in the State, similar to those belonging to their caste-men in Travancore, and one of their caste-men is their priest. They worship Kali or Bhagavathi, who is their guardian deity. Their propitiation of the minor gods and demons are in common with that of the allied caste-men.

Funeral customs.

The dead bodies of the Kammalans are either buried or burned; and the funeral ceremonies are the same as those performed by the Izhuvans. The pollution is for fifteen days, and the son is the chief mourner, who, during this period, is forbidden to eat meat, chew betel, have any kind of play or amusement, or go out. The *Kurup* is the priest who officiates at these and other ceremonies, and he is also their barber.

Occupation.

There is always a great demand for the labour of these artisan classes, the members of which earn comparatively higher wages, than other castemen, their condition being hardly one of prosperity and contentment. In the Cochin State, there is no general movement in progress by which the occupational castes are abandoning their traditional employments; and the village industries group themselves according to the purity of the occupation. In each village of the rural parts, a few families of each sub-caste, may be seen living together to meet the local requirements.

The carpenters who form a large and important community work, for their constituents, all kinds of agricultural implements, during the period of cultivation, and receive wages either in grain or in coin. During the summer months, they are engaged in house-building and in many other kinds of work, when they get high wages (six to eight or ten annas a day). The better class workmen often migrate to towns or other places, and do superior work of all kinds. The minor subdivisions among them cut timber, saw wood, and do less skillful work.

The Kallasaris or stone masons quarry stones for house-building, erecting walls, and for other purposes. The better workmen make stone images, and on that account demand a higher recognition. They are called Silpi Asaris.

Kollans or blacksmiths are engaged in making or repairing ploughshares, mattocks, weeding spuds, or other rude implements of husbandry for the village farmers, and are often remunerated with a dole of grain for each rude implement in return. Their workshops are mere flimsy sheds, erected by the side of their huts, and their tools very primitive. Their furnace is a small fire-place, and the bright red heat caused by the burning of wood charcoal, is often kept up by a pair of rude bellows which consist of two cylindrical leather bags about eighteen inches long and nine inches in diameter. The top has a slit, the edges of which overlap and serve as a valve. Each pair is placed on a small platform of clay, and a man, taking hold of the outer flaps of their upper ends in his two hands, alternately pushes them down to expel the wind, and draws them up to get a supply of air, the one end going up, and the other coming down. The air is expelled through a nozzle common to both bags. Each furnace has two pairs which require two men. The average earning of a skilled workman varies from six to eight or ten annas a day. There are many among them who possess fine mechanical aptitude, but remain in a backward state for want of opportunities.

Moosaris or bell-metal workers form a minority in the State, and hold a position as equally respectable as that of the carpenters or goldsmiths. They supply the villagers with all kinds of household utensils of their own manufacture; and every villager invests his surplus cash in purchasing them as their value is easily realized at the village pawn shop or at the factory of the brazier. The Moosaris are conversant with the preparation of the alloys in various proportions to form the different kinds of bell-metal for different vessels which they may have to make. The moulds for the vessel to be made are first

THE MOOSARIS (BELL-METAL WORKERS).

made of earth, which when dry are coated with wax. The melted alloy is allowed to run into them, which when cooled solidifies. The moulds are destroyed and the vessels thus formed are then polished.

Thattans or goldsmiths make the jewelry of the villagers which is partly worn as ornament and partly as talisman, and forms a convenient reserve of easily realizable capital. When need arises, the precious metal is promptly melted and sold. The function of the jeweler sometimes merges in that of a money lender who is often suspected as acting as a sort of fence, placing his melting pot at the disposal of the burglar.

Tolkollans, owing to the work in leather, are classed as the last among the artisan classes in social status. They make native shoes, and the skilled men make boots of European pattern.

The houses of the artisans can be recognized from their surroundings, that of a carpenter from the wood piled round it, that of a blacksmith from the flimsy shed containing a small furnace with wood charcoal by the side of it, and that of a Moosari with his small workshop containing the earthen vessels, just made or drying in the sun which are only moulds of those he has to manufacture. In this connection, it must be said, that these artisans have no capital whatever to work with. They are often engaged to work for those who supply them with the materials, when they obtain their wages slightly in advance. When thus employed by several men at the same time, they find it difficult to be honest and punctual to the finishing of the work. Very often some greedy merchants engage several of these men, furnish them with the materials, and have the articles made under their supervision and management, when they are given only the wages. With the necessary capital, there is ample scope in these parts for an organized industry.

It is said that Indian woman is the chief carrier and beast of burden. The remark is no less applicable to the women of the artisan classes, who do laborious task of husking and grinding corn, attend to all domestic work, supply fuel to the family, gather cow manure, convert it into cakes with the admixture of chaff and other refuse, and plaster them on a sunny wall to dry, weave coarse mats for their own domestic use, and also supplement the work of their husbands.

Social status.

Of the six subdivisions, the first five interdine, but rarely intermarry. Tolkollan is considered a degraded caste, probably on account of his work in leather, which, in its early stages, is an unholy substance. The members of other sub-castes do not even allow him to touch them. Again, among the Marasaris are included the Thachans, who are looked upon as a separate caste, the members of which cannot touch the members of other sub-castes. The stone working sections are the sculptors, some of whom have to carve the images of gods, and so earn a certain degree of recognition. The Kammalans generally do not claim to be Brahmans as their brethren of the Tamil districts where some from the northern parts of the State work for high wages. Of late, the Marasaris in the Chittur Taluk and some others in the Palghat Taluk of South Malabar have been advised by their caste *guru* (preceptor) from one of the Tamil districts to grow a tuft of hair on the back instead of on the top of the head, to wear the holy thread as their brethren in the Tamil districts, and to perform *Sandhia vandanam* (daily prayers) and other Brahmanical ceremonies. These innovations on the part of the carpenters are resented at by the *jenmies* (landlords) in whose lands they live, as also by the members of the higher and corresponding castes, who ridicule them for their exaggerated claims described above, without any attempt to elevate the status of their women. Their approach within a distance of twenty-four feet pollutes the Brahmans, Kshatriyas, and Sudras, whose food and water they are allowed to eat and drink; but they are absolutely forbidden to eat whatever is prepared by the barbers, washermen, and other caste-men

THE THATTANS (GOLDSMITHS).

below them in status. When the services of the members of all the subdivisions are required for the construction of a temple, they bathe early morning, go to the temple, and stand near the *bali kallu* (sacrificial stone), when the *tantri* (priest) gives them each a holy thread (*Poonanul*) and two garments, one of which is worn round the loins like the Brahman priest, and the other tied round the head. As they enter the outer enclosure, a cow that has just delivered a calf and is tied to a pole is let loose, and in the event of her attacking any of them, he is not enlisted for the work, which shows, that he is not fit to work in a holy place. Furthur, they also consult their mothers before going to work, and if they are not inclined to give them permission (which insinuates that their parentage is not genuine, and their work in a holy place is sure to endanger them) they stay away, pleading some excuse. Just as the Nairs have to use the language of respect and veneration in addressing the Namburies, the Kammalans and the members of the polluting castes have to observe the same formality and courtesy in addressing the Nairs and those below them.

END OF VOLUME I.

INDEX.

A

U

V

Printed at the Cochin Government Press, Ernakulam.